THE

ANGEL'S

DESCENT

Book Four of The Dark Angel series

COURTNEY LILLARD

Copyright © 2022 Courtney Lillard.
All rights reserved.

No part of this publication may be reproduced, distributed, or transmitted in any form or by any means, including photocopying, recording, digital scanning, or other electronic or mechanical methods, without the prior written permission of the copyright holder, except in the case of brief quotations embodied in critical reviews and certain other noncommercial uses permitted by copyright law.

ISBN: 979-8-8063359-8-3

Cover Design by Etheric Tales & Edits | MC Damon

ACKNOWLEDGEMENTS

This book is dedicated to everyone who contributed some fraction of their time to help shape the person I am today, including my parents, siblings, friends, teachers, and colleagues from across the country. I also must thank my husband, Darren, who not only gave me the push I needed to begin writing seriously and reads all of the drafts but who also listens to my ideas with honest, eager ears.

Contents

ACKNOWLEDGEMENTS iii

PART ONE

Prologue 1

1 28

2 40

3 55

4 68

5 86

6 102

7 114

8 130

9 140

10 157

11 169

PART TWO
Prologue 209
1 236
2 253
3 268
4 281
5 300
6 316
7 333
8 351
9 365
10 382
11 398
12 414
13 434
14 463
15 486
16 508
17 524
18 549
Epilogue 572
About the Author 589

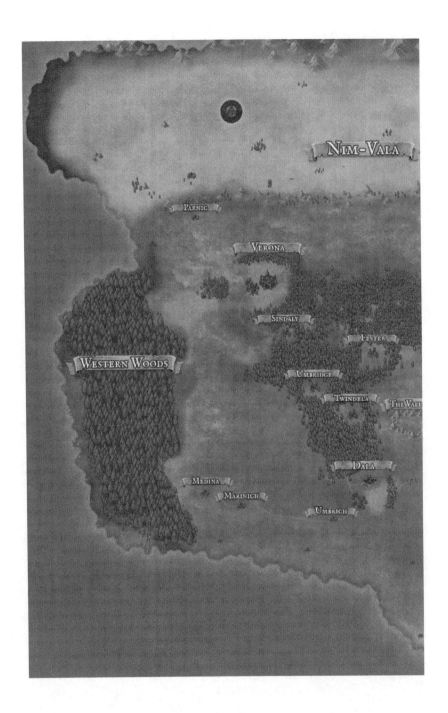

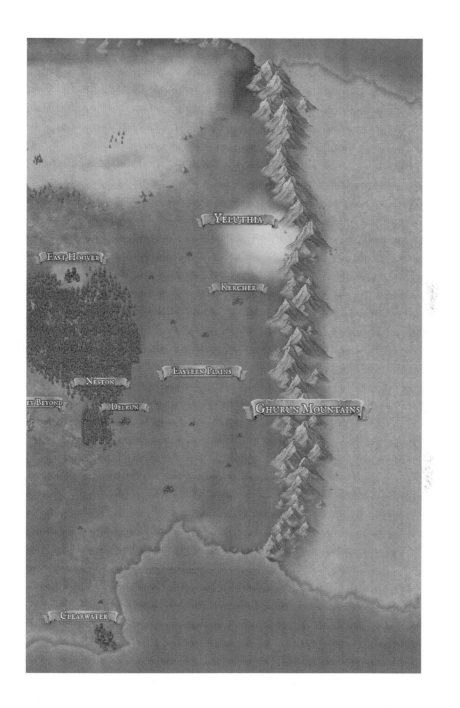

Part One

Prologue

Becoming a priest had never been a choice. Many people thought it required an incredible amount of magic; even more believed there to be some sort of connection to one or more deities. With a variety of religions, it was easy to assume much. Hendal stopped caring about such notions by the age of nine. If the gods couldn't answer his prayers, were they really worth his time? If he was forced to revere them, couldn't they at least free him from his life of servitude?

Even though he had been born in Kercher, he never considered the town to be his home nor felt any connection to its people. At some point in his lineage, the Yeluthians apparently blessed his family during Kercher's founding as a necessary means of communicating between the humans and angels. Only in their family did the eldest child carry the expectation to produce many offspring. All but the second child of the previous generation's first born were trained as messengers to travel across the country on Yeluthia's behalf and would raise their own families to grow the system. It became their responsibility to connect the two kingdoms, a task meant for no other household.

Meanwhile, the second child, the one considered a special gift, was given to the town's priest or priestess as soon as they could be separated from their mother. The church then accepted them as their mentor's replacement. Since a servant of the gods wasn't allowed to create a family, this ensured there would always be someone to honor Kercher's founding faith. The tradition continued for generations, even when the angels stopped visiting and the townsfolk began to leave and never return.

    Hendal's mother had been the eldest of three to his grandparents and bore a daughter at a young age. She loved the child dearly and spent much longer than normal training her. With a lack of news to spread, his mother felt less pressure to produce any more offspring. In fact, as far as he understood, the only person who harped about the tradition had been his uncle and the town's priest, Verdic. By the time Hendal came into the world, his mother nearly reached the age to no longer conceive and readily gave him away as soon as he could walk to silence her devoted brother. When Hendal turned three years of age, his sister, who was over two decades older, welcomed a second son. As per tradition, she passed off the boy when he seemed at the proper stage to join the priest.

    At first, the lessons Verdic taught emanated a sense of wonder and left Hendal in awe. He and his nephew, Wesley, learned about the angels and demons, the power of light and dark energies, the history of their town, and the god Summa and goddess Izina, who were said to be all-knowing life-bringers. The foundation of their town's church reflected the principles of Summa and Izina, stating all life is precious, the energies of the world are meant to be balanced, and tradition is necessary to honor the ancestors of Kercher. Since Hendal developed a better memory for studying the texts passed down by the priests, he helped Wesley along, and the two grew close enough to consider each other brothers.

    Eventually, the reading and memorizing became tedious. Hendal often stared out the church's window to watch the other children skip around and enjoy their freedom. The next day, when his uncle brought them in front to repaint the wooden building, he decided to bring up the subject.

    "Why aren't we allowed to play outside?" he asked Verdic after a pause to wipe away the beads of sweat trailing down his face. No matter the season, the priest still required them to wear gray, woolen robes at all times.

    "We were born different from the others in Kercher," his uncle answered without looking away from his work. "While they have their duties that allow for such activity, we must continue on with ours."

"But why?"

Verdic's lips scrunched up, as if he'd eaten a tart piece of fruit, then he glared down at his pupils. "What does Izina say about questioning one's life?"

Immediately, Wesley attempted a guess. "She says to live as though each day is a gift that will only last for-"

Hendal watched in horror as his nephew's sentence cut short when the flat paint brush in their teacher's hand struck Wesley across the face.

"The destiny of one's life is predetermined by the gods! As it is written in Nedian's journal seventy years ago, "...for the goddess herself cast upon me a vision of paradise and promised eternal bliss for those loyal to their human lives. One cannot hope to escape unless they wish to spoil the future of their people, and thus, end the line of Annonely, who spoke with Summa's ancestor..."

Wesley put a hand to his cheek, and Hendal could see his shoulders begin to shake. As the smeared paint began to dry, the two boys continued listening to the crazed priest spew verses and quotes from their studies. Verdic only stopped when he ran out of breath, but Hendal caught half a dozen sets of eyes on them from the children and adults nearby.

After the first incident, he never mentioned anything like that to his teacher again. He and Wesley worked diligently to avoid sparking the priest's wrath; however, Hendal would share his feelings with his only friend late in the night when the thoughts kept him awake.

"Why would Verdic get so upset?" he whispered to his nephew while shifting positions on the wide cot they shared in the attic.

"I don't want to bring it up again," came the soft reply. Wesley usually acted sensitive about the experience, yet Hendal grew more confused and frustrated by the unexpected outburst.

"All I wonder is why we have to be priests? Why is it necessary to keep the tradition going? Would something bad happen to the town if we didn't?"

"I don't like when you talk like that."

Hendal rolled over to turn his face toward Wesley. Even in the darkness, he caught the other's eyes on him. "I'm sorry," he offered in a sincere manner, "but do you ever consider what life outside is like? What could we do if we were not forced to be priests?"

"We would be messengers."

Hendal ended the conversation there since it became obvious his nephew didn't understand what he meant.

*

During the next couple of months, not a day went by that the boys didn't fear stepping out of line until a sickness spread throughout the area in early spring, causing Verdic to be bedridden. The man would only comment on how the gods destined their circumstances against a fever clouding his mind. Hendal's mother visited to give him medicine; otherwise, the two boys had been left alone. At first, all they could think to do with their new freedom was go outside and join the other children in their games until their uncle recovered. Wesley felt too concerned with being punished, though, so Hendal crafted a plan.

"We can take turns. I'll leave in the morning, and you can go after lunch."

"Won't someone tell the priest?"

"Not if we claim he let us outside in order to keep us from getting sick. We'll still study when we're here and at night together."

After some more persuading, Wesley nodded, albeit hesitantly.

The next morning, Hendal snuck through the kitchen's back door and, for the first time in his life, sprinted through town until he reached the fields beyond. His lungs burned once he slowed to a stop, then he spun around and walked back through Kercher. The few people tending to the fields and opening their shops gave curious glances, but no one spoke to him.

The sun's light shined bright and warmed his skin, prompting him to pause, close his eyes, and savor the sensation as much as he could. *Why would a priest not be allowed to enjoy this simple pleasure?* he wondered.

When he stumbled upon the children his age participating in a game requiring one person to chase and tag the others, he asked to join. Most of them mumbled their uncertainty while the rest remained silent.

"Aren't you living in the priest's household?" one of the youngest girls inquired without displaying more than genuine curiosity.

"Just because I stay inside to study doesn't mean I can't be here with you," he replied to reassure both the children and himself.

After accepting his explanation, they taught him their game and eased up enough for Hendal to have fun during the rest of the morning. Around noon, they scattered for lunch after he informed them Wesley would be there in the afternoon. He returned to his nephew and enthusiastically described what the town was like and the game he learned. Although Wesley remained uncertain, Hendal sensed excitement underneath the nerves. The other boy scurried away, leaving him to relax in the church's library with no small amount of envy.

Once alone, and for the first time in many months, Hendal put his hands together and prayed. Whenever his uncle led the action, Hendal knew Verdic could not control what he thought, so he often let his mind and imagination wander. He never believed Summa or Izina were listening because he hadn't experienced a moment in his life that he considered spiritual. This time, he tried to focus.

Please, he begged without addressing a particular deity. *I don't want the life of a priest. I desire to have choices, not people relying on me to stay here, study the scripture, and teach information I'm not sure I trust. Grant me this one request, and I will do whatever it is you need of me.*

Never before had he felt a desire to ask for more than his simple, methodical lifestyle. The game allowed him to express himself, and the children provided an opportunity to interact with other people. That taste for the world beyond his duties, beyond what he began to see as chains, stirred a restlessness previously sleeping within.

*

A week passed until Verdic recovered. Hendal and Wesley resumed their daily routine in the church, except their chores and lessons became tiresome. The priest noticed them fidgeting in their seats, glancing longingly out the windows, or slacking on their work and would yell or scold them into submission before they outgrew his vocal reprimanding. Then, he resorted to physical disciplinary actions. One morning, he started carrying around a thin branch as long as his arm and used it to strike their hands, or faces in severe instances.

Wesley ceased his misbehavior since pain influenced his mentality; Hendal reacted in practically the opposite manner.

Week by week, he hated his teacher and the life lined up for him more and would often bring about the punishments by questioning the material they were being taught. Verdic's denial about why they might not be needed as priests, along with his unwillingness to address any information other than Summa and Izina, led Hendal to consider the possibility of other religions and beliefs that did not align with his uncle's. Instead of following the assigned readings, he sought new sources, and what he found infuriated him. Dozens of books mentioned differing ideas from what Verdic preached regarding their gods and history while a few contradicted their ancestors' writings.

The next day, he approached his uncle at the priest's desk in the library, threw down the materials, and demanded answers. Hendal raised his voice without fear, asking the man before him what went on outside of Kercher's church and when they planned to lecture from the pieces in front of him. He expected Verdic to unleash his fury once the room quieted, but the silence stretched for an uncomfortable amount of time. While their eyes remained locked, Hendal could sense the rage seething within Verdic, and even Wesley's terror nearby, until the priest finally lowered his hands from where they had been folded in front of his nose.

"One chosen to worship the deities who blessed their people with life should never question the existence of secondary gods or goddesses who mind their own peoples. We were given our assignments by those before us as a way to be thankful for what we have and who we are, lest we forget the sacrifices, obstacles, and acts leading us to be the people we are today."

"A people who's dying away?" Hendal countered and avoided wincing when his voice cracked on the final word. At the lack of a complete, credible answer, he dipped his chin to stare at the ground.

"Changing, perhaps, but not dying," Verdic continued while showing more patience than Hendal expected. "You will understand in time. For now, Kercher needs someone to give them hope, to keep their faith strong, and to teach them how to live as Summa and Izina instructed the founders of our town."

Hendal refrained from letting out a long sigh in defeat and glanced up; however, the priest's eyes no longer rested on him but gazed over his shoulder. He glanced around to see Wesley sitting at the table behind him, watching their argument without expression. Then, Verdic stood, picked up the items containing writings from the line of priests before him, and spoke once more.

"I'll take a look at what you brought me. It is possible they were disregarded for false or inaccurate information by those who lacked the comprehensive knowledge of our beliefs."

Hendal held his tongue as his teacher exited the room.

He never saw those books, journals, or papers again.

*

For a time, Hendal abandoned his fight against the position fate demanded he accept. He and Wesley, who grew into a handsome man and adequate scholar, only left the church on Verdic's orders, which frequented as the priest's health declined. When Hendal was twenty-five years old, Verdic passed away in his sleep with Wesley holding his left hand and Hendal his right. They chanted prayers through the tears in their eyes and looked at one another helplessly before releasing the lifeless, limp hands. The man had requested he remain in his room during his final days, so announcing his death to the public fell to his successor.

"Hendal," Wesley muttered when neither moved.

"What is it?"

"You're the new priest."

"Yes, and?"

"You should go tell everyone what happened."

"I suppose I should, shouldn't I?"

"I will accompany you."

Hendal didn't answer but stood and wiped the tears away. Although he hated his uncle and always would for such narrow-minded actions and opinions as their caretaker, as a man, Verdic acted wholly faithful to the people of Kercher and their other relatives.

"Is that all it takes to be a priest?" he voiced aloud to nobody in particular.

"What do you mean?" Wesley asked in a soft, empathetic manner.

Hendal clenched his fists when a surge of old emotions welled. "He was a rotten teacher. He never listened to us or anyone who believed something different. We've been sheltered because it's tradition. We couldn't raise families or build friendships because it's tradition. There's so much to learn about the world, but he…"

Wesley rose to stand by his side and made a sound to interrupt, but Hendal continued.

"We never had a chance to live our lives. I want to blame him for that. Deep down, though, I know it wasn't his fault."

"Of course not," his nephew responded while sliding to stand in front of him in order to put both hands on his shoulders. "You're right. Our lives have been predetermined according to Kercher's religion and its god and goddess. We were not allowed to do much, yet you're still responsible for leading us forward. At least, unlike Verdic, we have each other."

Wesley let his arms fall to his sides before returning to their teacher to drape the blanket over the peaceful, gray face. After a moment, Hendal left his uncle and nephew alone.

*

The first month of heading the church began as a strange experience. Hendal and Wesley spent at least three days clearing out their old mentor's belongings, sorting through his writings, and moving Hendal into the priest's quarters. Although he missed the company, having a personal space to relax and think in private felt invigorating, and it inspired him to make additional changes to their routine. Once a week, he opened all the windows in the building and, along with his nephew, thoroughly cleaned the inside.

"I don't remember Verdic ever ordering us to dust and scrub so well," Wesley mentioned before he plopped down on a bench next to Hendal, who frowned at the memory of the previous priest.

"That's because he didn't care for much besides his duties as a holy man."

Wesley didn't comment. Soon after, he left for the kitchen and returned with two glasses of water. They enjoyed the peace for a while longer, allowing Hendal to consider what his nephew thought of their current situation and what he should do.

I'm in charge of how the church functions now. If I wanted to, I could introduce new ideas or traditions. Who would question me, aside from Wesley? He's technically my student anyway.

Despite his cynicism, the idea of abandoning the church's customs disturbed him. *No, I could never turn my back on what the people of Kercher consider sacred, even if I don't truly believe in Summa or Izina.*

"Do you think there's more we can do?" Hendal asked after scanning over the old yet somewhat brighter chapel.

His nephew gave him a sidelong glance. "What do you mean?"

Hendal couldn't help himself from running a hand through his thinning hair. He knew how Wesley felt about priesthood, how his nephew could embrace the writings and teachings, take them to heart, and discuss the lessons with the townsfolk whenever Hendal was busy. The young man at his side fit into the position and displayed more empathy and understanding than Verdic had.

"I guess I'm wondering is if there's anything else you can think of to improve this place. Could we encourage the townsfolk to join us here for moments of prayer? Can we find a way to help them see us as approachable instead of…of…"

"Instead of those who would verbally condemn them? Instead of speakers of the gods possessing some ability that makes us seem different than them?"

The accuracy of the guess startled Hendal, causing him to snap his head over to meet Wesley's understanding look.

"You forget I've known you my entire life," his nephew continued while raising his eyes to the church's ceiling. "I can tell what you're trying to do and agree our people should feel more welcome in our presence."

When Wesley stopped speaking, Hendal could tell the younger man began contemplating the request, so he pushed for more. "I won't judge you for new ideas. We're a team in this life. We might as well bounce our thoughts off each other. In fact, we'll probably be reigning ourselves in from getting too eccentric!"

His nephew chuckled and eased up enough to speak what was on his mind. To Hendal's amusement, the most daring suggestion involved creating a garden in the unused space behind their building. Neither of them could remember noticing life beneath the tall, wild grass filled with weed patches, and it seemed possible to do. Their other ideas branched off their current duties, such as re-categorizing the library and mending the worn or broken prayer books available by the entrance. They agreed to start the following morning since their conversation lasted until it became time to prepare supper.

*

Spring rolled over into summer, making the fall season quite pleasant. By that point, they accomplished their original goals and more. Wesley took a personal liking to the garden they established, even going so far as to use it as a space for outdoor worship. Plenty of the townsfolk would poke their heads around to see what was happening and accept his offer to pray together. Since the land proved less fertile than they expected, the two only successfully grew flowers during the first summer. Of course, Wesley expressed his optimism about continuing the following spring, and they savored the floral scent that found its way into the church.

While his nephew spent extra time in the garden, Hendal became invested in the library project. Seeing many loose papers gutted him because their bindings had been torn, poorly crafted, or worn down so the yellow pages crumbled between his fingers. He, and Wesley once winter showed itself, worked diligently to copy the writings onto fresh parchment, tie them together, and organize the completed pieces. At the end of the season, they burned the older papers at once while praying over the flames. To Hendal's amazement, several of the townsfolk who appeared here and there around the church and garden joined in. Wesley made sure to explain what took place afterward, then he learned their names and thanked them for participating in the process. Hendal kept smiling and greeted them when addressed, but for the most part, he remained behind his nephew.

That evening after lying in bed, he reflected on what took place and how the experience made him feel. It seemed as though he should be upset by Wesley's outgoing behavior because Hendal acted as the lone priest of Kercher. He saw no reason for his nephew to remember details, such as names and faces, greet the townsfolk in such a casual manner, or try to be liked.

Still, the negativity backfired immediately. He loved Wesley and would never shy away from how proud he was of the man his nephew had become. To criticize him for acting in an opposite manner as Verdic would be like admitting the former priest's methods should be tolerated, and Hendal could never do that. The more he considered what he believed a priest should stand for and what purpose they serve, the less he felt any sense of self.

Over the next few weeks, he stepped away from the church, often without announcing his departure to Wesley. Unlike when Verdic acted as the priest, Hendal had no qualms about moving through the town or allowing his nephew out as well. There were those who bowed or appeared shocked to catch them walking nearby, but more faces appeared friendly and gracious. Almost every time they ventured around, someone offered them a piece of fruit, baked goods, or spare change as a donation. At first, Hendal had his suspicion about the people hoping to bribe their priest for positive favor with Summa or Izina, so he would refuse in a polite manner; however, his efforts proved futile because those individuals became persistent, in a humble, kindly way.

"They didn't beg for acceptance, mercy, or forgiveness," he later shared with Wesley when his emotions grew complicated enough that he needed to vent. "I think they just wanted to offer those gifts to be nice. It doesn't make sense why they would do so when they spot us in town instead of stopping by to see us here."

His nephew laughed at his lack of understanding. "People can act out of the goodness in their hearts and souls because it helps them feel fulfilled. Isn't this what we preach about all the time?"

Hendal had mumbled his agreement yet did not fully comprehend the notion.

At the moment, plenty of people roamed about Kercher to bask in one of the first warm days of spring. He passed a trio of women around his age who smiled and greeted him. Although his heart fluttered upon catching their natural beauty, years of celibacy under his former teacher kept a wall between them. An older lady stopped him to chat, which turned into her complaining about her grandchildren spending too long away from the town. As he usually did in these instances, Hendal stayed quiet. In most cases, the person would request his opinion or a prayer to ease their minds and hearts, but the older woman sounded as if she just needed an ear to babble to.

Once that lengthy session ended and he wished her well, he moved to the empty fields beyond where he meditated until his legs grew stiff and evening approached. He and Wesley prepared supper when he returned, and his nephew questioned his whereabouts until Hendal refused to discuss what he had been doing. Every day after, he repeated this routine. The townsfolk came to expect him down the road, and his nephew became less dependent on him.

*

Eleven months after he began leading the church, he learned of the birth of Wesley's niece, the eldest brother's second child. The news didn't affect Hendal since he knew it would be at least a couple of years until they would be expected to raise the child, but Wesley acted distraught. His mother, the sister Hendal rarely spoke to, visited the church to announce the news with eyes red and swollen from weeping. The baby arrived too early and was underweight. Its skin turned a sickly, pale color, and it never cried, according to its mother. Based on the impression Hendal received after hearing this, they expected the child to die any day.

Despite the odds, Wesley would go to the family's home every morning to pray and ask for Summa and Izina's blessing. Hendal remained in the church until his nephew returned, then he left for his daily meditation. A sense of guilt hindered his otherwise emotionless reflection, though.

THE ANGEL'S DESCENT

I'm the priest here, not Wesley. He doesn't bear the responsibility to care for Kercher yet, so why does he insist on serving with more dedication than me? Could he actually care about the family he never got the chance to know? Does he wish for the child to live so he possesses a pupil to look after?

The next day, his thoughts expanded on those questions. *What will happen if the baby lives? It would be Wesley's duty to raise her, not mine. I've been spending more time away from the church so he has a chance to experience the lonely life of a priest and what one's tasks entail. Perhaps I went about this all wrong...*

That evening, Hendal sat with his nephew and shared his reasoning for being so distant.

"Wesley," he began after the lengthy explanation, "you understand I didn't want this life. When Verdic died, I felt too uncertain to abandon the church, and I would never leave you behind. So, I took up the position."

"Why have you abandoned your duties here then?" his nephew asked without placing any sort of blame.

Hendal swallowed around the lump in his throat. "I hoped you would experience this life for yourself. That way, you're justified should you wish to leave. If you're lonely or you hate it here and asked me to go, I would let you."

He couldn't stand to look at his nephew after Wesley's lips pressed together and the blue eyes watered, forcing him to stare down at his hands. Despite the stir of emotion, he spoke his remaining thoughts aloud in a gentler tone of voice.

"You are so unlike our teacher that my impression of a priest has changed. Where he was abusive and impatient, you're kindhearted and always willing to listen. Verdic would never hear anything having to do with another god's beliefs, or he would dismiss the writings I found containing blasphemous information. I've seen how you approach prayer with the townsfolk. You answer their questions after taking every detail into consideration and never shy away from what is new. You care about them, Wesley; that's the difference between us."

"Thank you, Hendal," he heard his nephew whisper.

For some reason, admitting his feelings lifted an unfamiliar weight from his shoulders. He tilted his head back and smiled at the dark ceiling. *Not only do I not understand his way of thinking, but I fear it is a process I simply can't comprehend. No matter how much work I do, I already set my mind on a life outside of the church. In my heart, I know I don't deserve this position.*

He took Wesley's closest hand in both of his and bowed his head as a warm energy filled his body. "Let us pray for the child," he ordered and dove straight into a chant asking the gods for healing.

*

Due to her daughter's weakened state, Wesley's sister didn't bring his niece to the church until the girl reached the age of four when she could act on her own, at least physically. Mentally, she spent more time learning words and behaviors and managing what she needed to in order to get by within her family. Her emotional state proved to be the worst hindrance, though. The child severely relied on her mother for everything and, at the mention of living somewhere new with two strangers, broke down in tears when Hendal and Wesley went to meet her. Although Hendal tried his best to coax the girl named Lyla into coming along, Wesley surprised him by arranging an agreement.

"If you visit me at the church every day, even for a minute, I won't make you live there unless you want to," he explained in a calm manner and without any trace of frustration or urgency.

Lyla nodded while her mother glanced at Hendal.

That's right. I'm the official representative of the church, he reminded himself and smiled as reassuringly as possible before adding a comment in support of the compromise.

As they left the home, Wesley lost his composure, blurted out an apology, and attempted to justify his words.

Hendal interrupted his nephew mid-sentence. "Every child is unique, and if you believe this is the best way for her to become accustomed to this life, then I trust your judgement."

"Doesn't this go against tradition?"

Hendal paused to consider his personal feelings on the matter, then he shrugged. "In some cases, traditions need to change for the times. How I see it, we're not going against any rules relating to Summa or

Izina. Updating our duties doesn't necessarily mean shunning the prayers or teachings. For example, you tend the garden space and invite others to join in the experience."

"I see. That sounds a lot like what Verdic used to say," Wesley mumbled just loud enough for Hendal to hear. They spent the rest of the walk contemplating this in silence.

The next morning, Lyla, accompanied by her mother, poked her head around the building's wall to where Hendal worked with Wesley to plant the bulbs and seeds from their garden last fall. Although he longed to become involved in kindling a relationship between the girl and his nephew, he allowed Wesley to act without his influence, which the man did regardless. They stayed for less than an hour to silently observe before taking their leave. The next day passed in an identical fashion, except Wesley convinced Lyla to bury the final bulb in the garden while he said a prayer over the space.

Every morning after remained similar. Lyla and her mother would stop by, the girl assisted with whatever project they were doing, the pair listened to the priests' chanting, then they left. Before long, Wesley's niece arrived at the church on her own and for growing periods of time. Hendal hardly spoke, but his nephew asked sincere questions to get the child to open up to them. He seemed patient, warm, and approachable without expecting Lyla to linger after every visit. Only when the two became fairly comfortable with one another did Hendal begin his treks outside of the building to meditate once more.

As the weeks turned into months and Lyla finally felt comfortable enough to accept her role as Wesley's apprentice by moving into the church, Hendal wondered about the world beyond Kercher again. He often sparked up conversations with messengers when they returned, using the excuse of offering a prayer of thanksgiving for their safe return. His few relatives delighted in the honor while Hendal learned about the cities to the south, those hidden in the woods, and the grand capital city. Just to keep the information coming, he would offer simple updates on Kercher and include bits and pieces of rumors about the angels, or rather the magically gifted beings from the mysterious place known as Yeluthia, before sending the messengers away. He figured no one ever questioned a priest when it came to religious intentions; no one except his younger self, then his nephew.

Once Wesley caught wind of what went on, he confronted Hendal at his desk in the library.

"I know what you're doing," his nephew began and stood frowning with arms crossed.

The years had been kinder to Wesley than Hendal. His chestnut hair trailed down his back in a neat braid while a strong jawline accentuated his stern expression. Not a wrinkle or blemish marred his fair skin either, though they were still in their thirties.

Meanwhile, Hendal already lost most of the thinning hair on top of his head and dealt with crow's feet. He tried not to think about those physical aspects as he pretended to read the papers in front of him.

"What are you talking about?" he asked, willing his voice to mirror innocence. On the inside, he had been dreading this conversation ever since he started sending the messengers out of Kercher. His nephew didn't speak again until Hendal raised his eyes.

"Lyla's mother stopped in to see her and mentioned you were giving the messengers news about Yeluthia. Why are you saying such things?"

Hendal licked his lips and contemplated an answer. It would be all too easy to avoid admitting the truth. Wesley would believe him if he claimed his meditating brought about a vision of the angels, especially if he acted passionate enough to defend the notion. Still, he could never forgive himself for lying to his nephew.

I spent days preparing for this moment, contemplating how to approach my decision. Even if I deviate from the reason, my actions and the outcome will probably be the same no matter how I respond.

"Come with me," Hendal ordered and rose from his seat. Together, they walked to the main chapel used for prayer and procured a bench in the front row.

"Do you remember why I make my daily route through town and leave you alone?"

The audible gulp before Wesley's reply showed his nephew became aware of what their talk was going to be about. "I do," came the quiet answer.

"You're not like me," Hendal started. "What I mean is, you're a better priest than I could ever be. That's because we both know my heart isn't in this. I never desired a life trapped in one place, forced into a position requiring me to believe in inexplicable deities. Actually, it's not so much Summa or Izina. I'm curious about the world. The more I hear from the messengers of our family, the more I long to learn what is out there. How many gods do the people pray to? What kinds of lives do they live?"

Wesley didn't speak during the following pause, though Hendal wished his nephew would.

"If I had a choice, I wouldn't have been a priest," he continued. "At least by sending the messengers, I'll hear their stories and enjoy what I can without leaving." With his explanation complete, he released a long sigh, leaned forward, and rubbed the back of his neck.

"Is there anything I can do for you, uncle?" Wesley asked.

Hendal clasped his hands together on his lap. Although he felt he shouldn't, he turned to glance over at his nephew, who stared with what he could only describe as incomprehension. *No, this is an issue I don't believe anyone in Kercher understands how to help with. A community rooted in tradition that involves appointed assignments should long to feel the freedom of making decisions regarding their lives. Still, no one expresses their disdain for Kercher's outdated positions, except for me. Maybe those who did are the ones who abandoned their homes for what's beyond the fields.*

Hendal wanted to tell Wesley this, to pour out his heart to the one person who would listen and not judge him for the way he felt; however, hope reflected in his nephew's pleading eyes. Not a hope for the new, though, but a wish for what had already been established. Silently, he begged Hendal to remain at the church.

After their brief discussion, which abruptly ended when Lyla entered the space to inquire about supper, the two dropped the subject.

*

Hendal continued his business despite a rising apprehension as he sensed some inexplicable force stirring. Soon, they learned about a sickness spreading in the northern cities, which did not bode well because of the approaching winter. The messengers refused to risk their lives, leaving him frustrated with their fearfulness.

Meanwhile, Wesley did his best to introduce subtle changes to their daily routine in an obvious attempt to make the life of a priest more tolerable. Dinner options rotated every week and often involved guests bringing their own, delicious offerings. It succeeded in cultivating more relationships during the usually basic meal, as well as require Lyla to interact with others in Kercher. His nephew also invited the townsfolk to prayer sessions or to join in chants. When that happened, they sometimes ended up with a large choir whose unified voice breathed life into the building.

If Hendal had not set his sights on life beyond the church, he might've been able to tolerate those changes and others they tried out. The most unavoidable one seemed to be Wesley's push for Lyla to spend more time with Hendal. Her mentor certainly influenced her behavior over the months; she always observed the world with wide, bright eyes and obeyed his requests. Despite that, she shared Hendal's sense of curiosity. Whenever the two sat alone, usually during his reading hours in the library, Lyla would ask several questions at once regarding a variety of topics in a gentle yet confident manner.

At first, he grew eager to converse. *If she is as interested in the world around us as I am, perhaps we do have something in common. Who knows what we could discuss and how I can help her cope with what I feel*, he originally thought.

Over the cold, snowy weeks, his excitement subsided. Lyla liked to hear information but was either not at the age or did not possess the ability to consider what she wanted for herself. She couldn't understand Hendal, and that fact put him in a sour mood. He soon gave up on replying to her questions with such encouragement.

In the months following spring, the sickness plaguing the rest of the country subsided enough for the messengers of Kercher to obey Hendal again. Life returned to normal while they were away, but each returned wearing the same, exhausted expression and announced a somber message. The king of Asteom fell ill during the winter and died, along with the palace's high priest and hundreds of citizens in the capital alone. A mourning ceremony and funeral took place before the next king had been crowned.

Hendal didn't recognize much from what they described about the events or people, yet the updates brought him a sense of comfort. Outside of Kercher, life continued on despite the circumstances.

The evening after hearing the news, while sleep evaded him, he thought about the piece of information that had piqued his interest the most. *The palace's priest is gone. They must have another to replace him, as we do here, but would they be willing to let me study there? Would one's death allow me to take a student's spot? As much as I hate the idea of spending my life as a priest, it would allow me to learn more than I ever could here.*

Even in his dreams, the idea persisted until he acted upon it. He called forth the eldest of the messengers, who happened to be Wesley's younger brother, and gave him a letter with the church's seal.

"Bring this to the palace and request it be presented before their new priest," Hendal instructed while showing what composure he could muster. "Tell them the priest of Summa and Izina in Kercher wishes to aid them during a time of loss, as instructed by the god and goddess."

The man's eyes lit up from some unspoken emotion, then he nodded and hurried off with the letter. Nearly a month later, the man returned with a notice.

Priest Hendal of Kercher,

Your letter has not been read by blind eyes nor heard by deaf ears for now is the time to start anew. A message from your gods cannot go unnoticed after the losses Asteom has faced, especially with many taking advantage of the uncertainty following those of us who were recently appointed. Because of this, I request your presence. It is imperative we find a high priest worthy of acting as a member of my council, and your letter reflects this. Show the king's seal to the guards at the palace's front gate. You shall be escorted to the proper person. Best wishes for a safe journey to Verona.

King Hernan

Hendal brushed a thumb over the golden wax stamped into a crest at the bottom of the page. He became too stunned to process the request and dismissed the curious messenger.

For three days, he spent every waking hour alone to reread the words and consider what to do. As the time passed, his initial shock faded to reveal apprehension, fear, and regret for his poor decision. To proclaim the gods spoke to him would surely backfire when those in the capital realized how clueless he was about the rest of the country. Still, Hendal remembered no one would believe he lied unless he acted suspicious.

No deity bothered to assist me throughout my life so far. I already renounced their existence, but no one knows that, not even Wesley, he reflected as his lips twisted into a frown. A minute later, they curved upward to form a wicked smile. *This is my chance to leave Kercher! Even if it only lasts for a few weeks, I must try to convince them to allow me to live among their people.*

For the rest of the day, he repeated the thought often and soon grew excited for the change. Wesley caught on to Hendal's secrecy after his brother's return, so Hendal showed him the message and explained the situation in order to avoid any arguments later on.

"My meddling led to an opportunity to help the people in the palace," he finished, letting his passion slip into his tone of voice. "I've been so selfish by sending the messengers. Perhaps this is a chance to atone. I'll never make up for my mistakes until I go there."

To his amazement, Wesley agreed, though with no shortage of mixed emotions spread across his face.

The following morning, Hendal prepared to depart. He summoned his younger nephew, informed the messenger of the king's request, and assigned the man as an escort. As soon as they were both ready, they left the church. Many lingering eyes forced Hendal to hold his head high and smile despite his nerves. He didn't expect to see

THE ANGEL'S DESCENT

Wesley that day since his nephew had not appeared throughout the morning; however, he spotted a figure wearing the gray robe against an overcast sky on the road farther ahead outside of town. Lyla stood at his side, though she looked clueless about what was taking place.

"Wesley," Hendal began before realizing he hadn't planned how to say goodbye.

His escort continued on to give them some privacy, and Lyla stepped forward.

"Have a safe journey, Priest Hendal," she offered in a rehearsed manner, bowed, then glanced at her teacher, who dipped his chin. At his dismissal, the girl left them to jog into town. Hendal watched her go while his nephew spoke.

"She really does admire you. I believe she noticed your interest in learning and tries to absorb as much as she can."

"I couldn't think of a better teacher than you for such an innocent child," Hendal admitted. He turned his back to the buildings while Wesley watched him with watery eyes. "I guess this is goodbye."

"You don't have to leave."

Hendal looked over to see the man, the *new* priest, squeezing his eyes shut and balling his hands into fists.

"Wesley…"

"You're in charge, and there's nothing else… We *need* you here! I can't…"

This time, Hendal's eyes welled with tears he refused to shed lest he give up his opportunity for a free life. He stepped closer to his nephew, laid both hands on the sturdy shoulders, and spoke his truth in a wavering voice. "You don't need me. For years now, you never needed me. Sure, you *want* me to stay, yet who would that truly benefit? I envy your commitment to this life; you're destined for it, and I can't imagine you doing anything else. Not only do you care about the people of Kercher, but you also bring about positive change for the present and the future of this town. You and Lyla will continue to do good here."

The tears Wesley repressed slid down his cheeks, though he didn't make a sound until after Hendal spoke. "Please…"

The whispered plea tugged at Hendal's heart. He inhaled through his nostrils and pulled his nephew in for a final embrace.

Although he kept still, Wesley's shoulders trembled as he tightened his hold. They remained shaking when Hendal broke away to walk toward the awaiting messenger without another glance at what he left behind.

*

Hendal had some idea of what the capital city would be like, though he never expected to pass through it on their way to the palace. Even with a sickness that killed hundreds, according to the messengers, people crowded the streets of Verona, moving in all directions on their own business. As daunting as it became, he forced himself to act as though he belonged while keeping close to his nephew, who led them straight to the tallest stone structure.

Once they hailed a guard and showed the letter's seal, the soldier guided the pair up a set of stairs and around the building's winding halls until a metal door appeared. Then, the stranger dismissed Hendal's escort before knocking. The idea of being in a tight, unknown space petrified him, but he pretended not to mind when his nephew thanked the man before disappearing down a different passage. Someone shouted for them to enter, yet he went alone while the guard remained at attention in the hallway.

The inside of the room elevated his discomfort. A circular table with several chairs rested at the center, and the only sources of light came from lamps hanging along the stone walls. To his right, a portion of the flooring had been raised so a throne could be positioned above everyone else.

"Priest Hendal, I presume?" someone asked to get his attention.

Hendal cleared his throat and stepped farther in. He took a moment to study each person's face as five sat at the table and one on the throne. He addressed the latter after swallowing his nerves. "I am Hendal, priest of the church in Kercher. His Highness summoned me, so I came as soon as I could."

"I believe we sent for you over a week ago with the expectation you would arrive sooner," the young man wearing the gold band on his head responded without allowing a pause. His attitude seemed to consist of annoyance, impatience, and an odd amusement.

The response startled Hendal, causing his mind to go blank. "F-Forgive me," he managed to bumble while keeping eye contact with the new king. "I wasn't prepared for your request." Only after he spoke did Hendal consider he might be disrespecting the group by making such casual remarks and glances.

In any case, the young man on the throne scratched his chin, which already displayed a full beard, and addressed those at the table. "We can pick up our previous discussion another time. Califer, would you explain to Priest Hendal what it is we are doing in regard to the high priest's position?"

Hendal watched as one of the older men rose in a slow, careful manner. His white hair had been trimmed to his shoulders, and he wore a similarly colored robe embroidered with golden thread only visible when he moved due to the lighting.

"Allow me to introduce myself," the man began with a hoarse voice. "I am Califer, the master mage of the palace. Our previous high priest named Ronaldo came from Clearwater and served the kingdom for forty-seven years before his death this past winter. We invited you, along with several other religious men and women who wish to take up the position, in the hope of finding someone worthy to fulfill this role, join our council, and assist King Hernan."

After each word the mage spoke, Hendal felt himself starting to sweat more. *This isn't what I expected*, he thought while fighting the urge to wipe his forehead with his sleeve. *They didn't already have a replacement chosen? Isn't their faith based on a religion requiring more than one leader of the church? Did he say other priests are here too? I'm not-*

"Well? Is this a job you believe you can handle?" the king asked, interrupting the mental concerns.

Hendal closed his eyes for a moment to consider what he planned to do, yet an answer poured forth without him fully understanding the offer. "I would be honored to receive an opportunity to serve in the palace and learn more about Asteom's religious cultures."

When he opened his eyes and bowed, he noticed the people at the table glancing at one another while the young man on the throne tilted his head a bit with what Hendal assumed was interest.

After the panic-inducing encounter, a servant led him to an empty bedroom and left him there. Just when he began to wonder about meals, another person entered bearing a tray of miniature, savory pies, fruits, roasted root vegetables, and a sweet pastry he never tasted before. Hendal cleared the platter, then he fell into a deep, comfortable sleep.

The next morning, a servant presented an invitation to tour the palace with the other candidates. No one spoke the entire time except for their guide, though another man around his age and a woman at least a decade older smiled warmly whenever he caught them staring. Otherwise, they kept to themselves. In the afternoon, the group reunited in the same meeting space Hendal had first gone to the day before. There, a guard stationed by the door instructed them to sit around the table, and they found Califer waiting inside.

The mage's presence made Hendal feel odd, mainly because he wasn't familiar with magic wielders since none lived in Kercher or visited, as far as he knew. Such a foreign topic intrigued and terrified him considering how dangerous such power could be in the wrong hands. Not only did he worry about that, but many questions surrounded the spellcasters. One thought related to the angels in their legendary city in the clouds and how they were said to use a different type of magic from a human's. He never considered the subject, yet he believed it would be necessary to understand should he remain in the capital city.

"It's a pleasure to see you all again," the older man started while offering a slight smile. "Our kingdom is fortunate to possess so many leaders of various religions to guide people to more fulfilling lives. Each one of you comes from a sect separate from those seated around this table. The representation from across the country is marvelous! With that in mind, I would like to take the time to inform you of what being the high priest entails."

Hendal expected a list similar to his duties in Kercher; this priest or priestess would need to participate in ceremonies, daily prayers and chants, visit the sick or whoever requests their blessing, and such tasks. In that case, he had little to worry about aside from studying their main deities and rituals. Instead, the description Califer gave wound up shocking him.

"The high priest was established as a figure of faith to stand beside the royal family because Asteom doesn't follow a single religion. Citizens are able to choose what gods or goddesses to worship, so the country is diverse. The high priest must be a representative of the churches across Asteom, no matter the religion."

During the pause after his statement, Hendal sat stunned, though not against the notion. The idea of requiring everyone to serve the same deities just because of the royal family's beliefs would not be tolerated by the established churches. Whoever suggested the palace host a single person to speak on behalf of both the rulers and the faithful had been taking precautions. Essentially, they avoid the kings and queens favoring one religion over another when making decisions, donations, or judgements and keep the leaders grounded.

Many in the room did not comprehend this, or they thought it to be unacceptable. The man to Hendal's right jumped to his feet, slammed his hands on the table, and announced his view.

"A priest's duties are to his church! If the king does not follow a religion, why is it necessary aside from keeping an image with the people? That's blasphemy!"

"I agree," the woman who smiled at Hendal during their tour added. She had been frowning ever since they entered the space. "You misuse the title so it seems as though the position pleases a religion when it just serves your needs."

"Not necessarily," Califer replied, surprising Hendal with his calm demeanor. Based on his behavior, the man had prepared for backlash against the explanation. "I cannot speak for the previously appointed high priests, so I shouldn't assume the motivations behind their decision to accept the position. Perhaps it is better to say this in plain terms. We're seeking someone who can keep their minds and hearts away from one particular religion or church in order to understand the rest spanning across the country. Whatever you choose to personally follow is your business, but the high priest must not be biased lest they betray the peace and freedom of religious beliefs established in Asteom. It is their sacrifice in order to assist the king. We also require the high priest to be an active member of the king's council because their knowledge could contribute to various efforts. Is that clear?"

A couple of people at the table grunted a response while the rest remained silent, so the mage dismissed them for the evening meal. When the candidates reconvened the next morning, only Hendal and three other men were present.

*

For four days, the remaining priests met with numerous people, both in groups and individually. He couldn't remember most of their names or faces and often wondered why he bothered to leave the safety of Kercher. The questions he faced focused more on his daily routine and how he felt about taking on extra responsibilities. Hendal made sure to give honest answers, even admitting his hope to learn about the world and how he thought the capital city would be the best way to serve the country. Only once did he mention something he later regretted, which had been when the master mage of all people asked about a city to the south and their religious affiliations. Hendal didn't understand the topic or what they wanted from him. Ultimately, he shared that he would not return to Kercher because of his interest in the world outside of the town, whether they chose him for the position or not.

Two more days passed, and he didn't hear from anyone. A knock at his door in the evening seemed to signal an update, especially when he saw Califer enter. The man greeted him with a wider smile than normal before cutting right to business. A decision had been reached, and the council selected Hendal as the new high priest.

He stopped listening once the realization dawned on him.

Califer noticed, shut the door for some privacy, and ushered him to the bed where they both dropped down. "I must admit, I expected this reaction," the man added and chuckled.

Meanwhile, Hendal instinctively brushed his hair down. "I can't believe it," he mumbled.

THE ANGEL'S DESCENT

"This is why I come to you now, before the announcement is made by King Hernan in the meeting tomorrow morning. After that, preparations will be arranged for your appointment."

Hendal kept silent.

"I also wish to explain the reasoning behind our decision," Califer went on. "You see, our two main qualifications involved someone familiar with the religious life who could also willingly set aside their own faith in order to study others for the purposes I've mentioned. Those not a part of any system of belief would never be able to understand its necessity regarding the royal family. On the opposite side, like many religious leaders, if the person is too stubborn to accept different faith systems in Asteom and why it is permissible, they will no doubt show preference to their community of followers."

"Yes, I figured," Hendal commented with a little more energy.

"Exactly! You comprehend the entire assignment and can leave Kercher in your nephew's care. Also, you expressed your interest in learning about our country."

So, my honesty worked in my favor. What luck!

"Out of all the priests and priestesses invited to the palace, you showed the least bias for your own gods too," Califer added, reminding Hendal of the outcome. "I want to prepare you for the council's presentation. Should you accept, we'll begin the transition immediately."

The two talked for a bit longer on the matter before the mage exited. Although Hendal contemplated what this would mean, he knew the offer was one he shouldn't refuse.

I spent my whole life trapped in Kercher as their priest, desiring nothing more than to escape. If acting as the king's servant means access to freedom, I think I can manage. Besides, I won't need to uphold my previous responsibilities and traditions anymore. This might be better for me after all.

1

In the dimming light surrounding the training ground, Byron observed the groups of three or four soldiers and mages working together in an exercise he devised before his reassignment but didn't perfect until recently. The rules involved each team attempting to capture a colored cloth dangling from an opponent's belt. Only a single member carried the rag, but the entire group would be eliminated if another team stole it. Those remaining on the field were the victors, reflecting how their strategy proved to be the best for that particular day. He permitted mages to use magic without the intent to seriously harm their opponents, and soldiers chose between a shield or wooden sword.

The original purpose of the exercise had been to spark their critical thinking, creativity, and defensive skills when facing multiple enemies. As his eyes glazed over the troops, Byron analyzed their positioning and tactics while keeping his mind as clear as possible. With the level of enthusiasm for a new training activity, at least two dozen groups formed throughout the afternoon. Byron alone contained any stray spells, declared fair or rough actions that could penalize a team, and ruled when a cloth had been captured. At the moment, half of the participants remained.

I don't know why I didn't start this sooner, Byron thought with a slight smile when he noticed a team creeping up on another, preoccupied one. *Seeing the different approaches has been enlightening for more than just myself. Most opted to order a mage to hold the cloth while surrounding them. Others separated and regrouped multiple times, giving it to the most skilled among them who could dodge or shield their body. Every time we do this, I learn something.*

Byron couldn't help but wince when a member of the sneaking group snatched the distracted trio's cloth without the target realizing it. "Meghan, Nala, and Uylan, your group has been compromised," he announced, to their surprise.

Although the three women appeared displeased, they accepted the loss and jogged over to where the eliminated participants stood as an audience. That proved to be all the excitement for a while.

The first time we experimented with this activity, it seemed to go by much faster. I suppose everyone understands how risky it is to act on impulse when an opponent has a variety of options.

"Master Byron."

A familiar, expressionless voice addressed him from behind, and he repressed the urge to roll his eyes while glancing over to see General Tont staring at him. As usual, the man's face revealed nothing more than a bored look. His eyes had glossed over to show his master still held control over his mind and body.

Byron knew what the general's presence meant and clapped his hands together to catch the soldiers' and mages' attention. "That's all we have time for today."

Many participants released a unified groan to show their dissatisfaction, though more, especially those on the sidelines, sounded relieved to be dismissed for dinner. They broke apart to chat and hurry inside, bowing or saluting Byron when they passed.

Again, his lips curved upward when most of what he heard were positive comments or constructive criticism. *It's been a few days since the council ordered me to supervise the training ground, yet I feel the troops' bonds strengthening. Perhaps we're closer to becoming connected like General Tio's base than I thought. Would he laugh at me for comparing the two?*

When he remembered who waited for him, Byron turned and followed the general inside the palace. Unfortunately, his step forward became overshadowed by the current, powerful enemies keeping him and his companions from doing much.

Even then, he kept the crumpled notice from Aaron, or rather Hendal, that had been sent to him a few days ago in his pocket.

Master Byron,

Due to your failure to capture and reprimand your former student, who possesses a threat to the safety of the kingdom, you are hereby dismissed from the king's council, per his request. Your reassignment has been taken care of, and General Tont will supervise your duties until further notice.

His hands clenched into fists at the reminder, which proved mild compared to his original, infuriated reaction. *Hendal's keeping Emilea under house arrest, leaving me to handle the mages' training with Tont, who's coincidentally preoccupied with Nim-Vala.*

The general didn't speak a word as he led the way to the private dining hall where Hendal required them to eat meals with King Aaron, General Casner, Grace, and the nobility. Byron's original concern had been hostility when they gathered together; however, with most of the people under the demon's influence, the whole affair seemed bleak.

The lone benefit became seeing Grace's recovery. Her paled complexion, thinner figure, and overall projection of gloom led many to doubt she left the palace of her own volition, yet she needed to play the part in order to protect herself and those under the demon's control. He caught her eyes light up from where she sat next to Hendal when he entered, though the high priest loomed over her like a shadow.

{*How did the training exercise go today?*}

He ignored the weary strain in her inner voice and smiled from across the room. *All is well, except there's less excitement and action as they grow more cunning.*

Tont moved straight to his seat beside Aaron, so Byron took the chair two seats from his right. The one in between remained empty for Marcus. The assistant general didn't stay in the palace anymore, claiming his mother requested his assistance with their family's business. The real reason stemmed from Byron's cautious nature.

THE ANGEL'S DESCENT

As soon as he suggested spying on his father or Aaron, I knew it would be too dangerous to keep him involved here. I'm just thankful he listened to my advice and is staying far away from Hendal. When the time comes, we'll need whatever help we can get.

The nobility's gossiping filled the hall with enough noise to help settle his nerves, allowing his mind to wander. *It's been six days since the ball. Hendal took advantage of our separation to make sure we remain away from one another. Emilea and her children are under watch with Aimes, Lady Katrina is still housing Marcy, Marcus is in Verona until I signal for him, and Clearshot traveled north in General Casner's company to scout for the Nim-Valan troops. Grace has been safe because she's out of the way, but at least we're able to keep in contact without Hendal's meddling. That leaves Will, who I spoke to during his training. I fear if we start acting suspicious or meet in secret, someone will catch on and silence us before I get a chance to plan accordingly.*

As if sensing his train of thought, the young Yeluthian's presence brushed against his mind, a sensation he was becoming more accustomed to every time they conversed. *How are you feeling, Grace?*

Their connection wavered a bit before she answered in the same, weary manner.

{I am better, though still afraid. My goddess gift is not as strong as it once was.}

So many times, she admitted her fear to Byron. When he discovered her alone and drugged but free from Hendal's clutches, she found comfort and protection with him. Everyone had, though he could supervise her light magic's progress and Will's combat work directly because of his assignment. Although he tried not to, he couldn't stop himself from recalling the instances after the ball when his companions begged him for a new strategy.

I understand it's difficult to relax, but just be patient a while longer. In time, we'll have another opportunity to rescue those who need us.

If that had been the first time Byron said those words to Grace, she probably would start protesting his decision; however, he felt her presence withdraw and chanced a glance over to her side of the table. A sense of pity and guilt rose while her eyes dropped to her untouched plate, and he wished he could suggest a better option.

They knew a second move against Hendal, the demon, or the hidden, rogue angels would hurt their limited group if they acted too soon. Not only did the high priest threaten the king, General Tont, and others under his control, but trouble in Verona could hinder the proposed alliance from Nim-Vala.

The last problem we need now is a war with the northern country when our leaders aren't truly available. It'd be foolish and selfish to risk it by causing an uproar in the palace. I doubt Hendal studied the art of war, so he also wouldn't ruin the chance to strengthen our kingdom. We should recover, regroup, and strike when the odds are in our favor.

As the remains of dinner were cleared for dessert, Byron inhaled slowly and mentally prepared to wait until that time arrived.

***

The forest outside Verona buzzed at a natural pace, filling the wooded area with the wildlife's chirps and calls. Despite the noise, the only thing annoying Coura happened to be what sunlight beamed down on her from where she had crashed through the canopy. She tried to ease the brightness blinding her vision by turning away, which was a mistake she made each time it peeked through. A surge of sharp pain stiffened her spine and forced her next breath to release in a hiss. While she steadied herself, she noticed her hands trembling and willed them to stop with the last shred of her self-control.

Her situation took a horrible, unexpected turn after she flew into the palace. When she could reflect on the memories, she replayed each encounter and movement over until her head pounded from the strain.

Thankfully, her mind worked better than her body. The fall broke bones, bending and twisting her limbs and wings in the air and only stopping when she slammed into the unforgiving ground. The results she conjured of what could happen if she released the spell on her wings in their condition terrified Coura, so they remained in a misshapen mass beneath her. Soirée's power started the healing process, but another, unknown force seemed to keep it at bay. She begged for it to let the demonic energy tend to her injuries, yet, for some reason she couldn't explain, she trusted the warm force that had been present ever since she escaped the palace.

The sun continued moving west, passing across the hole, and the canopy blocked its rays. A coolness swept over Coura, causing her entire body to shiver. For a while, she stared upward without a thought since they weren't able to develop into any worthwhile ideas.

I can't...stay here... I'll die if...I don't move...

The notion returned more than once during the following hours, though it sparked no motivation to seek help. When she considered her next, potential steps, her friends' possible situations, and what took place in the palace, a surge of emotion rose to bring her close to tears.

I'm too weak... Maybe I should just...stay here until I...

A sound within the regular noise not naturally heard in the woods drew Coura's attention. She strained her ears to listen, and this time she let the tears in her eyes fall when she recognized the distant sound of voices. Their soft, high-pitched quality seemed similar to a child's, and she considered if she began hallucinating.

Even as she wondered, she moved her mouth to call out only to find her throat dry and voice gone. The abnormal noise faded until she couldn't tell if the owners still lingered in the area or if the forest played with her mind. Still, the thought of being alone once more when an opportunity for aid presented itself forced Coura into action.

Using what dwindling strength remained in her aching limbs, she felt for the ground beneath her wings and pushed her upper body away. The spots where the frail pinions tucked under her legs and feet responded to the movement with furious shots of pain. Gradually, she shifted into a sitting position. Next, she pressed her wings to her back as tightly as possible in order to scramble around easier; that created the worst discomfort. Breathing came in short gasps as she grabbed onto the nearest tree trunk to pull herself up to stand. A grunt of frustration and agony escaped, and her legs trembled from the lack of use, but she made it.

Despite the need to hurry after the voices, Coura spent precious time catching her breath as she hugged the trunk until a tickle along her forearm had her staring at the source. A ladybug crawled down to her hand while avoiding the bruise-like markings before flying away.

Keep going, she ordered within her empty mind.

One wobbly step became two while her arms clung from one tree to another, and her nails dug into the tough bark. The aching throughout her body grew numb before a rush of demonic energy swept over every part of her. In response, the second, warm presence cut across her veins to halt the start of the healing spell once again. The sensation prompted a tightness in her chest, making her cough and taste blood.

If my body isn't recovering on its own, then these injuries have been worsening for days. My only chance is to find whoever wandered around here and hope they can help.

The distance stretched from where she started, so the mess was soon left behind. Unfortunately, the childlike voices didn't return to guide her.

Coura became preoccupied with staying on her feet and progressing forward to the point where everything outside of her direct line of vision blurred. Her uncontrollable panting burned her throat, yet nothing distracted her more than the struggle in her center. Both the demonic energy and additional presence rolled around, extending and recoiling at various moments in some sort of argument; she had never experienced anything like the clashing powers.

All of a sudden, a root above the grass hooked her outstretched foot, sending her face-first into the ground before she knew what happened. The world darkened as her nose and head throbbed, and her exhausted, hurt body refused to be pushed through more. She relaxed on the forest floor, letting out weak groans until she passed out.

***

Emilea kept a close eye on her children while they jogged ahead along a dirt path just north of their home. Behind her, one of their guards hid in the shadows of the surrounding trees, and at her side stood Aimes. She swallowed around the lump in her throat and yelled.

THE ANGEL'S DESCENT

"Mace! Lexie! It's time to head back!"

Against her better judgement, she glanced to the shaded man in the crimson uniform. His hollow eyes remained glued her, noting every movement, and she faced forward. Aimes studied her too with concern etched into his wrinkled features.

Nearly a week went by since she last spoke to her husband or Byron because the two had been forced to stay in the palace while a pair of soldiers escorted her home to resume her position as Hendal's pawn. The high priest's inhumane behavior after the ball and how easily he threatened anyone under his influence rattled her. She hadn't felt comfortable informing Aimes of what took place for three days and didn't allow him to travel to Verona, not that he seemed inclined to do so. The older man's decision became a blessing, though. He understood her fear and preoccupied himself with watching out for her and the children.

It's obvious we're in no position to stand against a demon's power. At least, I'm not. Hendal never commented on how I assisted Byron. His guards just ushered me home, like the first time, and patrol during the day.

Both of the men who observed her searched for rebellious intent, yet Aimes went unnoticed. The soldiers lingered outside her home during the day to monitor the area, then they disappeared toward the capital at dusk. Where they slept and when they ate, she didn't know, but they returned to their duty when the sun rose.

Emilea would have already submitted to Hendal's orders and acted obedient in order to keep her family safe, except Coura was still missing. The younger mage's familiar energy stemmed from somewhere nearby and continued emanating ever since Emilea's return.

Byron's plan included her retreat to my home if the situation grew too dangerous, which it no doubt became. So, she should have been here or met up with Aimes. The energy I sense isn't quite right either...

Hurried footsteps approached from farther ahead, and she moved to meet her children. To her relief, the guard seemed willing to give her some breathing room. With Mace and Lexie's lives at less of a risk, she trusted them to explore during their morning and afternoon strolls. The two could also pick up Coura's power and agreed to search for her without attracting any attention.

"Mother," came her son's voice as he emerged first to meet her before leaning forward with his hands on his knees to catch his breath.

"Where's your sister?" she asked a bit impatiently. When he glanced up, Emilea noticed his concerned expression.

"Lexie tripped and hurt her ankle up the trail."

While her son pointed behind him, she bit her lip. *Lexie should be able to take care of a minor sprain, or Mace could support her. Is it worse than that?*

Aimes moved to Emilea's side and shot her a knowing look. "I'll wait with the boy while you help Lexie," he offered.

She expressed her gratitude and nudged Mace toward the older man. As she hoped, the guard in the shadows stayed where he was with a blank expression as Emilea held herself to a walk. Soon, she moved beyond his line of sight.

"Lexie," she shouted and slowed when she still couldn't see her daughter.

"Over here!"

Emilea froze at the worried cry off to her right within the brush. Once she realized how tense the energy around her felt, her eyes went wide. *Coura? Did the children really find her? This power is definitely strange enough to come from her.*

It took precious time to maneuver around the overgrown bushes and branches clinging to her dress, yet she became more certain of her destination. Her thoughts were cut short once she made out Lexie kneeling in front of a silhouette on the ground.

Her daughter spotted her then and reached out, displaying the tears streaming down her face. "Mother!"

"What happened?" Emilea inquired as she continued forward.

The injured, black wings revealed the figure's identity. Both ends bent backward at an awkward angle, several spots had feathers broken or missing, and a handful of arrows were still embedded in them. When she knelt and touched one of the wings, it didn't move.

Why hasn't she dismissed the spell?

THE ANGEL'S DESCENT

Emilea mumbled Coura's name before examining the body. What she could see and touch were not nearly as heartbreaking as what she sensed with her magic. Meanwhile, Lexie fidgeted at her side.

"Can't you heal her?"

"It would take too much time to do something worthwhile if I start now," she explained and remembered the guards. "Her left arm and right foot broke in multiple places, along with her wings. It will be impossible to move her unless I can fix them. I'm not sure why her wings haven't disappeared, but that's not a positive sign. Her energy is already trying to heal the internal injuries, though, so we should return another time."

Lexie began to whine until one of Emilea's displeased looks hushed further protesting.

"I don't like leaving her here either," she reassured her daughter while rising and offering a hand. "We just need to believe in her will to live."

Together, they prepared to trek back to the trail, but not before Lexie spoke over her shoulder.

"Don't worry. We'll help as soon as we can!"

*

Emilea always found it difficult to lie to her children, but she refused to put them at risk even more than she already did. Aimes supported her caution after mentioning the possibility of the guards watching at night from a different location. She served dinner around sundown, and Mace and Lexie became too preoccupied with saving Coura to notice the sleeping potion mixed into their bowls of stew. Emilea tucked the two in early, promised to organize a rescue in the morning, then initiated her own plan. Aimes waited at the bottom of the stairs with his travel cloak wrapped around his shoulders and a lamp in one hand.

"Ready?" she asked.

The older man nodded and turned to head outside. "Don't you dare think of leaving until I return," he warned.

Emilea agreed, so he snuck outside. Throughout the evening, Aimes volunteered to wander around the home's perimeter in order to keep an eye on their guards. If Hendal could really communicate with the soldiers like he claimed, he would learn if she left and give the command to capture or kill her children.

She forced her beating heart to steady despite the nightmare her imagination conjured. *I need to calm down. Aimes saw them walking on the road toward Verona at sundown, so he should be able to follow them. I'll be safe to work on Coura then.*

Their one concern had been that Hendal or his companions would sense the demonic energy.

"If they didn't act before, what would prompt them to do so now?" Aimes had wondered earlier in the day. "When the creature attacked on your property, wouldn't the high priest, demon, or their lackeys try to eliminate the threat if they sensed magic being used? That right there makes me think they can't from this far away, especially since you mentioned Coura's power has been noticeable ever since you returned."

Emilea agreed and commended his ability to assess the situation.

An hour flew by before she heard a light knock on the front door. Aimes opened it a crack as she rose from her favorite armchair, then he gestured for her to join him.

"Those men went straight on to Verona, even after I showed myself. I'm guessing their minds are set on returning to their master or resting someplace. Of course, I didn't expect to follow them all the way into the city, but we're alone tonight."

When he limped toward the path leading north, she hesitated to go and called his name.

"You can wait here to rest if you need to. I won't force you to accompany me."

Indeed, he breathed heavier from the stroll and favored his right side, but he let out a dismissive huff, puffed his chest, and held his chin high. "Don't you worry about me! If I can't keep up, I'll catch you eventually. What's more important, you can't carry her back here on your own. In fact, why don't you run on ahead and start the healing. Time is precious tonight, unless you can wait until tomorrow."

Aimes would protest if she suggested leaving Coura in her condition and knew Emilea would too if their roles were reversed. After offering a nod, she jogged along the path with enough attentiveness to avoid tripping over herself while focusing solely on the demonic energy lurking deeper in the woods.

2

Nim-Vala proved to be a foreign land to most of Asteom's citizens, and many cowered in the face of the unknown future. Grace didn't allow her hopes to rise too high regarding the northern country as news returned from one of General Tont's messengers. It had been two weeks since word last reached Verona about their delay the evening of the eventful ball, which concerned her and others in the palace. Their general would continue to lead a reduced company of two hundred soldiers across the border to discuss a potential alliance. Now that General Casner, the assistant general, and Asteom soldiers joined them for the remainder of the journey, no one would question their intentions.

Aaron announced the Nim-Valans' anticipated arrival to those present in the dining hall during the evening meal. Every day after, she looked for some spark of emotion from Byron, an answer to her prayers so they would fight for Aaron's freedom and ensure a treaty under the real king; however, her optimism decreased when he avoided the questions in favor of inquiring about her physical and mental health.

When approaching him seemed to fail, Grace reached out to Will. He didn't even try to hide his fear through their thought-driven conversation. Her friend wanted to assist and supported her enthusiasm, yet he claimed they should trust Byron to know when the time was right to strike.

THE ANGEL'S DESCENT

{*Until then, I suggest you practice your magic. Let's hone our skills so we can do something worthwhile when we're needed. Does that sound fair, Grace?*}

She pulled her mind away in frustration without answering.

What would Coura do? Grace wondered as she contemplated who else she could trust to discuss such a risky subject. The outdoor hallway on the third floor remained mostly empty while she stared out over the training ground below. The humans sparred with one another, otherwise the world sounded peaceful.

Coura, where are you?

The desperate call echoed in her mind, signaling a lack of response. Three more times, she stretched her mind to grasp for any presence similar to her friend's, but she ended up sweeping over several strangers. Nothing important stuck out enough to push her to pry, so she gave up.

The following morning, the palace buzzed with news about the Nim-Valan army's entrance into the city. Just as they had done for Grace's introduction, the servants cleaned and polished the grand hall while the cooks busied themselves and their assistants with preparations for a feast. Every available mage and soldier hung decorations in Verona, spread out the lengthy crimson carpet cutting through the hall toward the grand staircase, and assisted friends and relatives in the city. Around noon, everyone hurried to dress in their formal attire before assuming their positions at the entrance.

Grace felt too weary to do more than don her pearl-colored gown, pin her blonde hair into a neat bun, and decorate her face. Once she finished, she sat on the edge of her bed until a knock at the door startled her enough to jump.

"Just a moment," she called. After peeking into her vanity mirror one last time, she opened the door to see the high priest. A handful of guards and Aaron stood behind while staring ahead with blank expressions. No matter how hard she tried to ignore the past, seeing Hendal's crooked smile and being close to him caused her arms and legs to tremble.

"Good afternoon, Lady Grace!" He feigned his cheeriness and bowed. "His Highness and I figured it would be proper for you to enter alongside us when the guests arrive. I don't believe the Nim-Valans have seen a Yeluthian before."

He waited for a response, but she refused to reply.

The man shrugged and began strolling down the hallway. She stepped out, closed the door, and followed as Aaron trailed on her heels. Again, she attempted to reach her mind toward him, yet the demonic presence shoved her away.

Aaron?

He ignored the thought, and the invisible force blocked her a second later. The sensation didn't hurt, but it continued to make her worry.

*

Hundreds of people filled the grand hall to the brim and conspicuously glanced toward the main gate. Aaron stood in front of his throne, Hendal lingered at the king's side, and Grace waited farther behind near their guards. At the bottom of the stairs, General Tont supervised the soldiers there with a hand on the hilt of his sword. Byron entered a minute later and moved to her left, positioning himself between her and the high priest. She caught the two men narrow their eyes at one another before resuming calmer appearances.

Hendal didn't mention many details about the welcome ceremony to her or Byron when the master mage inquired about it the night before at dinner. Neither expected any changes from Grace's ceremony, yet she couldn't stop herself from frowning as she eyed the entrance at the opposite end of the space. A loud thud hushed the chatting crowd, then the doors parted to reveal General Casner, three men in Asteom's uniform, and the Nim-Valan troops.

Despite her concern, Grace's eyebrows rose at the sight. Soldiers wearing dark colors lined the street in rows of five that extended far into the city. The spectators murmured below, and General Casner marched in with a stranger she figured had to be their commander. The three Asteom soldiers followed, though the Nim-Valans remained standing at attention just outside the palace.

Grace tentatively brushed against Byron's mind and felt his anxiousness. *What do you think?*

He didn't sound startled by her question and answered right away.

THE ANGEL'S DESCENT

{They must be trained well to stay put after traveling for so long. Also, the man approaching us holds the power since they're giving him their full attention.}

If the master mage intended to warn or prepare Grace for something, she didn't understand. They could only watch the tension in the room grow as General Casner halted at the bottom of the staircase. Then, his voice projected enough to perk everyone's ears.

"Your Highness, I present the highest ranking member of the Nim-Valan army, the Blockade Master of the North, the Winter Guard, General Harvey."

The strained silence continued when the stranger placed a hand over his breast and, to Grace's surprise, knelt before the stairs.

A man possessing multiple titles, like how the Sie-Kie warriors introduced themselves. I wonder if it is common in their country.

She shifted her focus to Aaron. Under Hendal's control, she found it difficult to tell if her friend remained aware of what went on around him, and what was at stake. She had been afraid of Hendal's plan to rule Asteom, but his power threatened Nim-Vala and terrified her because of the risk it posed, whether or not she considered the country her home.

"Welcome, General Harvey," Aaron picked up in an expressionless manner. "To welcome such notable guests in our capital under peaceful terms brings comfort to myself and the citizens of Asteom."

Grace resisted the urge to wince at how he delivered the greeting and noted the Nim-Valan's narrowing eyes. *He sounds condescending. I hope the general is able to see past the unflattering tone of voice.*

Byron cleared his throat, creating a slight growl directed at Hendal, and she imagined the high priest's resulting frown. Meanwhile, General Harvey rose and followed General Casner up the staircase.

Aaron continued when they approached and showed a bit more life. "My people, as you may have heard, the Nim-Valans wish to discuss an alliance between our two countries."

After the brief message, introductions took place in a similar fashion to when Grace first arrived. Aaron inclined his head after the general bowed but did nothing more. Hendal stepped forward next, pretending to be the kind-hearted priest by babbling blessings and gratitude before introducing Byron. At the mention of a master mage, General Harvey's eyes widened, and he expressed his sincere interest in magic. She watched Byron closely when his lips curved upward into a slight smile, as if the man's visible curiosity amused him.

"I wondered how familiar Nim-Vala is with light and dark energies," he responded. "If it's a display you'd enjoy, I would be willing to demonstrate my abilities sometime."

His words seemed smooth enough to consider as nothing more than an invitation, yet Grace remembered her lessons in political verbiage. *Byron confirmed their country's lack of magic and knowledge about both types of energy just by assessing the man's reaction. Instead of acting secretive, he volunteered to share the information in a setting he can control. The offer remained hospitable but left room for a sense of mystery. If I were in the general's position, I would note the mages' magic as an advantage Asteom holds over Nim-Vala, which must have been Byron's point in mentioning it.*

General Harvey's considerate expression appeared to reflect the same thoughts before he moved to face Grace. Doubt replaced the caution he showed during Byron's introduction, presumably because of her relevance compared to the adults. From a closer distance, she could assess his appearance better. Dark blotches of fur sewed onto the black clothing added extra padding and warmth to their uniforms or armor beneath; she couldn't tell which it was and considered the uncertainty to work in their favor. The man's amber-colored eyes matched his unkempt, dirty hair and beard while his long face and high cheekbones caused his eyes to sink inward, giving him an almost menacing presence.

An irritation rose inside her, one developed throughout her time in Asteom from being overlooked for her age, and she put extra effort into her low, poised curtsy. "It is an honor to meet a Nim-Valan for the first time. I am Grace Zelnar, the ambassador for Yeluthia."

Byron's position impressed the general, but the mention of Yeluthia had the man's eyes nearly popping out of his head, and he lost the intimidating presence.

THE ANGEL'S DESCENT

"Yeluthia," he muttered and paled slightly. "The city in the clouds? Stories of your kind are but mere whispers in my country. We believed the angels went extinct or fled from Asteom, yet you're here before me."

Grace savored the general's newfound admiration for her while he bowed. She said no more after, reinforcing herself as one without power over Asteom's business, though she always observed on her kingdom's behalf.

With the introductions complete, Hendal ushered the Nim-Valan toward Aaron. "A few more individuals aren't present, including another general and master mage, but I'm sure you and your soldiers are ready for a meal and some rest. We prepared quarters in the palace for two hundred, so if you would like to see them-"

"That won't be necessary," General Harvey interrupted and turned to Aaron. "Your Highness, my army and I brought tents for shelter and our own previsions. Mind you, we don't refuse your housing lightly. We were bred to withstand the conditions and instructed not to burden you. It would seem invasive to spread ourselves within your walls."

Grace gaped at him, and even Byron seemed shocked by the man's insistence.

The high priest glanced between Aaron, who didn't flinch, and General Harvey before responding. "I suppose there might be space in the southern field. Are you sure? His Highness is more than willing to house your troops here."

The man ignored Hendal and spoke directly to the unresponsive king. "Your open land in late summer is a blessing compared to the winters of northern Nim-Vala. We shall make camp at once and return for the feasting you planned."

With that, General Harvey bowed again to Aaron, spun around, and returned to General Casner at the bottom of the stairs. The two spoke for a few seconds, then they exited through the front gate. Grace heard Hendal release an irritated groan and clear his throat to address the waiting, confused crowd.

"People of Asteom," he projected, "our Nim-Valan guests offered to stay in the field just south of the palace. Let us give them our patience as they settle in before returning for the feast. In the meantime, we shall begin the celebration for their arrival!"

At the cue, servants slipped into the hall through every door lining the walls, bearing trays of finger-foods and drinks. Many murmured below because of the odd presentation, but they lightened up after a while. Grace stayed next to Byron because she remained unsure of what to do until her stomach growled.

The master mage must have heard since he glanced over with a smile. "Why don't we head down and grab something to eat?"

"I would like that," she replied while returning the gesture. As she accepted the arm he offered, the two descended to the crowd below.

Hendal remained at Aaron's side. Although he kept a grin on his face, Grace noticed how his eyes darted around the room in a nervous manner.

Byron led the way across the space, introducing her to the light and dark mages in their white and blue robes as they came over to greet him. Grace just listened and let the tidbits and treats she ate settle in her stomach to lull her into a lazy state of mind. Soon, she realized the previous conversation had ended, and the master mage disappeared from her side, prompting an embarrassed blush.

Where did he go? How long have I been lingering here idly? I hope no one paid attention to me.

It didn't take her more than a minute to spot Byron chatting with Emilea's husband, Clearshot, and join them. The former had said something funny, causing the soldier to chuckle before brushing off his wrinkled crimson coat in a rather informal way.

"You know, Lady Katrina's on the opposite end of the hall," Clearshot added to continue their conversation. "Perhaps you should greet her. She mentioned it's been years since you two talked."

"She always does," Byron replied and rolled his eyes. Then, he lowered his voice. "Is Marcy with her?"

In the days following the ball and Grace's rescue, Byron and Will informed her of their original plan to expose Hendal while Coura dealt with the demon. A pair of strangers, Coura's companions on her mission to search for the demonic creatures, had been involved as well. One was a shy woman who pretended to be Lady Katrina's cousin in order to relay information to Byron, Clearshot, Marcus, and Will while they waited in Verona. Grace's heartbeat sped up upon remembering the event and what each of her friends had gone through as well.

Clearshot, oblivious to her anxiety, dipped his head. "She's planning a trip outside of the city and asked about staying with Emilea while I'm away from home."

Byron contemplated the message before turning to walk toward the other side of the hall. Grace watched him but didn't want to be rude by intruding, especially when she didn't know the women.

A minute later, Emilea's husband cleared his throat to catch her attention.

She met the man several times in passing yet didn't learn more about him until her friends' reassignment to Dala when she communicated with him through her goddess gift. Her first impression had been that he represented what a soldier should be and always seemed present when new business came about. He and Byron proved to be close friends too, so he kept his ears open. Still, she did not expect him to show any interest in her.

"You're awfully distracted tonight, Lady Zelnar," he commented with a wink.

Grace offered a polite smile but didn't respond. She found herself looking to where Byron vanished among the guests, unsure of why she felt the need to do so.

"If I may," Clearshot began at a hushed volume meant for only her to hear, "I believe you're safe for the time being."

His words caught her off guard, and she stared at the man without hiding her confusion. "What do you mean?"

He continued in a reserved manner while gazing around the hall. "Byron won't admit it because that's just the kind of person he is, but I can sense how dependent you've become. Every time we spoke, you were brought up, usually when he expressed how obligated he felt to guard you and make sure you're uninvolved. Now, I see what he meant. After all, he did find you alone in the palace when chaos erupted and Coura fled."

His impersonal behavior and honesty stung, yet Grace struggled to justify her behavior once she realized the truth. *My fear lessens when I am with Byron or Emilea because they can defend me, and both were not afraid to stand up to Hendal. Even so, what is wrong with needing their protection after what I went through?*

As if sensing her thoughts, Clearshot placed a reassuring hand on her shoulder, leaned over, and used a softer, more comforting approach. "Please, don't misunderstand my intentions. Byron has a conscience that likes to push him toward anyone he believes needs rescuing."

"I do not understand."

His lips had straightened into a line to display his concern, which she understood was for Byron, but they curved upward as he stared at her.

"You're braver than those your age. You traveled to Asteom on your own and stayed after learning about the atrocities hiding here. Additionally, you went so far as to assist us when matters weren't technically your business. With that being said, Hendal and the demon left an impression on you, which might not lessen for some time. The night we lost will haunt us for different reasons, but we must strive to become stronger and focus on how to fix this mess."

Despite her wishes and Clearshot's encouragement, a wave of self-pity washed over Grace while they remained together in the crowded, noisy space. At one point, the Nim-Valan soldiers slipped into the hall and joined the festivities. Most lingered near the entrance and conversed with one another in hushed voices, but they appeared calm. A select few attempted to talk to Asteom's soldiers, though none approached the decorated citizens or mages. She didn't see General Harvey at all.

"They really aren't familiar with our language," Clearshot shared in a casual tone of voice quite unlike his previous, cautious one. "It's simpler by our standards and more common with citizens born into the lowest class."

"Class?" Grace felt compelled to ask.

Yeluthian society was no doubt less complex than what the humans in Asteom developed, consisting of the king and royal family, his chosen commanders and community leaders, then everyone else. Nobility could never exist because her people did not measure wealth. Citizens collected money or possessions and built homes however they liked, but regulations prevented a person from owning extra land when they didn't need or use it. She explained as much to Clearshot when he tilted his head to show his interest.

"Compared to ours, their class system sounds straightforward," he started after snatching a handful of cubed cheeses from a passing servant's tray and popping one in his mouth. "You already understand some of Asteom's, but in Nim-Vala, they established four rings branching outward from its center. The innermost circle is where the royal family lives in luxury with those they claim as their own kin. Surrounding the palace of sorts rests a massive city, and the well-off citizens can retire or manage their own trade. Everyone else is a commoner, farmer, servant, or soldier, and below that level are the slaves and social outcasts." He paused to offer her the handful of cheeses warmed by his palm.

She selected one to nibble on before pushing for more information. "How is their class system different than Asteom's?"

"I guess I could put it this way; status here is based on valuables. Money, property, livestock, and items of wealth contribute to how much power you hold in the area where you establish yourself. Fortunately, our land is expansive enough to where each city manages its own tiers."

"So, there are more opportunities to grow in status?"

"Exactly. Although, most people don't care since it doesn't impact our lives, unless your residence is located in the populated cities like Verona, Dala, Clearwater, or even Fester. Not to mention, there are those of us who serve the kingdom; however, possessing an extra, unique characteristic does recognize you as someone with the skills to contribute to your community."

"Such an idea sounds complicated," Grace admitted. She couldn't imagine how she would settle into such a system.

Clearshot shook his head. "Maybe. As I was saying, Nim-Vala's classes aren't based on wealth or property since their country values honor over all else. The ruler inherits his position and selects his generals and advisors by assessing their physical strength, ability to strategize, and knowledge of the country's politics through public tests. Losing brings humiliation and can tarnish their reputation. Everywhere else, a dishonored name or family lineage, deformed body, or other mark against a citizen is reason for the inner circle to cast them aside. Many of them join the army as foot soldiers hoping to work their way up in the ranks."

"What a primitive structure," she commented before considering those around the pair after her words were spoken.

Clearshot didn't seem to notice her lack of manners, though. "I did mention it's rather different. The point is, those of lesser importance join the army, meaning a majority of their troops are poor, possibly illiterate citizens who only speak their language."

As she reflected on the information, Grace found herself becoming more invested because she had never bothered to study any kingdoms besides her own when growing up. *If my parents did not hold such positions in Yeluthia to support the king, I would never have learned so much about Asteom before coming here.*

"I thought no one knew much about Nim-Vala," she muttered, more to herself than to Clearshot.

Still, he surprised her with an answer. "I happened to overhear General Casner's discussion with General Harvey. I believe he hoped to prepare our troops for what their men are like. Otherwise, none of us would have understood how to behave around them."

As Grace scanned the strangers' faces while they huddled together, she figured the Nim-Valan general made the smartest decision by explaining his soldiers' reserved mannerisms. "I am sure Byron is aware of their system as well," she threw in when their conversation seemed to end.

She didn't receive a verbal answer, but Clearshot sent a wary look her way, as if to halt any sort of plotting at that moment.

Hearing about their potential allies in the face of what danger lingered in the palace lit a spark inside her. *He said I am brave, so I must try to uphold his claim. If only we can start figuring out how to stop Hendal...*

Grace prepared to project the inquiry to Clearshot with her goddess gift in order to motivate the man when a voice chirped from her side, one with the power to make her involuntarily shudder.

"I'm surprised you haven't befriended them yet considering how much you've learned, Mr. Bayporter."

The slightly annoyed expression on Clearshot's face revealed his own feelings about speaking to the newcomer. "Why do you say that, Hendal?"

The tone of voice behind the question held plenty of venom, which made Grace's eyes widen in alarm. Although she sensed the soldier's muscles tensing under the uniform, his relaxed posture reassured her he wouldn't attempt to harm the high priest.

Meanwhile, Hendal chuckled. Hearing the deceiving sound she had come to associate with a kind personality brought her close to tears.

"You're such a social person is all," the high priest responded, seemingly oblivious to their strife. "I'm always interested in hearing about Asteom's allies, so my ears are open to these sorts of discussions. Now that I think about it, I don't believe you normally have an opportunity to talk with our Yeluthian ambassador. Isn't that right, Grace?"

She managed to avoid the urge to turn her head and raise her eyes to the man who kidnapped and drugged her, but no words would vocalize to reply.

In the next instant, Byron appeared. Somehow, he just slid next to Clearshot once Hendal answered without her noticing. Both relief and a mixture of guilt and shame washed over her then because of Clearshot's earlier message.

If I remain dependent on him and Emilea, they will keep protecting me, even if doing so hinders their attempts to help Asteom.

"To what do we owe the pleasure of your company?" Byron asked more casually than he appeared.

The master mage's eyes narrowed into a glare, though Hendal ignored it to exploit Grace's weakness. A heavy hand dropped onto her shoulder, causing her to jump at the touch.

"I quite enjoy listening to what's being discussed about our guests," the high priest continued. "General Casner is an intelligent man aiming to gather intel for our benefit. It's similar to how our young ambassador shares information about her home country for the betterment of Asteom's relationship with Yeluthia. The more we understand Nim-Vala, the easier it will be to work together."

He means to say it will be easier to manipulate their weaknesses, Grace realized. *I forgot he has ears all over the palace. I would assume Clearshot and Byron understand this as well.*

She longed to reach her mind to the two men, both for comfort and to see if they would defend her against Hendal. The idea reminded her of her helplessness, especially since hearing their support would change nothing except ease her fear slightly.

The hand on her shoulder gripped tighter as the high priest spoke in a sly manner. "You can always count me in on your conversations. I'm a trustworthy, virtuous man after all."

Grace watched as Byron and Clearshot pressed their lips together while their glares sharpened, prompting her to wonder what they thought of the lie. Even though she didn't seem to be in immediate danger, her body still shook like a terrified rabbit, and she begged for it to stop. Memories of Hendal's control over her weakened state came to mind, including when he dragged her to the council's meeting chamber by her hair. The demon had been there, waiting with Coura.

Her friend was much braver, mustering the courage to fight against the creature while shielding Grace, whose mind had been muddled and her body unable to stand without assistance. Coura's support pushed Grace to flee and hide until help arrived.

I did not possess the strength to stop what Hendal had been doing then, but I am becoming stronger.

The notion sounded fierce in her head and rang through the fear. Her heart thundered in her chest, and she did what she never would have dared to do until that moment. After apologizing to the goddess who blessed her with the mind-speaking gift, she used her inner voice to address the high priest.

Enough.

THE ANGEL'S DESCENT

This time, Grace glanced over while smiling as naturally as she could manage in order to appear as unphased as possible. She held a faint hope that the demon influenced his mind, urging him to act in such an unforgivable manner, but his thoughts sounded as normal as any other human's.

His smug grin faded, his eyes widened a bit, and the hand on her shoulder promptly lifted. The shocked, babbling voice resulting from her call sounded like the complete opposite of both the arrogant, pompous man and the jolly, composed high priest he pretended to be.

{*H-How are you... W-What are you-*}

My goddess gift is none of your concern, she hurried to respond before she lost her nerve. *I can assure you, we discussed nothing involving you, your demon, or your precious reputation. You are safe to return to Aaron and let us enjoy the limited freedom you permit.*

Over the years of training her ability, Grace found everyone's mind-to-mind speech reflected more natural emotions than those vocalized aloud. Her words were meant to be firm, like how she pictured Emilea or Byron when they scolded someone.

Hendal's face remained the same as he cleared his throat and paused to brush down his robe. Then, the good-humored features returned.

"Well, I wish you three a pleasant evening," he said to abruptly end their conversation before walking in the direction of the staircase.

Grace followed him with her eyes until he stood beside the king's throne; however, she hesitated to remove her presence from his mind. She wished she had sooner when he glanced in her direction and spoke through their connection in the same, demeaning manner he would use when she had been locked away.

{*Don't grow haughty because you have a gift like no other, and don't bother using it as a means of plotting with those two fools. If I catch even the faintest suspicion you are doing so... Well, let's just say my demonic companion has been asking for a plaything now that Coura has been disposed of.*}

She retracted her mind as Hendal looked away. Byron and Clearshot didn't speak while she trailed the man, but they settled down when she returned her attention to them. The latter grinned, and she understood why.

This is what he wanted me to do, to prove I can stand up for myself and leave Byron and Emilea alone.

Despite her mental outburst, the master mage frowned to project his concern. Grace smiled in return to show she intended to face the uncertain future with them, even if it meant risking her life.

3

As the days went by and Coura recovered on a hardwood floor, she pieced together where she ended up and some of what happened around her. The first time she woke had been because of discomfort stemming from her broken wings as someone dragged her through a doorway. The feathery limbs were unable to fold down enough to squeeze through the opening, so multiple people tried talking to her, but she felt too shaken and weak to answer. Finally, whoever was there stopped handling her gently and opted to push and pull her through instead; the force and resulting stabs of pain caused her to black out. She vaguely remembered stirring several times in a daze only to be given medicine that made her sleep.

When she could process the situation in a half-awake state, voices in the room made her freeze. She recognized Emilea's first, then Aimes'. They discussed her condition at a lower volume until Mace and Lexie leapt downstairs, and the whole group moved outside.

Against a pounding in her head and chest, she opened her eyes and blinked at the ceiling until her vision cleared. It proved to be morning since sunlight flowed in from the windows to brighten the sitting room. Coura had been placed against the far wall, hidden behind one of the armchairs with nothing but a blanket under her body and a pillow for her head. The black wings were still present to drape over her in a comforting fashion, but she winced at the unseen damage reflected by the odd, bending tips and spots of missing feathers. She fell asleep before the others returned.

The next morning, Emilea's energy poured through her wings in a strong yet gentle wave to heal their many injuries. After a break, the light mage continued until Coura felt less tenderness and could finally sleep peacefully for the remainder of the day.

She counted three more mornings of the sessions before she felt better, at least physically.

Despite being around friends in a safe, comfortable home, Coura couldn't brave her nerves and voice her questions during or after Emilea's healings. She pretended to rest through the afternoons in order to contemplate what she needed to do against the disorganized thoughts and emotions.

Coura woke before dawn the following day and discovered no one else was up, even though the colorful world outside sang with life. For a while, she remained still, unsure of why she grew so reluctant to ask Emilea or Aimes about Hendal and the palace. Her mind wandered back to the evening Soirée spent toying with her before Coura fled for her life. A familiar weight of guilt from her failure settled on her chest, stirring the unnatural power until it became difficult to breathe.

Not again... Why is my body behaving like this? Soirée must have interfered with the demonic energy before she disappeared since this started right after.

Recalling the memories also brought up the demon's confession.

I'm part Yeluthian.

Slow footsteps came from above, and after a minute, Emilea's figure appeared and moved into the kitchen. Coura shut her eyes, lightened her breathing, and pretended to sleep before the light mage proceeded with her healing; however, instead of the calm energy she expected, a hand rested on her arm and carefully shook it to rouse her.

Although the gesture startled her, she played the part by cracking open one eye at a time.

"I need you to wake up now," came the woman's voice, which teemed with worry.

As Coura croaked Emilea's name in response, she found her throat became dry enough to throw her into a coughing fit. The sudden, repeating pressure on her chest and abdomen brought about the pain from earlier, though the light mage helped her into a sitting position to ease it. She tasted blood on her tongue and saw the ruby liquid on her hand after she covered her mouth.

Didn't Emilea heal me? She wanted to ask, but a glance at the woman's face seemed to say she had been trying.

"I brought you some more medicine," Emilea responded before grabbing a mug and pressing it into Coura's hands.

While she choked the bitter-tasting drink down at a leisurely pace to avoid coughing it up, the light mage went on.

"I don't know where to begin," she admitted. "I suppose we should start with your injuries. The children found you in the northern part of the woods one morning on our daily stroll. I believe that was about a week ago."

The length of time that passed didn't bother Coura. *I counted five or six days in the woods, at least I think I did. That means I've been away from the palace for about two weeks. I wonder what happened since then.*

"Aimes and I retrieved you during the night to avoid suspicion. We had a difficult time bringing you inside, and your wings made it impossible to carry you through the stairway to a bedroom. So, I made do with this."

Coura recalled the foggy memory and how the physical force caused her to lose consciousness. Her wings twitched in response.

Emilea noticed and extended a hand toward their dirty surface. "Do you feel pain in them?"

Naturally, after what they endured, the wings flinched at her touch. The lack of any sensation except for Emilea's hand against the messy feathers proved to be a welcome surprise.

"They don't hurt," she shared while extending both as far as she could in the cramped corner. "Did you heal them completely?"

Before Emilea could answer, Coura attempted to stand only to be punched in the ribs by an invisible force, sending her doubling over in a coughing fit for the second time. More blood came up to decorate the floor with scarlet freckles. The master mage reacted by putting both hands around Coura's shoulders and guiding her to sit in a hunched position that wouldn't use most of her upper body's muscles.

"As I was saying," the woman continued while eyeing her impatiently, "your wings should be healed, but that's about all I can do."

When Emilea looked down at her folded hands, Coura sensed her despair and dreaded the explanation. "What do you mean?"

The light mage glanced upward before taking one of Coura's wrists to show her the arm. The rips and tears in her clothing let the markings peek through, but the blood had been wiped away to work on the wounds. Patches and bandages covered what Coura suspected were scrapes on the forearm Emilea held. As she examined the rest of her body, she discovered most of her skin hid beneath the wrappings, and her gaze settled on a cast covering her right foot, something she didn't notice until that moment.

"The bones in your foot shattered in several places," Emilea added in a less sympathetic manner while releasing her grip. "I cleaned a nasty split in the back of your skull that was close to infection too. Besides the external damage, you had several, minor puncture wounds to your lungs and stomach, as you may have noticed."

Even with the horrendous state her body had been in, Coura knew Emilea's following pause meant another issue took precedence. *What about the others who were in the palace that night? Did something worse befall them? I don't like this.*

Instead of picking up the conversation, Emilea rose to stand with the empty mug and ordered her to rest. The woman moved toward the kitchen when what should have been an obvious realization dawned on Coura.

"My power isn't healing me anymore."

The master mage entered the kitchen without a word, confirming the truth.

At first, Coura wasn't sure what to think because Soirée's demonic energy saved her multiple times in the past. Then, it became disheartening to imagine the recovery process for her current condition. She half-expected the power inside of her to stir, so she reached into her center for it once it started to hum in response. The tendrils of energy slipped through her invisible hands like water, leaving her unable to muster enough to cast a basic spell. She withdrew her efforts when Emilea returned carrying a plate full of sliced bread coated with an herb-butter spread.

"It's been a while since I tended to a patient without my magic," she commented and knelt next to Coura.

They nibbled on their slices in silence, unsure of what to say. At last, the quiet home grew too unbearable.

"Where are Mace and Lexie?" Coura asked after swallowing the rest of her meal.

"Aimes took them to the pond earlier this morning. I'm not sure when they plan on returning, but they'll be relieved to see you're awake."

The words sounded reassuring, yet all Coura could consider remained her inability to stop Soirée. Her lips pressed together as she averted her eyes, though the master mage read every movement.

Emilea reached over to place a hand on her shoulder. "What happened in the palace doesn't matter now."

Coura couldn't refrain from choking out a laugh that hurt her insides. *What do you mean? How is it not my fault we didn't stop Soirée or Hendal?*

The questions wouldn't vocalize. She decided she wasn't in the mood to face the past, and probably wouldn't ever be, so she started to clear her mind. This time, the new, brighter energy grew active, fluttering in her center like a swarm of tiny butterflies.

After a minute, Emilea removed her hand to grab another piece of bread. "Hendal threatened General Tont and everyone under his control. He forced them to put their own blades right over their throats to keep us from interrogating him before sneaking away."

"What?" Coura exclaimed while imagining the scene with disbelief.

"He took a coward's approach to escape, flaunting the lives of those who aren't able to fight," Emilea continued, allowing her frustration to show. "Because of Hendal's hold on my family, I need to remain here most of the time under the watch of two guards. As we speak, one is observing our home from nearby while the other trailed behind Aimes and the children. Even though I'm unable to go to the palace, to my husband's and Byron's sides, I can help a little here.

Aimes has been distracting the children and keeping them safe while I heal you. For some reason, the soldiers outside can't sense magic even though they carry the demon's power. I suppose that's all you missed."

A second later, the master mage remembered another item, which softened her serious expression. "I forgot to mention, Grace is safe. Byron promised he would look after her."

Coura's heart skipped a beat before she recalled the frail Yeluthian crawling desperately out of the chamber for her freedom. A surge of anger followed the memory before it became replaced by relief so deep, she dropped her face into her hands. "I'm glad," she replied after as exhaustion crept up once more.

"It's because you were there," Emilea added, startling her.

"I couldn't stop Soirée or the high priest."

"True, but your interference brought about her rescue. Who knows when we would have had the opportunity to save her if you didn't confront the demon. Besides, in addition to Grace's goddess gift, she told us what took place in the meeting chamber." Emilea's last sentence projected her sympathy, implying her knowledge of Coura's lineage.

"I told her to share what they revealed in the hope of figuring out their intentions." She didn't elaborate on the details and tried to push past her personal views on the revelation.

I'm just a tool, another subject for Soirée to test her power on...

"Do you want to talk about it?" Emilea asked next.

The question sounded innocent enough to tempt Coura. One part of her encouraged a discussion, especially with a light mage who would be supportive amid her internal pain. On the other hand, she didn't fully accept the demon's story, even though Soirée had never lied to her throughout their entire relationship.

"What's there to talk about?" she countered in place of an answer.

Emilea observed her for a few seconds until Coura felt uncomfortable under the woman's compassionate gaze and prepared to feign sleepiness. Then, the light mage spoke again.

"Relax," she instructed.

THE ANGEL'S DESCENT

Before Coura knew what was happening, Emilea shifted to lean over, wrap both arms around her shoulders, and gently pull her in for a hug. Instead of breaking it off right away, the master mage held on and started brushing her hair down in a soothing manner.

As soon as the woman touched her, Coura's body instinctively went rigid until she recognized the gesture. *This must be her way of comforting patients who need emotional support.*

When she remembered no one else would be wandering around until Aimes and the children came back, she caved into the voluntary, selfless act. As her body relaxed and breathing slowed, she let the tears slide down her cheeks without making a sound and dipped her head into the woman's shoulder. Emilea didn't comment or make her feel embarrassed in any way, though the embrace tightened.

Coura pulled away when the crying ended to see the master mage smiling in a friendly enough manner to prompt a blush. "I'm sorry," she mumbled and wiped her eyes.

Emilea shook her head. "There's nothing to apologize for. Now, Aimes, Mace, and Lexie should return for lunch soon, so I'll be in the kitchen if you need me. Try not to move around too much today, and stay as inconspicuous as possible. Hendal didn't order the guards to watch the inside of my home; don't give them a reason to suspect I'm hiding anything. Since your wings are healed, maybe we can move you upstairs into a proper bed."

The idea of sleeping without interruption on a feather mattress sounded like a dream. Coura lied down on the blanket after expressing her gratitude while Emilea walked away. Just when she grew tired, despite the wooden floor stiffening her muscles, Mace and Lexie burst through the front door and giggled gleefully.

"We won! We won!" they chanted and skipped around before taking their seats at the dining table. By the time Emilea emerged with plates of sandwiches and sliced fruit, Aimes stumbled through the door, huffing and holding his side.

"I can't believe you lost," Mace blurted out before his mother scolded him for speaking with a mouthful of food.

Aimes waited until after he seated himself next to the boy to respond. "No one has ever beaten me in a race before."

Emilea raised a skeptical eyebrow at the older man. "Is that right?"

"I didn't lie. Until this day, no one moved fast enough to outdistance me."

"We won!" Lexie sung to herself and bounced her head from side to side in between Aimes' words.

"And how many times did you actually race anyone?" the master mage inquired as she moved in Coura's direction.

"Let's see," Aimes began and counted his fingers. "The last time had been when I lived in Clearwater, though I don't agree to run often. They didn't need to know that, though."

He winked and chuckled when Emilea rolled her eyes, and she set a plate on the floor beside Coura. The room fell silent after the light mage took her seat with the others.

"How's she today?" the older man asked at a lower volume.

Although she couldn't see his face from her spot at the opposite end of the house, Coura figured he was referring to her. "I'm just fine," she grumbled loud enough for them to hear and strained to sit up. Her wings were still the only part of her body that didn't throb from the damage.

Gasps escaped the children, then they jumped out of their seats, scurried to her side, and spoke her name with a mixture of elation and concern. On the outside, Coura resumed her casual façade while her stress spiked on the inside, especially when Aimes hobbled over to start pressing her with questions.

"How are you feeling?"

"Sore."

"Is the leg any better?"

"I haven't tried using it yet."

"We heard what happened and what the demon told you. Is it stopping you from healing like you normally do?"

Coura opened and closed her mouth, uncertain of the reason.

Fortunately, Emilea came to her aid. "That's enough," the woman chided from where she remained at the table. "Coura hasn't eaten in days and can't recover on her own without a decent meal. Wait until after lunch."

THE ANGEL'S DESCENT

Aimes, Mace, and Lexie apologized for their nosy behavior and returned to their food yet did not hurry to finish. This left Coura alone to nibble on the edge of the bread Emilea had given her in place of the others' sandwiches. The peace also allowed her to consider her next move since she felt better.

It's no use trying to return to the palace, especially in the condition I'm in. Everyone knows what I look like too, and they'll attack me under Hendal's order, meaning I need to wait for Grace or Byron to contact me. Then, we can come up with another plan to lure Soirée away or figure something else out.

The idea gnawed at her for the remainder of the day and slipped into her dreams that evening.

*

Noise from the kitchen roused Coura the next morning. As she opened her eyes, she noticed her immense stiffness and groaned.

Why can't this be over already?

The thought had not been directed at any person in particular, yet both traces of energy in her center hummed in reply, leading her to confront what she didn't wish to acknowledge.

I should see what's going on with Soirée's energy before it drives me crazy. If I can also get it to heal the rest of my body, that would be even better.

The internal injuries prevented her from twisting around too much, but she managed to rest on her hands and knees before pushing up to balance on the latter without distracting the person in the other room. Then, she focused on releasing the spell keeping her wings manifested because she wouldn't be able to climb the stairs or move around inside Emilea's home with them present.

She began by analyzing the energy in each wing, which branched from her center to her shoulders and back; the consistent flow amazed her given their lack of use. At the reminder of the spell's disappearance, Coura remembered the annoying, itching sensation when it was inactive and sighed in resignation before reaching to cut the tie. She half-expected this to result in some sort of backlash, but the strands wouldn't budge under her pull. With every failed attempt, her mind and heart raced faster until, in a frantic effort, she threw all of her internal force at their weakest points located directly underneath the skin.

This time, the bonds severed. The wings disappeared in a silver shimmer, yet the energy binding them snapped to Coura's center like a whip, sending her doubling over while gasping from the sudden strain. The sharp gesture hurt her insides again, and she coughed up bits of blood while her vision showed nothing except colored spots.

"Breathe," a feminine voice ordered multiple times until she recovered.

It took a few minutes for her to calm down enough to glance at Emilea, who knelt beside her with an unamused expression.

"What happened?" the light mage demanded.

Coura's mouth worked, though her fraught mind struggled to discern an explanation. "I-I don't know," she admitted after.

The released energy stirred within her center, but the wings were gone, leaving behind the anticipated tingling. Emilea remained where she was, as if waiting for more, so Coura looked away, unsure whether to be concerned or embarrassed by the lack of control, or both.

At last, when it became obvious she opted for silence, Emilea produced an unsatisfied huff.

"Let me show you something."

Before Coura knew what the woman planned to do, she felt a hand on her back followed by light energy, which soothed her spirits. She closed her eyes and could sense it proceeding toward the damaged parts needing the most attention; however, as soon as it came into contact with one spot and began healing, the demonic energy inhabiting Coura's center lashed out to swipe it away. In response to the retaliation, the unknown, warm energy suppressed Soirée's power by expanding to swallow it up.

Emilea attempted her spell two more times only to reach the same conclusion, then the master mage removed her hand with another, less frustrated sigh. "This is why I haven't been able to heal you," she explained. "I would never ask Lexie to try and see if it isolates just me, but I believe the results would be the same for any light mage."

Coura wondered what could possibly cause such a disturbance in the balance of energy within her center. "Can you tell me what the second presence is?" she ventured.

The woman tilted her head. "What do you mean?"

"You can sense it too, right? Soirée's power rejects your energy, then there's another to counter hers. The sources seem to be fighting about whether or not your magic should heal me."

While Emilea paused to consider the dilemma, Coura waited, unsure of what the response would be. Finally, when faint footsteps on the floor above indicated the impending arrival of more listeners, the master mage answered.

"I think I have a pretty accurate assumption, but it might depend on what you tell me. When did you start noticing this second stream of energy?"

The question took Coura back as she never considered its appearance. "I remember noticing it before I became familiar with your presence," she mumbled, more to herself than to Emilea. "Ever since I woke up after the fight with the angels in Dala, I sort of felt it on and off. I stopped wondering about it once I tracked down the demonic creatures possessing Soirée's energy because it faded."

"You don't recall any recent moments?"

She ran through the previous months in her mind until reaching her flight from the palace, and she replied when the memory sent a jolt through her body. "It returned to me after I dropped into the woods. I can't remember much, except it behaved as restlessly as the demonic energy."

Emilea bobbed her head before wiping her forehead with one hand. "I don't know how else to say this. What you described seems to be what originally belongs to you, or rather the part of you that is Yeluthian."

Coura froze in disbelief, though the master mage ignored her alarm and stared at the floor while going on.

"From what Grace explained to us about the demon's experiments, it sounded used to humans who share dark or demonic energy. Similar sources of power can easily overshadow each other based on their strength. For example, when Grace utilized her goddess gift in order to contact your group in the Dalan base while you were unconscious, she needed an extra amount of energy to stretch farther. I could tell hers is purer than mine, yet I possess more power, so I remained in control of that spell's flow. Regardless of her intentions, she acted as a conduit for my magic. The demon probably overwhelmed your potential when you were too young to understand."

"Why did it start when I lost Soirée's power? I thought the ability to wield light or dark energy couldn't be gained after a certain age range."

"That's true, at least for humans. If I had to guess, it became active when the ancestral weapon stripped away the demon's hold. Your body had already been prepared to use magic thanks to your training at the academy. The issue we're facing is that the pair of energies residing within you are complete opposites, which is another reason why I believe the additional presence belongs to you. It mirrors Grace's. Not exactly, but close enough to where I would be shocked if I remained unaware of your lineage. The limited power a human wields becomes irritated by demonic energy, but it doesn't repel or repress them like what you're experiencing."

By the time Emilea finished explaining, Mace and Lexie descended the stairs to slip into the kitchen for their breakfast. Aimes appeared as well, stretching with a wince before noticing the women.

"Well, we can bring you into a proper bed then. It's about time! The ground is no place for a recovering patient."

"Would you like to move to a room?" the light mage asked to switch topics.

Coura shook her head, letting her dark hair fall over her face as she stared down at her hands. To her relief, Emilea and Aimes left her alone to join the children. While they ate together, she resigned to settling her mind and the resulting knot developing in her stomach that prevented her from consuming her lunch. Her caretaker glanced at the untouched plate more than once yet didn't bother her about it.

I don't know how I should feel, she realized as her eyes rose to stare at the world beyond the window across from where she sat. Her thoughts wandered from the possibility of possessing light energy to being a Yeluthian and allowing a demon to meddle with her life.

THE ANGEL'S DESCENT

One part of me is frustrated for losing half of my life, or what belonged to my father, and longs to get it back. I doubt that's possible, though. Soirée and the damage she caused are my problems to fix, and I need her energy, whether I like it or not. Can I still wield it? What am I supposed to do if I can't use my magic?

The final question proved the most difficult to overcome and kept her awake into the late hours of the night.

4

Despite his optimistic mentality, Will regretted stepping out from the warmth of his room and into the dreary corridor where he hurried to exit the palace. Nobody lingered in places they didn't need to be anymore since it began to feel as though an unseen set of eyes stuck to their backs. Even as he leapt down the stairs, that unpleasantness continued stalking him until he reached the well-lit grand hall. There, people wandered on their own business while guards rotated shifts around the wide space. They paid him no attention, so he slipped through the gate and emerged to find the afternoon air unexpectedly chilly.

The wind blew from the direction of the troops camped in the southern field. Like he did every time he went into Verona, Will turned toward the familiar buildings instead of the strangers. The Nim-Valan soldiers both intrigued and frightened him to the point where he figured it would be best to wait for their group to approach the Asteom citizens first.

It's obvious they're not comfortable speaking our language, or talking to other people in general. They might react negatively if I were to inquire about their culture at this point. Until a solid connection is established, we should give them privacy. In any case, I have more important issues to worry about.

Despite the cooler weather, the city showed plenty of life as it radiated excitement for the Harvest Festival about a month away. Between the celebration, the northern guests, and a possible alliance, he heard nothing else and didn't plan to for some time. If he hadn't been involved with Grace, Marcus, or his other companions, Will would probably be just as eager for the approaching weeks.

It's a shame this whole situation turned out the way it did.

In a matter of minutes, he crossed the main road, passed through a series of alleyways, and entered a shop displaying a sign reading Dandy's Clothing. The front of the inside stretched as wide as his own bedroom, which didn't seem like a comfortable fit when he considered standing with more than a handful of people. Thankfully, the space remained as empty as it always had been around that time, which was why Marcus ordered him to arrive then. No one waited at the counter, most likely because they needed every free hand to assemble the suites, robes, and dresses for the festival alongside the necessary items normally sold in preparation for the winter months.

Grace, are you listening? Can you tell Marcus I'm here?

His Yeluthian friend liked to keep an invisible eye on him during his ventures into the city and confirmed she was doing so again with her next message.

{*He is coming to the front.*}

As he smiled to himself, Will thanked the deity she served for the convenience of that gift since he knew their group's efforts wouldn't remain a secret if they couldn't communicate through the ambassador. This led his anxious mind to start considering the threats they faced by continuing to plot behind the palace leaders' backs.

Fortunately, Marcus appeared in the doorway to the room at the rear and gestured for him to follow before he could dive deeper into their problems.

This was Will's third visit, so his friend's family felt familiar enough with him not to ask questions. The first time he stopped by to see Marcus, he merely wished to speak with someone other than Grace, who projected her impatience and only contacted him through her ability. Those conversations, as well as the reminder of his previous encounters involving demonic magic, rattled him more than he would let on, especially since she expected him to help stand up to the evil plaguing Asteom.

Why would she think to ask me about stopping the high priest and a demon? I wouldn't even count on myself to assist in plotting something like that!

His mindset worsened when Marcus voiced similar ideas during his initial visit. Will didn't know what to make of their strong emotions, so he avoided bringing up the subject whenever possible, opting to study, train, or do whatever else could distract him until the impending moment arrived for him to be pulled into the scheming once more. With many individuals listening all over the place, it came as a complete shock when Grace spoke to him on Byron's behalf two days ago to introduce a new plan. Will didn't express his interest in their offer to join, though Byron must have sensed his hesitation because the master mage left the request open-ended so he could consider it further.

That night, he reflected on the ball and how frightening the ordeal had been. Marcus bolted from his side once Aaron announced the demon's appearance, leaving him to search for their friends alone. When he moved through the halls, groups of soldiers, mages, and various guests pushed and shoved him aside until he decided to return to the grand hall. There, Clearshot spotted him, dragged him away, then they met up with Emilea, Marcus, and Byron, who had located Grace. After, his life resumed without anyone thinking twice about their intentions. Combat training began in the morning, meals were shared between people he came to know and befriend over the months prior, and he studied whatever he could to keep his mind occupied during the rest of the day.

That routine of pretending like nothing had changed ultimately drove him to agree to help the master mage.

Dandy's Clothing belonged to an elderly man Marcus described as a close family friend who lived in an additional section of the building's back side while General Tont's family occupied the upper floor. Will didn't comment on how the owner gifted the more livable part instead of keeping it for himself. The children shared a room, Marcus' sister and her husband had their own, and his mother stayed in one meant for two people. When he visited, the assistant general used the room otherwise meant to be a play space for his nieces.

THE ANGEL'S DESCENT

Perhaps he prefers to live in the palace to avoid crowding the building.

Marcus also kept his mouth shut when it came to the relationships within the family. On multiple occasions, his friend mentioned his preference for relying on himself instead of his parents. They never talked about his sister, her husband, who Will had yet to see in the shop, or their children, but Marcus' mother had shown her caring personality. She gifted Marcus with new clothes throughout the year, wrote letters to him often, and addressed guests with a genuine smile. A part of Will wondered if the woman grew lonely without her husband present and how she would react if she knew what happened to him.

The shop itself expanded farther beyond the entryway and held raw materials, scissors, dyes, and various other tools scattered on wooden tables. As the two passed through, Will received a wave from Marcus' mother and sister, curious glances from the working children, and a nod from the owner while the man kept his eyes glued to the pattern he painted on a voluminous skirt.

Once the two climbed the winding steps, they entered a slim hallway, and Marcus held open the door to the room on their right. Will stepped inside and took his preferred place on the edge of the neatly made bed as his friend closed the door before positioning himself on a wooden stool in the corner. A basket of balls, dolls, and other toys sat at his feet, but nothing else decorated the space.

"I'm glad to see you again," he surprised Will by saying and crossed his arms.

"We met up a couple of days ago."

Marcus rubbed his neck in a bashful manner. "Family can be draining, though. Staying here stretches the days out. I feel I should be doing more."

To emphasize his point, he pretended to hold a sword and strike an invisible target twice.

Will laughed at the assistant general's behavior and shook his head. "We're complete opposites there! I could spend the entire afternoon reading, especially when the weather's poor."

"I don't doubt you're doing that already."

Marcus shot him a knowing look, and Will could only grin at the truth before Grace words reached them.

{*Are you two ready?*}

Given the magic surrounding the palace and the majority of his friends, Will took comfort in his and Marcus' shared lack of experience when it came to the subject. The assistant general never seemed comfortable speaking mind-to-mind, so he stared at the ceiling while Will confirmed their presence with the Yeluthian, who sounded more confident compared to their previous conversation.

{*Byron, Clearshot, and I are in the palace, so I will project to everyone and repeat Byron's thoughts at one time.*}

After a brief pause, her voice returned in a serious tone of voice, indicating the start of the master mage's message.

{*I wish we could speak together again, but as you know, it is far too dangerous. Grace is strengthening her ability, but she still cannot reach Emilea, Aimes, Marcy, or Coura. Our options are limited as to how we can stop Hendal because of his influence over many leaders in the capital. He has yet to reprimand us or go after the Nim-Valan army, which is what I fear may come next.*}

Will forced his body to relax by taking a deep breath. *That's our situation summed up*, he thought, along with how slim their chance of success was.

{*Should we choose to act instead of waiting for his next move, I believe luring him away from the palace is our best approach.*}

"What does he mean?" Marcus inquired aloud while turning to Will.

Grace went on before he knew how to respond.

{*Either we take the initiative or do nothing until he does decide to move forward with his own plans and adjust. To be honest, I am not certain which path to follow.*}

When Grace's voice withdrew a bit, the assistant general glanced at Will again with a concerned expression.

"I get the impression she didn't expect him to admit that," Will muttered.

Marcus shrugged. "I can't blame her for being surprised. From what you shared before, she's ready to retaliate."

THE ANGEL'S DESCENT

"Byron's never been the type of person to jump into action. She should have considered he wouldn't reach an immediate decision regarding our next move, or that he'd consult with us first."

Marcus opened his mouth to add more when Grace's voice chimed in their heads, reflecting a more positive attitude.

{*Byron requests to hear your thoughts and suggestions on what should be done. I am going to listen to Clearshot, Marcus, then Will. Without access to Emilea, Aimes, Marcy, or Coura, he insists the final decision rests solely on our shoulders.*}

Will couldn't help from gulping at the notion. *It's easy to offer ideas without consequences, but jumping into and following through with a strategy at the possible cost of our freedom, or even our lives, requires real courage. Can I agree to accept such a burden? Am I confident enough to say anything worthwhile, or should I observe and hone my skills before contributing?*

While his Yeluthian friend addressed the others individually, he rushed to answer the questions until it became his turn.

{*Will, I do not want to deter you, so I shall remain silent about what I collected already.*}

I understand. Based on her previous and current attitude, he figured she wished to move along with the plotting, though he didn't understand what prompted her shifting mood. *Normally, I would be against involving myself with such matters and stirring trouble in the kingdom, yet I remember those who are being controlled by the high priest. Without learning what his goals are, why he uses the demonic power, and what the rogue angels' assistance means, we're more likely to see the issues multiply rather than resolve in our favor. I also have a feeling Emilea, Aimes, Marcy, and Coura would share a similar opinion.*

{*Then, your answer?*}

I'm in favor of striking before Hendal moves forward with his own plan.

A surge of elation escaped Grace before she cut off the emotion; however, it proved enough to reveal that Will's input had been the deciding factor. Before he could begin doubting his choice, Marcus startled him by speaking aloud.

"You told her we shouldn't wait, didn't you?"

"How-"

The assistant general raised a hand to interrupt. "I'm not upset; it's just written on your face. Whatever route we follow, whether to be patient or not, has its risks and rewards."

Will could only mumble his agreement while fidgeting with his fingers until Grace's voice returned.

{*Byron will spend the evening piecing together our options. This gives me another day to practice reaching for Emilea, Coura, and the other two. Tomorrow, we can meet again at the same time.*}

After her dismissal, the additional presence faded again and disappeared, allowing Will to clear his mind as he and Marcus sat in silence until the latter rose and stretched his arms.

"I guess there's nothing else we can do. Were you going to stay for dinner? If so, I need to let my mother know to prepare an extra plate."

Will smiled to show he appreciated the new topic and shook his head. "Sorry, but one of the trios I've been practicing with invited me to eat with them. They want to discuss the activity Byron started since their group only has three people."

That sparked another conversation on the intriguing session and his weapons training progress. Marcus drilled him on what he learned, even going so far as to demonstrate the proper stances, swings, and physical counters while Will humored his friend. He found the assistant general's passion for combat rather entertaining, especially because it was the first time they behaved as friends and not coconspirators in a while. Unfortunately, the experience couldn't last.

In the windowless room, they had no means of tracking the time, so he judged the hour based on when hunger tightened his stomach. Marcus evidently felt the same and decided to lead Will back through the hall, down the stairs, and across the busy workroom. The two said their goodbyes in front of the store and parted ways.

The late afternoon meant the streets filled with vendors displaying their portable meals and treats for easy consumption in addition to the taverns, inns, and restaurants with doors wide open to let the tempting aromas waft toward potential customers. Will forced his feet to continue moving in order to avoid stuffing himself before the evening meal, thus disrespecting the invitation from his training partners.

His considerate mindset steadily broke down, though, and the scent of roasting meat at the shop to his left made his mouth water. *I'm sure they wouldn't mind if I grab a snack to hold me over until I reach the palace*, the weakest part of his mind pushed.

The internal persuasion became enough to adjust his steps until he stood staring through the window of the brick building. Inside, around a dozen people waited in line while a worker handed over paper-wrapped bundles to the figure across the counter. Before he could consider the products' popularity any further, the stranger with the bundle turned around, and Will's body went cold.

The sight of the individual's nearly white hair and blue eyes probably wouldn't attract much attention in Verona because of the light mages who frequent the city, but Will had seen that particular person before under less-than-friendly circumstances. He didn't think he could ever forget one of the angels who attacked the Dalan troops in the Valley Beyond, especially not the most vocal of their group.

Despite how conspicuous staring made him appear, Will couldn't look away as the dangerous, magical figure exited the shop and began walking down the road and away from the palace.

Why would one of them be out in the open? he wondered, accidentally allowing his mind to continue questioning the encounter. *Are his companions hiding around here? Did he recognize me? Would Hendal be going to meet with them? Should I follow?*

Will took one step in that direction, but it was too late. The rogue angel disappeared within the crowd, and it became impossible for him to discern where he should go. Every muscle grew tense, so he paused to calm himself down.

If I trailed behind, I doubt I could remain careful enough not to get caught, and they wouldn't let me go. Judging by that one's appearance and how much food he purchased, I'd bet the rest of his group is together in the city, or at least some of them.

He peeled away from the storefront since his hunger ebbed and resumed his return to the palace. Only when he stepped inside the grand hall and became surrounded by the soldiers and mages on his way to the dining area did Will relax.

The meal passed in a blur. He accepted whatever the server threw on his plate, plopped down alongside the group who invited him, and remained silent while they laughed and schemed, unaware of his concern. Whatever he did eat sat like a lump in his stomach.

No matter what, I must inform Byron of the angel's appearance, he concluded. *Tomorrow, or maybe before then, I'll check to see if he is in his quarters. Otherwise, Grace should contact Marcus and me. Perhaps we can avoid coming into contact with-*

"Will, aren't you hungry? You barely touched your food," one of the light mages named Clara asked from where she sat on his right. Her turquoise eyes studied him from behind cropped, golden-brown bangs and reflected her more mature persona, though she was just two years older.

He replied with a curt nod, then he shoved forkfuls of smashed potatoes into his mouth in an attempt to reassure those at the table. This caught the attention of Jean and Peter, two other mages who sat across from him, pausing their conversation.

"What are you doing?" Jean asked to draw even more eyes to him. "You're going to make yourself sick!"

Will shook his head, unable to vocally respond, and most of the table returned to their own meals after chuckling at his expense. Meanwhile, he noticed Clara and Peter exchange a look. The former leaned over to whisper into his ear when he swallowed the mouthful of food.

"Can we talk to you in private?"

He pulled away with a slight blush before glancing between both sets of eyes. "What is it?"

Without giving an answer, Clara rose to return her plate and silverware. Peter joined her after gesturing for Will to follow, and the three left the area together.

She led them to the third floor, wandered to Will's room, and stopped in front of it. "Now, if you wouldn't mind…"

He shrugged to cover his growing interest before unlocking and holding the door open for the pair to enter. Both mages remained standing, reminding him of how they probably hadn't seen how messy he kept his personal space. In addition to the stacks of books, misplaced papers, various herbal ingredients, and other items scattered around, the dimming light from outside seemed to highlight every crevasse.

Well, it's too late to hide it now, he thought as he decided to sit on the edge of his unmade bed.

When neither of his newer friends spoke, he initiated the conversation. "So, what did you want to talk about?"

"I'll say it," Clara began before Peter could utter a word. "Ever since you returned from the southern base with Master Emilea and King Aaron announced the presence of a demon during the ball, we mages have been sensing a strange, frightening energy within the palace."

Will held his breath and remained unsure of an appropriate response.

This allowed Peter to use the opportunity to share what they knew. "We're not fools. Most of us mages trained alongside each other long enough to trust our instincts. The newest recruits are questioning if this is normal and if they should ignore it. I informed them to discuss it with Master Emilea, or even Master Byron, before creating a panic."

"Emilea isn't here," Will mumbled when Peter fell silent.

"She barely spent enough time in the palace to begin with after the late king's murder. We need her guidance to deal with this problem, but all we've been told is that she has personal business outside of Verona. Since Clara's one of the senior mages, she tried reaching out to others for information, including the generals and their assistants." Peter glanced over to his partner, who stared down at her folded hands.

"I understand your concern," Will interjected against the guilt of hiding the truth, "but what does this have to do with me? I can't confirm or deny the magical energy."

"We want to know if Master Byron brought this up to you in the past. Several dark mages mentioned his suspicious behavior when your group returned and how he ordered us to be alert but not to act.

After that night, everyone fell silent, as though the situation couldn't be addressed."

"Some of the soldiers are being distant too," Clara added. "These people are normally social and helpful around us. I rarely see the generals anymore too. If this doesn't change, whatever is lingering in the palace *will* force the mages to leave, or drive us insane."

Although he sympathized with them, Will's main concern had always been jeopardizing any chance at secrecy by including more people, thus risking their lives in the process. He weighed his options in the heavy silence of the room until twilight fell upon the three and his belongings. Finally, he chose to reveal the bare minimum without mentioning the developing plan to stand against Hendal, the demon, or the rogue angels.

"If you hear too much, the creature you sense will threaten you," he prefaced to hint at the danger.

When neither mage argued, he dove into the limited amount of information based on his experiences. The only piece he regretted bringing up was how Coura became a target due to her demonic energy, which led to her be chased away from Verona.

The pair listened intently and didn't interrupt, though Will noticed their bodies stiffen and faces hold a tight expression, projecting their anger and a deep-seated fear. By the time he finished, he scrambled to light the candles placed around his room from the nearest lamp in the hallway since he forgot about the approaching night. The dancing shadows began playing tricks on his eyes while he waited for their response.

At last, Clara turned to Peter. "What should we do?"

Her fellow mage bit his lower lip before answering. "There's no doubt if we tell the others they'll either insist on joining us in killing the demon or leave the palace. I'm debating which would be the better option."

Will felt his eyes widening. "You're seriously going to fight the high priest, a demon, and hostile angels?"

"Why wouldn't we?" Peter countered. "If you could feel how repulsive this energy is, you'd be motivated to end it too. It grates on my nerves and simultaneously terrorizes me. My power keeps

THE ANGEL'S DESCENT

buzzing throughout my entire body, and I imagine someone brushing against my skin when I'm not looking."

The change in his attitude and the negative emotions had Will remembering how the rest of the mages were behaving. It also reminded him of the way Coura had been treated in the past.

It's no wonder she seemed to bother so many people, he realized. *She shares the demon's energy, so it makes sense anyone who feels so poorly about the creature now would have disliked her in an instant. It wasn't her fault, though. No one could know.*

Clara noticed him starting to sulk and closed the distance between them to sit beside him on the bed. "As blunt as his explanation was, Peter's right. It's unacceptable for us to live in the same place as a demon, let alone dismiss the trouble it's causing. I appreciate you trusting us."

"What are you going to do?" Will asked after recalling Byron, Grace, and the others and the risk of the mages' actions affecting their plotting.

"Spread the word," Peter answered for the pair while raising his chin. "I mentioned how most of us worked together at the academy, so I know it'll stay a secret. Anyone who wishes to flee can do so, and the rest of us will come up with a strategy to put an end to this mess."

"What about Emilea and Byron?"

This time, Peter hesitated to reply and glanced at Clara, who shrugged.

"They'll probably find out sooner rather than later," she admitted. "Besides, it might encourage them to communicate with us more often."

Will managed to repress the urge to smirk at her additional comment. *She's not wrong. Although, knowing Byron and Emilea as well as I do, I expect they'll be furious if the mages act without warning either of them. Maybe I should intervene in order to prevent further conflicts.*

Since the matter seemed to be settled for the moment, Clara stood, moved toward the door, and inclined her head at Peter, who caught her message to leave. Will stopped them before they could do so.

"Please, wait to act until you hear from me," he warned. "I didn't mention it earlier because I needed to hear your intentions, but I'm part of another group more invested in stopping the high priest. I'm not going to explain it tonight. If you return here tomorrow afternoon, I promise to give you more insight into our plan."

The hopefulness he tried to convey came through since both light mages nodded and agreed to visit again.

*

Will located Byron in the training ground the next morning, shared what Peter and Clara brought up, and anticipated the negative reaction. Despite appearing displeased with the news, the master mage's words during their resulting conversation reflected the man's compassion for his subordinates. They decided to allow the mages to share what they knew about the demon, and those who wished to assist in the future could do so; however, Byron agreed only on one condition.

That evening, Peter and Clara arrived after dinner. Will informed them of Byron's decision and mentioned a stipulation.

"What does he want in exchange?" Peter pressed.

"He agrees anyone informed of the situation should be allowed to leave the palace for their own safety but with guidelines."

"What does that mean?" Clara asked when Will paused to clear his throat.

"It'd look suspicious if a dozen or more mages abandoned their posts over the course of a few days. To remedy this, Byron suggests you keep everyone in the palace and arrange for a signal in case..."

"In case the worst happens," Peter finished. "I suppose it makes sense. If Master Byron and your group fail, the high priest manipulates our minds, or the demon goes on a killing spree, we can alert everyone to go at once."

Will frowned and saw Clara's face pale upon hearing the possibilities.

He sure gets straight to the point.

For the remainder of the evening, the three attempted to figure out the best way to manage the hundreds of mages, and possibly soldiers, who would fight or flee in an emergency. The conversation died down once they began nodding off, so Peter summarized their conclusions.

"In order to control the spread of information as best we can, Clara and I will tell a handful of our closest friends first. If they agree to help us and Master Byron, we'll share more. Then, everyone else can do the same while we come up with a solid escape cue they should watch for."

"If it does come to that," Clara added after yawning.

Will didn't feel confident enough to support her words. Instead, he agreed to act as a messenger between the two and Byron, decreasing their chances of being discovered.

The pair expressed their satisfaction with their progress, then they exited the room, leaving Will to slip into more comfortable clothing and crawl into bed. Every few minutes, his weary mind returned to the angels, high priest, demon, or the palace's future until he resigned to drink one of the sleeping potions he kept on his nightstand. At some point during the night, he drifted into an uncomfortable dream where he battled unseen foes in Verona's eastern square.

***

"Where could they have gone?" Hendal growled through his teeth as he paced around his lonely quarters on the highest floor of the palace. The space hadn't been cleaned since before he left the demon in charge of the Yeluthian ambassador nearly a month ago, but he possessed neither the time nor motivation to do so. He dismissed the idea of letting a servant in because of the secrets he guarded, including the many letters for Yeluthia from the previously disposed messengers.

"Are you referring to the pigeons you ordered to spy on the southern base?" Soirée's voice responded, rich with her characteristic, unwarranted humor. "Their disappearance shouldn't matter that much."

Hendal glanced over his shoulder at the shadowy figure leaning against the far wall and avoided the urge to disagree since he knew she was right. "It's been a few weeks, and they still haven't seen me," he continued instead. "If they insist on helping me unite Asteom, they should be putting in the effort to fulfill their roles and return as soon as possible."

"Why? Do you not trust them to wander through the city on their own?"

He eyed the demon carefully. *She understands I banished them into Verona to avoid dealing with them after they returned from Dala. Their appearance could connect them to Yeluthia, so they must remain out of sight until I send for them. Besides, they failed me multiple times already.*

"They couldn't bring me the head of that barbaric general," he muttered, ignoring her questions and his building frustration. "Then, they refuse to contact me after the Nim-Valans arrived."

"What would you have them do?" Soirée asked.

Hendal noted the edge to her voice before answering. "They would be my spies, of course. I can send one or two into the camp disguised as the king's messengers."

"Then what?" she countered. Her scowl suggested she disliked the direction of his idea.

After facing her while wondering what bothered the demon, he reminded himself of his position, straightened his shoulders to showcase his confidence, then scoffed. "I thought the reason would be obvious. There might be a few soldiers worth procuring for myself."

Possessing the Nim-Valans came to mind over the past week as he studied their camp from the outdoor hallway overlooking the southern field. Similar to Asteom's troops, the northerners acted independently, though they quarreled often, yet the only person the two hundred obeyed proved to be their general.

To control that man means commanding the Nim-Valan soldiers, he had realized with rising excitement. *What better way to establish an alliance than by using the one person who has influence on the king of their country?*

Knowing Soirée was clueless about his intentions made Hendal chuckle, at least until she strolled nearer, crossed her arms, and leaned forward to put her face close to his. No matter how hard he tried to remember her nature as a horrific creature, he would catch himself admiring her feminine, *almost* human features. Her violet eyes held him in place, leaving him dumbstruck.

"I bet you think you're *so* clever," she began at a lowered volume. "The one leading the Nim-Valan army will sway their country toward the peace you're orchestrating. After all, why would anyone suspect the high priest of aiming to cause the opposite?"

Hendal bit his tongue. He had cast aside the implications of his title for the betterment of Asteom, so to hear the demon referring to them brought about memories of the oaths he swore to uphold.

"However," she went on and pulled away with less hostility, "you forget the threats lurking in the capital."

An ugly laugh escaped him at the mention of those who stood against his vision, especially the master mages. He waved his hand in a shooing motion to dismiss it as a serious issue. "Are you really concerned about them? Emilea wouldn't dare risk the lives of her children, and Byron is in the same position, except with the general and his soldiers."

"And the Yeluthian ambassador?"

"Grace's abilities are troublesome, but I see the fear in her eyes. She understands we could always lock her away again."

"Another kidnapping would be too obvious," Soirée drawled as she crossed the room to stare out the window.

"As long as her freedom hangs in the air, I doubt she'll act out. Speaking of which, Coura shouldn't be a problem anymore either."

Hendal waited for confirmation from the demon, who, for some reason, took an interest in her half-Yeluthian pawn. To hear how Soirée put together a plan to capture the young woman as a child and force her to become part of such experimentation seemed cruel, even by his standards.

A coy smile spread across her face during the pause.

He groaned before grumbling a curse. "Judging by your silence, I presume she's still alive?"

"I wouldn't stay here if she wasn't."

The response tempted Hendal to inquire about her reasoning, but he feared the answer. In an attempt to return to the original topic, he turned his back on Soirée, cleared his throat, then clasped his hands in a casual manner. "No matter what, I must wait for Jaspire or one of the others to send word. I'll request they scope out the Nim-Valan camp, and we can lure their general away so I may grab hold of his mind."

"That's a foolish plan, one I am ashamed came from you."

Hendal spun around to see her inspecting a handful of her raven hair and opened his mouth to snap at her; however, she stopped him with her signature, petrifying glare.

"Did you forget how that spell works?" she asked after. "My energy is filtered through your body, thus allowing you to manipulate my power in such a way. When I use it to possess living creatures, I often drain their natural energy to sustain and increase my own. As a human, you do not share such an ability. Every person you control expends *your* energy alongside mine, which is not much in this case. Even if you do comprehend what I just said, what would you accomplish by simply taking over everyone in the country? How many innocent citizens are under your influence? You wish for Asteom to unite angels, humans, and demons, that's been my impression, but what you're doing defeats the purpose."

"No," Hendal snapped in reply as he became offended by her accusation. "Some people don't understand that what I'm plotting is for the greater good. Who can bring about change in a country where its leaders are not fit for their roles? These pompous fools would rather shun those of us with ideas to unite the humans, Yeluthians, and your kind."

"You intend to force these relationships upon them until they serve their purpose?"

"Yes," Hendal declared before pausing to reflect on what that meant.

Soirée tilted her head and appeared to want to press the subject, so he decided to leave his quarters for some fresh air. When he approached the door and reached for its knob, she spoke again.

"Remember what I said about my magic," she warned. "You're far too weak to handle what may happen if such a spell requires more of my energy."

He groaned at her claim. "What do you mean?"

"Try to think of it another way. If your servants are injured, what do you suppose will happen?"

The question startled him out of his annoyance, and he ventured to guess the first result that came to mind. "They'll die."

The demon giggled like a child at his answer, causing Hendal to hunch forward in embarrassment.

"Silly priest! My energy instinctively heals without needing to be ordered to do so."

"And that means?"

"Anyone under your control will recover from their wounds until the source fails."

Hendal spent a moment pondering what she revealed. The notion of soldiers who could not fall in battle had him feeling light-headed, and his lips stretched into a grin. "An unstoppable army obeying my orders would be useful in achieving my goals."

"Fool," Soirée growled maliciously, like a wild animal. "*You* are the source through which my energy attaches to those you possess. The more spells you cast, and the more power expended to heal, the greater the strain on your body and mind."

The direct threat to his life hadn't been something he accounted for, which led him to verbally lash out at the demon. "You... How could you do this to me?" he cried with a mixture of rage and terror and grabbed at his chest. "Your power is cursed!"

Once the words were said, he cowered away, expecting a physical blow for raising his voice at her. Soirée must have fulfilled her purpose in telling him that bit of information, though, because she resumed a bored expression.

"Your ability to predict the results of your actions is astonishing," she added without attempting to hide her sarcasm. "I forgot to mention, demonic healing takes as much of a physical toll on the body as a human mage's light magic. You might care to do some research on it before you start sacrificing those under the spell."

Hendal cleared his throat before muttering his agreement with her suggestion and prepared to exit his quarters. As he crept out of the room, he heard her mumbling to herself.

"Humans are *much* more interesting..."

5

Over the next week, Coura had no success figuring out what she should be doing while she hid in the safe location away from Soirée, Hendal, and the angels. While Emilea, Aimes, and the children often left the house or studied in their rooms, she snuck upstairs and found the space she occupied less than a month ago. The comfort of an actual bed relaxed most of the recovering muscles, yet nothing eased the burden of uncertainty about her future, or what she considered herself.

The idea of being half-Yeluthian didn't sit poorly, though she wasn't certain if she would ever accept it. Beneath the current situation and her own doubts lied thoughts of her parents, and she soon grew gloomy.

Why would Father leave Neston without an explanation? Perhaps he told Mother, but why keep his lineage a secret from me? Was he tired of living among humans? What about Mother and the others Soirée attacked?

She shook her head to clear the questions before forcing herself to stand and move around. The cast no longer bound her right foot thanks to Emilea and what limited control Coura had on her center. Despite the wild energies, she managed to restrain what she could in order for the master light mage to attempt another healing spell. The process took more time than either of them preferred, but if it meant lessening the pain and bandages, they were willing to try.

Just that morning, Emilea deemed the injuries in a well enough condition to not need any more sessions. "We pressed through the worst of it, and what's left can recover on its own," she shared. "You should focus on stretching, building, and utilizing those muscles. Knowing you, you'll want to be active anyway. Just remember, you need to stay inside until we figure out what to do next."

Reluctantly, Coura obeyed, not that she could do much else.

No noise came from the rest of the house, so she figured the four left for a walk. The effort it took to descend the staircase embarrassed her considering her training and honed skills, but she grit her teeth and forced herself to be thankful for the mobility, as limited as it was. Hunger didn't bother her, even though Emilea permitted more than the bread and herbal spread for meals, so she ignored the kitchen entirely to drop into the armchair farthest from the windows, the one she rested behind for days.

What can I do besides sit around? Coura wondered as she gazed around the space. *There must be more inside.*

In that moment, her eyes fell on a stack of books tucked away next to the unused fireplace. With no other immediate options, she sighed and limped over to them.

"Of course the only thing I can do is read," she grumbled along the way.

Twelve books without writing on their covers had been perfectly balanced into a neat tower. She picked up the one on top, opened it to a random page to read a paragraph, then set it on the fireplace's mantle to inspect the next. None sounded interesting until a word in the fourth book caught her attention; she stopped and put a finger on the spot.

The Mintelian people live in scattered villages throughout the Ghurun mountain range. Each specializes in a different type of craft. Those to the north primarily work with metal, those in the middle villages favor hunting for skins and trophies, and those to the south are known for their paintings, as they create seashell paints and color them with dyes traded from Yeluthia.

Coura continued skimming the chapter since it went on to elaborate the sections' crafting. Although the metalwork intrigued her because of the Mintelian man she met at the Harvest Festival, she focused on the southern villages.

The South-Hobs, unlike their sister-villages, are less tolerant of strangers. In order to make the seashell paints their villages are known for, each member must scout for the best materials, which often causes rivalries between the areas. Currently, seven known villages function by crafting and selling paints. Most remain within their possession for their own projects, including wall art, home decorating, paintings on a canvas or skin to be displayed at public ceremonies...

She skipped the process of creating the infamous seashell paint and hesitated at the next section titled "Yeluthian Ties."
Would this tell me more about their people? The following question she shoved to the back of her mind was if she *wanted* to know about the place her father came from.
Before she could begin reading again, someone started to open the front door while chattering ensued on the opposite side. Her instincts had her preparing to close the book and return the others to their original spots, but she realized it didn't matter since her host gave her permission to stay occupied.
Lexie noticed her first and pranced over while wearing a wide smile. Her palms were pressed together to tightly hold and conceal something within. "Look what I found!"
"What is it?" Coura noticed the edges of some plant sticking out.
Sure enough, the girl opened her hands to reveal bright orange, red, and yellow leaves. "Mace and I collected them on our walk," the girl explained. "Mother said we should have you choose the ones to use in this year's centerpiece."
Coura raised an eyebrow at Emilea, who pretended not to see, and avoided the urge to frown. *She's trying to cheer me up by involving me in whatever she can.*
Thankfully, the children didn't seem to notice the silent exchange and led everyone to the dining table. Coura placed both hands on its wooden surface, leaned forward to assess the colorful selection

without putting too much weight on her right foot, and considered what would please Mace and Lexie the most. Meanwhile, Aimes disappeared upstairs while Emilea prepared a late lunch. By the time she made her decision, which consisted of even choices between the two children, the older man returned to help carry plates and mugs from the kitchen. He joked with them about the process and what his ideal centerpiece would be before winking at Coura to show he enjoyed teasing the children. As they ate, she contemplated his desire to supervise Emilea, Mace, and Lexie and decided to speak with him later about his intentions to either continue living with the family or travel to Verona.

After the meal, Aimes took the children upstairs to supervise their studies, and Coura assisted Emilea with the dishes and some overdue cleaning. The master light mage expressed her appreciation, but Coura only dismissed the words while secretly feeling a sense of relief for an excuse to be moving, even if she had to avoid the windows near the guards outside.

The pair didn't talk except to communicate instructions. As Coura dusted above the fireplace, she wondered if she should bring up the stack of books with the information about Yeluthia; however, they didn't get a chance to relax until after dinner when they wore themselves out. Lexie warmed some cider as an official welcome to the fall season, and Coura drank hers right away so she could lie in the armchair closest to the others at the table.

"If you get too comfortable, it'll be difficult to force yourself to bed," Aimes warned after.

Coura waved a hand to dismiss his comment.

"What he means is, we're not carrying you if you fall asleep," Emilea added.

"I never asked you to," Coura replied before covering a yawn. "Perhaps I'll spend the night here."

"Speaking of carrying people to bed," Aimes interrupted and stood without finishing the thought.

Coura peeked around the back of her chair to see Lexie propping her head up with her hands and Mace licking the last of the cider from his lips. Both children stared at the adults as their eyelids drooped.

After chuckling at their weariness, Aimes shook the boy's shoulder a bit to rouse him and pointed at the stairs. Mace obediently trudged to climb the steps as the older man followed close behind while suppressing a yawn. Emilea did the same to Lexie, though she held her daughter's hand to lead the girl. Coura contemplated snuffing out the candles on the table and prepared to rise when she heard someone return to the first floor.

"Are you really planning on sleeping there?" the light mage inquired as she crossed the room to take a seat in the remaining armchair.

"I can't complain when I slept in the woods and on the floor for two weeks," Coura mumbled in answer. Although she meant it jokingly, the words sounded unpleasant.

They sat in silence for a while to savor the peaceful evening until Emilea spoke again. "He's sure grown attached to Mace, Lexie, and this simple life."

Of course, Coura knew who the woman was referring to. The reminder of Aimes brought her earlier intentions to mind. "Has he mentioned what he's going to do?"

"Not to me. Why do you ask?"

"Do you expect him to stay for a while longer?"

Emilea paused to consider the question. "I believe he feels this is the best place for him to be at the moment. There's never been any doubt in my mind to show he would rather be doing something else, especially since he has yet to discuss the subject with me or mention your other friend in Verona. With that being said, he's obviously concerned about Hendal threatening the children and I and the guards outside, though they leave us alone for the most part. Did you talk with him yet?"

Coura shook her head, unsure if she should venture the subject. *It's his life. Besides, Marcy's relatively safe with Lady Katrina. Emilea's right about him being able to do something here by watching her and the children.*

With the thought put to rest for the time being, she straightened to stretch her back, reached her arms upward, then noticed the books

THE ANGEL'S DESCENT

next to the fireplace. "I forgot," she muttered before stopping herself from saying more.

Does Emilea know Yeluthia is mentioned in those texts? Is it worth bothering her about?

Still, she already sparked the conversation, and the master mage stared at her with interest.

"What is it, Coura?"

"Nothing. I just flipped through that stack of books this morning."

Emilea's eyes lit up, signaling her understanding. "Grace lent those to me."

"She did?"

"When we began researching the ancestral weapons, she volunteered to find information in the palace's library and her own collection on whatever mentioned light magic or her people's history. What you see is the discarded pile, or what wasn't relevant to our dilemma."

"That makes sense." She prepared to end the discussion there and rose to her feet.

"Did you find any interesting information?"

A strange sensation came over Coura then, like anticipation masked by anxiousness. "Should I be looking for something?" she countered after the pause.

The master mage continued observing her instead of answering.

"Good night," she offered and started toward the stairs instead of pushing for an explanation.

"You should read them."

"Why? You already mentioned you didn't find them useful."

"I said they weren't relevant at the time. Besides, they contain pieces *you* might find helpful. I recall some mentioning Yeluthian culture on multiple occasions."

Coura wanted to roll her eyes and pretend she brought up the subject on accident, yet they knew she hadn't. So, she thanked Emilea for the advice and moved to her room for the evening.

*

The following morning, Coura discovered she was the last person awake. Despite that, it seemed as if the extra rest provided her with new strength because, for the first time in weeks, she could move without the constant aches and sharp pains brought about by jarring or jerky motions. Emilea and Aimes gave her curious glances when she joined them at the end of their breakfast in a much livelier mood than usual.

"What are you planning on doing today?" she asked before either could question her chipper attitude.

Emilea shrugged while Aimes discussed hiking to the pond for a swim before the cooler fall weather robbed them of the experience.

Coura nodded, went into the kitchen for her food, then joined them at the table. Once she felt satisfied with the first couple of bites, she explained her intentions. "I need to start my physical training again."

Emilea raised an eyebrow, presumably because she questioned the recovery process, but didn't comment, allowing Coura to continue.

"If the two soldiers stay with you when you leave, I'll be able to sneak off and work on my own for a while."

To her surprise and relief, neither objected nor requested more of an explanation. The meal concluded, and the adults led Mace and Lexie to the front of the house. Coura peeked through the window to see Hendal's guards trailing behind the four without saying a word, as if they were tethered to the group by an invisible rope. After waiting a couple of minutes, she slipped outside.

Watching the seasons change from indoors provided only a glimpse of the visual aspect, undermining the whole beauty of the natural phenomenon. A gentle breeze blew to carry the crisp scent of fallen leaves, decay, and dirt. She inhaled through her nose, savoring the moment as she smiled and remembered why she loved that time of the year.

It never lasts, but perhaps that's what makes it so special.

When she finished taking in her surroundings, she circled the building to inspect the open space in back. Plenty of fallen branches proved sturdy enough to act as a makeshift weapon, so Coura chose one she deemed the most fitting before facing a tree trunk within the wooded area. Its bark didn't chip off as she tested its durability, which meant it would handle her serious swings. The first few thwacks echoed at an uncomfortable volume, but they soon blended in with the woods' noises.

Her main goal for the morning hours became judging her current status after the damage to her body. Overall, it didn't seem as though she lost strength or speed, and Coura figured she still had Soirée to thank for those changes. What impacted her the most were the internal injuries and previously torn muscles that needed to grow accustomed to the movements again after the healing sessions.

Once the familiar motions returned, she worked hard enough to break a sweat. When her stomach tightened and growled, she went inside to prepare lunch. Emilea had brought a basket's worth of food along for their time at the pond, so Coura assumed the four wouldn't return to the house until suppertime. This left her free to procure what she needed from the kitchen for a decent meal. Nothing she made could ever compare to what Emilea cooked, or what the palace offered, yet just eating enough became a luxury as of late.

Despite the temptation to curl up and nap in the early afternoon, she dismissed the idea, cleaned what she had used, and moved outside once more to begin running through her exercises. The sunset stretched across the treetops to color the sky when Coura decided to call it a day. Her original, makeshift weapon broke earlier, and the two replacements followed suit. Fortunately, she spotted one thick enough to withstand the repeated contact and propped it against the tree, which bore missing patches where the bark broke off, before hurrying inside.

Emilea and Aimes didn't give an estimated time for when they would be back, but Coura imagined they wouldn't want to stay out past dark. After such a productive day, she was feeling generous and wanted to throw together their dinner. By the time the four walked through the front door with drooping eyelids and hunched shoulders to indicate their exhaustion, a simple layout of toasted meat and cheese sandwiches, boiled potatoes, and sliced fruit had been laid on the table.

At the sight, the master light mage placed a hand on her chest in disbelief. "You did all this?"

Their obvious, if not exaggerated, appreciation made Coura blush, yet the doubt in her ability to be unselfish and prepare a basic meal offended her a bit. "I don't know how to cook much, but you need to be able to feed yourself when you travel with Byron."

The adults chuckled at the comment as they took their seats and began eating.

After the first few bites, Aimes turned to Coura. "Speaking of Master Byron, have you heard from him or the Yeluthian ambassador?"

"Me? Why would I have heard from them? They should reach out to you or Emilea."

The light mage shook her head, revealing her nervousness. "From what I understand, Grace has to be somewhat familiar with the mind she wishes to connect with in order to communicate. She's never met Aimes, and my husband told me to wait until either he or Byron contacts us. Of course, Grace could talk to me, but I imagined I would receive a physical notice since she needed to recover."

"That's interesting," Coura mumbled as she picked at her remaining food.

They finished their dinner in silence, then the children were excused and played cards in the sitting room. Once the two went away from the table, the conversation continued.

"Am I to understand you haven't had contact with anyone in the palace then," Emilea said as more of a statement than a question.

Coura nodded. "I hate to say it, but I bet Byron is waiting for more of a reason to act."

"What do you mean?" Aimes asked.

"In all the time I spent with Byron, he's never been one to charge into an argument or fight unless he's sure there's a chance for success. He's not stupid, so why take the risk? Well, what happened during the ball was unexpected. We lost, plain and simple. We rescued Grace, which is important, but Hendal still has control, and now he knows we're aiming to stop him."

She paused to contemplate her next words. "I would say Byron's letting the situation cool down before deciding on what to do next. Grace needs to recover in order to be a point of contact between us while the others learn what opportunities are available. That's my best guess."

"It makes sense," Emilea added. "I don't believe I mentioned it yet, but the Nim-Valan troops arrived earlier this week to meet with the royal counsel about their alliance proposal."

"Do you think Hendal will go after them?"

An eerie silence filled the space before Emilea dipped her chin. "I'm not sure. When he shared the general's report with me, he seemed uncomfortable and nervous about their visit. He must not have been counting on controlling the king during such a crucial point in time."

The reminder of Aaron, helpless under the high priest's hold, made Coura's chest ache.

"Then, our only option is to wait," Aimes concluded in a gentle manner.

Emilea sighed and stood to begin clearing the table without voicing an answer. While she moved into the kitchen, Coura faced the older man.

"Aimes, what are you going to do now? You could easily reach Verona within a day, and-"

He silenced her by raising a hand. "I understand what you must be thinking," he started and offered a bittersweet smile. "With Marcy in the city on her own, should I go in search of the stable life we desired? Well, I've got a stake in this game too."

His eyes met Coura's after his statement. The edges crinkled from age and weariness, yet they appeared more full of life than she ever remembered. After, they slid to the sitting room where Mace and Lexie had sprawled out on the carpet to whisper and organize the playing cards.

"To abandon what you're apart of with the knowledge I possess would mean turning my back on what I hope to build for myself and who I wish to become," Aimes continued at a hushed volume. "Since I can't fight or use magic, I'm at a disadvantage when it comes to confronting trained combatants, angels, or demons; I'll leave that to you, the master mages, and Asteom's soldiers. What I *am* able to do is take care of these children while their parents are occupied with saving the kingdom. It's not as heroic as what the rest of you can do, but it's these actions that become the most satisfying to accomplish for the ordinary man."

"I'm sure Emilea and Clearshot are grateful for your willingness to save them the extra work," Coura commented and returned his widening smile.

"What about you?" he asked after.

"I thought we just discussed the issue."

"You plan to stay here until the Yeluthian reaches out to us with Master Byron's orders? What if it takes days, even weeks for them to contact you or Lady Emilea?"

Coura resisted the urge to lick her lips, which would reveal her anxiety. "I'm comfortable enough to focus on training until my body feels normal again."

Although he didn't appear convinced, Aimes left the conversation at that. Everyone moved upstairs soon after as the day's activity caught up with them.

*

The next morning was the complete opposite of the previous. When she woke, Coura found her muscles sore enough to require stretching before even attempting to move downstairs. While her body adjusted to the motions, the energies in her center riled in response despite being stable yesterday. She slept soundly throughout the evening but yawned and rubbed her eyes to the point where she contemplated returning to bed.

Once her limbs were sufficiently warmed up, she limped down the hallway and descended the stairs only to find no one else awake. The entire floor looked a shade darker due to an overcast, which persuaded her into making the day one for relaxing.

Coura fell into the nearest armchair facing away from the kitchen. *It must be mid-morning by now. Perhaps the long day of swimming wore them out more than I thought. It's not like they'll be doing much. I might as well wait for them before going to train this afternoon.*

Out of the corner of her eye, she spotted the red cover of the topmost book in Emilea's collection by the fireplace. Her hesitation lingered while she stared at the stack and wondered what answers she wished would be revealed. The initial idea became to seek information on the ancestral weapons' locations or spells similar to their sealing magic. Still, the master mage already attempted to find just that to no avail.

She tried to consider another reason to study them aside from her own curiosity before questioning why it seemed to be such a hindrance. Then, the explanation dawned on her.

Could it really be that simple? I'm afraid to learn about Yeluthia, about my own lineage. Ever since Soirée told me about my parents, I've been doubting who I am and what I should be.

The conflicting energies hummed in response.

I'm a disgrace to the Yeluthians because of what I've done. In that case, as long as I don't associate myself with them, I can consider myself human. Would those books even possess anything pertaining to me, or better yet, this mess we're in? If they do, can I ignore my emotions for my friends and the betterment of Asteom? I'm thinking too much...

Coura rose from her seat and grabbed the three books on top while opting to distance herself from the information. The first contained nothing more than reports from soldiers across the country, and she wondered why Grace thought that would be important to look into. When she progressed halfway through, the sound of footsteps on the staircase made her jump. Despite her desire to replace the books and avoid a confrontation, she forced her body to remain still.

If I refuse to study in front of others, I'll never find out what's in these texts. Besides, maybe I can recruit them into assisting me. The suggestion helped her relax and continue reading as the house steadily came to life.

Her optimistic attitude faltered as the process of skimming through reports made her want to quit altogether. That particular book had been written twenty three years ago and included simplistic numbers and notes over the course of the next five years, such as crop tallies, severe weather accounts, physical fights or arguments deemed severe enough to take to the city's leaders, and much more.

"Have you found anything to help our situation?"

Coura glanced to the right where Emilea moved to sit in the second armchair. "Not yet."

"Which one is that?"

The woman pointed to the text, prompting Coura to hand it over. "Just a bunch of reports," she added, shrugged, then opened the next book, which happened to be the one she began reading a couple of days ago.

Emilea flipped through the pages before closing the red-covered text. "I didn't notice much in this either. I asked Grace for one to see if the records' keepers add magic-related items for the general public."

"Why would they?"

"I never actually read through them before since I have access to those written by the upper-ranked mages and former master light mages. They're full of other accounts; however, if those same pages were referenced elsewhere, then that would be good to know."

Coura didn't quite understand, but she nodded anyway.

Mace and Lexie hurried downstairs and into the kitchen, so Emilea stood and returned the book to the pile. "Call me if you stumble across more," the woman urged and went after her children.

Although she wondered what the light mage assumed she would find, Coura continued reading and took a break to eat once she heard the three move to sit at the table.

"Aimes must still be sleeping," she commented with a glance at the staircase.

"He snores through the door," Mace muttered before sucking on an apple slice.

In response, Lexie covered her ears in a dramatic fashion. "That's what *you* sound like," the girl retorted.

"Do not!"

"Do to."

Coura found their bickering amusing while their mother ordered them to behave. She finished her meal and returned to her book only to have both children request to help in the search, but one glance at the lengthy, small-lettered pages had them changing their minds.

*

THE ANGEL'S DESCENT

The next seven days passed by in a similar fashion. When Emilea, Aimes, Mace, and Lexie left for a walk or participated in an activity away from the home, Coura trained on the opposite side of the building. She spent the rest of her time reading what she could about Yeluthia, the ancestral weapons, light magic, or anything else available within the stack of books. Meals and sleep aided her body's recovery, though the desire to manifest her wings returned to accompany the persistent stir of conflicting energies. In the middle of the night, the power began to suffocate her, forcing her awake to gasp for air and sweat profusely until her body stopped trembling enough to rest again.

On the eighth day, when Coura had gone through two thirds of the stack, an image in the text she currently skimmed sparked an unexpected, frightening idea. The book covered a more recent portion of Asteom's history, which no doubt would have been useful considering the alliance with Yeluthia. In fact, one of the middle chapters discussed it briefly and mentioned the gifted ancestral weapons. The final chapter explained the establishment of Clearwater and two other eastern towns named Rolian and Lyrt after the explorers who later became their founders.

After sharing the profits from the southern seaports, the final few pages held a collection of maps. Coura usually skipped them since she didn't care too much about old layouts when a current map of the country could be easily acquired; however, one within that particular book seemed different as it showed the eastern cities, the Ghurun mountain range, a handful of the Mintelian villages, and a blurred space near the eastern border. She scanned the rest of the maps, both in the text and others from the stack, but none displayed the unusual, foggy area.

It appears to be a smudge, though I doubt the owner would keep the page in with the other, clean ones instead of redrawing the image. If the marking was intentional, why is it absent everywhere else? Could it be a weather pattern? It does look like a giant cloud or storm system.

She traced the mysterious section with a finger until a sudden realization came to mind and sped up her breathing.

Yeluthia is sometimes described as a city in the clouds, and it's located close enough to the Mintelians to continue trading. Is this really...

At that point in the day, it proved to be late afternoon. Rain poured throughout the morning to keep everyone inside, except the guards who stayed at their posts with waterproof cloaks. Aimes sat at the table with Mace and Lexie and taught them a card game called Trick Play, which he learned when he worked on the docks in Clearwater. Meanwhile, Emilea curled up on the sofa with a mug of warm cider and a book.

Coura felt content spending the day indoors until the possible discovery sparked a series of emotions. She glanced through the final chapters and maps again, yet nothing supported her theory. Even so, she couldn't dismiss the notion.

What if that's where Yeluthia is hidden? No one knows for certain, besides the Mintelians and messengers in Kercher. If I can reach Grace, she could confirm or deny my guess. Still, what does it matter if I locate the city? She can't fly, so she would need an escort, and she's being held in the palace.

The shadow of an idea crept forward from the back of her mind.

What if I go to inspect this location? Would the angels uphold their end of the alliance? Would they believe me if I told them what's happening in Verona? Could they help our cause in any way?

Those questions and more swirled around her head, causing it to begin aching. She closed the book after taking note of the page and put one hand over her eyes. For a while, she focused on nothing except breathing at a steady pace to ease her flustered mind and tense body.

"Are we ready for a break?"

Coura removed her hand to see Emilea stretching while wearing a knowing smile and nodded. She volunteered to assist with preparing dinner in order to give herself something else to think about. When the time came for them to eat, she poked and pushed her food around with a fork. After, she offered to clean the dishes, which the master mage appreciated, and dropped into her preferred armchair once more.

THE ANGEL'S DESCENT

Later in the evening, Emilea poured mugs of steaming tea before sitting between her children on the sofa, and Aimes took the second chair. They managed a little conversation, emptied their cups, then traded off yawning until deciding to go upstairs. Coura offered to bring Lexie to bed, Emilea led Mace upstairs, and Aimes made sure the lamps were snuffed out.

"Goodnight," Lexie mumbled as she crawled under the covers.

Coura repeated the word and slipped into the hallway without a sound. There, Emilea stood waiting for her.

"Thank you for helping Lexie," the light mage said quietly and flashed a genuine smile as they approached the door to Coura's room.

"It's nothing," she replied while reaching for the knob.

"Are you feeling all right?"

"I'm fine."

"You didn't eat much at dinner," the woman commented, as though she just became aware of Coura's reserved behavior. "If your stomach is bothering you, or perhaps your head from the reading, I can grab you medicine."

The offer sounded tempting, yet she knew in her heart what bothered her wasn't a problem herbs or potions could fix. When the light mage moved closer, she opened the door with a glance over her shoulder.

"I think I found where Yeluthia is."

Emilea gasped and prepared to speak, but Coura hurried inside her room while she had the chance to stall the inevitable questioning.

6

Coura expected the master mage's reaction to be similar to her own, which had been why she opted to reveal her findings the following morning after breakfast. Aimes offered to supervise Mace and Lexie on a walk through the autumn woods, giving the women time alone. In a way, Coura grew jealous of them. The rain from the previous day ended early enough to create a beautiful scene with droplets reflecting the many colors of fall, and it warmed up thanks to a clear sky beaming sunlight down on the forest.

As she sat in silence, Emilea flipped back and forth through the pages while keeping one finger on the blurred spot the entire time.

"You didn't find any notes regarding this?" the light mage asked without looking away.

Coura released a frustrated breath as she repeated herself for the third time. "No. Nothing hints at a mistake on the map."

"What makes you so sure this is it then?"

"I already told you."

This time, Emilea glanced at her. "It's a bold assumption. Anyone who has heard of Yeluthia will know it's near the mountains, and the city in the clouds title might be for show since they *are* referred to as angels. I can see how you might believe this spot represents their location, but it's not enough evidence to convince me."

Coura frowned but didn't argue. In order to avoid spreading rumors or jumping into action, she needed to hear Emilea's professional, calculated observations. Her resulting shrug signaled her resignation.

"You're right. I got ahead of myself."

"To be fair, if I took the time to glance over the final pages, noticed this, and made the same connection, I'd seek a second opinion too."

"Thank you for that." Coura made to take the book back, yet Emilea hesitated before returning it. "Is there anything else?"

"Say it's true, that this is where Yeluthia lies. What would it mean for us? Could we use the information to help our situation?"

"I'm hoping to discuss their involvement with Grace when she decides to contact us," Coura added in place of an answer.

The questions continued and soon reflected her own, solidifying her original idea to communicate with their people. When Emilea fell silent to contemplate the concept, Coura realized none of the master mage's comments had been directed at or regarded her specifically, which proved to be the complete opposite of what filled her head.

I can fly. I can go there and see if it really is Yeluthia. But, what then? They must keep scouts on patrol and defenses in place, so it'd be dangerous. Why should I risk my life and their secrecy by leaving? If it's only for the sake of being right, that hardly seems fair to Emilea and Aimes, especially when Grace or Byron could contact us at any moment. How would anyone be able to reach me?

She caught Emilea rising from the armchair with a slight wince and waited to hear more.

"What would you prefer to do if that's where Yeluthia is located?" the light mage startled her by asking in an innocent manner.

"What do you mean?"

"Would you be willing to go there?"

Coura opened and closed her mouth, unable to brave a response until Emilea repeated the question.

"I don't know," she admitted. "It's smarter to not act until we communicate with Grace or Byron. Then, I wouldn't be abandoning you." She paused, lowered her eyes, and ventured a personal remark. "Anyway, what could we gain if I went? One look at me and they'd label me as a threat."

She regretted those words almost immediately and raised her gaze to Emilea's face. The woman's mouth hung open a bit while her expression turned sympathetic.

"I'm sorry, Coura. I had no intention of pushing this on you if you feel uncomfortable. It was more of a hypothetical suggestion."

"Isn't that a little reckless?"

"Perhaps, but it has the possibility to yield fruitful results," Emilea replied in an odd, controlled tone of voice.

Coura raised an eyebrow to hide her growing curiosity. *As allies of Asteom, would their leaders trust me if I explained our request, even though we haven't established a consistent relationship?*

The warm energy in her center hummed, as if in confirmation, so she voiced the thought. "Do you believe the Yeluthians would answer a call for aid from the palace?"

"If they were willing to send Grace to reestablish the old alliance, it's worth a try. Remember, the capital is sheltering the Nim-Valan troops as well. I shudder when I consider what Hendal could do to their country in addition to ours."

"I might not discover anything new. If I do, though, it can help our cause."

"The journey will be satisfying for you as well."

Although Emilea didn't elaborate, Coura knew what the master mage hinted at.

*

In the end, only they would know where Coura planned to go. The two reached a mutual agreement that the less people who were involved with the venture, the better, especially if the altered spot was Yeluthia. Their hesitation to wait until Grace contacted them lingered, but time didn't favor those in the palace.

Preparing for the near future proved more difficult than Coura expected. One part of her urged for caution because of the risk to her life in case the Yeluthians became hostile. Another, greater side overshadowed that, though. An eagerness to be in the sky, as well as contribute to stopping Soirée and Hendal, rose with each passing hour. Still, if her fear caught up to her, she would abandon the trek and stay in a safer location to figure out what she should do then. Of course, Emilea wasn't aware of the backup plan.

"When do you intend to leave?" the master mage asked once they sufficiently discussed their business through the entire afternoon.

"Tomorrow."

"So soon?"

"Why are you surprised? The point is to contact Yeluthia before the worst happens, assuming where I'm heading is the correct location."

"I suppose you're right."

Emilea appeared to want to say more, but Coura had grown tired of wresting with their doubt, which motivated her to depart next day. Together, they moved into the kitchen, prepared supper, and laid the dishes and food on the table as Aimes, Mace, and Lexie trudged inside through the front door.

The children began recounting a tale of their adventure in the woods without any sort of prompting while the adults ate. Mace foolishly chased a deer away when he practiced a fire spell, then the trio noticed a fawn hiding in the foliage and waited for the mother to return. When it didn't, Aimes suggested they lead it in the doe's direction. The story concluded with the two animals reuniting before disappearing into the trees. Lexie's exasperation and description of the young deer's timid behavior reminded Coura of her once-suppressed memories of being a child full of wonder.

"What an honorable decision," Emilea commented while giving her son and daughter a pleased smile.

From across the table, Aimes let out a groan. "They forgot to mention we chased the blasted animal to the eastern edge of the woods. For once, your guards showed some emotion; they didn't look too thrilled."

"I hadn't thought about them. What a shame they must follow us *everywhere* outside."

A full stomach accompanying their tired bodies became enough to send them to bed early. Despite how much she longed for a full night's rest, Coura lied awake to imagine what she should expect during her flight.

The morning revealed an overcast promising rain, but she intended to be gone before it began. No leftover traces of drowsiness remained, allowing her to focus on readying herself for the journey.

First, she needed to dress properly for the frigid winds and lower temperatures, which had been normal when she passed above the clouds before. Emilea provided enough clothing throughout Coura's stay to warrant a pile specifically for her, so she threw on a dark gray, sleeveless shirt, a charcoal-colored sweater on top, and finally a worn pair of brown pants. In the closet, she found a hat and scarf and procured those as well.

The sun hadn't risen yet, so she descended the stairs at a slow pace. Next, she fumbled in the kitchen for breakfast and double-checked the pouch Emilea gave her the night before, which held coins for purchasing food along the way. There wasn't a need for her to bring much, something she spent half the previous evening worrying about. The book containing the map would be extra weight, so she memorized where to explore, and her magical sword and spells could protect her.

Once she felt ready, she used the back exit to sneak outside in case the guards already arrived to stand in the front. Inhaling the fresh air, stretching her limbs, and manifesting her wings filled her with new life after the weeks of recovering.

I'm free!

The words triggered Coura's determination, propelling her into the sky for the first time after the damage her body endured. Still, the last thought she had after climbing higher was how Emilea planned to explain her disappearance to Aimes, Mace, Lexie, and their companions in the palace.

*

With the clouds acting as a veil below, Coura soared east at a leisurely speed. Despite the protection from any wandering eyes, the air became too thin to stay there for more than a few minutes at a time. Every so often, she dove under, caught her breath, then moved upward once more. She hoped if anyone noticed they would see her as a speck in the sky, like a bird.

The additional clothing proved their worth against the freezing wind and water, which clung to her every time she passed through the clouds. Late in the morning, when she started shivering from the nonstop pressure and temperature changes, a break in the trees revealed a wide pond. She pulled her wings in tight to dip lower before fanning them out near the canopy.

For a moment, Coura recalled the fall that resulted in her injuries and hesitated to drop through the trees. The recently healed bones didn't protest as she transitioned into a glide before gently controlling her wings by shifting the angle. When her feet touched the ground, she steadied herself and released the manifestation spell. The landing felt sloppy compared to what she had perfected in Dala, but after the past month, she was just glad she stayed upright.

A scan around the area showed it didn't possess a station for a rotating guard, meaning no one supervised it. The uncut grass displayed weeds and wildflowers wilting in the autumn weather while fallen branches and mossy logs covered with mushrooms sat nearby. She walked over to the water, found a patch of dirt at its edge, and sat for a break. A moment later, her stomach growled, and she wrapped both arms around her midsection.

How long has it been since I traveled on my own? she wondered as she stared at her reflection in the water. The surface wobbled when a breeze blew by, one far more merciful than those she encountered in the sky.

Coura began to mentally measure how far she could fly before the end of the day and the layout of the country's eastern half until movement in the image on the pond caught her eye. She glanced up to see a silhouette pass by in the trees ahead. Then, it shifted directions to come near her location. The possible threat had her springing to her feet and preparing the spell to summon her sword; however, the second set of energy, presumably from her lineage, hummed, as if commanding her not to act yet.

"Who's there?" she called instead, causing the shadow to halt.

She expected the stranger to flee or attack, or an ambush, yet they moved closer, approaching with visible caution to stand on the opposite side of the pond. The cloaked figure removed their hood, revealing the face of an attractive, middle-aged woman with blonde hair that trailed down her shoulders.

I recognize her, she realized but could not remember a name.

When the stranger didn't speak, Coura addressed her again. "Who are you?"

The woman stared, tilted her head, then seemingly ignored the question. "Where's Byron?"

At first, the mention of her former mentor startled Coura, but it sparked a memory to reveal the woman's identity. "You're from the tavern in Fester."

Their previous exchange came to mind, as well as how she needed to drag Marcus and Byron to safety before rescuing Will from the pair of angels. Most of that night still remained hazy.

The woman nodded and placed a hand on her chest. "Forgive my caution. I'm Cintra, a friend of Byron's. You're his student, correct?"

Coura wondered if she should answer truthfully or not before deciding it wouldn't matter what she said if the woman intended to search for Bryon. "He's not here."

"I was afraid of that when I noticed you were alone."

"What do you mean? Why do you need him?"

Cintra began to circle around the pond. To Coura's satisfaction, she stayed a respectable distance away once they stood closer.

"It's much easier to speak without shouting at each other," the woman explained, smiled, and tossed her hair casually over her shoulder. The natural-looking makeup she wore accented her light blue eyes, ruby lips, and rose cheeks.

Coura considered her own appearance and grew self-conscious about her wind-blown hair and bland face. "Why are you looking for Byron?" she asked to distract herself.

The woman's lips curved downward into a frown, and she sighed before replying. "Byron and I have always been friends, but there are times when he reaches out to me for help. I possess a rather unique ability passed down from my angelic ancestors. It allows me to draw upon visions of the future. I can't predict what will happen because life constantly changes, but I see faces or places with omens associated with them. Does that make sense?"

Coura nodded. Somewhere in her once-lost memories, an elderly woman from her hometown could use a similar spell, though it had never been on such a grand scale. Others from the Magical Arts

Academy could do the same if they chose to, but the instructors discouraged the practice.

When Cintra paused to rub her hands together in an uncomfortable manner, Coura understood why she didn't continue.

"What did you see, and why does it involve Byron?"

"If I focus on a person intensely, I often lean one way or the other and sometimes prompt visions," Cintra responded while lowering her voice in a way that fueled Coura's worry. "I love Byron, but he likes to use my ability when he's truly concerned. Every instance I receive a letter, I know he'll request I use my power."

She reached under her cloak to remove a crumpled piece of paper from a satchel and handed it to Coura.

Cintra,

It's rotten of me to ignore a proper greeting, especially considering all you've done for me, but I'm afraid time is of the essence. My work prevents me from leaving the palace, and I'm in desperate need of your help. If you remember my last visit and what I requested of you then, I ask that you repeat your marvelous assessment and respond with your findings. Truly, I am at a loss for company and options. Otherwise, I would never press such a thing upon you. I love you and am thankful to have grown with you beyond your gift. When I am able to, I will visit to express my gratitude in person.

I eagerly await your response. Byron

"A messenger delivered it two nights ago," the woman explained once Coura returned the letter. "I don't know what to make of it."

"He'd only write in a cryptic manner if someone is keeping a close eye on him. It also sounds like he wants you involved as little as possible."

"Byron has always been considerate like that. Ever since I refused to accompany him to the academy in East Hoover, he promised to respect my decision to leave this ability a secret, except at my discretion. I appreciate his thoughtfulness more than he will ever know."

"If he's asking you to report the most recent visions you've seen, why not respond instead of hiking toward the capital?"

Coura became so preoccupied with the note that she hadn't noticed the single tear sliding down the other's face until it glittered in the sunlight.

"I'm so sorry!" the woman exclaimed and pulled a handkerchief from the pouch.

While Cintra composed herself, Coura waited despite her rising impatience, curiosity, and sympathy. The woman continued after a moment, though her voice wavered.

"The last time you were in Fester, Byron requested I use my ability to see the future of the country because of those creatures wandering around and killing people or their livestock. I couldn't make out much in the resulting darkness. It was as if some power greater than mine had swallowed me. In the midst of my fear, a person with wings emerged, an angel bearing a dim, golden light."

"That's amazing," Coura mumbled before reflecting on the vision's meaning.

Byron met with Cintra, then Will encountered two hostile angels. My life changed that night, and this woman had seen what I would be up against. I wonder if a demonic creature blocked her foresight, or perhaps Soirée.

"As soon as I read this letter, I focused on Asteom, specifically the capital city."

"And?"

"All sorts of spells involving fire, ice, and lightning clashed, like balls of colorful lights. Usually, the scenes and images are clear, but this time was different. Hundreds of people marched against each other in a battle, and a shadow loomed over them all. Seeing such conflict scared me. Then, the brightest lights descended from the sky."

"What does that mean?" Coura pushed when silence followed Cintra's description.

"I assume fighting will take place near Verona. The shadow haunting my vision felt similar to what drowned out my ability when I spoke with Byron during your visit. I could never forget such a sensation since it's what I *can't* see that frightens me the most."

"So, you left to tell Byron about this."

To Coura's dismay, Cintra shook her head.

"I chanced a look at his future. It's easier to focus on a wider scope than a single person, but I felt his presence. His power was at work before everything cut off..." The last sentence ended on a chocked sob before the tears started again.

Meanwhile, Coura's mind went numb. *Is she implying he's...or he will...*

She clenched her hands into fists, digging her fingernails into her palms. "Look again."

Cintra blotted her face with the handkerchief. "What?"

"Look again," Coura repeated and stepped forward when the woman continued to stare at her. "I don't believe Byron's been killed, or will be. Other forces are at work in the palace, and they're stronger than your magic. Perhaps the connection cut off. Tell me what you see now so we can figure out what to do."

When Cintra didn't react, Coura refrained from muttering a curse. Her heartbeat thundered enough to cause her chest to ache, but something began to stir within the woman.

The weak energy trail felt similar to Grace's because of their shared, light nature. Cintra closed her eyes, allowing any sorrow to leave her features. Her power stretched beyond the clearing and returned at a steady pace over the course of a few minutes. After, she opened her eyes, which held uncertainty instead of the previous hopelessness.

"What did your ability pick up?" Coura prompted in a gentler manner since she didn't want Cintra to cry again.

"He's alive," the woman replied slowly, as if each word carried a weight to it. "His presence wandered through the same darkness that shut me out. I think...he will be hurt. If he remains where he is, we might lose him."

Coura lowered her eyes to stare at the grass around her feet, uncertain what Cintra's message hinted at and what she should do about it. When she raised her head, the woman's eyes were shut, and she felt the light spell for a second time.

"What are you doing?"

A minute passed by before Cintra relaxed, opened her eyes, and answered. "I hoped to test if I would have the same issue when I use my ability on someone else. The same darkness shrouded the vision, so perhaps it's everywhere, hindering my foresight."

Coura's initial reason for the spell's problem revolved around her relationship with Soirée. *I would believe her power can bother light energy, even indirectly.*

Cintra studied her as she considered whether or not to let the woman go to the capital city and find Byron. Hendal would be a threat to her safety if he connected her to the master mage. Because of that, Coura had a feeling Byron would not wish for anyone to pursue him.

Evidently, Cintra realized that as well. "I must return to Fester," she began while placing the handkerchief and letter in her satchel. "You have my message, so I trust he'll hear it soon."

Coura voiced her agreement and promised to describe the issue at the first opportunity.

This caused the woman to smile. "Also, I wish to share the vision I had regarding you."

"What is it?" Coura asked hesitantly.

Cintra shifted her gaze to stare into the pond. "I can tell you're nervous about the future. What I see is never certain, but it always includes a bit of truth. You should find answers in the direction you're going. What those are, I can't say, except I advise you to search for a golden weapon."

"A golden weapon?"

"It shines beneath the palace, cutting through the darkness I sense there and around you. Although I can't promise how the future will play out, I believe you need to try and locate it."

The cryptic message held no answers but acted as a warning of sorts. Coura expressed her gratitude for it anyway, which seemed to please the woman.

Cintra pulled the hood over her face, returned to the opposite side of the pond, then waved before shouting a parting message. "Take care of yourself, and Byron too. He's a good man!"

"I know," Coura muttered as the woman disappeared into the woods. When she stood alone once again, it became impossible to dismiss the fact that his life remained in danger.

7

With the Harvest Festival less than a month away, the city and palace started preparations for the event since the Nim-Valans had settled into their camp. Rain and dropping temperatures threatened to hinder what progress had been made, motivating the citizens to act with fervor.

Despite the weather and positive attitudes of his fellow mages and soldiers, Byron needed to spend additional time outside and away from the excitement to cool his head. He trekked across the training ground to the stone wall lining the area where the northern forest stretched beyond and leaned against it with his arms crossed. He remained there for a while in a partial meditation to clear his mind as the afternoon turned to evening. So much happened behind his daily routine that he wished someone else was in his place and he could just worry about the upcoming holiday.

Over the last week, he spent whatever time he could spare devising a plan to lure Hendal away from the palace without facing the demon or rogue angels too. Challenging him indoors again would be out of the question. To keep the high priest there not only endangered the lives of multiple residents who had nothing to do with the situation but also limit what he could do.

My magic is dangerous in closed spaces, he explained when their group met for a second time. *Clearshot's strength is useless in the dark, and Marcus wouldn't be able to wield his sword properly in a cramped room. The demon can remain inconspicuous in the shadows, adding an extra risk. It might leave Hendal alone if we approach from outside. If we expect retaliation, we shouldn't be going into this alone anyway.*

No one disagreed with his logic, not that he expected them to.

Once a location had been settled, they began considering how to go about a resolution. Several ideas came to mind, which ranged from involving General Casner, General Tio, and possibly the Nim-Valan general, searching for a binding spell to capture the high priest and forcing him to remove his hold on everyone, and even killing the man to see if the spell would break. Byron didn't mention it, but he thought the final strategy would be the most successful should they capture their target.

In the end, he left the decision to his co-conspirators because they would be supporting each other throughout the plan. Marcus, true to his noble nature, voted to use a binding spell instead of taking drastic measures. Despite his prior involvement with the rogue angels and his encounter with one in Verona, Will seconded the idea. To Byron's surprise, the herbalist also suggested they include volunteers from the mages. Grace had no preference, which reflected her neutral position as a representative of her country. Finally, Clearshot provided the lengthiest explanation that favored trying a binding spell first before resolving to kill if it failed.

Developing the actual approach based on their discussion ultimately became Byron's responsibility. It took two days to formulate a solid, organized outline, yet the outcome still would not favor them.

He gazed around the training ground and reviewed the next steps when he couldn't relax. His hands were buried in his armpits for warmth, and he hugged himself tighter against the crisp wind while wishing he brought a jacket or cloak.

Still, once Hendal emerged from the palace, the internal flame would spark to life.

{*Byron, are you outside?*}

Grace's mental voice teemed with nerves that had him feeling concerned for her position, so he attempted to sound reassuring. *I am. Are you ready?*

{Clearshot and Marcus should be leaving now. Will, his friends, and I are waiting for their signal.}

Just remember to stay calm and out of the way as much as you can.

Grace's presence disappeared, taking the negative emotions with it. Another breeze cut through his clothing, and he swore under his breath.

Waiting is always the hardest part, like the anticipation before a storm. Let's hope our actions here impact what Hendal is doing.

He sent up a silent prayer as Clearshot and Marcus entered the training ground from around the front of the palace. Both dressed in dark colors with daggers and swords dangling from their belts, quivers on their backs, and bows in hand. Byron waited until the pair approached to acknowledge them.

"Are we ready?" he asked through chattering teeth.

The assistant general nodded before turning to walk west along the stone wall where the pair would hide in the shadows. Clearshot looked after him instead of following. When the younger soldier moved out of earshot, Byron's friend faced him.

"I didn't tell them what we should do if we fail to capture Hendal," the man revealed, showing a rare glimpse of the vulnerability he usually locked away. "They seem distracted enough by what they're supposed to do. Besides, who among us is the likeliest to…"

Byron bit his tongue to stop himself from berating Clearshot. "You should have told me sooner. It's realistic to organize a backup plan, especially given our chance of success. Marcus and Will should contribute input from their experiences as well."

"I know, but I doubt Hendal or that creature would allow an escape."

The statement hung in the air ominously while the two stared at each other. As they contemplated what would take place, another, unforgiving wind howled.

"I'd better get going," Clearshot commented. "I'll make sure to get word to the Dalan base if we do need to scatter. They might be our only allies if the plan fails." With that, he hurried after Marcus.

What Byron didn't get a chance to mention was how he already prepared for that scenario. The previous afternoon, he explained the situation in a letter to General Tio and urged the man to bring as many soldiers as he could spare to the capital. The request had been sent through a messenger, and with a dual purpose. Of course, his troops would provide extra support for their cause to rescue those within the palace; however, should Hendal be restrained, the Dalan general would need to be present in order to judge the high priest, especially since the demon's power controlled Aaron, Tont, and others in the capital. Because the two communicated often enough, the letter wouldn't seem suspicious either.

I ordered Clearshot to head south anyway and asked him to tell Marcus and Will to do the same if the plan doesn't work. I don't want them to think I'm betting against our chances. The letter should serve to move the process along, no matter what happens.

He resumed his position, practiced his breathing exercises, and reviewed the next steps. During the action, he didn't believe he'd get an opportunity for such a leisurely break.

*

"This is what I suggest we do," he had shared with Clearshot, Marcus, Will, and Grace once the details came together. "Hendal has never been one to shirk his responsibilities, and we'll use that to lead him into the training ground. If someone asks for a prayer or blessing, I wager he'd come alone instead of including others unaffiliated with his duties. Grace, Will, and the recruited mages can act as a barrier to prevent him from running once he sees I'm there. Clearshot and Marcus will be our scouts for the same purpose, except they'll be armed with arrows since they'll hide at a distance."

He didn't elaborate on the implied measures to use should they lose the chance to capture Hendal, or if the demon or rogue angels appeared.

"If you wish to involve your comrades in our business, warn them first. They have every right to decline. Remember, what we're plotting must stay a secret, so those you disclose the information to should be trustworthy," he concluded.

Against his resulting nerves and suspicion, the amount of support from the mages proved staggering. Will's friends didn't seem to understand the impact of their words because they gossiped behind his back without him catching on. Grace had been the one to break the news to Byron, and he grew upset until he remembered the paranoia at the welcome ball.

Even then, those with the ability to sense magical energy felt the demonic power at work, he reminded himself. *I guess that swayed them to help. They know more is going on beneath the surface and didn't receive confirmation.*

Still, he made it clear they would not include more people than he deemed necessary. The rest of their group agreed, yet he worried about Marcus, Will, and Grace conspiring without his knowledge. After a chat with Clearshot, Byron decided to leave it alone.

"If anyone else intends to support us, I'm sure they're smart enough not to directly interfere," his friend had commented. "Besides, Hendal won't have any doubt about the mages we can send to fetch him."

*

The area emptied throughout the evening, except for a trio of mages who practiced sparring with wooden swords. Will assigned all three to put out the lamps around the center stable, then they would patrol the perimeter for any intruders once the confrontation took place. Due to the previous murders and intimidating, unnatural energy, most people who lived in the palace didn't venture outside of their quarters after the sun set, which Byron learned during his observations over the past week.

He studied the mages to distract from his shivering body until one of the doors leading into the training ground opened. Two people emerged, along with the high priest whose white robe stood out against the dimming twilight. Byron froze since he hoped to remain as inconspicuous as possible while the selected mages led their target farther away from the building.

To his dismay, Hendal noticed something wasn't right far sooner than they anticipated. He halted and addressed the two mages, prompting them to urge the high priest to go near the stable. When he still hesitated, they started walking back toward the palace.

THE ANGEL'S DESCENT

I guess we'll adjust, Byron decided before pushing off the stone wall to cross the open space. *Will and his friends should already be preparing to move outside as well.*

Even at a distance, he noticed Hendal frown upon spotting him and expected to pursue the man should he attempt to flee. Surprisingly, the high priest began strolling toward him instead. Soon, they stood face to face in the middle of the training ground.

"Am I to assume you wish to speak with me alone, Master Byron?" Hendal asked in a nonchalant tone of voice quite unlike the personable manner that made him favored in the palace for years. "You should be above treating your subordinates like servants."

Although Byron understood how precious their time was, he vowed to offer the man a chance to surrender before opting to restrain him. "Enough is enough. Asteom has more to lose than just the royal family. Our ties with Nim-Vala and Yeluthia are at stake, and you have no right to fill the role of our kingdom's leader. Please, step down now before someone gets hurt."

Hendal rubbed his chin, as if pondering the plea. Then, his shoulders trembled while a chuckle rose from the silence into a wicked laugh. "I believe you finally lost your mind!"

The high priest's behavior didn't startle Byron, but he continued to prepare for any sort of sign that the man would move to run or attack.

"You've always been a person I admired, Master Byron," Hendal continued, emphasizing the title. "Ever since the late king proposed the Mage Service Law, I envied the way you stood up for your students and defended their integrity. That's why I'm hurt you do not share my values."

His words tempted Byron enough to question their validity. "What do you mean?"

"Just as you desire the best for your trainees, I want what's best for the people of this country. The Magical Arts Academy feared the future because they doubted their students' preparation, which motivated you and your fellow instructors to try and prevent the law from being passed. Do you feel the same as you once did? If not, why do you attempt to thwart the outcome you don't want when it'll benefit Asteom. You can solidify the safety of the entire country by joining me."

As much as he longed to scoff at the notion, Byron held his irritation in check and straightened. "You're right about the results of the service law. I never would have predicted such a successful turn of events. In *your* case, other factors are at play. Influencing rogue angels, conspiring with a demon, and using its power to manipulate people is inexcusable."

"Is that so? How is it any worse than what you've done to your possessed protégée?"

The question caught Byron off guard. Despite being aware of the man's attempt to spur a reaction, he couldn't help letting his temper show. "Coura has nothing to do with this," he growled in response.

Hendal laughed again. "How can you stand there and lie to a priest? The young woman's been blessed with extraordinary power, yet she placed her faith in those who would limit her abilities to serve their own intentions. King Hernan viewed her as nothing more than a weapon, and so did General Tio and the Dalan army. In fact, you encouraged her to live as a soldier, even though you knew the risks."

Byron's repressed doubts drifted to the surface of his conscience as the man went on.

"How can you act like you weren't the least bit relieved when she reclaimed the demon's magic? After all, with a powerful pupil like her, your name should be well known to the common folk. It's a shame she's no longer here to support your efforts."

I won't fall for his silver tongue, Byron thought against the triggered memories of bloodstained stone and black feathers lining the palace's hallways the night of the ball. *No matter what happened to Coura, I must fulfill my role and capture Hendal. I'll worry about finding her later.*

"This is your last warning," he stated. "Do not resist arrest, and you will be given a fair trial. Release your hold on the minds you control, and no harm will come to you."

The high priest muttered to himself before reaching into a fold in his robe and removing a knife. As far as Byron knew, the man hadn't been trained for combat, yet Hendal held the weapon with both hands and an unwavering glare.

In response, Byron stepped closer while unsheathing his steel sword, which served him well over the years. *The plan is to immobilize. I won't harm him unless I need to, but I might not have a choice.*

He halted to point the tip of his blade at Hendal's face. "If you refuse to cooperate, I will use force."

The high priest opened his mouth to respond when the whirl of an arrow sounded above their heads. Byron hurried to track its destination since that had been the agreed-upon signal for outside interference.

On the upper floors of the palace, the outer hallways' glassless windows loomed over the training ground, and five figures observed the conversation below. The world seemed to pause until three of the silhouettes leapt from the openings, one after the other. Before their feet touched the ground, they manifested white wings that appeared to glow in the night, landed as a unit, and released the spell to a shower of glittering, silver light.

{*Byron!*}

Be ready to create a shield, he ordered as Grace shouted in his mind.

"I sometimes forget you met my companions in Dala," Hendal commented while the newcomers moved to stand behind him. "Yeluthia desires peace too, but I'm told their ruler cannot fathom the value of his citizens' freedom. The same can be said for the Nim-Valans. Just as we demonstrated how meaningful sacrifice was to the academy, I intend to reunite all beings by any means necessary."

As if Hendal's final sentence had been a cue, the angels drew their swords and charged.

Byron would have panicked if he needed to fight the trio at once, but he prepared for as much. He outstretched his free hand in front of him to craft a wall of dark energy, surrounding his body on all sides except from behind.

The angels slowed their steps, shared an amused look, then the tallest struck the shield with his weapon.

Although the blow caused his ears to ring slightly, Byron exaggerated the impact by stumbling backward, as though he had been physically pushed.

"Has the famous master mage lost his footing?" the one in the middle teased.

"Perhaps remembering our last fight makes his knees quake," the shortest added, causing all three to snicker.

Still, Byron remained patient. *They're believing my feigned struggle and underestimating my abilities. Arrogance seemed like their group's major weakness last time, so I'll take advantage of it to draw them away.*

Once their noise ceased, they rotated striking at his shield in a lazy attempt to break it. Anyone familiar with magical energy would notice the power in the shield didn't waver, but Byron staggered after each hit. Before he moved too far, he formed another wall, released the first spell, and repeated the process, drawing the three away from Hendal and the palace. They neared the perimeter soon after, and he shifted to the next phase, trusting Grace, Will, and the assisting mages to fulfill their assignments.

The middle enemy raised his blade in preparation for a slash, so Byron dismissed his shield as soon as the sword was in mid-motion. This caused the angel, who anticipated some sort of resistance, to lose his balance when his weapon passed through nothing but the shimmering remains of the spell.

With one opponent distracted, Byron focused his attention on the tallest and burliest of the trio, calling forth a wave of energy from his center. He shaped the power into lightning aimed at his target and launched the magic forward.

A blast of bolts connected with the unsuspecting angel, and his companions threw up their hands as they scrambled in the opposite direction. Bright flashes of white light and deafening cracks stunned them momentarily, and when he could look over, Byron saw the victim sprawled out on the ground with smoke rising from his charred body.

THE ANGEL'S DESCENT

I can manage them for now, he noted. *The main issue is finding the one responsible for healing their group at a distance. Otherwise, I risk draining my reserves to cause useless damage.*

"You are a clever human," the middle angel shouted while grinning and rubbing his left arm. A thin stream of blood trickled down a patch of red skin to indicate the lightning had spread wider than intended.

What the remaining two failed to notice until that moment was why Byron lured them to the edge of the area. The third angel who hadn't been affected by his spell slid to the ground while producing a gurgling noise and clawed at his throat. Protruding from his neck and chest were a set of arrows expertly released by the hidden soldiers.

Byron silently thanked Clearshot and Marcus for their accuracy, even in the limited light, though he expected nothing less from the former.

Two down...

The lone angel mumbled his fallen companions' names as a new shielding spell appeared behind him, thanks to Grace's magic. The Yeluthian ambassador's task consisted of holding the wall so the three combatants wouldn't be close enough to interfere with Hendal's capture. This limited Byron's line of sight, but he understood his value as the bait in their strategy and accepted that he wouldn't be the one to restrain the high priest.

"How shameful," his opponent began while raising his voice into a shout and glaring. "We aim for peace, and you support murder."

Somehow, Byron knew the angel would charge, so he cast another shield to stop the impending strike. "Clearshot! Marcus!" he called to the nearby soldiers.

At his signal, he heard footsteps as they sprinted behind and toward the palace. The angel's eyes darted to the pair, but he didn't pursue or attempt to break the shield again.

"What's your name?" Byron asked to keep his opponent's attention. Already, the pure light energy from the healer stirred around the fallen bodies, and he remembered that magical power would disappear once Clearshot and Marcus succeeded in fulfilling their responsibility.

"Are you truly worthy of my name?" the angel countered, though he lowered his sword and spoke with less ferocity.

Byron responded by removing his shield. Neither glanced away from the other despite the rising sounds of voices and clashing spells closer to the palace.

"We met before and never had the opportunity to converse," he continued. "Hendal claims you're helping him achieve his goals, so a mutual understanding can do more than combat."

The angel's eyes narrowed, though he answered after pausing for a moment. "I am Drake, and these are my brothers. On my right, acting as your cohorts' quiver, is Hector, and the one you injured on my left is Urvin."

"Why did you come to Asteom?" Byron pressed.

"We hope to establish a world where our kind do not hide from the tyranny of kings and tolerate the destruction from demons."

"You side with both then?"

"A human cannot comprehend the potential we bring as members of the Yeluthian race," Drake retorted. "Disappearing shows we are weak, feeble creatures. We deserve the freedom to go where we wish and act as we desire. Less aggressive measures may be preferrable, but that is not always the case."

Byron sensed more emotion simmering beneath the bitterness in the angel's voice, yet any hope to stall their fight vanished once those on the ground started moving. The bulkiest of the trio, the one introduced as Urvin, pushed himself to his feet with some effort, but he didn't seem to be in pain. Meanwhile, Drake removed the pair of arrows from their final member named Hector and tossed them aside.

The newly healed angel nodded to his leader, who grinned before both turned to stare eagerly at Byron.

"Enough words, master mage. Show us the power you possess!"

***

When Will volunteered to guard Grace during their attempt to separate and capture the high priest, he expected to be thrown into combat. He didn't doubt the rogue angels would interrupt because of their contact with Hendal and their appearance in Verona, but they were targeting a fellow Yeluthian. Byron prepared for their arrival and many other possibilities, including if they did not appear, if the demon joined instead, or both.

During the scheming, he tried his best to remember everyone's positions and duties in each scenario, even after he recognized how ridiculous that was. Fighting never seemed to follow what one could plan for, which he remembered from the incident in the Valley Beyond, so he trusted Byron's knowledge and experience. Keeping track of himself proved to occupy his mind as he and Grace snuck outside to meet up with Jean, Clara, and Justin.

Their group huddled together against the palace and watched the high priest near the stable. Already, Will noticed beads of sweat sliding down the man's forehead and neck to display his uneasiness. Whatever their companions, Peter and Diana, said to bring Hendal outside must have been convincing enough not to warrant his concern until that moment.

"Do you think he fell for it?" Clara whispered and leaned in closer.

Will didn't answer.

The high priest came to a halt, conversed with the pair of mages, and remained behind while Peter and Diana trudged back to the group's location. Then, they all spotted Byron approaching.

"What did he say?" Justin asked when their companions returned.

Will hated to peel his eyes away from their target, but he was glad he did once he caught Peter and Diana's expressions. Over the months he became familiar with the two light mages, they never openly displayed negative emotions. The worst had been when they grew nervous about some relationship or training conflict.

Diana didn't, or couldn't, hide her fear. She glanced at the ground, rubbed her hands together, as though they were cold, and visibly breathed faster.

Meanwhile, Peter, who showed the least amount of emotion out of Will's new friends, seethed. His hands balled into fists at his side, the muscles in his upper body tensed, and his eyes darted between each of their faces.

"What did he *say*?" Justin repeated after they realized the voices were too far away to understand.

Diana cleared her throat before answering. "The high priest accused us of treason even before he guessed we lured him there. He claimed if we value our lives, we would make sure he never recognizes us after he leaves the training ground. His behavior became so erratic."

"Who does that monster think he is?" Peter grumbled in an uncharacteristically bitter manner. "For him to abandon his responsibilities as an advisor is blatant heresy. What kind of person lets their morals be corrupted in such a position?"

The hushed outburst startled Will, and he involuntarily gulped at the looming possibility of failing his friends and the kingdom. Those around him seemed to behave the same, projecting regret for choosing the same path.

Grace's voice cut through their doubt. "A virtuous man has nothing to fear, but a man who believes himself to be virtuous fears nothing."

"What?" Will felt compelled to ask in the resulting silence as they stared at her.

"It is a saying among my people," she explained. "The high priest should act as an advisor, healer of hearts, leader in worship, and much more. Hendal took advantage of our faith in the position and controls the helpless to force his will upon Asteom. Remember that, or your emotions will overwhelm what hope we have of stopping him and the demon."

Will realized his jaw had dropped a bit while she spoke and snapped his mouth shut. *Because of her age, I forget she's been trained to be an ambassador. I expect such authority and composure from Byron or Aaron, but never Grace.*

"She's right," Jean added after. "We need to stay focused on the plan."

The group's following nods and mumbles of approval lifted Will's spirits, and he drew the sword at his waist as quietly as possible in preparation for their moment to jump into action. Although the others carried knives, they would be relying on their magic.

Seconds crept by while they observed Byron and Hendal. The discussion led to the two wielding their weapons, and Will wondered if it would come down to a physical scuffle. Unfortunately, the sound

THE ANGEL'S DESCENT

of an arrow soaring overhead and crashing into the palace's wall far above them signaled trouble.

"Oh no," someone muttered as a wave of dread fell over him.

They're here...

"Do it now!" Justin ordered in a harsh whisper while turning to Grace.

The Yeluthian closed her eyes and bowed her head after their three light mages, Clara, Jean, and Diana, placed their hands on her shoulders. Although Will didn't possess the ability to sense magical energy, he knew they were lending Grace their power. She then reached her palms outward toward the training ground as three of the rogue angels landed behind Hendal.

I remember them, Will thought upon recognizing the males. *Another could heal from a distance, and a female had been there using spells too. I wonder if Hendal will stay once they begin fighting, especially since he avoids dirtying his hands.*

"Wait," he began and held out an arm for the rest of his companions to stop. "Let's see what he decides to do."

No one acknowledged Will's interruption, but Grace didn't cast her spell, which he felt grateful for when his judgement of the high priest proved correct.

Hendal said a farewell, spun around, and moved toward the entrance he had been led through. Meanwhile, Byron's shielding spell entertained the rogue angels enough for them to pursue him as he retreated toward the perimeter.

So far, the plan was going as expected. Will readied himself for his role by evaluating the high priest. *We were informed of his lack of combat training and magical energy. Unless he's keeping some ability or spell a secret, we should only worry about if he lashes out sporadically.*

Upon noticing their group in the limited lighting, Hendal paused, but he appeared unphased by the additional people in the area. Grace used the opportunity to cast her spell, creating an amber-colored, shimmering wall behind the high priest. Its height and width continued to expand until Will guessed it to be as tall as the palace and wide enough to cut through the entire training ground. He also knew better than to doubt its strength, even though it looked just like a thin sheet of glass.

With the shield in place, Justin stepped forward, Peter hurried to stand in front of the door, and Will sidestepped to put his body between the high priest and Grace, who remained focused on holding the spell with the three light mages' assistance.

Nothing about Hendal reminded Will of the high priest he had seen in the months prior. The man's face turned scarlet as he fumed and glared between those who blocked his path. No trace of the friendly smile or professionalism he was known for remained.

"Have you no shame!" he roared and made a sweeping motion. "Coming between the high priest and palace is treason. I'll order you all to be arrested for this!"

"What about you?" Justin retorted at a matching volume. "Robbing the kingdom of its rightful leaders isn't what a priest should do, let alone the high priest!"

Hendal audibly inhaled before releasing the breath in long sigh. Some of his frustration simmered, but his next words still held their previous heat. "You couldn't possibly understand what it is I'm doing to rescue this country. Arguing with an impudent soldier is beneath me. Now, *move!*"

The high priest stepped toward the door, and Justin stopped him again by raising a hand to send an apple-sized fireball at his feet. The spell had been aimed to land in front of Hendal, not hit him, but the man stumbled backward and growled a curse anyway.

Before either could continue the verbal bout, a gust of wind had everyone covering their faces as two other angels dropped to the ground. Will remembered both from the Valley Beyond, which caused his body to tremble, yet he pushed the memory away and set aside his feelings by focusing on protecting Grace.

The wings disappeared once the two figures descended, and the female planted herself in front of Hendal with a sly grin.

"What should we do with them?" she asked without so much as a glance at the high priest.

A wave of dismissal followed and proved to be the signal she waited for. Just as Justin had launched his fireball, she threw up a

THE ANGEL'S DESCENT

hand to release a single, slim bolt of lightning toward Peter without warning. Will could only react by covering his head with his free arm as the spell crashed mere feet away in a clap of thunder that shook his entire body. Smoke clouded around from the charred earth and damaged stone wall, and he, Grace, and the light mages began coughing.

The eerie silence lasted until the air cleared. Then, Will froze when he saw a magical shield in front of him. Before he could question its appearance, Justin moved in front of him and dismissed the spell with a flick of the wrist.

He protected us.

"You seem reasonable. Why don't we take this somewhere else?" the dark mage offered, though his serious expression reflected his intent to accept only one answer.

The question had the angel chuckling before she crossed her arms. "You are a brave human."

"Entertain these fools," the high priest ordered, though the two didn't seem to be paying attention to him anymore.

If Justin can distract her, Peter and I should be able to corner Hendal, Will thought and gripped his weapon tighter. *Would the angels surrender if we threaten his life? I hate the idea of hurting a defenseless person, but if we must...*

With no better options available, he braced himself and raised his blade.

8

Justin's taunts successfully interested the female angel enough to give chase when he took off at a sprint along the palace's outer wall. More smoke stirred once they began exchanging spells that lit the growing darkness with flashes of red, yellow, and white.

In the midst of their fight, Hendal resumed walking toward the door Peter guarded with his chin held higher. The second angel, the male responsible for healing his companions, had his back to them and arms crossed as he observed whatever took place on the other side of the amber-colored shield.

If Justin handles one and the other isn't interested in us right now, I can't let Hendal get away.

Will glanced over his shoulder at Grace and the light mages and deemed them safe to leave alone for the moment. The distance from the high priest to Peter proved just far enough for Will to slip in between, halting the man for a second time.

Hendal scoffed and rolled his eyes, again behaving in a completely different manner. "What's this?"

"Give yourself up, and we won't harm you," Will stated and held his breath.

During his last visit to see Marcus, he requested the assistant general help him find the best approach should he need to address the high priest. His lack of muscle, skill, and magic put him at a severe disadvantage, but his friend's reassurance boosted his confidence.

"You're in better shape than him," Marcus had explained. "What you possess is experience when it comes to combat. You've seen how the flow of a fight progresses, whether it's real or a sparring match, and you're not expected to be the one to capture him. Since that's the case, flaunt your blade. People who lack our training fear pain, so never underestimate a scratch on the arm or leg. Include some bluffs to keep them guessing too."

Will had faith in his friend, and his trust solidified when the advice worked. The high priest tried to pass around him only to retreat when he used slow swings to herd the man backward.

At first, Hendal pretended not to be bothered by the threat; however, after two more failed attempts, he became angry and demanded Will stop. The third time, he lunged forward instead of taking methodical steps while raising his arms with the intent to shove the obstacle in his path.

Will chose to retaliate then, just as Marcus advised. In a faster and more controlled swing, he scratched the tip of his sword across the high priest's right forearm before resuming a defensive position. The attack succeeded in drawing blood, though he knew from practice it wasn't deep enough to be a serious injury.

Nevertheless, Hendal panicked, grabbing the spot and cradling his arm as though it would fall off. Will attempted to ignore the nasty glare shot his way and opened his mouth to warn the high priest again, but an explosion from the direction of Justin and the female angel had them both glancing that way.

Something glittered in the air within the resulting cloud of dust and smoke, and Will's insides tightened when he realized it had been part of the dark mage's shielding spell. As he began to wonder if his friend weakened enough already to need support, he spotted Justin being thrown back by a barrage of ice-coated wind.

What should I do? I don't have magic, and Hendal can't escape...

Movement to the left caught his eye, and he shifted to see Jean and Diana abandoning their positions behind Grace in order to sprint over to their fallen comrade. Together, they raised their hands in sync to conjure a gold-tinted shield, separating all three from the immediate danger.

The female angel paced in an impatient manner before throwing more spells at the shimmering wall. Unlike Justin's shield, the one the two light mages created absorbed whatever slammed against it, rippling like a pool of water in the rain.

With his friends taken care of, Will faced the high priest once more. Hendal hadn't tried to slip around him, but he seemed to be considering it.

"I remember you," the man started and twisted his lips into a displeased frown.

Will remained silent, though mostly because the comment took him by surprise.

"You accompanied Byron during his last visit before the service law passed. I assumed you were one of his other students, but he never introduced you as such. How someone lacking the power of a mage and the skills of a soldier managed to scrape up a life within the palace is beyond me. You should be a servant, at best."

Although the insult stung, Will didn't reply. The high priest had resorted to using words instead of actions, which he could handle better anyway by not arguing. *I already know my worth, thanks to Byron and Marcus, and I'll prove it by assisting them now.*

A cry from nearby interrupted his reflection, but it abruptly cut off as he prepared to spin around. Hendal took advantage of the distraction to run toward the entrance, leaving Will grasping for a method to stop him again. Despite his normally reserved behavior and habit of thinking through a problem, the fear of failure pricked him like a thorn, initiating his instinct to act.

Just as the man passed by, Will lunged, placing both hands on the hilt of his sword and moving it upward in a slash across Hendal's left pec and shoulder. Unlike the first cut, this proved deep enough to need stitches and bled profusely, but he knew from his years of medicinal experience it would only be fatal if left untreated. Fortunately, it yielded the desired result.

The high priest screamed, clutched the wound, and froze in place. His eyes darted around, and he gasped for air.

Meanwhile, Will stood stunned by what he had done. The action succeeded in what he needed to accomplish, but he couldn't tell if

THE ANGEL'S DESCENT

Hendal's behavior reflected horror, terror, or rage. Before he could consider the matter, a male voice spoke from behind.

"You would believe he is dying with such a dramatic reaction."

The sound caused him to jump and awkwardly twist around to raise his blade in preparation for an attack. Until that moment, he had forgotten about the fifth angel, the one with the ability to heal from farther away. His heart dropped as the figure observed him.

Peter didn't warn me? Will wondered before his gaze fell to where his friend's body lay in the grass next to the door the mage guarded. *No! That cry...*

He had no time to process what happened next. The angel removed a short sword from the sheath at his waist while charging, forcing Will to attempt a block; however, his timing didn't line up with the attack.

The figure feigned to the right, a motion Will normally would counter because of its poor execution, but he felt overwhelmed by the additional opponent, leading him to strike with a vertical slice to mirror what caused Hendal's injury. The other blade moved faster, though. In a matter of seconds, a sharp pain rose from a slice across his chest, and scarlet liquid poured forth from the open wound to coat his torso. Will dropped his weapon in order to cover the spot in a feeble attempt to avoid losing more blood.

"On the other hand, *your* injury is grave enough to give you reason to panic," the angel started in a condescending tone of voice. "Go ahead and beg for mercy." Instead of a follow-up strike, he inspected his blade and presumably waited for a response.

Will didn't believe the words would form even if he intended to surrender. His heartbeat drummed in his ears, pounding faster and pumping more blood onto his chest. It didn't slow despite his efforts to calm down, ultimately leading him to search for help.

He glanced around to where Peter had been ambushed and saw Diana on her knees in the middle of a healing spell. Clara and Jean traded off creating a shield for protection against the female angel's attacks while Justin leaned against the palace's walls with blood coating the right side of his head.

All of this left Grace alone. The Yeluthian swayed as her raised arms wavered, and the dazzling shield she produced dwindled instead of towering over them. Losing the extra power from the other light mages also made it more transparent, so Will could distinguish movement from the shadows on the opposite side.

We're going to die here if something doesn't change. The hopelessness in his thought, accompanied by the blood loss, sent a wave of dizziness over him, and he focused on not collapsing.

During his struggle, Hendal snapped at the angel for taunting Will, then the two conversed as the high priest pulled himself together.

"I want this mess cleaned up before the entire building is out here asking questions," the man muttered before limping toward the unguarded door.

Will managed one step, but his legs locked and refused to move after, allowing Hendal to pass without giving him a second glance.

I...can't let him get away...

The pain in his shoulder began to grow numb. Although the concern for his life matched his worry about losing the high priest, all of that disappeared when the nearest angel turned to stalk in Grace's direction.

"No," he groaned and reached for the figure with one hand.

He understood Hendal wouldn't kill the Yeluthian ambassador because she remained too valuable as a pawn. That fact compelled him to go to her and attempt a rescue, despite his limitations.

Each limb protested the forced movement, yet Will grit his teeth and continued as the angel reached his friend, who kept concentrating on her spell until the threat stood in front of her. Only then did Grace open her eyes wide, drop her arms, and begin backing away with a frightened expression. Her shield dissolved into a mist-like cloud, revealing more action on the opposite side of the area.

When Will neared the two, he remembered he dropped his weapon and blushed with both shame and frustration at his stupidity; however, once the male angel seized Grace by the wrist to keep her in place while she shouted for help and attempted to free herself, his instinct kicked in again. A surge of adrenaline rose to push him into a charge, and he released a cry as he threw his body forward.

His lack of muscle and strength wouldn't result in a successful tackle, but the sound caught his target's attention. The figure spun around, noticed Will, then started to laugh while Grace still tried to tug her arm away to no avail. Before Will could lay a hand on her captor, though, the angel's head dipped sharply until his chin touched his chest, as though something struck it from behind.

The sudden jerk had Will slowing to a stop out of caution, and he watched as the hold on Grace loosened enough for her to break free. Her captor's body fell to the ground after where it didn't move, then they noticed an arrow protruded from the back of the angel's head. Two more rested in the center of the torso.

What happened? All of the swelling emotion cooled to leave Will unable to muster more than mere curiosity, even when he neared the enemy.

"Stay back!"

He glanced up to see Marcus approaching. The assistant general kept his bowstring drawn with another arrow pointed at the lifeless body, only lowering it once he came close enough to nudge it with his boot.

"Did *you* do that?" Will blurted out, making his disbelief evident.

Marcus ignored the question and instead peered around at the rest of their group before fixing his eyes on Will. "All of you need to retreat," he ordered in a serious tone of voice quite unlike his usual, easy-going manner.

Although he longed to protest, Will understood the situation. "Fine. Where should we go? Where can we meet you, Clearshot, and Byron afterward?"

The assistant general winced and paused to contemplate an answer.

Will caught the message. "You three aren't coming with us, are you?"

"No."

"Why? What are we supposed to do?" he whined against his better nature. It wasn't the time or place to be doing so, yet the idea of dragging their battered group away without additional protection concerned him. Luckily, Marcus wasted no energy reminding him he couldn't argue with the decision.

"Bring them into the city, to my home if you need to, but you can't stay here. Hendal might send someone to finish us off or label us as traitors. It's more dangerous, and the rest of the rogue angels are still here. With their healer gone, though, Byron, Clearshot, and I still have a chance to reduce their numbers. Our main objective is lost, but that doesn't mean we can't accomplish something tonight."

Marcus lingered until Will agreed before raising the bow again while hurrying over to where the mages still held off the female angel. The elemental spells had diminished since she first began attacking, which allowed the assistant general to easily stand nearby and begin firing arrows.

Whether or not they landed, Will didn't know. His eyesight grew blurry, and the darkness prevented him from seeing much. The additional opponent had the remaining angel debating if she should abandon her current prey and chase after Marcus. A moment later, she decided. Just as Justin had done earlier, the assistant general led her across the training ground toward the ringing of metal and flashes of dark magic spells.

A touch on the shoulder drew Will away from the sight, and he groaned from the pain that arose when he flinched. At his side stood Grace, who fixed her eyes on his wound.

"Hold still," the Yeluthian instructed while placing both hands on his chest.

A warmth reflecting her gentle nature spread to envelop his pain and dull it significantly. It ended in an instant, leaving Will to marvel at how the open injury thinned into a shallow cut. "Did you—"

"I mustered what I could to prevent it from bleeding," she interrupted, closed her eyes, and dropped her head into one hand, as though the healing drained her magic. "The rest can mend on its own."

"Thank you. Let's share Marcus' order and find someplace safe to rest." Will hoped he sounded more confident than he felt because his body began trembling from both the physical and emotional toll the day took on him.

Together, the two leaned on each other and limped over to where Clara, Jean, and Justin huddled near the palace. When their faces turned to the pair, he noted how pale and bloody they appeared, reminding him of the cost to wield their energy to such an impactful extent.

THE ANGEL'S DESCENT

Clara noticed his chest first and came closer to meet them. "You're hurt," she commented, yet she didn't reach out or say more.

"We need to get away from here," Will responded to dismiss their concern and uncertain looks. "If the rest of the angels attack, we can't protect ourselves, and it'll distract Byron, Marcus, and Clearshot."

"Where's Hendal?" Jean asked before anyone else could speak. One of Justin's arms was slung around his shoulders to support the dark mage's body, which slouched forward.

"He escaped inside," came Diana's voice from where she steadily trudged nearer to join them. "I lost track of the high priest while treating Peter."

Their aforementioned friend walked behind her with his hands on her shoulders; the entire front of his shirt and neck were splattered red.

"Don't call him that," Justin grumbled and stood straighter. "I will *not* abandon Master Byron."

"I refuse to leave either," Grace startled Will by adding.

I would stay too, if I could help, but we'll get ourselves killed, he wanted to say, yet his mouth went dry and the shaking continued. Fortunately, Diana saved him the trouble of convincing the group.

"Are you that stupid?" she shouted at Justin. "Can't you see Peter and Will are hurt, and how drained the rest of us are? You should be close to exhausting yourself fending *one* off. What makes you confident you can keep up with more?"

Everyone dipped their heads in defeat, snuffing out the argument. Diana seemed satisfied with this.

"Let's move," she suggested after and turned to head toward the palace's entrance.

Jean ordered her to wait. "We can't go back in there. Hendal will capture or kill us as soon as someone notices what we did. The halls are crawling with the demon's presence."

"What do you suppose we do? We can't just run like fugitives."

"Isn't that what we are now?" Justin muttered, silencing the group.

Will recalled Marcus' message and how the assistant general offered his home as a hiding spot. Still, he refused to put his friend's family at risk. After considering more options, including Emilea and

Clearshot's home and Lady Katrina's estate, a wave of dizziness clouded his mind.

"We need to decide," he began to distract from his weariness. "The best place for us to hide is in the city. Even if Hendal pursues us, which I doubt, we'll be protected by the civilians as long as we stay in a busier area."

Jean gave him a sidelong glance. "This many people, let alone injured mages, is pretty conspicuous."

"We can split up then," Will agreed and prepared to share his suggested locations until Diana cut him off.

"Don't worry about us," she said with a tilt of her head as a gesture to Peter. "My father owns a house down one of the alleys behind the eastern square. I healed his injury, so we'll reach it tonight and recover until we hear more from you."

Even as she finished her last sentence, the light mage moved toward the glowing lamps on the outskirts of Verona.

"The rest of us need to recover as well," Jean picked up where the conversation left off. "Did you have a place in mind for two or three people?"

Will considered what he had thought of earlier and weighed the risks once more.

"I know where we can go," Clara told him and stared across the clearing. "Sorry, but your silence isn't reassuring. A friend of mine owns a flower and décor shop with her father. It's on the main road, but we'll need to sneak around if we're avoiding the guards."

After sharing the directions, she requested Jean accompany her before offered Will an apologetic look. "Are you and Grace going to be able to-"

"Yes," he answered before she finished the question. The lack of noise from across the training ground didn't go unnoticed, and his chest started to ache.

Clara and Jean accepted his response without another word. They adjusted Justin's arms around their shoulders and turned around to follow in Diana and Peter's wake.

As he watched the trio leave, Will felt feverish and attempted to clear his head by taking a deep breath. His mind wandered to Marcus,

Clearshot, and Byron, and he wondered how they were faring. "We'd better get moving too."

"Where are we staying?" Grace asked as they began walking at the fastest pace he could manage.

"Emilea and Clearshot's home."

"Absolutely not."

Her firm response had Will looking over. "Emilea can help us, and we wouldn't put any innocent civilians in danger."

"You will not reach the edge of the capital city in your condition," she chided. "It is late as well, so we would not get there until the sun rises. Besides, Clearshot mentioned Hendal is keeping an eye on Emilea and their children. Our unexpected visit could put their lives in further danger."

Will couldn't come up with a rebuttal.

"What other options do we have?" she inquired with less hostility.

"Marcus suggested we use his home, but his mother, sister, and her family live there. I also considered Lady Katrina's estate."

"After all she has done to aid Byron, I feel as though she would believe our reasoning and allow us to rest there," Grace concluded. "Once we recover, then we can visit Emilea. My goddess gift is also able to reach the palace if we are in Verona."

With nothing else to decide on, and barely enough energy and motivation to keep one foot in front of the other, the pair forced their eyes to remain on the lights ahead.

9

Byron already knew he pushed his luck by expending more than enough energy to distract the angels. The loss caused his center to feel hollow for the first time in years, which acted like a signal for when he was reaching his limit. Still, the plan deteriorated as time passed until he fought to survive instead of just hold the enemy's attention.

The shield Grace created with the light mages' support had been a barrier meant to separate Hendal from his guards, but the spell noticeably wore down after the sun set. The next time Byron glanced in that direction, it vanished. He considered calling out with a mental shout yet refused to draw her away from what took place closer to the palace.

Even if she wasn't in harm's way, he didn't get an opportunity to spare a second. The leader, Drake, and his companions kept him busy until Clearshot and Marcus were able to jump into the fray. Until then, he focused on using his magic to prevent the three from coming too close, and the shifts between elemental spells and shielding often surprised them when they expected one or the other. This switch in the pattern resulted in disabling and lethal strikes, which would have been enough if they weren't being healed. When one fell from a serious blow, they returned in a matter of minutes.

To Byron's credit, he avoided their weapons until Clearshot and Marcus appeared to begin sending arrows through the air, nipping at the angels like biting flies. He knew his friend would be accustomed to working alongside dark magic, but he paid attention to how the assistant general moved because he didn't believe Marcus ever fought alongside a mage before. This became evident when the young man continued to put space between himself and the shields.

Movement to his right had him preparing for another attack. Urvin, the tallest of the three angels, charged even as an arrow found its way into his back. Instead of bringing up a shield, Byron held his ground until his opponent neared. With another tendril of energy from his center at hand, he adjusted to plant his feet firmly while the angel lowered his weapon, signaling an upward swing.

As he predicted, the sword's tip grazed the grass as it rose in a curved arch aiming for Byron's chest, but the blade didn't go farther than his knees. A horizontal shield manifested at his command to block the attempt, producing a metallic ring and chipping off a part of the blade's top half.

Urvin stepped backward, visibly startled by the spell and resulting damage to his weapon, and retreated to stand beside his two companions. Without a retaliation in mind, Byron chose to pause the fight in order to catch his breath.

Grace never replaced the barrier, he noted after sparing a glance at the opposite side of the training area. *I should assume the worst since she hasn't contacted me either.*

His gaze returned to the three angels, who panted from their efforts while wearing smiles, as though this became the evening's entertainment. Approaching footsteps from behind reminded him he wasn't alone, though only Clearshot moved to stand by him while their opponents huddled together.

Byron caught Hendal's name being thrown around but ignored the voices to address his friend. "Where's Marcus?"

"As soon as the shield disappeared, he sprinted over to help Grace's group," Clearshot replied. "I'd bet the rest of the rogue angels from the Valley Beyond are there, or maybe some of the soldiers under Hendal's control."

"What do you think we should do?"

"I'm out of arrows and not exactly gifted at wielding a sword. We're much slower than them too, so unless you plan on dying here, I suggest we run."

Byron bit back a curse. "What would that accomplish if they pursue us?"

A flash of light and thunder interrupted their conversation and drew all eyes in the direction of the palace where two shadows crossed the open field. As they neared, Byron saw Marcus in front leading someone throwing inaccurate spells in an attempt to hit the assistant general. He recognized her a moment later as the angel he faced in the Valley Beyond, which explained her inability to land an attack. Whoever trained her had not been a skilled mage, or she wasn't fully trained, because every spell she cast utilized raw energy instead of filtering it through natural channels. This wasted plenty of power, and the result became sporadic instead of precise. The only instance Byron could remember this method working had been when he ordered Coura to unleash all her energy against the serpent-like demonic creature on their way to Clearshot and Emilea's home. Even then, she became useless for days after the encounter.

The female angel chased Marcus until he adjusted to rejoin Byron and Clearshot. Both anticipated lashing out to stop her, yet she slowed to a jog before halting in line with her three companions. Fortunately, the rest continued their private discussion and included her, extending the break in their fight.

"Are you crazy?" Clearshot snapped while snatching the assistant general by the arm to emphasize his frustration. "You could have been killed! Did you forget we're supposed to stick together?"

Sweat slid down Marcus' face as he tried to catch his breath. "Just...a minute..."

In the resulting pause, Byron watched their four opponents and noticed the previously amused expressions turned grim while they conversed. *Where's the fifth, or is this it? What's keeping them from attacking?*

Marcus' next words seemed to follow that train of thought. "Hendal made it back into the palace, but the angel responsible for the continued healing is dead."

"What?" Byron and Clearshot exclaimed at once.

"I hit him when Will became a distraction," the assistant general shared with a slight, exasperated grin and brushed the hair out of his eyes. "One through the head, and more in the chest. The first shot should've done it, though. I made sure it was clean in case he could heal himself."

Just to be certain, Byron performed a mental scan for any lingering trace of the angel's light energy and found nothing. As dazed as he felt by the turn of events, he realized the implications of the healer's death provided another opportunity. *Without a way to avoid permanent injury anymore, these four won't take as many risks if they stay, and they'll try to disarm, immobilize, or outright kill us instead of playing around. The odds of eliminating more of their group, and lessening Hendal's personal forces, just grew immensely.*

He met Clearshot's eyes, then Marcus', and the pair nodded, as if they reached the same conclusion.

"I can keep her occupied," the assistant general started and gestured with his chin toward the female angel. "I've been able to avoid the worst of her magic, and that's about all she can do from what I could tell."

"Come by me once you're finished," Clearshot added before turning to Byron. "If you take the two on the left, I'll occupy the tall one."

Byron raised an eyebrow at his friend's decision to fight the most formidable-looking opponent but let his doubt slide. "Just don't get killed," he told them. "It's either them or us at this point."

The time for talking ended after their acknowledgement. All four of the angels faced the humans, yet only the three combatants charged, leaving their spellcaster to observe alone.

"Let's spread out," Marcus suggested and sidestepped to the right.

Clearshot did the same, except to the left, so Byron remained in the center to await whichever angel chose to strike first. All three sets of eyes were on him, and they approached warily to show their new, cautious mentality.

In a single, fluid motion, he drew his sword. Using magic over his weapon always seemed tempting, but he felt another strategy might change their view of how to fight him, especially since he had yet to prove himself adept at both to their group. It would also allow him more options for defense given the lack of sunlight in the early evening.

The trio hesitated to attack until their leader bolted toward Clearshot, ruining any chance for Byron to initiate targeting them individually. As soon as someone moved, Marcus took off in an attempt to reach their female companion; however, the tallest angel intercepted him. This left their final member alone. Instead of waiting, Byron walked toward his opponent and halted before assessing the angel, who did the same to him.

Nothing noteworthy stood out to warrant caution, but he knew not to underestimate a Yeluthian. *Although this one kept up with the others, he always followed behind and never came close enough to threaten me. Either he chose to stay back or the fighting became too advanced for his abilities.*

With that observation at the forefront of his mind, Byron raised his blade and lunged for a horizontal swing. He purposefully put less weight behind the attack in order to gauge the angel's strength and allowed his sword to be pushed away. He used this tactic often in order to create a fake opening for his opponent to retaliate. To his relief, the angel took the bait and stabbed for Byron's torso.

The strike came less forcefully, and he wondered if it would be a misleading thrust he should dodge. Still, years of training reminded him to avoid taking risks when his gut told him to be wary. He sidestepped to avoid the other's blade, which passed by a second later to show the attack came at full force, and opted to trade blows in an effort to become accustomed to his opponent. Once he felt satisfied, and beads of sweat tickled his brow, Byron retreated to distance himself and pause the fight.

The decision appeared to irritate the angel, who began pacing, as if debating whether or not to pursue.

I naturally lack the speed and strength he has, Byron reflected. *I also used my dark energy earlier. For now, it would be best to avoid prolonging the combat. These shorter trades should hold his attention, and I can utilize whatever openings he provides since he isn't being deceitful with his attacks.*

THE ANGEL'S DESCENT

He charged a second time and performed the exact same attack, swinging wide from the left and letting his opponent shove the blade away. This time, though, Byron didn't dodge during the retaliation. One block exposed the angel's chest, so he attempted a killing blow.

To his dismay, this brought about the other's speed. The angel twisted to avoid the sword while immediately following with a downward slash that had Byron scrambling backward. Again, his opponent fidgeted restlessly but didn't attempt anything while he caught his breath.

If I moved a second later, I'd have earned a nasty scratch across my chest, or worse. At least I can expect more than barbaric hacking and slashing. I'm curious why he seems so hesitant to come after me when I pause the combat, especially since he's growing upset. Can I use his emotions to my advantage?

Twice more, Byron refused to expand on their series of strikes after continuing the fight and opted to separate following a close brush. As he expected, the fluctuating and releasing tension between them succeeded in drawing out more of the angel's impatience. Based on his experience mentoring the younger mage trainees at the academy, he knew more pressure would cause his opponent to snap sooner or later. Then, he'd have his opening.

Another horizontal swing from the right picked up their bout, and after a few more blocks, he prepared to step away. Fortunately, his taunting finally spurred a reaction.

The angel retaliated with a lunge and multiple jabs to prevent a pause, scowling in the process. Byron found he had less time to position his sword and received several cuts as a result.

I need to wait, he repeated in order to focus on each movement. *Don't go on the offensive. Each blow followed through as intended, so he wouldn't try tricking me when I'm at his mercy.*

The clashing metal rang in his ears before his opponent's blade grazed his left hip, then his right bicep a moment later. Despite knowing he would be overwhelmed soon, Byron ignored the consistent stings and watched the other's weapon.

No, not the sword...

In a sudden realization, his eyes darted to the ground just barely visible in the near darkness. The angel hadn't stayed stationary except when the two broke apart, so his feet were never firmly planted. This method benefited from the fighter's speed and stamina, yet it prevented powerful attacks and increased their loss of balance should the terrain become uneven. Byron recalled explaining his decision to teach a more grounded technique to his students for those reasons.

He intended to take advantage of the fast-paced steps and acted as soon as the other's stance narrowed. Using every ounce of his strength, he blocked the other's blow, pressed one hand against the flat of his sword, and shoved with a grunt.

The physical change in their confrontation startled his opponent, and the lack of a defensive position caused the angel to stumble backward, just as Byron expected. He used the other's lack of a serious block to stab for the chest and pierced through the heart.

For a moment, both combatants froze. The angel's mouth opened and closed before his body relaxed and slid to the ground. Only then did Byron remove his blade. His previous experience with their group had him eyeing the limp figure, though nothing suggested his opponent still lived. Exhaustion dropped onto his shoulders while he lingered.

This one looked younger than the others, he thought absentmindedly. *I can't give up now. We need to take care of the rest.*

Byron peeled his eyes away from the corpse to search for Clearshot, Marcus, and the three remaining angels. He noticed his friend struggling to his feet while someone, presumably the leader who went after him, stalked forward. Meanwhile, the assistant general held his own against the one who intercepted him earlier, and the female was nowhere to be seen.

Why didn't she intervene? he wondered as he tried to decide who to assist. *Could there be a trap laid out for us? If that's the case, should we retreat? I felt optimistic after hearing about their healer's death, but I don't think we can keep up at this point.*

Already, he began walking toward Clearshot and mustered the resting energy within his center to send two balls of fire ahead. The sudden brightness drew their attention, and the angel leapt away to avoid being hit, though Byron hadn't used enough power to do more than give minor burns to the intended target. As the spell dimmed, descended, and disappeared in a flash of sparks, he neared Clearshot and circled around to stand beside his friend while keeping his eyes on his new opponent.

"Are you hurt?" he asked at a lower volume.

Clearshot shook his head. "Not badly enough to whine about."

The lead angel, Drake, glanced around before facing them again. "Where is Hector?"

The voice, controlled and unsettlingly calm, sent a shiver down Byron's spine. He assumed the question related to the person he defeated, so he pursed his lips together, uncertain of how to respond.

"Did you not hear me, human? Where is my brother?"

Again, he refused to answer.

"You did not kill him," Drake continued while moving closer and speaking in that same, disturbing manner. "You *could* not kill him because I trained him myself."

His mind isn't right, Byron realized and lifted his sword. *If they really were related, or close enough to feel like it, his grief might make him more dangerous.*

While he considered responding, Clearshot turned to the right and shifted his blade.

"He is gone, Drake," came a feminine voice from that direction. The spellcasting angel who disappeared earlier approached, and her bored tone of voice suggested she didn't share the same sentiments about her fallen companion.

Her appearance made Byron start to sweat again, and he debated whether or not to split up from Clearshot. Before he could decide who he would rather challenge, the distraught angel sprinted forward to attack him, closing the space between them in a matter of seconds. The wild swings that followed held enough rage-fueled strength to drive him backward step by step, and he couldn't spare a glance to see what happened to Clearshot.

"You will not live!" Drake growled like a vicious animal before raising a fist.

Byron could only watch as the unexpected punch struck him in the stomach, causing him to bend forward before a blow to the back of his head sent him to his knees. Once he dropped down, he knew he became vulnerable. The fist connected with his jaw next, rattling his teeth, and he brought up his hands for protection. In the next instant, Drake raised his foot to kick them away.

The impact and resulting broken fingers had Byron releasing the grip on his sword. By that point, multiple voices began shouting only to fade into a mass of noise as the angel grabbed a fistful of Byron's hair to hold him in place while beating the left side of his face. The first strike bruised his cheek while the next landed on his temple with the same amount of force. He swore he would lose consciousness and fully expected the hitting to continue.

When it didn't and the angel let go of his hair, Byron sagged forward and waited for his senses to return. Any attempt to move his jaw or hands brought about pain.

I'm going to pass out at this rate...

The noise grew louder once Drake started shouting curses, and a deeper voice tried to calm him down. Byron cracked open his eyes, raised his head to see what had happened, and saw the other remaining combatant, the one Marcus had been fighting, standing in between him and the lead angel.

"Get a hold of yourself," the bulkier figure ordered.

Drake snarled yet didn't go after his target again. "Out of my way, Urvin! Hector, he-"

"The master mage must be kept alive."

Hendal won't have them kill me? Byron grasped against the throbbing and aches. As pathetic and weak as he felt, an unsettling sensation stirred to amplify his fear once he connected the information to what he already knew. *If they intend to take me prisoner, I'll serve as another political tool without my free will, like King Aaron and General Tont. My disappearance would raise as many questions as if I turned up dead, but the others who participated in this plan don't possess the same influence. We need to accept our losses. I might be captured, but there's still hope for the future if everyone else can escape.*

THE ANGEL'S DESCENT

As the angels' argument cooled into bickering, he hurried to locate Clearshot and Marcus. Their third opponent, the female spellcaster, stood in their way of reaching Byron, though he caught the frantic concern each projected in their expressions. He accepted the pain of moving in order to gesture for them to flee, waving one hand toward the city and its twinkling lights.

His friend noticed the message first. Although Clearshot seemed conflicted, Byron saw his mouth work as he spoke to the assistant general. Neither appeared pleased, but they backed away before spinning around to run for Verona. Their speed decreased almost immediately, becoming an awkward jog to display their own exhaustion.

To his relief, the female angel didn't bother chasing after them. Instead, she returned to her partners and pointed a thumb over her shoulder. "Should we worry about those two?"

"Why bother?" the tallest responded. "Our assignment is complete. Go find the high priest."

Without another word, she began heading toward the palace. A heavy silence descended upon the field when she left them, but Byron vowed not to let the current circumstances break his resolve or diminish the trust he had in his companions.

***

As uneventful as the trek to Lady Katrina's home was, it became one of the most frightening experiences of Will's life. His body's condition prevented him from doing more than stumbling along, and Grace's weariness left her trailing behind. The people who wandered around didn't pay them any attention, mostly because they avoided who they could by creeping in the shadows, and he thanked their luck.

The paranoia didn't lessen, though. His imagination explored various instances where the angels, the demon from outside of Dala, one of its creatures, or someone under Hendal's control came after them. Every flicker of movement had him questioning their safety, and his sanity, yet nothing happened. Still, the knowledge of his place in the issue hung over him.

Grace would be captured and held prisoner again, but I'd be left for dead without question, he thought while on the verge of tears from his hysteria. *I'm not a mage; I'm not even a real healer. I'm useless in a fight or as a spy. All I've done is throw myself into danger and distract everyone else from the task at hand. That's my reality.*

Once they reached the western main road, the well-lit, extravagant homes eased some of Will's tension. Metal bars in front of the lady's estate sealed her property for the evening, and he rapped on them to alert those on the opposite side of their presence. The ringing and clanging succeeded in drawing someone outside.

"Who goes there?" a man demanded as he hurried over while hugging himself from the chill.

Will thought he recognized the servant as the lady's butler and addressed him as politely as he could given his mood and appearance. "This is the Yeluthian ambassador, and I'm her guard. Master Byron sent us for Lady Katrina."

"Master Byron? At this hour?"

"It's urgent." Will avoided rattling the gate further to express his desperation.

The man contemplated the request, then he nodded and unlatched the metal bars. Once he saw how they struggled inside, he seemed to understand their need for assistance and called for three other servants to lead the pair to the bathing area.

Time flew by in a blur after they took Grace aside before scrubbing Will clean and applying medicine to his tender wound. He remembered meeting the lady and hearing her shrill voice as she left their care to her staff. Somebody poured a scolding, overly sweet drink down his throat, and they brought him to a spare room, which he hardly had time to assess since he passed out on the featherbed within seconds.

***

Faint echoes of distant voices haunted Hendal while he hid in the hallway just inside of the palace. His previous, authoritative behavior in front of those who cornered him earlier had been an image he felt proud to uphold. Then, the magicless, young man injured his shoulder, and any attempt at keeping his composure crumbled.

The fear of being discovered overwhelmed him as he bled until Jaspire arrived to close the wound and ease his pain. The effort it took to not blow up on the fool for waiting so long to intervene added to what already strained his concentration. One part of his mind stayed on the soldiers under his control, forcing them to guard the doors leading to the training ground and the upper floors' outdoor walkways. He could sense the concerned individuals moving toward their locations in order to learn what caused such a ruckus, but no one evaded his guards.

Jaspire's group worried him as well, leading to him linger near the scene. His trust in the angels hindered on their ability to finish a job and clean up after themselves, which they proved incapable of doing on several occasions.

So, he remained in the pitch-black hallway until he believed he was safe. Without the regular servants and guards on patrol because of the various tasks he assigned, the lanterns had burned out. Hendal grunted, pushed off the wall he leaned against, and rubbed his shoulder.

Someone should be around to light these hallways. I tasked them with making sure no one exited on this side, but I said nothing about shirking their responsibilities. It's as though I must do everything myself.

His newly healed muscles began to ache, and he rubbed his chest before resigning to stumble around in search of a servant to properly light the space. For a while, his annoyed thoughts kept him occupied in the silence. He became so accustomed to the lack of noise that Soirée's familiar laugh from farther ahead caused him to jump and press his back against the stone wall.

"It's a shame," she began as a shadowy figure parted from the darkness. "With all that power, you can't send somebody to fill these lanterns."

Hendal scoffed at her comment. "It's the servants' business to attend to such mundane tasks. In fact, I might put in a word with their master if such laziness continues."

"Perhaps you should beckon one here now?"

"What do you mean?"

"If you follow the mental connection and trace the tendril of demonic energy, just as you do when you control a person's mind, you should find it possible to sense their locations. Did I forget to mention that?"

He already expected her to chuckle after explaining what he hadn't known about their connection, but the sound still aggravated him. In a brief moment, he tracked down the nearest guard under his influence and sent a silent command for the man to light all of the lamps on the northern side of the palace's first floor.

"There," he muttered before proceeding to continue down the corridor. Even with a hand on the wall, though, he fumbled without a clear destination.

"Would this help?" Soirée asked after he tripped and caught himself on the wall.

Before Hendal could question her intentions, a flash of red illuminated the space, blinding him momentarily. He blinked to clear his eyes and glanced to his left where the demon stood. In her hand, a fireball the size of an apple floated above her palm.

"Why couldn't you do that earlier?" he grumbled to suppress his genuine amazement and appreciation for her assistance.

As usual, she shrugged off his inconsideration. "I'm surprised you didn't return outside yet. They're waiting for you."

"What do you mean?"

Soirée responded by turning around to head in the opposite direction, taking the light source with her, and he scuttled behind to avoid becoming lost in the darkness. They reached a familiar part of the floor just when his patience wore thin, then she stopped. Hendal decided to proceed ahead in order to resume the lead until they approached one of the doors to the training ground. As he expected, a handful of soldiers guarded the exit, so he waved them away before passing through.

The area appeared empty, though the moonless night didn't help to identify anyone or anything aside from the stable. One concern had been emerging to find a dead body, or multiple, but he saw none and breathed a sigh of relief.

"Where could Jaspire and the others be?" he wondered aloud while peering around. Movement across the field caught his eye, and soon he recognized Thelma strolling over as carelessly as ever.

"High priest, the master mage is in our possession," she shared without sparing a glance at Soirée.

The unexpected news had his jaw dropping until he snapped it shut. "You do?"

"Yes."

"Take me to him."

The thought of capturing the man who had been hindering his plans put more energy into Hendal's steps. Soon, he stood alongside Drake while Byron knelt on the ground with the tip of Urvin's sword pointed at his throat to dissuade him from trying to fight or flee. Seeing the mage so helpless and beaten brought Hendal immense joy.

"Well, it seems your attempt to avoid the inevitable failed," he taunted; however, the rest of his gloating ceased once he met Byron's glare, and his tongue refused to work.

For the first time in months, he felt intimidated because of the ferocity burning behind the emerald eyes, which appeared red-rimmed thanks to the flame Soirée held. Even with all of the anger the master mage projected, they still reflected the man's sanity. Byron tipped his chin up to display his defiance.

Hendal stepped backward instinctively, turned away, then brushed down his robe. "Y-You're defeated," he managed to stutter and kicked himself for faltering. No other words came to mind, so he cleared his throat instead.

Fortunately, Urvin assumed he finished speaking and didn't hesitate to progress with the conversation. "What should we do with him?"

"We shall add him to our numbers," he replied, nodded in confirmation, then faced his angelic servants. "The sooner we leave this place, the better."

The blade at Byron's throat remained as Hendal came closer to extend his right hand and place it on the damp head of the master mage while averting his eyes. Soirée's power leapt forward as soon as he gave it permission to, and his victim's expression settled into a neutral gaze. Only when he felt no further resistance did he withdraw.

Excellent, he exclaimed to himself with a poorly concealed grin. *Both master mages obey me now. This will make the upcoming changes much easier to implement.*

A displeased growl from Drake stole his attention as new ideas sprang to mind. "Is something the matter?" he demanded.

All three angels stared at each other, but Thelma answered at a quieter volume.

"Jaspire and Hector were both killed, and the rest of the master mage's group escaped."

"What? How could they let themselves be..." He stopped himself from berating the deceased members aloud. Until that point, he hadn't noticed their disappearance.

I figured they were all capable of staying alive, especially Jaspire. Without his healing ability, I doubt the rest will be as useful. Perhaps I must reevaluate their strengths before allowing them to assist me.

Hendal prepared to voice the order to finish cleaning up and hide in the city again, but Drake cut him off while glaring at Soirée.

"Where were you, demon?" he spat. The anger in his eyes gave him a crazed look.

Urvin mumbled for their leader to deal with the matter at another time, but the words didn't sound persuasive. Still, it proved enough to provoke Soirée into responding.

"Me?" she asked, feigning innocence and flashing her signature, wicked grin. "I promised myself I wouldn't become involved with your kind, which I'm sure you appreciated until your precious healer decided to lower his guard."

"Jaspire knew what he was doing," Thelma interjected.

"He behaved like a fool; however, I'd say it's only the second worst decision of the evening, right next to sending just one of you against a master mage. He had been the weakest too, possessing no magical gifts or talent with a weapon."

"What did you say?" Drake snapped and gripped the sword in his hand tight enough to cause the blade to tremble.

As Hendal sensed the tension growing, his regret for remaining outside doubled, and he found himself at a loss for how to manage the angels and demon. If it came to blows, he would be utterly useless.

THE ANGEL'S DESCENT

"I wonder if it had been *your* idea," Soirée went on in a vicious tone of voice, directing every word at the group's leader. "Did you place too much faith in your brother? Could it be you wanted an easier opponent? That makes the most sense; send him off to die so you can live to present the prize. I suppose I would do the same if I were-"

"Shut up," Urvin growled as a warning. Both his blade and Drake's rose together after.

In response to the pair's movement, Soirée manifested a slim, dark sword in her free hand while the fireball resting above the other dimmed.

Hendal's mind raced at the danger he found himself in. *This is terrible. She pushes their sorrow, hate, and guilt in order to amuse herself. Disgusting! What if she goes too far?*

"I've been waiting for this," the demon purred.

Her eyes danced with anticipation while Drake's seemed to widen from his burning hostility, and Urvin and Thelma appeared ready to strike as well. Before Hendal could figure out the best way to diffuse the situation, and avoid becoming a target in the process, Soirée closed the open hand holding the flame, snuffing out their light source and making it impossible to see everyone. He blinked several times to help his eyes adjust, but that did nothing. It didn't matter anyway; the fighting already started.

Sporadic ringing of metal had him flinching, along with the grunts of both frustration and pain. His breathing picked up once he realized how vulnerable he'd become. If a single, stray swing came near, he would be utterly helpless.

What do I do? How can I... Byron! Where is he?

Just as the demon showed him earlier, Hendal traced the connection between the demonic power and master mage. To his dismay, Byron's magical energy had been exhausted during the fighting, though the mage managed to produce a sputtering, candle-sized flame in response to the order. The attempt wound up infuriating Hendal more, and his paranoia caught up with him.

"Stop this!" he demanded to no one in particular. "I am in charge here, and I will not tolerate this behavior! There is far too much at stake for us to be discovered because of your stupidity."

The shuffling, growls, and clashing of weapons ceased abruptly, creating a deafening silence. Then, the ball of fire returned in Soirée's hand. Her sword had vanished, but dots of blood decorated her left cheek. Although she displayed no injuries and appeared calm, Hendal swore the demon trembled.

Thelma stood farther away with her sword drawn, and Urvin had shifted to the right, bearing a scratch down his right arm. Drake remained frozen an arm's length away from the demon, holding the tip of his blade at her throat. A thin scratch stretched across his forehead, his clothing had been torn in half a dozen places, and ruby blood peeked out underneath.

She did all of that in the two minutes of darkness? Hendal didn't know what else to say, so he held his breath until his lungs ached.

"I suppose I got ahead of myself," Soirée began. Her body relaxed, and she resumed an indifferent stare at Drake before pushing the angel's sword away with one finger. "Don't you think we should let the high priest take his new toy inside? The curious humans will soon come to investigate the area as well. Even with guards posted, it won't be impossible to stop those who are determined to find out what happened here."

Hendal cleared his throat and rubbed a hand over his bald head. "Yes, of course. Quarrelling can often attract the ears you wish to overhear the least."

When nobody else added to his comment, he beckoned the master mage to follow him inside. The dried blood on Byron's face reminded him of the fallen angels, and he made sure to sound respectful while issuing his next order.

"I will return to the palace and release the guards while you take care of the bodies. Remain hidden in the city for now, and I will send Soirée to fetch you when I have need of your abilities. As unexpected as this evening's event turned out, it ended in our favor."

Without a reason to linger outside any longer, he began heading toward the palace. The aching in his chest returned, prompting him to massage the spot while reflecting on what the day had brought. *There's much to address if my plan continues smoothly. First, I believe a hot bath is in order as a means of rewarding myself.*

10

The third day of Coura's flight brought her within sight of the Ghurun mountain range looming over the horizon. After talking to Cintra and hearing about the woman's visions, her priority became reaching Yeluthia as soon as possible, even if it meant avoiding stops. Soirée's power continued to ebb her hunger, thirst, and weariness, but the lack of a break from the wind's force strained the muscles in her wings.

Keep moving, she told herself before descending below the clouds. *According to Cintra, I should find answers in this direction, which reaffirms my suspicion about Yeluthia's location.*

The rest of what she learned, specifically regarding the golden weapon, needed to be pushed aside for the time being. She believed the woman had been referring to one of the ancestral weapons, but she could do nothing at the moment if it remained within the palace. So, her attention returned to the journey at hand.

In order to pass the time, Coura reflected on the closest she ever traveled to the mountain range. The Magical Arts Academy in East Hoover lied farther north, and she didn't consider her life in Neston because of her once-lost memories. This meant the grasslands and farming fields were completely new, a fact that made her eager to explore.

Bunches of trees appeared every so often to interrupt the bland color palette, along with towns holding no more than a few dozen people. As she adjusted to fly south, fewer appeared, prompting her to consider the many texts Byron assigned to her in the past about Asteom's geography, landscape, climate, and crops.

If I'm remembering correctly, the eastern third of the country contains villages and farmers who rotate growing beans, corn, and wheat. Without the cover of the woods, no wild game would venture into the open. They lack a water source for fishing as well, except maybe those closer to the southern cities. Still, the weather stays mild enough with the exception of windstorms during the spring. This seems like such a simple life. Then again, mine isn't exactly a normal one to compare it to.

The sun stretched across the land to the west, casting an array of colors across the sky. It hadn't rained since Coura left, but gray clouds hovered around the direction she intended to go in. The idea of traversing through a storm didn't sound appealing, and she began to consider her options. After gauging the sunlight, which would last another hour or so, she decided to delay a landing in favor of shifting to the east at a leisurely pace.

For a while, she became lost in her thoughts as the wind drowned out any noise. The sight of a town below, one more spread out and active than the others before it, startled her enough to try hiding from their view in case they could distinguish her from the usual birds.

She glanced upward before rising only to notice a shadow above. It grew until she realized how similar it looked to a raincloud; the revelation had her snapping her wings open with a gasp to halt. Because of her speed, though, she wound up passing through the next layer, which left her clothing and hair damp. Coura released a groan, fixed her position, then followed a path around the potentially dangerous section.

Once she felt safe from the weather, something whirled by her head. The sound had her stopping in place to scan for the source.

"Remain where you are!" a baritone voice shouted at a distance from behind.

Coura's heart skipped a beat. A glance in the opposite direction revealed a man wearing brown, leather padding floating at the same level and pointing a loaded bow at her. Behind him, a pair of pure white wings beat to keep him in the air, blending in well with the surrounding clouds.

The sound of ruffling feathers had her facing forward. Two more men in the same outfit and with the same, snowy wings descended. She noted how all three appeared identical, sharing gem-like blue eyes and sun-kissed hair.

Could this...really be...

"State your name and business," the angel on the left ordered. His firm tone didn't seem rude, though he had to raise his voice above the wind.

The demonic energy in her center crawled forward because of the opposing power, causing her fingers to twitch in anticipation for summoning her weapon. As her heart continued pounding, she couldn't figure out the words to explain her situation despite rehearsing a greeting over the past three days.

Another arrow whirled above her head. The sudden noise caused her to flinch and disrupted her balance.

"This is your final warning," the leftmost angel called with an arm raised as he prepared to cue the next strike.

To avoid giving them a reason to attack, she raised both hands slowly in a gesture of innocence before saying the first words that came to mind. "My name is Coura Galdwin. I'm a messenger sent by King Aaron from Asteom. I bring news for your leader."

Based on her lack of experience as an authoritative figure, she expected them to question her claim or dismiss her outright if they were feeling merciful. The leader appeared to be contemplating both options, so she summarized the issue.

"A demon is controlling our high priest, the generals, and more innocent civilians; consider me proof of her existence. I come seeking aid for my country under the order of both master mages, who are residing in the capital city as prisoners. If you won't allow me to speak with your leader, at least pass on this message to remind them of our alliance with Yeluthia."

Coura understood the risk she took by assuming the strangers were Yeluthians. If they were, they would likely have little to no influence over their ruler. In any case, she knew she had one opportunity to convince them, and keeping silent would make her an enemy.

The two angels didn't show a hint of emotion during or after her explanation, but they remained silent for a while. Only when the deeper voice from behind addressed the pair did the discussion move forward.

"Night will be upon us soon," he informed his companions.

The one on the left narrowed his eyes at her while the other leaned over. "What say you?" Coura heard him mumble to his partner.

At last, the first resumed speaking to her. "Your message will be brought before our king," he concluded. "You are free to return to your country below, unless you wish to come as a representative of Asteom."

The invitation caught Coura off guard, especially because of their defensive behavior, yet she nodded before committing to an answer. For a moment, she swore the Yeluthian appeared relieved by her cooperation, though his next words suggested otherwise.

"Because you are an outsider, you will remain in our custody until we receive further orders. Your hands and feet shall be bound, and you are to not speak unless spoken to. Any resistance or disobedience may result in imprisonment, or worse."

He raised an eyebrow, as though he expected her to disagree or change her mind about going along. When Coura did neither, he motioned for the man at his side to go to her. After removing rope from the satchel he wore, her hands were tied close together in front of her, though he gave her feet enough leeway so she would be able to walk.

Despite the circumstances, she couldn't stop from marveling at how fluidly the angel moved in the air. Each motion seemed effortless, no matter how simple the task, yet she never saw him falter in his flight. Meanwhile, she struggled to hold herself still and keep her wings from disrupting his work.

His final knot around her wrists left some extra rope, which he used to lead her along. When he approved of his restraints, he signaled to each of his companions, then the one in front pumped his wings to climb higher before shooting away. Coura and her guide followed, though at a much slower pace, allowing her to ease into the flight. The third angel stayed at a lower level and kept a close eye on her from below.

*

They soared for less time than Coura expected as the sky turned a shade of lavender to signal the end of the sunset. Soon, the Yeluthian farther ahead disappeared. She assumed he intended to warn their people of the suspicious-looking guest from Asteom and prepared for the curious, frightened, and disapproving stares she would inevitably receive.

Although she couldn't see much, the person holding the rope began to go faster until they neared a swirl of clouds. They ascended for another minute before he dragged her through the mass. Coura hadn't encountered a thicker patch during any of her ventures through the sky, so losing her vision to the wall of white whisps felt unnerving. She hesitated to continue only to have the rope around her wrists sharply yanked to move her forward.

Then, it ended so abruptly she thought it had been a hallucination. Like drawing a curtain, they emerged into clearer air, and what she saw she could only describe as something so abstract it seemed to have been stripped from a dream. Various colors stood out against the cloudy backdrop to catch her attention first. Emerald grass covered most of the ground except for lines where dirt paths had been established as walking trails. Some stretched wide enough to fit a carriage while others thinned out near the buildings, which differed in structure. Those farther away stood three or four stories tall and had been crafted from a smooth, white material, but the rest of the area consisted of huts with stone walls, thatched roofs, and space for gardening.

Before she could process her surroundings in detail, Coura found her arms being pulled downward as her guide descended. He reached the ground first and released the spell on his wings instinctively, resulting in a display of miniature crystal shards that faded away. The beautiful, rehearsed display left her envious of his control and embarrassed by her own, or lack thereof.

She did the same once she landed but found the demonic energy returning to her center instead of dispersing as it normally would. In her mind, the city's rejection of the opposite type of power proved she stood in Yeluthia.

Dark energy is supposed to return to the planet, but we're high above Asteom, she realized. The idea left her dazed. *I think such pure light power is possible because of that fact.*

"This way," the angel said to get her attention as he gently tugged on the rope to nudge her on.

Coura nodded, followed, and forced her eyes to focus on him instead of the distractions. Already, dozens of people noticed the newcomer, leading them to investigate from a safe distance. Although she would have rather dipped her head to hide her face, she ignored her discomfort and held her chin high as they proceeded into the busier section of the city.

There, they went toward the largest structure where a staircase led to a silver-colored gate between two pillars. In front were a pair of guards clad in polished, bronze armor, and they gripped the spears they held tighter when she neared; however, neither moved from their rigid positions as Coura's guide brought her inside.

Four more soldiers waited alongside the leader who addressed her earlier. Her eyes fixed on the swords at their waists as the group continued through the hallway.

They have no reason to hurt me, she reminded herself to quell a growing anxiousness. *I'm a representative of Asteom, so attacking would risk the peace their leader established. At least, it should...*

The walls appeared as white as the outside had been, and lanterns hung from the ceiling. Their light revealed glimmers of gold and silver etched into the stone in no particular pattern. Portraits and paintings of people and places appeared to share some of the city's history. Beneath their frames, plaques described each scene, though she found them impossible to read without stopping.

Soon, the guards halted in front of a set of bronze doors. Coura inhaled while her guide knocked three times and held her breath until the metal parted inward to let them into the space. What lied beyond proved to be the throne room, which was organized to reflect as much, more so than what she became familiar with in Verona.

Aaron once explained how the palace's original throne remains in the king's meeting chamber because it had been designed as a private area not meant for everyone to view. The grand hall became utilized for ceremonies in order to accommodate more people, so really there is no special room. Remembering her friend's words and the meals they used to share made her wish for the days when her life seemed less chaotic, and his mind was his own.

Her dismay faded once her guide began walking toward the opposite end, allowing her to observe her new surroundings. The walls stretched wide enough to encompass hundreds of people, and a circle of glass on the ceiling let in the natural light, which faded into twilight. Metalwork framed the window and bent inward to continue into a basic design of an angel reaching for the sun. The lone pieces of furniture consisted of the throne on an elevated pedestal, two rows of benches on either side, and a handful of wooden chairs lined up against the back wall. Coura instinctively noted the two sets of doors there as well, which were guarded by a pair of armored soldiers.

The angels leading her along stopped a good distance away from the throne, and the scout in command of the three lowered himself to one knee.

"My king, we present Coura Galdwin, a messenger of Asteom, who brings news from their kingdom."

Once her eyes fell on the ruler of Yeluthia, she felt several strings of emotion while they stared at each other. Firstly, and most prominent, was fear. She didn't even know his name, history, or abilities, but he appeared formidable without lifting a finger and revealed no detectable trace of magical energy.

Jealousy lied underneath. The king reminded her of Hernan, except in a godly sort of way. His golden hair and eyes matched most of the Yeluthians she had seen, though a well-trimmed, blond beard covered part of his long face. His clothing also suggested a clean, presentable nature as he wore a white shirt bearing bronze buttons, charcoal-colored pants, and brown boots; all stood out against the scarlet cushions of the throne. Finally, a thin band of bronze adorned his head to display his status.

Coura avoided the urge to look down at herself and further acknowledge how horribly out of place she was with the purity of the building. No doubt she appeared worn and tired from the trip, but her unpleasant demonic and human features didn't belong.

If I really am half-Yeluthian, shouldn't I have inherited something beautiful?

A tiny voice called out amid the self-loathing to remind her of her purpose for visiting the king. *If I fail to explain the situation, no help will come from these people. They couldn't communicate with us because of Hendal's meddling, and us with them. I need to put aside my doubt and act as a representative should.*

From the king's wary expression, she knew he would not be swayed easily. Coura racked her brain for the memories of her time watching Byron address Hernan, Emilea, and other figures of importance in order to use them as a reference for behaving properly.

Pretend to be Byron, she told herself with a shred of hope. *He always sounded polite yet stood his ground, and he got his message across without hesitating. Listen, watch, and adapt to the Yeluthians' behavior.*

With as much grace as she could manage, Coura bent low in a formal bow. Until anyone spoke to her, she remained in that position, even against the protesting muscles in her legs.

A new male voice, articulate and powerful, filled the room after. "What news do you bring, messenger?"

At the response, Coura rose before answering. "The palace in the capital city of Verona has been compromised by a demon who corrupted our high priest." She went on to explain how the letters between their kingdoms were intercepted, then she skimmed over the demonic creatures, omitting her involvement with their elimination. Lastly, she shared Byron and Emilea's attempts to catch Hendal and hers to stop Soirée.

"I was injured in the process," she concluded. "After recovering with our master light mage's help, we discovered an older map

THE ANGEL'S DESCENT

containing a clue to Yeluthia's possible location. I'm the only one capable of making the flight, though I never felt certain of anything."

"Now you stand before me, asking for aid," the king finished without a hint of emotion.

Coura nodded. She told them all she could; whatever else needed to be discussed or resolved became his responsibility to bring up. It comforted her to see his sharp facial features soften as he seemed entertained by the information; however, his following questions were harsh and his tone dismissive.

"Tell me, why should I send my soldiers off to fight a war that does not concern them? After years of inactivity between ourselves and the humans, do you think it is fair for us to come at Asteom's beck and call? What can you offer in return?"

The resulting silence grew deafening, especially since Coura's mind went blank. Her job had been to inform Yeluthia of the danger, not bargain for their service. In order to stifle her rising panic, she again turned to her former mentor.

What would Byron say? How did he tolerate Hernan's constant interrogating? In fact, most people I know deal with similar pressure on a regular basis. Grace has to be brave despite her age and country's absence, Aaron needed to prove himself because of his parents, and Marcus has to live up to his father's expectations. Will even learned how to fight and defend himself despite his lack of interest in combat. The least I can do is stand my ground.

"You have many reasons to not assist a country that ignored your existence until recently," she began with a calmer heart. "Your ambassador had been treated poorly because of her age and first appearance until we realized something was amiss. Instead of striving to find out what happened to your letters and fix the issue, we were lazy. It proved to be our worst mistake since it allowed the high priest time to build his power, a demon to invade our nation, and her creatures to infest the land. I've seen firsthand the effects of what that's doing to the people of Asteom, our king, and your ambassador. I'm not the person to offer riches or goods for your assistance because I'm as trusted there as I am here. So, in answer to your question, no. I don't think it's fair for you to help Asteom."

Coura purposefully paused to let her words sink in. The king's eyebrows raised a bit, as if her response surprised him. Only after she noticed this did she continue.

"Despite what I shared, I believe if your kingdom was willing to reach out after nearly a hundred years and send an ambassador to live among us, you're looking to reestablish ties with Asteom. Grace told me as much. In that case, let King Aaron repay you later. Ask for whatever is equivalent to your soldiers, and our country will more than give you their worth. You've been given the first opportunity to show this alliance still stands."

"Those are bold words," he replied quietly, like a low rumble from the back of his throat.

"War and death do not wait for bargains to be made, Your Highness."

The rich, sapphire eyes full of wisdom watched her without wavering. Coura kept her chin raised and refused to look away, no matter what his answer would be. After an uncomfortably long wait, the king's posture relaxed. He leaned an elbow on the arm of his throne before resting his head on that hand while gesturing to her guards.

"Remove the restraints. I see no reason to keep her bound when she is supervised."

"Yes, my king," the lead scout muttered, then he undid the knots on her wrists and ankles.

Coura rubbed the skin on her arms, ignoring the slight irritation caused by the rope's material, and glanced at the king, who wore a thin smile. The evening's darkness crept into the space despite the many lanterns keeping it well lit. Still, it proved enough to remind her of the late hour and her weariness from the day's flight, in addition to the lack of a decent meal or sleep during the past three days.

The Yeluthian king asked a few more questions about the soldiers in Verona, the Nim-Valan general and his troops, and what magic Asteom possessed. She couldn't provide the information related to the palace due to her absence, which he seemed to understand, so he accepted what she offered. When they finished, he leaned back in his throne while wearing a thoughtful yet satisfied expression.

"I must apologize," he added. "I do not believe I introduced myself. I am King Arval, son of King Mercius and Queen Terilia. You sound as though you are acquainted with our ambassador, Grace Zelnar."

She allowed herself a smile and nodded. "We're friends."

One of the guards huffed a laugh and another coughed in an awkward manner. Coura did her best to pretend not to notice.

I don't blame them for doubting our friendship. With my dark energy and appearance, it might be shameful for Grace to associate with me.

King Arval turned his gaze toward the armor-clad soldiers surrounding her. "You are dismissed for the day."

Every guard saluted by placing two fingers on their left eyebrow, then they spun around and crossed the room to exit. As they took their leave, the king signaled to one of the figures posted behind the throne, and the guard disappeared through the nearest door.

"I will have one of my commanders escort you to where you can stay during your time here. As you might imagine, it is necessary for me to hold a meeting to discuss what you presented, but I expect to reach a decision soon. I shall request your presence again when that time comes. For now, I invite you to explore the city and let the commander know if you have any questions."

After Coura thanked him, he rose with poise only royalty could master and proceeded to exit through the second door with the last guard, leaving her alone. It took a minute for her mind to catch up to her current situation, but her lips curled upward into a relieved smile.

That seemed too easy, she reflected while throwing her head back to gaze at the sky through the ceiling's window. *Either I made enough of an impression on their king or Yeluthia really wants this alliance. Also, why would they leave a stranger alone and unsupervised after one introductory meeting? Even if they send someone to look after me, it's just one person. If I wanted to, I could stir up trouble.*

The click of a door opening drew her attention, and the soldier she assumed to be the commander entered from the left. They wore the same bronze armor as the others, including the helmet, but carried no weapon. Coura intended to wait for them to approach; however, they didn't move, prompting her to walk over and join them in case they exited through the same door.

I wonder if anyone told them about me, she thought all of a sudden when the soldier remained frozen, even as she stopped in front of them. *I've been repressing my energy naturally, but every look I received shows their people know what kind of power I possess.*

"Good evening," she offered tentatively. "My name is Coura, and I-"

The commander leaned forward and raised one hand in a sharp gesture that startled her enough to step backward and abandon the greeting. A moment later, when the hand didn't lower, she realized they were reaching out to her. The soldier must have become aware of her confusion since they jumped a bit and grabbed for their helmet. Bronze passed over their head before a pair of glittering eyes met Coura's, and her world froze once she recognized the familiar face.

The man standing in front of her was her father, Evern Galdwin.

11

As she continued staring at the Yeluthian soldier, who let tears stream down his cheeks, Coura became more confident in her childhood memories of living in Neston with both her parents. No other person had *his* blue eyes or *his* cropped hair, which crept down the front of his ears into short sideburns. In fact, the only new features seemed to be a few wrinkles lining his eyes and mouth. The more she studied him, the surer she felt.

How long has it been? I couldn't even remember him until recently…

Evern dropped his helmet with a dull clang and cautiously came closer until she found herself gazing up into his face. In a single motion, he wrapped his arms around her shoulders to pull her into a tight embrace before pressing his face against the top of her head, muttering her name, and weeping without shame. Coura didn't recall ever seeing her father cry.

"We thought you were lost," she heard him mumble. The sound of his voice snapped her mind back to the present, and she returned the hug.

It's him, right? Father is… This isn't a dream?

When tears began welling in her eyes, she caved into her heart's desire and released the sobs blocking her throat. They held each other for what seemed like the entire evening until their emotions quelled. Coura pulled away from him then to wipe her face and catch her breath. After her father did the same, he took her hand in his.

"Come," he began while bringing her toward the door. "Save your tears."

Evern led her out of the throne room and through a maze of empty hallways until they exited the building. The sun had finished setting, so the sky above came to life with twinkling stars. Coura inhaled the crisp, clean air and felt thankful for the lack of wind after her journey, as well as the peaceful atmosphere and inactive landscape reflecting a calming stillness.

Her father was alive; he was *with* her. Those notions sent her heart thundering from a joy she hadn't experienced in her entire life.

The building containing the throne room appeared to be one of many filling the center of Yeluthia. As they strolled farther away along one of the dirt paths lit by lamps on wooden posts, the wider structures soon disappeared. Dozens of stone huts spread as far as Coura could see, bearing lanterns to light their walkways. She studied them and noticed no two were alike. Some utilized extra space for a garden, laundry line, or children's toys, and most had additional rooms built to expand the inside. Puffs of smoke floated out of chimneys to carry delightful aromas around the area.

These must be houses, Coura thought as people entered and left alone or with other adults or children.

Evern shifted his direction to approach one of the extended structures sitting atop a hill, which seemed to have at least four separate rooms judging by the outside. Although she didn't understand his need for so much space, she kept quiet. Instead of a typical door, a piece of cloth hung over the opening, reminding her of the Sie-Kie's treetop huts, but they passed by to move around the front. The backyard revealed a view of an empty field below, as well as a community of buildings beyond.

"Beautiful, is it not?" Evern commented to break the silence. "I spent much of my time working for this location, but the effort was worth it."

"It's amazing."

"I want you to wait here."

Coura prepared to protest but paused when she noticed him fidgeting. "Sure."

THE ANGEL'S DESCENT

He offered a smile, spun around, and hurried to the front of the house.

Although she expected an explanation for his disappearance, the moment alone gave her a minute to breathe. *After all those months, we assumed he died. Mother and I waited. She always acted so hopeful, and when he didn't return...*

The memories of their time in Neston threatened to cause Coura to cry again. In order to dismiss her stray emotions, she focused on the scenery. Light bugs flickered below to mirror the star-filled sky, and the vague sound of people chattering in the distance added another sense of life to the environment.

This land radiates peace. In Asteom, the citizens constantly worry about being drawn into conflict, whether with Nim-Vala, the demonic creatures, or some other threat. I would bet the residents of Yeluthia don't experience anything worse than a squabble between neighbors.

Comparing the two mellowed her attitude. She wondered if they knew about demonic creatures, paid attention to the fighting below, or simply shut themselves away to keep the established harmony. The last reason gave her mixed feelings because the angels swore to protect Asteom's citizens in the past, yet Soirée freely roamed the country.

Footsteps from behind distracted her from such negative thoughts, and she heard someone gasp. When Coura turned around, she saw Evern next to a shorter woman she recognized immediately.

"Mother?" she whispered, too captivated to speak louder.

The shock of seeing another familiar face felt like a blow to the stomach. Her mother, Paulina, wore a plain, tan dress and a scarlet apron spotted white with flour, and her chestnut hair had been pinned into a messy bun on top of her head. The woman's delicate hands covered her mouth as tears dropped from her hazel eyes when she shook her head in disbelief.

Unlike Evern, Paulina didn't hesitate to rush over and throw her arms around Coura, who had no restraint this time. She hugged her mother so fiercely she was afraid of snapping the slender woman in two. More crying ensued from them, and her father joined in.

When they seemed to feel satisfied with the reunion, Coura's mother broke away, though her eyes continued shining. "I cannot believe it! You are alive!"

"I am, but I doubt I look like what you remember," she replied with a chuckle. The joke had been meant to poke fun at her age since they were apart for years, yet it dawned on her that other, unnatural changes altered her appearance and presence as well. Judging by how her parents' smiles faltered, they took it as the latter.

Paulina put a hand on Coura's cheek. "What happened to you?" she asked in a concerned manner.

"It's a long story."

Before anyone could say another word, a girl no older than Lexie ran around the corner of the house.

"Mother, Odell is sneaking into the cookies before dinner!" Upon spotting the trio, her eyes widened, and she ducked behind Paulina while grabbing the woman's skirt.

Coura didn't even attempt to hide her surprise. "What did she call you?"

Her parents shared an amused look, then Evern responded.

"I suppose we should sit down and talk."

*

With a sigh, Paulina dropped into one of the remaining two chairs placed around a circular, wooden table in the middle of the kitchen. The inside of the house had a few ornamental pieces to decorate the walls and countertops, but it lacked any sort of personality. As Coura clutched her cup of tea while ignoring the jam-filled pastry her mother set in front of her, she noted how nothing reminded her of Asteom or her childhood in Neston.

"Where to begin?" her father mumbled with a frown that accentuated the wrinkles around his lips. He removed his armor after they went inside, revealing a lean build with less muscle than she imagined considering the metal outfit.

"Did we ever tell you how we met?" Paulina picked up and tilted her head.

Because of her memory loss, Coura couldn't recall much in the way of information. Even if they did mention it, she shook her head.

THE ANGEL'S DESCENT

"I am originally from Tremple, the fishing town on the southern border to the west of Clearwater. My father worked on the boats, so he never lingered for long, and my mother cooked at the local inn. By the time I was your age, they had passed away. I lived with my brother for a few months after."

"I had an uncle?" Coura muttered aloud, unsure if she knew before or not.

"We rarely talked because of our differing views on life and work. He loved the sea and wished to be like my father by spending his days on the water; I became the complete opposite. Fortunately, your father arrived to sweep me away." Paulina laughed, a sound that warmed Coura's heart, then looked to Evern as a cue for him to continue the story.

"I was born here but had been raised in Verona," he began. "My parents started a carpentry business and kept our lineage a secret because they did not want the humans to bombard them with questions or threaten them for our people's absence. Instead of learning the family business, I trained to become a soldier for the city's guard by studying combat and wielding the light magic I possess. When I informed my parents, they were proud I embraced my abilities and explained our family's lineage. They encouraged my curiosity, and I knew I wanted to visit Yeluthia one day."

Coura noticed her father's gaze go elsewhere for a moment, as if he pictured the conversation.

"After serving in Asteom's capital for several years, I decided to travel the country for a few months. As fate would have it, I ended up in Tremple and met your mother." He reached over to grab one of Paulina's hands.

"Your father and I settled in Neston," she added. "We stumbled upon it during our travels, got married, and had you."

Both faces turned to Coura. Their genuine smiles made her feel loved, yet she couldn't forget the point in her life where they separated.

"Then what happened?" she pressed while meeting Evern's eyes. The pain and bitterness that arose from the resulting sense of betrayal because of her father's departure came across more than she anticipated. "You left. You abandoned us without saying a word."

He shifted in his seat before looking at his wife, who winced.

Coura understood what their behavior meant and stared at her mother in disbelief. "You knew?"

Paulina nodded before raising a hand to prevent an outburst. "Yes, but let me explain."

Reluctantly, Coura closed her mouth and listened.

"We received a letter from Evern's mother. His father fell ill, so they were selling their business in order to leave Verona and move back to Yeluthia where he could spend the rest of his life. I knew of this place from the stories, but your father's desire to return dwindled once we started raising you."

"My mother included a map with its location and requested I join them," Evern added. "She figured it would be my last opportunity to see them, and I should experience the place where I was born."

"How did they reach the city?" Coura asked, unable to refer to them as her grandparents.

"We met in one of the villages along the bottom of the mountain range. There, they tested my magic to see if I could manifest wings since only a select few can. Because my father could not, we trekked on foot."

"Then, you really chose to go…"

"Let me finish," he coaxed. "I had every intention of returning in a few weeks. Your mother agreed to stay with you while I went away."

"I understood his reasoning," Paulina interjected. "It was a mutual agreement. If I remember correctly, I did tell you he would be gone."

"You never explained why he left," Coura retorted. "I never knew I'm half-Yeluthian or had living grandparents. Neither of you bothered to mention Yeluthia is real."

"Then, I owe you an apology. I did not believe you needed to learn about any of this until you were older."

Coura considered holding onto the grudge directed at her mother but ultimately failed and let out a frustrated sigh instead. In the resulting pause, she caught Evern smirking in her direction.

"While I stayed here, my parents had been cared for," he shared. "I fell in love with this city and its people. Because of the atmosphere, I desired to bring you and Paulina here. I am sure you understand how rare this peace is."

She recalled how he watched her study the city earlier and nodded. *The perfect home to raise a family.*

"I wrote about it to your mother. Once she gave me her permission, I sought an audience with King Arval. Although the idea made him wary, he shared the details of a law regarding human exceptions." The burden placed on Evern became evident in his last sentence.

"What did you need to do?" Coura ventured.

"The policy requires the individual making the request to serve the kingdom for three years, and they must not have penalties against their family's name. There are a variety of assignments, but I informed him of my experience as a guard. Once the position had been arranged, I wrote to your mother again."

"Neither of us felt too attached to Neston," Paulina admitted. "I agreed to wait with you until we were ready."

"Why didn't you tell me?" Coura asked without hiding the turmoil their planning caused her.

Her mother glanced away while her father lowered his eyes.

"You were just a child," he began. "The secrets we learned about Yeluthia needed to remain as such in order to protect their people. If anyone overheard or read the letters, their people and culture would have been at risk, in addition to our future. We hoped to test your magic too, as my parents did to me, and determine when to reunite since at least one of us could not fly."

"Regardless, we never could have anticipated what took place," Paulina concluded. "We sensed no urgency to move or tell you about Yeluthia, so we chose to wait. We discuss the past often and agree you had a right to know."

Evern put an arm around his wife to comfort her, yet she didn't go on, forcing Coura to press the unpleasant subject.

"I suppose that's when the attack on Neston happened." The memories remained foggy despite their return, so hearing about

Soirée's rampage had been a topic she didn't feel entirely comfortable with.

Her mother inhaled a shaky breath. "Your father had been gone for a year and ten months. Nothing out of the ordinary raised the alarm, but Widow Marie became frantic."

"Widow Marie?" Coura muttered. Her recent conversation with Cintra reminded her of the older woman. "She could use a foresight spell, right?"

"That is correct. Normally, she would only predict the weather or see minor accidents, but that day she warned us of a terrible creature on its way to Neston. What she described sounded like the beasts we would see wandering through the woods during the evening."

Widow Marie warned the town before Soirée arrived? They wouldn't know what she did after...

Her mother's face paled. "She claimed we needed to leave immediately. Some people fled north while others went south. It all happened so fast. No one helped me look for you; they assured me you would hide in the woods until it ended."

Her voice cracked on the final word, severing the dam keeping her emotions in check. When she started weeping again, Evern held her against his shoulder.

Meanwhile, Coura couldn't stop herself from replaying Soirée's confession in her head. The demon stalked her parents, targeted her after her father's disappearance, then confronted her as a child, resulting in her ability to wield demonic energy. She accepted what the past did to her, but now she saw the effect it had on those closest to her at the time.

I'm the one who went off on my own, causing them heartache. They've been carrying around the guilt of losing me and blaming themselves. I should mention what took place with Soirée, at least to Father, though now isn't the time.

Evidently, her mother and the townsfolk escaped the attack. Many questions remained unanswered, so she waited a few minutes for Paulina to calm down before pushing for more.

"I followed the group heading south," the woman explained at a lower volume while toying with her apron's strap. "Night already descended, so I figured there would be safety in numbers. Widow Marie also urged me to stay close to her. She comforted me and promised you would be fine. I hated her ever since because I never heard from you."

"Where did you go?" Coura asked to keep the conversation on track.

"Delrun. It is a farming town outside the woods if you go southeast. We hiked through the night, and their guard spotted us just before dawn. As soon as they heard about Widow Marie's warning, they offered what they could in the way of sleeping spaces and food. They were kind, understanding, and generous people. We stayed for four days, just to be safe, before venturing back to Neston. The town remained empty in our absence, though we found scorched roofs, broken windows, and scattered debris. I set about searching for you but saw no clues."

"She wrote to me as soon as she could," Evern picked up. "Once I processed the situation, I begged King Arval to let me leave in order to be with her. He appreciated my service and honesty, which is why I think he promised to still honor our agreement. With his blessing, I returned to Neston. Paulina and I scoured the area for days to no avail, leading us to assume the worst. We lost hope in ever reuniting with you."

Byron investigated Neston and once told me he sent messengers to follow up since he brought me straight to the academy, Coura reflected. *The distance between the two requires at least three days of traveling on foot, and he waited to question me until I settled down a bit. Because I lost my memories, I felt no attachment to my old life. Soirée's power needed training too. My future relied on me living at the MAA.*

"I take it you didn't tell anyone where you were going when you returned to Yeluthia?" she inquired after.

Her father shook his head. "At the time, I still hoped to avoid drawing suspicion. We left without mentioning a destination, breaking off what ties we had established. During the next few months, I extended my flights to scan the area from above, just in case."

Hearing about how he hadn't given up pulled at Coura's heart, though she reluctantly dismissed her sorrow to recognize the present. *My parents created a fulfilling life here, even without me. Our paths crossed again; I refuse to let Soirée's meddling make me less grateful for that. Besides, who knows what she, or anyone else, could have done if they discovered where Yeluthia is. I'd have no experience with demons or knowledge of my abilities, but I wouldn't have met Byron or any of my friends and traversed Asteom.*

Somehow, everything seemingly fell into place; the realization both comforted and discouraged her. The damage needed months to heal, if it ever could, yet she set aside her personal feelings to support the two people in front of her who wore dejected expression.

"So, King Arval welcomed you to Yeluthia with open arms?" she asked while forcing a smile.

At the sight of it, her parents returned the gesture, appearing more optimistic.

"We informed him of the situation, including losing you," her mother answered. "He was sympathetic, and I doubt he ever forgot what we went through."

"I think your full name jogged his memory," Evern interjected while rubbing his chin. "Unlike in Asteom, the people here consider their family's name sacred, so it is not mentioned often, except in important circumstances. King Arval remains one of a few who know ours, so hearing Galdwin connected you to me."

"I see."

He chuckled softly, lightening the lingering tension. "I prepared to head out for the evening with my scouting company when his guard found me. He announced your arrival, and I dropped everything to sprint to the throne room. Then, I saw you…"

Paulina squeezed his hand in a reassuring manner as he rubbed his eyes. "We accepted our new lives," she added. "We have not left Yeluthia in years."

"Speaking of which," Coura began, leaned back in her chair, and glanced at the nearest doorway leading farther inside their home. Throughout their conversation, she noticed the light footsteps and clustered breathing of those on the opposite side of the wall.

THE ANGEL'S DESCENT

Her mother gasped and raised both hands to her rosy cheeks. "My goodness, how could I forget! Odell, Jackie. Come here, please."

At the request, two children hesitantly sidestepped into the opening before Evern urged them to approach the table. The boy couldn't be older than five or six, yet he seemed to be the spitting image of Evern. Sandy hair grew to brush over his nose as he kept his head down a bit, though the thin locks couldn't hide his freckles or the light blue, almost silver eyes. Behind him, the girl from earlier clutched onto his shirt. They shuffled to stand in between their parents, and Coura observed the four together for the first time.

Even if she didn't learn they were related, their similarities made the familial resemblance obvious. Paulina beamed at her youngest daughter while Evern placed a hand on his son's head, causing the children to glance up. In that moment, they created the perfect family portrait.

Coura held her smile against a tightness gripping her chest. "They look just like you."

"Children," her mother began in a gentle tone of voice. "This is your older sister, Coura."

Both sets of eyes stared in disbelief, darting between her and Paulina, who laughed at their reaction.

I doubt anyone informed them I went missing. They're still young, so why not wait a few years to tell the full story? Besides, no one expected us to ever meet.

"What happened to her hair?" the boy, Odell, attempted to whisper to Evern.

Coura's smile widened at his innocent behavior while her mother reprimanded him for what she deemed an inappropriate question.

Without dark energy around, it wouldn't surprise me if most Yeluthians never encountered a human like me. I've been repressing my power, but can anyone here sense it? She made a note to ask her parents about the topic and realized they had yet to question her about her life in Asteom.

The girl, Jackie, gazed at her father with a perplexed expression. "Sister?"

"We planned on telling you when you were older," he explained. "Coura went away for a while, but all that matters is she returned to us."

"Okay," Odell muttered to no one in particular.

While the children lowered their eyes to the ground and remained silent, Paulina frowned, shook her head, and sent Coura an apologetic look. "They usually are not this shy."

"It's fine. I'll need time to adjust too."

In order to calm down from the excitement, her mother suggested they save the rest of the talking until after dinner. Her parents ordered their youngest children to show Coura to the guest bed while nudging them toward the inner doorway, and the pair obliged.

Children's toys and art projects littered the room, though the bed had been left untouched. A lone window near the ceiling didn't let in any light because of the hour, so Odell went to fetch a lamp from the kitchen. When he returned, she observed some of the items before picking up a crafted picture woven using dyed string and sturdy twigs.

"Who made this?" she asked, projecting as much of a friendly attitude as she could manage.

"I did," Jackie replied so quietly Coura strained to hear the words.

"It's beautiful. I wish I could do this, but I don't have the patience."

"Mother taught me."

She offered the piece to Jackie, outstretching her arm until the girl decided to step closer and accept it. Then, the children scurried out of the room.

Take it slow, Coura told herself with a sigh, rose, and picked up the lamp to move back into the kitchen.

Paulina went about warming an orange-colored soup, Evern sliced a loaf of bread, and both shooed her away after she inquired about assisting. The children were busy gathering napkins and utensils, so she resigned to sitting at the table where an extra, mismatched chair had been added.

*

Dinner proved to be more relaxing than Coura anticipated. Her first taste of the earthy and rich soup was the only spoonful where she hesitated because of its odd appearance, and the bread complimented it as well.

Her mother filled the silence by describing the community garden she volunteered at in her free time, which yielded the vegetables she used that evening, and her position as an overseer for a selection of houses used by the elderly. Most couldn't clean or cook for themselves, so she completed the tasks and kept the people company. Coura admired the passion in Paulina's eyes when she shared the names and personalities of the Yeluthians she had grown close to over the years. In her opinion, no other job would be as rewarding.

On the other hand, her father didn't speak much. He served as one of three commanders under King Arval, managed a scouting party, and organized the city's defenses alongside his comrades. The responsibilities sounded like what the generals in Asteom handled, except with fewer soldiers and mostly light mages.

His mention of a scouting party led Coura to ask about Yeluthia's location.

"This city rests on an upper plateau along the Ghurun mountain range," he shared after scoffing at the idea of a floating kingdom. "Several more branch off farther north and higher up, but this is what is considered Yeluthia's center. Because these plateaus lie above the lowest cloud level, they remain invisible to the people on the ground in Asteom. The mountain range also provides extra cover and attracts fog."

Paulina called for seconds then, preventing Coura from clarifying their position in relation to the places she knew, such as East Hoover and Neston. When everyone ate their fill, her mother began the dishes, and Odell and Jackie jumped up to help. Meanwhile, Evern cleared his throat to get Coura's attention, gestured to the front doorway with his chin, then rose to exit the house with her close behind.

The temperature grew chillier than what she expected for late fall, though she appreciated the lack of insects. Hardly any night creatures scampered or soared to produce noise, which bothered her more than she thought it should, and she hugged herself as she followed her father around to the back side overlooking the field below. He stopped near the edge, crossed his arms, and gazed ahead without a word.

As Coura mirrored his stance, she noticed how balanced her center had become. *Emilea's prediction must have been true. My Yeluthian power belongs here, and Soirée's energy is suppressed for once. I can't remember the last time I felt this relaxed.*

Neither of them seemed inclined to speak, so she leaned against the house before glancing at the starry sky for a few minutes.

"My king offered us another house much grander than this one when he promoted me," Evern mused, breaking the silence.

"Really?"

"Yes, but your mother and I did not want to abandon this spot because it reminds us of the hill outside Neston."

Coura recalled watching the sunset above the eastern woods as a child, often with her parents. Her lips curved upward at the memories, and she turned to see him eyeing her fondly.

"So many years have passed. My daughter is now a young woman."

The smile she wore faded as she returned to admiring the view. Being beside her father provided a sense of comfort where they didn't need to talk; simply standing in the other's presence proved enough to satisfy their relationship. Still, time went on while they were apart, shaping them into different people.

"I hope your life has not been too difficult without your mother and I," Evern commented, as if sensing her train of thought.

Coura recognized the invitation he offered. She could share her past, inform him of her troubles, and provide a warning for what was to come, yet the fear of how he would react to Soirée, including what the demon did to her, outweighed any perceived relief.

She planned to thank him, but Paulina called the pair inside before she had the chance.

Part Two

Prologue

Over the next fifteen years, Hendal watched the world around him change from inside the palace where he fulfilled his duties as Asteom's high priest. Hernan developed into a man with an iron will, married a nobleman's daughter the year after Hendal's appointment, and they welcomed a son, who shared much of his appearance with the king. Califer acted as Hendal's mentor until the master mage's health declined, forcing the older man to retire to his home out west after naming a successor. During the following months, Hendal grew fond of Califer and wrote to him often, though this led him to neglect his nephew. Wesley's letters arrived frequently for a while, then they tapered off before stopping altogether. He assumed Kercher's priest understood they both had more important matters to attend to.

The days flew by, especially since Hendal spent most of his free time reading about Asteom's geography, history, and various religions. Once he lost interest in what the palace's library held, he sought knowledge elsewhere, but his position prevented him from leaving the capital unless King Hernan approved the trip. The world he had seen as limitless steadily narrowed, preventing him from obtaining knowledge outside of books.

My escape from Kercher only ensnared me in another trap, he reflected one evening as he paced around his room. *This position is nothing more than a puppet for the king and his council. I possess no authority, yet I must attend their meetings and be present to the citizens. Those people are human too; the lone difference is what families we were born into. It reminds me of the system of priests in Kercher. Without an opportunity to speak for myself, I remained sheltered. Now, I see the country for what it is, and what it could be.*

The following afternoon, he received a message from Califer. The former master mage's health took a turn for the worst, and he requested a final blessing from Hendal. His message moved Hernan enough to permit the high priest to leave without a fuss.

Two guards accompanied Hendal toward the northwestern region to a town called Wailon, which proved to be nearly half the size of Kercher, and its people brought him before the frail, bedridden man. Califer greeted the visitors, then they were left alone. Because of his profession, Hendal grew accustomed to acting as a friend during a person's last moments in life; however, seeing the master mage so weak after all the man had done for him hurt.

"I was beginning to think King Hernan wouldn't let you come," Califer commented while lifting his head a bit.

Hendal smiled, sat in the lone chair placed by the bedside, and took the former master mage's hands in both of his. "The news of your condition troubled us," he responded before changing to a lighter subject.

They talked about what went on in the palace, especially surrounding the people Califer would know, until they wound up discussing the additional defenses along the northern border. Hendal didn't mind doing most of the speaking, though he understood less about the military's business because of the generals' secrecy.

"Rumors of conflict make their way into the council meetings, but that's all they seem to be," he concluded.

Califer paused to cough and shook his head. "I'm thankful I don't deal with the politics and troops anymore. It's too much to keep up with when you're older. You start to realize what is most important."

"I can understand how you feel."

The man's eyes drifted around the room until they fell on Hendal again. His next words carried an oddly serious weight. "Have you any regrets in life?"

Over the course of their friendship, Hendal revealed his distaste for his position in Kercher as its priest and his aspiration to learn. He recalled how Califer never judged him for his opinions, yet the question made him uneasy. "What do you mean?"

"I remember you mentioning your desire to explore the country. Although the high priest is provided for, as is the master mage, they're confined to the king's side. Sometimes, I wonder if I could have had a family here to the west. What about you?"

Hendal shook his head. "I never considered such a path in life."

"Interesting," the older man muttered. His attention seemed to go elsewhere. "Once the time comes for a person to stare death in the face, they can reflect on who they are, or their true self. Were their goals fulfilled? Did they leave behind a legacy worthy of their name? Will their regrets tie them to this world after they pass on?"

Hendal didn't know how to respond, so he remained silent.

The former master mage coughed again, wheezed for a moment, then continued with less enthusiasm. "I suppose I'm saying you shouldn't waste what time you have left. Even if you're not living your ideal life, you can still get fulfillment out of it."

"You should relax," Hendal felt the need to recommend.

Califer smiled in his ordinary, gentle manner while squeezing the hand in his. "If only you could've been able to study magic with me. Despite the circumstances being out of my control, it will forever be one of my greatest regrets."

The mention of magic caught Hendal's interest, in addition to the older man's indirectness. "What?"

"I sensed your potential during our first encounter. Perhaps that explains why I favored you above the others."

"I can't wield magic."

"Not anymore. At least-"

"No one in my family has ever been able to," Hendal interrupted after remembering Califer's explanation of how light and dark mages inherit their abilities.

"Are you that familiar with your family's lineage?"

Hendal pressed his lips together and couldn't defend his previous statement. Because he had been separated from his parents when he was young, he never knew most of his other relatives. Verdic also considered the topic of magic irrelevant to their duties, thus dismissing it.

"A mage at the master level must possess the power to sense energy within others," the older man went on, straining his voice until it grew hoarse. "I noticed a spark in you, but your body already developed, making it too late to start working on it. You would've been a wonderful healer, full of compassion. I'm just glad...I could form one...worthwhile connection and help...those I did."

"Wait," Hendal practically shouted when Califer's eyes closed and his breathing became shallow. "I was supposed to be a mage like you?"

The pale man cracked open one eye after the other. "You had the potential," he whispered. "If that power doesn't act on its own, or if it's not trained, the energy seals itself away. I believed you'd found your calling as the high priest, so I left it alone."

Hendal's chest ached until he realized he'd been holding his breath. *I would have had another life...a better life, without Verdic trapping me in their cycle...*

"Please," Califer begged before falling into a coughing fit. "Give me your final blessing. Give...me hope for...the afterlife..."

Seeing the man so weak and helpless brought out an uncharacteristic, primal sensation from within Hendal. *He possesses the power to heal yet is unable to fight off this sickness. We're not so different, and we'll both die when our time comes. Doesn't this prove how equal human lives truly are? At least, they are when we're given a fair chance.*

The older man watched him with a hopeful gaze and tear-filled eyes.

"You asked me if I have any regrets," Hendal managed to say against his mixed emotions. "I had the opportunity to live another life, but it was stolen from me by those who believe their worth enables them to manipulate others' freedom. In a way, you held me back by never mentioning my potential or bothering to train me."

Califer mumbled what sounded like an apology before his hand went limp and dropped out of Hendal's.

THE ANGEL'S DESCENT

The high priest turned away without pity or sympathy. "If we're all meant to die, why must we be restricted by those with more authority? Why should they claim the innocent civilians' futures by neglecting their potential and limiting their opportunities?"

He received no answer, not that he expected one. With nothing else to say, he rose and exited the room.

I might be forced to act as the high priest until my death, but my eyes have been opened. Califer, I shall use you as an example. My loyalties will lie with my own heart and mind, not someone else's, especially people who were gifted a position of power. I vow to change this kingdom so it is possible for everyone to choose the life they want to lead.

*

Califer's death, as painful as it was, solidified Hendal's goal to help Asteom and support the people who wish to escape a predestined fate. If ever his faith in the idea faltered, he would simply remember his late uncle, Kercher's traditions, and his lost future.

Even if his resolve held, he needed to understand what actions he could take. He considered this while staring through the window of the fourth floor's outer hallway where he often came to think without disruption.

How can I possibly convince other people that the leaders they follow might not be the most qualified or the best suited for the position? Can I use my limited authority as a priest somehow? If I do, they might consider me a hypocrite for acting as high priest and staying in the palace. I suppose I would need to make them aware of my past, in addition to how I earned this role over several priests chosen by the king and his council. I'm discovering too many moving parts and conflicts right now.

Hendal released a weary sigh, stood straighter to stretch his back, and slipped inside using the nearest doorway. A meeting had been arranged for that afternoon to organize the kingdom's next steps regarding the northern country's actions near the border, and for some reason they needed him present. His frustration with his unnecessary involvement quelled suddenly when a servant stumbled into him in an intersecting hallway.

The boy didn't appear older than thirteen, but he blurted out an apology and bowed upon realizing his rude behavior. "My apologies, high priest!"

"Where are you going?" Hendal asked without attempting to hide his annoyance.

"To find His Highness. A messenger from Kercher arrived with news from the city in the clouds."

Hendal frowned. "City in the clouds? Do you mean Yeluthia?"

Evidently, the servant didn't know the proper title of the kingdom said to house the angels of legend. He tilted his head from one side to the other while tapping a foot. "The messenger claims the news is from the city in the clouds and requested an audience with King Hernan. That's all I know."

When the boy bowed again and attempted to hurry by, Hendal reached over to grab the servant's shoulder. An itching sensation compelled him to not let this opportunity go to waste, so he intended to take on this task instead of involving the king and his council unless they were needed.

"We mustn't bother His Highness right now. You see, he's leading a rather important meeting. Allow me to speak with this messenger. I am from Kercher after all; perhaps I know them." In reality, Hendal had not returned to his hometown since he departed fifteen years ago.

In any case, his poorly contrived excuse succeeded. The servant's eyes widened, he bobbed his head twice, then he spun around to escort Hendal to the grand hall at the front of the palace.

Soldiers, servants, and well-regarded civilians scurried about on their own business when they entered, though one man stood alone. As they neared, Hendal admired the stranger's blond hair and toned physique but hesitated to approach when he caught the odd sense of urgency behind the man's blue eyes. His guide didn't stop, so he continued.

The boy introduced the messenger as Jaspire before considering his duty complete and leaving. Hendal stared at the stranger until the other spoke once they were given some privacy.

"I believe I requested the king's presence, not another one of his servants."

THE ANGEL'S DESCENT

Hendal raised his eyebrows to emphasize his surprise at the disrespect. His mind filled with replies, both polite and equally rude, yet he grew curious about the messenger's identity since he doubted Jaspire was really from Kercher. Because of the town's tradition, he assumed no one trained to present information at the palace would speak so unkind, let alone not recognize his position.

"King Hernan is in a council session and sent me to inquire about your arrival," he lied. "After all, you wouldn't give details to a servant or myself. We don't know if you're a spy or an assassin."

"I am neither," the stranger snapped in response.

"How interesting. I offered to speak with you first as the palace's high priest, a trusted source in Verona, and because I was born and raised in Kercher. Whose household do you belong to?"

Hendal decided to suggest a few names to demonstrate his knowledge of the town's residents. If the man really came from Kercher, he could have easily corrected or added more information given how Hendal spoke based on the experience from over a decade ago.

The stranger kept quiet, though he did lower his gaze slightly.

"Is there anything you *can* tell me?" Hendal pushed while taking advantage of his title. "People come to me all the time to share their secrets, sorrows, and regrets in confidence. It's my duty as the high priest of Asteom."

Nothing in the man's facial expression or body showed what he thought, but he did raise his eyes to meet Hendal's before clearing his throat. "You may call me Jaspire. I traveled from Yeluthia to pledge my service to your king."

Growing up in the town connected to the angels' home provided plenty of fodder for Hendal's imagination as a child. He learned about the Yeluthians through his studies, including how they wielded a unique type of light magic and could manifest wings, and he fanaticized about meeting one someday. Over the years, that dream faded.

"I don't believe you," Hendal responded to cover his shock. "No one has heard from Yeluthia in nearly a century, yet you expect me to accept your claim? Somebody would send a *real* messenger ahead to inform King Hernan. He doesn't meet with just anyone wandering in from the street."

Jaspire inhaled through his nose and opened his mouth, as if to retort, but he paused. His eyes darted around the hall where people continued walking or conversing nearby, revealing his intent to keep his presence a secret to the public.

Hendal took advantage of that behavior to establish his authority within the palace. "Why don't we find a better place to discuss what brought you here."

He motioned for the Yeluthian to follow as he crossed the hall. They passed through one of the doors lining the wall, and he purposefully used an extended route in order to avoid giving his guest an opportunity to memorize the floor's layout. After a few minutes, they entered a decorated room used by the royal family for their social gatherings, which remained unguarded when not in use.

"Now, let's talk," Hendal began when they were both seated in two of the cushioned chairs. "Why are you actually here?"

Jaspire still appeared displeased since he kept dealing with someone besides the king, yet he caved into the request to discuss his business. "It is as I said. I wish to serve Asteom's ruler."

"Why?"

"Are you humans familiar with the class system in Yeluthia?"

The question startled Hendal, and he shook his head.

"One's birth determines if they will be given the chance to lead, or if they must follow," Jaspire responded. "I am from one of the upper families you might consider nobility."

When he didn't go on, Hendal sensed the Yeluthian contemplating his next words and ventured a guess. "So, you would pledge your loyalty to the king of Asteom in order to give your family's name more value?"

"Yes, that is correct."

His eyes narrowed at the immediate response. "Why did your people not send any prior messages?" he countered. "Surely they would bother to communicate beforehand."

Again, Jaspire fell silent.

THE ANGEL'S DESCENT

Hendal took advantage of the pause to share his own opinion. "If I were to guess based on your behavior alone, I would say you haven't mentioned your departure to the Yeluthian leaders."

The sapphire eyes darted to the door and back. "In a way, you are right."

"What's that supposed to mean?"

Jaspire slid a hand into his pocket to remove a knife no longer than those found in an ordinary kitchen. Its dull blade didn't shine at all but displayed patches of rust. Still, the Yeluthian admired it as though it were a prized weapon.

Meanwhile, Hendal squirmed in his seat. He had a feeling his guest lied about pledging his service to Asteom's ruler, yet he hoped to utilize Jaspire as a resource if he was connected to the city in the clouds.

"Explain yourself," he demanded with more courage than he felt.

"I did not intend to interact with anyone other than your king," Jaspire began, his voice threateningly calm. "I believe I can make an exception."

"You're wrong."

The Yeluthian tilted his head, giving Hendal time to continue saying whatever came to mind.

"If you kill me, my body would be discovered before you reach King Hernan. Also, you wouldn't be allowed near him without someone like me escorting you."

"Clever, human. I am pretty adept at cleaning up after myself, though." Jaspire leaned forward yet made no attempt to attack.

Wait a moment, Hendal thought once his mind caught up to the situation. *If he came here to murder the king, his goals might align with my own. He hasn't tried to strike, so he must be providing an opportunity for me to apologize, leave him alone, or do something to provoke him into killing me too.*

The notion provided a sense of strength, and he cleared his throat while forcing his body to relax. "Perhaps we can help each other."

"What can you possibly offer me? My people do not value coin, property, or possessions except for sentimentality."

"I have a presence in the palace, one established over the last fifteen years. The people here trust me, and rightly so. Your actions are a means to a finite result, which makes sense, unless you want more." As he expected, his words proved alluring enough to tempt the Yeluthian.

"What are you saying?" Jaspire asked next.

Hendal held his chin high, smiled, then leaned back in a position reflecting his confidence. "Why don't we start over? Tell me, why do you wish to eliminate the king of Asteom?"

The resulting silence lasted longer than the previous, yet he dared not interrupt because he knew his guest used the time to debate revealing the reasoning. In the end, it paid off.

"I mentioned my family's status," the Yeluthian began, showing less intensity. "Our lives and responsibilities involve serving the citizens. Since most assignments are decided at birth, promotions are few and far between unless someone dedicates their entire being to another, but demotions are enforced easily. Those of us who fail expectations, even accidentally, even if it is *one* incident in twenty years, find ourselves branded as less than deserving of better. When I learned this, I sought vengeance."

"Why give up what you had to travel through Asteom?"

"From my understanding, violence in my country results in a similar punishment to what happens in yours."

A shiver went down Hendal's spine at the icy reply, and he attempted to hide his discomfort. "So, you hurt one of your people, and they tossed you out."

Jaspire scoffed at the assumption. "I left of my own volition."

"Then, murder here will redeem you? Is that what Yeluthians believe?"

"No, quite the opposite. My sacrifice shall be our revenge."

In that instant, Hendal understood why Jaspire targeted King Hernan. "By killing the leader of Asteom, you hope to place the blame on Yeluthia."

He received a sly, disturbing smile in answer.

It's not a horrible idea, yet he can't do this alone. Firstly, even if he claimed to be from Yeluthia, I doubt the generals would go to war over a stray dog. His reputation in his home country would vouch for his insanity and thirst for blood, succeeding in uniting us instead of dividing the races. That is, unless others support his cause.

"I have one final question," he continued once the situation became clear. "What change are you trying to bring about?"

The question seemed to confuse Jaspire, who narrowed his eyes and frowned. "A war between humans and angels is not enough?"

"No one will fall for such an obvious trap. You may have friends to take more lives, but Asteom would label your rebel group as the problem, especially if they contact Yeluthia to confirm their lack of knowledge about what goes on below their kingdom. In this scenario, murdering the king won't do much."

Jaspire's eyes widened, as though the honest criticism offended him. Instead of lashing out, which Hendal expected, he returned the knife to his pocket before folding his hands together and speaking at a lower volume.

"What I do is for the people praying for better. The blind citizens revere their leaders while remaining stagnant, accepting their lives because it does not bring about conflict. I desire change and redemption, even if it means resorting to violence."

Hendal stared at the Yeluthian and recalled his final conversation with Califer. The reminder of the future he envisioned, where opportunities would be available to all regardless of their status, education, talent, or other classification, lit a flame under him.

"The king, his council members, and the nobility behave similarly to those you describe as stagnant. Most stand above the weak because they formed connections with those in powerful positions or were born into their roles. They base their status on who they know possessing riches and influence over the capital city and other locations around the country, denying those beneath them the chance to learn and develop their potential. All of that is to hold onto their comfortable, peaceful lives. My goal is to end such delusions. As a victim of their carelessness, I claim it as my right." Hendal went on to summarize his childhood, duties in Kercher, and eventual transition to high priest before sharing Califer's betrayal.

"Our ideals can converge here," he concluded. "Once Asteom is liberated, then we'll possess the means to do the same in Yeluthia. We need each other, Jaspire. Join me, and let us fulfill our destiny."

The Yeluthian's expression shifted from suspicious to dubious before appearing uncertain. Then, he pressed his lips together and nodded.

*

The others Jaspire referred to consisted of Yeluthians who had also been shamed for their beliefs, according to him. Hendal didn't care who assisted them, but he insisted they gather followers before attempting to go into action.

"It won't happen right away," he warned the newcomer. "It might take years. As long as we remain steadfast, though, we can succeed." After, Hendal sent his assistant out to collect the Yeluthians exiled from their home.

A little over a year later, he heard from the angel again.

Jaspire communicated with a letter addressed to the high priest, describing the location of a meeting space in the capital city. During his next period of free time, Hendal snuck through Verona until he found the seemingly abandoned, one-story building that looked to be about as large as his quarters in the palace. He knocked and waited.

Not a moment later, Jaspire opened the door. He hadn't aged at all; if anything, he appeared younger and wore a robe similar to a priest's. "Please, come in," he said by way of greeting while gesturing Hendal inside. "This home may be cramped for twelve people, but it is cheap enough. The owner does not ask questions either. Allow me to introduce you to everyone."

Seven males, who looked physically stronger and meaner than Jaspire, and three, beautiful females in dresses stood around. None of them paid Hendal any attention while they were introduced.

"We make up a wide range of skills," Jaspire added once the group assembled. "Four among us can wield magic, including myself and my goddess gift, and the rest are trained warriors. I think you will find this suitable for our purposes."

THE ANGEL'S DESCENT

"What have you told them?" Hendal asked, ignoring his curiosity stemming from what Jaspire referred to as a "goddess gift." Those present had to know the angel's plan to go against Yeluthia's rulers.

Their leader confirmed this.

Before Hendal could consider more, one of the males stepped forward with a scowl. "Let us get started already. You gathered us here, so tell us what to do."

Jaspire opened his mouth in preparation to scold him for the outburst, but Hendal spoke first.

Over the months, he spent the evenings alone to plot where his personal scouts would be placed based only on the mentality and skills best suited for each area. Now that he could do so, he explained this, leaving the group to figure out who would fit at these locations. Essentially, the major cities needed to be under their watch since they'd provide precious information. Then, when the time felt right, they could strike.

Hendal kept an eye on Asteom through the group planted across the country. Those in the south sent updates to Jaspire, who remained the lone member in Verona in order to avoid any direct connections with the palace. Three took cycles in and around the Dalan base, which proved to be the second most guarded area. The others scattered east as nothing worth the trouble would be to the west.

He didn't receive news from Jaspire for a while until someone near Kercher reported seeing another Yeluthian flying high above. In their report, the messenger carried a letter addressed to King Hernan regarding an arrangement to reestablish the old alliance. Hendal could hardly believe the news and ordered future disruptions, both from Yeluthia and Kercher, to be silenced.

Either the first attempt hadn't been serious or their people were cautious because Hendal didn't hear about the alliance again for many months.

*

At long last, their patience was rewarded. After four years of studying the country from the comfort of the palace, the council dragged Hendal into a discussion about their military. Normally, he had no interest in such matters because the king never requested his opinion, yet that day proved to be the exception. The temperamental generals shouted over one another when he entered the space, giving him some idea of what took place. Their concern arose from the number of troops available if most were to be sent away from Verona, especially the mages. They debated how to solve this, even going so far as to invite the nobility Hendal distasted for their greed and prideful nature.

Fortunately, their presence didn't seem useless that day. Someone familiar with the Magical Arts Academy in East Hoover knew about the opportunities offered after a mage graduates and suggested King Hernan take advantage of the system.

"If most of the trainees request to be stationed somewhere around Asteom, why not ask them to serve their country first?" the nobleman threw out with a foxlike grin.

"Would this make them more or less fearful of the army?" another added. This one appeared much younger and acted oblivious to the others' interests.

"What do you even know about the army?" the first sneered, causing the second to cower.

Everyone else in the room ignored their behavior.

"I like it," General Tont continued and tugged on his beard. "I doubt they do much physical activity anyway, so this'll help them prepare for the world outside of their academy."

Evidently, King Hernan sided with that rationality after more input. "I will send for a representative to collect their thoughts and opinions on the idea," he concluded, ending the matter for the time being.

A mage instructor named Byron Rinod arrived a few days later and traveled back and forth from Verona to East Hoover under the king's orders. From their first encounter, it became obvious the man was capable of speaking in a professional manner on behalf of the academy's headmaster and faculty. He proved intelligent enough to hold his ground without lying, instead countering points the council made in favor of what King Hernan deemed the Mage Service Law.

Hendal soon grew envious of the master mage's ability to manipulate the flow of a conversation. In fact, it prevented the proposed law from taking place for months. Still, the council's frustration entertained him, especially their king who couldn't do much with words alone.

With the tension building, Hendal privately recommended they use a more direct tactic. During one of the mage's visits, he arranged for a breakfast with the nobility and announced the future plan to enact the service law. While they flocked into the grand hall, Hendal took pleasure in seeing Byron attempt to keep his composure. The lords and ladies worked perfectly, believing their king's proposal as fact and spreading the news throughout the city. Further word on how excited the people were to have the prospect of mages to keep them safe sealed the deal. The academy could not turn away such a request without appearing selfish and inconsiderate. Instead of severing their relationship with the palace, Byron agreed to return to the academy with his tail between his legs.

The evening the master mage was scheduled to leave, a sudden concern about the magic users living in Verona struck Hendal, so he hurried to see Jaspire. Three others from the group were present and glanced at him after he barged into their building.

"Can a mage sense your power?" he asked just after the Yeluthian spoke a greeting.

Jaspire pointed to the opening in a silent request for privacy. "What do you mean?" he countered once the door closed.

Hendal proceeded to explain the service law, finishing with the idea that brought him to their abode. "I heard mages can sense another's power. If dozens more are wandering through the city, what are the chances they'll figure out you're here?"

Jaspire didn't reply right away. One of the two females in the room stared at him with an expression Hendal couldn't read while the other male threw in his opinion.

"Is there not a master light mage in the palace already? If they have not felt our energy by now, I doubt anyone else will."

"Unless we cast a spell near them," Jaspire added after nodding to himself. "The only power we expended for some time has been for our wings, and that is beyond the city. Perhaps it is similar enough to a human's light magic, so anyone who senses it thinks nothing of it."

Hendal still wasn't convinced. "Perhaps, but be careful. I want an update sent to your companions as well to inform them of this new law."

"It shall be done."

"Good." Hendal self-consciously brushed down his tattered cloak and prepared to leave; however, a feminine voice filled the space before he reached the door.

"Did you say the law *will be* passed without issue?"

Hendal glanced behind and noticed the others staring at the female beside Jaspire. She seemed frail and physically harmless, but her eyes glowed with a mischievous interest.

"Once Byron, the mage I mentioned earlier, brings the documents to the academy's headmaster to sign, they'll begin the transfer."

"So, the law is not complete," she added with a sly grin rivaling any nobleman's.

"What are you getting at, Elsa?" Jaspire asked.

She stuck her chin up. "This could be our chance! If these mages are a necessity to the palace, would it not be suspicious if the master mage is killed and the important documents disappear?"

"We want to avoid any involvement with the humans' business," the other male replied in an annoyed manner.

Elsa merely shook her head, opened her hands in front of her, and chuckled. "Drake, if no one knows about our presence here, what would they assume if they catch one of us flying away?"

Hendal heard himself gasp as the idea clicked into his mind. "Yeluthia!"

She snapped her fingers so abruptly that Hendal jumped. "Exactly! Not only do we weaken the defenses in the palace by delaying this law, and possibly causing conflict between the two human cities, but we can also frame Yeluthia for intervening."

"We would need to leave the master mage alive in order for it to work. Then, he will be the first to report," Jaspire added.

The angels' willingness to accept the plan right away startled Hendal, but he found he liked the idea. *Not only will this initiate distrust between Asteom and Yeluthia, but I will also rid the palace of Byron and prevent him from interfering anymore. I do recall two students with him. General Tont's son is also acting as a guard for their return.* He shared this with the others in the room.

"I guess we will only need one alive," Elsa finished with a chilling calmness.

The other female rolled her eyes. "I think you just keep talking because you want to get out of here."

Elsa flashed her a smile and stood. "Would you like to accompany me?"

"No," Jaspire interrupted. "Thelma is a magic wielder, not a fighter. Devan, I am sending you along. Keep an eye on your sister."

The other male grunted his confirmation. Hendal remained with the group until well after midnight when the assigned pair left to hide in the woods before Byron departed in the morning.

"That Elsa is one scary woman," he mumbled to Jaspire and Thelma when the three were alone.

"I have known Elsa my whole life. She enjoys the freedom Asteom provides," Thelma shared.

"Was she always...like that?" Hendal felt compelled to ask, even against his better judgement.

The female tilted her head. "Yes, I suppose so; however, it grew worse when we were banished. Elsa, Devan, and I found pleasure in killing animals for sport across Yeluthia and the mountain range. Every so often, a Mintelian or a farmer ended up in the wrong place at the wrong time. That gave her a thrill. I am sure you can imagine the rest."

Hendal had not cared to hear about any of the former Yeluthians' histories for that reason. Some, like Jaspire, had been cast aside for their beliefs while others were demented.

Instead of continuing the conversation, he brought up various ideas, such as luring the Yeluthian king to Asteom for an assassination and blaming it on King Hernan, or something less drastic to sever the alliance between the two kingdoms. After, he would be able to help Jaspire and his companions without being a threat to his own country. It seemed the details were falling into place, and Hendal rested well that evening.

*

"We have a problem."

Hendal frowned at Jaspire's words as the angel stood in the high priest's quarters. He knew some part had gone wrong not only by the tone of the statement, but also because of the fact that the Yeluthian snuck in to visit him. "What is it?"

"Our attempt to kill the master mage and those accompanying him failed. They will probably reach East Hoover within the next two days."

At first, the update shocked Hendal, and his face paled. He prepared to demand an explanation for their failure before voicing his regret for not learning the angels' skills. Jaspire's glare suggested more, though, so he pressed his lips together to avoid blowing up until he could handle the rest.

"What else?"

This time, Jaspire let his internal hatred seep through, biting off each word as he spoke. "A demon became involved. It possessed the young woman traveling with the master mage, killed Elsa, and took Devan's right foot."

Any emotion heating Hendal drained from his body, leaving him shivering. "A d-demon?" he stuttered, unable to pull himself together at the thought.

Demons were a subject no one wished to venture into. Thankfully, the topic of possessions and rituals had been constituted as a magical matter for the master mage in the palace and their assistants to handle. Sometimes, though, people requested him to exercise spirits believed to be influencing a person into committing crimes or catching an incurable sickness. Matters relating to the creatures, even bringing up the word in most places, became taboo.

"Devan is frantic," Jaspire went on, too caught up in his fury to consider Hendal. "He will not sit still long enough for the wound to heal and demands we avenge his sister."

"We can't do that…"

"I said the same, but he does not listen! Besides, Thelma and I are in Verona. No one else will be returning unless I call for them."

"Yes!" Hendal yelled from the fear creeping up on him. "Inform the others. Fill them in on the situation, and I'll stop by after. We can decide our next steps then."

"What about *it?*" Jaspire growled through his teeth while narrowing his eyes into a glare.

Hendal held his breath. *I don't understand his reaction. Something else is creating these deeper emotions, and it's going on beneath our scheming. This will distract his group and thwart my plans if I don't handle it properly.*

"Whatever your feelings are on demons, you must put them aside for now," he replied. "Its meddling has led to the end of our opportunity to use the Mage Service Law. If Byron is still alive, he'll see his duties through and most likely notice the connection between Devan and us if we do more. Gather the rest of your companions, then send for me."

Jaspire tried burning a hole through Hendal's head with a furious glare but never attempted to interrupt or deny what needed to be done. The Yeluthian left without so much as a nod to let Hendal know he would follow orders.

*

The hectic days after their meeting passed in a blur. Even before he saw Jaspire and the other angels again, Hendal learned of Devan's fate and cursed their rotten luck. The injured angel acted on his own without consideration for what his actions would do to his companions. He got himself killed, confirmed the presence of his race in Asteom, and still couldn't kill the master mage or demon. The law passed, but that news had been swept under the rug when General Tont received a letter from his son, which he flaunted to the council and his men. Apparently, he claimed a rogue angel wounded the young man, though his son had been aided by what the assistant general referred to as an individual with unique, powerful magic being kept at the academy.

As Hendal listened to the general read the letter word for word, he began to put the pieces together. *The demon possessed Byron's student, but it hasn't completely taken over her mind or body. Worst of all, she can manifest wings now and fight someone like Devan while remaining sane.*

Once he finished, General Tont laughed in a condescending manner. "Who here scolded me for appointing my son as an assistant general? Now you heard it! He's done some sneaking around, and we can bring their weapon here for us to use."

"You would want such a creature in the palace?" the master light mage named Emilea asked without hiding her disbelief. "Demons are terrible beings that cause nothing except pain and destruction. There *is* a reason why any involvement with them is against the law."

Hendal nodded and voiced his agreement, noting this moment as the first the two ever spoke in favor of the other's stance. "I concur. Lady Emilea has worked with conflicts regarding demonic possession, so it would be ignorant to push aside her experience. We should end it while we have the chance."

Somehow, he knew his words didn't hold much weight when it came to discussions relating to military power. General Casner, the harsh-looking man who always sat directly across from the king's throne, pounced on that notion.

"Easy for someone uninvolved with the soldiers to say. We organized just enough in Verona to get by, but our worry is for the future, more specifically, for the worst scenarios."

"It's only the north we're focusing on, though," General Dillon offered. He proved to be the least explosive commander, emphasized by his soft demeanor and clean-shaven face. "I highly doubt we'll see any armies climb over the Ghurun mountain range or cross the western or southern seas. Besides, we're welcoming dozens of mages from the Magical Arts Academy."

"They'll need training too," General Tont countered. "I'm not saying we need a possessed mage in order to survive. We should just be making moves to see if it's willing to fight on *our* side before killing the person."

Hendal caught Emilea sitting up straighter. "That's insane!" she exclaimed with hands balled into fists. "You don't understand how unpredictable the creatures manipulated by demons can be. Everyone's life is at risk, as well as the sanity of the mages. Demonic energy puts us in a state of unease because of the opposite nature. Even the dark mages would find it unsettling."

General Tont frowned while General Casner huffed a laugh. Hendal half-expected the master mage to slap the soldier for his disrespect if he didn't sit out of reach. He glanced at King Hernan, who typically watched the meetings while processing what the council said. Only when the man felt a sufficient amount of information had been presented did he state his conclusion. It drove Hendal crazy at times like these when the king would not share his opinion aside from asking a question or two.

When the space fell silent, Hendal chanced a peek into what their leader thought.

"Your Highness, do you feel the risk of keeping one possessed by a demon is worth the reward of another, skilled combatant?" he asked in his gentle manner to suggest concern. Underneath the facade, Hendal hoped the young woman responsible for losing him two angels would be executed. Without her around, Jaspire and the others under his command could focus on starting another plan.

Unfortunately, King Hernan typically sided with the generals.

"I don't care for sharing the same roof as one touched by a demon," the man began in a firm tone of voice. "I trust the concern of the mages as well as the direction of my military leaders; however, I also have a strong feeling the renowned academy would take measures to eliminate anyone who poses a threat to our kingdom, lest they be punished for their negligence. I will leave it up to them, then. Should they leave her alive, we can assume they relinquish the demon's power to us." King Hernan finished that sentence by nodding to General Tont.

The news disgusted Hendal, yet his disappointment continued to grow when the man went on.

"Lady Emilea, keep watch and handle any disruptions if the mage becomes a threat. I expect the academy will send Byron Rinod as their representative since he is most familiar with Verona and the palace. He's also capable of holding himself accountable, especially when his students and reputation are on the line."

Hendal managed to resist the urge to groan and sensed the light mage doing the same. The king dismissed everyone, and Hendal saved the information to share with Jaspire whenever the Yeluthian sent for him.

*

If the situation with Elsa and Devan did something for Hendal, it solidified their companions' resolve to stand behind Jaspire, and thus behind the high priest. They all managed to gather together just after the Harvest Festival took place, which had been much later than Hendal preferred.

By then, a Yeluthian child acting as the ambassador for their country slipped past their patrol because she didn't fly, though the letters their group confiscated and another messenger from Kercher mentioned her arrival beforehand. Jaspire confirmed her position, adding how she was the king's niece and used a goddess gift for mind-to-mind communication. That had been when Hendal learned what the term meant, as well as his assistant's ability to heal another's injury from a distance. The high priest soon acted as a guide for the young Yeluthian named Grace. She would remain in his sights, but more importantly, she would not see him as a threat or connect him with Jaspire's group.

Meanwhile, the demon-possessed mage named Coura worked closely with Byron, who became the second master mage in the palace, and did little aside from make everyone uncomfortable. Hendal wished she would slip up and lose control of her magic just so King Hernan had an excuse to get rid of her. During their council meetings, he, along with Emilea, questioned her progress and behavior. Byron always eased the tension with his smooth explanations, providing plenty of detail as he admitted his own concerns. Eventually, he managed to get Emilea to trust him, forcing the high priest to intervene.

When the opportunity presented itself, Hendal approached King Hernan with the idea to inquire if Coura could demonstrate the demonic magic. Byron danced around the subject again during their council meeting, but after more pushing, their ruler caught on to the master mage's avoidance. Hendal pounced on the king's doubt.

"If it distresses the people here, why not send her away?" he suggested when he got a moment alone with the man. "An area with less mages could allow her to practice the magic. Besides, if she does lose control of herself, there will be less people around to harm."

King Hernan raised an eyebrow at that, so Hendal pretended to babble an apology for being so insincere. Despite that, after a moment to contemplate the idea, he caved in. "That would be a feasible way to rein her in. I've been meaning to send someone to Dala for months now too. General Tio heard about the service law and requested we bring mages south for their base. I would guess you heard the shadow creatures are roaming the country."

Hendal nodded. Whispers here and there came from soldiers and citizens traveling outside of Verona, yet he actively tried to stay away from what could hinder his work, specifically an issue that would distract Jaspire again. He needed the angels to focus on the rest of his plan.

"I can spare those with adequate physical skill," the king went on. "After all, we underestimated the combat training offered in East Hoover."

"Yes, Your Highness. How were we supposed to know without a means of communicating between the capital and academy?" Hendal added before noticing the man hesitate to speak, which was a rare feat. "Is there anything else?"

"You're right. I feel like I've been neglecting the citizens outside the capital city. Several people propose I do some readjustments to how soldiers and mages are placed in the cities and towns across Asteom. I believe now might be the best time to do it."

"Who would you send? One of the generals or their assistants?"

The king contemplated this just as they reached his quarters. "Aaron might enjoy leaving the palace for a while. I won't risk those necessary here or in Dala."

Hendal's mouth fell open to reflect an inner sense of disbelief that the man voiced his willingness to send his only heir away from the safety of the palace. He understood what this meant for his cause and composed himself before replying with fervor.

"That is an excellent idea! Prince Aaron is of the age to explore on his own, though with a few guards of course. I'm sure as long as only a handful of people know he's gone, and he doesn't flaunt his position, the matter should turn out fine."

Despite the enthusiasm he projected, King Hernan frowned. "As a ruler, I concur. As a father, I'm not sure about it. I haven't even told Freya yet, but I can hear her harping at me."

Hendal involuntarily winced. The queen proved to be a woman with little capability for deep thought, so sending her only child away would not go over well. He patted the man's shoulder to express his genuine sympathy before moving on.

On the evening of the prince's departure, Hendal kept a close eye on the young man before he and his guards set out. The web of his plotting steadily weaved together, which shouldn't have put down his spirits; however, it felt as though a foreign presence lurked around every corner. The unknown eyes on his back were enough to make him anxious and quick-tempered. During the night, he called Jaspire and the remaining angels to a private space in the palace for fear of wandering through the city alone. He knew the evening meal took place at that time, so the least amount of people would be roaming the halls.

The meeting went according to plan, even with their sour attitudes. He sent the four possessing the greatest speed and ability to blend into their surroundings to Kercher, Clearwater, and the northern border in order to patrol the country's perimeter. They had all agreed it would be dangerous to stay grouped together and lead to suspicion if any were caught. That consideration seemed important once Jaspire, Thelma, and three others named Drake, Hector, and Urvin flew to Dala. Hendal would still utilize those whose faces would not be exposed to the southern base. Once away from the city, he entrusted the assignment to Jaspire. All their group needed to do was take down the troops and its general, then capture the prince.

"The backlash on Yeluthia for his kidnapping will bring about the end of that petty alliance," Hendal concluded with a glance at the nine sitting around him. "We can kill him later once the hostility is strong."

"What about the demon?" the bulkiest of the bunch asked.

"What about it?"

All eyes slid to Jaspire, who reached into the satchel at his side and removed a bundle. With a wide, wicked smile, he unwrapped a dagger seemingly made of gold. Hendal wasn't familiar with weaponry, yet he couldn't mistake the glorious craftsmanship humming with an unseen power.

"This is an ancestral weapon," the angel explained and held up the dagger, which glistened even without a direct light source nearby. "Our ancestors crafted these weapons as gifts for the humans once they rid the land of demons. It amplifies light magic, allowing one of our people to use several spells compared to one or magnify a single casting. Yrian brought it from Umbrich's underground market. With this, we can get our revenge."

Hendal frowned despite the malicious smiles of the others in the room; worrying about a demon gave him a headache.

"We should leave now before the sun sets," Thelma suggested. "Then, we can catch that group on the road."

Silently, most of the table moved to rise.

I can't let them ruin this, Hendal realized. *There's no chance of hiding their wings, and they'll reveal themselves to Byron and those with him by attacking his student. We'll lose our element of surprise on the Dalan base.*

"I tell you when to go!" he blurted out in a rage before slamming his fist on the table, causing the angels to freeze. "This is our final opportunity to make progress on our plan to frame Yeluthia and spark tension between your people and Asteom. We need to organize this business, or else they'll catch us. I think it's best you leave tonight, under the cover of darkness."

Those standing returned to their seats.

"You are certain he will leave tonight?" the outspoken Drake asked, referring to the prince.

"Do you question my sources?" Hendal snapped to emphasize his rising temper.

The shortest person in the room named Hector put a calming hand on Drake's arm. Hendal knew the two were related, yet their facial shape hardly suggested it. "What about the royal family?"

Hendal brought his fist down on the table once more. "Your main concern for now is the base! You have your orders and a leader." He expected someone to continue the questioning, but thankfully they didn't.

"We understand," Hector ventured to speak on the others' behalf.

"Good. Now, get out of my sight."

Jaspire took over the meeting then, leaving Hendal to put his throbbing head in his hands. The four monitoring the perimeter would travel on foot to their destinations while the remaining party headed south for the woods near Dala. He offered to stay behind and arrange the kidnapping with Hendal.

"It would be too obvious we know more than we should about matters in the palace if we attack right away," the angel explained. "Not only that, but it would be smarter to focus on both goals once the prince arrives in Dala."

Hendal could not find any reasoning against this decision, so the discussion concluded there. They all left, except his assistant.

"High Priest, is there something wrong? You appear distressed." The question wasn't as sympathetic as it sounded, instead reflecting Jaspire's annoyance with Hendal's behavior.

"It's nothing. I'm just nervous because we're acting again."

Jaspire raised an eyebrow before carefully removing the golden dagger and running a finger back and forth across the edges to caress the metal. "We hate being in this palace too," he startled Hendal by saying. His voice remained soft yet still full of venom. "It is irritating to say the least. That is why I am going to seal it away with this ancestral dagger. The creator placed an old spell on it to keep the energy inside the demon's physical body, essentially killing it. As I mentioned earlier, the essence it holds also amplifies the power in my people's blood. I already feel my energy swelling. The lone drawback is it really can only be used once, for if the blade is removed, the seal is broken. Who knows how disastrous that could be. Demonic energy latches onto a host for more power. They are truly disgusting creatures."

He hid the dagger in its wrapping before returning it to the satchel. Jaspire's fierce attention relaxed as he turned to leave the room. "I want to be near here for a while, probably until spring. Then, you can expect us to return."

Hendal couldn't think of a response. His eyes followed the angel out of the space before he decided that returning to his quarters seemed like a better idea than lingering alone in empty places.

1

During the years spent living in the palace, Will grew accustomed to the darkness and warmth he awoke to in the morning. Normally, with nothing except his own schedule to keep him busy, aside from afternoon training sessions alongside the newer mage recruits, he could rise whenever he pleased and at his leisure. He sensed something wrong when sunlight shined into his eyes. When he attempted to roll over and bury his face in the pillow, a dull yet recognizable ache in his left shoulder reminded him of the last time he had been awake.

Will's body grew tense, and his mind cleared almost immediately. *What time is it? Where am I? Where's Grace? What about Marcus, Clara, Byron, Clearshot, and the others? How bad is...*

At the thought of the wound inflicted by the angel, he reached over his bare chest to brush his fingers along the skin. No marks or bandages reflected the previous damage. He chanced a peek down at himself and shuddered with relief, irritating the still-sensitive muscles.

I'm alive, he realized. *Grace and I reached Lady Katrina's home.*

Despite the obvious healing done to his body, Will proceeded to sit up with caution while squinting to observe the room. A cream-colored bedspread lay on top of him, along with soft, matching sheets, and a set of four, fluffy pillows filled the top third of the mattress. The walls were the same shade, though the entire space appeared gold against a ray of sunlight streaming past silk curtains. Everything else in the room was shaped from a fine wood painted a dark cherry color.

THE ANGEL'S DESCENT

An armoire stood opposite from the bed, a rectangular chest with gold latches sat on the floor to its right, and a nightstand had been positioned to Will's left. On it rested his glasses, which he promptly returned to his face. Finally, a rug at the foot of the bed covered most of the wooden floor underneath. Compared to his own, gray space in the palace, this seemed unbearably luxurious.

I should get up and figure out what's happening.

His concern eased when nothing besides his shoulder bothered him enough to protest, giving him the boost he needed to crawl off the oversized bed. Whoever put him in there stripped off the torn, bloody shirt and cleaned the mess but left a fresh set of lavender-scented clothes on the chest. For a minute, Will fidgeted in front of them, unsure of whether or not to seek out a bathing room before or after donning them. In the end, he listened to his inner voice and opted for a more mindful approach considering his mild familiarity with the lady. Had his caretaker removed his pants as well, or more, he never would have thought to explore. So, he scooped up the clothes before sneaking into the hallway.

The layout of the upstairs reflected its owners' mindset for a cozy home. The flooring continued from the bedroom, yet floral wallpaper coated the walls in colorful roses against a pearly backdrop. Two end tables painted gold had clear vases holding lilies and fern leaves for decoration. Will secretly admired whoever's consideration it had been to choose flowers that lived without sunlight as he wondered how much attention they put into the design.

Most importantly, and to prove his point, he found a bathing area in the room next to his with an indoor toilet and hot water through a pump and copper pipes. As he laid a hand on the golden knob, he imagined what the value of such a place would be.

Now that I think about it, I don't believe Lady Katrina ever mentioned what her husband does. Whatever it is, he must be pretty successful to be able to afford all of this.

In no time, Will found himself feeling clean and much more active than earlier. He hurried to the previous space where a servant began making the bed. Before he could offer a greeting, the girl, who didn't appear older than Will, looked him over before extending a hand with the palm upward.

"The lady and her guests are in the tea room. If you exit to the left and take the staircase at the end of the hallway, you should hear them to your right."

Will nodded before realizing the servant waited for him to relinquish the dirty clothing in his arms.

"Oh, thank you," he bumbled as he handed them over.

The servant gave a curt nod before returning to tidying the bedspread. Meanwhile, Will followed the instructions to move toward the tea room. Other servants wandered around and minded their own business, which felt odd to him. In the palace, he saw maids, pages, laundresses, and more people with their own duties, yet most managed a smile, greeting, or even a brief conversation. They never insisted on assisting anyone unless they were ordered to do so, but they acted more than willing to adapt should someone ask. It proved an interesting concept, how palace servants behaved compared to those in the homes of the wealthy.

Will stepped into the common hallway and paused. Months earlier, he and his friends were preparing for the funeral procession of the previous king and queen. At the moment, a group of noblemen and ladies mingled with one another inside the sitting room. Each of the dozen or so finely dressed men and women held saucers and tea cups while chatting in a casual fashion. A girl in a white dress with yellow flowers and a bonnet played with a doll on the floor at some woman's feet, but she appeared to be the only child aside from two, younger servants. One held dainty foods on silver platters while the other stood as still as a statue with a teapot that matched the china.

Who are these people? Will thought when none of the faces looked familiar. He lingered in the opening while each set of eyes looked him over before dismissing him just as seamlessly.

When he decided to turn around with the intent to abandon the nobility, he nearly bumped right into his hostess. Lady Katrina gasped, then she giggled in her high-pitched manner. Surprisingly, her outfit showcased less frills compared to the other ladies. Her sky blue dress had lace trimming on the sleeves, neck, and skirt edges, she wore a silver bracelet on each hand, and her hair fell down her back in curls.

"You're finally awake! Let me introduce you." With a smile and a wink, she spun him to face the room once more. "Everyone, this is William Shairp. He's an herbalist from the palace and friend of my cousin, Marcy."

At first, Will couldn't remember meeting the lady's cousin, but he nodded anyway. The name sounded familiar, and it soon fit together with the face in his mind. He noticed a bit of recognition in the guests' eyes before they resumed their conversations, though a handful sent him polite smiles.

Lady Katrina leaned forward once the noise picked up to speak at a hushed volume meant for only Will to hear. "Now you don't need to worry about avoiding them. Your friends are in the backyard with treats of their own."

With that, she moved to enter the crowded area and hop into the nearest conversation. He appreciated the dismissal and stepped outside through the glass doors farther down the hallway.

During his previous visit, Will spent a majority of the passing time exploring the garden space. He had fawned over the various plants' proper treatment and remembered the layout well enough. That happened during the spring. Fall became abnormally cold for the season, causing the garden to wither away until the following year. Decorative chips of wood, dead leaves from the trees, and dried grass made the yard seem eerie.

Against the dull colors, two figures he recognized as Grace and Marcy stood near a metal set of outdoor benches with a table in between. The pair looked relieved when he called from the entrance before he walked over to meet them.

His Yeluthian friend wore a casual, white dress with none of the jewelry the ladies inside displayed. Meanwhile, he hardly recognized Marcy from their introduction. Her raven hair had been pinned on top of her head with several strands loose to trail over her shoulders. Will assumed her elaborate outfit belonged to Lady Katrina since they both appeared to be about the same size. Silver beading along the neckline accentuated the evergreen color, as well as emerald earrings and a necklace to match. She fit the role of a lady's relative yet looked indifferent about the disguise.

Grace smiled when he joined them. "Good morning! How are you feeling?"

"Better than before," he replied and avoided the urge to rub his left shoulder. "What about you? What happened after we arrived?"

"Why don't you eat first?" Marcy interrupted with a gesture toward the table. A tray of untouched pastries sat beside a teapot and three cups. "It should be cool enough to handle now. Also, I wouldn't use either of the benches. The frost this morning left them damp."

Will snatched a handful of his favorite item, sausages covered with a pastry dough, and nibbled on one until Grace and Marcy had a chance to eat as well. Only when they polished off the tray did he begin to feel a chill beneath the sun's warmth.

"Why are you outside anyway?" he asked as Marcy poured him more tea.

"This is one of the few places we can get some privacy. Lady Katrina likes to host a weekly brunch, so it would be rather strange if I ever declined an invite extended to me through her." She paused to sip her drink, and Will could sense she wasn't as disappointed by this life as she acted. "Anyway, you've been in and out of sleep for a couple of days."

"That's all?" Will wanted to exclaim. It felt as though he woke much later and in a distant place. Instead, he asked about Grace's condition.

"I exhausted myself," she explained with a frown. "The worst part had been coming here with you because I used the last of my energy to close your wound."

This time, Will didn't hesitate to massage the tender muscles and roll his shoulders. "I appreciate it. I don't know if we would've gotten help if you didn't."

Grace blushed at his gratitude, but the downward curve of her lips remained as she glanced to Marcy.

The woman released a sigh and set down her empty cup. "I can tell you what little changed, and then we should probably move inside before we end up sick."

At first, Will mentally prepared to hear worse news than what he remembered in the training ground. Perhaps someone died, or Hendal took over the palace and let the angels roam the city. In actuality, Marcy heard no news while they were recovering. She requested an innocent, trustworthy servant recommended by Lady Katrina to deliver a message to the palace yesterday and watch for suspicious activity. The young man returned later that day and explained how life stayed the same, as far as he had seen.

No word came from Diana and Peter or Clara, Jean, and Justin, which Will assumed was for the best since most of them had been in worse shape. His hopes plummeted when nothing came from Byron, Clearshot, or Marcus either. Marcy went on while Will hugged himself tighter in an attempt to savor the sun's heat.

"The lady is worried too," she added while jerking her chin toward the home. "Lord Donovan doesn't tell her about where he goes. I guess they keep to their own business."

That confirms my suspicion. The lady appears to be in her late thirties while I believe her husband is well past his forties. He married for a younger, pretty wife, and she married for money and status. What a pairing, though it works for them. He could never imagine spending his life with someone he barely saw or who only wanted to be with him for his belongings.

A gentle yet icy breeze reminded him their breakfast ended already. "Is there anything else?" he asked when Marcy stopped talking.

She shook her head. "It seems we can only sit around and wait for an update."

"How about we do so inside?" Grace added before taking a couple of steps toward the entrance to usher them in that direction.

*

The lively group in the tea room remained, but the lords and ladies ignored the trio as they passed by to head upstairs. Marcy led the way, taking them farther down the hall than the room Will stayed in. At the end, she opened a door on the right.

Her quarters were twice the size of Will's with the same, softened colors and added furniture, including a set of rose-colored, cushioned chairs. Marcy moved to the first while Grace took the second, leaving him to hop onto the edge of the bed. Two windows on either side of the headboard had their curtains drawn to reveal the road below.

"What should we do now?" he couldn't stop himself from mumbling.

The resulting silence didn't feel as unexpected as he imagined, though it lasted for a few minutes. Grace yawned, politely covered her mouth, then spoke.

"What options do we have?"

"Not a lot," he answered while removing his glasses to wipe them clean. "Separately, we're weak. I don't mean just us either. Everyone in the training ground two nights ago was worn down, injured, or both. I don't believe the three of us can do much against Hendal or the rogue angels. Perhaps our best chance involves not acting until we learn more from the others."

"We cannot do that," Grace practically shouted, revealing the buried emotions from their fight. "I refuse to abandon what we started."

"Aren't you the ambassador for Yeluthia?" Marcy interjected before Grace could dive into her rant.

His friend held back whatever she prepared to say and nodded.

"Why do you want to help Asteom? Correct me if I'm wrong, but I thought ambassadors act as a bridge between nations. Why not report the issue to yours and stand aside? Is the high priest after you because of it?" Marcy's voice sounded innocent; no hostility or sarcasm marred her general curiosity.

Grace heard this too and glanced down at her hands with a deflated expression. "I... Hendal hurt me, though that is not why..."

Seeing the Yeluthian torn between her kingdom, duties, and personal experience pushed Will to intervene on her behalf. "Grace is our friend," he began, using a calm tone to emphasize his sincerity. "She always represents her people, but her life was on the line when Hendal kidnapped her. I believe she deserves the opportunity to stop the high priest as much as, if not more than, either of us."

Marcy's eyes widened a bit to show she remembered what Grace had been through. He recalled his companions mentioning the

THE ANGEL'S DESCENT

Yeluthian during their journey from Dala, but he wasn't certain if she put the entire situation together.

With that in mind, he moved away from the touchy subject. "Besides, our attempts to reach Yeluthia were foiled by the rogue angels who serve Hendal."

"Where would Asteom's messengers be sent?" Marcy countered. "I didn't know the king was aware of Yeluthia's location."

Will opened his mouth to answer before realizing he had no idea either.

Grace giggled upon seeing his clueless expression. "I would be amazed if you actually found out."

His cheeks heated while he responded with a bashful grin.

"Messengers loyal to our king would make the flight to Asteom," she went on. "Kercher, the town below Yeluthia, was named after King Servian Kerch, who had been crowned after the founding of our kingdoms' alliance. He suggested we establish a solid method for communication not so reliant on an individual's flight. The King of Asteom at the time agreed and built Kercher from the ground up, placing trusted households there to live a quiet life while serving the nations. Ground messengers from your country would transfer letters and news to Kercher, then ours would make trips to collect them."

"What happened?" Marcy asked when Grace fell silent.

The Yeluthian looked between her and Will. "We do not know. Less and less came from Kercher over the weeks. Our king did not wish to waste his messengers' time and effort, so they were sent sporadically. I assume the connection stopped altogether after."

"I would bet the people in Kercher either chose to leave or disappeared over the years," Will picked up despite the melancholy feeling her explanation spurred. "If the Yeluthians didn't need to visit, the messengers' entire purpose just faded away."

"How would the recent king of Asteom send letters?" Marcy pushed.

Will turned to Grace for the answer.

"I cannot say for certain because I was never involved with King Hernan's council meetings, but my guess is his messengers attempted to go to Kercher after learning someone interfered with our communication." She summarized how the Yeluthian leader sent letters to announce her arrival in Verona, and how they had been intercepted before reaching King Hernan. When he became aware of the issue, he sent messengers to reestablish the connection, though they didn't return.

"That explains why none of your people came here after you, or why it would be dangerous to visit Kercher," Marcy mused with upcast eyes.

Will had not considered involving the Yeluthians until that point because he didn't know about the town. He rolled the idea over in his mind for a moment. "Grace, what if we try it? Would you go to Yeluthia on Asteom's behalf?"

She stared at him and tilted her head yet didn't respond right away.

"Is it safe?" Marcy started, expressing more concern than he expected. "What if the angels you met are keeping watch? One might be manageable for the three of us, yet the rest of them…"

"True, but I don't think we should stay in Verona," Will added.

Grace agreed and appeared to be contemplating their situation.

"Should we return to Dala, or another southern city?" Marcy asked him after.

"No, I mean… I don't know."

"Then, why not stay here for the time being? You both could use more rest, and if your friends are still in the city, it would be safer for them if we don't draw attention to ourselves."

"We're not helping by remaining nearby, though," Will protested. "If we assume the worst, that Hendal did send someone under his control into the city to find us, then we should leave and use Grace's ability to gather everyone when they're healthy."

"Yes!" his Yeluthian friend exclaimed, startling him.

"What?"

"We should go see Emilea. With her additional energy, I might be able to project my goddess gift to my people. Then, I can inform them of the situation. They are more likely to assist Asteom if they hear about the problems from me."

"That is a lot safer than trekking across the country," Will muttered. "Her house isn't too far out of the city that we can't return if something were to happen, and you can always speak to the mages in the city."

Grace nodded eagerly while Marcy appeared uncertain, though the woman didn't mention any thoughts against the suggestions. Will figured she wouldn't object because of her ignorance regarding a Yeluthian's goddess gift.

He sighed with a glance out the window. "When should we leave?"

There came a knock at the door before they could move further with the discussion. Marcy hurried to open it, revealing a man Will remembered to be Lady Katrina's butler. Unlike the younger servants, he dressed in a clean, navy blue suit with his dark hair slicked back. Based on his regular, professional presence, his job demanded a formal appearance.

"Forgive me for interrupting, Lady Marcy. I was requested to pass along information from Lady Katrina."

Marcy caught the hint and moved aside so the butler could enter before closing and locking the door once more. "What is it, Leo?"

The man gestured for her to sit and only cleared his throat to begin when she did so. "Now, the lady asked me to listen in on your previous conversation, so there is no need to fill us in on your leave."

All three sat up straighter.

"You eavesdropped?" Marcy cried to express the trio's disbelief.

Leo ignored their alarm. "Although one may try to remain secretive, the servants of any noble household are taught to keep our ears open. Don't worry, I'm alone and would not have done so if the lady did not send me."

"So, why did she?" Will pressed. It seemed odd to him that Lady Katrina would intervene. She left them on their own in the morning, and neither Marcy nor Grace mentioned her interest in matters relating to what took place in the palace.

To his relief, Leo seemed more than willing to be patient with them. "Lady Katrina is not inclined to participate in whatever rebellion you're a part of. Both her reputation and her husband's are pristine, so mucking around would only tarnish them; however, we became involved when you showed up. She grew concerned about bringing you into her home because your presence could raise questions regarding her allegiance to Asteom and the credibility of Lord Donovan's trading."

He's a merchant, Will noted. *That explains why he's never around.*

"You want us to leave as soon as possible," he stated, voicing what the butler's words implied.

"Correct. Of course, Lady Katrina understands the pressure on each of you and values your relationships to her."

"Which is why she sent you to spy on us and listen for when we might leave her alone," Marcy concluded.

Leo nodded. "When you mentioned your intentions, I figured I would share this so you can consider the lady's mindset."

A gentle smile spread across Marcy's face, and she stood to approach the man. "Thank you. The last thing we need is to bring trouble to Lady Katrina after all she's done for us. Can you send that along as well? We should be heading out before noon."

He placed a hand over his heart and bowed. "Of course, Lady Marcy. Please, allow me to finish. What I shared with you was not why I had been sent here. In actuality, the lady requested I tell you a tidbit of information from the party downstairs. She believes you might like to hear it."

Will glanced over to Grace, and the two shared a look.

"Let's hear it," Marcy urged when he didn't go on.

"As you know, none of our household servants reported anything out of the ordinary in the palace. It is more noticeable for the wives of noblemen who do business there to catch wind of their unusual behavior. Lady Katrina meets with various parties throughout the week, gathering as much as she can with the facade of concern for her own husband. Fortunately, Lord Donovan's work brings him to Verona a handful of times a year, so her observations are more for your group. Many of the people she speaks to have been noticing their spouses acting unfeeling and impersonal. Their responses are dull, behavior is sloth, and activity is limited to using the least amount of effort."

Will began holding his breath throughout Leo's summary and let it out during the pause. *This must be a result of Hendal taking control of their minds. At least this is suspicious enough to bother the nobility.*

THE ANGEL'S DESCENT

"What does Lady Katrina think?" Grace asked with a serious expression.

Leo didn't hesitate to respond. "Other than affiliating with the nobility, she has no reason to care what takes place in the palace. As I mentioned earlier, she has no interest in becoming involved with matters regarding a rebellion for or against the kingdom."

How does she not possess a drive to help her country? Will longed to demand. With how much he learned throughout the years about demons, the monstrous creatures, and angels, he felt obligated to do so.

Despite his passion, he focused on the wider picture. *Lady Katrina must be starting to worry about the future. She knows she can't fight or resist should anyone threaten her household, so the best option is to support us. The more she hears, the greater a target she becomes. Using her home as a sanctuary will put everyone's lives at risk, which is why she's hoping to give us what she can before urging us to leave. After all, it would be better for her to shut out the danger than continue digging just for our benefit.*

"I see," he said aloud to break the silence.

While Grace and Marcy shot him curious stares, Leo nodded, as if reading his mind.

"Thank you for understanding," the butler added. "Whatever is going on in the palace has seeped into Verona beneath the surface. I haven't heard talk of a battle, but should it come to that, most citizens will hide at the unknown rather than jump in."

"That's fine," Will responded immediately. Who better to relate to what the people felt than him.

I grew up ignorant about my patriotism, he reflected while recalling his first experience in the capital with Byron and Coura. *They protected what they cared about and fought for their academy. After encountering the angels who hurt me and almost killed Coura, I just didn't want to be alone, especially the way I was. From then on, with Byron's permission, I trained to use a sword and continued my own studies to better myself. In the Valley Beyond, I abandoned my efforts. I became paralyzed with fear when I saw the fallen soldiers, and I lost hope. It wasn't until Coura distracted me enough to consider the problem that I understood what I could do. Dragging the injured into the cave may not have been much, but I contributed to saving their lives. No one in Lady Katrina's home, or probably even in the city, possesses the power to fight, let alone without being told what to do. That's why we need to strategize without them in mind. I doubt Hendal would attack the people he wishes to rule too. With the rogue angels and a demon in mind, it would be best to keep what we know to ourselves.*

"We don't expect any unarmed citizens to be involved," he continued to ease any tension. "Please, tell Lady Katrina to stay safe. Ask her to spread the word to the other nobility on our behalf. There *is* a threat in the area. They should stay away from the palace, remain deeper in the city, or head south for the time being. None of us want innocent people getting hurt."

Grace said his name in a reassuring manner, but he ignored her eyes and Marcy's as his cheeks heated from an unexpected blush.

To his surprise, Leo offered a smile. "That's exactly what I hoped to hear. I'll bring your message and what we discussed to the lady."

"Thank you," Marcy said while the butler bowed again before turning to unlock and open the door. "Make sure Lady Katrina understands how grateful we are as well."

The man acknowledged her additional comment with a wave of his hand. "You will find your original clothing clean, mended, and packed outside of the rooms you stayed in. Lunch is in the kitchen. Lady Katrina will be away for the afternoon, so I suggest you slip out then. No further servants shall question your departure. Farewell, from both me and the lady."

*

Will, Marcy, and Grace had no more to talk over, leaving them to separate for their own quarters to find the promised items, change, eat, and hurry to the front of the house. The temperature outside warmed slightly, but the servants still left fur-lined cloaks with their clothes. They voiced their appreciation with one another as they bundled up and moved onto the western main road.

Around midday, traffic grew busier because the travelers and citizens headed toward the center of Verona on business or for their noon meals. The trio exited the capital without speaking to one another until they were on the path to Emilea's home.

The cold kept them awake and moving to stay warm, no rain or snow hindered their progress through the bland scenery, and night only approached when they neared their destination. Their conversations remained limited to what they felt comfortable discussing in the open, which proved to be simple topics.

"We should almost be there," Grace mentioned after a break.

Marcy shaded her eyes from the dimming sunlight with one hand and squinted ahead. "You're right. I think I can see the brick walls in the distance."

"Let's go," Will urged. His impatience stemmed from how thin their lunch stretched.

To his dismay, Grace called for them to wait. He slowed to a stop behind Marcy, who glanced over her shoulder while he turned around.

"What is it?" he asked when she didn't elaborate.

"I would prefer to inform Emilea of our arrival."

Marcy and Will nodded to one another before backtracking as the Yeluthian closed her eyes to focus. He didn't think much of the moment until he noticed her eyebrows raise and lips purse together. Once she opened her eyes, he inquired about Emilea's response.

"She is there with her children and someone named Aimes," Grace began. "They will wait for us, but Hendal assigned a pair of soldiers to monitor them."

The update concerned Will because of the master mage's defiant actions in the past, and Marcy voiced the question on his mind.

"How are we supposed to get inside?"

Grace pointed toward the building. "She assured me they leave around nightfall and return to the city until morning."

"Hendal must've set them on a routine, though I'm not sure why it must be every night," Will mumbled. "They probably switch soldiers to keep the guards fresh." The notion piqued his curiosity regarding the high priest's abilities and how much effort it took for him to control multiple individuals.

His companions didn't appear as considerate about the subject. Instead, they selected a convenient hiding spot in a circle of pine trees and waited. In the midst of twilight, two silhouettes grew closer before passing by along the path toward Verona. The trio remained in place until both figures were out of sight.

Marcy emerged first to race toward the lit house with Grace following and Will on her heels. The front door swung open as they neared, releasing light from inside while a familiar, older man waved them over. Will recognized Aimes and picked up his speed, along with Marcy, but Grace, who had yet to meet the stranger from Clearwater, slowed her pace to stop farther behind. After Marcy wrapped her arms around Aimes and kissed his cheek, Will found himself shaking the man's outstretched hand.

"How wonderful!" he exclaimed with an infectious grin before leading the three through the entrance.

A mouthwatering scent caught their attention first, but it proved to be the only part that remained of an earlier dinner. Fortunately, Will's hunger became overshadowed by overdue greetings and an introduction for Grace. She upheld her polite nature even when Aimes fumbled for a response upon meeting a Yeluthian. Will decided to save the older man from further bumbling by asking for something to eat. While Aimes offered to grab what he could from the kitchen, Emilea led her new guests to the living room for a seat near the crackling fireplace. All they could snack on right away were cured meats, cheeses, berries, and raw vegetables, but no one complained.

"I'm glad you made it here without trouble," Emilea commented and sighed with relief. "Hendal must be too preoccupied with his business to consider changing his protections on me."

"Then, he never figured out you were working with us?" Will inquired as the realization dawned on him.

Emilea's resulting smile confirmed it. "He never guessed I would be doing much besides meet my husband. When that evening quieted down, I stayed the night with Clearshot and was escorted home with the assigned guards the following morning."

Will took the opportunity to summarize their planning for the welcome ball to Grace since he could see she desired an explanation but didn't feel compelled enough to ask.

"It sounds like nothing went according to what you hoped," his Yeluthian friend concluded with a downcast expression.

Emilea reached over from where she sat next to Grace to place a hand on the other's. "That may be, yet not all of it ended up for the worst. Coura managed to help you escape so Byron could find you. We also learned more about Hendal's intentions, so don't feel distraught about how everything turned out."

Her reassurance lifted Grace's spirits, prompting his friend to smile.

"Well, what brings you here?" Aimes asked to move the conversation forward.

"I'm afraid we don't bring better news," Will started with a displeased groan. For the remainder of the evening, he shared Byron's strategy to catch Hendal by surprise, lure the angels away, and deal with them all before the high priest could cause more damage to the palace. Then, he explained what actually happened, ending with their reunion at Lady Katrina's. He left out the part about Leo's message and their decision to ease the woman's troubles by not staying; to him, what he brought up seemed to be enough for the time being.

About halfway through, they paused so Emilea could put her children to bed, and Will grabbed a drink to ease his hoarse voice. Neither Grace nor Marcy interrupted with additional information, which he figured meant he covered the details. He wanted to question Coura's location after since he remembered she was supposed to return to the house, yet Emilea needed to understand their current situation first. When he finished, Will sipped the last of his water and waited with heavy eyelids. It grew far later into the evening than he wished to be awake.

"I see why you chose to come here," Emilea replied. "For as long as I've known Katrina, she avoids the politics in the palace, which is odd considering how much she thrives on currying favor with the other nobility. Besides, it's better for us to regroup, especially if Hendal does consider sending someone to look for you and the other mages hiding in Verona. I believe they'll be fine so long as they don't act."

She covered a yawn after, giving Marcy a chance to remind them of the hour.

"We're in no rush," she told Emilea. "I, for one, would prefer to sleep now and speak tomorrow with a clear head."

Aimes agreed immediately, stood, and ushered them upstairs to the spare bedrooms.

2

For the second morning in a row, Will woke and found himself bewildered by his unfamiliar surroundings. Once he remembered the previous evening, his mind settled before he dragged himself up, dressed, and went downstairs. The sore shoulder felt better, so much so that he would assume he slept on his arm incorrectly if he forgot about the injury. The almost normal sensation, and the smell of cooking ham and eggs, made him optimistic for the day.

Aimes showed Mace how to fry the food in the kitchen while the boy sliced bread for toasting. In the seating area, Lexie read to Emilea in one of the armchairs, leaving Will to procure a spot nearby. Marcy joined soon after, and Grace descended when Mace began to set out the dishes. Together, they ate a quiet meal until the master mage picked up their conversation from last night as casually as if she were asking about the weather.

"What are you three planning on doing now that you're here? The guards ignore Aimes, so I predict they should do the same to you. I haven't heard from my husband, the assistant general, or Byron, and I don't expect we will anytime soon." She couldn't hide the pain beneath her words.

She accepted the worst, Will reflected with a heavy heart. *Either those three fled like us, have been taken over by Hendal, or were killed. As much as I want to show faith in their abilities, they faced the retaliation by the rogue angels. I guess we're on our own...*

"We have an idea," Grace added. "If you lend me your energy, I think I might be able to reach my people in Yeluthia to tell them what has been going on in the capital city. If they heard about what happened to Aaron, I doubt they would let a demon continue to meddle when we are out of options. Besides, they are more likely to listen to me than anyone else. We would not need to risk our lives or time by going…"

She paused when Emilea shared an unsettled look with Aimes.

"What is it? Did I say something wrong?"

"Oh, no," the older man replied to offer reassurance. "It's just…"

"I don't know if that will be necessary," Emilea shared while rising from her seat. "We could focus your gift on finding recruitment to the south instead."

The master mage moved to the corner of the space where a stack of books laid away from the morning's fire and selected the text on top. Then, she informed the three of what took place in her home after the ball, flipping through the pages and handing the book to Grace as she did so.

*

"Where is she now?" Marcy inquired once Emilea finished. She had been listening intently after leaning forward and placing her chin on her intertwined fingers.

Will became too stunned by Coura's condition, discovery, and decision to explore with the hope of finding Yeluthia to come up with additional questions. Despite Emilea's lengthy explanation, he still felt the master mage didn't share all of the details.

"We don't know. It's been six days since she left. That's why I'm glad you made it here. Grace, can you confirm your country's location on the map there? Was Coura's guess accurate?"

The book Emilea passed along laid open on Grace's lap, making her already petite figure appear even slimmer. Will craned his neck toward where she sat in the opposite armchair from Emilea in an attempt to glance over the pages, which appeared to display a map of Asteom. Her index finger brushed along a part he couldn't see too well.

"Of course," Grace practically whispered, seemingly overcome with emotion. "Those texts are from the palace's library, but this one I lent you from my personal collection. I used to study this in order to become familiar with your kingdom and blotted this area using white paint so I would never forget my home. I have not seen any other documentation of Yeluthia's location in the capital city."

She passed the book along to Marcy, who positioned herself near enough to Will for him to read the pages. The yellowish parchment bore slight tears and wrinkles from years of handling, which didn't surprise him, but the right page possessed a blurred spot. It appeared faint enough to be mistaken for a stain from a spilled liquid or an incorrect marking the creator wiped off.

Will glanced at Grace. "This is where Yeluthia is?"

His friend nodded.

Emilea released a sigh and rested a hand on her cheek. "I must say, I'm relieved to hear I didn't let Coura go chasing after nothing."

Will felt the same until he recalled the danger her demonic magic brought when she ventured on her own. He turned to Grace and saw her knitting her brow in thought. As he opened his mouth to ask what Yeluthia would do to an outsider in their country, she answered the question on his mind.

"Even if Coura goes to that location, there would be scouts posted above Kercher who can sense her. I do not anticipate them harming her unless she attacks first. If she convinces them to listen, then they will learn of Asteom's troubles."

"Would they help?" Marcy pressed.

This time when the Yeluthian nodded, she flashed a proud smile. "My people were fully committed to support Asteom before I had been chosen as the ambassador. Actually, if King Hernan seemed hesitant about reestablishing the alliance, my king planned to utilize the looming Nim-Valans to the north to persuade your leaders."

She said the last part with some reluctance, making Will wonder if she wasn't supposed to share the information, or even know it in the first place.

"I suppose we should be thankful the only conflicts we're facing are internal ones," Emilea commented. "In any case, Coura went toward that area, so I think it would be better to try speaking with the Dalan base's general. We can alert them to the threat and ask for advice on what to do next."

"Will Coura be safe on her own?" Marcy practically interrupted.

"She'll be fine," Aimes answered. "She sounded confident, claiming she could convince those people to send help. Besides, she's got half their blood. They can't just throw her out, right?"

He directed the question at Grace, who confirmed his claim.

"See? Why not contact the Dalan base, send some soldiers to the capital, then worry about Coura?"

Aimes appeared satisfied with what he said, easing the tension, yet Mace muttered from where he and Lexie sat at the kitchen table reading books of their own.

"You weren't even awake when she left," the boy clarified loud enough for everyone to hear.

"No. I wasn't, but… I didn't…" Whatever rebuttal he attempted to provide melted into a jumble of incomplete sentences.

Will, along with Emilea, Grace, and Marcy, allowed themselves the pleasure of laughing at Aimes' expense while the older man rubbed his neck and continued grumbling.

"Why do I ever believe anything you say?" Marcy asked, rolled her eyes, then sent him a smile to show the jest had been in good fun.

Their joking behavior relaxed Will's nerves. "If you agree it would be worth the time and energy to contact General Tio first, then I agree," he added. "Knowing Coura, she'd berate us for wasting our efforts on her."

Those around the room agreed before Emilea and Grace prepared to contact the southern base. He watched as the two moved closer to hold hands before closing their eyes and letting their expressions fade.

After a moment, Aimes reassured Will and Marcy they wouldn't be a distraction before urging the pair to go on with their day. They lazed around with an eye on the mages until the hands broke apart nearly an hour later. Grace dropped onto the couch next to Will, huffed a breath, and closed her eyes again. He would have been concerned if her lips didn't curl upward into a sly smile.

THE ANGEL'S DESCENT

Emilea's body slouched at the same time, and she opened her eyes to stare at the Yeluthian. "Why did you do that?" she asked in an annoyed tone of voice.

"Do what?" Will inquired.

They both ignored him.

"I figured we could send both messages right away," Grace replied to the first question.

Emilea frowned. "We had the opportunity to do so tomorrow, or even later tonight. Now, you stretched your ability and used up your power and mine. I expect the headaches will be twice as painful as last time."

"What happened? Don't leave the rest of us in the dark," Aimes threw in.

Grace opened her eyes a bit. "I spoke with General Tio and warned him, like we planned. Since I already cast my spell, I adjusted to search east for Yeluthia."

Will's eyebrows rose upon hearing her reckless decision. "Really?"

"Yes, but unfortunately I did not possess enough energy to seek out a familiar mind. I settled on a soldier near the center of the city."

"What did he say?"

"He did not get a chance to respond. Once I introduced myself, I told him about the demon and Hendal. I hoped to mention Coura, but the connection grew too weak to hold."

"That second stretch drained both of us," Emilea added with a displeased expression. "Please tell me you didn't rush your conversation with the Dalan general."

The Yeluthian shook her head, seemingly either too tired to vocalize more words or unwilling to further upset the master mage.

Will turned to Emilea. "What did General Tio say?"

She gave him an odd look before presumably remembering no one else understood a mage's spellcasting process. "Allow me to explain. When we made physical contact, I could lend Grace my light energy to amplify her goddess gift. I can trace her power yet do nothing else. Her mind-to-mind conversations are between her and those she addresses."

"I see." He shifted his attention to the Yeluthian at his side.

She noticed how they waited for more information and took a deep breath. "He was not in the base where I spoke to you last time."

"What?"

"At first, I felt just as confused. I had to spend precious time skimming the area and finally resorted to listening in on a soldier's thoughts. I do not do such an act carelessly, but I could not think of another option. When I caught the hints in the man's mind, I understood. I did not notice how few people wandered inside the base because I remained focused on only one."

"He left the base," Emilea concluded for them. "His troops are already moving north.

***

For days, Marcus could consider little aside from keeping Clearshot's pace as the two led their mounts south. During that time, the hours blurred together until it became either morning or night. Physically, he grew so exhausted his aching muscles and deep cuts from the rogue angels went numb. Nothing would stay in his mind besides an immense sensation of guilt. His loyalty to the palace, and those inside it, conflicted with what he figured Clearshot planned to do. Lastly, a small part of him pitied the animal underneath his body; the filly seemed just as unprepared for the journey.

They rode through the first night until reaching Sindaly near dawn. Clearshot wordlessly slipped the innkeeper some coins before the sleepy man led them to a room. Marcus didn't remember much of the place, and his companion shook him awake around noon that same day. As the innkeeper brought them packaged, portable meals, Marcus did his best to solidify his resolve. Together, the two soldiers moved outside to where their horses were already fed and saddled and took their positions once again despite the animals' reluctance.

I understand, he thought, as though he were speaking to the creature, and nibbled on his breakfast while Clearshot led them through town. *I'll try to slow us down a bit today, if only to get a word in.*

Despite the promise, as soon as they moved onto the road toward Umbridge, Marcus felt himself fall back into a dazed, unaware state that made him oblivious to the world around them. Greens, browns, and grays blurred by for hours, and Clearshot continued his breakneck speed. If other people traveled on the road too, they were smart enough to stay away. Soon, he abandoned his attempt to focus altogether. He wrapped the reins tighter around his hands, gripped the saddle horn, and closed his eyes.

Sometime later, his filly began to slow, drawing Marcus out of his feigned rest. The sky had darkened with brighter colors hiding behind the trees to the west when they stopped. He heard the trickling of a stream and understood why they paused their journey. Clearshot swung off his mount while dropping the reins, letting the horse follow him farther from the road. Marcus did the same, though with less grace, but his cramping legs had him struggling to keep up.

I'd be laughing if I didn't feel so miserable, he reflected while standing next to his companion.

The horses bent their heads low to gulp down the clear water snaking through the forest while the two riders grabbed their waterskins and meals before scarfing down the latter in silence. Marcus hurried to finish first in order to address their situation because he believed he wouldn't get another opportunity that day.

"Why are we going to Dala?" he asked and drank from his waterskin. It became obvious where they were headed, and he knew why, but he needed an explanation for the rush.

Clearshot paused his chewing for a moment, then he answered around the mouthful of food. "We're getting General Tio to send his army north."

Marcus heard the disgruntled tone in the man's voice and ignored it. "Why the hurry?"

The animals finished drinking and began to nibble on the grass in an urgent manner, as though they understood their limited time to eat. When Clearshot crossed his arms without replying, Marcus' dormant temper sparked, prompting him to continue speaking.

"We failed, and Byron's gone, but what about everyone else? Hendal can't be plotting another scheme so soon, right? Why not regroup and send a messenger south, or at least take our time with this?"

"We don't *have* time to lose." Clearshot moved to grab the reins of his animal and began leading it back toward the road.

Marcus contemplated holding his tongue, yet his companion's dismissive behavior struck a nerve. "Look at us!" he practically shouted. "We're in no condition for this. It took four days for Aaron and me to ride from Dala to Verona at this pace. This is the second day, and I can tell you, we'll regret continuing if we reach the southern base alive. Our wounds need attention. We're risking more if we don't stop."

Clearshot spun around to level a glare at him. "If you would rather return to Sindaly, that's fine with me. It only takes one person to deliver a message."

"No," Marcus answered almost immediately. "I'm just saying, there's no reason for us to kill ourselves by hurrying."

"This was our backup plan," his comrade grumbled, reflecting his sour mood. "Byron and I decided we would make a break for Dala if the plan went wrong before Hendal had a chance to send someone after us. If he stops you and I, no one will know what's going on in the palace."

"I understand the need for a fallback, but that doesn't mean we need to sprint ahead. Why not try being secretive and hide ourselves? You're forgetting Will and the mages."

"You said they were injured, and I bet they exhausted themselves like Byron did too," Clearshot countered. "They wouldn't survive a journey to Dala. Sneaking around will take even longer."

When Marcus couldn't come up with another argument, his companion resumed their return to the road. He led his horse behind while being sure to give it plenty of well-deserved neck scratches.

It's crazy to push ourselves so hard after what we've been through. Could he be driven by Byron's sacrifice? That idea made the most sense. Instead of continuing the discussion, Marcus kept his mouth shut as the pair went on.

*

Because Umbridge would be the next town they'd pass through, which was another day away at their pace, Clearshot stopped when a convenient resting spot appeared. He remained alert enough to discern a clearing just beyond the first few bushes along the path.

Marcus stopped thinking in favor of keeping his body in the saddle. If a packaged meal didn't wind up in his hands thanks to the other soldier, he wouldn't have realized how desperately his body needed the sustenance. They ate while securing the horses to a grounded tree trunk, then the pair curled up to sleep.

For some reason, his mind became active the next morning after being rustled awake; however, his body felt the opposite, proving to be in a worse condition than the previous days. Clearshot said nothing as he removed the last of their food before preparing to ride once more. Marcus trailed in his wake, wondering how he managed to do such a hectic trip with Aaron half a year ago.

At least I could convince him to stay at an inn every night. While Clearshot expresses his emotions, Aaron had no idea how to respond to the news of his parents' murder.

He replayed the memories in his mind during the ride despite the reminder of his best friend's current imprisonment. When the pair reached Umbridge during the late afternoon, Clearshot surprised Marcus by taking them through town to a tavern and purchasing a hot lunch consisting of a brothy stew and bread. He savored the warmth and shelter, especially after they ordered portable meat pies, extending their stop. When the two were left alone to empty their bowls, he decided to chance a conversation.

"You must have been carrying around your money pouch before heading out to the training ground," he started.

When he didn't receive a response, he assumed the man at his side still didn't seem ready to speak casually. Then, Clearshot leaned back in his chair, letting his weariness show as he replied.

"You're wrong. Why do you think the horses were already saddled when we got to the stable?"

"You mean, you set all of this up?"

Clearshot dipped his chin with a sigh. "Just in case. I wouldn't tell Byron, mostly because I knew he already understood the risk. When the angels showed up, our chance of success became even slimmer. At least the demon kept out of it; otherwise, we'd be done for."

"Did you plan anything else?" Marcus asked with a sliver of hope.

Unfortunately, Clearshot shook his head. "Whenever we talked about it, Byron just ordered me to do whatever needed to be done with whoever could help. It wasn't like him at all."

"So, you kept your money with the stable worker and had them prepare our mounts beforehand"

"That's right," Clearshot answered as their eyes caught a server approaching. "I figured other business occupied his mind if he didn't organize an escape route. Either that, or he had a secret, foolproof strategy."

The woman handed over a bundle of the wrapped meals, and they thanked her as they rose to exit.

*

Despite their progress, the chilly weather steadily irritated the pair's wounds. Marcus forced himself to bite back several nasty comments about how poorly thought out Clearshot's actions had been as he tore off strips of his clothing to act as makeshift bandages during their next break. He wondered if they would ride until they reached Twindela since the sun began to set, yet the pace took a toll on their horses. When the animals weren't being pushed into as much of a gallop as they could manage, each bent their head low and panted. Even Clearshot rubbed his mare's shoulder with a sympathetic expression while mumbling something Marcus couldn't hear.

Perhaps this means we'll stay at an inn. I can't imagine going on like this. It's enough to trouble ourselves, but...

The notion disappeared after he glanced up the road and caught several figures coming their way. Twilight's creeping darkness made it difficult to see the strangers clearly, but dozens more appeared behind the initial ones, walking shoulder to shoulder and spanning the entire width of the road. The path moved on an incline to hide the rest of their numbers.

Clearshot noticed too and ushered him to the edge where they waited instead of hiding in the trees.

"Who do you think they are?" Marcus asked after.

His partner's stern gaze relaxed enough for him to see the genuine uncertainty beneath. Whatever the man thought, he kept to himself.

THE ANGEL'S DESCENT

The figures stopped, huddled together, and produced a flame to illuminate the nearby area, revealing their identities as armor-clad soldiers. While they lit more torches and broke apart, Clearshot urged his mare forward while Marcus lingered on the side of the road. The filly must have sensed their interest, for he stamped and snorted until his rider started moving too.

"Hey!" one of the soldiers called with gesture for them to stop.

Clearshot did so and waited for the individual and one of his comrades holding a torch to approach. By then, Marcus caught up to stand at his side.

"Who are you, strangers?" the soldier bearing the light inquired and tilted his uncovered head. None of the others wore helmets either, though Marcus knew the metal grew confining after a while.

"My name is Cornelius Bayporter, and this is Marcus Tont. We're soldiers from Verona," Clearshot answered. His baffled tone matched the confusion he showed. "Where do you hail from?"

"Tont?" the same soldier replied, ignoring the question. "You're General Tont's son?"

Marcus nodded, unsure of how to respond.

The two newcomers shared an amused look before chuckling.

"As luck would have it, we're from the Dalan base," the second man clarified before turning to walk back toward the others.

"Dala?" Clearshot mumbled.

The first soldier waved them ahead. "I'm guessing you'd like to speak with General Tio then? Just head toward the center; you should hear him."

Marcus thanked them with a relieved smile as Clearshot went ahead.

Many of the faces they passed looked at least a little familiar, yet everyone grinned in their direction to show the troops recognized the pair. Hundreds of individuals filled the road, settling down just off the dirt path to relax and begin meal preparations. A slim strip of open space remained in the middle, but nothing else.

Men and women in suits of armor, padded clothing, or simple cloaks built fires, cooked supper, set up sleeping rolls, or gathered firewood in seemingly assigned groups. Marcus found himself enjoying the hustle and bustle since it reminded him of his normal, palace life. The nostalgia settled before a sudden bellow from farther down the road alerted them of the general's location.

"How many nights have we been camping out? Most of you sad excuses for soldiers *still* can't manage to build a fire without rubbing up to a mage! Didn't anyone throw you into the woods for the night? You know what, your sniveling is answer enough."

Marcus stopped beside Clearshot to dismount and watch the burly figure berate a handful of young, bewildered men. After another minute or so of the general's ravings, Tio dismissed them. Although several people surrounded their leader to wait patiently for his attention, he happened to spin around in the newcomers' direction before addressing anyone else.

Out of habit, Marcus straightened and prepared for a loud greeting while Clearshot stepped forward.

"General, we're-"

"*What are you two doing here?*" Tio roared, interrupting the introduction with his face glowing red in the torchlight.

The yelling took Marcus back, and he glanced at Clearshot, whose mouth hung open as he attempted to decide how to answer.

Meanwhile, the general crossed his arms and continued ranting. "Are two notices not enough anymore? Do the featherheads in Verona think I'm too stupid to listen to even one person? You both look unfit to be out here, even by my standards." He paused to wait for some sort of reply.

The others standing around chose not to pursue their requests, either because of his shouting or their business, and disappeared into the groups of people staring at the remaining three. Marcus struggled to ignore the urge to stare down at himself to see if he appeared as horrible as he felt. Fortunately, Clearshot paid more attention and found his voice again.

"Two notices? What are you talking about?"

This time, the general studied them for a moment before opening his mouth with less ferocity. "Calin! Where are you?"

As if Tio's voice were a summoning spell, the assistant general appeared at his side seconds later.

THE ANGEL'S DESCENT

"Here, sir!" Calin offered his superior a salute with a grin that leveled the general's frown.

"Give me the letter." The man extended a hand while Calin dug through his pockets for a folded piece of paper. "Leave it to Byron to muddle the situation," Marcus heard the general mutter before he opened the page and handed it over to Clearshot.

"It's from Master Byron," Calin began, then the assistant general paused to count with his fingers. "The messenger arrived six days ago now claiming this letter needed to get to the base as soon as possible."

"Six days ago," Marcus repeated and eyed the paper. "What does it say?"

Clearshot's eyebrows furrowed together, either to help him read in the poor lighting or in annoyance. Then, he relinquished the page to Marcus, who skimmed it as best he could.

Byron must have been informing General Tio about our problems in the palace earlier because he jumps right into the details of our plan. The message explained their intentions and strategy, except for the addition of Will's friends, then went on with a plea for the general to bring as many soldiers as he could spare to Verona.

If we succeeded in capturing Hendal, Byron and Emilea would still need another general's authority since my father, Aaron, and most of the other figures of power are under the demon's control. In our case, with Hendal running Clearshot and I out of the city, only the Dalan base possesses the amount of soldiers necessary to stand against him. That's all without mentioning the Nim-Valans and how they would react knowing about the threats within Asteom.

"Byron's one wordy mage," General Tio started, interrupting Marcus' thoughts. "For months now he's been sending the same messenger with an update and asking about those demonic creatures around the southern towns. If I didn't admire his consideration for others, I'd hate his guts for bothering me so frequently."

"What about the second notice you said you received?" Clearshot pressed.

"That Yeluthian girl reached out too, the one who speaks with her mind."

"Grace?" Marcus supplied.

General Tio made a shooing motion. "Sure, her. I knew her voice meant the warning had to do with your group; I could never forget the first time she popped into my head. Anyway, we were approaching Umbridge, and I heard her. I started glancing around, which made me look like a fool, but we talked. She seemed as clueless as you two when I finished explaining. Byron didn't inform anyone about our communicating, I guess."

"Then, this means you're bringing your troops to Verona?" Marcus felt compelled to ask, even though he expected the harsh response.

"Why else would I haul two thousand of my own soldiers out of the base? I'll tell you the same thing I told the Yeluthian ambassador: You can quit fussing about the capital city! Calin also gathered another five hundred from around the south, and the base is protected. Don't be sympathetic when I'm being nice. Unlike the soldiers in the north, we Dalans know how to get business done, and get it done right!"

Shouts in agreement rang down the road from those awake and within earshot, causing Marcus to grin. The weight and fears pushing down on his shoulders lifted, and he shrugged, as if he could slide the pressure off. "I just needed to make sure," he commented.

Calin caught his eye and spoke before General Tio could offer another passionate response. "You both look like you could use some food and rest before we continue in the morning. Let me see if we can find you a couple of bedrolls and blankets."

The general huffed and addressed the people who approached again while Calin led Marcus and Clearshot along the road until they reached a horse-drawn cart monitored by two, stout women. Clearshot relieved his mare, telling the keeper he wouldn't need it anymore, and Marcus decided to do the same after offering to brush his animal in the morning. They were given bundled bedrolls in exchange, grabbed their remaining food, and found an open space nearby next to a bonfire. The soldiers seemed more than willing to sacrifice the extra room, so Calin left them alone for the time being. As they finished their meal, Marcus sensed his mind drifting off until a woman wearing a white robe knelt in front of the pair.

THE ANGEL'S DESCENT

"The assistant general requested I treat your injuries," she explained in a soft voice that lulled Marcus into a calmer state. "Please, lie down and relax. I can work while you rest."

Her words were like an answer to some unspoken prayer, so he accepted the offer. She began healing Clearshot first, at Marcus' request, leaving him to drift into sleep with the anticipation of waking up pain-free, less exhausted, and with a drive to save his home.

3

No news came to Coura from King Arval during the seven days since she arrived in Yeluthia. In fact, her parents didn't mention her meeting with their ruler or inquire about her past, not even the dark energy or bandages hiding her markings.

I know they want to ask, she reflected as she neared the centermost building holding the throne room. *They stare and act like they're going to but don't. Are they worried about what I'll say? I don't understand their behavior, and that's without mentioning how they avoid my questions.*

She regularly rose at sunrise, along with her father, which provided an opportunity to discuss what the king would do. Before he left for his daily duties, Evern promised he would inform her when King Arval reached a decision; however, when he returned in the evening, he admitted nothing changed.

Bringing politics up with Paulina resulted in odd looks before the woman brushed the topic aside.

"You are worrying far too much," her mother would respond and switch the subject by encouraging her to explore the city.

It's as though they don't want to talk about the problems in Asteom. Sometimes, they look at me like I'm a stranger.

After her father departed that morning, Coura felt she needed to see King Arval in order to move the process forward. The idea of abandoning the family she just found hurt, but the condition of her home and her responsibility to her friends outweighed any stray emotions.

THE ANGEL'S DESCENT

I'm one of the only people with the power to defend the palace. If I run, how long will it be before Soirée can strike against Yeluthia too?

Those thoughts drove her to visit the king in his throne room. The city appeared active around that hour, as Coura discovered after wandering in her free time over the past six days. Curious and fearful glances met her everywhere, yet no one addressed her with ill intentions, so she could study the area as long as she minded her own business. At the moment, she focused on returning to the hall at the center of Yeluthia.

Because of its size, she found the building without issue and decided to approach from the front to avoid raising suspicion. The two guards straightened when she ascended the polished steps.

"What business brings you back?" the one on the left asked in a more casual manner than she anticipated.

"I wish to see King Arval again. Can you take me to him?"

"I can," the other guard replied while gesturing toward the entrance.

The first soldier gave his comrade a sharp glare, though Coura pretended not to notice. She thanked them before moving inside with her escort.

The Yeluthian continued to be friendly as he guided her through the decorated hallways. Whenever he caught her studying one of the many paintings, he halted to let her read the plaques and explained what he knew of their history.

"This is one of my favorites," he began after Coura slowed to admire a portrait of a former queen.

"You don't need to stop at every one," she added, letting her impatience show a bit.

His smile widened as he shrugged her comment off. "You are Commander Evern's daughter, correct?"

Is my father's reputation why no one questions where I go or what I do? she wondered before nodding when he seemed to be expecting a response.

"My name is Coura."

The guard removed his helmet, held the metal under one arm, then shook his head to ruffle the neatly trimmed, white hair. "My name is Lavine. I work directly under your father and have for months. We were all surprised to hear he has another daughter."

His younger age and following wink startled Coura enough to spur a blush. Even in a suit of armor, his arms and chest looked burly enough to make him a formidable fighter. Against his square face, the pearly smile outshined his stark, blue eyes.

Lavine acted genuinely playful, if not flirty, during the rest of their walk to the throne room, sharing his positive impression of Evern and the city with her. He also revealed how her father mentioned her arrival to the other commanders and his troops to avoid hiding the information.

All of a sudden, they were standing in front of the double doors.

"Here we are," Lavine announced while reaching for the door handle. "I suppose we should have asked before bringing you here, but why do you wish to speak with King Arval?"

"I brought him a message from Asteom about the capital city but didn't hear a response yet."

"I see." He rubbed his chin, as if contemplating her reason. "We were not informed of such news. It must be important if he spent so much time seeking the advice of his commanders and the city's leaders."

"It is," Coura added to emphasize her need to move forward and end the conversation.

Lavine knocked three times, then the soldier pushed the bronze door inward. In the afternoon light, pieces of the metal built into the foundation glittered against several stone benches placed in neat rows before King Arval, who remained seated as she approached. Three other soldiers in the same armor stood beside the throne with two more posted at the doors beyond. Once they reached the opposite end and bowed, the king looked Lavine's way to dismiss him, leaving Coura alone.

Her father stood to the right and addressed her first. "What are you doing here?"

"I came to press the need for a response from King Arval," she answered before turning her attention to the royal figure. "With all due respect, I can't wait around while my friends are struggling in Verona."

Evern's stoic expression softened to reflect his internal pain, but she stood her ground and ignored him.

I'm sorry, Father. I already made my decision.

King Arval scratched his cheek with an unreadable gaze before nodding, as though he reached a conclusion about something. "I apologize for the delay," he began in a strangely calm tone of voice. "I believe my commanders and I have all reached an agreement. Firstly, you should know we discussed your place in our city. It is only fair to Commander Evern that you be welcomed as one of our own. He has served Yeluthia for much longer than necessary until he earned his position. You might appear human, carry a distasteful power within you, and bear half our bloodline, but I permit you to live among us so long as you honor our kingdom's laws and customs."

The idea of being considered a Yeluthian seemed almost as unbelievable as meeting her parents again. Her nerves rose at the realization in a similar manner to when she found out about her lineage. To remind her of the moment, the repressed energy along her shoulder blades caused her back to itch; however, Coura forced her mixed emotions away.

"Thank you, but what about Asteom?"

Her father offered a genuinely proud smile, stepped forward to place a hand on her shoulder, then spoke at a lower volume meant only for her to hear. "Do you understand what an honor it is to be recognized as a citizen? It took the contributions of your mother and I, as well as several friends who do not distrust outsiders as much as most. One even suggested you visit a sage who lives in a Mintelian village. He specializes in soul cleansings that could heal yours, and it is no more than a day's trip away. You can still live here with us."

A lump swelled in Coura's throat. *This should be what I want, to stay with my family. I would never be alone or fighting for my life, but Soirée is out there causing mischief. It's because of her intervening that I wound up training under Byron too. If my life was meant to be simple, Evern and I would have found each other after what happened in Neston. I'm destined to be an outcast. No one else should pay for my mistakes, especially not my friends.*

Coura removed her father's hand from her shoulder, met his eyes, and turned her attention to Yeluthia's leader. "What about Asteom?"

The king's mouth tightened, yet he showed no other hint of displeasure. "My decision regarding your country is to wait for now."

His answer wasn't what she wanted, nor one she could accept. "Why not?"

Evern's smile disappeared as he said her name, but Coura refused to back down.

As if expecting a reaction, King Arval sat up straighter before elaborating. "Our lives and concerns outweigh those of another land despite the alliance, which has been shaky as of late. Until we suspect trouble greater than your ruler and his soldiers can handle, my order stands."

"They need your help," she couldn't refrain from adding.

"Should you wish to stay until that time comes, if it does, you are welcome. I only ask that you not interrupt my meetings again."

"You don't need to worry," Coura began before she really knew what she was saying. "I won't be here long."

Her father tilted his head. "What do you mean?"

"I was sent to seek aid for Verona. If I find none here, then I'll return to do something. I'm one of the few who might be able to prevent the situation from getting worse."

"You should not leave," one of the guards interjected when she stepped away to exit.

Evern made as if to follow until King Arval spoke once more.

"If you are certain Asteom cannot defeat the demon plaguing your country, perhaps we can reconsider our initial conclusion."

That stopped Coura from storming out, and she heard her father release a quiet, relieved sigh.

"I will call for a council gathering tomorrow morning," the king went on. "I ask you remain patient a while longer. Commander Evern shall inform you of our decision when the time comes, but I will not promise when that will be."

She bit her tongue to keep from arguing any further. *I may be in a hurry, but their troops are far more valuable than my presence around Verona right now.*

"What do you say, Coura?" her father pressed.

Her gaze shifted between him and the king. "Thank you," she added with a bow. "I always heard stories about the bravery and compassion of angels toward humans. I hope they're not as made up as we believed the demon was."

While her father's eyes widened a bit at her comment, King Arval's narrowed before she took her leave, praying the two weren't just wasting her time on false hope.

***

Evern stood staring after his daughter for several seconds in order to sort through his mixed emotions. As elated as he felt about their reunion, her words and unplanned visit became marks against him. In any case, his superior stayed true to his word, despite her rude behavior.

"My King, I am deeply sorry," he apologized while turning toward the throne.

The figure leaned forward with his hands together. "If she had not introduced herself with your family's name during our first encounter, I never would have guessed you two were related," he responded with a faint smile.

As Evern returned to his king's side, he felt his face flush with embarrassment, shame, and annoyance due to his eldest child's behavior.

"Are you sure you do not want to reconsider bringing her along?" his fellow commander and closest friend Detrix asked.

Both Detrix and Isan, the other, much older man present, took him under their wing after his promotion nearly a year ago. They raised families larger than his, so when he shared who Coura was, they were in favor of whatever ideas he had, including acknowledging her as a citizen of Yeluthia.

Evern shook his head to dismiss any notion of going back on his decision. "She always was headstrong and enthusiastic about becoming involved in what my wife and I do. Paulina is adamant

Coura remains here while we seek out this demon, and you know I cannot refuse her requests."

The two commanders chuckled in response; even King Arval, who rarely showed his humorous side, cracked a smile.

"I assume we should still plan on your wife joining us," their leader added with a knowing look at Evern.

"I tried to persuade her from going, but I respect it is her home country and that she feels obligated to assist. If she stays out of the way, which she will do, her addition does not bother me."

"You are certain your daughter will remain here then?" King Arval asked next with a frown. "I do not intend to put her or your youngest children under guard if you trust them."

Evern nodded. "Until she hears from someone or grows impatient enough, Coura will stay in the city. I already ordered a couple of trustworthy soldiers to look after them until our return."

"I only hope we will not be staying in Asteom for too long," Isan grumbled. Those like him who knew little about the world below had no interest in risking their lives for it. Thankfully, they were too few in number to worry about.

Their ruler was not one to ignore a call from Asteom either, especially after hearing word from his niece, the ambassador representing their kingdom.

"I cannot in good conscience wait until it is too late for our friends on the surface," King Arval had announced over the chattering during his earlier meeting. "We initiated contact with them and know a presence is interfering with our communication. It is only sensible to prepare for the worst, which seems to be a demon worming through their capital city. Evern's daughter is proof enough that her explanation is true."

Ultimately, she had been the reason for their agreement since they all sensed the sickening, slimy energy. Even with how far down the power settled, it proved off-putting to be around her long. A demon really lived on the surface, and it instigated the fighting their people steadily learned of.

Since the council remained hesitant to allow Coura to leave in case her ties with the creature stretched farther than they could fix, Evern had voiced the difficult resolution. For her safety, and the sake of their journey, she would stay in Yeluthia without knowing of their plan to fly that night under the cover of darkness. Some of his soldiers would supervise her to make sure she behaved, against her will and the demon's.

Telling Paulina had been the most painful part. Hearing about how the creature influenced their daughter terrified his wife. She would never turn her back on Coura, not that he would either, so they agreed to visit Verona and ensure their eldest child's future.

I could not bear to lose her again in such a way, he reflected as the other commanders and their king wrapped up the previous discussion.

"You will each command thirty soldiers," King Arval repeated and looked them over. "Detrix, you shall lead the charge at sundown, followed by Isan, then myself with Evern once evening is upon us. It is a three-day flight to Verona, so scouts must be sent ahead to spot open space for resting. I doubt we will run into trouble before reaching the city, but in case we do, we shall regroup before venturing to their palace. Are there any more details before I dismiss you?"

"No, my king," all three answered in unison.

I never forgave myself for losing her...

"We will gather together later, under the sky."

Evern, Isan, and Detrix placed the first two fingers of their left hand over their brow in the Yeluthian salute before exiting.

This time, I will show you how much I love you and your mother by bringing peace to your home country. Wait for me to return so we can live as a family again.

***

No matter how hard she tried to take her mind off the problem at hand, Coura found herself considering it as she wandered the city. She turned over the idea of leaving anyway to avoid losing precious time, yet doing so would betray the king's trust in her, and by association, Asteom and Aaron. Not only that, but she struggled to come to terms with her parents being alive, her new siblings' existence, and Yeluthia accepting her as a citizen. When her thoughts shifted to Soirée and Hendal, she wondered what she should do when the conflict ended.

Do I resume my life as a soldier in Verona or join the angels here? Would they expect me to stay? I might not have a home to return to given how the palace chased me away.

That started the vicious cycle over.

Plenty of shops kept her attention otherwise. Bakeries, craft tables, welders, carpenters, and more were organized down the roads leading from one section of homes to another. The world around her appeared so bright and colorful in contrast to the towns in Asteom, though no one approached or addressed her, which she expected. Despite their wariness, she wished to learn about the city.

During the afternoon, Coura found herself moving in the opposite direction as her parents' home. Before long, she reached the valley directly below their property and could spot the structure in the distance atop the hill. It would have been possible to cross the grassy area and hike up, but some sort of game was taking place there, drawing a sizable crowd of onlookers.

Out of boredom more than curiosity, she snuck behind to peek over the heads of those in front. The people who were able to sense her sidestepped away with bothered looks, but she ignored them, opting to study the new activity a group of children in heavy padding demonstrated.

She picked up on the basic rules and ways to score in a matter of minutes. Each of the three teams consisted of two players on foot and two flyers with the former unable to use their wings while the latter had to stay off the ground except in certain resting spots. Breaking either rule resulted in a penalty, which happened often because of how young the participants were. Three posts taller than everyone in the field stood an equal distance apart in a triangle, and three balls traveled around to represent each team. An official awarded points when one of the objects hit another team's post. It took Coura a moment to notice the colored lines on them, and she figured they represented how many points were earned.

The game involved a lot of passing and kicking because of the limited mobility as the children attempted to attack or defend. Every few minutes, one player whined or complained about a call or hit they claimed shouldn't be permitted, but they hurried into position again in order to avoid costing their team when the game didn't pause. By the time the official whistled for a break, Coura felt exhausted just from watching them.

It's a worthwhile training exercise, she realized as the children collapsed onto the ground, stood panting, or huddled with their teammates. *Those in the air practice manifesting their wings for periods of time while those on the ground work their arms and legs. Everyone builds stamina, each team learns to strategize, and it brings about competition.*

The pause lasted for five minutes, then they dove back in. The onlookers cheered for their team or child with more excitement, leading Coura to believe it neared the end.

"This is the final quarter," a familiar voice said from behind to confirm her assumption.

She glanced around to see Paulina slide beside her while carrying a basket of fruit. The woman wore a faded, green dress and didn't remove her eyes from the activity as cheering erupted from a handful of people in the crowd when one player kicked the ball against the middle of another team's post.

"What is this?" Coura asked amid the noise.

Her mother smiled. "Crusader's Ball. It is a sport for children interested in honing their physical abilities. Instead of requiring work at home after their primary years, Yeluthia has an academy to continue their education until they are old enough to become apprentices. Students begin enrolling in private courses related to their skills, such as crafting, history and geography, scouting, research, and healing. This is one of those classes for students interested in becoming a soldier."

The idea of an academy like that amazed Coura and reminded her of the months she spent struggling to figure out her future. With the service law in place, not to mention the demonic energy she discovered, her options had narrowed significantly.

How many children in Yeluthia are naturally gifted with magical abilities? She prepared to ask but reconsidered when a flashy maneuver earned one team another point, and more cheering ensued.

"Have you seen him yet?" Paulina yelled over the crowd.

"Who?"

"Your brother, Odell. He should be guarding the southern post."

Coura spent the rest of the game's duration trying to locate the boy until the final whistle sounded. The players immediately began removing their padded helmets to reveal pink, sweat-covered faces, and she learned Odell had been a flyer on the winning team. He celebrated with his teammates through high fives and hugs, which felt strange to see given his normally reserved behavior at the house.

The onlookers parted ways at the conclusion, and parents led their children away. Odell was one of the last to leave because the winning team became responsible for returning the game's equipment to its place in a nearby shack.

Paulina shared her day with Coura while they waited, explaining her duties and describing some of the elderly residents she looked after. As she listened, Coura realized she had yet to ask about her grandparents and felt somewhat disappointed upon hearing of their passing.

"They were the first people I worked with when I arrived," her mother shared with a bittersweet smile. "They took a liking to me because I left our old life for Evern. They knew about you, too."

"I wish I could have met them," she admitted.

Odell jogged over after and boasted about the victory. Any trace of his previous shyness vanished as they started up the hill while discussing the experience. Once they approached the entrance, Coura found a moment to compliment his aerial skills, causing the boy to blush.

"I studied how Father moves," he explained. "My dream is to be a commander like him when I grow up, so I need to practice every day."

"You're definitely on your way."

She offered a smile and risked ruffling his hair in a playful manner. To her relief, he ducked away from her hand with a grin instead of becoming tense or looking to Paulina for help.

I'd like for him and Jackie to warm up to me. It's a start for missing out on the first few years of their lives. Once again, her heart tugged in opposite directions upon considering the invitation to live in Yeluthia.

To keep her mind occupied, she assisted her mother with preparing supper, which involved slicing fruit for a salad while a stuffed goose roasted on the fireplace. Jackie scuttled inside at some point during their conversation on volunteering in the community, which Paulina did often, and they had dinner ready shortly after.

Coura ate about half of what she put on her plate, despite the effort she contributed to the meal. Once everyone else finished, she excused herself for a breath of fresh air. Thankfully, Odell grew so eager to tell the table about his game, and Jackie about her embroidery project, that their parents were too preoccupied to follow.

She sat on the grass with her back against the cool stone building to contemplate the day and her current situation while expecting the stress to build up, like it did earlier. In actuality, laying out every thought without any distractions proved refreshing. When the sun set and the surrounded area quieted, she moved back into the kitchen.

As Coura slipped around the doorway's curtain, she discovered her parents talking in hushed voices with only a lantern on the table for light. The slightly concerned expressions they wore projected their reason for waiting around.

"I figured you would be in bed," she commented and began to move toward her room.

"We wanted to talk with you since we will not be here for a few days," Paulina responded with a glance at her husband.

Coura stopped mid-step. "What do you mean?"

Evern cleared his throat. "One of the residents your mother cares for has taken a turn in his health, so she will be going over in the morning. I am scheduled to take my scouting party around the southern mountain range starting later tonight. It is usually a week-long trek."

"We normally let the children stay here under a friend's watch or accompany me; however, I do not wish for them to be around such an illness," Paulina continued. "We were hoping you would be willing to care for them while we are both working."

Coura avoided the urge to roll her eyes yet didn't hold her tongue. "What if I hear from King Arval about Asteom?"

"Just let your mother know if you need to leave when the decision is made," her father interjected, as if expecting the protest. "With that being said, it might be a few days if the leaders change their minds."

Paulina nodded in agreement before sharing more details. "There is enough food to last a week. Otherwise, we can pick up more later. We informed the children just before bed as well. They know to behave, get to their classes on time, and prepare decent meals for themselves."

Although she had more questions, Coura assumed the answers were already waiting and released a sigh in resignation. "I suppose I can look after them."

Her parents visibly relaxed before expressing their gratitude, yet the lengthy silence afterward told her they intended to ask more. At last, Evern addressed her again, visibly choosing each word carefully.

"There is another subject we wish to discuss. It may feel like people are uncomfortable around you, and they might avoid speaking with you because of your appearance. Most Yeluthians have never been to Asteom, so your features are odd to them, as well as the energy you possess."

Coura rubbed her arm and glanced away, unable to hide her nerves. *I've been dreading this...*

"Those of us who can sense your power understand it is dark in nature. Paulina and I are curious why you carry it and why you cover your arms in bandages, but we have no right to demand an explanation. Just know your mother and I will listen when you feel ready."

"You grew into a beautiful young woman, and I cannot wait to hear about what your life is like," Paulina added with more optimism.

This is worse than I imagined, Coura thought as she met each set of eyes. *Instead of directly asking me to reveal my past, they're leaving it in my hands when I decide the time is right. What if that moment never comes? What if they hate me for what I did, or for what I am?*

She thanked them anyway and went to her room, knowing their short-term disappearance would allow her to sort out her current emotions before preparing for the future.

4

The days spent among General Tio's army crept by as Marcus struggled to come to terms with what awaited them in the palace, no matter how much he enjoyed the company. He expected Clearshot to complain about their pace since moving so many soldiers took extra time, yet his companion kept close to the general and even went so far as to assist him when needed. Calin also remained preoccupied with serving the needs of his comrades, so Marcus hardly saw him.

The men and women of Dala were always interesting to converse with because of their positive, loyal attitudes and blind expectations of what Verona would be like. Based on General Tio's descriptions, many prepared for people dressed in flamboyant outfits to ignore or criticize them. Marcus made sure to provide plenty of reassurance, which proved easier than expected when he mentioned their general's personal experiences might have caused such dramatic impressions. Evidently, the soldiers understood their leader well enough to laugh.

Talking kept his mind off his nerves while some physical labor, including keeping his promise to the filly, made sure Marcus' body didn't grow stiff. It wasn't until Clearshot approached him during the afternoon of their fourth day of traveling that Marcus realized how close they were to Verona.

"Do you have a moment?" the man asked after Marcus finished brushing his horse when they stopped.

"Sure. What do you need?"

For the first time since before their escape, Clearshot shot him a smile. "How would you like to help me with a side project?"

Marcus raised an eyebrow but didn't turn away the offer. "What are you talking about?"

Whatever Clearshot's intentions were, he kept them hidden for the time being and began heading toward the front. To Marcus' surprise, both Calin and General Tio stood alone farther ahead of the troops.

"We're ready," Clearshot said by way of greeting as they approached the pair.

"It's about time," the general grumbled yet faced them with his signature, broad grin. "How soon will it take for you to set out?"

Marcus couldn't hide his curiosity any longer. "Set out? Where are we going?"

"What? You didn't tell him!" General Tio shouted at Clearshot and threw his hands up in an incredulous fashion.

As usual, Calin continued the conversation after his commander's outburst to answer Marcus' question. "We're nearly two days from the capital; however, the scouts we sent ahead aren't confident we'll be well received by the people. Then, there's the matter of a resting location once we reach our destination. I doubt the palace would welcome us if what you faced is true and the high priest controls everyone. The Nim-Valan soldiers will be suspicious as well, so we're aiming to be within distance of the city without appearing to be a threat."

"So, where do I fit in?" Marcus added during the following pause.

"Clearshot gave us an idea," the general began. "There's a field to the south of the palace far enough away from Verona and along the edge of the woods. The northern troops are stationed just outside of the city, so if we keep against the trees, we should be able to give them plenty of space."

What he neglected to mention is how suitable the extra room is for a battle.

"How do you plan on marching your soldiers to that location?" Marcus asked instead of voicing the thought.

"That's where we come in," Clearshot replied. "Do you remember the narrow path we took with Byron, Will, Coura, and her friends once we ventured north from Dala?"

It seemed like years ago, but he nodded.

"I've tracked several others over the years, and one in particular leads upward to the southern field. It's only wide enough for three or four people, or an animal-drawn cart, so it'll take time to get the troops through."

The general scoffed. "Time doesn't matter."

Marcus held his tongue despite knowing his father, comrades, and best friend struggled under the demon's hold.

On the other hand, Clearshot offered no such restraint. "Unfortunately, it *does* matter, but this route will prevent you from spending extra hours heading to Verona before marching south."

The plan sounded decent and accounted for all sorts of options based on the best, and worst, possible outcomes. Still, only part of Marcus' question had been answered.

"What are we going to do?" he inquired and glanced at Clearshot.

"You and I must make sure no spies, guards, or creatures are hiding on our way to my home. If the coast is clear, we'll recruit Emilea."

At first, he felt uncertain about dragging the woman into their scheme, but soon he understood the reasoning. *She's a master mage, meaning her skills and insight are invaluable to our cause. Aimes should also be there. I doubt she'd have a problem joining us once she hears about Byron too...*

"When do we leave?"

*

Since Clearshot knew the area, he took the lead after the debriefing. The pair grabbed only their cloaks before hurrying beyond the soldiers in front as fast as their feet would take them. With most of the day gone, they needed to travel through part of the night if they hoped to reach their goal.

The previously discussed path appeared invisible due to the knee-high grass and overlapping branches, but the trail widened as they went on. For the most part, it remained clear from sticks, roots, and other obstacles that would have otherwise hindered their progress when darkness covered the land. Before long, they entered a clearing. It took Marcus a moment to recognize it as the spot where the serpent-like demonic creature cornered their group.

"You know, I used to have fond memories of playing with the children here," his companion commented. "Now, I don't remember much aside from the blinding pain, though I won't ever cross through it unarmed."

Marcus frowned and didn't know how to respond. He didn't realize until that moment how much of a toll the demon's presence was taking on Clearshot, but he hoped his comrade would be able to keep composed until they resolved the issue.

Once they reached the home, Marcus stayed behind his fellow soldier as they stood in front of the entrance. No light came from anywhere except the moon, which hung directly above them to show how late into the evening it had grown. As expected, the door was locked, so Clearshot pounded on its wooden surface with his fist. The resulting thuds silenced their part of the forest, and Marcus pulled his cloak tighter. Since they stopped moving, his body began to feel the chill once more.

"Come out, Emilea," he heard the man grumble before proceeding with a second round of knocks.

After a minute passed by, Clearshot started pacing.

"What do we do now?" Marcus asked. His question sounded rather loud in the lingering stillness.

Suddenly, they heard the door's lock click.

"Who's there?" came a soft, feminine voice.

Instead of replying, Clearshot sighed and put a hand on the door, steadily pushing it open a little until they could see a set of eyes glinting in the moonlight.

"Cornelius!"

The door flung open to reveal Emilea in a loose nightgown. She put a hand to her mouth to reflect her amazement, then she wrapped her arms around her husband before the two shared a kiss. Marcus felt himself blush and looked away until they were comfortably greeted.

The master mage started a question after but must have felt the cold and ushered them inside. While Clearshot and Marcus removed their cloaks and shook off the chill clinging to their bodies, Emilea locked the door. Only a lone lamp sat on the dining table to provide light.

"Should I warm you some tea?" she asked quietly with a glance between the two soldiers.

Clearshot shook his head. "All we need right now is some rest."

"Are you at least going to tell me why you're here?"

"It can wait until morning," the man replied before looping his arm through his wife's and taking the lantern to head upstairs.

Marcus trailed behind with the assumption that at least one of the rooms would be open. Once the couple disappeared into their own quarters, he slipped through the first door on the right, which happened to be the same space he used in the past. There, he stripped off his clothing and tucked himself in until he felt comfortable. He slept rather soundly considering what the previous week had been like, and all that was to take place the next day.

When he woke, Marcus could hear several voices from the nearby staircase and decided to return to business; however, the amount of unexpected faces at breakfast raised his spirits. He greeted Aimes and Marcy, who sat together at the table, as Clearshot and his children set out plates of food and dishes. He didn't think anything of the woman's appearance because of her association with Lady Katrina, but a sense of relief washed over him once Grace joined them, and Will soon after.

"Where did you go?" the herbalist asked after the three expressed their joy upon being reunited.

Emilea interjected before Marcus could answer.

"I don't want to hear any of this until we're done eating," she stated.

When Clearshot announced breakfast was ready, Mace, Lexie, Grace, Will, and Marcus took seats in the living room with their plates on their laps while the older adults caught up at the table. Once everyone finished, Marcus and Marcy volunteered to collect and wash the dishes, leaving Clearshot to begin filling the others in on the meeting with General Tio and his soldiers.

"They really are going to Verona?" Grace asked as Marcus and Marcy dropped into the chairs at the table.

"The general brought two thousand of his troops, and his assistant recruited another five hundred men and women from around the area. They're going to be camping in the open field south of the palace by following the trail through these woods."

"If you're referring to the path I remember, it will take them a while," Emilea commented and returned to the professional personality Marcus became used to seeing. "With that being said, I like the idea of avoiding Verona. From what Marcy told us, Katrina mentioned rumors of trouble throughout the city stemming from the palace. If soldiers start parading through, it could cause people to panic."

"True," Clearshot added with a nod. "General Tio plans to make an appearance in the hope of startling Hendal out of whatever he's planning. The high priest isn't familiar with combat, so I doubt he would know what to do if the Dalan army goes to arrest him."

"There are the other enemies to worry about, though," Will reminded them in reference to the demon and rogue angels.

A pause followed his words as they contemplated what course of action to take.

"What about the Nim-Valan troops?" Clearshot said to break the silence. He looked at Emilea, then Marcus, as if expecting them to know.

In actuality, Marcus had no idea what to expect from anybody and voiced as much, to his companions' disapproval.

"It's not like we can do much on our own," Marcy startled them by commenting. "Aside from Emilea and Grace, none of us use magic, so acting in the palace is out of the question. Unless we learn of a way to stop the demon, it doesn't sound like there's much for us to do."

"Perhaps, but that's foolish thinking," Aimes picked up before anyone else, including Marcus, could voice their disagreement. "You're talking to some of the most strong-willed people I've ever met. Not to mention, what we lack in magic we *do* have in other skills. Marcus and Clearshot are both soldiers from Verona, so who better to know the layout of the land than them? Will's able to patch the wounded and holds his own with a sword, and so can you with a bow and arrows. I possess some experience with taking care of people too. There has to be someone who needs an extra hand in a campsite."

"It sounds like you want us to join the Dalan soldiers," Marcus concluded and knit his brow in thought.

That wouldn't be a bad idea. After all, everything we've done up until now has been based on Byron's planning. Without him, I believe it would be better to add what we can to General Tio's troops. Besides, nothing is prompting them to fight right now.

"Well, I'll tell you what I'm going to do," Clearshot went on in a confident manner. "Aimes is right. General Tio's going to need all the help he can get, including some insight into the palace."

"I agree," Marcus added before he fully committed to the decision. His concern for Aaron, his father, and the other soldiers he knew and his frustration stemming from their failure gripped his heart. A strange, new sort of anger, one that made him determined not to lose again, sharpened the thoughts that lingered in his mind over the past few days.

"We can't pretend like our presence alone will turn our luck around," he continued. "If anything, those angels, the demon, and Hendal will recognize and target us because of how we stood up to them. I trust General Tio's motivation to help, but he'll need the extra support to bring them down."

He met each set of eyes after and sensed their matching resolve. At last, he glanced at Grace, who covered her mouth with a hand and giggled.

"I have never heard you talk like that," she said despite Marcus' seriousness.

He felt his cheeks grow warm and turned away, but not before noticing the others in the room relax as well. "I *am* an assistant general. My father addresses his soldiers in a similar fashion."

"In any case, I agree too," Emilea picked up. "If anyone can get through to Byron, Aaron, or General Tont, it would be one of us."

"We're forgetting about General Casner and the people in the palace," Clearshot reminded them, though he spoke slowly, as if putting together an idea.

Thankfully, Will understood the direction the discussion seemed to be heading in. "Clara and Peter, the two light mages who approached me about the demonic energy, agreed to spread the word about what's been happening. If we reach out to them, we should be able to recruit whoever is willing to join the Dalan soldiers."

"They could speak to the soldiers on our behalf too," Clearshot concluded with a slight smile.

Marcus noticed Marcy straighten before the woman shared her input. "I'm going too."

No one protested. In fact, Clearshot offered to let her use one of his bows.

"Will, what are you going to do?" Marcus asked his friend next. He truly expected Will, Grace, and Aimes to act hesitant and offer to stay behind; however, they proved more resilient than he gave them credit for.

"I might not be skilled enough to fight, but if I can help in the camp for a while, and even use my medicinal knowledge, I want to try. Besides, Grace and I are the only ones here who are familiar with Clara, Peter, and the others who worked with us before."

"I am also the only one here with a goddess gift," Grace added and crossed her arms. "Emilea trained me, so I learned basic light spells too. Once we are closer to Verona, I will try contacting those in the palace, like you suggested."

Marcus caught himself smiling because of their dedication. *I don't know why, but hearing their commitment to our cause makes me feel reassured. Perhaps I just trust them enough to not worry.*

A grumble from Aimes brought his attention back to the matter at hand.

"Of course I wait to be the last one to speak up after claiming we should go."

"What do you mean?" Emilea asked with a tilt of her head.

"It's like I said, each one of us can find a place there. I didn't volunteer yet, but I'm the only one left to watch over those two," the older man replied with glance at Mace and Lexie, who sat on the couch between their parents.

Even though they remained silent, the two appeared to be absorbing the information each person presented.

Clearshot raised his eyes to the ceiling. "I suppose we shouldn't bring them along," he muttered, which earned him a glare from his wife.

The master mage addressed Aimes after. "It's not your responsibility. You have a right to do as you please."

"What about Lady Katrina?" Marcy interjected.

"I doubt she would deny our request, but that puts them even closer to the conflict. We already mentioned the possibility of danger in the city if Hendal decides to attack innocent people."

"Isn't there anyone else to watch them?"

Marcus kept his opinion to himself since this didn't seem to be his business. To his amazement, their son spoke after.

"Mother, please let Aimes go," the boy blurted out before someone else could comment. "I'll watch Lexie. We've been alone before, so why should this time be any different?"

"It's too risky," Clearshot responded firmly. "Have you forgotten about the guards outside? What if more come here after we leave?"

"No one should stay if they need all of you! We know how to lock the doors and make food for ourselves. The soldiers might not even notice we're still inside."

"This isn't like what we faced before," Emilea began. "We don't know when we'll return, and there's a chance they'll be ordered to force their way in."

Ultimately, the discussion remained within the family. The debate continued as Mace, with Lexie's support, voiced their desire to remain on their own so their parents would be able to help. Emilea remained adamant about keeping them safe, but their pleas soon reached Clearshot. Once he voiced his change of mind, it became impossible to accept another option.

"Are you sure you'll be all right?" Emilea asked when she accepted she was outnumbered.

Both children bobbed their heads with reassuring smiles.

"I suppose I can't argue with you anymore then." The master mage faced the rest of the room. "What's left to cover?"

"You brought up the guards outside," Will replied and pointed to the front door. "I doubt they'll let us leave without putting up a fight."

Clearshot scratched his head with a groan. "What's the easiest way to dispose of them?"

"Is it possible to avoid killing them?" Grace countered, making her discomfort obvious.

Marcus closed his eyes to consider the situation since he also hated the idea of harming his mindless comrades. *Luck brought Clearshot and I here during the evening when they were away. Now, I'd bet they'll pursue us if we flee. That is, after they alert Hendal. It would be best to end the problem to avoid that.*

He voiced as much, and his companions agreed.

"What if we capture them instead?" Grace continued with a glance at Emilea.

The Yeluthian's question sparked an idea.

"Can you cast a binding spell, like the one the demon used on us outside of Dala?" Marcus asked the master mage.

She appeared contemplate it before dipping her chin. "A binding spell is a type of advanced magic requiring the wielder's full focus, so I won't be able to go and cast it without them realizing something is going on. Also, it isn't reliable, which is why it's never used."

"What do you mean?"

"I'm sure you're more familiar with dark magic because of how much time you spent with Byron."

When Emilea raised an eyebrow at him, he agreed.

"That's what I thought. The two types of magic are completely different to cast. To put it simply, dark spells are manipulated into what the wielder shapes them to be before their release. The only control the mage has is how much energy they pour into the spell. On the other hand, a light mage must release the energy he or she wishes to use, *then* they adjust what they want that spell to do."

"Interesting," Will mumbled. "I never imagined there would be such a difference between light and dark magic."

"Most people don't. Not even the advanced mages usually know this because there's really no reason for them to. If someone could wield both types, it requires an extreme amount of concentration and control over each pool of energy. Returning to my original point, once I release the spell, it would be mine to manipulate. Anyone trapped will attempt to worm their way free, and that movement adjusts the bindings. I need to be willing to adapt."

"So, the spell won't hold together if you can't monitor the energy the entire time."

"Exactly."

Marcus contemplated this as a chill ran through his body upon remembering the demon and its hold on their group. *It kept us in place for a while, and I remember Byron and Emilea talking about how strong the binding was. That means the creature's control is greater than either of theirs.*

"Could you restrain the guards until the rest of us are able to do more?" Clearshot asked his wife with more enthusiasm in his voice.

Emilea stared at him for a moment. "If someone distracts them, I can cast the binding spell, but I'm not sure how long I can hold it…"

"That's fine," he practically interrupted and looked at Marcus. "Even if it's only for a few seconds, we'll hurry and tie them up."

The idea sounded strange, but Marcus felt willing to try. "Do you actually believe it'll work? We can't predict how strong they might be, or how they'll react."

Movement drew their attention when Aimes pointed at the master mage. "Emilea didn't have any trouble using magic to heal Coura."

"You're right," she confirmed before elaborating. "If they can't sense magical energy, they won't see this spell coming. None of the following guards will be able to tell what happened or where we went either. As long as Mace and Lexie stay out of sight, they might assume we're hiding inside."

"We also don't know if they're able to contact the palace, "Marcy added with a concerned expression.

"It's best to assume they'll be attached to the high priest, no matter what," Marcus went on. "They might inform Hendal, or they might not. It comes down to what needs to be done. Since that's the case, using a binding spell and physical bonds to keep them from stopping us is the best option, in my opinion."

Grace shared her agreement first, then the rest of the room followed suit.

*

Given how much discussing they did beforehand, the actual capture later that day went smoothly. The Dalan soldiers would reach the southern field within three days at their previous pace, so if their group intended to meet up with General Tio and his troops when the army made camp, they would need to leave in the morning.

Clearshot led Marcus to the back of the house where they waited around the corner to listen and peek at the front yard. Emilea ordered Mace, Lexie, and Grace to stay inside while Will, Marcy, and Aimes volunteered to be the distraction. The trio walked farther away from the targets, who didn't pay them any attention aside from a lazy glance, and pretended to argue with each other; however, the men remained stationary and uninterested. Only when Marcy came closer with a raised fist to threaten the guards did the two turn to face her, letting Emilea slip outside. The master mage outstretched her hands toward them and began her part immediately after.

Marcus had no notion of the spell's accuracy, yet her stance acted as his and Clearshot's signal to go over and tie their targets up with lengthy pieces of decorated rope taken from the curtains. He caught the guards stiffen before falling over, giving him an opportunity to pounce on the one Clearshot didn't claim and bind the man's hands and feet.

After securing the final knot, he copied Clearshot by shoving the guard onto his back. Only then did the two soldiers start to wiggle uncomfortably.

"That felt almost too easy," Marcus commented and let his unease slip into the words.

Clearshot nodded. By then, Emilea, Marcy, Aimes, and Will joined them to surround their captives.

"Who are you?" Emilea asked with her hands on her hips.

Neither spoke as they stared ahead while feebly attempting to free their limbs.

THE ANGEL'S DESCENT

"I don't think they know what's happening," Marcy shared with a glance at the master mage, who shook her head.

"I hoped it might be worth asking."

The sun dipped below the tree line, casting a shadow over the grassy area. Clearshot's following sigh seemed to reflect their uncertainty regarding what to do next.

"We can't leave these two outside like this overnight," Aimes stated. "Who knows if their bodies can take the cold or live without food or water until their minds are free."

Emilea shared her agreement before turning toward her husband, then the two began to discuss where to keep the bound men. In the middle of their conversation, Marcus caught the nearest captive start to jerk his shoulders around violently.

"What's going on?" Will exclaimed as the second guard joined to perform the same, sporadic movements.

Their group stepped away, though Marcus made sure to keep himself in between just in case the pair somehow got free. This prompted the men to snarl, growl, and sneer at him with narrowed eyes.

"They've gone mad!" he heard Aimes shout from behind.

In the next instant, it ended. Both heads snapped to look at the sky, as if they were struck by an invisible force, then their bodies went limp. Marcus held his breath and leaned forward in preparation for something to lash out. He heard someone make a startled sound, but no one moved for a minute after.

Will took a step forward first, and Emilea followed.

"Be careful," Clearshot cautioned, though he remained where he stood.

Marcus did too while his friend and the master mage knelt beside the bodies and checked for a pulse.

"They're still alive," Will announced before glancing at the rest of them. "Unconscious, but alive."

"What do we do now?" Marcus asked and reluctantly abandoned his defensive stance. Although he appreciated how they settled the matter so fluidly, the guards' behavior still bothered him.

Emilea stood, brushed the dirt off her knees, and wiped her forehead. "I'm going to bring Grace outside to look into their minds. As they struggled, I sensed the demonic energy stirring, then it disappeared."

"What? How could that be?" Clearshot demanded.

His wife didn't reply, but he let her hurry into their home. Soon, she emerged with the Yeluthian ambassador.

Marcus noticed Grace's perturbed expression as Emilea led her in front of the two bodies and requested she inspect them. His friend closed her eyes to presumably use her ability before she nodded and opened them wide.

"Each mind is inactive, though not blocked off like when I reached out to Aaron," she admitted. "We will not know if they are still sane until they wake up."

Her diagnosis had them all glancing at one another in disbelief.

"How can we tell if they're not under Hendal's control?" Marcy was the first to ask.

"Why don't we see for ourselves?" Will countered and knelt once more to shake the nearest guard's shoulder.

Marcus prepared to order him to stop in case the pair were being manipulated, but the limp figure groaned and cracked his eyes open.

"Who…are you?" came the raspy, weak response.

Will offered a smile. "I guess you could say we're the ones who freed you."

"Then, why am I…" The man glanced down at the ropes binding his hands and feet.

Emilea stepped forward to rouse the second soldier as she began the questioning. "Do you remember anything before this moment?"

The guards glanced at each other before the first responded.

"It's difficult to explain," he began. "It seemed like I had been dreaming, and I could only watch the images. My body moved on its own, walking, standing, eating, and sleeping when it was supposed to."

"It's the same for me, except I would be standing at attention and black out," the second commented. "When I came to again, night covered the woods, and we always left at night. Sometimes, we waited in our room for days doing nothing."

Emilea and Will rejoined the others lingering behind. As they put their heads together, they concluded the two were no longer under Hendal's influence.

"What should we do with them?" Marcus eventually asked.

When neither Clearshot nor Emilea replied, Aimed voiced his doubt.

"Do you really want them in the house unbound? They could snap right back into that state again."

The master mage raised an eyebrow at her husband, then the woman looked to the Yeluthian, who shook her head again. "Grace doesn't sense the demonic magic in their minds anymore, and no trace of it appears to be influencing their bodies. Unless Hendal is able to control a person from any location without seeing or touching them, we should be safe."

When no one voiced additional concern, they broke apart, and Marcus and Clearshot went to work untying the bonds on the guards. After, he helped the man to his feet and noticed the soldier eyeing him as they moved inside.

The well-lit, warm interior eased the remaining tension, though the children stayed upstairs and away from any possible danger. Emilea and Clearshot guided the men to sit on the couch before taking the armchairs. Marcus remained standing near the fireplace, Marcy stood behind Clearshot's seat, and Will and Aimes occupied two spots at the dining table.

Before everyone seemed settled, Marcus noticed the guard's eyes on him.

"What's wrong?" he finally asked, drawing everyone's attention.

"You... You're one of the assistant generals, correct?" the soldier inquired in a tentative manner.

The question startled Marcus a bit. "I am. I'm Marcus Tont, and I serve my father's company."

His confirmation had the man staring for several seconds before replying. "I know General Tont. I mean, I worked under him until my reassignment to General Dillon, and he... Never mind. You look alike."

The bumbling yet sincere words caused Marcus to smile, and he thanked the guard; they also gave him an idea of how to go about questioning the pair. "What are your names?"

"I'm Joseph Minera," the one who recognized him shared before glancing at the second man.

"My name is Stephen Oldune."

"Were you both under General Dillon's command before his death?" Marcus asked next.

Joseph nodded. "I am...or, I was, sir."

Stephen mumbled the same response.

Do they remember what took place before Hendal controlled them? he wondered. *Did they sense the change in my father as well?*

Marcus cleared his throat before continuing. "Let me explain what happened to bring us all together..."

He proceeded to reveal the demon's existence, its conspiring with the high priest, the rogue angels' involvement, and Hendal's ability to take over a person's mind. Then, he finished by mentioning their position guarding Emilea. The others in the room remained silent, though he sensed at least one person wasn't pleased with his choice to share the information.

Meanwhile, the men grew more uncomfortable as the time passed.

"You were two of a few soldiers forced to come here," Marcus concluded. "For some reason, rendering you unable to move released the hold on your minds."

"Are you sure?" Stephen asked. The soldier's already pale complexion lightened significantly by that point.

To Marcus' relief, Grace supported him by describing her goddess gift, confirming the lack of demonic energy.

"I can't believe it," Joseph muttered before dropping his head into his hands.

Neither guard raised their eyes to meet anyone else's or questioned the past, so Marcus moved forward and revealed the group's decision to join the Dalan army. Clearshot added a few points, such as the length of the trip and the camp's intended position, but Marcus did most of the talking.

"If you wish to accompany us, it's your choice," he continued. "I hate to be brash, but you can't stay here. I'd suggest you return to the palace, but you might face trouble if Hendal or another person under his control recognizes you."

"What are our other options?" Joseph asked without hiding his desperation.

"Unless you feel like exploring these woods, there's Verona or the Dalan army," Clearshot replied.

During the following pause, Marcy emerged from the kitchen and suggested they take a break to eat. Marcus noticed her exit earlier with Aimes, yet he didn't realize how hungry he'd grown until that point. The children descended the staircase once everyone received a piping hot bowl of a broth-based soup, and the dishes were taken away soon after.

The late hour coupled by the mentally exhausting day led each person to retire for the night after Emilea instructed them to prepare to depart in the morning. The master mage took Mace and Lexie upstairs, then Marcy, Aimes, and Grace went to their rooms. Marcus understood this would be their last opportunity to recuperate, let alone sleep in a comfortable bed for a while, but he refused to leave until Joseph and Stephen responded.

Clearshot apparently thought the same since he occupied the armchair without giving the impression he would get up soon.

When Emilea returned, she stood next to Will by the fireplace and looked the two men over. "Well? Have you reached a decision?" she asked them.

Joseph nodded and met her gaze. "I've served in the palace for thirteen years, so I refuse to dismiss a serious threat to our kingdom. With that being said, I won't raise a weapon to my comrades. It doesn't matter if their minds are not their own."

"What will you do then?" Clearshot pressed.

"I will accompany you to the southern field and head into Verona to protect the people there. From what you explained, assistant general, the citizens are not aware of the danger they're in."

"We need to avoid creating panic," Marcus commented, though he did not dissuade the soldier.

Joseph seemed to understand and offered a bow from his seat.

"Allow me to go with you," Stephen interjected, directing the words at his fellow guard.

"You would help me in the capital?"

"Of course." The man turned to Emilea, yet he avoided raising his eyes. "I must atone for my actions. Even though I was being manipulated, I still disgraced my country and my family by making you a prisoner in your own home."

The master mage's lips curved into a gentle smile. "Thank you. I believe that would be the best path for you two."

To Marcus' surprise, Will chimed in after. "You won't be alone. Several mages in Verona joined our cause, and more are waiting in the palace for our signal to act."

"They are?" Joseph asked and raised his eyebrows when Will nodded.

The message lifted their spirits and seemed to be the perfect way to end the evening. Will volunteered to lead the newcomers upstairs, though Marcus had no idea how much sleeping space remained available. As long as no one requested he move, he assumed there was enough.

Emilea and Clearshot snuffed out the lights, but the latter caught Marcus' arm to hold him in place while the master mage climbed the stairs. The grip released once the two were alone.

"Is there something else?" Marcus inquired with a bit of concern.

Even in the dark, he caught Clearshot grin before his fellow soldier placed a hand on his head to ruffle his hair.

"Not really."

"Why did you-"

"You handled this situation like a true professional," Clearshot interrupted. "I behaved impatiently after we left Verona and dismissed you during that time. Still, you kept your head. I owe you an apology."

Marcus couldn't think of a reply, so he mumbled his thanks.

"We're going to need your leadership when we get to the camp. Remain confident, no matter how you might feel, and we'll follow you."

Although he didn't fully understand what Clearshot meant, the message echoed in his mind and through his dreams.

Everyone stirred around dawn the next morning. After they ate breakfast, Emilea and Clearshot gave instructions to their children before saying goodbye, Marcus helped Aimes lock every door and window, and the rest of the group moved onto the road. They prepared beforehand by bundling up against the brisk wind, then the group set out.

5

Hendal rarely let himself become worked up to the point of hysteria, but today challenged every bit of self-control he developed over the years. That evening at dinner, a strange, ever so slight tightness stretching from Soirée's gifted power alerted him of something, though he didn't know what. It grew distracting, like an insect bite, and pulled his attention away from the conversations taking place around him. So, he cut off the connection and let the thin strands of energy return to him. He planned to ask the demon about it when she appeared that evening; however, for some reason, she seemed to be avoiding him. Her disappearance infuriated him, but dealing with her would need to wait.

Before he could consider his plans after he reached his chamber, Drake appeared with an unexpected update.

"The southern troops are on their way here?" Hendal repeated in disbelief.

The angel nodded from where he stood near the window. "I noticed them on my patrol for the humans who escaped. They are marching north through the woods. I might not have noticed if their numbers were fewer due to the canopy, but their armor caught my eye in the moonlight."

Hendal avoided the urge to grind his teeth in frustration. "Who are they?" he demanded, though he already assumed the answer.

"I would guess soldiers from the Dalan base." Drake shrugged to show his indifference.

If these useless angels properly attacked and killed the general, we wouldn't be in this mess!

Hendal prepared to say as much but stopped himself. *Scolding them would be a waste of time at this point. Perhaps I can order them to cause a diversion to lead the soldiers away from here. Would that work? Does General Tio know that much about who I control? I might be able to pass the blame along...*

"Whatever you're considering to distract them from the palace, I suggest you abandon it," came an all too familiar voice from behind.

Hendal turned to see Soirée's silhouette emerge from the darkness beyond the door she opened. The creature slipped inside, closed the door, and strolled past Drake to lean against the windowsill with her arms crossed. The angel's eyes narrowed as she entered, reminding Hendal of the tension between the two.

"Where have you been?" he asked after.

"I did a little investigating on my own." She paused to study them, as if hoping to see their reactions.

Hendal waited for her to continue since he knew it would be meaningless to demand the details when she merely intended to spur his temper. In the next instant, she closed her eyes and froze, like a statue, and he understood she was seething.

"It seems we have a couple of issues," Soirée went on in an annoyed tone of voice. "As you no doubt felt, high priest, two of the soldiers whose minds you controlled were put under a binding spell."

He found himself rubbing the center of his chest when he remembered the earlier irritation. "Binding spell? Is that what that was?"

Soirée nodded, opened her eyes, and held him in place with her venomous glare. "Did you consider where they were placed when you released your hold or what that might mean?"

"I did not. Can't you tell what happens to those under my influence?"

"I can, but I thought you might be intelligent enough to see what might be putting tension on those connections *before* releasing them," she practically hissed.

He couldn't keep himself from gulping once he understood his mistake and racked his memory for the direction of the two tendrils of energy.

"Don't bother," Soirée spat, as if she read his mind. "I'll be the one to inform you of your mistake. Those two soldiers were with the group farthest from the palace, which you ordered to prevent the master light mage from leaving her home. You might not have realized it right away because any power weakens over distance, especially a spell that doesn't require a lot of energy to begin with."

Hendal clenched his hands into fists. "Emilea struck back!"

"Didn't you hear me? That wretched mage used a binding spell to keep the guards in place. The contact with light energy bothered my demonic power."

Curse that woman! I bet she'll attempt another plot against me or assist the Dalan soldiers. How could I be so careless?

"Why is this a problem?" Drake asked, interrupting Hendal's thoughts. "We have the other master mage under our control, and she might not even leave her children. You can always send the other guards."

Soirée chuckled and threw her hands up in a dramatic shrug. "There are so many issues with what you just suggested, pigeon."

"Why is that?" Drake growled in an attempt to not raise his voice at her snide remark.

In return, she met his dirty glare with one of her own. "Firstly, the bond humans develop with their children is much deeper than what you or I ever experienced. I've seen it numerous times, so I doubt she would think to use a spell on the guards just so she could remain in her home. Nothing would have happened if she didn't retaliate. Secondly, given her past resilience, do you really believe she wouldn't attempt to escape to Verona again, or even join the troops heading here?"

"Then, you know about that too," Hendal interjected.

The demon ignored his comment yet glanced his way. "My third point is that you shouldn't consider sending more guards if she won't be there anyway. I already doubt the two will return here. When you released your hold on their minds, they became free men again."

This time, Drake frowned and asked what she meant. Soirée pointed to Hendal in response, making him jump.

"Talk to the high priest. In a way, I lent him my power, meaning any spells he casts are through his own actions. I possess the ability to merge my energy with another creature's until they become one, then I take it back into myself. That ability kills. Hendal isn't a demon and cannot change or accept the power. I'm allowing mine to be used through him under his control and showed him how to manipulate another human's mind."

"Then, when he cuts off the connection, the people are of their own mind again," Drake finished with a thoughtful expression.

Soirée nodded. "That's right. Also, as the high priest is well-aware of, the energy heals, meaning no one under his control can sustain damage; however, the physical toll falls on him, not me."

Drake fell silent for a moment, seemingly pondering the information. When Hendal prepared to move the discussion forward, the angel spoke again.

"Did you make this arrangement with the human we fought in the Valley Beyond? Is that why her energy kept changing?"

The sadistic grin on Soirée's face after the questions sent a shiver down Hendal's spine.

"No, not exactly," she responded. "I refuse to speak about our bond until my experiment comes to an end. You can relax, though; she doesn't know how to cast such a spell, let alone possess the cruel desire to manipulate another human against their will."

"So, she can only use elemental and shielding spells, manifest wings, and heal herself with your power then?"

"That's right. I figured you'd like to know how much of a threat she is." Soirée resumed her impassive expression as she turned toward Hendal. "Back to my point, do *you* understand what all of this means?"

He scoffed. "Of course. Those two soldiers are no longer under my control, so I can't use them anymore. Emilea will most likely leave before I can send more to guard her. I believe she'll appear again, then we can deal with her permanently. Now, did you find information relating to the troops heading for Verona?"

"Nothing more than what I'm assuming you can figure out on your own."

When she glanced at Drake, he picked up the conversation.

"Based on what I could count, I estimated two thousand soldiers. It is safe to assume they contain dozens of mages among their ranks as well because of the recent transfer. They appeared to be about two days away from the edge of the southern forest."

"That close," Hendal grumbled, revealing his pent-up anger. "They must know what's been going on around the palace if they're eager to move. Either that, or there's some ridiculous reason for them to abandon the base."

"I favor the former explanation considering the lack of space here for an additional group that numerous," Drake added.

"There must be a traitor within our walls feeding General Tio information," Hendal continued while beginning to pace. "Considering the number of mages who tricked me into approaching Byron, they're probably working together. Could one of them be behind this? That Yeluthian brat's ability might've allowed her to speak with the base, or-"

"How amusing," Soirée murmured loud enough to distract him.

"What?" he snapped.

"People move in and out of the palace all the time, so dozens of insects can slip through your fingers. How many men are under your control? You have the king, a general, the dark master mage, plenty of the nobility, and the soldiers who happened to stumble into the wrong place at the wrong time. Then, consider who actually knows the truth about us."

"What of it?"

"I just wonder how you expect to convince the Dalan general, someone who's heard enough through the master mage, and his troops that nothing is amiss. You can't forget about the northern country's men right outside your window either."

Hendal felt himself starting to sweat. *Everything she said is true. It'd be one thing if the Nim-Valans weren't involved, or if I could learn who's heard of Soirée to silence them. Unfortunately, that makes everyone in the palace a suspect...*

Suddenly, a certain realization dawned on him once he considered her words further, and it brightened their cloudy future.

"That's it!" he cried without hiding his relief.

"You have an idea?" Drake asked while Hendal took a moment to consider the necessary precautions for his latest scheme.

Instead of answering the angel, he smiled in a proud manner at the demon. "I finally understand what you want me to do."

She raised an eyebrow to express her doubt yet didn't comment.

Hendal clasped his hands behind his back and straightened. "Your power may flow through me, but I decide how it is used. If that truly is the case, I'll share it with the Nim-Valan soldiers so they can act as our main defense should the southern troops attack. King Aaron will suggest they support us against the traitors who wish to control the capital, and the people here should understand and join to aid their kingdom. With Byron under my thumb and Emilea still away, the mages won't know any bet-"

"What did I tell you about wielding that power so foolishly?"

Soirée's words cut him off, leaving him to gape at her while she stared him down.

He paused to skim his memory for her previous warning before venturing a guess. "Doing so requires more energy."

"That is true," she began slowly. "I also specifically mentioned the toll for using so much power. The more minds you possess, the more energy will be taken from me through you, which exhausts your weak, human body. It's the same for the healing ability. Those under your control might not be able to comprehend how they need rest to fully recover, but some of that exhaustion will trace back to you."

As Soirée explained the consequences, Hendal became afraid, yet hearing it again allowed him to see beyond his emotions. *Taking risks is necessary to bring about change. I must accept my role as a tool through which peace is achieved; however, Soirée has never cared about me. Why would she be concerned if I fail?*

He dove deeper into that question while Drake asked for details regarding her bond with Hendal, such as the number of people he can control, any additional repercussions, and her influence over him. To the angel's visible displeasure, Soirée dismissed each one.

"Let me make this clear," she offered to quell his curiosity. "I hardly ever associate with humans because most don't survive the initial encounter."

"Is it that, or are you concerned about what harm should befall you?" Hendal chose to ask. "Why would a demon worry about the fate of one man? Unless, she must be risking something as well…"

Her following glare proved difficult to ignore, and he expected her to argue; however, Drake defended his accusations first.

"I agree with you, high priest. Your ability to control another human's actions is necessary at this point, especially because we agreed we cannot fool both the Dalan general and Nim-Valan leader without influencing them."

"My main concern is your life," Soirée said to Hendal. "I just admitted I don't know what might happen if you exceed your mental capabilities. You won't be able to sway everyone with that spell. Others will come for you too, and I refuse to become involved in your petty games."

"You're just worried you might lose what power you allow me to use," he countered.

She remained silent.

"It would be wise to help me then. I refuse to flee, and this is our chance to squash any resistance and rise as a new nation."

Drake stepped forward and dipped his chin. "I will inform my companions and prepare for the battle ahead."

Soirée rolled her eyes and scoffed before putting her back toward Hendal to stare out the window. After a moment, she spoke in her usual, bored tone of voice. "If that's what you intend to do, I'll continue on my own for a while. Use my power if you must, but be wary of the potential results."

"You will not fight with us?" Drake inquired, though he seemed to be fine with her decision.

"I would never lower myself to do battle alongside your kind; it goes against my very nature. Although, I'm extremely interested to see how this ends."

The angel shook his head, displayed his disgust with a frown, and glanced at Hendal. "Why bother relying on a demon at all?"

While Hendal cleared his throat without an answer in mind, Soirée looked over her shoulder and snickered.

*

The following morning, Hendal extended an invitation to General Harvey for a private meeting with the king. He sent a servant to the Nim-Valans, but they returned empty-handed, claiming the northern general had no interest in leaving his camp. As much of a nuisance as it was, Hendal forced himself to walk outside into the brisk temperature with Aaron and several guards during the cloudy morning. Stares came from the soldiers as they muttered in their own language, but nothing sounded hostile.

When the two reached the centermost tent, they saw the opening flap tied back, allowing the man to spot them before Hendal needed to interrupt any business taking place. He stopped, offered a polite smile, then began his rehearsed excuse for the intrusion.

"Good morning, General Harvey. I hope we're not disrupting you."

The Nim-Valan leader didn't appear pleased, but he gestured for them to enter anyway. A blanket covered the ground where he sat, preventing him from sitting directly on the dead grass, and a fire had been built in the center. The top of the tent had been designed with holes to vent out the smoke, though their angled shape would prevent rain or snow from entering. Lastly, Hendal spotted a bedroll behind the general and several papers in a pile at the man's side.

Without an additional, designated space for guests, Hendal remained standing. "His Highness wishes to discuss our annual Harvest Festival with you," he began. "This event will take place six days from now and allows us to celebrate the year our laborers have had."

He shared part of the history, the activities, and how the Nim-Valans would be welcome to participate. Meanwhile, in the back of his mind, Hendal considered the right moment to get close enough to place a hand on the general's head. To do so without warning would bring about the northerner's instincts and most likely harm him or Aaron as a result.

When he finished, Hendal bowed and waited for a response.

General Harvey remained silent throughout the explanation. He had been glancing over the papers in his hands, seemingly oblivious to his guests, then it took another few minutes for him to complete his reading. After, the tough-looking man set the documents aside, crossed his arms, and stared up at them with an unfriendly gaze.

"You visit only to share news of a celebration among your people? The festivities in Nim-Vala are held at the king's estate or within the inner circle. Those of us who train to survive as soldiers and who guard our borders do not get such privileges. In fact, it's an insult to the families of those serving our leaders if their sons drink and dance instead of fight. Our goal is to establish peace between nations. Why are you shaming those in this camp in such a way?"

Hendal felt his fingers twitching as he stood stunned by how much offense the general took and how fluently the man spoke Asteom's language. The worst part about the scolding was how General Harvey ignored him to speak directly to Aaron, letting the question hang between them. The king, unaware of what took place, stared ahead while Hendal tried to step in.

"P-Please, we meant no disrespect..."

The Nim-Valan stood then to tower over the two and talked down to Hendal.

"Religious affiliations and their gods are pleasantries most Nim-Valans can't afford to worship. Your title and words mean little to me, but you seem to be your king's mouth. Is he not able to speak for himself on these matters?"

By that point, Hendal started fuming and couldn't put together a coherent, appropriate reply. He wordlessly commanded Aaron to babble an apology while he cooled his head.

The alliance he mentioned is at risk of crumbling. Should he escape, I fear what might happen to me. What would draw his attention away from us? He acted surprised when he met the mages and the Yeluthian ambassador...

"Forgive me," Hendal blurted out, interrupting the king's insincere-sounding expression of regret to draw the general's attention. "I forgot to mention an important aspect of the Harvest Festival. It's tradition for me to say a special blessing upon our people, which was the main reason King Aaron and I came to visit you. We would like for your group to participate, especially since the Yeluthians will be in attendance as well."

The Nim-Valan's eyes widened a bit. "A blessing?"

"Why, of course!" Hendal purposefully elevated his feigned enthusiasm. "It might not mean much to you that I lead it, but the magic we perform is real. If it would help, I can demonstrate the prayer right now. I understand your doubt and respect if you distrust our intentions or are uncomfortable with my work."

Internally, he laughed when General Harvey paused to consider the offer. *Either he lets his cowardice show, or he caves into a polite present from Asteom. Will he rely on pride or gut instinct?*

During the silence, Hendal decided to push the request further. He asked the king to bow so he could show the movements since the general seemed shy around magic. As he expected, the Nim-Valan overcame his suspicion in favor of appearing brave.

"Fine," the man grumbled. "If you're adamant about this, then I will allow you to recite your blessing, if only to explain to my troops what they should expect."

Hendal felt no remorse as he approached the general and placed a hand on top of the unkempt hair. "This will only take a moment," he promised and felt the demon's power reaching outward.

*

With General Harvey now in support of the fictitious blessing, Hendal spent the afternoon in the Nim-Valan camp building his defenses. The soldiers' leader spoke in their language to instruct each person to approach the high priest, bow their head, and accept the blessing in order to respect the country's tradition. Many sneers, looks of disinterest, and what Hendal could only assume were blasphemous comments reflecting their view on religion followed; however, not one man went against their commander, which he felt willing to take advantage of.

While Aaron stood at his side, Hendal placed a hand on each head, extended the demon's hungry power, and mentally ordered the individual to obey him through their general. No one expected their mind to be swept away, so he sensed no internal or physical resistance to reveal anything was amiss.

By the time the entire camp fell under his control, it proved to be well past noon.

Wonderful! No one ventures into their camp or knows their behavior, so this won't be noticeably out of character, Hendal thought as he moved inside. *Should someone question our time spent there, I can say the king and I were telling them about the Harvest Festival. I might even mention the general requested a blessing in case they noticed the dramatics. How ironic! Now, if I can just find General Casner and do the same to him, we should be fully prepared for those Dalan rats.*

After dining with Aaron and whoever arrived in the private dining hall, including several, loud ladies who remained blissfully unaware that their friends and lovers were not themselves, Hendal called a servant over and ordered her to find the general.

"Please inform him we received news from General Tio in the southern base, and we must talk in the council chamber," he lied to the wide-eyed woman before she disappeared.

Hendal moved to the space after, yet he found himself waiting nearly an hour for a response. The servant appeared just when he prepared to leave and timidly reported the general hadn't been seen in the palace for days.

"What do you mean by that?" he practically snapped.

"My apologies, high priest. We're still searching, but no one seems to know where he went."

With a wave of his hand, he dismissed the woman before taking several deep breaths to avoid overreacting to the news. *I never considered Casner much after the other generals' murders, but he didn't appear to be avoiding me, as far as I could tell. Could he be the one feeding information to the southern base? I should have ordered Drake and his comrades to eliminate any messengers sent to Dala. Either way, Casner is gone for now. If he appears, I'll hear about it; if not, then I can only assume he's hiding or assisting the traitors. I can't afford to wait for his return.*

Fortunately, word spread easily under one roof. He called Tont, Harvey, Byron, the nobility under his control, and the servants' masters together and shared the Dalan troops' intent to march north and most likely attack the palace. Then, he emphasized how the Nim-Valans would act as their first line of defense before commanding the rest to rally the soldiers and mages and inform them of the situation. Hendal sent everyone away after, let the king wander on his own, and found a servant to bring him a late meal. Once in his quarters, he spent the remainder of the day tracing the many connections he manipulated.

***

The trek to find the Dalans proved both easier and more difficult than Grace imagined, though she refused to voice her discomfort. The fierce wind somehow cut through the trees, and her lack of experience traveling on foot drained her physical energy. Still, she slept well the first night.

The morning of the second day proved much better. They awoke to a clear sky showcasing faint stars until the sun eventually climbed its way above the canopy to warm them. The wind died down too as Clearshot continued to lead them on with some pointers from Emilea until it became evident they were not alone in the woods. By late afternoon, voices, clamoring armor, and shuffling feet were audible, even at a distance.

"Come on," their leader urged. "If we don't hurry, we might have to wait until morning or risk getting lost."

That thought worried Grace since she had no idea where they wound up in the slightest. He made several, similar comments until their lean path intersected a wider, well-worn road bearing fresh footprints. The trees steadily grew apart while they moved, then the dirt merged with grass to reveal the southern field beyond the final wall of trunks. In the distance, the structure Grace had become familiar with stood like a pillar above the hundreds of homes and shops nearby. The last time she saw it from that angle had been when she first arrived in Asteom's capital city.

Fires were being built one by one all around to shed light on the space, and the smell of roasting food lingered to cause her stomach to growl. Groups of men and women huddled together in preparation for the evening, discarded pieces of armor lay in piles next to tents, and bags and sleeping rolls were scattered between. It seemed everybody worked together on their own tasks for the evening meal, including cooking, handing out metal or wooden bowls and mugs, pitching the remaining tents, or tending to the fire. Some wore smiles as they joked with one another while others silently relaxed or frowned and slouched forward to show their weariness.

Grace stayed behind Clearshot, who moved farther into the center of the camp. Many people recognized him, Marcus, and Will, and even a few of the mages in their robes approached Emilea to greet her. No one seemed to care about Aimes, Marcy, or the two soldiers, though the four didn't appear displeased about it.

Their group moved away from the woods at their backs until they spotted several individuals on top of a lone hill overlooking the surrounding area. One man noticed their arrival, said something to those around him, and strolled over to shake Clearshot's hand with a grin.

"Glad you made it," he commented as he wiped his forehead and laughed.

Based on his voice, Grace assumed he was General Tio. Another man came over to stand behind, like the Dalan leader's shadow, yet he made no attempt to interrupt.

"Make the introductions short," the burly figure stated while adjusting his feet into a broad, proud stance. "I haven't eaten a decent meal in days, so I'm rather impatient."

While the others laughed, smiled, or shook their heads in response, Grace genuinely wondered if that was how he normally behaved. He already acted short-tempered during their previous conversations through her goddess gift, so she remained quiet.

The general acknowledged Emilea from her time in the southern city and offered a nod to Marcy, Aimes, and the two guards when Marcus introduced them. All four appeared nervous, though no one commented on it.

At last, the man faced her.

THE ANGEL'S DESCENT

"This is Grace," Clearshot began. "She's the ambassador from Yeluthia, the one we spoke to at the base."

Grace expected some surprise, yet General Tio's expression only softened. He placed his right hand, or lack thereof, over his heart and bowed at the waist in a flattering gesture compared to what he offered the others.

When he rose, the man groaned. "I beg your pardon. You assisted us earlier, though that gift of yours startled me the first time. I hate the idea of dragging outsiders into our mess, so allow me to thank you and apologize all in one."

His words and polite behavior shocked Grace, especially after how rudely he spoke to her on his way north. Nonetheless, she expressed her gratitude and blushed when he grinned in response before addressing their entire group.

"Calin will tell you what our plans are," he shared before stepping around them to head back into the camp.

The second man saluted his superior and chuckled. "Sorry about that. I think he forgot about my introduction. For those of you I haven't met, I'm Assistant General Calin. Why don't we find someone to take you in for supper while we talk."

He apparently knew people willing to accept the company since he led them to the center of the camp where three men sat wrapped in blankets. Each held a mug and raised it in welcome before offering the rest of their leftover, oatmeal-like mixture, which satisfied the newcomers' hunger. The assistant general nearly inhaled his supper, disappeared into a nearby tent, then returned with a bundle under one arm.

"Once you're finished, you can find extra bedrolls and blankets there," he explained. "As you might have guessed, we brought many supplies for additions to the camp."

"You mean to say, you expected our return," Clearshot commented matter-of-factly before rising.

Calin shrugged with a poorly concealed smile as Grace and the rest followed suit. In another few minutes, she was snuggled underneath a couple of blankets. The camp quieted as well, and fires here and there were no longer being fed, leaving their flames to dwindle.

"There really isn't much to tell you," Calin started once they all seemed comfortable. "Our scouts arrived here late in the morning, so we spent the day setting up. The general watched the palace while I led the establishment of the camp. Nothing happened from across the field the entire time."

"Did anyone see the Nim-Valan soldiers?" Marcus asked when his fellow assistant general took a moment to cover a yawn.

"No. Their tents and smoke trails are visible in the distance, but no movement indicated they even took notice of us. That's partially why we avoided hiding ourselves. If our noisiness and the sight of our camp doesn't alert them of our presence, then the smoke should do the job."

"Are you sure that's wise?" Aimes asked in a bashful manner, as if he felt ashamed to speak up.

Calin noticed the tone of the older man's voice too and offered a reassuring smile. "Some of us weren't certain that would benefit our cause either; however, the general is not one to spy or sneak around, especially when we're dealing with a demon's power. Besides, I believe those behind this already knew we were on our way. We're still soldiers of Asteom, so they shouldn't have a reason to be hostile toward us."

"In that case, what will General Tio have us do?" Emilea inquired from her spot to Grace's left.

"Tomorrow will be the true test of what we can expect. One hundred of our troops are guarding the perimeter as we speak and will raise the alarm if anyone, or anything, approaches. The morning is for preparations, including sending messengers into the city to ask for aid and urge the citizens to hide or flee, if possible. We aren't sure how everyone will react, but I don't expect resistance. At least, not against us. We'll line up by the afternoon."

"The general intends to fight then?" the master mage responded with an edge to her voice.

Calin nodded. A more serious expression cast a dark shadow over his face. "Sitting around and waiting for them to attack is foolish. We didn't bring the supplies to stay outdoors like this for more than a couple of weeks. If they don't plan on sending us away with force, then it's up to us to invade and put an end to the madman."

"At least we know General Tio isn't getting soft," Will muttered loud enough for Grace to hear.

"That's plenty for tonight," Clearshot concluded, signaling for them to lie down and sleep. "Everything else can wait until dawn."

6

Grace found herself awake just as sunlight peeked above the trees to the east. Already, dozens of people rose to start up the fires again, stretching, yawning, and grumbling as they worked. Without a proper bath, or at least a way to wash her face, she felt dirty, especially since she wore the same clothes from yesterday. No one had packed more than was necessary to survive outdoors, so she refused to embarrass herself by claiming to need more.

Breakfast consisted of a warm oatmeal heated just enough to be edible. She sat between Will and Marcus close to the flames with a blanket around her shoulders and her hair tied back. All the while, she considered her responsibilities for the rest of the morning.

I expect I will be reaching out to the mages in the city, as well as whoever is in the palace. If that is what I can do to help prevent further conflict, then I can manage the strain.

As Grace wiped her eyes in an attempt to ward off the lingering weariness, General Tio's assistant gathered their group together. Only the shadows under his eyes seemed to reveal his lack of rest given his activeness.

"The troops have been ordered to line up according to their predetermined squads," the man began. Using the dirt in front of his feet, Calin drew three, vertical lines with a circle in between each and a squiggle behind those. Once finished, he stood and wiped his hands on his already dust-covered pants.

"The three lines are our foot soldiers, who will move first to attack with weapons. They know to close the gaps, circle around, or retreat when the general or I give the signal. The circles represent our combat mages. Some shift between their magic and a weapon, so they can choose to come forward or stay back to launch projectiles. Behind the circles are the archers. For the most part, that group is independent since they move with the tide of the fighting. What you don't see are healers. We arranged for a medical squad and light mages to be at the ready, along with volunteers to carry the wounded to camp. About a quarter of the healing mages are comfortable doing their work on the battlefield; most will wait here. Is everything clear so far?"

Their group nodded.

"Right, then let me tell you where you'll be positioned since you're not part of any squad. Clearshot and Marcy, I'd like you both with the left wing of archers. Master Emilea and Will should remain in the camp for treating the injured. Aimes, you're welcome to assist them or the others keeping this place running. They could use an extra hand with cooking, gathering water and firewood, and the more mundane tasks. Marcus, you're with me. Joseph and Stephen, the general's counting on you to help organize defenses in the city."

As he spoke, Calin made eye contact with every person until his gaze fell on Grace. "General Tio would like for you to remain here. Your gift is too valuable to risk losing, and you're still Yeluthia's ambassador."

She dipped her head to acknowledge his reasoning. If she were harmed or killed by an Asteom or Nim-Valan soldier, it would send a negative message to her people.

The assistant general lingered to answer their following questions and inform them of who to report to, where to find armor, and the timeframe they were looking at.

"If that's all, I must be going," he said at last. "Before I forget, we're leaving contact with those in the city and palace to your group. General Tio only requests you inform him of what takes place, especially if it involves adding to our numbers."

They thanked him and watched as he snaked his way through the many, moving individuals making their own preparations for the future. Grace noticed the faces around her becoming grave as the idea of a violent conflict inched closer to reality. Emilea was the first to speak after the group rose and turned her attention toward Grace.

"We should begin, if you're ready. Joseph, Stephen, you'll be coming along as well. We can head to the eastern part of the camp closest to the city and away from the commotion here."

Both men voiced their agreement, and Marcus and Will offered to join too.

"Just remember, this is where we gather during the evenings," Clearshot added. "If the situation grows worse, we probably won't see each other often, so don't be afraid to lean on the people in this camp."

He appeared to be contemplating whether or not to say more, but a carefree chuckle from Aimes cut through the tension.

"Let's be on our way," the older man ushered in a calm manner. "I saw these soldiers take down a creature the size of a house that could've destroyed their city in one afternoon! Most of you were there too, so if we do our part to assist them, there's nothing to stop us."

"Don't forget who we're fighting for either," Marcus commented with a glance at the palace in the distance. "Aaron, my father, Byron, and other, innocent people are trapped in there. Remember how much they need us."

Marcy stepped forward, nodded to Clearshot, then held her chin higher before pressing them on. Her fear crept through her mask of bravery, though she refused to acknowledge it. Aimes departed next with a wave over his shoulder before Emilea led the rest away from the fire.

Along the way, Grace reflected on each person's emotions and how they compared to what she had been exposed to growing up.

Yeluthians experience the same emotions as humans, though they allow more of a variety to show. My people focus on logic and use what needs to be done as a guideline. By keeping our minds occupied, we set aside emotions, which prevents them from distracting or immobilizing us. On the other hand, they lead humans to fight with more passion. This proves to be a weakness, yet it also seems to be one of their greatest strengths. Learning about them has proved quite interesting.

THE ANGEL'S DESCENT

Grace caught herself yawning and put a hand over her mouth before rubbing her eyes.

"Are you sure you're going to make it?" Marcus joked from her left side. "You can always go back and take a nap by the fire. That is, if you're able to ignore everybody else."

She smiled and shook her head.

"Please don't say such tempting things," Will picked up and readjusted his glasses. "It doesn't take much physical activity to wear me out anyway."

His following grin sparked a laugh from Grace and Marcus, which lightened the mood a bit as they went on.

*

Only when they reached a spot receiving plenty of sunlight and sufficiently away from the camp did they halt. No wind chilled them any more than normal, which Grace felt thankful for, so they sat on the most comfortable-looking patch of dry grass. She knew this process would be draining, even with Emilea's help, which meant her well-being was the key to her body enduring the passing time. Otherwise, it distracted her mind, thus disrupting her goddess gift.

Once everyone appeared settled, the master mage began the discussion.

"With the city close by, we shouldn't need to strain Grace's ability; however, that doesn't mean we won't be discovered if people start acting at once. I suggest we plot out who we want to speak with before starting."

"Are you going to tell them about us?" Stephen asked and pointed a thumb at Joseph.

Grace tilted her head before recalling their shame after discovering how Hendal manipulated their minds. "I will share how you two are on your way into the city to assist with protecting the people there. They do not need to know what the demon did to you."

"She's right," Emilea interjected. "Besides, our goal isn't to involve them. Those are innocent people, and in situations like this…"

"The less they know, the better," Joseph finished with a nod. "We understand. Just find out where those friends of yours are hiding."

The light mage turned to Will next. "Can you tell us where they are?"

He removed his glasses to rub his eyes while considering an answer. "Diana was going to her father's house near the eastern square, I remember that much. She took Jean along…no, Peter. Justin had been seriously injured, so Jean and Clara took him to a flower shop off the main road."

"Did they provide any more details?"

Will shook his head.

During the following pause, Grace cleared her throat to get everyone's attention. "I usually try not to pry into a person's mind in order to respect their privacy, but I can linger over the citizens in those areas of Verona to see if someone might reveal any information."

"Do you think that would work?" Marcus asked without hiding his doubt.

"It should narrow down the details. Then, I can gently project their names. If a person recognizes one, I should be able to tell by their stream of thoughts." Although she sounded confident when suggesting this method, she had never attempted such a thing before.

"Why don't you start to locate the mages while we figure out what to say?" Emilea recommended.

Grace agreed, closed her eyes, and reached into her center of Yeluthian power. The familiar, stretching sensation eased her back into the process of searching for a target as she passed dozens of active minds. Like a gathering of light bugs in the night, each glimmered in varying degrees of brightness, and their surface thoughts whispered to no one in particular. She imagined the layout of the city and found the main road based on how populated it was.

How will I ever sort this out? she wondered distantly.

For some time, she listened to the voices around her. Most of their comments related to mundane tasks or the Harvest Festival preparations, though a few seemed worried because of the state of the palace. She honed in on those individuals in particular. One woman's relative claimed the mages were abandoning their positions, and another's husband served as a soldier who shared his fear of a spirit haunting the palace. Plenty of the citizens had grown annoyed with the lack of activity from their king and the generals because of how little the leaders contributed to the festivities so far.

When Grace felt a headache approaching, she decided to skip ahead along the main road. Once the activity lessened, she scanned where she had just been. Again, nothing stood out, except something about the soldiers startling a handful of the citizens.

One more time, she urged herself half-heartedly since she expected similar results. It wasn't until she reached the end and began to return again that someone's distress caught her attention, so she decided to track down the source and listen.

{I must make a selection! What would she like? What if it wilts too soon? Should I just bring her tomorrow?}

His fretting and anxious questions continued until he projected a dramatic cry, which startled Grace until she realized he intended to impress someone with a gift. Two people lingered nearby, so she eavesdropped on their thoughts out of curiosity.

The first mind belonged to an older woman, who pitied the man before considering an alternative to his selection of yellow and orange mums. It took Grace a minute to recognize the name as a type of flower, and she found her hope renewed.

The other individual proved to be a man with less compassion than his coworker. He grumbled about the lack of activity in the shop before considering searching for someone named Crissy.

This may be my chance, Grace realized. *I noticed several other flower shops, but none were directly on the main road. Perhaps one of these two will give me a hint about Clara, Justin, or Jean.*

Despite her enthusiasm, nothing happened for a while after the customer took his leave. A few people entered and departed, and the older woman moved into a back room to continue an order of decorations for the Harvest Festival. Grace enjoyed listening to the pleasant thoughts and ideas that followed since she didn't usually interact with humans who genuinely care about their craft and succeed because of it.

Two people entered to draw her attention away after she noticed how fatigued she'd grown. The man at the counter mentally expressed his relief, but she ignored him to assess the new pair. Both were young women and didn't share much besides minor annoyance.

With no other leads and a limited amount of time left to use her goddess gift, Grace decided to intervene. She began by softly projecting Clara's name to one of them, like a whisper of a thought. If her attempt didn't reveal any new information, she wanted to avoid scaring the women.

The first shared some curiosity yet ultimately dismissed Grace's voice, so she moved on to the second. This time, she sensed a bit of alarm and caught the resulting thought.

{Did someone say my name?}

It became difficult for Grace to hide her resulting elation. She paused to rein in her emotions before approaching the figure once more in a gentle manner to avoid causing a panic. *Clara, this is Grace Zelnar, the Yeluthian ambassador.*

The response sounded afraid and came immediately after her introduction.

{How are you able to talk to me? Can you hear me?}

We can communicate through our thoughts thanks to my goddess gift, Grace replied patiently. *It is a type of spell unique to my people. I am using it from the field to the south of the palace with Lady Emilea's assistance.*

She stopped to let Clara process the news before contemplating how to go about approaching their situation. Thankfully, it didn't take long for the light mage to understand.

{Let me go somewhere more private so I don't seem crazy for brooding by myself.}

Grace accepted the proposal and waited until her contact addressed her again. The resulting relief in Clara's voice warmed her heart.

{We didn't know where you went, and we didn't hear from you before now. I assumed... Never mind. Is Will with you? Please, tell me he's safe!}

After reassuring the light mage, Grace did her best to explain their decision to stay with Lady Katrina and recover before going to Emilea's home outside of Verona. She then shared their reunion with Clearshot and Marcus, the Dalan troops' intention to cease control of the palace in order to stop Hendal, and the resulting journey to the field near the capital.

I feel the citizens' nerves all around Verona, she concluded to segue into her final item to discuss. *Are the people aware of the demon's appearance or Hendal's betrayal?*

{*Not that I know of. I believe their fear stems partly from the mages departing the capital or choosing to live outside of the palace. You see, our group arranged for a signal so the others there would know when to prepare to fight or flee. If no one from our group returned after three days, they were to assume the worst.*}

Grace couldn't hide her surprise. The decision was risky since such an order would require an enormous amount of trust between the individuals; however, the transition seemed to be flowing without issue at the moment.

The mages who do not wish to remain were given an alternative, she summarized. *Will they defend the city or fight alongside General Tio if the conflict continues?*

{*I won't speak on their behalf, but everyone has their reasons for staying in the palace, escaping to the city, or leaving this area altogether. Just be aware, not all of the mages and soldiers are on the same side because of their limited understanding of the situation.*}

Their connection wavered, revealing Grace's lack of energy to continue the spell. Any further discussion on the subject would need to take place at another time.

Clara, please help protect the people in the city. I have a bad feeling about the coming days, and those who are nearby may become involved or get hurt. If the soldiers or mages in Verona would like to assist you, the general encourages it.

{*I'll do my best. You take care of yourself too.*}

Grace retracted her mind from the light mage and returned to her body. A slight dizziness welcomed her once she opened her eyes, prompting her to drop her head into one hand. Those around her had been talking, but their voices stopped abruptly before Emilea addressed her.

"Are you all right?"

She nodded while noticing how bright the area had become. The sun rose above the buildings to signal that at least a couple of hours went by, and she rubbed her temples to ease her dull headache.

Fortunately, the others gave her a proper amount of time to recover by remaining silent until she felt prepared to speak. No one interrupted her report or brought up additional questions once she finished.

"At least Clara's cooperating," Emilea commented with a sigh. "I'm embarrassed to admit I hardly know much about her. Diana has always been outspoken, and Peter's proved himself a natural leader. I think Jean became quite personable as well. I can see how you came to make friends with them, Will."

"They sort of took me under their wing and let me train with them," he responded a bit bashfully. "Anyway, it sounds like we should leave Verona to them."

"And us," Joseph startled everyone by adding.

The man stood after to stretch his legs with Stephen mirroring the movement, then they turned east.

Marcus jumped to his feet once they began to walk toward the city. "Where are you going?" he demanded.

"Forgive me, assistant general, but I refuse to sit around and wait to learn about those in the palace," Joseph replied with a rueful expression. "Our people will need guidance to quell their fear when the time comes."

"Don't you want to wait until we learn how many plan to support us?"

This time, Stephen answered him. "I'm afraid time might not be on our side. If General Tio intends to organize his troops at noon, we need to set up near the city in case anyone from the palace decides to act against them. Let us ease a portion of the pressure on you and your companions."

Marcus appeared displeased, yet he accepted their reasoning when no one else complained. "Fine. Grace can find and update you if anything important happens here or involves the city."

Both men placed a fist over their hearts and bowed to express their gratitude before continuing on.

THE ANGEL'S DESCENT

With her first assignment complete, Grace prepared for more work and cleared her throat before addressing her friend as he lowered himself into a sitting position once more. "You mentioned contacting someone in the palace too, right?"

He scratched his cheek, glanced at the master mage, and shook his head. "I'd like to, if only to hear what's going on, but I honestly don't know who to have you speak with. My first choice would be General Casner or one of the other assistant generals; however, I'm not certain if they're still in the palace, where they would be, or if Hendal's manipulating them. Another concern is whether or not they'll discover you and retaliate."

"From what I have experienced, they might be able to sense my magic and repel it, but they cannot harm me through the spell."

"I agree with Marcus," Emilea shared. "If enough mages are in the city already, they can tell us what we need to know about the soldiers. I would also guess a majority of people will remain loyal to the crown. What good would it do us at this point?"

Will voiced his own thoughts on the matter, which related to the group in Verona and keeping them safe. The three continued to repeat the same ideas about contacting various individuals when and where, but Grace had no preference for their next steps. A break would allow her time to rest, so she remained passive during the discussion.

"I think we just need to trust General Tio and Calin," Marcus concluded with some reluctance. "Let's check in and move forward with their orders."

***

The four returned to Aimes heating the leftover oatmeal in a pot as the energy around the camp seemed to pick up. Marcus raised an eyebrow at the older man when he ushered them closer to the fire with a grave expression.

"You might've caught wind of this already, but the general ordered the troops to be in their positions by noon," he explained once the four accepted the bowls he offered and began slurping down the tasteless meal. "They're going to send a messenger to the palace then, so we're supposed to be ready in case the enemy doesn't surrender."

Despite the sudden news, Marcus wasn't surprised since he figured as much when they returned to plenty of activity. People rushed from one place to another to acquire armor, weapons, shields, bandages, or whatever supplies they would need in the near future. In the distance, he could see hundreds of men and women gathering together and decided to prepare before their downtime ran out.

He thanked Aimes for the food and information, though he only ate half of his portion, and rose to stretch. "I'm going to find some gear before I meet up with Calin and General Tio. Grace, feel free to check in on me every so often in case we need your ability. Make sure not to overwork yourself."

The Yeluthian's eyes widened and her lips parted a bit, as if she hoped to add a comment. That was when a certain realization dawned on Marcus while he looked from her to Will.

If the palace retaliates, we're essentially at war with ourselves, and possibly the Nim-Valans. The three of us may not speak to each other again; at least, it'll be a while before we can relax. Who knows if the next time they see me will be when they tend to my injuries, or worse...

He caught Emilea smiling at him and lost his train of thought.

"Be careful," the master mage warned as she stood. Then, her attention shifted to Will. "You should come with me to arrange the necessary medical supplies."

Will bobbed his head and jumped to his feet before casting a glance at Grace.

"Do not worry about me," she said before anyone could inquire about her intentions. "I will stay here with Aimes for a while. That way, I can focus on Marcus without becoming distracted."

"You can contact me if you need my assistance," Emilea added as she gestured for Will to follow her.

Together, the pair moved south, leaving Marcus to walk north alone.

Individuals in tents or next to wagons handed out pieces of armor and weapons while the remaining soldiers finished getting ready. The kingdom provided its troops with a set of metal armor after they passed their introductory instruction, and in Dala, any untended dents, rust, or scratches became their responsibility to fix. The wagons brought along extra items for at least two hundred people and whatever else they could collect.

In Verona, various shops had been established to maintain the soldiers' armor, and the basement space in the palace became a storage area for weapons and armor. Marcus' family used a section to house their belongings for decades, though he had only been there once or twice in his life. At the moment, he found it difficult to dismiss his own armor sitting unused in his room.

It took him a few tries to find a set of leather padding to fit his arms, legs, head, and stomach and plain luck for the man assisting him to dig out a metal breastplate. Once equipped, Marcus positioned a decent sword comfortably around his waist, selected a wooden shield from a pile nearby, and hurried to locate the other assistant general. He pushed his way through the clusters of Dalan troops standing around chatting with one another and wondered how they could be so calm. Nothing suggested they felt concerned about challenging their fellow soldiers, which both interested and frustrated Marcus.

Soon, he reached the front row and spotted Calin over to his left. The assistant general noticed him a second later and waited to speak until they were face to face.

"I've been looking for you," Calin started. He wore silver armor covering every surface of skin except his head since he held his helmet in one hand. "Anything to report?"

Marcus took the opportunity to mention Grace's conversation with one of the mages hiding in the city, as well as Joseph and Stephen's departure.

"What of the palace?" the Dalan soldier asked next.

"We chose to wait for now since those in Verona plan on organizing a system to defend the people there. What we do depends on how this afternoon goes."

Calin chewed on his bottom lip and frowned. "It's foolish to postpone communicating with the palace; however, I won't argue when the Yeluthian is lending us her power. Let's approach General Tio with this and see what he says."

As usual, they heard the general before spotting him among a dozen troops bunched together, so they waited for an opening to slip into the huddle. Their superior noticed their appearance immediately and ended the previous discussion.

"There you are," the man shouted at his assistant. "What've you got for me?"

Calin briefly touched on what Marcus shared regarding the citizens in Verona and Grace's position within the camp.

General Tio crossed his arms and nodded. "What about a messenger?"

"Orin volunteered, just as you said. He's on his way with a horse."

"Good. It's time we learn what they're up to."

The general turned around to face the Nim-Valan camp in the distance, leaving the conversation there. A stillness seemed to float over everyone's heads as an eerily quiet moment gave the impression that this would be their last break. Like an upcoming storm, their actions would either bring relief or destruction in its wake.

Noise from behind had Marcus and Calin looking over their shoulders to where the nearest troops parted for a soldier and his horse to approach the front.

"We're ready for you," Calin said to the newcomer as he shaded his eyes with one hand in order to stare at the sky and judge the time.

The soldier previously referred to as Orin acknowledged the assistant general's words by dipping his chin before leading his animal forward. General Tio grumbled something to him as he passed and mounted his horse.

Then, the three could only watch as the messenger rode toward the palace.

"Now what?" Marcus asked in the lingering silence.

Calin's eyes continued to follow the lone rider until he disappeared around the Nim-Valan camp. "Now, we wait."

*

Instead of remaining stagnant, the Dalan troops actually relaxed while waiting for Orin to return. General Tio never looked away from the opposite side of the field, yet the soldiers behind Marcus talked with one another, lowered their arms and shields, and even paced or stretched to keep their muscles warm.

Marcus upheld his appearance as he considered their messenger's goal while shaking out the tension in his arms. *Without Dala's purpose for being here completely clear, Hendal would only complicate the issue by ignoring our messenger. I can tell General Tio won't act until he understands our opponent, which seems smart. Still, Orin's vulnerable. Hendal might reject whatever terms the general instructed him to pass along.*

As the minutes crept by, nothing changed. Every so often, a flock of birds soared above, but no movement came from across the southern field. Even the sounds from the city seemed to hush while they stood at the ready.

It wasn't until the Nim-Valan soldiers emerged, like hundreds of shadows in their dark clothing, that a lone figure parted from the group to close the distance between the palace and the Dalans. By the time Marcus recognized the individual as Orin, the northerners had lined up at the edge of their camp.

Did Hendal order them to defend the palace on Aaron's behalf? Marcus wondered as he watched them march forward.

Calin muttered a curse under his breath after when more people began emerging from the looming structure in suits of armor and white and blue robes. When they stopped behind the Nim-Valans, Marcus' stomach dropped.

Emilea mentioned their loyalty to the kingdom might impact their decision to say, but I can't believe so many would choose to fight before hearing the truth. Unless... How many humans can a demon manipulate?

Concerned murmurs echoed within the groups behind him, raising his anxiousness until General Tio balled his left hand into a fist and raised it above his head. Their entire side of the field fell silent in response. Not even a whisper reached Marcus, leaving him to stare in awe at the influence the general had over his troops. When he glanced at Calin, he found the man beaming.

"Unlike some of those soldiers marching toward us, our minds aren't swayed by magic," the assistant general explained at a lower volume. "The general embodies the spirit of Dala. He's part of the city and base's foundation. Without his leadership, courage, and honesty, what would distinguish us from the rest of Asteom? As long as he stands tall and assures the people who support him of a better future, there is no hope lost on the fear of failure."

In that moment, Marcus understood Calin's resilience and admiration for what General Tio, a true leader, was capable of. He began to consider what drove him to want to become a general like his father and what he contributed to Verona.

A glimmer of light from Orin's armor caught his eye, so he made a mental note to ask his father about the matter in the future.

Their messenger halted quite a distance away from the front line, though many sighs of relief welcomed the soldier back. This report would help them formulate a plan, so Marcus intended to hear every word, prompting him to slide to General Tio's right side as Calin did the same on the left.

After a pause where Orin stared blankly ahead, the man spoke in a dull tone of voice. "How brave of you to sacrifice one of your men on a wasted warning."

The words rang in Marcus' head until he understood what they implied. Any trace of optimism dwindled when he realized Hendal didn't expect to avoid conflict, and his hands instinctively clenched into fists.

General Tio replied afterward in a surprisingly tame manner. "You dismiss my offer then."

"You Dalans have no place in the capital city unless you decide to support the rest of the country. Swear your allegiance to the king and his vision for Asteom. Only then will you avoid bloodshed."

"You don't speak for Aaron," Marcus longed to retort, though only a growl escaped his lips. He ignored the general's following glance in order to continue glaring at Orin, or rather the high priest manipulating the messenger.

This time, the response from his superior contained the man's normal forcefulness that actually quelled Marcus' rage. "We didn't travel north to avoid bloodshed; we're here to rid the palace of leeches. If it's a fight you want, then that's what you'll get!"

THE ANGEL'S DESCENT

As if the statement was a cue, Calin drew his sword, pointed it at the sky, and let out a battle cry. The sound traveled through the lines to grow louder as the Dalan troops answered with their own supportive shouts and gestures. Marcus joined in with a grin as Hendal, through Orin, snarled.

"I suppose I have no option except to oblige," their possessed comrade added once the cheering died down.

Before anyone could react to the comment, Orin's hand snapped to the hilt of the dagger strapped on his belt. Calin shouted for him to stop before reaching forward in a feeble attempt to prevent the man's next movement; however, the soldier had the blade at his own throat before the assistant general finished the warning. No one could prevent the slice that left Orin to fall to the ground with a clamor. Scarlet blood covered his throat, then it was over.

Marcus stared at the lifeless body, and his mind went blank. Sweat began to trickle down the back of his neck before he tore his eyes away. "Why?" he wondered aloud without directing the question at anyone in particular.

"He wanted to send a message," the general answered in that strangely calm, uncharacteristic manner. "Orin knew what he was risking when he decided to do this, so don't bother pitying him. It would only insult his actions."

"Yes, sir," Marcus replied and decided to face their leader.

His shock lessened when he noticed General Tio's hands trembling. *Is he... The general doesn't show his fear or anguish. This is something else entirely, something frightening...*

"Let's get on with it," the man bellowed as he spun around and drew his sword. "Those who raise their weapons to you deserve no mercy. All the allies you need are at your sides and in our hearts. Only when we free our king from that imposter can we reunite with our brothers and sisters; only then will peace between nations be possible. Fight with all the skill and intelligence you've built your entire lives around, and don't you dare disgrace the pride of Dala!"

The resounding cries lightened Marcus' attitude.

Calin moved to stand at his side after. "Stay by me. We'll follow behind the first lines and hang in the middle with General Tio," he ordered above the noise.

Marcus' heart pounded beneath the rumbling of the hundreds of voices around them. When the general pointed his blade at the sky and arched it toward the palace, the troops began their march.

7

Once the Dalan soldiers moved across the field after a rousing cheer sparked by something she could neither see nor hear, Grace wrapped a blanket around herself and attempted to get comfortable next to the fire. Aimes didn't request her help or bother her even though the clashing of weapons roared in the distance. The humans were battling one another, and she could hardly imagine what took place while she rested. It all seemed like a dream.

Her lack of usefulness, both physically and magically, soon irritated her, yet a part of her felt relieved to be out of the way. This proved especially true when the results of the fighting returned to the camp. It started with shouting from the people around her, then light mages hurried toward the retreating soldiers to carry the wounded. Grace had never seen so many injured, bloodied bodies in her life. The new sights startled, disgusted, and horrified her until the healers and their assistants were able to create a balanced system based on who returned to the camp. No instructions came from Marcus either, so she decided to check in throughout the day instead of lingering within the conflict.

That was when Aimes recruited her to hand out mugs of tea or medicine to the recovering men and women. She managed to keep away from the worst of the wounded, where she assumed Emilea and Will were working, and wondered if she would recognize anyone among the injured.

By dusk, more soldiers populated the area than available healers, forcing her to step in and assist where she could. One mage asked for her to press a rag against a bleeding stab wound in a man's leg until a healer became available. She had no choice except to help, though her body quivered the entire time while the soldier groaned in pain. After, Grace found herself pulled into similar situations that required little out of her other than stomaching the task.

During a break, she went to the buckets of water used for washing and scrubbed the crusted blood off her shaking hands. She continued doing so even when her skin was clean because she could only imagine the ruby-colored liquid covering her body. Fortunately, Aimes found her then to tear her attention away.

"If they can spare you here, we need help lighting torches and fetching more of these," he said while pointing to the bucket. "It seems the troops are retreating for the night, so it won't be long before the camp fills up again."

Grace stared at the older man in disbelief. In the blink of an eye, evening crept upon the land. "I can fetch water," she replied. The simple job promised a moment of peace to ease her mind.

Aimes told her where to find a supply station near the edge of the forest before disappearing into the crowd around them. When she arrived, a muscular woman wearing a deep frown looked her over, huffed, then pointed at a narrow trail merging in with the trees.

"Do as much as you can," the woman ordered. "The path is clear through there. Fill up whatever is in the pile next to it and just leave the water here." With that, she turned to yell at a lanky man nearby about meal preparations and lighting.

Grace hated how she had been spoken to but dismissed the feeling and approached the buckets, which were stacked to stretch above her head. She grabbed a pail in each hand, trekked through the brush on the narrow trail, and found the stream to her right. After filling each, she walked back to avoid spilling any. Two people approached her then to take the buckets before she could even consider setting them down, so she shrugged to ease the tension in her shoulders, picked up another pair, and repeated the process.

Soon, her mind focused solely on the laborious task. It's importance came to light each instance she returned because someone waited to take the water and hurry away. Only when the forest grew too dark to safely reach the stream did Grace stop, let her arms drop to her sides, and pant until her chest relaxed.

"That's enough," someone called from the supply tent.

The woman from earlier came over to shove a bowl of something warm into Grace's hands and give her a gentle push in the opposite direction as a clear dismissal. She believed another individual or two would continue to fetch water in her place, leaving her to return to the bonfire her friends had claimed.

Will sat alone eating his supper, yet he smiled when she joined him. Neither spoke until their bowls were empty and set aside.

"I'd bet everyone else is too busy to rest with us right now," her friend commented in an attempt to make conversation.

"I did not realize how cold it grew," she added. Because her job required her to continuously move, Grace had been warm enough to ward off the night's chill. Now, it returned to force her into bundling up so only her face was exposed.

Will didn't respond. He copied her position, then she fell asleep.

*

A clank of metal woke Grace what felt like seconds later, and her entire body became tense as she remembered the battle across the field. Whoever moved nearby gasped, but they shuffled around some more until she heard them plop down to her left.

When she craned her neck around, she saw Marcus sitting close to the fire with his eyes closed and rubbing his forehead. Their fire still went strong, allowing her to make out Emilea and Clearshot snuggled together on the opposite side. Meanwhile, someone else, presumably Marcy, and a snoring Aimes rested behind her and Will.

Everyone is here, she thought with a yawn and adjusted her position, which caught Marcus' attention.

"Did I wake you?" he asked at a lower volume while glancing over. Exhaustion darkened his features and made his eyes sink into his skull. Drops of dried blood decorated his clothes and neck, but worst of all, his expression appeared defeated.

"What is going on?" she whispered for fear of bothering anyone else.

The assistant general released a long sigh. "It's late."

"Can you tell me anything?" she practically begged. She needed to hear him say the Dalan troops were doing fine, if only for her own morale. That feeling, as well as his resulting silence, compelled her to sit up with a wince as her sore muscles protested.

At first, he said her name and told her not to push herself; however, once he realized she intended to wait for an answer, he rubbed his eyes and lied on his back to gaze up at the sky.

"The Nim-Valans are being controlled and have the demon's healing power."

Grace's eyes widened in alarm. That was all she needed to hear to understand the troubles they faced.

"We don't know what to do," Marcus went on. "The soldiers from Asteom are hanging back to act as both a net to keep us from slipping through to enter the palace and a second wave when the Nim-Valans fall. All General Tio can order is to hold our lines and use magic to hinder them so they don't trample us. If we aren't able to figure out how to break their formation, then they're going to wear us down."

Grace's hands began to tremble. "How many..."

"It doesn't matter," he interrupted.

No more words were spoken between them that night, and she fell asleep again shortly after she heard his light snoring.

*

In the morning, Grace had a feeling the day would be similar to the previous afternoon. Everyone around their fire rose at the same time with visible weariness. No one talked as Aimes put the pot over the dwindled fire to reheat breakfast. While they ate, Clearshot and Emilea mumbled about the undying Nim-Valans, leading Marcus to confirm the news. He also mentioned the general's order that the troops be in their positions at noon again unless the Nim-Valan's acted first. Silence fell over the group while they glanced at one another, as if expecting someone to come up with a solution.

"Did their soldiers follow you during the retreat?" Emilea inquired a moment later.

Clearshot shook his head before looking at Marcus. "They halted when we pulled back. Perhaps Hendal doesn't want to try his luck by pursuing us."

"Either that, or the power he uses needs recovery time as well," Emilea responded and combed her fingers through her hair. "The energy necessary for healing has to be expended from someone. Even if it's the demon, I doubt it would be willing to attack unless it meant a sure victory. If Coura were here, we could ask her."

"What do you mean?" Marcy pressed without hiding her anxiousness.

"The demon's power allowed her body to instinctively heal any wound. I wonder if she would know more about it, such as if there's a limit to the amount of energy or a timeframe for the process to take place."

Marcus swung his head over to stare at Grace. "Can you reach her? Would your gift allow you to go that far?"

Aimes expressed his agreement, but Grace shook her head in a sympathetic manner.

"I wish I possessed more energy to do so. The truth is, I could only reach Yeluthia with Emilea lending me her power."

"All of the light mages in this camp are practically drained, including myself," the master mage added to snuff out any remaining questions. "I doubt we would do more than waste time and energy by trying."

Marcy mumbled a curse as Clearshot groaned to show his irritation.

"We should've thought about this sooner," the man growled before taking a deep breath.

"There was no way we could have predicted this," Emilea replied to calm the pair down as she placed a hand on her husband's back.

While they discussed the situation, Grace considered the limits of her goddess gift and remembered those in the city. "What about Clara?" she wondered aloud.

The others paused to look at her with mixed expressions.

"She was supposed to build up defenses around Verona. Would she know about those in the palace or if the soldiers fighting against you are actually under Hendal's influence? Perhaps if they learned of the demon's existence, they would not wish to fight."

Will encouraged the idea when no one argued. "It's worth a shot. The soldiers and mages in the city might join our efforts here if the people are safe. The least we can do is explain the issue."

Grace's lips stretched into a weak smile once the rest of their group began to support the reasoning. She hoped she projected a sense of reassurance because she honestly wasn't certain how much of a strain it would cause. Still, no one questioned her.

They split apart for their assignments, allowing her to position herself comfortably enough next to the fire before activating her ability. Her familiarity with Clara's mind would help her locate the light mage, but she worried her target wouldn't be at the flower shop. When she reached the location, she found the building empty and searched the surrounding area.

Where could she be?

With no direction to go in and her body needing to utilize every bit of energy, she prepared to return to the camp. Her mind swept over the main road upon her retreat, which showed clusters of people staying indoors and sharing their doubts and fears about the future; some even claimed they would leave the city before the end of the day if the conflict continued.

I suppose I should not be surprised these people noticed the fighting outside the palace. I only hope Clara and her friends are doing their part. Maybe I should explore a bit in case they do have soldiers and mages gathered to protect the city. I do not wish to return empty-handed.

Although her head began to pound from the strain of using her gift over such a distance, she circled along the perimeter instead of following the main road. She lost track of the roads and shops as she sped by until her presence darted straight into the midst of hundreds of other minds all active and filled with various emotions. Grace reeled back in order to shield herself from their thoughts.

What is this? Who are these people?

When she could compose herself, she began skimming over the individuals without directly reading their minds; however, what they let slip through to her promised an answer to her previous questions.

THE ANGEL'S DESCENT

Soldiers, mages, and even ordinary civilians crowded what she discovered to be the eastern square in preparation for orders from the person who informed them of the situation. It took her a while to find the aforementioned leader since they stood at the front of the crowd, but she wasted no time introducing herself after.

***

Although the troops had another hour before noon to prepare for the upcoming combat, most were already in position as Marcus and Calin remained at General Tio's side to listen and add input to his planning session. Dozens of ranked individuals shared their reports with the trio and one another so they could each adjust their provisions, actions, and scheming, if necessary. In the end, the worst of their problems stemmed from being unprepared for the demon's healing power.

Less than a hundred died because of the light mages' response, but they won't be able to perform as well as the days pass if they can't recover what energy they expend. The supplies were also only meant to last about a week or two, so the longer this drags out, the worse it'll become.

"That's enough for now," General Tio said to the group and scratched his chin. "Make sure we're ready as soon as possible. There's no telling if that traitor will have his troops make the first move today or not."

"Yes, sir," they replied in unison before separating.

He watched them go before glancing over his soldiers while still rubbing his chin and wearing an unreadable expression.

"General," Calin began to get his superior's attention. "Do you believe the Nim-Valans will strike first? If so, shouldn't we make haste with our preparations?"

When the man didn't give a response, Marcus met his fellow assistant general's eyes. Calin's frown deepened, and he seemed to say, "I don't know what he's thinking, but I don't like this."

Marcus dipped his chin to acknowledge the unspoken words. He opened his mouth to address the general until the burly figure turned to stare at the palace with his arms crossed.

"I can tell you're both concerned, but we shouldn't resort to using our strength up at once," General Tio said just loud enough for them to hear. "There's no telling what's going to happen. No one reported any suspicious activity overnight, and nothing's moved at all this morning. My guess is Hendal won't attack us unless he believes he won't lose. Or maybe he's going to surprise us."

"What will you have your troops do, then?" Calin pressed.

The general groaned in answer, and Marcus prepared to hear the worst.

Do we continue to act like we did yesterday or wait until someone comes up with a better plan? Unless we stop Hendal or the demon to end their control over the Nim-Valans, I wonder if-

"Marcus!"

A female voice called his name, pulling him away from his thoughts. He, along with Calin and General Tio, spun around to see the soldiers sidestepping so a petite figure could run forward. Marcus recognized Grace and walked over to meet her.

"What's wrong? Are you hurt?" he asked when he noticed how she held her head with one hand.

He prepared to request a healer until she looked up to smile at him.

"I found General Casner. He is waiting in Verona with more of Asteom's troops."

Marcus' mouth hung open in disbelief. "Why is he in the city? What did he say?"

Grace took a moment to catch her breath before answering. "I tried to find Clara, like we agreed, but no one was at the shop. I decided to explore the city and found hundreds of people in the eastern square. General Casner acted as their leader. After I revealed my presence, he requested a favor."

When she paused to shift her attention to General Tio, the Dalan commander's eyes narrowed.

"Well, out with it then," he pressed, though in a gentler tone of voice.

"He wanted me to tell you the citizens are safe. Hendal has not attempted to do much there except spread a rumor about how your soldiers are trying to take over the palace. Of course, most people do not seem to believe it. Anyway, he spent time away from the palace to recruit soldiers from out west. They gathered in the square once they noticed the fighting in order to prepare to travel to our camp."

"Aha!" General Tio exclaimed and threw his fist into the air. "That sly dog!"

While the man laughed, Calin cracked a smile and allowed his shoulders to slouch with relief.

"Did the general mention how they escaped into the city or how many he's bringing?" Marcus asked next. He felt too stunned to react unwarily.

His Yeluthian friend lowered her gaze. "I am afraid not. I lost the connection after he finished his explanation, though he claimed he would tell you more when they arrive."

Only then did Marcus allow himself the pleasure of a grin. He wanted nothing more in that moment than to wrap his arms around her, but he refrained when she winced and rubbed her temples. "We can't thank you enough," he said instead. "Go back and rest. That's an order."

While she disappeared into the nearest line of troops, Marcus asked General Tio if he could do anything for the time being. A sense of anxiety still held its grip, nagging at him to ensure they were prepared before the afternoon.

The general seemed to understand and requested he and Calin spread the word to avoid startling those in the camp. By the time the two completed their rounds, the Nim-Valan and palace soldiers began to line up across the field. A shadow also crept toward them from the west, revealing the troops General Casner had promised.

Seeing the hundreds of people emerge from Verona lifted the Dalan soldiers' spirits, and they cheered as their allies approached. It seemed not everyone in the palace stood against them.

Amid the noise, Marcus remained at General Tio's side with Calin as General Casner led the newcomers. Despite the support, the second commander looked annoyed when he stopped in front of them.

"It's been years since I've seen your face," the Dalan general said to initiate a greeting. His signature, hearty laugh followed while he extended his only hand.

General Casner's frown deepened, but he accepted the handshake. "I see you haven't changed," he replied before straightening. "I also see it's too late to diffuse the situation…"

"There's not much anybody could've done," General Tio interrupted with less enthusiasm. "The high priest is working with a demon to control the Nim-Valan soldiers and some of the others inside the palace."

Marcus caught General Casner's eyebrows rise in surprise. "A demon? So that's what's been happening."

"A portion of the soldiers and mages are still willing to follow the king despite our attempt to notify them of the danger," Calin added. He proceeded to share what they knew before hinting at the enemy troops across the field.

General Casner fell silent to contemplate the news, so Marcus took advantage of the opportunity to learn what led to the man's sudden appearance.

"How did you escape and recruit this many people from within the city?" he asked while considering Joseph, Stephen, and Will's friends.

The general stared at him for a few seconds with an expressionless mask. "Assistant General, I'm glad you were one of the few soldiers able to see through the problems and get help. Like you, I've been sensing a deeper, malicious power and noticed how your father, His Highness, and others were behaving. My hope in the palace's future wavered until I heard the mages began disappearing. That evening, I decided to travel into the capital city with my most trusted assistant in order to track down someone to provide more insight. Every mage or soldier I spoke with shared their growing fear of an evil presence within the palace; however, I soon understood they left without intending to abandon their comrades and king. This problem became much worse with each passing day, so I took it upon myself to manage the placement of those hiding in Verona. When we noticed your arrival, we decided to act by establishing a defensive system before agreeing to fight."

"That's fine, but I don't believe our Nim-Valan friends will wait much longer," General Tio interjected. "How many came with you?"

THE ANGEL'S DESCENT

General Casner's irritated expression returned, making Marcus wonder if the two didn't care for the other's personality. "About seven hundred foot soldiers, including two hundred of the Sie-Kie men from the Western Woods, nearly two hundred mages, and more civilians who offered to join our efforts. I figured your camp could use the extra hands, and we only brought those willing to fight. My assistant general is taking care of those staying in the city."

"Let's get them lined up," General Tio said while turning to Calin, who caught the message.

The assistant general offered to provide direction for the additional combatants while ordering Marcus to organize those who would act as healers or help with supplies in the camp.

***

Being in Asteom again seems so surreal, Evern thought as he inhaled the earthy scent that drifted upward when he flew closer to the ground for the first time in years. Although their soldiers had been on the move for half the afternoon already, the past two days of straight traveling began to wear on his senses.

Meanwhile, Paulina clung to the harness keeping her tied to the front of his body. Unlike what he believed when he was a child, about two-thirds of the Yeluthian population could manifest wings, and only about half of those who could were able to work or train them to hold more than their body weight.

Evern found the experience indulging, which led him to enjoy his position so much. What he told Coura about having to scout often for nearly a week straight had been the truth, but he did not mention the many times he volunteered to do so in a comrade's place. On the other hand, his wife found pleasure in their peaceful flights through sunlit areas instead of the fast-paced, heart-pounding journeys he made.

Unfortunately, we both are aging too rapidly. I would never risk a flight now without making sure she or either of the children were safely strapped tight.

He gazed down to take her in, avoiding the rope-like braid she tied her long hair into at the start of the day. The harness, as awkward as it was to get into, consisted of a sturdy leather pad between his stomach and her back and straps to go above their shoulders, around their waists, and through their legs. The front clipped at Paulina's stomach, pressing them together with belts to hold every limb in place.

I remember when Isan first told me about this contraption; I had been so ignorant that I could not comprehend carrying myself and another person like this. If she did not agree to try it out, I never would have believed him.

Of course, the added weight meant twisting and maneuvering would be impossible, so bringing along an extra body limited a flight to either slow soaring, the kind his wife enjoyed, or straight, consistent, and in his opinion, boring treks, like their current predicament.

Evern returned his eyes forward. As much as he hated the straight hours of such a consistent pace, he had been trained for such work while Paulina remained on the ground. She continued to brave this trip more than him, and he loved her for it despite their more frequent stops so she could catch her breath and avoid fainting at such a high altitude.

A wave of exhaustion passed over him, yet his wings beat on as he became lost in his thoughts. *This should be the final evening before we see the city. I assumed three days would be long enough, but I have never traveled with dozens of soldiers, King Arval, and Paulina. There is no reason to rush when we must stay together and remain out of sight from the humans below.*

For the most part, their company passed over empty fields, then the woods beyond. As he flew over the trees yesterday, Evern wondered where Neston lied beneath; Paulina had shared his curiosity that evening when he brought it up, claiming she felt certain they went over it already. Later, she asked if he felt excited to see Verona again.

The idea of returning to my original home occurred to me before, but I expected it would happen when I retire. We possess no ties to the people there, and Yeluthia is still unknown to most of the country. I would go anywhere for her, though. Evern told his wife as much, which earned him an appreciative kiss.

The scout farther ahead veered right as a signal to their group that a resting point was within sight. Because Isan and Detrix's troops remained ahead, they would already be descending. He obediently cupped his wings a bit to dive downward since the woods didn't allow for an extended landing, and his company reached the ground a minute later.

Paulina wiggled like an impatient child until he helped her loosen the straps keeping her in place before glazing around at the field they found themselves in. A brick home stood in the distance, but nothing else suggested any humans lived in the area. Once he and his soldiers dismissed their wings, he approached King Arval and his fellow commanders, who waited at the edge of the group with thoughtful expressions.

"Detrix, why did we stop here?" he inquired when no one addressed him.

"Verona and its palace lie northwest. I sent my scout ahead to see if it would be clear to land, but he returned immediately with a warning."

"It seems we were too late to prevent a battle," King Arval said in a voice strained from indecisiveness.

"An open field stretches south of the palace," Detrix went on in the same, serious tone. "The level of demonic energy made my scout frantic. He claims he saw two armies, both similarly clad in silver armor or dark uniforms, numbering four thousand on one side and five hundred less on the other. Those defending the palace radiated the hostile energy while the other humans created a camp across the field. They were in the midst of fighting, but no one appeared to notice our arrival. I aimed to regroup as soon as possible to discuss our next course of action."

"What about that?" Evern pointed to the brick building.

Isan shook his head. "We have more pressing concerns."

"Should we at least make them aware of the Yeluthians on their land?"

"They might offer some idea of what is happening outside the city," the king added as he stroked his golden beard.

"I will go," Evern offered. "Any attempt at an attack is idiotic given our numbers and skill, though I am more than prepared to handle a few reckless humans."

No one argued, and Isan gave a curt nod. "We will wait until you return in case you learn additional details."

Their meeting ended then as each commander returned to their awaiting soldiers to issue the usual orders. Evern explained his intent to seek assistance in the nearby building, prompting several of his more loyal subordinates to request they accompany him or take his place. In the end, he went alone, or at least he thought so until a pair of footsteps joined his as he crossed the clearing.

"I can do this by myself, Paulina," he began with a glance over his shoulder. None of his comrades would disregard his previous words, and they would hurry or call to him if it were an emergency, which narrowed his follower down to one person.

His wife strolled up to his side and sent him a knowing look. "How can I doubt you?" she joked with a smile. "I am here for their sake since you can be rather intimidating. You all look the same too. Perhaps some familiar features like mine can persuade them to trust us if they are fearful."

Evern raised an eyebrow. "Not a bad idea."

He sensed her pride grow after his comment as they approached the home's front door. One of his hands instinctively slid to the hilt of the sword at his waist, and his muscles tensed in preparation for a sudden attack. Nothing would be left to chance, especially with Paulina by his side.

With his other hand, he knocked three times on the wooden surface and waited.

"Did you see that?" his wife whispered before lightly tugging on his arm.

"See what?"

"A shadow moved in the window."

"Are you sure?"

"Someone is inside," she stated while creeping over to peer through the glass. "Perhaps we frightened them."

Evern prepared to tell his wife not to venture too far when the knob turned with a click. The door opened slowly enough for Paulina to return before they saw the person on the other side; however, neither expected a child to be the one to answer. The girl half-hiding behind the door appeared a year or two older than Jackie and studied him with wide, round eyes.

"Hello," Paulina began in her gentle tone of voice while leaning forward with her hands clasped in front of her. "Are your parents home?"

Without taking her eyes off Evern and his shiny armor, the girl shook her head.

"You cannot be all alone."

Again, she moved her head from side to side. "My brother is here," came the mumbled response. Then, she spun around to disappear farther into the house.

Evern made a move to go inside until his wife placed a hand on his shoulder.

"We should wait," she warned.

After a minute of silence, they heard footsteps, and the girl returned with her aforementioned brother, who seemed to be in shock rather than awed by the strangers.

"What are you doing here?" the boy blurted out, directing the question at Evern.

That did not take long, he thought with a casual smile before answering.

"Our soldiers needed a break in your clearing is all. Are you the only two here at the moment?"

The boy's eyes widened, as if he realized the strangers were not a hallucination.

"Everybody went to fight," his sister replied. The following sniffle released two tears that slid down her cheeks.

Evern ignored the behavior. After years of Odell and Jackie's crying fits, he'd grown immune to tears when children used them for dramatics.

If his unaffected mood portrayed him as the unforgiving sun, Paulina acted as soothing as the full moon on a serene night. The woman naturally had a way with children and somehow knew exactly what they needed. If their own children threw a tantrum, she projected patience; if they were truly afraid or hurt, they received comfort.

Without prompting, she knelt in front of the girl and offered a reassuring smile. "Come now, wipe away your tears. Tell me your names."

"I'm Mace," the boy surprised Evern by saying first. "That's Lexie. Our mother is a light mage, and our father is an archer in the army. They left to join the other soldiers."

"Are you angels?" the girl asked immediately after her brother's explanation.

Evern suppressed the urge to laugh at the word, mostly because of their hopeful expressions. *Angels... What an odd term considering we are merely another race of humans. Do they expect us to call them "mortals" in our presence.*

"Yes, we are Yeluthians," he corrected with a nod. "We departed once we heard from your king. We were hoping someone could share what has been happening around your palace, but-"

"We can help!" The boy nearly jumped with anticipation as he interrupted Evern, who could only stare in response.

"What can you tell us?" As kind as he tried to make his question sound, he couldn't mask his doubt.

The children glanced at one another yet didn't seem offended. They took turns throwing together what they picked up on from their parents and the other adults, and what they mentioned proved to be the same as what Coura told King Arval.

There really is a demon manipulating the humans...

"Our parents left right away to meet up with the soldiers from Dala," the boy continued. "We said we would be fine by ourselves so they could go. Maybe, since you're here, we can still help."

The resulting looks on their faces reflected their desperation and worry.

Paulina shot Evern a concerned look, which he half-expected.

She wants to take them along, but I refuse to risk the lives of children near a battlefield. He countered with his own, serious expression and prepared to end the conversation when the girl spoke up.

"I could sense you're angels," she added and twirled her blonde hair around one finger in a nervous manner. "I can wield light energy, and Mace can use dark magic. I opened the door because I knew you would help. We know a shortcut through the woods to the southern field that leads to the palace."

"We can guide you to their camp," her brother summarized.

Evern's mouth turned downward into a frown while he met each set of wishful eyes, including Paulina's. *Why is she so eager to bring them along? They would be safer here, and we should be able to find our way. Then again, it might be wiser to avoid flying right into the fighting. We would lose our element of surprise and possibly startle those we are trying to assist. I suppose they can return here after directing us.*

"It is not solely my decision to make," he shared and turned to face the rest of the Yeluthians. "If you children wish to guide us, you must present yourselves to our leader, King Arval. He will listen and decide our next course of action."

With that, he started his walk back to the three men who watched from a distance. His king would listen to his opinion above the children's desires, but dragging them over would save him from having to explain the situation. Once he heard the door close, Paulina returned to his side while the children lingered a few steps behind them.

They reached Detrix, Isan, and King Arval, he introduced the boy and girl, and they repeated what they told Evern and Paulina. After, his wife guided the two away so the three commanders could converse with their leader.

"Your daughter spoke the truth then," Detrix was the first to say with a slight smirk. "That means we can accept the children's story."

Isan groaned in dismay, crossed his arms, and knit his brow. "I agree with Evern. To approach from the sky would confuse our allies and be suicide if they possess more than arrows and elemental spells. Besides, it is foolish to enter a battle without a clear sense of what has happened and what is currently taking place."

"I concur," Detrix added. "The children might also recognize someone who can act as a resource."

The three commanders faced their king to hear his thoughts. In the silence, new ideas and concerns rolled around in Evern's mind until he heard his wife speak. She usually kept her opinions on politics or plotting to herself unless he requested she share them with him.

"Allow me to accompany them first," she began. "I will scope out the area and deem it safe for the troops before returning. That way, we avoid the risk of revealing too much information to an unknown army."

The idea of Paulina putting herself in harm's way didn't sit well with Evern. He prepared to say as much until his king addressed her.

"Would you be willing to do that?" The implication of his words was clear in his ominous tone of voice.

If this backfires, our people will not come to her rescue. At least, King Arval and his company will not. They would probably try to stop me from going to her...

Paulina nodded, leaving Evern to accept her selfless decision. She ushered the children over to inform them of the Yeluthians' intentions, and they agreed to guide only her to the campsite. With the matter settled and the day growing later, the boy jogged back to his home to prepare for the journey; however, his sister lingered with nervous glances at each of the adults.

"Do you still wish to leave?" Evern asked when he got the impression she was hesitating. He figured her nerves had caught up with her, which would inevitably became a distraction for Paulina.

To his relief, the child shook her head before her eyes slid to the soldiers nearby.

"I was just looking for someone," she admitted.

Before he could question her further, the girl bowed and took off after her brother.

8

The second day of combat between the Dalans, their allies, and Hendal's forces became a blur as Will collapsed onto the ground in front of their fire. Twilight settled upon the camp by the time he left the medical station, and he felt as though his arms and legs would fall off at any moment.

Unlike his previous time spent tending to the wounded where he could keep up with the mages' ability to heal using magic, that afternoon proved to be nearly the opposite. Light mages worked themselves to exhaustion, even with the additional people from Verona refilling their supplies and assisting when necessary. Since many needed rest in order to recover their lost energy, those who could still stand turned to him for guidance due to his extensive medicinal knowledge.

Most of Will's day consisted of instructing groups on how to stop a bleeding injury, bind or stitch it up, and various other life-saving procedures, demonstrating them on the worst of their patients, and delegating tasks to those capable of committing to his orders. This system proved useful; however, by sundown, their losses proved to be greater than the first evening. At some point, he learned about General Casner and the additions to their troops through the talk surrounding him, but it seemed as though the new soldiers were only meant to even out the number of troops from when they started.

The effects of the fighting evidently left their mark on those who were not on the battlefield as well. Will would force himself to focus on each individual to avoid letting his emotions swarm him like they did in the past. Emilea, of all people, had placed a hand on his shoulder to shake him out of that mindset. Then, she ordered him to leave the rest for the overnight healers. He wanted to ask how she was doing, especially since she didn't stop moving either, but the master mage disappeared before he could find the words.

He reflected on this while he took his time eating whatever Aimes handed him moments ago. The older man became a blessing because he somehow knew to prepare whatever was needed for the approaching individual, whether it be food, a larger fire, extra blankets, or something else. Amid the negativity, he never complained and kept his chin held high.

When he returned with additional firewood, Will made sure to thank him again. Aimes responded with a weak yet sincere smile before heading south through the camp on more business.

Will finished his meal and paused to savor the warmth it brought to his stomach. Soon, footsteps drew his attention. Marcus and Clearshot came into view from the opposite side of the fire to join him. Their hardened expressions dissuaded him from inquiring about the battle.

The pair took a seat to Will's right and proceeded to glare at the flames without moving or speaking. With a grunt, he stood, walked over to the nearest supplies cart, and retrieved enough sleeping gear for the three before dropping to the ground once more. That drew Clearshot out of his slump, though the soldier still stared at Will with a half-attentive gaze.

"Where's Aimes? Is there anyone available to bring us something to eat?"

"He walked farther into the camp," Will replied. He prepared to rise and grab them food until a familiar voice from behind offered instead.

"I can fetch your dinner."

Clearshot gave a weary smile. "Thank you, Grace."

While the man lied on his back, their Yeluthian friend circled around the fire and blankets to head toward a designated kitchen of sorts established at the center of the camp. She appeared a few minutes later carrying three bowls in her hands and handed two off to

Clearshot and Marcus. They ate in silence, so Will wrapped his body up in the blankets with a yawn. Grace tried to make conversation, but neither soldier seemed inclined to talk.

A lull loomed over his mind, which beckoned him to sleep, yet some inclination tugged at his heart, preventing him from properly resting. It grew to be a nuisance when he peeked around and saw everyone else settling down. He repressed a displeased groan, tossed around on the ground, then considered rising to find a task since he apparently had the energy to stay awake.

The sound of approaching footsteps at a running pace distracted him from the issue. He jolted upright and prepared for the worst news he could come up with in that moment, which happened to be an emergency in the medical station. Those around the dwindling fire also sat up as Emilea rushed into their area to seemingly confirm Will's suspicion.

"What is it?" he asked and scrambled to his feet.

Marcus and Clearshot did the same while Grace remained seated, though the master mage went to her husband.

"It's the children," she said between breaths.

Clearshot placed his hands on her shoulders. "What about them? What happened, Emilea?"

She shook her head, inhaled through her nose to take a deep, calming breath, then her eyes shifted to Grace. "Our children led a woman through the woods who claims to be from Yeluthia. They brought troops to support us. I thought you could confirm her identity before we proceed with…whatever it is we do next."

Will still needed a moment to process the news, but Clearshot reacted instantly by taking his wife's hand and ordering her to lead them to the stranger. The pair departed without another word, leaving Will to hurry after with Marcus and Grace.

The closer they moved to the edge of the forest, the more crowded the space became. Both eager and doubtful onlookers spoke in hushed voices around them until someone near the front recognized Emilea and instructed everyone to clear a path. The awaiting children stood in front of the aforementioned Yeluthian just beyond the trees.

Mace came forward first when his mother and father stepped closer, then Lexie followed. Clearshot knelt to welcome the girl in his arms while Emilea hugged her son. Before either parent could berate their children, which Will fully expected given their hope to keep the two safe, Lexie pulled away to gesture at the lone woman.

"This is Paulina," she shared. "The angels sent her with us to discuss bringing their soldiers here to help."

Her brother agreed as the stranger closed the distance between herself and the camp. Will sensed the tension growing and understood the onlookers' concern. None of the woman's features matched Grace's or radiated any hint of magical energy, which meant she could be lying in order to cover her true identity.

Still, Mace and Lexie were in control of their minds and behaved normally. If they brought her to the camp without coercion only so she could talk, he didn't see the harm in giving her a chance, especially when so many combatants would step in if trouble arose. He also hoped the offer was genuine, if only for the sake of peace.

It's too late to waste our time considering every possible outcome, Will concluded and turned to Marcus. He caught his friend's uncertainty, as well as Clearshot and Emilea's, and decided to save them some time by beginning the conversation.

"One of our assistant generals is present with the Yeluthian ambassador," he started and looked at the woman in an attempt to ignore everyone's surprise. Of those present, he had the least amount of authority to speak on behalf of the camp's leaders, yet his next question tumbled out of his mouth anyway. "Would you consider discussing your business with them?"

"Both are here?" the stranger asked without hiding her disbelief. When she glanced over the people surrounding her, Marcus took a couple steps forward.

"I am Assistant General Marcus Tont. You can trust whatever news you bring to be accurately delivered to our generals through me."

Before the woman could respond, Grace followed suit. "As a true Yeluthian, I will also vouch for these people's integrity. Are you truly from my city?"

"I am but not as some might see it." She placed a hand on her chest and smiled at Emilea and Clearshot. "Your children are extremely brave and kindhearted. They explained the situation to my husband, his fellow commanders, and our king before offering to guide me here."

"Why didn't the rest join you?" Marcus asked.

"No one felt certain your people would accept us, mainly because of the demon lurking around this area. On the other hand, we did not know what to expect. I volunteered to approach you because I am not Yeluthian by birth, as you may have guessed already."

"You must be Commander Evern's wife," Grace commented. "Few humans ever become citizens of Asteom, but I remember my father mentioning you and your husband."

The woman dipped her chin. "Should you accept our offer to assist you, King Arval will give the command for his troops to march here at once."

Plenty of whispered conversations began when no one spoke after. Will looked to Marcus since his friend would either make the decision or postpone it and inform the generals.

"I trust her," Grace mentioned at a lower volume for those around her. "What she said is accurate, and darkness does not cloud her thoughts."

"I don't sense any malicious energy in the woods beyond," Emilea added before addressing her children. "Did you actually see their soldiers?"

They nodded and remained quiet.

Marcus thanked them for their input and faced the woman again. "Tell your people to join us when they can, and I'll discuss where you can stay with my superiors. They'll want to meet your king and the commanders first, though."

A smile crept across her face before she bowed with the promise to return as soon as possible. When she disappeared into the woods, Marcus departed to locate the generals.

Many of the onlookers snuck away to spread the word, but Will remained where he was, unsure of what he should do. He noticed Clearshot moving to trail Marcus and figured he would follow since

Grace, Mace, and Lexie appeared to be doing the same; however, Emilea cleared her throat in a testy manner to halt their progress.

"Where do you think you're going?" she asked them all at once. "Marcus, Calin, and the generals can handle the arrangements without you gawking over the Yeluthians."

Clearshot pouted. "We just…"

"You just what? You want to see their reaction? You intend to size up the new soldiers?"

No one argued with her assessment, and even some of the people surrounding them paused to hang their heads.

"Leave them be. We need to rest for tomorrow; otherwise, you're going to complain about how tired you are. That can cause fatal mistakes."

Will understood her cautionary message and thought about the lives he helped save over the past couple of days. "I'm sure Marcus will tell us all about them later," he commented with a wave toward their fire.

"You're right," Clearshot admitted in defeat as he took his daughter by the hand to guide them in that direction. "I suppose we have to keep the children in mind now too."

With that, they returned to their designated area amid the gossip spreading the news faster than any messenger could.

***

As soon as Paulina passed safely into the trees once more, Even slipped out of his hiding spot to join her on the path toward where King Arval and his company waited in the clearing to the south. He hadn't told anyone about his plan to stalk his wife and the children to make sure they found their way, but nobody stopped him. Many seemed anxious to emerge from the claustrophobic forest, so he indirectly supported the cause.

He avoided looking at Paulina or commenting on the conversation he overheard with the Asteom soldiers; however, she was ready to scold him for following her after she convinced the other commanders she could fulfill her role.

"Did I say I needed your help?" she started to show her rising temper while keeping her eyes forward.

THE ANGEL'S DESCENT

"No," he replied sheepishly. "You did a fantastic job."

"Well, your actions sure do not reflect your faith in me."

"I am sorry for doubting you." He knew the pause after an apology usually meant she prepared to forgive him; her next words confirmed it.

"At least I have company on the way back from someone who can provide light."

Evern grinned and called upon the energy slumbering within to create a flame in the palm of his hand so they could see around the uneven path. That earned him a smile from Paulina. As they walked back together in a comfortable silence, Evern wondered what kind of spells the human mages could produce and if such magic would compare to his or the other Yeluthians' power.

When they returned and shared what took place, the tension he sensed earlier eased drastically. The pair then led everyone north while Detrix and Isan proposed questions about the camp, soldiers, palace, and more. The former genuinely acted curious, if not a bit excited, and the latter stayed true to his cautious nature. King Arval didn't comment on the update after Evern finished explaining the situation. The king merely nodded to confirm their next move and trusted in his commander's judgement.

The crescent moon rested high in the star-filled sky when Evern, with Paulina at his side, emerged from the forest. Four men in mismatching suits of armor stood apart from the camp to greet the new troops. Each displayed lines of weariness on their faces, but they appeared attentive as he halted the company just beyond the trees. Farther back, he noticed quite a few humans watching their arrival with wide eyes. None came any closer than the four.

"As promised, I delivered your message," one of the soldiers said before gesturing to his comrades. Evern recognized the voice from his wife's conversation and recalled mention of an assistant general. "This is General Tio, General Casner, and Assistant General Calin."

"It is an honor to meet you and be welcomed as your allies," he replied to identify himself as their group's spokesperson. "I am Commander Evern. If I may make a request, we would like to set up our camp for the evening before discussing what is to come."

One of the men in the middle, the one introduced as General Casner, stepped forward. The lack of proper lighting prevented Evern from noticing any unique features to help put the name with a face. In fact, the man appeared as generic an Asteom soldier as he could visualize. "The area to the east should be sufficient for your troops. We'd prefer to hold a meeting with your king as soon as possible in order to cover what's been going on."

I figured as much. Although we can prove ourselves and our motives to earn their confidence, it would be wise to understand the entire problem. Perhaps the enemy has a history of sneaking around at night to provoke more conflict.

Evern nodded. "That is acceptable. Allow us a moment to converse. We will join you here after." With that, he turned to address his soldiers. "Go and build the tents and fires, then you can settle down for the evening. The assigned night patrol will continue to rotate as they have already."

Those who heard him acknowledged his orders and proceeded to march to their right. Paulina took his hand, squeezed it once, and left his side to assist with the preparations. As the rest followed, he approached Detrix, Isan, and King Arval.

"I hope this is brief," Isan grumbled and covered a yawn.

"As do I," their king surprised them by adding.

Evern followed his ruler's gaze to where the four humans waited and noticed the two generals bickering with each other in hushed yet fierce voices. When they came forward, the men ceased their argument, and General Tio spoke before anybody else could.

"I'm going to be honest with you because I'm just that kind of guy; every one of us looks like he'd rather be sleeping," the general stated and scratched his scraggly beard. Then, he pointed a thumb at his comrade. "I tried telling that to Casner, but he insists we don't waste time, and I agree. He volunteered to talk with whoever wants to now. We can hack out a strategy in the morning since the enemy hasn't attacked before noon, and our scouts are posted on all sides to raise a warning if that changes. At the moment, I won't stay awake long enough to care."

With that, he spun on his heel to walk into their camp. Evern watched in disbelief, unable to process how anyone could be so lax during such a time. The other general crossed his arms with an annoyed expression to reflect similar feelings.

"Calin, Marcus, you're dismissed for the evening," the man said without looking at either of the soldiers.

His assistants appeared startled by this, but they obeyed, leaving their superior alone with the Yeluthian commanders and king. Evern expected a long conversation and mentally prepared to go somewhere immediately to begin the long discussion; however, Detrix faced his comrades with his usual smirk and addressed them then.

"The first man had a point. We are going to need all of our strength tomorrow when we reveal ourselves during the battle. Let me discuss matters with the general while you supervise the camp and recover from the journey."

"Detrix, that is not the way things are done," Isan warned. "We trust you, but we should be present to process the information individually."

"You will get the chance, only with a clearer mind. There is no reason this requires all four of us to listen at once."

Evern understood his fellow commander's intentions, yet his dedication to their mission because of his past in Asteom and loyalty to Yeluthia would not allow him to willingly shirk his responsibilities.

King Arval must have known this would lead to an argument because he cleared his throat to draw their attention. "I concur. Let us focus on our own wellbeing while Detrix gathers the information."

"Your Highness," Evern all but blurted out as he caught Isan open his mouth to protest too.

Their king raised a hand to gesture for them to be silent. "Not only will one of us do, but to send three commanders and a king away from our troops around strangers would be intimidating, as well as foolish. Besides, I am exhausted from the flight. The scouts should suffice as guards, along with the humans keeping watch."

"Yes, sir," all three commanders replied in unison.

With that, their king began heading in the direction of the newly lit fires illuminating the pitching of tents, stripping of armor, and other tasks in progress.

Evern moved to follow a second later.

"You better not daydream while you are here," he heard Isan tell Detrix in a harsh tone of voice yet not without a bit of humor. Then, the older commander caught up to Evern so they could walk in sync toward the shadows making up their camp.

*

The sun stayed hidden behind a wave of clouds threatening rain when Evern woke. Paulina curled up against him as they relied on each other's body heat to sleep comfortably at night. He wrapped his arms around her to stall rising since it felt frigid enough to bring about ideas of snow and ice.

Since Yeluthia was a part of the mountains, and thus elevated above the lower layer of clouds, they saw plenty of snow during the winter; however, the constant shielding spell his ancestors wove to surround the main city attracted a swirl of clouds for cover while still allowing people through and preventing the worst gusts of wind from ruining the season. At the moment, Evern was not looking forward to spending winter in Asteom.

Should this fighting continue any longer than a couple of days, I worry we may grow uncomfortable, he thought and tightened his hold on the woman in his arms. It seemed like he would remain undisturbed in a half-awake state until the others around them stirred.

Paulina groaned with displeasure matching his own and rolled onto her back before tilting her head to stare at him. "Good morning."

Her grumble sounded nearly incomprehensible, and Evern answered after a yawn. "I suppose we should go too."

His wife nodded and sat up to rub her eyes and retie her hair into a bun at the nape of her neck. Meanwhile, he stood, stretched, and offered her a hand, which she accepted so he could pull her to her feet. Their soldiers were either working to rekindle the fires for a decent breakfast or preparing their weapons and bronze armor for the day to come. Beyond their camp, they heard more activity from the humans.

I should hurry and find Detrix. Without a word, he stole a kiss from his wife, took a drink from his waterskin, and made his way around their space.

One of the first lessons Evern learned as a Yeluthian soldier was how leadership remained central to a well-functioning system, both literally and metaphorically. This meant King Arval and the commanders stayed close to the middle of the camp for their protection and to relay messages and orders efficiently. Those surrounding them were expected to stay alert in case danger threatened the group. It only took a matter of seconds for Evern to spot his fellow commanders standing close to one another next to a fire. He jogged over and nodded when they noticed him.

"It took you long enough to wake up," Detrix said by way of greeting. Shadows under his eyes emphasized his lack of sleep, though he seemed otherwise unaffected.

Isan buried his hands in his armpits, and Evern matched the position after apologizing.

"At least you are not as lazy as His Highness," Detrix went on after covering a yawn." Of course, I would never disrespect him by saying so."

Evern chuckled and stepped closer to the flames to savor what warmth they provided. "Is there much to report?" he asked instead of commenting on their leader's absence.

Detrix's discontented sigh revealed enough to cause Evern and Isan to glance at their fellow commander. Still, no one spoke as they observed the sunrise until King Arval emerged from the lone tent across the fire.

"Forgive my tardiness," the royal figure offered and held open the tent's entrance flap. "Come inside."

A few minutes later, the four sat together with extra blankets draped over their shoulders.

"Now then," the king started. "Detrix, what did you learn about the enemy in the palace?"

The commander shared the details of his discussion with the Asteom general, including some items Evern had considered, such as using the Nim-Valan outlanders as a first line of defense before sending out the soldiers and mages. Other ideas never crossed his mind. For example, the horse stables were located in the city instead of on palace property, allowing the stablemasters to move the animals to a range outside the capital when they grew too restless to manage. General Casner also warned of trouble while he hid in the city, but nothing their people couldn't hold off. The most troubling part, and what became the Asteom troops' greatest struggle, was the demon's extensive healing ability.

"Let me get this straight," Isan cut in as soon as Detrix concluded his report. "Their priest is working *with* a demon to possess Asteom's king, one of their generals, a dark master mage, and the Nim-Valan troops. Those under the creature's influence possess the unnatural energy and can heal from any injury, which the traitor is using to protect the soldiers closest to the palace. The people here are essentially being whittled away to nothing by a lack of healers, sleep, supplies, and a means of stopping the forces coming from the palace. The only consolation is the enemy has not attacked before noon or after the sun sets."

Detrix nodded. "That is correct. The other complication General Casner mentioned is a group of Yeluthians, or what these people refer to as angels, who are loyal to the priest. Their numbers are unconfirmed, and they apparently have a habit of showing up to a fight."

"How ridiculous!" Isan rumbled. "Why would our people side with a demon?"

When no one could answer, they dropped the subject.

As Evern noticed more noise from outside, King Arval stood to tower over his trio of commanders with an expression projecting confidence. "Whatever the reason, we cannot allow Yeluthia to be insulted by their behavior. Isan and Evern will accompany me to visit the generals. Detrix, you are relieved for the morning."

The latter expressed his gratitude before the four exited the tent together. Most of their troops' armor shined in whatever rays of sunlight reached beyond the clouds, making Evern feel as though he stood naked in the sea of bronze.

"Your Highness, I believe we should prepare ourselves before seeking the Asteom generals," he proposed.

"I agree," Isan added with a bow while their king nodded.

"As do I. Meet me here once you are suited up and armed."

*

The remainder of the morning proved to be quite interesting. Although Evern preferred more time with the Asteom generals and their assistants in order to sort out the near future, he soon found himself lowering his expectations.

Once their trio stepped into the adjacent camp, it became obvious how much the humans were struggling. People sprinted from tents to fires to others huddled in groups of a dozen or more, as though an unseen force pressured them into action. Some carried bundles, weapons, bandages, or various items with pale faces, and they sensed light energy from the mages who worked on the wounded.

No one appeared to notice the three, lingering Yeluthians.

"What do you suppose has them so riled up?" Isan leaned over to mumble.

Evern shrugged despite his muscles growing tense, and King Arval dismissed the question by leading them farther into the camp.

When they reached what they believed to be the generals' tents based on the bonfire at its center, they paused to wait for someone to take notice of them. Instead, the humans continued to scramble around. Evern decided to grab the arm of the nearest man and ask for his superior's location.

The person looked as old as Isan with unkempt, graying hair and a matching beard, though his arms were scrawny and face worn thin. His eyes went wide, his mouth hung open, and his shoulders slouched, so Evern repeated his question.

"They should be at the front," his target answered in a wavering voice.

"Thank you. By the way, what is happening to cause such stress?"

The man pointed in the direction of the palace. "The enemy's troops are already lined up!" As if his own words acted like a physical nudge, he jogged away into a crowd marching in the same direction.

Evern spun around to face his king. "I thought Detrix said their soldiers did not line up until noon."

"He did." King Arval's face darkened as he brooded over the sudden update. "Why they have not informed us before now, I cannot say, but we should not waste whatever time is available to us. Isan, ready our soldiers. Send half to the healers while the others join the Asteom troops. Line them up in the back for now. Evern and I will meet you there."

The commander saluted and sprinted back to their camp, making the humans nearby look slow and uncoordinated in the process. At the same time, their king hurried north, leaving Evern to catch up.

9

Three more days in Yeluthia seemed to be all the time Odell and Jackie needed to get an understanding of who Coura was and why she stayed with them. They shared meals together, which tasted lackluster compared to their mother's cooking, and she made sure to ask plenty of questions to keep building their relationship, as well as her knowledge of the city. Most of the children's answers sounded simple, especially considering the life Coura lived, but they were entertaining nonetheless. Each morning when her brother and sister were away at their classes, she seized the opportunity to stretch and practice what movements and magic she could in the kitchen while suppressing her energy and avoiding any wandering eyes.

If someone caught me working on these types of things, especially dark magic, they might report it.

At first, Coura remained hesitant about casting the basic spells since the last two times she used magic scorched her arms and chest, and before that, she couldn't control the power; however, the two pools of energy inside her center reached a balance during the time she spent in Yeluthia. When the wild, demonic side threatened to spark out of control, the natural, fluttering side swarmed the former to straighten the spell, resulting in a less powerful yet manageable wave of magic. In the two days of practicing, she felt more confident in herself than she had in months. The effort left her less time for physical work, but the sacrifice proved to be worth it.

At breakfast on the third day since her parents left for their duties, Jackie suddenly became interested in Coura. The girl asked a handful of questions at once about life on the surface, such as where she lived and what she did every day with an enthusiasm that startled her. Odell only rolled his eyes, but she could tell his curiosity piqued, especially when she mentioned the Magical Arts Academy.

"Your school was just for teaching magic?" he asked during a break in the conversation.

Coura nodded and pushed her mostly empty plate aside. "Anyone with the potential to wield energy must attend to train their power."

"We are in similar classes," Jackie added and smiled. "Does that mean you can cast spells like we can?"

The question took Coura back, but she chuckled to cover the unpleasant feeling that followed. *Are they aware of both types of energy? They've spent their whole lives in Yeluthia, so it should be new, unless someone mentioned it before.*

"Mine isn't exactly the same. Its essence is dark instead of light." Their resulting looks of confusion provided an answer to that thought.

Thankfully, the hourly bell rang throughout the city to save her from explaining since it served as a beckoning call to the students. Odell led Jackie away after making Coura swear to finish telling them about it once they returned. On the outside, she waved them away with a smile, but on the inside, she went cold at another reminder of just how different she was from the people who were supposed to be family.

The morning dragged on, so Coura decided to get some fresh air by strolling through the city. Stares still followed her everywhere, but now she found them to reflect the people's inquisitiveness instead of fear or concern. When she spotted a middle-aged man possessing hair as dark as charred wood, she began to wonder how many others had been brought to the city like her mother.

I wonder if she knows? Would I be able to pay her a visit?

Despite not committing to the idea, Coura later found herself in the area below her parents' home where the children began to set up for their next game of Crusader's Ball and decided to ask for directions. Eventually, an older woman who reminded her of the Sie-Kie's *shalma* offered to guide her there. They walked in a casual silence before the woman stopped in front of a sign that read Full-Heart Community.

"This is where I leave you," the elderly Yeluthian announced with a genuine smile and pointed down the dirt road. "The volunteer station is farther along and on your left."

Coura bowed at the waist while expressing her gratitude, causing the woman to laugh and make a shooing gesture with her hands.

"There is no need to thank me," came the response. "Please, do not take up too much of their time, though. They have been a bit shorthanded, which is why I am spending more time with my brother. Although, he much prefers his keeper Paulina's company. Well, those with family members or friends here were asked to take care of their own whenever possible."

Coura tilted her head at the mention of her mother's name. "Paulina? You couldn't mean Paulina Galdwin?"

"I only know of one person here named Paulina." For a second, the elderly woman's smile deflated slightly. "She has taken some time off, but you can see when she will return."

As they parted ways, Coura stood alone on the path. *Mother... Did she lie about her work?*

Just to be certain, she hurried to the volunteer station to inquire about her mother. The attendant informed her of Paulina's requested leave without a return date in mind.

When nothing more could be gleaned from that location, she made her way toward the center of the busy city. People went around on their own business, including children who were released from their classes. She ignored them all to tackle her own emotions.

Mother lied to me, and Odell and Jackie too. Why wouldn't she wait to take time off until Evern returns...unless she left with him. How do I know if he was telling the truth either? If anyone could tell her, it would be his own soldiers stationed at the main building housing the throne room.

Her intentions must have been as clear as the sunny day, for one look at her had the fully clad front guards fidgeting. After eyeing the pair up, Coura crossed her arms.

"Are either of you under the command of Evern Galdwin?"

The man on the left immediately shook his head, as if he expected the question; however, the one on the right dipped his chin just enough to give it away.

"Where is he now?" she asked that guard.

"He is away with the scouting party," the first answered instead. "They left three days ago and will not return for another few.

Coura hesitated to accuse her parents of more when she didn't know exactly where they would be going. In response, she sighed, relaxed the muscles in her shoulders, and opted for another approach. "Please, I need to find him. My mother is missing, and my siblings and I are concerned. At least let me speak to your king if you can't help. I might be able to go after him, or we can send a scout to inform him of the situation. I searched everywhere; my last option is to see King Arval."

Evidently, the plea resonated with the pair better. The first guard grumbled an apology while staring at the ground, possibly while contemplating a response. His partner glanced at him without a word.

Will they let me near their ruler? Even another commander would do. I hope they weren't careless enough to return to Asteom on their own, especially without Yeluthia's support. Maybe I'm overthinking this, but no one disappears from a city without telling anyone.

Coura waited for a reply.

At last, the guard on her left cleared his throat, resumed his straightened position, and spoke in a sympathetic manner. "I am sorry, but there is nothing we can offer you at the moment. King Arval and his commanders will be attending meetings with various representatives throughout the day. We can bring up your request, but I suggest you continue to watch over his other children until we hear more."

That was far from the answer she hoped for, but Coura bit her tongue to avoid lashing out at them and thought about what she should do next. *No matter what I decide to do, Odell and Jackie need someone to look after them. That comes first since they'll be returning home this afternoon.*

"I wish you were more useful," she admitted without hiding her bitterness. "Still, I understand. Is there someone you can recommend to watch the two children while I'm away for a few days?"

Again, her seemingly harmless question had them pausing to contemplate the best answer.

"No one is better suited than their older sister," the first said. "We will let you know when King Arval is available or Commander Evern returns. Until then, I urge you to relax, enjoy the city, and spend time with the young children."

Coura raised an eyebrow before turning toward the second guard, who acted less convinced than his fellow soldier. "What about you?"

"My comrade is correct," he answered. "Place your faith in our leaders."

Although she avoided the urge to groan with displeasure or roll her eyes, Coura thanked them for their time and started down the stone stairs. As her feet touched the dirt road below, she heard footsteps from behind and turned to see the guard on the right descending as well.

"Did you remember something?" she asked sarcastically once he reached her.

He surprised her with a chuckle and removed his helmet, revealing the grinning, young man who led her to King Arval's chambers when she last visited. "No, but I thought you might like an escort home."

Coura didn't reply as she tried to recall his name. *Lav...Laverne? Lavine, that's it! Why would he offer to walk with me? I'd bet his superior requested he makes sure I avoid getting into trouble.*

They moved through the city together, though Lavine seemed as social with others as he had been with her during their first meeting. Many people, mostly women, greeted him warmly or stopped him for a brief conversation. Coura had no reason to converse, so she kept going, leaving him to catch up if he truly expected to be her escort. She wasn't sure whether or not to be glad when he rejoined her every time, though she didn't expect to be friends with the Yeluthian. Regardless, Lavine kept coming back.

Once they were away from the wider buildings, he inquired about her interests and what she liked most about the area. It sounded casual, but Coura acted indifferent and reminded him of the problem at hand, resulting in a pregnant pause.

"Maybe one day, when you return to the city, I can give you a proper tour," Lavine said while gazing at the sky before rubbing his neck.

"What do you mean?"

"I imagine you will leave when I tell you where your parents, my king, and a portion of his army went."

Coura stared at Lavine in disbelief. "Where are they?"

"I am a member of your father's company, so we were informed of the situation in Asteom after I brought you to King Arval."

"Where are they?" she repeated in a growl and narrowed her eyes.

He met her gaze without a hint of worry. "Their fleets were hand-picked to utilize our best flyers. The rest of us remained to ensure the safety of Yeluthia, but no one knows their goal or when they will return."

"They went to Verona."

He didn't appear certain, but Coura was. She would be the only person in Yeluthia who understood what awaited them in Asteom, and the following sense of urgency pushed her into a sprint toward her parents' home.

Lavine cried for her to wait, yet she didn't stop until she stood in front of the entrance's curtain. A twinge of guilt arose when she remembered the armor the soldier wore, which led her to pause until he caught up.

"There is one other matter I must share," he added at a quieter volume while panting. His eyes slid to the opening at her back. "Commander Evern ordered us to keep you in Yeluthia under his personal authority."

"Why?" Coura growled. Anger fueled by her parents' lies started bubbling to the surface.

"He did not say it outright, but he wants to keep you safe. Since you live in Asteom, I believe he feared you would return amid the threats looming there. Also..."

"What?"

Lavine frowned. "The commanders, our king, and the leaders of the city are nervous around you because of the strange energy you possess. They wish to avoid bringing you closer to the creature in case the connection runs deeper than you know."

He said no more, but Coura caught the message. *They think I serve Soirée, or I belong to her, and bringing me near her would be risky in case I can't control myself.* In her heart, she could not blame them for believing that since they weren't familiar with Soirée and her power to manipulate others.

"Lavine, is there anything else you can tell me?" she added after a moment.

The Yeluthian shook his head.

"Why *did* you tell me?" she felt compelled to ask after.

He rubbed his neck again with a slight smile. "I guess I considered what I would think if I stood in your shoes. You sounded so passionate when you requested our king's help and remained persistent. I knew you would leave once you caught wind of their plan. Besides, Commander Evern always says we should trust our instincts."

Coura realized then how much Lavine admired her father. "That's still pretty thoughtful of you, to support a stranger from Asteom."

Her comment seemed to make him nervous. "After you arrived and met with King Arval, His Highness and the commanders reached an agreement to aid your people because of our alliance and the demon's involvement. The rest of the details regarding your father and mother's excuses were according to his orders. They did not want you to follow."

Somehow, the blow came lighter than she expected, which she figured was because she understood their actions. She thanked Lavine once her mind processed the information.

"What will you do?"

She proceeded to hold open the curtain and usher him inside without giving an answer. Odell and Jackie were already busy preparing some sort of potato dish Coura didn't recognize, but they froze when they caught sight of the soldier in bronze armor.

"Who is he?" the girl asked with more interest than alarm.

"My name is Lavine," he introduced himself before Coura could. "You may not remember me, but I work under your father."

"You all look the same," Odell mumbled indifferently. He blushed when Lavine laughed at his comment and agreed.

Coura leaned forward and met the two sets of sapphire eyes. "Odell, Jackie, I need to go away now."

In the brief amount of time she spent with the children, she must've made a larger impression on her new siblings than she realized, for they grew concerned and questioned her decision. It became difficult to avoid lying as she desired nothing more in that moment than to keep them uninvolved, but somehow she managed.

"Don't worry. I'll be back in a few days after I take care of my business. Then, I can tell you all about Asteom. Does that sound fair?"

Jackie nodded while Odell shook his head, though they didn't protest. Coura moved straight to her room, rummaged through her few belongings, and dressed in the outfit she first wore upon arriving in Yeluthia. Once she felt sufficiently bundled with the scarf wrapped around her neck, she looked over the room before returning to the kitchen.

All three had taken a seat around the table and continued to watch her. To her relief, they were either too stunned or uncertain to question her anymore, allowing her to exit the house without issue.

She glanced around until she felt confident in the direction she selected. Before she could go, a hand grabbed her arm just above the elbow.

"I will send someone to look after them," Lavine said from where he stood outside the doorway.

Her eyes studied his face until he released his hold. "Thank you, for everything."

The soldier offered a smile but didn't say another word.

With matters in Yeluthia settled for the time being, Coura hurried across the city until she reached the grassy space she set foot on days ago when she first arrived.

My flight from the woods outside Verona lasted about three days. How long will it take if I don't stop?

THE ANGEL'S DESCENT

She focused inward on the energy in her center and prepared to trigger what tingled along her back when another power fluttered to life. This second surge flared against the invisible barrier keeping it within, startling her into abandoning the previous spell. After a moment, Coura recognized it wasn't the demonic energy, meaning it had to be what Emilea claimed belonged to her.

I don't have time to fool around, she thought, as though she were addressing a living creature that could be scolded. *I can return here once I deal with Soirée.*

The uncertainty underneath her statement lingered as she departed Yeluthia.

*

For a while, her surroundings distracted her. She dove under the clouds when she had the opportunity, paused to figure out the direction of the capital, then shot forward to set a brisk pace. Nothing below caught her eye, allowing the previously slumbering power to rise again once she could acknowledge it.

Instead of lashing out, like the demonic energy did in the past, this kind settled to fill her body with a familiar warmth.

I remember this, Coura realized. *Outside Verona, when I fled the palace, this presence comforted me when Soirée's power wouldn't respond. Although it prevented the demonic energy from healing me, it never seemed hostile.*

The memories of that night and the resulting pain she experienced led her to reflect on what that night meant, and what her return would bring. A wave of sadness came first, leaving behind a burning hatred for the demon. Throughout the process, the soothing energy never faltered.

I have to stop Soirée. If killing her means hurting myself beyond repair, I'll gladly do so. She imprisoned me, forced me under her control, and ruined my life, my family's, and so many others'. I accept what happened to me... I need to in order to create a better future.

The fact that her involvement with Soirée would lead to further suffering, and probably her death, surprisingly never bothered Coura as long as she kept fighting. What she failed to come to terms with in the past, and what she didn't let trouble her until she left Yeluthia, was what it would be like for everyone else to live without her. That became the worst burden for her to bear.

Memories of her time at the academy, Verona, Dala, and all over Asteom, the friends and comrades she met and fought alongside, and now her reunited family appeared in her mind no matter how hard she tried to force them away. Her imagination began to play possible outcomes for defeating Soirée, then she pictured her friends moving on without her.

Coura rubbed her eyes when the thoughts prompted tears, which irritated her more because of the flight, and she glanced up to see a dark gray cloud right in front of her. Before she could change directions, her body passed straight through it. Seconds later, she emerged and found herself drenched from the water it held.

Despite her intent to avoid wasting time, the resulting chill and suppressed emotions forced her to land when she could. An opening in the trees allowed her to climb down to the ground where she dropped to her hands and knees to catch her breath. The creatures and insects ceased their calls and chirping, so the area fell silent.

The unpleasantness didn't go away; in fact, it grew worse with each second. Her throat burned from repressing a sob as she squeezed her eyes shut. At last, a tiny voice from within destroyed what little control she had on herself.

I don't want to leave them...

She began to tremble while the words repeated in her mind until she hugged herself and wept. During the moments when she felt afraid, someone else had been present to force her to put on a brave face and dismiss her emotions. Now, nobody could distract her from the pain.

For a while, Coura remained in that position, unable to calm down until she wallowed enough to ease her heartache. She wiped away her tears with Emilea's scarf and took comfort in the lingering energy resting like a hand on her shoulder.

When I return, I refuse to let anything hold me back. Doing so might harm or kill me too, but I vowed to be the one to put an end to her cruelty.

She steadily rose to her feet and stretched to lessen the tension in her muscles only to find the warm energy still humming inside her center. The sensation felt familiar, yet she couldn't remember where or when she experienced it before. None of her recent memories in Emilea's house nor those spent in the woods prior to that time made the energy as active, and even then the presence merely observed and reacted to Soirée's power.

The connection to her Yeluthian lineage diminished when she tracked down the demonic creatures, leading her to look further into the past. Finally, she remembered what originally caused the energy to stir, and she shuddered as one hand slid to her left side where she had been stabbed with the golden weapon.

When Soirée was gone, I sensed this same presence. I lost consciousness, but I do recall falling somewhere cold and dark. Was that part a dream...

The light energy jittered again, and Coura waited to see what would happen. It spread through her entire body all the way to the tips of her fingers and toes, forming a spell in the process. While the power continued to radiate in preparation to be released, Coura hesitated.

I didn't know Yeluthian spells acted this lively. Grace never mentioned experiencing anything like this with her magic.

Cautiously, she extended a hand while glancing around to make sure the area remained empty. This led her to consider her interaction with Cintra when the woman seemingly appeared out of nowhere and wonder if it would be safe to wield her magic without supervision.

In response, the enthusiastic humming became a ringing in her ears. She decided then to cast the spell, if only to rid herself of the persistent sound.

The prepared power leapt from her outstretched palm, causing the air in front of her to shimmer. Unlike a shield, though, it didn't remain transparent as it expanded into an oval shape from the ground to just above her head. It seemed comparable to a mirror for a moment until its surface rippled and grew foggy. When an image solidified, Coura noticed tress and a pond beyond before she recognized it as the location where she took a break in her flight and spoke to Cintra.

This...can't be right... Is it really some sort of portal?

When the leaves and branches in the spell swayed from a distant breeze, she understood it wasn't a mere trick. Wielding the power also required her to maintain control over the light energy, whereas she'd learned to cut off the connection when casting a dark spell. This required her to ignore her shock and focus.

Coura approached the contrasting image, but it took another couple of minutes before she could convince herself to pass through. Nothing felt any different from walking through a doorway until her entire body entered. Then, it was as if she had been thrown forward before an invisible force pressed down on her shoulders. Although it didn't cause any pain and ended in an instant, she stumbled, doubled over, and held her stomach before dropping to her knees.

"That was awful," she groaned as she ended the connection to the spell.

The light energy didn't pester her afterward, which she appreciated since she needed to catch her breath until the nausea ceased. When it did, and she could look around, her heart skipped a beat. Just as the image showed, she wound up in the exact spot she had been in beside the pond a few days ago. No additional time seemed to pass by either.

"It worked," she mumbled in disbelief before a smile tugged at her lips. "I can't believe it!"

The possibilities of her newly discovered ability stretched before her, such as returning to Verona in a matter of seconds instead of continuing to fly; however, Coura felt how significantly the spell depleted her reserves.

There's no point in wearing myself out before I reach the palace, she told herself despite her enthusiasm. *I should save as much of my power as I can. Not only that, but I'd hate to show up in front of everyone without being able to stand my ground.*

With the original plan in mind, she manifested her wings and moved into the air again. The sun began sinking at her back as she moved northeast, yet she inhaled the crisp air and pressed on as the evening darkened the land ahead of her.

***

In the midst of the turmoil taking place outside the palace, Hendal remained poised from where he sat on the meeting chamber's throne.

THE ANGEL'S DESCENT

A lantern on the floor at the center of the room lit most of the space, revealing the charred remains of the furniture Soirée destroyed weeks ago. Even the burning smell still lingered to irritate his nose.

Each elbow rested on the chair's arms, and his hands clenched and relaxed repeatedly no matter how hard he tried to fight the urge. He ordered the young king to bring him some wine a while ago, though the single goblet remained balanced on a tray Aaron held to the right of the throne. The idea of such an influential figure being forced to serve him had Hendal rumbling with laughter before; now, he simply chuckled under his breath.

"To peace and prosperity," he muttered while extending a hand for the glass cup.

Aaron placed it in Hendal's hand without disturbing the silence. That was the one reason they stayed there instead of his quarters. From deep within the palace walls, the sounds from the battle became faint enough to dismiss as a hallucination. At the moment, he wished the situation proved to be his imagination instead, for all that he strived for threatened to crumble.

Someone banged on the door unexpectedly just as Hendal raised the goblet, causing him to jump and spill a bit of the ruby liquid on his white robe. Without waiting for his permission, whoever stood on the other side burst into the room. Drake entered first, followed by Urvin, Yrian, Kline, and Gerald with Thelma and Ester keeping close to the door.

"High priest, we need to plot out our next steps," their leader declared in a neutral voice to mask his intentions.

Hendal inspected his cup, swirled the wine around, and took a sip. "What is it you wish to discuss?" he asked without removing his eyes from the glass.

"You know what is happening out there," Drake answered. "The Yeluthians are here, aiding the Dalan troops along with the Asteom soldiers who slipped away from you. Your troops are not getting anywhere with them."

Hendal remained silent.

"The evening approaches, and they could breach the palace through the air if they wish. Only the shield your mages conjured prevents them from breaking in."

That new piece of information caught Hendal's attention. His head snapped up so his eyes could meet Drake's. "Shield? I didn't order our mages to create a shield. They should be nearest to the wall using elemental spells to kill the Yeluthians who get too close."

"Yes, but we-"

"Shields will do nothing except make us appear weak," he interrupted and raised the volume of his voice. "If the Yeluthians wish to invade our palace, they'll become enemies of Asteom, just as the Dalan soldiers are. Our troops and the Nim-Valans have the power to keep up with them. Why hide behind a shield when we're already in plain sight? Surely they would understand the need to bring us together to unite the kingdoms…"

Drake let Hendal continue to share his annoyance for another minute, which he soon directed at the demon once he realized it was most likely her doing. Then, the angel found an opportunity to interject.

"High priest, we wish to fight instead of hide away inside. Allow us to strike down the Yeluthians who cast us aside."

The others nodded while Hendal frowned.

"Send *you* out there? You mean, waste my only protection and our most skilled fighters?"

"Use one of your possessed soldiers," Drake retorted. "I believe a few of the humans would gladly remain here to guard you as well."

Hendal huffed a laugh and shook his head. "Servants are useless when it comes to war. Trusting them to protect me would bring upon my death sooner, and the combatants are necessary outside."

The angels stared at him for a moment before each set of eyes narrowed.

"Do you remember why we joined forces with you?" Drake asked next without hiding his irritation.

If he were to be completely honest, Hendal had quite forgotten the details beneath his own desire for power. The longer they stayed, though, the less of a grip he had on both the situation and his temper.

"Now is not the time to reminisce. I order you to find Soirée and bring her to me."

It's her fault, he realized while ignoring the angels' mumbling and protests. *She won't let me work on my own, and now she expects me to act as the scapegoat for her plotting. I'll wear myself away because of her power too. The demonic energy makes me a target for the Yeluthians; they wouldn't harm me otherwise. Still, that shield is the main problem right now.*

As he searched for a solution, he noticed a greater pull from the center of his torso, signaling more of the demonic energy being used. This always resulted in a wave of dizziness and limited his mind's ability to process information.

"We cannot succeed unless we rid ourselves of that shield," Hendal announced. "Drake, you are to find the demon and eliminate her."

"Without the spell's protection, the palace will be overrun," Thelma added.

Her snarky tone of voice and objection pushed Hendal to react violently. He jumped to his feet and threw the goblet in his hand at Drake's feet. None of the angels so much as flinched, yet the wine splattered on multiple boots and spread along the floor.

"Perhaps you don't care, but we humans value rules and laws," he shouted after. "Anyone who enters the palace to harm me will be tried for their crimes."

"How well will that statement hold up when they press a blade against your throat?" Drake countered at a quieter volume.

Hendal ground his teeth without replying. His mind became too flustered for him to deal with intruders, and he blamed the demon for his misfortune.

Evidently, the group in front of him sensed he wouldn't give them the answer they desired. They turned toward the door as a single unit and moved to exit until he called for them to wait.

"You seek revenge for being cast aside by your king. I understand your loathing, but we must also consider the matter from a strategical perspective. If you wish to go out there and fight, you must defend the palace as well and kill Soirée when you find her. That's all I ask."

Drake frowned but nodded on behalf of his group.

"We should not leave him alone," Kline commented while facing his companions. "If something happens to him, we will lose the soldiers restraining the southern troops."

Thelma scoffed in response. "Why do we care about the humans again?"

"They support Yeluthia and need to be punished for choosing the wrong side."

Hendal dropped onto the throne and observed their interaction while they spoke as if he weren't in the room. For the first time since they worked together, he felt like a means to their goal instead of their partner or superior.

"Kline has a point," Ester added. "I prefer to fly without worrying about archers and mages firing at me from below."

Drake moved past them to exit. "Do what you want. We can draw lots on the targets."

All except Kline and Urvin followed.

"Stay here and protect the high priest," the latter ordered before leaving without so much as a glance at Hendal.

Kline scratched his head, paced, then turned to Hendal. "I will patrol these halls," the angel decided before disappearing through the open doorway.

Hendal could only stare at the wall across from him while his emotions wrestled with each other. He felt stressed, and it frightened him how easily his assistants dismissed him. The strain of Soirée's power weighed heavily on his body even though he could tell the healing continued on the battlefield.

I'll keep the mages against the palace walls with Byron just inside in case the enemy tries to sneak through one of the entrances. The servants are smart enough to stay out of the way, and everyone else has fled already. I suppose there's nothing I can do about the shield except use it to my advantage. With this power, I should be able to influence the Nim-Valans enough to ensure everything goes the way I plan.

After a moment longer to reflect on his resolve, Hendal cleared his throat and leaned back in his chair with a content smile as the demonic energy's presence settled his nerves and eventually erased his doubts.

"I'd like that mess cleaned up," he said with a gesture at the broken goblet and wine.

The king approached the glass, lowered himself to his knees, and began picking up the larger bits while Hendal savored the sight.

10

After another day of flying, Coura couldn't mistake the location of the capital city. It felt as though a hundred spells were happening at the same time, overwhelming her senses with harmless jolts. Because of the chaos, it proved impossible to identify Byron, Emilea, or any other mages individually. She did recognize the Yeluthians' energy, which she knew all too well; their power irritated her just as the hostile angels' always had.

The closer she got to the palace, the worse she saw. A camp had been established near the woods possessing dim fires and tents looking to hold over a thousand people. Figures moved frantically in various directions, like panicked insects, and she sensed faint healing magic at work.

Farther north, a mass of soldiers, who were no doubt the Dalan and Asteom troops, fought in the middle of the southern field. Colors flashed when mages used spells, yet the energy felt too weak to manage much. A Yeluthian in their bronze armor would leap into the air every so often only to be brought down by either another angel siding with Hendal or a blast of fire or bolt of lightning that came from near the palace.

Soirée's unmistakable presence covered the entire area as well.

Coura held her breath as she glanced around and wondered what she should do. Her entire body went numb at the reveal of a civil war, but the fading sunlight reminded her of the limited amount of time she had left to reach her destination.

I can't charge in without learning who is who, especially since Yeluthia's involved now. My best option is to find someone below and have them explain what happened.

To avoid detection, she stopped to hover just above the canopy beyond the camp where she could observe without being seen. She slipped into the trees after to weave her way down to the ground before dismissing her wings and sprinting in the direction of the noise. The trunks and brush thinned until she eventually burst straight into the activity.

All around, people focused on their own tasks, such as carrying the wounded or supplies. Someone nearby shouted for a healer. A woman cried in the shadow of a tent while the ringing of weapons echoed from the clearing. Movement continued everywhere Coura looked, yet she had no idea where to start. The reality of their struggle hit hard enough to stun her body, though her mind compared the chaos to the vision she experienced of the demons beneath the surface who danced and ripped each other to pieces. That would always be a different sort, yet the madness remained present nonetheless.

A blood-soaked man limped past and glared at her, but no one else paid her any attention. She forced herself to concentrate on the matter at hand by heading toward the combat while allowing her repressed anger to slowly creep to the forefront.

Anyone in the camp not recovering appeared preoccupied, leaving her little choice except to press on. A weak barricade had been put together consisting of random pieces of wood and armor, dwindling bonfires, and bandage-covered troops kneeling with wooden shields in hand. This gave her the impression a retreat was not too far behind.

Coura stood behind a guard and noticed his shield arm shaking. "What's going on?" she shouted to make herself heard above the noise.

The man's head swung from side to side, then he resumed his position, as if he didn't believe the question had been for him.

In response, she knelt beside him in the grass and asked again. "Tell me what's happening out there."

Based on the bloody bandages wrapped around the top of his head, she understood he had been injured and probably would be mentally unstable as a result. The guard stared at her for a few seconds with one eye wide and the other squeezed shut. When he answered, he yelled louder than she had.

"They're pushing us back. This is it! They're going to run down the camp."

She shook her head. "Start from the beginning."

"What? What beginning? It's been just like every other day up until an hour ago, except they aren't stopping!"

Coura paused to contemplate whether or not to seek a conversation with a different person; however, the guard continued talking while facing forward.

"The generals aimed to cut through the possessed northerners since nothing can be done with them, and they'd get our troops in the palace. I guess that's where the high priest is holed up. Seemed like a decent plan, but they heal too fast. Why, I'd bet-"

"Who's healing?" she interrupted. If the rogue angel from the Valley Beyond was present, or more with a similar ability became involved, she imagined the additional problem their side faced.

"They say it's a demon. I don't know for sure. The priest's got control of the soldiers, and there's no way to kill them for good. Someone claimed a slice through the neck would do the trick, but I didn't get that far on account of this." He pointed to his head and went on with his rambling even as Coura rose to step beyond the barricade.

The soldiers must be like me, she thought absently. *Soirée's power heals them while using their lives as a source of energy. That must be this lingering presence of hers covering the field. I have a feeling Hendal's as unaware of her intentions as we are if she's been constantly using her ability. At this rate, more people will die before the fighting resolves.*

Once again, the opposing types of energy pulled for her attention. The warmer presence called to her like it did when she left Yeluthia, reminding her of the new ability that could lead her into the palace instantly. It fluttered, as if reassuring her she wasn't alone and her father's people were present to help; however, not even the goddess who watched over Yeluthia could restrain Soirée's primal instinct, which rumbled throughout her body. The unnatural power growled to awaken every part of her being and evoke the sense of betrayal stemming from her own friends and family. She became livid in response.

Worst of all, she knew the demon was watching her, waiting within the palace walls and silently encouraging the energy stirring in her center. Instead of attempting to free herself from Soirée's influence, Coura embraced that power just as she did in the Valley Beyond. The strength it provided helped to steel her nerves and narrow her focus.

I should assist the Dalan forces if they're retreating first. Then, I'll head straight for Hendal and Soirée. Anyone with any sense left won't pursue, but I shouldn't have to restrain myself if the Nim-Valans can heal.

The demonic blade appeared in her hand, and she felt the weight of her wings a second later; their feathers bristled from a mixture of anticipation and rage.

I can't wait to hear the explanation for this...

***

Marcus' arms and legs burned with exhaustion, but his senses went numb from the sounds, sights, and smells around him. Amid the pain, death, and destruction, he kept swinging and blocking whatever came at him.

A Nim-Valan soldier in leather armor approached with only a battered shield. The northerners' padding and clothing practically hung off their bodies after being brought down multiple times in one day. Marcus squared up and easily stabbed under the curved metal protecting the stranger's torso. Before his opponent dropped to the ground, he had already backtracked to take on another carrying a spear.

If anything went right for him and the Dalan troops, it was that those under the demon's influence were not fighting seriously. They acted like sleepwalkers as they wandered aimlessly, though these men still swung dangerous weapons. He sliced through his target without a second thought and ran his blade across the throat for good measure. It would be easy to detach himself from his humanity and consider their enemy as something other than human, yet what unnerved him were the eyes of the defeated soldiers. Their dull gaze reminded him they couldn't control their actions, and the real enemies hid in the palace just out of reach.

Marcus twisted behind one of the Nim-Valans to knock the man on the back of the head with the pommel of his sword, sending his opponent to the ground. The resulting pause left him panting and glancing to observe his comrades holding their ground. Too much time had been spent recovering from the initial push, then it happened again when Hendal made it clear he intended to keep fighting the entire day. This revealed the high priest's intent to stomp down their resistance that evening.

Flashes of magic came from every direction and stood out against the darkening overcast sky. One of the Yeluthian soldiers flew just above him in a tangle with another angel Marcus thought he recognized. They danced closer to the palace before one of Hendal's mages created a shield for them both to slam into. Dozens of the flying soldiers had tried to breach that shimmering, violet shield to no avail while being attacked by those with arrows or magical projectiles below. Marcus already gave up hope that someone could slip by. As if to emphasize that specific failure, a lightning bolt struck one of the Yeluthians across the field, knocking them out of the air.

How much longer can we keep this up? If King Arval and his troops hadn't shown up when they did, we would never have been able to restrain the Nim-Valans. Still, unless we figure out a way to break through to the palace, they'll continue to come at us with their regenerating bodies.

The reminder had him studying the men he struck down mere minutes ago. Already, the first climbed to his feet and brought the bloodstained shield up to mirror what he did earlier. Marcus matched the position, noting the soldier's movement.

The only consolation for inflicting damage is they're getting up much slower and attacking with less strength. We could use that tactic if only we weren't so beaten down. In fact, I should find Calin. Maybe someone can make it to the palace if we form a line and attack together.

He disabled the Nim-Valans once again and turned to head back into the mass of his own troops.

Ever since the Dalan's first charge, the assistant generals kept close to one another, so it only took a moment to spot Calin. Three soldiers with curved knives and shields surrounded him, forcing Marcus to hurry and stab one in the back, kick the shield of another so the man fell backward, and end with a slice across their throats. When he spun around, Calin brought the third opponent down.

"Thanks for that," his fellow assistant general said in between breaths.

Marcus shook his head and wiped at the sweat-drenched hair sticking to his face. "Don't thank me yet. We still need to survive this fight."

"It's not survival I'm worried about," Calin surprised him by replying with a glance across the field. "Neither general has ordered a retreat, so they must understand what the enemy's doing. If we can't figure out how to counter the healing, they're going to chase us into the woods."

Marcus frowned while preparing to voice his suggestion. "I have an idea, but I don't know how many more soldiers we can gather together."

Calin opened his mouth and started to answer when a flash of lightning erupted to blind the two momentarily. Not even a second later, a rumble of thunder had them, and everyone else, pressing their hands to their ears.

"What was that?" Marcus yelled after the sound.

Another bolt struck the ground near the palace with just as much strength, throwing Nim-Valan and Asteom soldiers into the air. He noticed something slide across the gray sky to his left before fire reigned down to the west. A silhouette appeared against the flames and smoke rising on the ground. Once he recognized the black wings and sword, Marcus felt a part of his exhaustion fade, and a weak smile tugged at his lips. In the next instant, his friend dropped to the ground, and he lost sight of her.

"Was that Coura?" Calin asked him without hiding his disbelief.

"She made it."

"Finally!"

Marcus noticed the other assistant general grinning, but their excitement was short-lived as several of the Nim-Valan men spread out around them. Several blasts from nearby caused the ground to tremble while they fought off their next opponents, and the spells continued after they finished. Then, the pair turned their attention to where Coura darted through the air to reach one of the angels floating high above the battlefield. Despite the fireballs and ice shards the enemy rained on her, she managed to land a strike. The angel grabbed for its throat before wobbling to the ground, like an injured bird. Coura swooped to follow and disappeared again.

When Marcus took a step in her direction, Calin grabbed his elbow. "What are you doing?"

"Look," the Dalan soldier ordered and pointed north with his sword.

When Marcus became distracted by his friend's appearance, the Nim-Valans began trudging toward the palace while the shield in front of the structure returned.

"They're retreating," Calin concluded as he released Marcus' arm.

Together, they watched the enemy soldiers return to camp underneath the new barrier. It took a few minutes for some of the fallen to rise and move away, yet they decided not to pursue, especially since the lack of Nim-Valans on the ground revealed just how many Dalan and Asteom troops had been killed or wounded.

Their comrades naturally approached them in search of direction. "Should we go after them?" someone asked Calin.

To Marcus' surprise, the other assistant general looked to him for the answer. *It's probably because I know Coura better than any of them*, he realized.

"No," he shared at a louder volume for those nearby to hear as well. "Consider this the enemy's retreat for the evening. Now is our chance to recover the injured and dead and get them back to the camp. Besides, I don't like the look of that shield."

Calin nodded and began issuing an official order. Throughout their conversation, none of the remaining Nim-Valans paid them any attention, so he made sure to remind everyone to stay alert but ignore the urge to continue the combat.

THE ANGEL'S DESCENT

After the group broke apart, Marcus found himself staring in the direction where he last saw Coura. Plenty of noise continued to show the fighting hadn't completely stopped either.

"Go on," Calin said and gave him a shove. "We can handle ourselves here. Spread the word about the retreat."

Marcus promised to do so before jogging ahead at a sorry pace due to his exhaustion. To distract from his physical condition, he shouted instructions at every person he encountered, telling them not to follow him toward the frontline and instead carry the wounded away. He sensed their suspicion regarding his announcement to abandon the battle for the evening, yet something told Marcus the fighting ended as soon as the Nim-Valans returned to the safety of their camp. At least, that was what he thought until he found Coura.

He'd only seen the demon causing trouble for them once in Dala when it used what Emilea and Byron called a binding spell to keep their group from attacking. At the time, its magic terrified him since he didn't believe he could harm or defend against it. The creatures that spawned from its power were frightening enemies because they possessed speed, strength, and ferocity. Although they proved to be tough opponents, they didn't have the instinct he imagined the demon did.

Watching his friend move became the closest comparison to his expectation of how the being fought. He remembered her engage the rogue angels in the Valley Beyond and her skill then; at the moment, she appeared far less merciful.

With twilight shrouding the field in a dim light, he struggled to locate her for more than a few seconds at a time. Her black wings also disappeared when she fought on the ground, so he gave up trying to separate her figure from the hundreds of other bodies flooding the area.

Many of his troops heard him earlier and went to work clearing their fallen comrades. Marcus did his best to focus on supporting them verbally until he noticed someone shouting his name. He recognized the voice as General Casner's and waved his superior over. The general heavily favored the left side of his body, and his armor looked crimson because of the amount of blood on its surface.

"Assistant General, what's going on?"

"The enemy is returning to the palace," Marcus explained. "We thought about pursuing, but we're worn and need to tend to the injured. They also placed a shield around the front, which I planned on inspecting to see if it would even allow us through."

General Casner peered north to stare at the remaining troops. "That was a smart call. We wouldn't have lasted much longer if they didn't retreat; however, we might be dealing with another issue. Let's see what that shield is all about and confront our intruder."

Marcus remained at the general's side as they closed the distance between their location and the latest spell. More than anything, he wished to speak with the friend he hadn't seen in weeks.

Unfortunately, a proper reunion would need to wait. He noticed how Coura paced along the shield without giving anything or anyone her attention. No enemy troops remained on their side, yet she seemed determined to give chase. As they neared, she slowed to a stop before facing Marcus and General Casner. Even at a distance, her furious expression wiped away any hope for a casual greeting.

"General, perhaps we should focus on returning everyone to camp," Marcus suggested and halted.

At the same time, Coura stormed forward to address them. "Does anyone want to tell me what's going on?" she practically demanded. The volume of her voice didn't raise to a full shout, but it held plenty of repressed frustration.

Either General Casner couldn't hear that or he didn't care. "What are you doing here?" he asked in an unfriendly manner.

When Coura narrowed her eyes, Marcus' stomach dropped. Based on what he knew about her, she wouldn't be the first to back down from an argument, so he decided a challenge between the two would do nothing to help their current situation.

"We don't have time to explain now," he interjected before Coura could reply. He even went so far as to extend his left arm between them to physically break up the foreseen conflict. "Everyone's exhausted, it's getting dark, and we still need to tend to the wounded and dead."

He prayed the general would remain silent while he met her eyes to project his plea. Although her intimidating stare seethed with vexation, she turned away and crossed her arms instead of continuing the verbal bout.

"Fine," she snapped. "Go take care of them. I'll be waiting here when you can talk." With that, she spun around to return to the glass-like wall looming over the field.

General Casner took his leave as well without a word, allowing Marcus a moment of reprieve before he moved to begin retrieving the limp bodies littering the area. At that point, it became a routine before the troops settled down for the evening.

Whenever he returned to that spot for another person, both the shield and his friend remained. Coura started pacing again, though with less vigor, and he wondered when he would be able to speak with her. Calin found him later when no one remained, and they led a scouting party to double check the area.

Once that was complete, Marcus stared up at the cloudy sky, which threatened rain or snow, then he held his torch a bit higher. "We'll meet you back at camp," he told his fellow assistant general without attempting to hide his weariness.

Calin nodded and called to the others around them as Marcus walked toward the palace. Part of the reason why he didn't look forward to returning was that General Casner usually held an impromptu meeting at night to organize the troops before morning. This evening would be no different, except Marcus planned to bring Coura along. If he couldn't calm her down before they saw the general, the two would keep everyone else up, and he didn't believe arguing would benefit anyone.

***

When a single ball of flame parted from the half a dozen remaining on the battlefield, Coura knew Marcus was on his way over. It hadn't escaped her notice how everyone exhausted themselves just to stay alive, and that made her blood boil.

If I didn't leave Emilea's home when I did, this might've ended differently. If I hadn't been lied to by the Yeluthians, this problem could already have been resolved. Now, Soirée's keeping me away to draw the fighting out. I can't see how she finds entertainment in this.

She inhaled through her nose in an attempt to calm down, but the iron scent of blood filled the air; the smell lingered in her nostrils and the back of her mouth to add to her frustration.

"Do you want to stay here or head back?" Marcus called as he approached.

Coura avoided wincing at his harsh voice, which sounded sore from days of use at a raised volume. She truly pitied all of the soldiers strung into Hendal's plans. Unfortunately, expressing her sympathy would have to wait.

"That depends on if you can stand without falling over," she answered. The thought of being gawked at by everyone, including her friends and parents, would only continue to sour her mood, yet she left the decision up to him.

Marcus stopped, gestured for her to follow, then turned around to move toward the camp. "I know you'd rather hear this as soon as possible, but I'm so tired that if I stand out here, I won't be able to walk on my own. Besides, you should be around when General Casner and General Tio discuss our next course of action."

Hernan used to refer to me as, "a tool and nothing more." I guess he was right after all...

In the meantime, her friend explained what took place during her absence. Hearing about Byron's attempt to corner Hendal didn't surprise her, yet their plan's failure did, resulting in the group's separation. Still, her former mentor remained sharp enough to outsmart Hendal by sending letters to Dala in advance, leading to the southern troop's arrival. The rest of what Marcus said contributed to the rebellion led by General Tio. The other general arrived with reinforcements from Verona, the Sie-Kie, and all over the west, and the Yeluthians joined to combat the rogue angels and mages.

"There's not much more than that," he concluded as the pair passed the first line of guards patrolling the area. They appeared pathetic as they leaned on their spears for support, and Coura doubted they could hold back any creature larger than a wild dog.

"What about the enemy troops?" she asked after.

"As I'm sure you've noticed, the Nim-Valan soldiers are under Hendal's control and heal from our attacks. That's partly why I'd like you here. Emilea mentioned wanting to discuss that ability with you."

Coura said nothing since she refused to acknowledge what similarities she had to Soirée's mindless servants. They could see the bonfire ahead surrounded by half a dozen people anyway.

Marcus went straight to an open spot and started to strip his armor. She stood behind, too anxious to sit beside him.

The energies in her center began reacting to the environment again, tearing her in half. The dominating part belonging to Soirée made her feel intoxicated by the demon's lingering power, and she desired nothing more than to return to the gleeful slaughtering of enemy soldiers. The Yeluthian side grew repulsed by this and found comfort in being around other people, particularly those she recognized. The imbalance twisted her insides, reminding her she hadn't eaten for days.

Next to Marcus sat Calin, then the presumptuous man from earlier referred to as General Casner. Tio was nowhere to be seen. Emilea also occupied a spot on the ground with her legs stretched out in front of her, and King Arval remained standing across the flames. Behind him, her father and a similarly aged Yeluthian hovered to guard their ruler.

She avoided eye contact with everyone by opting to stare into the fire instead.

"Let's get started," the Dalan's assistant general began with more strength in his voice than she would've given him credit for. "Hendal's troops pulled back and are protected by his mages' shielding spell. They're-"

"That spell is from the demon named Soirée," Coura heard herself correct with a glance down at Calin. "From what I can sense, their mages are probably as weak as yours."

"Really?" he asked yet with shock rather than skepticism.

After a pause for the Yeluthian king to confirm this, the assistant general continued.

"I see. Then perhaps something else is going on, and he needed to call upon its magic. In any case, without Coura's arrival or that shield, they would have pushed us farther."

"We must organize a retreat order for those in the camp," Casner added. "If that happens again, our troops need to know when to flee."

Coura glanced at the palace as she listened to the group discuss the topic. Tentatively, she reached out for Soirée using their shared connection; however, she felt no response.

It seems strange she would interrupt Hendal's expected victory just because I arrived. Then again, I bet she doesn't care too much about him so long as she gets what she wants. Why is she hiding when she's dangerous enough to impact this fight?

Next, she focused on the shield's energy. The structure appeared to protect the palace from a direct attack yet didn't stretch to cover any other side except the south. What startled Coura the most happened to be its increased durability.

The power going into the shield is balanced, like an undisturbed puddle of water. If there's a change, it can be easily detected as a ripple in the steady amount. It takes immense control to manage that, but why? What's the purpose? Unless the spell is meant to be up for a while...

From a dark corner of her mind, she sensed the demon listening and turned her attention to the group when nothing else could be gained from her inspection.

"How many did we lose?" Marcus inquired with a frown.

Calin winced before answering. "It's too early to tell, but I would guess at least three hundred troops."

"Twice as many are being treated, and more need to recover," Emilea shared. "Our greatest enemy right now is time. The injured need to heal, we mages need sleep, and the foot soldiers need rest from the combat."

"It seems they just gave you the opportunity," Coura said in the resulting silence.

Emilea met her eyes for the first time that evening while everyone else looked her way. "What do you mean?"

Coura jerked her chin over her shoulder to gesture at the shield. "Even a beginner mage should be able to sense the amount of energy in their spell. Why would they use that much power just to keep it up for less than a day?"

"Could it be an intimidation tactic?" Marcus suggested.

To her surprise, King Arval supported her assumption before she could reply. "No, she is right. For a magic user, at least one of our people, spells do not drain more energy than the wielder puts into it."

"It's the same for humans' light magic," Emilea confirmed with a nod. "It should be a similar principle for spells using dark energy."

Coura intended to say more when Casner scoffed to draw her attention.

"Of course *you* would say that," he began, directing the words at her. "Lure us into a false sense of security by claiming the demon is sealing them up. Why would we let down our guard like that?" His following glare was nothing short of saying, "I don't like or trust you."

She fully expected a confrontation with at least one person that evening, especially since she had been declared an enemy to the kingdom when she last stayed in Verona. Even with that in mind, though, she disliked the general from the moment he addressed her in the field. "Based on the situation, you should consider yourselves lucky and use whatever time is available to be productive instead of point fingers," she replied while returning his glare.

"What if they do catch us off our guard?" he retorted while leaning forward. "What if they notice movement and decide to sweep through while we recover? I think the shield is working for their benefit so we can't try to sneak inside."

"Believe me, that spell wasn't cast to stop your troops."

The lack of a response from anyone let her know the others understood that fact as well.

After the pause, Marcus cleared his throat to move the conversation along. "In any case, it's keeping our side apart for the time being. It might be best to place several scouts nearby to patrol in case the enemy changes their strategy."

"I agree," the general added without any of his spite from earlier. "We'll keep watch for movement. If the mages are able to notice a shift in power too, we can only act to recover, organize our defenses, and discuss a plan to get inside the palace in the time we've been given."

"Allow my soldiers to guard," King Arval interjected. "Those among us are more sensitive to demonic energy and will confirm more or less activity. Most of us can still fight if necessary as well."

The general nodded. "All right then. I'll leave the surveying to your people."

The rest of the conversation revolved around an escape plan mainly for the weak and wounded should Hendal remove the shield and send his troops across the field. Coura didn't add any additional input, and she crossed her arms to keep her hands from twitching while she listened. She knew Soirée's barrier would only come down when the demon willed it to, not Hendal. Of course, it would be a waste of time to try and convince everyone.

The meeting lasted until well past midnight, which seemed unfortunate since those present appeared ready to pass out from exhaustion. When no one brought up more to discuss, the general dismissed the group. Calin helped the man to his feet while Evern did the same for Emilea, who smiled and apologized for her lack of physical energy. Meanwhile, Marcus went to Coura before anyone else left and gestured for her to follow him.

"You can stay with the rest of us," he said in a weary manner. "They should all be asleep now, so they won't be bothering you until morning."

She wasn't certain who he referred to, yet she turned down the offer anyway. "I'm going back to watch the palace for the time being."

"Why? Don't you trust the Yeluthian scouts?" he asked as they slowed to a stop. Based on his half-hearted attempt to question her intentions, Coura got the impression he figured she would go off on her own once they separated.

THE ANGEL'S DESCENT

"An extra magic user could help detect a change in the shield's energy. Besides, I might be able to sense more beyond the spell." She avoided going into detail, which proved to be enough for Marcus.

His expression softened when he dipped his chin. "Fine. I'll send someone to bring you food when the sun's up."

Her friend continued alone without so much as a wave over his shoulder. Although that bothered Coura, she made her way to the northernmost point of the camp instead of reaching out.

When was the last time I saw Marcus? she wondered while wandering into the open and claiming the top of a slight hill as her scouting spot. *I can't even remember when we talked or the look on his face before this mess. I haven't seen Will either, or Marcy, Grace, and Clearshot.*

Her heart ached at the reminder of Byron and Aaron. Not only were her friends in danger, both under Hendal's control and with the Dalan troops, but now her parents became involved. They left Asteom to have peaceful lives, yet she dragged them and their people into the heat of a civil war.

Coura sighed and tried to stand as still as she could. Despite the chaos that took place in the area mere hours ago, a strange stillness preserved the land. It felt pleasant, and she enjoyed the cool breeze passing by. As the night stretched into the first minutes of dawn, she considered if something as vicious as a battle between humans, angels, and a demon would continue to result in a similar peacefulness.

11

Sleep did not take Coura while she stood guard. There were moments when she closed her eyes and meditated to relax her muscles, but all the while she remained conscious of the energy around her.

The Yeluthian scouts stayed at the edge of the camp, or she assumed so when she didn't spot anybody beyond the hill. In her mind, as long as Casner and whoever else acted suspicious of her knew others watched the palace, they wouldn't bother her. On the other hand, someone would seek her out eventually.

She continued to observe the unwavering shield blurring the figures on the opposite side until mid-morning. An overcast hid the sun and chilled the earth, but the lack of wind made their conditions a bit more comfortable.

Her thoughts wound up on the Harvest Festival since it usually took place around that time of the year when the sound of footsteps approached from behind. Coura glanced over her shoulder from where she sat cross-legged in a cleaner part of the grass to see Grace, wide-eyed and holding two, wooden bowls of steaming food.

It had been months since the two were together in a friendly setting. She remembered the Yeluthian ambassador crumpled on the ground after being held in captivity by the high priest; the infuriating memory made her want to strangle the man. Grace's weeping played over in Coura's mind to remind her of the cries for help she couldn't provide.

THE ANGEL'S DESCENT

When Grace set the bowls down to hurry over, Coura felt obliged to stand and face her friend; however, instead of showing pain or remorse, the Yeluthian appeared relieved and laughed as she wrapped her arms around Coura's waist.

"I am so glad to see you!" she exclaimed after a moment.

Before Coura could respond, her friend broke off the embrace to retrieve the bowls and hand one to her. Then, they dropped down into the grass to converse.

"How are you?" she began while attempting to hide her concern. Grace's chipper attitude wasn't necessarily unwanted, but it startled her, given the circumstances.

Nonetheless, the Yeluthian ambassador straightened and tilted the bowl upward to slurp the oat-filled porridge before answering. Meanwhile, Coura held hers with both hands to savor its warmth.

"When I heard you arrived, I could only recall the night you helped me escape from Hendal and the demon," Grace replied. "I was afraid and lonely, even after my rescue. Emilea explained what happened to you, and I felt better."

"That's good." Coura stared down at her meal, unable to think of what would be best to say. When she looked up again, she noticed Grace eyeing her bowl and held it out to her friend.

"Are you not hungry?"

"Someone brought me food earlier," Coura lied. The last thing she needed was to be scolded for not eating.

Grace accepted the offer and emptied the bowl before leaning back on her hands with a content sigh. After, they talked about the past few weeks. Coura became reluctant to describe her time in Yeluthia because that new part of her life still needed time to settle in her mind. Her friend caught on to her avoidance and didn't ask specific questions relating to her lineage. By the time they concluded their discussion, dusk crept upon the field.

"I always forget how soon the evening approaches near wintertime," Coura commented with a glance at the gray clouds, leading her to wonder if it would snow within the next few hours.

When Grace didn't answer, she lowered her gaze to see the Yeluthian ambassador pointedly inspecting the grass with a frown.

"I must apologize," her friend began after a moment. "I did not know about your family or bother to ask, and I was not aware of Commander Evern's family name either. You would not have had to worry, but I..." Her voice trailed off into mumbles.

Coura had shoved any thoughts about her parents into the back of her mind where they would stay for a while. Still, the reminder hurt, but that was her burden to bear, not Grace's. She made that clear when the full-blooded Yeluthian stopped speaking.

"Trust me when I say there were many opportunities for my life to change depending on what I said or did. You had no reason to know my last name, so don't blame yourself. Besides, I've been able to speak with my mother and father already. Nothing else needs to be addressed until we finish this fight."

Her friend's sorrow shifted into a mixture of resolution and pity, but she thanked Coura afterward. Another, familiar voice from behind prevented them from beginning a new discussion.

"I thought I would find you here."

Both she and Grace turned at the sound as Clearshot waved his right hand at them. His left arm rested in a sling, and his forearms had been bandaged.

"It's time for dinner and another meeting," he shared.

The Yeluthian ambassador hopped to her feet at the mention of their next meal and grabbed the empty bowls. Although she felt less enthusiastic about returning to camp, Coura stood and walked over. She fully expected Clearshot to spark up a conversation and mentally prepared for the questions, yet he made no attempt to do so. Instead, the soldier asked Grace if she intended to join the gathering.

"I have been away from Aimes and the medical station for a while," she responded with a bashful smile.

"Go on then. Make sure the man isn't running himself into the ground," Clearshot added before Grace took her leave of them.

He led Coura across the campsite, which looked reasonably more active than the previous night. With the majority of people awake, more eyes wandered to stare at the newcomer possessing demonic power and unnatural markings. The energy couldn't be helped, but she had been in a rush to leave Yeluthia and forgot to grab wrappings for her arms. The original bandages burned off, along with the skin underneath, when she arrived and unleashed several, elemental spells.

I've got more to worry about than my appearance, Coura thought as they merged into the group huddled around the centermost bonfire.

Calin and Casner occupied one side and chatted with another man she didn't recognize. To her amazement, Barnelus knelt behind to listen in on their conversation. The Sie-Kie warrior wore leather protection for his chest, arms, and legs and only briefly glanced at her without recognition. King Arval sat off to her left with her father and the other two commanders on each side. Lastly, Emilea and Marcus stood together, and the former waved her husband over.

"What about General Tio?" Clearshot asked without attempting to lower his voice.

The master mage shook her head. "I ordered him to rest for the time being."

The three took seats nearer to the Yeluthians, leaving a lone spot open next to Calin, who shot her a sympathetic smile. A pair of strangers passed out bowls of the same mixture for dinner, and she again kept hers in her hands to savor the heat. When everyone began to finish eating, Casner started the meeting.

***

Calin took up speaking first in order to recap the day's activities within the camp. Marcus had been with his fellow assistant general as they inspected the supplies, sought updates from Emilea at the medical station, and directed a team to gather and ration their food and water. Every person present received an assigned duty while the soldiers had the luxury of a free day.

In the meantime, General Casner met with General Tio, who was recovering from a stray lightning bolt to the chest, and the pair organized a retreat plan for the site. When he first heard about the general's injury three days ago, Marcus expected news of his superior's death at any moment; however, Emilea reported their leader would live if the man didn't push himself. They thought Calin would faint with relief as General Tio's second in command, yet the assistant general chuckled before mentioning the experience would be all he'd hear about for months.

Clearshot, at his wife's request, gathered help for the medical staff tending to the wounded, which included the Sie-Kie men and citizens of Verona still at the camp that morning. The Yeluthians tended to their own first before moving to work on the human soldiers while also patrolling the palace from above. Coura also kept watch throughout the day; Marcus trusted her senses, even though some others, like General Casner, did not.

The initial reports took up the first hour, starting with Calin, then Emilea, Clearshot, the oldest of the Yeluthian commanders named Isan, and ending with General Casner. Overall, the news sounded positive. There remained no sign of a potential attack from the opposite end of the field and no changes to the shielding spell. The supplies had been counted and rationed, water and foraged food items were being collected from the woods, and the wounded seemed taken care of. Letting everyone continue to recover became all that was left to do.

"Now that we're settled, it's time to hatch a plan for when their shield goes down," the general concluded and folded his arms before scanning over those sitting around the fire.

Marcus liked how General Casner thought. The man acted practical and had a forward approach to problems. Unlike General Tio, who wasn't afraid of showing his emotions, Casner typically stayed in the background until the conversation needed his input. Marcus didn't get the opportunity to work with him until the current conflict, though.

"What we need is a different strategy than earlier," Clearshot began. "If we continue fighting like the Nim-Valans are normal troops, we're going to find ourselves right back where we started."

"He's right," Marcus added. "We intended to go after Hendal, but their soldiers' healing power is too much. The rogue angels also prevent the Yeluthians from using an approach from the air. I believe we have all of the allies we're going to get, so we should plot out the best option with what we possess."

He made sure to meet everyone's eyes to emphasize the notion before finding himself looking to Coura. The others followed suit until she noticed and pulled her head back, as if offended.

"Why are you staring at *me*?" she snapped.

"You know the demon," General Casner answered, though he seemed to be accusing her of it more than stating a fact. "What can you tell us about its plan?"

She frowned and offered a sarcastic retort. "That's right! Did I forget to mention how she shared all of the details with me? Then, we had tea and cake with the nobility in the dining hall."

Marcus winced, fully expecting the backlash of the general's words, and heard the man grumble a curse.

Coura waved a hand in front of her face to dismiss the concept before clarifying her connection with the creature. "I can sense her energy better than any mage here, but I can't tell what she's thinking or what they're doing inside the palace."

"Take it easy," Emilea cautioned. "We're just looking for suggestions."

"You want a suggestion? How about we focus on weakening her power without needing to confront her or Hendal yet."

Even if she meant it out of spite, Marcus got an idea. "If we can figure out how to take apart Hendal's strongest pawns, then we may hinder his control over the troops."

Unfortunately, General Casner wasn't ready to dismiss the previous subject. "How is it you aren't being controlled like the rest of them?" he demanded while turning to Coura.

She pinched the bridge of her nose in irritation. "All you need to know is that I can sense what she does and that's it. I'm not about to explain my whole life story, especially not to you. I have my dark magic, and I'm on your side."

"I don't care whose side you're on! I'm trying to protect my troops by making sure you don't snitch on us to your friends across the clearing."

"They are *not* my friends! You don't-"

"Please, that's enough," Emilea interrupted and raised a hand, catching everyone's attention. "Each person here is trustworthy. I will vouch for it."

Her eyes moved between General Casner and Coura until the latter crossed her arms with a displeased huff. Marcus still wasn't certain the situation wouldn't heat up again until he heard the Yeluthian king speak.

He always thought Aaron's father had been the perfect image of royalty given his projection of strength and merciful personality toward his people. The former king's presence practically demanded all eyes and ears, and unlike Aaron, King Hernan acted completely confident in his words and actions. When Marcus first saw King Arval, the lead angel reminded him of those qualities, in addition to many others. The Yeluthian's motions looked smooth and gentle, though he proved to be a tough combatant on the battlefield, and an intimidating intellect matched the king's keen eye.

"The ancient magic of our people kept the demon race at bay long ago. Perhaps there is a way to seal the creature or exorcise it from your people," he suggested with a glance at the older commander to his left.

While they contemplated this, Emilea gasped and turned toward Clearshot. "The ancestral weapons!"

"That's right," Coura added and raised her eyes. "Cintra told me about a golden weapon in the palace after I left Verona."

"What good will that do us?" General Casner responded with a frown.

"If we can get someone in there to retrieve it, at least we'll have some advantage," Clearshot commented.

The general didn't appear swayed by the idea. "Suppose we do get inside. Do we know where it is? What if there are more guards? Besides, who is this person you mentioned anyway?"

Marcus expected Coura to start yelling again. Instead, she surprised him with a softened expression. "She's a close friend of Byron's. He wrote to her because she has an ability to see visions of the future. Not clear ones, but enough to give her an idea. She mentioned the golden weapon, so I would imagine that part is true."

"I'm afraid I agree with General Casner," Calin added. "It's too risky to send a group inside with so little information."

Marcus found himself watching the Yeluthian king while Clearshot, Emilea, and General Casner discussed the possible location of the object in question.

He seems like he's waiting for us to realize something. Perhaps he wants to chime in but knows it's not necessarily his people's battle. What he, or any Yeluthian, says and does without permission may be taken out of context or hinder their relationship with Asteom. It seemed ridiculous to him that such political notions remained at play even on the verge of their defeat; however, if another kingdom meddled with the state of affairs during such an important moment, it would ultimately hurt the countries' alliance.

With the proposed reasoning in mind, Marcus cleared his throat when the conversation ended. "Your Highness," he began while addressing King Arval, "is there any information regarding the ancestral weapons or your people's magic that could help stop the demon from controlling the Nim-Valan soldiers?"

He thought he caught a glimmer in the king's eye as a brief expression of gratitude before the angels' leader answered. "If the weapons you speak of are truly able to seal away a demon, I believe there may be a way to remove its presence from those under its influence."

Everyone except the Yeluthians murmured their disbelief before the king nodded to the older commander on his left, who picked up the explanation.

"The weapons gifted to Asteom's royal family had a sealing spell engraved on them. It sounds as if you are familiar enough to know this, but the spell itself can be used without the need for a medium, or a physical item."

"That would be useless, though," Emilea interjected. "Once a spell is cast, it would need the user's constant attention in order to maintain its shape. A dark mage can pour more into it, but light magic requires manipulation after casting. If the sealing spell were to be used, it would break once that source of energy runs out."

The Yeluthian commander nodded, as if he expected her to describe the process. "This is correct. If the sealing spell is focused on one possessed by demonic energy, it would merely keep that power within its host."

Marcus followed the master mage's gaze over to Coura, who hugged her legs and stared at a point across the fire. *Emilea and Byron told us about that in Dala. If the dagger one of Hendal's angels struck her with in the Valley Beyond wasn't removed, the demon would have been sealed away.*

"We ran into that problem in Dala," he felt compelled to say before sharing the demon's power would be released once the weapon is extracted. He made sure not to go into detail, or mention Coura had been the one directly involved.

The Yeluthian commander rubbed his chin thoughtfully. "I have never had the displeasure of using the spell on a demon, so this is new to me. Since that is the case, it would be useless to try a normal sealing spell. I do have another idea I think can help." He closed his eyes for a minute, leaving everyone to wonder what he could be planning.

Marcus stifled a yawn and caught Clearshot's wandering gaze. The man shook his head and rolled his eyes, making Marcus smile. After all, they were soldiers, not mages.

At long last, the commander grunted in confirmation with a nod to seemingly confirm his aforementioned idea, then he opened his eyes. "The answer we seek lies with a combination of spells."

"A...what?" Emilea asked without hiding her confusion.

In response, the Yeluthian's lips curved upward into a slight smile. "We were on the right track with a sealing spell because it contains energy, but the downside is it does not extract or do anything with it. Tell me, what is normally cast to purge a demonic possession?"

"I always relied on a sealing prism to limit the power's movement before trying a healing spell. Unfortunately, the person usually doesn't survive. If they do, their mind is lost."

"It is a start. My suggestion is to use the sealing prism first, as you mentioned, then an extraction spell, and finally what is known as goddess fire to purge the demonic energy. The only problem is a mage can rarely cast more than one spell at a time since it requires dual focus. Performing three at once is impossible."

"Impossible for a *single* mage," the younger commander next to the first started with a hint of eagerness.

"Even so, each spell requires all of the wielder's magic," the older Yeluthian commented before turning back to Emilea. "Most of our soldiers and yours have exhausted themselves. That does not even include those working to heal the injured. This is the route most likely to stop the man controlling the enemy troops, but it will require preparation and cost all of a person's energy. Also, I would advise against trying this on the demon immediately. It is meant to counter possession, not eliminate the creature altogether."

There it was, their solution to stopping Hendal. Marcus wanted to accept yet held his tongue. It seemed obvious Emilea would be the only non-Yeluthian involved. Even with others to guard her, she would need to infiltrate the palace and face the man who threatened her family. It would be her decision.

The master mage stared into the dying flames with an unreadable expression.

"Would you like the evening to consider?" Clearshot asked his wife. Marcus had a feeling if Emilea accepted, her husband would insist on going as well.

"No," she replied before releasing a sigh. "If this is the best option, we must try it. I still need to practice the spells with a Yeluthian mage in order to make sure it'll work and build up my reserves in the time that's left."

King Arval nodded. "Commander Detrix will accompany you and your chosen guards."

The younger-looking Yeluthian placed two fingers on his left brow in a sort of salute. If he had any quarrels with the assignment, it didn't show in his expression or body language.

"Lady Emilea, please report who will accompany you at our next meeting," General Casner said to conclude the topic. "Our immediate issues are solved for tonight. Unless there's any change in the shield, I think we should recover our minds and bodies. Tomorrow morning we can focus on a specific plan for her and Commander Detrix to get inside the palace."

Marcus heartily agreed to calling it an early night after the progress they made. He was one of the first to stand and stretch his tight back and leg muscles and the first to leave that area after wishing Calin a restful evening. Emilea and Clearshot wouldn't be far behind, but he remembered Coura and stopped.

I forgot she hasn't been over by our fire. Hopefully she didn't wander off so I can still catch her.

By the time Marcus neared the meeting spot, he heard his friend and slowed his steps. A moment later, he contemplated leaving as both Coura's voice and an unrecognizable man's sounded like an argument, but he waited until the sound of footsteps came his way.

***

Throughout that evening's discussion, Coura forced herself to remain neutral, especially when it came down to sending Emilea with the Yeluthian commander. The strategy of attacking Hendal with light magic would be risky, but the payoff more than made up for that. They also had to figure out a way to stop Soirée while avoiding Aaron, Byron, and the Nim-Valans until their minds could be freed. Worst of all, she felt the demon's presence. It took all of her concentration just to avoid thinking in case Soirée could hear her thoughts. The last thing she needed was to confirm the general's suspicion that she acted for those in the palace.

To her relief, the fragment of Soirée disappeared just as the Yeluthian brought up the idea of using multiple spells to stop Hendal. It sounded like an interesting idea, though Coura wasn't familiar with that type of magic.

It would be better to leave this to Emilea, she concluded once the matter seemed settled.

Emilea and Clearshot went to the commander named Detrix, Marcus, Barnelus, and the other man with him all disappeared into the camp, and Calin helped Casner to his feet. She had no intention of staying around and managed to take a few steps into the surrounding shadows before someone caught her arm. Even without glancing behind, she knew only a handful of people would want to talk to her, and only one possessed the skill to slip up silently.

"Your mother and I need to speak with you," Evern began at a low volume while keeping his grip.

Out of everyone in the camp, Coura wanted to avoid her parents the most, both because of their protective nature and the fact that she still had not made up her mind on how to address them. She glared at him in an attempt to convey the repressed anger directed at them.

"I have nothing to say to you," she responded with a hint of impatience. Evern kept his hold on her when she half-heartedly tried to tug herself free.

"What are you doing here?" he countered sharply. "Paulina and I left because we intended to help Asteom without endangering you. Not only that, but look at yourself."

It took Coura a second to realize he referred to the previously covered markings. This time, when she pulled her arm away, Evern let her go.

"I know how I look," she retorted. "Asteom is my home. My friends are here and trapped inside the palace. Did you really believe I wouldn't return to fight?"

"I do not think you understand what you being here means. We might not know your whole story with that demon, but it is clear it still holds some influence over you. From my view as your father, you should want to stay away until we take care of this. I would like you to at least be grateful for my consideration."

Coura couldn't stop herself from letting out a dry laugh. "Nothing makes me more willing to forgive you than to be abandoned again.

Her words visibly struck Evern, yet the dam had been severed enough that she continued without pausing for his reply.

"You had no reason to lie to me, especially since we were together for only a brief amount of time. Asteom is my home, not Yeluthia. These people became my family when you weren't there. I can't just turn my back on them."

Coura's lungs burned, leading her to end her rant there. The two were not shouting at one another, yet the strain of lowering their voices felt worse than screaming.

Evern's scowl deepened. "Our family is a much smaller part of this situation," he went on at a slower pace, as if every word became an added weight on his shoulders. "I promise to make it up to you, but that is not important now. People's lives are on the line, and having you here is a risk Yeluthia was not willing to take. Now that I have seen you fight and the way you behave, I could never imagine you controlling yourself around a creature that feeds off negative emotions. *That* is why your mother and I decided not to tell you about leaving. It was never fully because you are our daughter but because you are a danger to yourself and everyone in this camp."

The following pause left Coura feeling cold inside. Her jaw grew tight enough to ache as she kept her whole body still. Never in her entire life had she been lectured so sternly. Not even Byron had been that honest; he usually said just enough for her to learn a lesson on her own and feel guilty for her behavior later.

Evern's gaze remained unwavering.

Is he waiting for me to agree to leave with my head bowed? Coura wondered while sinking into her bitterness. *Unless he has something else in mind to keep me from interfering...*

She inhaled through her nostrils and exhaled in a stretched out sigh. "I'm here now, and I will continue to assist for as long as I can, whether you like it or not. In my eyes, you're a Yeluthian commander until this is taken care of, not someone I should prove myself to. Until then, I won't be waiting around for an apology."

Coura didn't give Evern a chance to respond. Instead, she turned around and began walking away. In her mind, she expected him to pursue her; a part of her wanted him to. Yet when she glanced behind, there was nobody there.

As she went on in that direction, Coura replayed the conversation over in her head. She thought some words had been too brutal, then others didn't sound meaningful enough, and she changed her mind again and again. The whole night gave her a headache.

A minute later, she realized someone had been calling her name. As soon as she stopped, the source appeared at her side. "Marcus?"

"Do you know where you're going?" he asked with a bit of surprise.

"No," she admitted and glanced around. Every fire and tent looked the same to her whenever she wandered inside the camp.

He chuckled before leading her forward. "You were heading straight to our spot."

"*Our* spot?" Coura gazed ahead while accepting the direction. Wherever they were going would provide a distraction from her feelings toward her parents and the Yeluthians.

"It's where I stay with Clearshot, Emilea, Aimes, Grace, Marcy, and Will. Calin comes over occasionally, but now he's usually guarding General Tio at the medical station. They're excited to see you."

At the thought of facing the group, Coura's feet slowed to a halt. It took Marcus a few seconds to realize she wasn't following.

"What's wrong? Are you not feeling well?"

"I should go back to guarding the shield." Inside, she dreaded being bombarded with their questions and emotions.

Marcy will hang on me just like Grace did. Will is the one I'm worried about interrogating me, and probably Clearshot and Aimes too. Emilea would do both. I shouldn't remind them I'm here, especially since I'll have to face Soirée and...I might...

"Here."

Marcus startled her by offering his hand, which she stared at without comprehension.

"Everyone's worried," he added a bit sympathetically. "It'll only grow worse until you show them you're still you."

She wanted to reject the offer but figured it didn't matter. What she told her father about Asteom being her home wasn't something she needed to hide or deny; the same proved true for his words.

"They're going to be pestering me," Coura added.

"All the better to get it over with right away." He shook the open hand after until she accepted the gesture.

*

As expected, the group felt the need to greet her with hugs and pats on the back before they sat around the dwindling bonfire to fling question after question her way. They mostly wondering about her previous injuries, journey to Yeluthia, and what the angels and their home were like. Then, they asked about the meetings, King Arval, and his commanders. She did her best to answer each one until her patience ran out.

"Why don't you ask Marcus any of this?" she demanded and pointed a finger at where the assistant general sat across the embers.

Everyone either looked his way or down at their hands.

"We try not to bother him or the other leaders in the camp," Aimes answered with a weak smile. "They're the ones who're up all day and night making sure the rest of us stay together."

Although she appreciated their consideration, Coura felt they had been drawing out the evening. "There really isn't that much to tell," she admitted while stretching her arms upward. "I just arrived yesterday. You should be telling me what you've been up to. Actually, let's leave it in the past."

"I agree," Clearshot commented before yawning. "It's late, and we're supposed to be recovering our strength."

"Do you need a blanket?" Grace asked from where she sat near a supply tent.

Coura shook her head and moved to her feet, to her friends' curious or disapproving stares. "Thank you, but I should head back to the front lines to keep watch."

"You aren't under orders," Emilea added.

Marcus sat up straighter and waved a hand at the spot she had occupied. "How about I order you to stay here and rest until morning. The Yeluthian scouts are on duty anyway."

She shrugged. "Sorry, but I don't trust them to sense the slight changes that could happen if Hendal decides to send a spy or assassin across the field."

"Would he really do that?" Marcy asked Marcus, who nodded.

"I wouldn't put it past him to try."

Will addressed Coura next. "Can't you sense the shield from here?"

She rubbed the back of her neck and contemplated a lie about the distance between the camp and spell. To her dismay, Emilea called her bluff before she got a word out.

"If I could yesterday when I was nearly drained, she should have no problem. Sit down and relax. If something does happen tomorrow, you're going to need your strength."

Reluctantly, Coura obeyed. Grace brought her two blankets, and one by one everyone else drifted off to sleep. She debated rising to return to the clearing yet thought against it.

Marcus was right; we need each other to stay sane. If being here helps them to feel at ease, then I can manage. Besides, I'm much warmer, and I can still sense the demonic energy.

For a while, she cleared her mind in order to listen to the gentle humming emanating from the shield. Perhaps it was her connection with Soirée, but Coura couldn't feel anything uncomfortable or malicious coming from the demon's spell. She became tempted to let sleep take her because of this, for it would if she stopped trying to stay awake.

When was the last time I could truly rest? In Yeluthia, I didn't even know this conflict was taking place. Now, look where I am. I doubt their people will continue to be welcoming after hearing about me from Evern and their soldiers.

Her mind went to the palace next, including the soldiers, servants, Aaron, and Byron. She wondered what would happen if the Yeluthian commander and Emilea failed to stop Hendal, which spurred the worst scenarios. At last, she decided sleep would be better than contemplating the possible outcomes.

12

"I see someone finally learned to listen to us," Clearshot commented with a snicker as he handed Marcus a bowl of their breakfast before taking a seat around the fire.

"Thank goodness for that," Marcus muttered and tipped back the wooden dish to slurp down his meal before it grew warm and soggy.

That morning proved to be the coldest since they joined the Dalan soldiers. The two kept blankets around their shoulders, yet every once in a while, an unforgiving wind cut through to remind them of the approaching winter.

"I couldn't imagine being in the open field. I'd freeze to death," his comrade added in between a mouthful of food.

Marcus followed Clearshot's gaze to where Coura lied on the ground in a warm-looking bundle. Everyone else was already up and gone on their own business, but he woke a few minutes ago to an empty stomach and found it to be late morning. Clearshot had been tending to the fire and offered to grab them breakfast.

"I bet she'll sleep all day," he thought aloud.

"Have you seen her?" his fellow soldier commented while showing some disgust. "Grace mentioned she gave up yesterday's lunch, and I didn't see her eat dinner. Emilea's really worried, though mentioning it would only bother her."

With the blankets wrapped around her body, Coura stayed hidden except for wisps of her black hair, though the middle part raised and lowered slightly because of her deep breathing. Considering he had only seen her during the evenings, Marcus could only imagine how exhausted she would appear in the daylight.

"At least we know her heart is in the right place," Clearshot mumbled before taking the empty bowls away while keeping a blanket on his shoulders, like a cloak. "I volunteered for a shift supervising at the front this afternoon, so don't wait up for me."

Marcus waved a hand as the man walked away, then he covered a yawn. *I wonder how Calin would feel about me napping until someone fetches me for the meeting*, he thought with a tired smile. The day would be a repeat of the previous one with the other assistant general until dinner; at least, as long as there remained no hint of an attack from the palace.

His eyes drifted down to the mass of blankets covering his friend, reminding him of her lack of knowledge about the camp. Without any assigned responsibilities, he figured she wouldn't be familiar with its layout and contemplated waiting for her to wake up before deciding what to do.

How long should I let her sleep? I could always return to check on her after another hour or two. Either that, or I can let her wander on her own until General Casner sends for us. Marcus doubted the general would want Coura present because of his impression of her. That was why he chose to bring her there two nights ago and show them her mentality.

I used to get upset when she went off on her own or avoided the normal life of an Asteom soldier. I don't remember when I realized that's simply how she is. If anyone tries to hold her back, she works harder to prove herself and protect the people she cares about. I suppose not every person is meant to fit into an organized line. Actually, Byron's like that too. I care about my position too much to act so recklessly.

Coura rolled over to reveal her face, which remained set in the peaceful expression of someone comfortably asleep. When she didn't stir, Marcus continued to watch her until he realized he'd begun staring. Memories of his own comrades, especially Clearshot, poking fun at his unintentional enamoring came to mind.

I don't feel that way toward her, he told himself when his cheeks began to heat up and his heart beat a bit faster. *She's a close friend. Of course I think she's amazing, as a fighter that is. I couldn't imagine her feeling the same way when this is over. Besides, she's never given me any reason to believe otherwise…has she? Wait, what am I doing trying to convince myself? This isn't the time to fret over our relationship!*

Marcus jumped to his feet, spun around, and hurried farther into the camp to seek out Calin. He decided then to leave Coura until he had the time to return for her.

***

A rejuvenating night's sleep had always been a luxury for Coura, who never thought she would enjoy lying on the ground outside, and in fall for that matter. She woke to memories of her only time camping out in that same field with Byron and Will during her first visit to the palace.

Oh, how my life has changed since then, she reflected in an oddly satisfying state of mind before steadily becoming aware of her surroundings.

It had to be late afternoon based on the activity taking place around the area. Still, she didn't feel compelled to rise. Doing so would forfeit the warmth of the blankets covering every part of her body except her face, though the smell of cooking meals made her stomach growl enough to consider eating the mushy food served at that time of the day.

After a few minutes, she realized no one had disturbed her; that proved worrisome, and she moved into a sitting position to rub her eyes.

Did they really leave me alone just to catch up on sleep? I'm slightly concerned I didn't wake up when they started walking and talking. Am I losing my touch, or did I really need to rest that badly?

No matter the reason, she pushed herself to her feet, stretched her muscles until she felt prepared against the conditions, and combed out the tangles in her unkempt hair as best she could. Emilea's scarf and sweater had been burned to scraps when Coura first arrived on the battlefield, but she didn't recall that detail until a sharp wind blew by.

She hugged herself and muttered a curse while moving her hands up and down her arms to keep them warm. Without anyone around, she suspected the camp was free to explore.

When I run into somebody, I'll see what I can do to help. Otherwise, I might return to the shield, Coura decided, though the idea of sitting out in the open exposed to the weather made her wince.

Her senses picked up the demon's spell naturally as she started walking around. The humming seemed as normal as the previous day, meaning it remained stable. If any part of that changed overnight, there would be a noticeable difference to her, and the Yeluthians would have been able to see or sense anyone passing across the field.

Even though that observation meant nothing endangered their safety for the time being, Coura felt a familiar energy farther into the camp, which froze her in place. If the shield's power reflected consistency and stability, this reminded her of a mouse that scurried and jerked its head from side to side in order to scan the area. She closed her eyes, extended her senses as far as she could, and found another source on the northern side closer to the front line.

Just to be certain she hadn't lost her mind, Coura reached for her connection with Soirée and identified the tendrils tracing back into the city.

Those sources of energy aren't normal, she realized with a start. *I knew they reminded me of something! They're like the demonic creatures that have been roaming the country. The connections lead back into the city but are no doubt connected to Hendal.*

Without losing another second, she bolted in the direction of the nearest source, managing to startle the people near her in the process. The midday activity slowed her enough to consider shouting a warning, yet questions filled her mind, such as if the creatures could sense her approach, if they would flee into the city or forest, and what form they took to avoid rousing suspicion from the soldiers.

The trail brought her to what looked to be a makeshift kitchen area as several, low fires held cauldrons and pots of the same meal Grace brought her yesterday. Men and women huddled over them with ladles to serve the dozens of soldiers wrapped in whatever spare clothing and blankets were available. Her stomach rumbled at the sight of food, yet she subconsciously suppressed the hunger by sinking into Soirée's power.

Although Coura tried to avoid creating too much of a scene, she failed miserably. She ignored the people's resulting glances to push her way through the mass of bodies, earning herself shouts and curses for her rude behavior.

Where is it? she wondered frantically while glancing around as the creature's presence continued buzzing in her mind. *I think it knows I'm here...*

She followed the tendril of energy to a space behind the nearest tent where three men carried empty, food-crusted pots away. A hefty woman at one of the fires told her to leave them alone and began to come over with a raised, wooden spoon, but Coura already spotted her target. Each of the male helpers faced her when she approached, and one wore an uncertain expression with crazed eyes that made her hesitate.

It wasn't a demonic creature she pursued but an Asteom soldier under Hendal's control.

Before she could decide what to do, the man dropped the pot he held with both hands and took off in the opposite direction, leaving Coura to catch up. He stood no chance of escaping given his slower speed, and the demonic blade appeared in her hand as she neared to stab at his chest. The man turned as soon as she lunged, revealing a hunting knife, and swung for her neck. Its tip managed to scratch her right cheek while her sword slid in between his ribs before he fell to the ground.

Those close by cried out and rushed over to either help stop the bleeding or raise their weapons at her.

"Get a healer!" one of the men yelled and knelt with hands on the wound.

There's still one more, she remembered and reached out for that connection. *It's near the edge of the camp.*

As she stepped away from Hendal's spy, the demon's power began to visibly heal the injury she inflicted. "Get away from him," she ordered and pointed her sword at the possessed man's throat.

Those around her with weapons in hand took a step closer instead.

"What's going on here?" a feminine voice from behind demanded.

Coura looked over her shoulder and saw Marcy approaching with three other women. All were decorated with spots of food and placed their hands over their mouths at the sight.

"Marcy, good timing," she began. "Get some rope and tie this man up."

"What are you doing?" her friend asked with less authority when she saw who caused the commotion.

"She just killed one of our helpers!" a nearby soldier shouted and brought his spear closer.

Coura debated staying to clear up the situation, but the second spy definitely sensed her and started heading out of the camp already. Meanwhile, the newly healed man on the ground tried to sit up. To many gasps and a woman's scream, she stabbed once more to buy them time.

Marcy squealed her name in shock and came closer.

"This man is a spy who needs to be restrained before he heals again. Don't let him get up or try to run."

Before anyone could question her response, Coura took off to sprint toward the western side of the camp where the second of Hendal's pawns was trying to escape. If they worked their way into the city, it would be difficult to find and capture them, especially if they neared the palace.

She moved as swiftly as she could manage without slamming into anyone, which drew plenty of eyes and concerned comments. Once she reached the end of the camp, she skidded to a stop in order to survey the open area. Except for a space to the south where she recognized the Yeluthians' bronze armor, it consisted of flat grass dried into spikes that crunched beneath her feet. The layout helped her identify the other possessed man, who scrambled away and tripped multiple times while attempting to move faster.

As soon as she spotted him, a minimal chase ensued. Coura hurried directly behind him when he seemed about halfway to the city's perimeter, and a slash across the back of his thighs had him falling face-first into the ground. She slid to a stop beyond where he fell, retraced her steps, and lowered her sword to keep him in place. Like a wild animal caught in a trap, he snarled and pulled himself forward despite the injury, then he stared daggers at her.

"That's enough," she muttered and stood still to catch her breath.

The wind cut across the field to carry the noise from the camp, which increased since she left. By the time anyone made their way out to where she waited, she began shivering.

Soirée, I played your game. Let these men have their minds back, she thought with a gaze at the building beyond the shimmering wall.

The presence swallowing the men didn't change, but she swore she heard faint laughter in the back of her mind.

"What are you doing?" a deep voice growled to signal the arrival of Casner.

Marcus, Calin, Emilea, Clearshot, and about a dozen other soldiers with weapons at the ready followed behind. From the south, half a dozen unarmored Yeluthians approached led by Evern and the commander named Detrix. Their faces looked horror-stricken when they came close enough to see the bloodied man at her feet, who still attempted to crawl away.

Coura fixed the general with an unamused expression. "Were you aware you had two spies in your camp?"

Casner went a bit pale. "We didn't hear any news about the shield," he replied less forcefully and glanced at the Yeluthians.

Evern stepped forward after. His facial features displayed his, and probably everyone's, doubt. "The demon's spell has not changed at all, according to our scouts."

"They didn't enter from the palace," Coura explained.

"You mean, they came from the city?"

"Either that or the woods. I thought they might be soldiers, but neither looks physically capable of much more than an ordinary servant's work."

"How did they get past us and the human mages with the ability to sense demonic energy?" Detrix asked next. When he spoke to her, Coura found he was the only person who didn't look at her like a criminal. Even Marcus, Clearshot, and Emilea appeared uncertain about her intentions.

She paused to consider his question. "If no one noticed a disruption in Soirée's spell, that proves the pair came from the city or snuck through the forest to infiltrate the camp. It would be easy with people going there to forage for food or collect water."

"What about the demonic energy?" Emilea countered. "I might not have all my strength back, but I felt nothing out of the ordinary."

"Can you sense my presence without me using magic?" Coura responded.

Emilea considered the question before shaking her head. "Usually your power conflicts with my own, but ever since that shielding spell was cast, its energy overshadows yours."

"There's your answer. They were just listening for information and acting as volunteers while everyone recovers. I doubt they would attempt using magic around us."

"How is it you knew who they were?" Evern interjected without hiding his displeasure.

Coura narrowed her eyes in aggravation and placed a hand on her chest. "Do any of you *listen* when I talk? My connection with Soirée leads me to the creatures she manipulates. I knew where they were by following that resting trail of energy. There *is* a reason I offer to keep watch."

"Are there any more in the area?" Marcus threw in.

"No." She bit her tongue to keep from saying more.

The possessed man at her feet shifted to his hands and knees yet still crawled too feebly to be a threat.

"What should we do with him?" Casner asked while facing Evern.

Before her father could respond, the other commander spoke without projecting any negative emotions.

"Might I offer a suggestion? The master mage and I could use some practice with the…" He paused to glance at the man on the ground before changing his words. "What I mean to say is, he and his partner could prove useful. I will take full responsibility for their lives, of course."

"Would the demon notice?" Clearshot asked at a lower volume.

"Not if we keep them unconscious."

After another moment, Emilea nodded and stepped forward. "I like that idea. If anything, it will prevent Hendal from knowing our business."

"We can take this one to our camp," Evern said to his fellow commander. "I will recover the other and bring them along."

Detrix nodded and moved to stand beside Emilea in front of the crawling man. Coura thought about incapacitating him once more, but the Yeluthian drew a knife from his belt and was able to deliver a gentle yet deliberate knock to the back of the man's head to render him unconscious.

"Allow me to accompany you," Calin said to Evern. "I heard complaints from the mess area on the way here, so someone will need to explain what happened."

While everyone else seemed to establish their next direction, Coura remained where she was and released the spell on her sword. She watched as Detrix carried the limp body away while sending her a sympathetic smile when he caught her eye. Emilea walked close behind him, and Evern dismissed the rest of his soldiers before following Calin into the camp where dozens of heads poked out to watch them. Casner and the lingering troops returned as well, though at a slower pace due to a strain on the general's left side, leaving Coura alone with Clearshot and Marcus.

"Can you believe they won't even thank me?" she asked after.

Neither said a word.

"What? Did I do something wrong by saving the camp?"

"You could've warned us before running around and stabbing people," Marcus retorted while crossing his arms.

The lack of gratitude annoyed her, and she threw her hands up in a defeated shrug. "Fine, I get it. Next time, I'll make sure one of you stands in the heroic light so nobody has to suck up their pride and thank someone like me."

"That's not what he meant," Clearshot interrupted before Marcus could respond. "You should know better than to worry everybody. Not all of the soldiers trust you yet, and not all of us possess magical abilities. Believe me, you saved us from more of Hendal's trickery, but we're here to help too. You don't need to take on everything by yourself."

Coura found herself looking at the ground while remembering a familiar conversation she'd had with her former teacher. "You sound just like Byron," she mumbled as her anger simmered at the memory.

"Hey, don't say things like that!" Clearshot yelled in a mock-offended tone of voice. "If he *ever* hears me talk like that, I'll never hear the end of it."

Marcus shook his head with an eye roll, and Coura felt the corners of her lips raising.

Instead of moving into the camp, she started strolling north with the intention of monitoring the palace and its barrier. The two men looked after her but didn't comment. Because of the commotion her violence caused, in addition to the news of spies entering from the forest, she planned to stay where she felt most comfortable, which was alone on the empty battlefield.

In order to keep her body moving in the dropping temperatures, she wandered across the area and only expected to return when someone came for her, because someone *would* come for her. The real question was whether she'd be in for a calmer discussion or an interrogation.

*

Her self-isolation lasted for part of the afternoon until she heard a pair of footsteps crunching behind where she stood on the hill overlooking the area. When Coura turned around, she felt a bit startled to see Will. His face appeared worn, faded stains covered his clothing, and the mop of hair on his head had grown to just above his shoulders.

"You're awfully quiet. You weren't expecting someone else, were you?" he asked with a sheepish grin while polishing his glasses on a spare cloth.

"Not you," she answered honestly.

He returned the spectacles to his face and stuffed the rag into his pocket but didn't continue the conversation. Instead, he plopped down on the ground with his legs stretched out.

"What are you doing here?" she asked when he stared ahead in a relaxed manner. During the following pause, she moved to sit beside him, still uncertain about his oddly reserved behavior.

"I thought you might want some company. That, and the healers said if I don't get away from the medical station they would tie me up and throw me into the woods."

He acted like he took the threat personally; that, coupled with what she knew about Will's character, made her chuckle.

"You know they aren't saying it because they don't want you there," Coura replied to reassure her friend. "From what I can tell, everyone's been struggling, and I would imagine you and the other healers need rest, especially if you're tending to those who need your attention and steady hands."

"That's true…" He hesitated to continue but did so anyway. "Then again, look at what happened when you weren't available."

Coura felt her lips curve downward. "I'm different."

"I've been thinking like that even before today," he went on while staring down at the palms of his hands. "A lot of my work hasn't been practical. I never regretted putting my research above anything else because it's what I enjoy the most. In fact, the potions I craft became a sort of justification. I would assume it was my contribution to people who left me alone. Now that I see what real healers do, how serious their jobs are, I just don't know."

Coura longed to interrupt and defend Will's work, yet something told her that wasn't what he needed to hear. She realized then he didn't look for sympathy but reassurance in the path he took, and she listened with a little more interest.

"Although I can't use magic, my years of studying medicine and treatments really came in handy when everyone else exhausted themselves. Emilea asked *me* to instruct the mages. Can you believe that? Hardly any of them could set bones or stitch up a wound. Of course, there's more to it." Will tilted his head back to stare at the clouds with a weary yet proud smile.

I was wrong. He's aware of the impact he's had here. I'm much less concerned about his mentality in the face of others with the power to heal.

The pair talked for a few more minutes after about various topics. Coura felt amazed by how little needed to be said about the days, weeks, and months leading up to what currently took place on the southern field outside the palace. Finally, when the sun loomed over the horizon, Will made a move to rise.

"I'm starving! Why don't we head back?"

"You go on ahead," Coura answered with a wave. She still wasn't in the mood to return despite the temperature drop that left them both shivering.

He circled to stand in front of her and offered a hand. "Marcus said you might want to be present for their meeting. It sounded important, which is why I'm supposed to bring you there at sundown."

Coura accepted his hand and got to her feet. "He told you to come get me?"

"Yes, though he sent me over an hour ago."

"Why did you wait until now to tell me?" she asked with a hint of bitterness. Not only would arriving later make her look less important than some of them already deemed she was, but they might need her input.

Will scratched his head and began leading her away from the hill. "Marcus found me at our fire after lunch and told me what happened with the spies who snuck into the camp. When I inquired about your location, he told me, so I offered to talk to you. He went to figure the agenda out with Calin and the generals beforehand. I guess everyone wanted to give you some space, though I haven't seen you in a while. It gets rather lonely staying out all by yourself."

Coura raised an eyebrow but said nothing since she believed there had been more to their conversation. At the moment, it didn't really matter. *At least they still understand me well enough to care about my mental health.*

Will brought her back inside the camp's limits to a familiar path leading to the evening's meeting.

***

As the regular group members began to assemble for another night, one topic continued to make Marcus feel anxious, and he decided to bring it up with General Casner. He and Calin spent the afternoon with both generals in the medical station where General Tio remained under Emilea's orders. Together, the four of them drew up an outline of a plan to break through Hendal's forces and allow Emilea, Commander Detrix, and their chosen guards into the palace. Marcus had some inkling the master mage would request he join, so they plotted out various tactics if he or another leader figure were necessary off the battlefield. Not that long after, they sent for Emilea to inquire about her decision.

In addition to the answer they sought, she and the Yeluthian commanders expressed their certainty regarding one item.

"We don't want Coura coming inside with us," the master mage stated. "For one thing, she's too valuable as a fighter to waste. Secondly, it would be noticeable if she disappeared. If the demon can sense where she is too, there's no point in bringing her unless we want to get caught before finding Hendal."

Marcus and those present voiced their agreement, yet no one volunteered to tell Coura, for obvious reasons.

I can hear her yelling already, he thought and rubbed his right temple. There was no doubt in his mind she would argue with the strategy, and when she grew upset, everyone else tended to find themselves with a short temper. That had been why he intended to warn General Casner before his friend arrived, leading him to request Will's assistance with calming her down.

"Sir," Marcus began at a lower volume while facing his superior.

The general sat to his left, and Calin occupied the spot on man's other side. He had a feeling the Dalan assistant general was listening, though his comrade appeared fixated on the fire.

"What is it, Marcus?"

"I have a favor to ask," he began. "It's about Coura."

The general raised an eyebrow to show his intrigue before his features reflected his annoyance; however, he didn't give any indication for Marcus to stop.

"I'm hoping to avoid an argument," he continued, "but I've known her for years. She isn't going to approve of being left behind. Believe me when I say that."

THE ANGEL'S DESCENT

General Casner's expression didn't change. If anything, Marcus thought the man grew interested in what direction this was going in.

"All I'm requesting is that you allow me to explain. Emilea might be able to help as well, but I don't want Coura to get the impression we don't trust her. She's a tough, brave soldier."

"What if she lashes out at me for the decision?" the general asked in a relaxed manner.

His rationality startled Marcus, especially given his previous words to her. "She might, but it will most likely be toward the people she knows, those of us who *should* defend her desire to accompany us."

He paused to wait for a response. It was out of Marcus' character to ask anything of his superiors because he trusted in their intelligence. Still, their situation involved someone he cared deeply about being kept away from where they could protect each other.

"Thank you for your insight," General Casner replied as the circle of mages, Yeluthians, and Asteom soldiers filled. "I expect you understand nothing you say can change my attitude toward someone connected with a demon. I'll never feel comfortable enough to let down my guard or reign in my suspicion. That's just the kind of person I am. I also care about my country, which is why I think she can be of assistance as long as she understands her position here. If you can vouch for her sanity and that she prioritizes the well-being of Asteom, then I'm willing to give her a chance. If she shares her input, even if it's negative, I will allow you to handle the matter."

Marcus sighed in relief and thanked the general. He figured that was the best outcome, though it did put pressure on him to control Coura.

From farther to the left, he heard snickering and glanced over to see Calin rubbing his nose with a grin.

"You won't have to worry about her sharing any input. Just be prepared to hear an earful," the Dalan soldier warned.

Minutes later, Marcus caught two shadows approaching and recognized Will and Coura. They conversed before Will walked away, and Coura stepped into the light of the fire.

"I think we're ready to start," Emilea shared with a glance at General Casner, who nodded for her to continue. "Commander Detrix and I made a decision regarding who we would like to accompany us through the palace. The fewer, the better, essentially. We already discussed bringing Marcus along as a guard and guide, but I would like another one or two people."

"What about Grace?" Coura added into the following pause.

"I thought about her, but aside from her goddess gift, she wouldn't contribute much. Besides, she has been using her energy here and there and might not have the power we'd need to communicate with anyone."

"I can accompany you," the other Yeluthian commander named Evern offered.

The third grumbled something inaudible from where Marcus sat.

"I think it might help to hear the proposal for how the two of you will enter the palace and what will be done inside," King Arval interjected above his commanders' murmuring.

General Casner followed the statement by nodding with a grunt, clearing his throat, and explaining the most basic plan that would only require minor changes based on who came along, if something happened to Emilea or Commander Detrix, and so on.

At some point, a pair of women passed out the usual dinner, and Marcus enjoyed the hot food while he half-listened since he became familiar with their plan by that point in the day. A distraction in the form of a charge would need to happen first, then the troops could steadily retreat to lure the Nim-Valan soldiers away and keep the enemy across the clearing. During the first march, Marcus would lead Emilea, the Yeluthian commander, and whoever else accompanied them around to the left near the front of the palace where they could enter through one of the side doors used by the laundresses. To ensure they were not followed, the remaining Yeluthian commanders and their troops would strike from above to draw out Hendal's rogue angels. They hoped this might focus the demon's shield up in the air instead of on the ground, allowing their group to sneak by. If that option failed, they would attempt a retreat into Verona in order to come in through the front gate or training ground.

Once inside, it was a matter of locating the high priest and performing the spells. Without any insight into the demon's location, the creature proved to be their main concern. As much as Marcus, Calin, and the generals tried to consider every detail, it remained impossible given the circumstances. They might run into worse than the Nim-Valan troops inside or nothing at all.

When General Casner concluded his summary, silence followed while he dug fervently into his untasted food. Coura was the first to voice a comment.

"It's not horrible," she said with a shrug.

It's a start, at least, Marcus wanted to grumble.

Thankfully, King Arval agreed. "I must say, your strategic sense is unique given what we are up against. If this is what we agree upon, there needs to be additional steps for those of us on the battlefield and the people left in your camp."

"You're right," General Casner replied. "As I'm sure you noticed, what we're expecting is a final confrontation. Should our attempt to reach Hendal fail and we lose those sent inside, I doubt we'll be gifted another chance to regroup."

"Even so, we must make sure those in the camp are taken care of," Calin continued.

Plenty of suggestions were thrown around to solidify that notion. In the end, Calin offered to lead a retreat into the forest with General Tio. Nothing more could have been said as they all understood that if it ever came to running away, anyone who got caught would be killed.

"Once the enemy nears our camp, Commander Isan will assist in evacuating the space," King Arval offered after. "That way, they have a chance to gain some distance as they move south. I also suggest sending away the noncombatants as soon as possible to avoid a scrambled escape."

The older commander appeared surprised at being volunteered before he accepted the order with a hint of irritation. With the matter settled, Emilea shifted the conversation to another subject.

"We should figure out who is necessary in the palace. Aside from myself, Commander Detrix, and Marcus, I would like my husband along as well."

The master mage glanced at Clearshot, and Marcus caught the soldier's returned gaze that practically said, "I'm not letting you run to your death alone."

"What do you think, Evern?" Commander Detrix asked his comrade with a glimmer of amusement.

Whatever took place between the two, Marcus didn't understand.

"I believe I would be more useful with my troops," the second Yeluthian responded and raised his chin a bit.

While Emilea continued throwing out other names, Marcus watched as the commanders continued to stare at one another in a sort of challenge. At last, the one addressed as Evern broke the eye contact, and Detrix's normal smile widened.

"We might be fine with just the four of us," Clearshot commented after some more discussion and rejected suggestions. "Think about it this way; if we don't want to get caught, why barge in with a number of people who might draw attention?"

"Will that be enough to protect you? That's the real question," Calin added. "No one here can predict what's waiting inside. It could just be Hendal with a guard or two, but we still haven't seen King Aaron, Master Byron, the handful of rogue angels, or the demon. Then again, we want people familiar with the building's layout and who are capable of putting their lives on the line without losing their minds."

Marcus considered the few soldiers he knew well enough in the Dalan army, as well as the ones who escaped the palace to join in their rebellion. Evidently, he could think of only one other person to join them, and it was someone he wasn't certain would want to participate. "What about Will?" he asked Emilea.

She tilted her head with a doubtful expression. "He's been extremely helpful at the medical station, so I'm hesitant to take him away. Aside from that, he isn't as skilled with a weapon or as experienced as you. I'm curious, though, why bring him up?"

Marcus pondered her question for a moment to prepare an answer when Coura spoke in their friend's defense.

"You say Will has no experience, but he's been involved as long as Marcus and me. Besides, I doubt you want to use your energy if someone gets hurt. He can act as your healer while holding his own with a sword."

"She's right," Marcus said with a nod. "It's worth a shot."

Emilea still appeared uncertain yet agreed to his request. "Fine, but I won't be responsible if anything happens to him. If he agrees, I believe that's enough support."

The matter seemed to conclude the remainder of their planning until Coura cleared her throat to add more, and Marcus immediately grew tense at her displeased tone of voice.

"If that's the case, then let me bring up two other, apparently forgotten, details. What about the ancestral weapons, and why am I being left out of this plan?"

Since he expected her to protest, Marcus was quick to reply. "Without a clear idea of where the weapons are, we would be wasting time by searching."

"So, you won't send anyone to bother looking?"

"That could take hours at the soonest."

"It's the only way to seal Soirée. Without it, she'll continue to hinder what you're working for."

"You want to go after it," Commander Evern interjected before Marcus could counter that idea.

Coura directed a glare at the Yeluthian. "I might as well since it seems I haven't been invited to storm the palace, even though I can sense demonic energy clearly. My body also heals, so there's no need to worry about-"

"We're just after Hendal," Emilea interrupted. "For now, we can stop him, and thus his hold on the Nim-Valan soldiers and King Aaron. Once we establish peace, we'll regroup to discuss what to do about the demon, if it's still in the palace."

"That won't work."

"Why not?"

Coura paused to take a deep breath, seemingly to avoid blowing up on anyone. "Do you really think you're the only ones who consider this the final chance to end this battle?"

No one commented.

"I can guarantee they see it the same way we do, which means they won't be running away. I would assume going into the palace will be more dangerous than staying on the battlefield."

"If there is a space in that building where the weapon could be kept, I suggest seeking it out," King Arval said after a moment. "Those gifts were crafted to stop demons from tormenting the humans living on the surface. Even if it means sacrificing the time, it could save your lives."

Marcus turned to the general at his side as he considered where the ancestral weapon could be. "Sir, do you think the royal family keeps them somewhere special? The only place I know of is the basement level reserved for the troops' belongings, but no one really uses it that often."

General Casner frowned. "To my knowledge, King Hernan has never mentioned such a thing. I would say, if you have the opportunity, visit the lowest level and search as thoroughly as you can. Once the high priest is dealt with and our troops swarm the palace, we'll make it a priority to find one of the legendary weapons."

"Why not send me?" Coura asked the group.

Marcus prepared to recite the reasons he prepared ahead of time, but General Casner apparently forgot his agreement and answered instead.

"We need you to stay outside to join in the distraction. It would be noticeable if you disappeared, especially with your connection to the demon."

"That doesn't matter. I'll go after Soirée to keep her from interfering with your plan to stop Hendal. Unlike him, she could care less about keeping or losing the palace so long as it means we'll continue to kill each other for her amusement."

"If what you say is true, then the creature shouldn't become involved at all."

"Not when there's someone holding her attention."

Their bickering went in circles as neither felt willing to give up on their point of view. Marcus found himself wondering what Byron would say if he were present and used what he experienced of the master mage's mentality as a focal point.

He said Coura's name calmly when an opportunity presented itself, drawing her eyes away from the general. "I understand you want to stop the demon," he began. "We're not saying it isn't going to happen or you can't do it, but you need to be patient. If you help defeat the angels working with Hendal, that gets us one step closer to the ultimate goal. Once we end Hendal's hold, we'll work together."

As he spoke, her frustrated expression softened.

"If fighting them didn't sound so tempting, I'd find my own way inside," she replied.

The thought gave Marcus an idea.

"Do it," he urged and caught some surprised expressions, including hers. "If you happen to get past the shield, go after Hendal or the demon. That would be a useful distraction for us."

Coura stared at Marcus with an unreadable gaze for a few seconds. Then, she rolled her eyes. "It sounds like that's the only option you're going to give me."

The corners of his mouth twitched at her resignation while he tried not to show his relief.

A few more comments were addressed regarding various parts of the overall plan and responsibilities to be assigned to others not currently present. Evacuation of the camp for those unable to fight or who were not necessary during the conflict would begin in the morning, just to be safe. The general dismissed the group shortly after and worked with Calin to organize messengers to share their orders. When everyone else rose to take their leave, Marcus glanced over to where Coura had been and found the space empty.

13

Preparations for the retreat began the following day. Non-combatants were expected to move into the woods or city, including those too weak to fight or still recovering. Of course, many human soldiers in either position protested as their loyalty to Asteom outweighed everything else. Their resilience always surprised Evern, at least until he spoke to Paulina. She acted just as stubborn, which had been why he made sure to make time for a conversation early that morning.

She shared the people's pride in her home country once he requested she leave with the others heading south, as well as a loyalty to him and their eldest daughter; however, one mention of Odell and Jackie had his wife reconsider risking her life. Then, the tears he expected fell while they said goodbye. She would travel with the other humans because no Yeluthians were retreating; those who could not fight already died, and they totaled a dozen.

During their time assisting the Asteom soldiers, Paulina performed tasks for their camp and worked at the medical station whenever they needed an extra set of hands. Her worn yet genuine smile upon his return every night kept him hopeful, despite the rough situation. Now that she would be gone, he at least had the motivation to end the battle sooner.

Around a hundred humans already made their way through the forest's edge when Evern and Paulina walked over hand in hand. Most were either carrying or supporting the injured with everyone else hauling bundles of supplies. Where they would end up, he wasn't certain.

"I suppose I should move along," his wife mumbled before embracing him one more time.

"Be careful," he ordered with a fitting expression of caution once they broke apart.

"I will, but please watch out for Coura. I want to see my daughter again."

He nodded and promised to do so, as he did the first two times she asked it of him. "We will be together soon. Make sure to take care of yourself, Paulina."

That earned him a slight smile before she adjusted the satchel hanging off her shoulder and hurried over to where supplies were being handed out. Evern remained still as he watched his wife gather a bundle in both arms and disappear into the trees.

***

At the sound of the camp stirring that morning, Marcus made sure he was up and prepared for the day. His companions rose as well, though with less enthusiasm.

Today is the beginning of this conflict's conclusion, he reflected solemnly.

The previous night, he told his friends and comrades what would happen. Emilea took the message to the medical station since those unable to fight needed to be patched up and sent out as soon as possible, allowing the healers time to recover. The camp's mood became peaceful, in a melancholy sort of way. Everybody understood what was at stake and if they were necessary in the camp or not. When the shield around the palace went down, there would be no turning back and no room for concern over casualties or saving supplies.

While those around the fire sat in silence, Aimes placed a pot on the coals to heat up their breakfast. Marcus stared at Will from across the flames until his friend noticed. "Can I ask you something?"

"Of course." The round glasses reflected the sunlight peeking through the looming clouds.

"Emilea and I will be heading for the palace as soon as the charge is sounded. I told everyone here about that plan last night. Would you join us?"

Will's eyebrows shot up and his mouth fell open a bit. "You want *me* to go after Hendal with you?"

Marcus nodded and explained his, or rather Coura's, reasoning. After the meeting, she hadn't returned to where they were gathered.

"Who's all going with you?" Aimes inquired as he filled and handed off the bowls of food.

Marcus looked to Emilea.

"It will be myself, the Yeluthian commander named Detrix, my husband, and Marcus," she replied while accepting her share of their breakfast.

"What about Coura?" Grace added. She appeared to be the most exhausted of the group.

He scratched the back of his neck. "She's going to stay on the battlefield with the others. We agreed it would be suspicious if she disappeared."

"I see."

They paused for a minute to begin eating.

"Do you want more protection?" Marcy asked.

Her question startled most of the group.

"You aren't thinking of going too!" Aimes was the first to exclaim.

"Why not? If what they're doing is that important, you shouldn't put so much faith into the mages being unguarded. Besides, would it be any safer for me out here?"

The older man's face scrunched up, giving Marcus the impression Aimes expected her to leave with him. Marcy ignored his silent plea and glanced at Marcus.

"We need to keep the party small," he shared. Internally, he felt uncertain about how to handle any soldiers or mages wandering the halls of the palace, especially if Emilea and Commander Detrix were preoccupied. That thought had kept him awake during the previous night.

"Marcy's a better fighter than I am," Will muttered without meeting anyone's eye.

This spurred a reaction from Grace. "If Will and Marcy go, I want to help too. You will need my goddess gift inside in case you face an unanticipated problem."

"That's enough," Clearshot barked with an annoyed expression. "General Casner and Calin are going to need all the assistance they can get out here. Grace, as a political figure I'm sure you understand why we won't put you in danger. The fewer who accompany Emilea, the better."

Marcus caught Clearshot's glare around the fire and held it for a moment. "It's not *your* decision to make," he felt compelled to add.

Marcy voiced her agreement with arms crossed and stared at Emilea, who pressed her lips together. Despite her intent to rest as much as possible, the master mage appeared even more tired than before. No one pushed the subject until an added comment from outside their circle caught their attention.

"Why not let them go? Maybe it'll ease some of your nerves."

Marcus' shoulders slouched once he saw Coura standing nearby with a bored look on her face. Like a ghost, she managed to approach without anyone noticing until she spoke and waited for an answer. Still, he didn't feel like arguing with her anymore.

"We went over this last night," Clearshot replied with a shake of his head, though he projected exhaustion rather than bitterness. "It's too risky."

"I'm not talking to you," Coura responded before stepping just behind where Grace sat. "Emilea, I thought of something this morning. Remember when you couldn't heal me right away because of the clashing energies in my center? Well, up until that point, I've always gotten a similar feeling whenever I'm around a Yeluthian."

Marcus had no idea what she was getting at, but Emilea seemed to understand. Even Grace gasped while glancing upward.

"I felt the same," his Yeluthian friend added. "I could always sense the demonic energy within you, yet I never acted on it because you were not…"

"I bet it became just as irritating," Coura commented with a raised eyebrow and crooked smile.

Grace lowered her eyes to stare at the ground with less amusement.

"What does that mean?" Marcy asked on behalf of the non-magic users.

"The uncomfortable sensation is mutual. If Commander Detrix, or any Yeluthian for that matter, goes into the palace, they'll be subjected to Soirée's malicious power."

"The demon will know he's near," Emilea concluded for the rest of them.

Coura nodded. "Hendal might too since he's using demonic energy."

"I get it," Will surprised them by adding. "Even if none of the troops outside see or sense the group moving around the palace, the demon will. If that's the case, there should be enough people along to protect Emilea and the Yeluthian commander because it might go after them."

Marcus wished he skipped breakfast then as the meal turned in his stomach at the thought of having to hold back the creature. Clearshot muttered a curse under his breath, and Emilea went a bit pale.

Meanwhile, Coura stretched her arms up in the air with a smirk. "So, who wants to go along now? I would, but for some reason, I'm more useful fighting soldiers instead of a demon."

"Don't fret," Aimes commented. "You'll still be contributing to the cause."

"Marcus gave me permission to enter on my own if I stop the rogue angels. If Emilea and the others with her can wait until then, I'd be happy to keep Soirée from interrupting your work until you find the ancestral weapon."

"In any case, the only certainty is that those in the palace will sense our arrival anyway," the master mage responded after a pause. "Perhaps it would be better to expand our company. Not too many more people but those here who are willing to risk death."

"Count me in!" Marcy exclaimed while practically cutting off Emilea's final words. "I've had to deal with being controlled all my life, so it's about time I help someone else in that position for a change."

Marcus didn't know about the woman's background and became curious because of her age, which he figured was a decade or so older than his; however, no one could deny the emotion behind the brave face she wore.

"I want to go too," Grace added timidly. "Perhaps I can find a safe area to stay. That way, you can speak with the generals through me."

"There might not be a safe area for you," Coura responded without rejecting the idea.

The more Marcus thought about their Yeluthian friend, the better he felt knowing they would not be completely isolated from the outside battle. He voiced as much to those present. Even Emilea appeared less concerned with a bridge between everyone.

"I guess that doesn't leave me much choice," Will said after. He didn't elaborate, but his weak smile provided an answer.

To Marcus, the group appeared satisfied. "Would you like me to tell General Casner?" he offered.

After a moment of thought, the master mage shook her head with a glance at Coura. "I get the feeling he might not approve of the risk we're taking based on the demon's ability to sense Yeluthians. Besides, they'll have enough to worry about here. We're not adjusting the plan either."

He nodded in understanding.

"Well, before I go, I'm going to make sure to leave you with a fresh pot of food," Aimes began while rising with a grunt, signaling the end of their brief discussion.

The rest of them shifted between talking, napping, and preparing their own armor and weaponry. Eventually, the number of people moving around the camp trickled down to handfuls at a time instead of dozens, significantly decreasing the noise compared to earlier that morning.

When it was the older man's turn to take his leave, he made sure to thank them all for their service. He bowed to Emilea and Grace, shook hands with Clearshot, Marcus, and Will, and wrapped his arms around Coura, who chuckled awkwardly at the unexpected gesture. Marcy stood nearby with the intent to walk to the forest's edge with him.

"Thank you," Aimes said once more, addressing their entire group. The scar on his face scrunched as he squeezed his eyes shut and bowed.

"We should be the ones thanking you," Will commented.

Marcus felt compelled to express his gratitude as well. "Never underestimate your ability to maintain a fire, cook meals, or take care of the tasks we're too preoccupied to do. Without your assistance, who knows how long we would have lasted! We really owe you."

"That's not all he did," Marcy snapped, as if his words were an understatement.

"It's all right," Aimes interrupted with watery eyes. "Just make sure to save this palace of yours so I can see it for myself one day!"

Marcus couldn't keep from grinning at the man's following, broad smile before he went over to Marcy. The pair strolled away together with Marcy's arm draped over his shoulder.

While the others began to go about the rest of their day, Coura stepped up to Marcus' side. "That was nice of you to say," she commented in a gentler tone of voice than he'd heard from her recently. Her gaze lingered on the trail the pair left from before she turned around to sit by the fire.

He had no idea how his words could be so meaningful, especially since he didn't know Aimes well, but he didn't ask her to elaborate. Intentionally or not, he wanted to avoid spoiling the moment by admitting his incomprehension. She departed to monitor the shield soon after, and Calin found Marcus to go through and supervise the camp.

***

After more time than Coura thought Hendal would allow, enough movement came from the other side of the glittering shield to draw her attention. That morning, the fourth since she arrived, was the only one with a clear sky, so the sunlight reflecting off Soirée's spell played with her mind. When the shadows continued moving and growing, she knew the wall would disappear soon after and sprinted back into the mix of tents and bonfires.

My best option is to find Marcus, Calin, or even Casner, Coura thought while hurrying in the direction of the meeting area. She hoped any one of the three would be there and found the general and Calin sitting around the fire.

"There's movement from across the field," she blurted out before they even noticed her.

"Is the shield down?" Casner demanded, projecting a sense of urgency rather than his usual distain toward her.

Coura shook her head. "No, but I've never seen that much activity before. We should at least prepare for-"

Calin took off at a sprint without letting her finish.

"Spread the word," the general ordered before running in the direction of the Yeluthian's camp.

Coura remained still for a moment to listen to the undisturbed humming emanating from the demon's spell. *As long as I feel the same amount of energy, they aren't passing through yet. I wonder how much longer it'll take for them to prepare a charge.*

With that in mind, she began circling around the camp to tell every person she saw to get ready for the inevitable fight ahead. Their initial, alarmed expressions were replaced by a resolute nod in confirmation each time, and soon the entire camp consisted of soldiers suiting up before jogging north while carrying swords, shields, spears, bows and quivers, and even a mace or two.

Coura stood alone once she fulfilled the general's request. No one had assigned her to a specific location, but something compelled her to find the Yeluthians instead of joining the mass of Dalan and Asteom soldiers. Their bronze armor caught her eye as they moved to the front, and she slipped alongside the nearest group.

The angels stationed themselves behind the human troops, who looked just about set in a block formation, so she found a spot in the middle and planted her feet firmly as the rest of the soldiers spread out. All the while, she continued monitoring the shield for changes in the energy's output.

"Are you ready?" someone to her left said while glancing over.

She didn't respond. Given her exposed skin decorated by the bruise-like markings, black hair, and lack of a proper uniform or armor, she knew she stood out terribly among their people.

Eventually, once everyone settled into position, they quieted enough for her to hear shouting from farther ahead. Coura figured Casner or Calin were barking orders or yelling to raise their troops' spirits, then the soldiers cheered as one unit. Even some of the Yeluthians raised their weapons or hollered in support, easing her rising nerves.

Hopefully the people outside can hold up their part of this plan. Once I break through in the air, I'll go after Soirée so Emilea and the others can stop Hendal.

She repeated this in her mind to keep from caving into her fears, which included if the others would survive, where Byron and Aaron were, if they could be rescued, and what else waited for them in the palace.

Without any immediate activity, everyone started shifting in place or stretching to keep their muscles warm and loose, but no one spoke. At last, a slight quiver came from the shield before the spell released completely. Those who could sense the magic felt the balanced set of energy dwindle until nothing remained except for a slight tingling sensation. Visibly, the wall shimmered like shattering glass, breaking into pieces and glittering as it disintegrated. The area went quiet once the ever-present humming ceased only to be replaced by the shouts and stomps of a charge that made her whole body vibrate.

She forced herself to clear her mind and breathe steadily against Soirée's growing bloodlust deep within her center. *This has been a long time coming for both of us*, she reflected when those in front of her began to move. *It's about time I face her. Then, we can stop Hendal and this madness for good!*

The Yeluthians jumped into the sky one after another until only Coura remained. With a nod and a silent wish for her friends to succeed on their own path, she manifested her wings and sword and leapt into the air.

***

Because of his earlier placement among the healers at the medical station, Will remained inexperienced when it came to fighting for his life and killing those who stood in his way. When he was preparing the day before, Marcus helped him and Grace find the proper armor and weaponry while offering advice for mental and emotional support.

"When the generals sound the charge, run at the pace I set. If you can, try to slip past the Nim-Valans' sloppy swings. If that isn't an option, go for the neck or legs. That should slow them down enough for us to continue. Remember, we're not supposed to stay on the battlefield."

Will recalled what he learned from his training with the assistant general and soldiers at the palace in order to focus. Although he grew so afraid his arms and legs trembled, he found his mentality ready for what was to come.

I've been around the wounded and dead for days now. What I see and hear won't bother me if I don't get distracted. Coura chose me to train the mage recruits with her, and Marcus spent his time working with me. I can do this… I just wish my body would cooperate!

He stood in between Marcus and Clearshot with Emilea and Grace in the middle, Marcy at the rear, and Commander Detrix in the lead. The Yeluthian apparently possessed the strength and speed to cut a path ahead while the trio at the rear would protect the sides and prevent the enemy from following. Aside from Grace, Will felt he had been put in the safest position.

General Casner managed the western half of the troops while General Tio and Calin led the Dalans on the eastern side; Detrix stood on the front line with the rest of their group behind. Each general shouted instructions while everyone waited for the shield to fall. Meanwhile, the mass of shadows beyond expanded, causing Will's anxious twitching to grow into frightened shivering.

"Don't worry about them," Clearshot said in a reassuring manner as he removed the bow from his back and slipped an arrow out of his quiver. Just that morning, the archer abandoned the sling for his left arm, which seemed to cause him no pain. "Remember to breathe, keep a clear head, and follow Commander Detrix. You won't be dealing with an entire army, maybe one or two soldiers at a time."

Will nodded and drew the sword Marcus found for him earlier that day. Although no shields were available, he didn't feel familiar enough with one to make it as useful as someone else would. He had just been thankful for the weapon and what armor could be scrounged together to protect his head, chest, and legs.

On the other hand, Grace needed to settle for leather padding that proved to be a bit big for her body. Will took comfort in knowing he wouldn't be the one their group needed to worry about the most, much to his chagrin.

His Yeluthian friend had no training, which was why she'd been given a dagger to use instead of a larger blade, and possessed little skill with light magic. He believed her only experience when it came to combat consisted of their attempt to capture Hendal in the palace's training ground. Even then, she focused on the shielding spell. Will vowed to keep an eye on her and used that as motivation to fight the enemy Nim-Valan soldiers.

Nobody could predict when the shield would come down, so all they could do was wait and watch the expanding shadows ahead. He hated the tension that caused.

Suddenly, a shout came from Detrix before anyone seemed to notice a change in the area.

"The spell has been released!"

"Prepare yourselves!" General Casner yelled and followed with a bellow echoed by his troops.

The glistening magic appeared to collapse into fragments of light before disappearing and revealing the hundreds of soldiers on the opposite side. The general then called for a charge, which would bring Will and those in his group closer to the building. He swallowed, forced his legs to move, and followed behind Emilea, who led Grace by the hand.

Inevitably, their enemy attacked from all across the front line. The clashing of metal sounded oddly reminiscent of a rain shower as one ring came after another, like the first drops of a downpour. Despite the many Nim-Valans blindly marching forward, Will didn't need to raise his sword for a few minutes as the Yeluthian commander sliced through the throats of those ahead. If any approached from the right, Clearshot halted their progress with a lethal-looking shot, and Marcy did the same to those at the rear. That left the remaining side for Marcus, and Will when he felt courageous enough. After his first stab through a man's chest, the rest became a blur of repeated lunges, stabs, and dodging.

The seven of them made it a few paces before pausing to deal with a handful of Nim-Valans, then they went on. As expected, those the group left behind began to close them in, but Will caught movement in the air followed by a red glow and a wave of heat to his right. The Yeluthians flying above dove in waves to fight on the ground while those in the air cast fire spells in a line to slow the enemy. He thought he spotted Coura among them, yet he didn't get the time to confirm her presence.

"We have to push through!" Emilea shouted from farther ahead. She held a dagger as well and slashed it across the nearest man's face before pulling Grace along.

Soon, Will noticed they were near the brick wall, though the possessed soldiers stopped pursuing, leaving them to face the palace's combatants and mages. Every person he cut down stayed on the ground, which grew to be a burden hindering him from inflicting a killing blow. Twice, he received a cut serious enough to warrant his attention: one across his left arm and another on his left calf, which his armor didn't cover.

He tried to avoid limping after the latter but couldn't. Marcus noticed and hurried over to drag him along.

"I'm all right," he protested and pushed his friend away.

"Then move," Marcus ordered before going on ahead.

Will struggled to match the others' pace; however, they paused a few steps away from the palace's stone wall to glance around, allowing him to catch up.

"What's wrong?" he asked when no one spoke.

A comfortable amount of space kept them a safe distance away from the nearby conflict, though the enemy mages crept closer. When one raised their hands to attempt a spell, Clearshot launched an arrow into their chest.

Meanwhile, Detrix looked between everyone else. "Where is the closest entrance?"

Marcus pointed to his left. "If we don't find an open door, our best chance is to use the main gate."

The Yeluthian nodded before leading them on.

"What about the shield?" Will heard Marcy ask. "Won't they see us?"

Detrix glanced behind to flash a grin. "You did not notice yet?"

"Notice what?"

"The human soldiers are already drawing our enemy to the camp, but my people and your friend are making a spectacle of themselves in order to hold the demon's attention."

He slowed to a stop and looked east, so the rest of the group did the same. The flashes of magic Will tuned out from the beginning came from the Yeluthians, who launched their spells toward the palace instead of at the ground. To his surprise, the previous shield returned, yet it only appeared to block the attacks in midair before they could land.

They aren't preoccupied with the people on the ground since the Nim-Valans are driving our side back, he realized with rising optimism.

"Don't let that fool you," Emilea responded, as though she sensed his hopefulness. "I don't expect Hendal or the demon to let us through so easily. They probably already know we're here."

Will nodded, along with Grace and Detrix. Their group continued at a slower pace, allowing him to keep up without straining his body, and Clearshot and Marcy dealt with the remaining enemy troops at a distance.

A wooden door along the wall came into view, though several mages in white robes guarded it with arms extended and palms facing them as they approached. Detrix stepped forward with the intent to disable the people who stood in their way, but Emilea ordered him to wait. When he backed away, the master mage confidently strode ahead and out of their formation.

Will noticed the startled expressions on the mages' faces and heard one cry out Emilea's name. This caused the rest to lower their arms, yet none moved from their spots in front of the door.

"Let us through," Emilea commanded.

"What are you doing here?" one of the women asked before she pointed at the rest of the group. "Who are they?"

THE ANGEL'S DESCENT

"We're here to rid the palace of the demon plaguing the Nim-Valans' and our comrades' minds. I'm sure you understand that's the source of our problems."

The mages nodded hesitantly, but they continued to glance between Emilea, Commander Detrix, and the others without obeying their superior's request.

To Will's surprise, Marcus lowered his sword and took a couple steps closer.

"If you need more proof, I'm Assistant General Marcus Tont," his friend offered while mustering an authoritative tone of voice. "My father is being kept inside by the creature, and General Casner is fighting with us across the southern field."

"Please," Emilea begged desperately when they heard shouting from behind to signal another wave of enemy soldiers.

"Let them through!" one of the mages snapped, leading the rest to scramble away in order to clear the path.

So, not everyone is being controlled after all, Will reflected with a bit of dismay during the brief pause. *They aren't bold enough to abandon their positions or home, or perhaps they don't know the truth. That isn't fair...*

The Yeluthian commander resumed taking the lead when the opportunity arose, so their group slipped inside and pressed against the chilled, stone walls before Marcus shut the door with a loud boom. The echo reverberated down the corridor until it blended into the noise from outside. To their relief, the lamps posted in the hallway remained lit, despite the conflict, and they didn't see anybody else.

"We actually did it," Clearshot mumbled without hiding his shock.

That seemed to be their signal to peel themselves off the wall and continue.

"Who will take the lead?" Detrix asked as they huddled together.

Emilea volunteered first. "I recognize the area since I spent so many years moving through here," she commented while gesturing for them to follow. "These first few rooms are for the laundry, so I doubt we'll run into much trouble."

After a couple of minutes, they reached a fork in the hall.

"Which way?" Clearshot inquired. He aimed his nocked arrow down the left path while Marcy mirrored his stance in the other direction.

"The entrance to the lower level is at the rear of the palace," his wife explained. "The servants' quarters are to the left. If we head right, we can move through the medical stations to the back staircase."

"I would be amazed if anyone is using those rooms," Marcus added when they continued through the latter option.

The sounds of the ongoing battle became muffled by the walls, yet every tremor from a destructive spell vibrated the stone surrounding them. They seemed to be the only people in that area of the palace, yet Emilea didn't move faster than a hurried walk, both for their safety and stealth.

Will kept to the rear with Marcus behind him and found himself gripping his sword tighter. *Something doesn't feel right. If Coura's assumption that the demon would sense the Yeluthian commander and Grace is correct, why haven't we run into anyone? I would think they expect us to go straight to Hendal's location, so maybe that's why. Does this mean we won't face any enemies until we get closer to him or the demon?*

He prepared to bring the topic up when Grace stopped suddenly enough to cause him to bump into her back, and Marcus into his as a result.

"Why'd we stop?" the assistant general demanded as the two of them recovered.

Will looked to those at the front and noticed Emilea standing rigid. Clearshot stepped around her with his bow raised, and the group crept onward in silence.

Soon, Emilea halted their progress once more; however, this time they could all see a magical shield blocking their path, which reflected the light from the nearest lamp.

"What should we do?" Marcy was the first to ask.

Will glanced at the nearest door to Emilea's right. "Can we go through there?"

The master mage didn't comment and kept her back to the rest of the group.

THE ANGEL'S DESCENT

In response, her husband lowered his weapon. "What's wrong?"

Will caught the master mage mutter something about the shield, but she didn't address anyone in particular.

When it didn't seem like they were getting anywhere, Detrix began discussing the possibility of an alternate route with Marcus. Will already knew they would need to backtrack to the grand hall in order to avoid the maze of hallways should they attempt to continue through the medical stations. The assistant general started retreating after mentioning this, but Emilea interrupted his next order and turned to face them; her expression reflected concern and uncertainty.

"This room is the entrance to the central portion of the medical station. It runs the length of the outer wall and exits farther down this hallway."

"Then, that's our best route," Marcus responded on the group's behalf.

When Emilea didn't reply, Will understood the route through the wide room was what bothered her. "Why are you hesitant to go on?" he decided to ask.

She pursed her lips together and placed a hand on her chest. "The energy making up the spell belongs to Byron."

The news shocked everyone except Detrix.

"What?"

"Does that mean he's here?" Clearshot exclaimed.

Emilea nodded. "It has to, but I believe entering this room will bring us to him."

"Who is this man you speak of?" the Yeluthian commander interjected.

"He is my equal in wielding dark magic and a close friend; however, his mind is under the high priest's control. If we interact with him, we're in for a battle of spells."

"Can you use a binding spell to stop him?" Clearshot practically begged, yet his wife shook her head.

"I don't have a lot of expendable energy."

"Neither do I," Detrix added before anyone could ask the same of him. "Should we find a different path?"

Marcus chimed in his agreement. "If we want to avoid harming Byron, it'd be best to avoid confronting him."

"I don't think that's what we need to worry about," Will shared. "I assume he has the demon's healing ability and enough power to seriously hinder our progress. Perhaps we could create a diversion to rush by."

His friend rubbed his chin yet didn't dismiss the suggestion. "That may be our safest option. It's definitely the fastest."

"Fine," Clearshot stated with his eyes on the nearest door. "Will and I can distract him while the rest of you cross the station."

Emilea frowned. "You won't be able to keep Byron's attention for long. There's no guarantee he won't go after Detrix or Grace while under the demon's influence either."

"We will not know this until we act," the Yeluthian commander said firmly enough to cease any further arguments. "I will not interrupt if you wish to keep him from harm, but we must focus on our ultimate goal, even if it means stopping the pawns he throws our way. Those outside this building are still retreating, so we are on our own."

At the reminder, their resolve strengthened. Clearshot moved to open the wooden door to the medical station, then he returned his hands to his weapon and led them into the room.

The space stretched along the outer wall with rectangular windows close to the ceiling. Through them, the distant battle waged on. Two dozen cots had been placed in a line with the pillow side against both the outer and inner walls to create an isle in the center wide enough for four of them to walk in a row, and short tables sat in between. None of the lamps were lit, making their only source of light the sunbeams that found their way inside through the windows.

Aside from the beds and tables, huge cabinets occupied the back walls by the doors on both ends of the station. During his first months in the palace, Will had learned they contained common medicines, bandages, and other items for those who needed easy access to the supplies.

"It looks like no one is here," Grace practically whispered to break the silence.

"Let's keep moving," Emilea urged, pushing her husband to continue.

As the group tiptoed warily across the room, Will felt a strange humidity in the air and opened his mouth to comment; however, the door on the other side of the room opened to halt their steps.

"How clever," a familiar voice grumbled to freeze them in place.

A figure emerged from the opening, and despite Emilea's warning, Will couldn't restrain his dread upon recognizing Byron. The dark mage's appearance seemed normal, from his clothes to his black hair, yet his eyes proved dull, reflecting nothing like his usual intelligence.

"Using your allies as a distraction to sneak into the palace," he continued, though they knew the monotone words belonged to Hendal. "Either every person out there consented to being used as a decoy or you're all extremely selfish."

"You coward," Clearshot growled through his teeth while aiming his arrow across the station.

Will and the others followed suit by bringing up their weapons.

Byron tilted his head before his hand raised in a sudden jerk to release a lightning bolt in their direction. Will instinctively glanced away at the initial brightness before the resulting crack of thunder had him covering his ears while the building trembled. When he looked up, he saw Detrix had created a shield to stop the spell.

"Scatter on my move," the Yeluthian commander ordered once the sparks vanished.

Someone grabbed Will's left arm a second later. A brief glance showed it was Grace who gripped his forearm, so he told her to stay close to him before the wall of light energy faded.

As soon as Detrix rushed forward, Will took a defensive stance and backtracked with Grace beside him until they returned to where the group had entered. Then, he ducked behind the last bed in the row and pulled his friend down into a crouch.

In the time that took, the others in the room went all over the place. The Yeluthian commander avoided Byron altogether in order to slip to the opposite side, and Marcus tried passing on the right, but a blast of fire from the possessed mage prevented him from continuing. Marcy crossed in the meantime to stand beside Detrix. Unfortunately, she proved to be the only other person to succeed. Emilea returned to the entrance with Clearshot, who had yet to release his nocked arrow, once the spells blocked their intended route.

Will hoped to find an opportunity to sneak around with Grace, or at least send her across while he became the distraction, yet Byron's magic kept him from predicting a safe path through the station. In addition to his mental struggle, he watched as Marcus attempted to dodge the relentless attacks.

I have to help him and get Emilea to the other side so they can exit this room.

Grace's hold on his arm tightened as the minutes passed, revealing her concern. Will removed her hands to free himself and met her eyes when she turned toward him.

"I'm going to join Marcus. Stay here until I can come back for you."

Once she nodded, Will shoved aside his ever-present worry about his inexperience with combat, stood, and hurried to stand behind Marcus.

His friend didn't notice his presence and tried to strike Byron with a horizontal swing. The master mage sidestepped to avoid the slash while wearing a blank expression, reminding him of the Nim-Valan soldiers. Instead of pursuing, the assistant general paused to create a standstill between the two.

In that moment, Will caught movement from where Detrix and Marcy waited on the other side. The former stalked forward while the woman at his side raised her bow to launch an arrow into Byron's back. Will flinched when the dark mage jolted as a result of the shot.

"Hurry!" Detrix shouted in Clearshot and Emilea's direction and took a couple steps closer.

Marcy aimed her next arrow at Byron, then she and the Yeluthian disappeared behind a violet wall of energy. Will didn't see the dark mage raise a hand to cast a shielding spell, yet the station became separated at Byron's back, trapping the pair on that side of the room. Their muffled shouts and strikes against the barrier did nothing to disturb it.

"He's separating us," Will told Marcus as a chill ran down his spine. "We have to try something else."

The two began retracing their steps until they were lined up with the final cots where Grace, Clearshot, and Emilea waited. Meanwhile, Byron didn't move.

"What do we do now?" the assistant general asked no one in particular.

A slight gasp from Emilea caught their attention. They followed her gaze to the door their group had entered from, which became blocked by a second shielding spell.

"I guess we just have to do this the hard way," Clearshot said next.

As if he recognized their cornered position, Byron cast a blast of fire from each hand to set the cots on both sides of his body ablaze. The top covers popped as the flames spread before he walked forward to scorch the next set.

Will glanced around the claustrophobic area available to them in search of a way to escape. *This isn't good...*

"Byron, stop this!" Clearshot yelled. "We know your mind is still in there. You have to fight against Hendal's control!"

Unfortunately, the words did nothing except make the dark mage frown.

"It was worth a try," the archer offered before finally releasing an arrow into Byron's right thigh, causing their opponent to stumble onto one knee.

Without missing a second, Marcus sprinted to close the distance, raised his sword, and brought it down into Byron's shoulder. Will scrambled behind after remembering this would be their best opportunity to immobilize the threat. When Marcus withdrew his sword, Will mirrored his attack by slicing through the opposite shoulder. Then, the pair retreated.

At some point, Clearshot sent another arrow into Byron's left leg; however, just like the Nim-Valan soldiers, he rose slowly while tearing out the arrows, as if they were mere thorns.

"Keep him down!" the archer ordered from behind.

"Then what?" Marcus snapped over his shoulder in response.

Will understood their frustration given the circumstances and coughed as the burning furniture created a swirling cloud of smoke above their heads. *Unless Emilea is willing to use her magic to free or bind Byron, which I'm not sure she's going to do, we need to find another way to incapacitate him.*

"Go for his legs," Marcus offered at a lower volume. "If we can stop him from moving, or even knock him out, Hendal might release his hold like he did with Joseph and Stephen when they guarded Emilea."

Will nodded before they approached Byron once more; this time, Will acted first. Just as he did with his previous attack, he swept his blade horizontally to cut deep into the master mage's left leg. His target wobbled but remained standing as Marcus stabbed for the chest.

Unfortunately, Byron was prepared for their plan. He shifted to avoid the strike while swinging a fist into Marcus' stomach. Even with armor protecting that spot, the assistant general stumbled backward and winced.

Next, the dark mage went for Will, who naturally raised his sword to take a defensive stance. Instead of a frontal blow, which he fully expected, Byron kicked him in his right thigh before he could anticipate the movement. The force sent waves of pain through Will's leg, and he involuntarily leaned forward to stay on his feet as a result; however, this exposed enough of his upper body for Byron to follow with a punch to the side of his head. The strength behind the attack felt like it sent Will's body flying through the air as his vision filled with colorful spots momentarily.

He blinked for a few seconds to clear his vision and let his mind settle from the shock. The left side of his face hurt, and he tasted blood, but any concern for his wellbeing was brushed aside when he saw Byron marching toward where Clearshot stood in front of Emilea. Grace had crossed over to join them as well.

Marcus recovered better than Will and continued to swing and jab at the dark mage. In between the strikes, Clearshot launched more arrows.

THE ANGEL'S DESCENT

I should back them up, Will thought through the dulling pain as he rose to his feet. The motion caused him to waver, and the ringing in his ears only eased when he decided to remove his helmet.

Clover tree bark, mint leaves, or even some lavender flowers would be perfect right about now, the herbalist in the back of his head muttered. Those three items had saved him from many headaches over the years and tasted better than the bitter, alternative plants. That same part of his mind wondered if he could find some when the fight ended. With how the situation progressed, he believed that would be the least of their problems.

Marcus continued aiming for limbs while Clearshot's arrows burrowed in Byron's chest, yet the dark mage remained resilient. He started another cot on fire while scorching the stone around Marcus before adjusting his magic to send a blast of lightning at Clearshot. Before the bolts could reach their target, Emilea cast a shielding spell to protect that side of the room. This left the assistant general to dodge whatever flames were thrown his way as Byron removed one arrow at a time.

Will continued looking between Marcus and the trio while attempting to ignore the growing flames until the cabinet at the back of the station caught his attention, giving him an idea. When his friend went on the offensive again, he forced his legs to bring him to that side of the room.

His companions noticed the movement, as did Byron, and the latter shot a ball of fire in his direction. Will paused to duck and let the spell fly by with a wave of heat before resuming the trek to his objective. Because of the others' attacks, nothing else hindered his progress, and he threw open the wooden doors once he reached the cabinet.

"Watch my back!" he shouted in Emilea's direction while pushing up his glasses. As soon as he saw her nod, he faced the assortment of items and began his search.

At least two dozen shelves contained various glass bottles, paper bags, bandages, and other necessities for a regularly used medical station. What he needed would be in a bottle, though he knew he might not find more than one or two.

Will had become familiar with what potions the healers kept in the area because he often found himself volunteering to forage for ingredients while conducting his own research. From what he understood, most light mages refused to treat simple ailments, such as head or stomach aches, muscle fatigue, and minor scratches, for personal reasons. He always figured the simple tasks were beneath their skill level; either that, or they wanted to teach their patients a lesson in self-care or raise their pain tolerance.

The noise continued while he scanned the handwritten labels glued to the shelves and recalled the mixture he remembered restocking months ago at a light mage's request. *Valerian root steeped in boiling water…grind with the rose-colored petals. I added a few ripe cherries for color…*

That narrowed the assortment down considerably as only several proved to be the same, ruby color. At last, in the bottom half, he spotted the label VALERIAN ROOT: MILD SEDATIVE. Five bottles as tall as his finger sat above the name, so Will snatched them all and spun around to find Grace at his back. She had crafted her own shield to protect him, though it rippled instead of remaining solid like the master mages'.

"Go back by them," he told her and gestured at Emilea and Clearshot with his chin.

She looked over her shoulder to stare at him and the bottles. "What are you going to do?"

"These should keep him down long enough for Emilea to try and release Hendal's control over his mind. If anything, we'll get an opportunity to escape." He didn't elaborate since his main concern was figuring out a way for Byron to drink the potions.

"How is he going to take these?" she asked, echoing his thoughts.

Will decided to pass the bottles over to her with an explanation as it formed in his head. "Marcus, Clearshot, and I should be able to immobilize him. We'll need you to bring the sedatives when that happens."

His friend began voicing her doubts, but Will remembered how precious every second was going forward and began to walk toward the continuing combat; however, when his hand reached for the sword previously at his waist, he realized he left it across the room after Byron punched him earlier.

Now what?

"Take my dagger," Grace said after noticing his hesitation. She dismissed her shield, passed along the weapon in her hand, and returned to Emilea without another word.

Will forced himself not to consider what needed to be done as he approached the dark mage. His instincts needed to lead his actions if they were to successfully restrain Byron.

Marcus backed up against the nearest wall where he continued dodging the fireballs being launched at his limbs. One blast caught the assistant general in the right arm, causing him to transfer his blade to the opposite hand with a pained expression.

Don't worry about Marcus, Will tried to tell himself as he prepared to charge. *If I go for the legs, he might get the hint.*

He made that his goal and ran to meet Byron. Although the dark mage turned upon hearing the footsteps, Will plunged the dagger into the possessed man's right thigh. A second later, his body was shoved backward in retaliation. He expected the physical push to be followed by a spell, so he darted to the side, just in case. The resulting flash of lightning confirmed his prediction, as did the smoke rising from the floor where he previously stood.

Thankfully, Marcus resumed his attacks and managed to cause some injury that created a puddle of blood at the dark mage's feet. Clearshot also jumped in by finding an opening whenever Marcus retreated.

Since Will had released his hold on the knife after his stab, he found himself without a weapon once more.

Just move! some part of him shouted, so he did.

Once Byron's back was to him, he charged with as much speed as he could muster. Marcus saw him coming and swiped across Byron's knees before sidestepping to avoid the resulting punch. In the next instant, Will threw all of his weight into their target's side while using his shoulder to deliver most of the blow.

Either Marcus and Clearshot's strikes weakened Byron or the dark mage didn't expect Will, for he fell onto his side without attempting to protect himself from the tackle. Will landed on top of the wounded legs and remained there to catch his breath, too dazed to realize his tactic had worked. The assistant general appeared after with his sword over Byron's chest and brought it down into the flesh with a squishing sound that made Will want to throw up.

"Grace!" he cried instead and remained where he was to wrap his arms around the legs beneath him.

Byron feebly reached his arms upward to grab at Marcus and attempted to kick at Will until their Yeluthian friend appeared.

"What do I do?" she asked with a terrified expression.

"Pour them all into his mouth," Will ordered.

She knelt, uncorked one of the bottles, and tried to follow his instruction. To their dismay, the dark mage spit it out and growling in frustration. When he stretched his hands for her, Marcus kicked them away without remorse.

"He will not swallow the potion," came Grace's distressed response.

Will considered what he could do in his position before he heard footsteps and saw Emilea and Clearshot hurrying over.

"Give them to me," the former said while throwing herself to her knees beside Grace.

When Byron began to struggle again, Will focused on maintaining his hold, though he noticed the kicks steadily grew weaker as the seconds passed by. Whatever the light mage was doing, it seemed to be working, and she let them know when the bottles were empty. They waited until the sedative kicked in and his body completely stopped lashing out to rise.

The dark mage looked horrific with his chest and legs wounded, his bruised hands at his sides, and the potion smeared all over his face. His head shifted from side to side, and he wore a grimace while squeezing his eyes shut.

"What did you plan on doing with him?" Marcus asked in between breaths while they waited in silence.

Will felt lightheaded then since he no longer needed to rely on his body's natural adrenaline to survive. "I figured Emilea would want to try getting rid of the demon's hold," he answered without considering if his friend addressed someone else.

Before the master mage could reply, a voice from nearby interrupted their conversation.

"Is everyone all right?"

The shielding spell Byron used to separate the room had vanished, allowing Detrix and Marcy to rejoin their group.

"We're fine," Clearshot answered for them. "Byron's been drugged, so he's not a threat, for the time being."

The Yeluthian commander approached the bloodied body on the floor with an unreadable expression. "I see. Are you planning on leaving him like this?"

"We can't," Marcus said with a frown, as if disgusted by the idea.

Will felt the same, yet neither of them wielded the magic to heal Byron. They glanced at Emilea, who shook her head.

"If I use my energy here, I may not have enough when the time comes to face Hendal or the demon. We *need* more than one light mage for the set of spells."

"Is there nothing you can do, Commander?" Grace asked with wide, helpless eyes.

This time, Detrix offered a sympathetic smile. "I will assist if it is what you all decide, though I agree with the lady that we should not waste our time healing his pawns. After all, cutting off the head of the serpent is more useful than the tail."

"Byron can help us when we find Hendal," Marcus protested. "He's a master mage, and he knows the palace's layout too."

Detrix shrugged. "As I said, I can perform the extraction at the very least to free his mind from the demon's hold. That power would go back to the enemy, and I refuse to use the goddess fire since that will drain me of my energy."

When no one else added any additional comments, the Yeluthian commander asked Marcus to remove his blade from Byron's chest and Clearshot to gather the remaining arrows before ordering everyone to stand farther away. Then, they watched and waited as Byron's injuries began to heal on their own.

"What are you waiting for?" Marcy demanded when the dark mage began to sit up.

Detrix never removed his eyes from Byron and knelt to place both hands on the bloodied torso. "I thought you would want your friend healed before he returns to you."

Will could never usually see light magic at work except for glowing spots on a mage's hands or their patient's body. This experience seemed similar as the Yeluthian commander's hands became enveloped in a golden light, yet a warmth radiated from them to gently brush along Will's face. It comforted him, especially when Byron's body relaxed and his face no longer appeared pained. The whole process took less than a minute.

"There," Detrix said as he wiped his forehead with the back of one hand. After he inspected the result, he stood while the rest of their group circled around Byron.

"Do we just leave him here?" Marcy was the first to ask.

"I suggest we move on," the Yeluthian commander offered. "Your friend is breathing, but there is no telling what the experience did to him, both mentally and physically. Besides, once word reaches the high priest, he will likely send others after us."

"What do you think, Emilea?" Marcus grumbled. It was obvious no one wanted to abandon Byron in his condition.

"Commander Detrix is right. We must remember everyone is still fighting outside, so time is limited."

A grunt from below startled their group, and most of them said Byron's name while the dark mage sat up and rubbed his eyes.

"What's...going on?" he mumbled, reminding Will of the sedative.

Emilea knelt and laid a hand on her fellow master mage's shoulder. "Are you hurt? Do you feel any pain?"

Although he looked dazed, her questions brought more life into his expression. He began patting down his chest and arms to check for an injury before shaking his head. "No," he concluded. "Nothing's wrong."

The room quieted as one of the burning beds collapsed with a snapping sound.

"We should keep moving," Clearshot said as he stood to offer his wife a hand.

She stared at it, sighed, and accepted the gesture.

"What should we do with Byron?" Will asked, even though the dark mage watched. "I doubt that much medicine will wear off shortly. Unless, I can stay here."

"Are you sure you'll be safe?" Marcus countered.

Before Will could answer, Grace offered her support. "I sense no trace of demonic energy around here anymore and can remain too, just in case."

"Let us be off then," Detrix urged. The Yeluthian commander turned to exit through the other door with Emilea, Clearshot, Marcus, and Marcy behind.

Now that the excitement died down, Will's temple resumed throbbing. His helmet still sat near the windows where he removed it, but he didn't intend to use it anymore since it hindered his senses.

Grace must have mistaken his pain for worry, though, because she glanced around the room before voicing a question. "Should we move to a safer location? The smoke is not as thick, yet if you think someone might find us…"

Will could hear the nerves brought about by her suspicion and prepared to plot out their next steps. Once Byron returned to his senses, they could reunite with the others or work on their own. Until then, it was his responsibility to defend them with Grace monitoring the area.

Before he could voice his conclusion, though, the master mage spoke in a surprisingly gentle manner.

"We should catch up with the rest of your group. If they're going after Hendal, they'll need our help."

"You must rest," Grace persisted.

Her words were brushed aside as Byron attempted to stand on his own. He wavered until Will moved to place the master mage's arm over one shoulder and support some of his weight. Together, they managed to walk near the exit.

Before they could leave, Grace slid in front of the doorway. "Are you sure about this?"

Byron met her concern with a smile so familiar it was hard to believe he had been under Hendal's possession at all. "Thank you both for offering to stay behind with me. Once my mind clears and my body can move freely again, I'll be strong enough to assist in your efforts; however, we don't have time to waste. I refuse to sit around while that happens. If you can help me a little longer, we'll do this as a team."

After a moment to contemplate his plea, Grace hesitantly agreed to go forward.

The trio left the medical station and continued along the right path leading toward the back of the palace. Since the area housed the royal family and their private rooms, Will wasn't as familiar with the layout, but Byron seemed confident in their direction. The master mage even began striding and relieved Will of his duty as a support crutch.

"Grace, can you contact Emilea to let her know our location?" Byron asked after they turned another corner. "Tell her we're on our way to meet them."

She nodded and closed her eyes to relay the message.

In the meantime, the master mage sparked up an unexpected conversation with Will.

"That was some quick thinking, using potions to slow my movements. I couldn't control my actions, yet I remember everything through a haze. Also, I'm sorry for that bump on your head."

The strain beneath his words had Will wondering what kind of internal struggle went on in the heads of those under the demon's influence. To keep himself from considering it too much, he listed off the ingredients in the mixture, and Grace interrupted to confirm a response a minute later.

"They are slowing enough for us to catch up," she explained before sharing directions the light mage provided.

"We better hurry then," Byron responded with a nod. With every passing second, he seemed more and more like his former self.

14

How long has it been? Coura wondered as she hovered above the ground just beyond what remained of the front line. Until that moment, she hadn't found a break to observe the battlefield.

Dozens of soldiers, both belonging to Dala and Verona, scattered along the gray grass; however, from what she could tell, the generals' plan moved along without issue. The troops under their command just reached the outer part of their camp, though only the Nim-Valan soldiers truly pursued. Coura noticed hundreds of enemy soldiers pausing in the middle of the clearing below, as if either confused or disheartened by how easily the fight turned in their favor. Steadily, they crept farther from the palace.

Meanwhile she, along with the Yeluthians, continually attacked the shield Soirée summoned to protect the palace. Most of the bronze-clad troops pushed the hesitating Asteom soldiers south in order to create a wider separation. Fortunately for Coura, that was when Hendal sent out the rogue angels to keep the dozen or so Yeluthians around her company. She didn't recognize some of the flying enemies from their previous appearances, yet it became evident they held a grudge against their own people. Each sparked vicious words with another in bronze armor, but given the situation, nothing came across clearly enough for her to understand.

This frustratingly hindered Coura's progress. When she moved to take on an opponent in the air, they cast her a dubious, spiteful glare, turned in another direction, and darted away. If she pursued, they kept their distance and circled the area; when she came within striking distance, the rogue angel shifted to head for the palace. Just as Soirée's power blocked any offensive spells, the violet wall appeared once again to seemingly halt both flyers. While Coura opened her wings to slow down and avoid ramming into the spell, her opponent soared faster as the demon released her magic to let the angel slip through before bringing the wall of energy up again a second later. Twice already, it prevented Coura from following, so she decided to keep her distance for the time being.

Ever since the battle began, it felt as though the time shifted between the passing seconds speeding up and the minutes crawling by. At the moment while she surveyed the clearing, it was the latter.

What can I do? she wondered and tried to calm her rising sense of impatience. *I should already be inside the palace. If I can just figure out how to get past that annoying shield, then I might-*

A flap of wings to the left instinctively had Coura spinning around and raising her blade in preparation for an oncoming attack. Instead of an enemy, one of the Yeluthian troops moved to her side, though their blood-splattered helmet prevented her from knowing their identity.

"What is wrong?" came a tired, male voice she didn't recognize.

"I need to get through," she replied while pointing her sword at the ever-present shield. In her mind, she recalled how little the Yeluthians knew about her past and expected their dismissal due to that lack of understanding.

"Leave them be," the stranger said, proving Coura's point. "Our orders are to capture or eliminate the outlaws."

"Outlaws?"

"The scum who act against us. Did you not figure that out yet?" The soldier all but grumbled the question before hurrying to where three of his comrades engaged with a pair of rogue angels in silver armor.

Coura remained where she was, contemplating her predicament until something struck her right calf and left wing. The force proved minimal enough to keep her position stable, and she glanced down to see a pair of Asteom soldiers directly below with bows aimed upward.

Then, she noticed the warm blood dripping from her wounds. As she descended to the ground, she removed both of the deeply embedded arrows, tossed them away, and dispatched the two soldiers when they didn't retreat. Part of her felt guilty for their deaths, yet her focus shifted to the next objective.

"You are as merciless as ever!" someone shouted from above.

Coura looked up at the source of the condescending words to see one of Hendal's angels, the leader named Drake. Just like his companions, he wore silver armor presumably belonging to the Asteom soldiers, though no helmet hid his smirk.

When she kept silent, he lowered himself to the ground and stood across from her while continuing his chastising. "I have been waiting for you, but I must apologize. My companions and I hold a slight grudge against the Yeluthians who banished us, and that revenge comes before anything else."

The piece of information didn't surprise Coura based on her previous observation. She half-expected the angel to go on with his rambling; instead, Drake charged. She brought up her blade in order to knock his away, then she followed with a horizontal slice; however, he retreated to manifest his wings and beckoned her closer.

"Come," he cried as the smirk stretched wider. "Join me in the air where we can fight freely! Do not worry about me fleeing either. I promise to dedicate as much time as necessary to put an end to your pathetic existence."

After his taunt, he leapt into the air and climbed higher while Coura followed at a safe distance. The frigid air was no more tolerable with a clear sky than during an overcast, and the sunlight served no other purpose than to make her squint when it reflected off her enemies' silver armor. The sound of their wingbeats as they reached an appropriate height drowned out the clashing of weapons below.

"Why is it you were banished from Yeluthia?" she felt compelled to ask during the resulting pause.

Drake's grin faltered for a moment, then it returned while he shrugged. "If you can defeat me, perhaps I will tell you."

With no other words to distract from the inevitable, Coura chose to go on the offensive first. She had only experienced combat in the air less than a handful of times, and it started to show once Drake backed away from the attack. In the past, Soirée had usually offered a warning if Coura didn't catch an opponent's movement. The lack of such assistance resulted in a pair of cuts across her wings after the strike, which set the tone of their fight.

For several minutes, she struggled against his brute strength while blocking since sidestepping, ducking, or any other form of dodging proved difficult to manage in the air. When she tried, he noticed and either prepared another attack or retreated upon sensing her retaliation.

Why is he so much faster than before? Coura wondered through the pain of another, deep slash through her forearm. *I hurt him and the other rogue angels last time in the Valley Beyond. Then again, the one with the goddess gift healed them instantly, so I guess they didn't need to worry about losing their lives.*

Drake raised his blade above his head to catch the sunlight and reflect it into Coura's eyes momentarily. A hint of fear gripped her heart during that instance of blindness, and she adjusted to block the vertical slice that followed.

An ugly laugh escaped the angel as he barbarically struck her sword again and again, like a hammer against a nail. "What happened to your ferocity?" he demanded to mock her current position. "I acted carelessly before because of the circumstances, but I expected more out of you. Even the weakest of the Yeluthian scum put up more of a fight!"

Coura grunted as she stabbed for him, but her sword passed through the air as Drake swept his wings in order to slide backward in an arch, leaving her panting in frustration and confusion.

"What is the matter? Have you depleted your energy?" he taunted.

She tried her best to ignore him, settle down, and focus before attempting another attack. *Why can't I hit him? I thought it had to do with speed, but I'm starting to realize that isn't the case. He slips away from every attack, so I can only defend.*

A stray cloud passed above to shroud the land in a cool shadow, which eased her eyesight. Without turning her attention away from her opponent, she noticed the rogue angels and Yeluthian soldiers darting around the clearing. A thought flickered in her mind as she watched the bronze suits of armor darting from one location to another. The scene vaguely reminded her of when Drake and his companions pursued her around the Valley Beyond.

They never stay in one place, and they don't stop moving to defend against attacks. By constantly dodging, they allow themselves the freedom to move without any sort of boundary, she realized.

A glance at the battlefield below showed she had been unintentionally keeping to one spot.

That has to be it. My training never prepared me for fights in the air. Byron, the other instructors at the academy, and even my old teacher in Neston always taught me to stay grounded while using a weapon. Blocking prevents a combatant from giving up space, and dodging or sliding out of the way should still allow them to remain within a sort of invisible circle. I'm almost certain Soirée is as clueless about this as I am considering she never had wings. Otherwise, I'm sure she would've instructed me differently.

She thanked her luck for that moment of reflection as Drake sprang at her after. For the time being, Coura kept her attention on maneuvering her wings and body out of harm's way while going against her instinct and distancing herself from her original starting point. Although maintaining a speed to match her opponent and avoid his sword felt natural, the effort it took to force her body to disobey one of the basic rules of hand-to-hand combat proved great enough to make her sweat.

"Where is your bite?" the rogue angel demanded with a wide swing to the right.

Coura grit her teeth and chanced going on the offensive. Using her wings, she created a blast of air by thrusting them forward while propelling herself back, then she twisted around to soar away in the opposite direction. The palace and violet shield stood in front of her, and she sensed the demonic energy supporting the nearly invisible spell. Even without looking behind, she knew Drake followed at her heels. The mages and archers below were too far away to interfere, but several Yeluthians engaged in combat close enough to be of concern.

I need to finish this, she told herself as the cloud passed across the sky and let the sunlight continue shining on the chaos.

It was too risky to halt right away, and slowing would allow Drake to catch her, so she decided to pull in her wings while spinning her body around. As expected, her opponent lunged with the tip of his blade pointed at her heart. A slight adjustment to the right had the weapon sliding straight through Coura's left bicep instead of her chest.

She accepted the inevitable pain and used the sacrifice as a chance to retaliate. Before Drake understood what she let happen, Coura slashed across his body from shoulder to hip with all her strength. Blood poured forth from the wound, and his expression fell into utter shock. His right hand held his blade in her arm while his left hand fruitlessly tried to stop the bleeding.

"You might not have your healer anymore, but I don't mind sacrificing a limb or two," Coura admitted with some smugness while they hovered.

The rogue angel gazed around frantically, looking anywhere except at her. Movement continued all around them, yet his eyes caught and held something over her shoulder. His pleading expression had Coura turning her head in an attempt to face the potential danger. She saw a set of silver armor and someone in bronze before her head was violently yanked forward again.

Drake twisted the blade in her arm and used his other, bloodied hand to grip her hair close to the scalp. "I refuse to die," he growled through his teeth in rage. "I refuse! I refuse!"

His sudden aggression took Coura back until whoever appeared behind her clashed in a series of ringing metal, grunts, and a screech of connecting blades that resulted in a pause. Coura tightened her grip on the hilt of her sword before bringing it up to punch Drake on his left cheek. He reeled backward and bobbed up and down, as if struggling to stay in the air. Meanwhile, she removed the sword in her arm and threw it away before assessing the figures behind her.

A Yeluthian covered head to toe in bronze splattered with crimson floated at her back. Two of the silver-clad angels watched him with their weapons at the ready. Coura recognized one from the Valley

THE ANGEL'S DESCENT

Beyond because of his unusual, cropped hair, but she didn't recall engaging with the second male.

"Are you hurt?" the Yeluthian soldier asked her while glancing over his shoulder.

She recognized her father's voice, though his sudden appearance left her dumbfounded. "Evern? What are you doing here?"

"I have been monitoring the front line to keep an eye on you and deal with these few."

In that moment, Coura understood he had just saved her from being ambushed by the pair in silver who were coming to Drake's aid. The notion gave her a mixture of pride in her father's speed and strength, as well as some embarrassment for her lack of skill against the rogue angel. Reminding him of her healing ability would express both of those emotions, so she thanked him curtly but not without sincerity.

"Keep an eye on that one," he said after. "King Arval requested we apprehend those who resist unless death is the only option."

"Shut up!" the unfamiliar angel yelled at Evern. "Your king is nothing but a tyrant! At least here we are given the chance to change how we are viewed."

"Would you rather be regarded as the criminals you are in Asteom than face justice in Yeluthia?" Evern responded in a cold manner, which made Coura flinch.

His question visibly upset the pair, and they raised their weapons again as a threat. Coura did the same with the intent to join her father until he extended his arm in front of her in a gesture for her to stop.

"I will take care of these two," he stated. "Bring the one you injured down to be restrained, if possible. Wait there for me after."

She opened her mouth to oppose his decision to fight alone, and possibly address his consistent lack of trust in her actions, but he shot forward to initiate the combat.

As Coura noticed mere minutes earlier, everyone in the air never followed a boundary while trading blows, and she grew envious of her father's ability to float, spin, dodge, and perform numerous aerial maneuvers without showing much effort. His opponents fought similarly yet not as smooth. Their armor protected against scratches, which meant mere stabs or lucky swings did no real damage.

From out of the corner of her eye, she spotted Drake where she left him. Without his weapon and bearing a bleeding wound, Coura figured he would either give himself up or eventually lose consciousness. Neither seemed likely to happen when he snarled at her, though he panted and struggled to stay steady. Before she could request he admit defeat, the rogue angel tightened his wings to dive through the air beneath her; a slight adjustment in his direction put him on a clear path toward the palace. Coura pursued him a second later.

Even in his weakened condition, Drake could still pump his wings and tighten them in a rhythm only mastered through experience. This kept him ahead of her as they approached Soirée's spell.

Where does he think he's going now? she thought and slowed her pace after remembering the barrier. *If he passes through, I'm going to lose. I doubt Soirée would let me follow if she hasn't before, meaning this might be my only chance...*

With that reasoning in mind and an understanding of the shield from the previous enemies' passings, she felt confident increasing her speed.

Drake never slowed nor did he bother glancing behind as he approached the shimmering wall of demonic energy. Coura strained the muscles in her wings to launch herself forward just as the spell waned enough to let him pass. In those precious seconds, she kept her body just above his in order to slip through too.

The energy shifted to presumably seal the hole, but she didn't dare look away from the rogue angel to confirm the adjustment. He hadn't noticed how close she remained, giving her an opportunity to surprise him. Unfortunately, the palace's wall rushed at them to spoil the moment.

We're moving too fast! she realized in shock before attempting to snap her wings open. *I became so focused on catching up that I didn't pay attention to what was beyond the shield.*

Drake's white feathers puffed in a similar, flustered manner as Coura braced for the inevitable impact by raising her arms to her face and turning to the side as much as she could manage. In the next instant, her vision went completely dark when her body connected with stone. A disorienting, falling sensation, accompanied by a throbbing in her head, both arms, and right hip, resulted in another blackout.

*

After what felt like hours of sleep, Coura regained consciousness and found her body curled up on one side. A wing wrapped underneath to keep her from lying directly on the stiff ground, and the other draped over her. The demonic energy in her center hummed in response to the pain, initiating its automatic healing. She sat up slowly, unable to hide a stretched hiss as she did so, and put a hand on her throbbing temple.

My head... It feels like it's going to burst. How long has it been?

Coura noticed a warm liquid dripping down her face and removed her hand to find the palm and fingers red with fresh blood. Although the healing already began easing the damage, her stomach still dropped upon understanding the extent of her injury.

Glancing around hurt as well. In the distance, she could vaguely make out the figures in the sky and a mass of people farther away on the ground. Any light that reflected off the metal weapons or armor stung badly enough to have her squeezing her eyes shut.

Once the disorientation subsided, Coura pushed herself to her feet where she wobbled and searched for Drake.

He couldn't have landed far.

As expected, the rogue angel fell closer to the palace in a heap of feathers, and his wings acted like a shell to cover his entire body. She made to investigate when something struck the back of her left leg, sending her to one knee.

"You'll stay down if you know what's good for you!" came a shout from behind.

Throughout the day, Coura became familiar with the sting of an arrow and winced as she removed the one in her calf. A group of mages in white and blue stood nearby, though their robes blurred together into one swirl of color. Out of pure instinct, she raised a hand and unleashed a lightning spell in their direction, spurring shrieks beneath the crack of thunder. Once the air cleared, she watched the remaining mages pick up their companions or begin healing spells; none so much as looked her way afterward.

Coura rose and walked over to stand next to Drake, who wound up on his side with a pained expression. Already, her body felt completely healed, though her eyesight remained hazy.

"Are you still alive?" she asked without hiding her dislike for the rogue angel.

Drake cracked one eye open. It stared at her feet before wandering up her body until it reached her face. Then, he grinned and chuckled weakly.

"I should have known," he started. Each word sounded raspy, as if it were an effort to speak. "You are a monster, like that demon."

For some reason, that was funny to him. Coura waited for more while his snickering turned into genuine laughter despite the obvious injuries hindering his breathing. When her temper simmered enough, she brought her leg back and kicked him in the stomach. Even with armor, the impact had Drake pressing both arms against the spot while lying flat on his back. The laughter continued in between fits of coughing and gasps, but it became evident he would no longer be a threat in his current condition.

Coura let her eyes wander from his position to search for some way into the palace until the rogue angel spoke again.

"I really hoped...to see how this will end. I still...wonder if..."

"What are you talking about?" she responded with a frown.

Drake's breathing grew labored, yet he went on with eyelids half closed and humorless lips pulled thin. "I suppose it does not matter what I say now."

"Should I wait until Soirée heals you?" Coura asked sarcastically; however, when his expression didn't change, she felt a bit guilty for the snarky question.

"None of us will accept assistance from that creature. We would lose all honor as beings of light, bestowed with such power by our goddess. I believe the demon understands that as well, though I have never known her to be sympathetic toward our kind. That is, except for you."

Despite the vulnerable person in front of her being an enemy, Coura felt herself pitying him. "Why did you work with Hendal? What was your goal?"

The seemingly lifeless eyes raised to meet hers once more. "You could never understand what it is like to be trapped. Not all of us were; some are just crazed murderers who wished to see Yeluthia suffer for their punishments. The rest of us were not happy with the lives we lived. We prayed for change, and for that, we were either cast out or chose to leave. For a time, that man in the palace had the same ideas. We were going to establish a world of freedom for those oppressed by traditions and birthrights. A country where no one is forced into a life they do not wish to lead, and one where positions can still be available to those who made mistakes in the past or are from a family with a troubled past."

Coura hadn't expected an answer, or at least one that personal, and found herself at a loss for words as Drake's eyes closed. *How could their answer to injustice be violence? Then again, what they believe is unfair might be how their society has lived for decades. Still, what would changing anything in Asteom do?*

"You're right," she muttered as more questions came to mind. "I don't understand."

Only when his chest stopped moving and his face went pale did she step away to take on the next part of her mission.

Coura remembered her father's order for her to remain in the field until he finished his fight with the two others. Staring at Soirée's ever-present barrier, which hovered between solidified and transparent, had her dismissing the idea.

Marcus said I could join their group once the enemy is taken care of and I passed through their defenses. I suppose my next move is to find the ancestral weapon. We're going to need it once Soirée shows her face. Then, I'll search for Emilea and Detrix to make sure Hendal is brought down first.

Mages, archers, and soldiers in Asteom's silver armor ran, limped, and lied all around, yet none were close enough to be of concern. After walking to the palace wall, she stretched her limbs and shook her head to find no lingering pain or side effects from her collision with the stone exterior, though her forehead itched enough to remind her of the drying blood along the right side of her face.

I'd hate to encounter anyone besides the Nim-Valans, Hendal, or the rogue angels, Coura thought with a wince at the foggy memory of when she struck down the mages earlier. *Since I'm sure Soirée knows where I am, I could use the outdoor hallway to avoid any confrontations here. As long as I hurry and focus on finding the basement space, I can leave anyone inside alone.*

The outer hall spanned most of the width of the third and fourth floors, meaning an entrance would be accessible from her location. Coura moved away from the wall until she nearly backed up against the demon's shield and summoned her wings. One leap with their support carried her to the bulging section on the third floor where she slipped through a glass-less window opening. As soon as both feet touched stone, she crouched in case anybody noticed and planned to launch an attack, yet nothing passed above, not even a breeze to carry the sounds and smells of the battle.

From her time in the palace, Coura had heard of the basement area reserved for soldiers to store their armor, weapons, shields, and other items since their bulk took up plenty of space in a regular bedroom; however, with no belongings of her own, she never bothered to look into the area. That lack of knowledge left her fumbling for a way to access the lowest level.

I need to get going, she decided after another moment of contemplation. *I should keep moving down, then I'll find the stairs leading there. As a last resort, I suppose I could just blast a hole in the middle of the first level's floor, but I'd rather not draw attention to our efforts. We would all be in serious trouble if Hendal or Soirée found out about the ancestral weapons.*

Coura released the spell on her wings before creeping to the nearest door and slipping inside the palace. Her footsteps hardly made noise, especially with the commotion outside, allowing her to jog to the nearest staircase despite the dimly lit hallways. The stairs were within sight in another minute, and she descended while skipping two steps at a time.

THE ANGEL'S DESCENT

The staircases leading from the fourth floor to the third and the second to the first are on the south side while the one I just went down is on the east side. If the pattern continues, the set from the first floor to the basement should be in the same direction.

Soon, she spotted her goal and descended to the ground level. Unlike the previous two floors, this one proved to be completely lit, so she slowed her pace until she reached an intersection with three other hallways. She knew continuing forward led straight to the kitchens and mess hall, and heading right would bring her toward the front of the building. This meant she needed to go left; however, voices echoing from one of the paths had Coura pressing against the wall under the nearest shadow.

As the sources neared, the individual tones and pitches became clearer, and she recognized one after the other. She stepped out of hiding to wait in the middle of the intersection since the voices grew louder to signal their arrival at her location. A minute later, their silhouettes came into view down the western hallway.

Whoever was in front paused before she heard Clearshot.

"Coura, is that you?" he asked with more amazement than uncertainty.

Casually, she waved a hand and moved to stand near the closest torch.

Meanwhile, the group approached with less hesitation. Emilea, Clearshot, and the Yeluthian commander assumed the lead, then Marcus and Marcy followed with Grace in the middle. She figured Will held up the rear but didn't expect anyone else, so upon seeing Byron, Coura felt a weight fall off her shoulders.

"What are you doing here?" the Yeluthian man in his full bronze suit asked first.

Those who knew her well enough expressed their surprise, relief, and worry after. Once they completed their brief reunion, including mention of the dried blood across half of her face and arm, Coura brushed aside the concerned comments to share her intentions.

"I'm going to search for the ancestral weapon. Can anyone tell me where the set of stairs leading to the storage area is?"

"It's good we met up with you then," Clearshot responded in his carefree manner. "We're heading that way right now."

"Another pair of eyes would help," Marcy added with a nod.

"Fine, let us move," the Yeluthian commander said to take control of the situation. "Coura, I would like to hear how the battle fares outside. Walk beside me, and Lady Emilea and her husband can resume guiding us."

While he spoke, Coura glanced over the others. She could practically feel the mixture of emotions radiating from their expressions, which included an acceptance of what they would be facing next. In a way, it comforted her to know how mentally prepared they were when it came to risking their lives.

"Come along," Emilea said while passing by with Clearshot to resume their walk through the opposite corridor.

*

The Yeluthian beside Coura expressed his thanks for the news she provided regarding his fellow commander and their troops. While everyone else listened, no one commented on her update. After her report, they saw the descending staircase near the back of the palace.

"From what I remember, there should be a set of doors directly at the bottom," the master light mage commented as they went down together. "We may need to break the lock, but I don't foresee any trouble."

"The weapon might be easier to find than you think," Byron added from his spot.

"What do you mean?"

Their group reached the bottom of the stairs as the light mage voiced her question and saw the aforementioned metal doors flung open. Since there were no windows or lit torches, a still coolness carrying dozens of years of must greeted them. Both Coura and Byron cast controlled fire spells to create a ball of flame in the palm of their hands. The red glow looked eerie in the seemingly abandoned place, yet it provided enough light for them to make out their surroundings.

"I'll return upstairs for a torch," Will offered while the others went inside to survey the messy space.

Coura expected a somewhat organized collection of weapons, shields, suits of armor on fitted stands, crates or armoires, and wooden posts for displaying more objects. With how large the area was, perhaps spanning the entire length and width of the palace above, there seemed to be enough room for thousands of items to be kept. Even so, it appeared as if a windstorm blew through, ravaging whatever stood in its path. Weapons, both metal and wooden, and random pieces of armor had been discarded all over the floor. The cabinets had been thrown open and emptied, stands were tipped onto their sides, and she didn't see a single shield in the piles. Will reappeared then and began lighting any torches he could find lining the walls, which were few and nearly useless in the dampness, while the others followed.

"Hendal ordered the Nim-Valans and Asteom troops to raid this place for weapons and armor to replace their own equipment," Byron explained with a touch of sadness. "I vaguely recall the command. Once they were satisfied, the mages could scavenge through the rest."

"How could he allow this?" Marcus demanded. "He robbed the soldiers of their own belongings. Those people entrusted them to the army and royal family!"

"Even so, we must focus on the goal at hand," the Yeluthian commander reminded them. Unlike everyone else, he seemed unaffected by the sight, making Coura wonder if he anticipated something like this to happen.

Their route to light the torches stopped about halfway across the space when Will turned to face them. "It's going to take hours to search through all of this."

Coura rubbed the back of her neck to try and ease some of the growing tension in her body. *There's a chance the ancestral weapon might not be here or was never in the palace to begin with too. I just need to trust Cintra's foresight.*

"Does anyone have any suggestions?" Clearshot asked while glancing over the group.

"We should split up," Byron said after the pause. "In pairs, we'll be able to spread out enough to cover the entire area. One person can carry a light source so the other can search freely."

"That sounds like the most productive method," Marcus added with a nod. He reached over to grab the nearest torch. "Clearshot and I will take the front by the entrance and keep an eye out for the enemy if they come our way."

"Grace, why don't you join me?" Emilea said next with a hand on the ambassador's shoulder.

Byron offered to go alone since he could produce his own light source, leaving Will and his torch to guide Marcy and Coura with the commander they addressed as Detrix. The name sounded familiar, eventually leading her to recall it being mentioned back at their camp. He acted comfortably enough around her to avoid forcing a conversation while they began looking over the nearest items.

For what felt like hours, their group combed through the mess in search of the ancestral weapon. Any talk died down with the consistent sounds of metal, wood, and leather being pushed around or thrown into a new pile and armoires sliding along the stone floor. Even with only one hand available, Coura dismissed dozens of pieces littering the space as none shined any brighter than a dull reflection, which certainly meant anything worth its value had been taken. Still, no one mentioned ending the scavenge.

She bent over the final weapon in the nearest bunch, a mace with a broken handle, and kicked it aside before standing straight to stretch her back. It was tempting to quit in favor of saving precious time, and she seriously contemplated bringing it up. Still, the quiet emphasized her friends' intense focus, and that would be best left undisturbed for the moment.

So, the search went on. Her partner, Detrix, remained at the edge of the circle of light Coura provided, though she had no idea how he could see in the dim setting. The thought prompted her to rub her tiring eyes before starting on her next target of interest.

An armoire of a rich, dark wood stood two heads taller than her and bore intricate carvings of a forest landscape on its sides. As with the others, both doors were thrown open, though one hung downward unnaturally because of its damaged hinges, and nothing remained inside. Coura sighed a bit dramatically at the results but decided to continue being as thorough as possible. On each side were dull blades better suited for practicing than actual combat, which she dismissed altogether.

Finally, she peeked around the back. There, she spotted the unmistakable shadow of a sword sheath hanging at eye level. It took some effort to push the armoire forward with one arm, but once she did, there proved to be enough room for her to grab the hidden item. Its location piqued her curiosity, and she found it caught on something. Her hand raised with the coarse material until her fingers brushed against what felt like a rusted nail. With the eagerness of anyone who stumbled upon what they believed to be actual treasure, Coura grasped the sheath and yanked. She heard the cloth rip as it tore away in one pull, nearly making her fall backward at the unexpected release.

The excitement her discovery built disappeared with one look at the bundle of ragged cloth poorly sewn into a makeshift sheath. Her eyes scanned the material before lingering on the hilt. Similar to the carvings on the armoire, there was no doubt its surface had been crafted with care, even if a sheet of cobwebs and dust clung to it. The guards curved upward a little with feather-like indents, and the red glow of the fire spell played tricks on her eyes until she blew away the debris. Then, she couldn't mistake its golden color.

This is it! Coura's disbelief left her speechless. A sense of hope welled inside her chest, solidifying her determination.

Since her left hand held the ball of fire and her right the weapon, she placed the sword underneath her left armpit to cease the hilt and shake off the sheath after. Its loose wrapping slid to the floor, revealing an untarnished, clean blade matching the hilt in color. She raised it closer to the light in order to admire it further, too awestruck to move.

Suddenly, a pain lanced up her right arm, slithering from her fingers to her shoulder. Once it registered, Coura let out a yelp and dropped the sword to let it clatter on the ground. Her spell abruptly released, so the circle of light disappeared. In the darkness, someone shouted in her direction, yet she fell to her knees and cradled the arm. Despite that being the only part afflicted, she remained frozen in shock, quivering from what just took place.

What was that? she wondered while gently rubbing her forearm, tracing the burning spots with a finger. Her whole body went cold once she realized the pain came from the markings tattooed by the demonic creatures' energy.

Detrix was the first person to come over. "What happened?" he asked as he knelt beside her.

Coura bowed her head and shook it. In response, he left her alone for a moment while the rest of their group rejoined them.

"What's going on?" Byron inquired from where he stepped up to her other side.

Coura rose to her feet then as the pain subsided. "I think I found it," was all she said in an unimpressed tone with a gesture to the discarded sword at the center of their circle.

Emilea released a gasp as Detrix whistled.

"That fits the description and what I know of fine metalwork," the latter commented with a slight smile. "I would imagine a protection spell was placed on it."

"What happened to you, Coura?" Marcy repeated to bring up the earlier question.

"I don't know," she admitted with a glance at her arm. "One second, I was holding it up to the light, then my arm felt like it was on fire."

"A sword did that to you?" Grace asked in disbelief.

Emilea crossed the gap and took Coura's right hand to inspect the forearm. "Are you still hurt?"

"The pain's gone," she assured the master mage.

At the same time, Marcus went to one knee and bent over the sword. He tapped it with the back of his left hand, but nothing happened.

"I would venture to guess it only reacts to opposing energy," Detrix added. "You should be fine to wield it."

Marcus wasted no time picking up the sword, weighing it in his hands, and taking a few practice swings. All the while his expression gradually grew more enthusiastic. "It's wonderful!" he exclaimed and again held out the weapon for all to see, much to Coura's envy. "This is the most balanced sword I've ever held."

"That would be Yeluthian metalwork for you," Detrix said with pride. "The entirety of it was especially treated to repel and seal demonic energy on top of being a quality above normal weapons."

Will tentatively reached for the sword, which Marcus passed along before removing his own and discarding it into a nearby pile. "I can't believe we actually found it," he muttered in amazement.

Byron crossed his arms and leaned in with obvious intrigue. "At least now we have two advantages in this fight: the sealing spell and ancestral weapon."

"Unfortunately, Coura won't be able to use this," Clearshot added, pointing out their next concern. Without it, she had no chance of defeating Soirée alone.

"What matters is it's ours now," she concluded while attempting to mask her disappointment.

Will returned the prized sword to Marcus, who sheathed it promptly at his waist.

"I can hold onto it for now," the assistant general commented, to the others' approval.

*

The hopefulness brought about by their prime advantage over Hendal and Soirée dwindled as the group returned to the entrance and glanced upward at the uninviting hallway above. The time was near for their battle to end, though it remained far too soon to tell which side to favor. Coura reflected on that as the Yeluthian commander returned to the stairs. He paused, perhaps to let someone else lead, when Grace's gentle voice piped up from her position in the middle of their pack.

"Commander Detrix, are you familiar with demons?" Her question revealed her fear, though not the kind reserved for physical scares.

Detrix frowned and paused to contemplate his next words before answering. "I am familiar enough to know about them as creatures. If you are wondering about my experience, I have none. Yeluthia has been separated from the surface world for as long as I have been alive. This is my first time dealing with any sort of demonic energy."

He waited for more questions after. When she had no intention to speak again, he smiled in a friendly manner.

"Do not be disheartened. Your friends are most likely more knowledgeable on the subject. If you have anything to ask, why not share and see what we can come up with together."

"In the meantime, you can follow my lead to the meeting chamber," Clearshot added. Byron joined him, and the two began their procession to the first floor and beyond.

"I just wonder what would happen to the Nim-Valan soldiers, and anyone else under the demon's influence, if the creature is sealed away," Grace continued at a softer volume, as though her words would summon ill will upon them. "Would the energy remain with them forever, or are they going to suffer?"

Detrix shook his head. "I am afraid I do not know the answer to that. I would venture to guess the energy does not return to the demon, but where it goes and the results are a mystery."

"The last time we dealt with an ancestral weapon, its energy scattered, resulting in the creatures we had to hunt down," Byron picked up after. "If my mind was left alone, I assume the same is true for the Nim-Valans, King Aaron, General Tont, and any of the other, possessed humans. Any thoughts, Emilea?"

The light mage didn't meet anyone's eyes as she spoke. "From my experiences, this demon merely lent its power to Hendal, and in turn the soldiers. As long as their intentions are to control and not to damage the body or mind, the energy should return to the source."

The answer sounded satisfactory enough, yet their responses all bothered Coura. As they approached the next staircase to the second floor, she caught Grace glance at her with a look that seemed to say, "What about you?"

She found herself wondering that too. *Byron is okay, and I'm sure Aaron will be too, but their souls were never bonded with Soirée's like mine is. I'm not possessed by her or Hendal. She stopped lending me her power because it's shared between the both of us; these markings are proof enough. Does that mean, if our souls are shared too, that when she's sealed away...*

The familiar grip of terror returned until she slowed her breathing down enough to calm her nerves.

THE ANGEL'S DESCENT

After dismissing the idea, Coura was reminded of how tightly bound that connection ran as Soirée's presence loomed nearby. The group approached the second and final staircase leading to the throne chamber and began to climb up, though she paused on the first step to focus on the menacing source. Like a stone in the river, she remained firm as the demon pulled her toward the corridor leading north. It persisted as she followed the others to the top until she understood she couldn't reject the confrontation without endangering everyone.

"Wait," she called to those ahead. No one hurried enough to be out of earshot, so they returned to where she stood glancing over her shoulder down at the previous floor.

"Is something wrong?" Will asked as the group retraced their steps.

With a sad, crooked smile, Coura returned her gaze forward. "I think this is where we split up."

Her response took them all by surprise, though most recovered right away.

"You can't leave us now," Marcus said while pushing his way to her.

"It was what we planned, wasn't it?" she countered. "I can already tell Soirée's going to interfere if she's left alone. While you take care of Hendal, I'll hold her off until you're done."

"Are you sure about this?" he persisted with more understanding when no one else protested her decision. "Plans *do* change."

Despite the constant fear of an uncertain future, Coura felt the energies within herself, both demonic and Yeluthian, settle to ease her nerves.

It's time, she told herself and nodded.

Of course, no one appeared pleased with her decision, but Detrix moved their group along.

"Let us be on our way," he ordered and looked at Clearshot.

The archer dipped his head, turned, then walked away with the Yeluthian behind. At the same time, Marcus stepped forward to pull Coura in for a brief embrace and tell her to be careful before continuing down the hall.

Emilea took his place in front of her to hold both her hands. "We'll be there as soon as we can," she offered with a gentle squeeze.

Coura returned the light mage's attempt at a smile before watching her leave.

While the others' faces projected courage, Grace's seemed distraught. "If anything happens, I will be listening for you," the young Yeluthian added. She remained where she was until Will went to lead her on with a reassuring glance at Coura.

Marcy also hesitated to speak. After a moment, she hurried to follow, as if she were afraid to be left behind. Her footsteps tapped on the stone floor as Byron and Coura stood alone. He watched her with an odd expression, prompting her to raise an eyebrow until he addressed her.

"Coura..."

She sensed a confession of his regret and concerns and decided to interrupt. "I'll be fine. I promise not to try too much on my own, especially since Marcus has the ancestral weapon. We work better as a team anyway."

"That's not what I was going to say," Byron admitted with a shake of his head. He raised his eyes to meet hers, and behind them lied a warmth of familiarity reflecting the years shared between them, something Coura hadn't seen in a long time. "I should've told you before, but no time ever seemed appropriate. When Hendal had control of me, I felt so helpless. I knew what I was doing was wrong, yet I could only watch from an uncorrupted part of my mind. It reminded me that I'm human. I was afraid, which is hard for me to admit, and I experienced a lot of pain, both physically and emotionally. During that time, though, it made me wonder if that's what you've had to deal with all these years."

The words conveying his vulnerability and the indirect question about her inner conflicts caught Coura off guard. She fumbled for a reply as he approached to put his hands on her shoulders. Their eyes met once more as she looked into his calm expression.

"You don't need to tell me," he continued. "Just know, no matter how this turns out, I'm proud of you. You're the strongest person I've ever known."

Then, while she felt her face flush upon processing his honest remark, Byron wrapped an arm around her shoulders to pull her in tight and kiss the top of her head before turning to jog down the corridor.

Coura stood looking after him and noticed how light her chest and shoulders felt.

Thank you, Byron. I didn't know I needed to hear that until now. I promise, to you and to everyone who helped me get this far, I won't rest until we put an end to Soirée. After sealing the words away in her heart, she descended the stairs with a clearer mind.

15

Walking through the empty, torch-lit halls was a surreal experience. For years, Coura roamed the palace freely as a citizen, soldier, and mage and never once did it feel as haunting. The battle waging on outside in the daylight became nothing more than a memory, which grew fainter with every step. The images of fighting for her survival, entering the palace, reuniting with her friends, and finding the ancestral weapon started to fade while Soirée's leash tightened. The demon still kept an invisible hold on Coura's center and used that to lead her wandering to the training ground on the opposite side of the palace.

Of course, Coura figured out the direction immediately, which left her time to mentally prepare. Their previous confrontation had been interrupted by Hendal before, but with everyone else occupied, she understood Soirée's desire to pick it up once more; however, even as she stepped out into the blinding sunlight covering most of the area, the only thing she wasn't certain of proved to be the demon's true intent for drawing her away.

Coura continued to walk forward before the hold released when she moved about halfway across the field; Soirée already waited farther ahead. The creature's physical appearance looked the same, except for an unnaturally wide grin dancing on her lips.

"My, so much has changed in such a short amount of time, Dear One," the creature purred from where she stood.

Coura remained silent. Her chest fluttered and tightened with an anxiousness she dared not show, and thankfully none of the energy inside stirred in response.

The demon put a hand to her cheek in a pompous manner. For a moment, they studied each other.

"I hope you know, none of this was my doing," Soirée continued with an indifferent shrug.

"I find that hard to believe."

The smile vanished. "After all of my honesty, do you truly doubt my words now?"

"Always," Coura answered while clenching her hands into fists. "It sounds like you never intend to do much, yet there's trouble brought about by your presence. Hendal is attempting to cause a civil war, demonic creatures wandered the country before that, and rogue angels from Yeluthia are attempting to kill their own kind. Can you really say you didn't do any of *that*?"

"Yes." The response sounded as dismissive as Soirée appeared. "Humans are tempted by power, especially that which is beyond their control. The high priest said he understood this when I asked to assist him. One show of my magic had him gaping and scrounging like a rat hungering for food from a silver platter. I did nothing to corrupt his beliefs.

As for the creatures, they are going to be around even without me present as long as demonic energy finds its way to the surface. You can thank the Yeluthian scum for stabbing you and releasing my power near the southern base, resulting in the ones you so graciously defeated. I also have nothing to do with those disgusting light-blooded angels you mentioned. Their troubles are between their own people. Is there anything else you want to blame me for?"

Coura paused as Soirée raised her chin in a proud manner.

I believe what she says. None of what the others are battling is directly under her control. Still, there's one problem I do know she is responsible for…

"What about me?" she asked and placed a hand on her chest. "What do you want me for? Why did you stalk my family and make a deal to share my soul? Are you planning something against Yeluthia or Asteom?"

Until then, Soirée displayed no outward emotions, but upon hearing the list of questions, she began chuckling. "You're too much. It's amusing how protective you are of such mundane interests. I despise the light-blooded, and humans are merely objects for study. You were different, which I believe I explained some time ago. Do you remember?"

"You wanted me to share your power," Coura picked up. "By possessing living creatures, you take their energy for yourself. Is that all I'm good for?"

For once, the demon seemed offended by the accusation. "Not at all."

"Then tell me why!" Coura shouted in the abandoned clearing. The feelings she suppressed for months slipped through to embellish the outburst.

Soirée stared at her for a minute without moving or making a sound. The violet eyes, like the demon's shielding spell, hid much more than they revealed.

"If you recall my confession, I consider myself a creature of experimentation," she began again. "In order for you to comprehend such a title, I will share a piece of information regarding a demon's behavior. We are independent beings who thrive on gathering what makes us strong. For some, that requires training the body in physical combat; for others, that involves manipulating energy into spells. I consider those necessary but dull after so much effort. You've seen how primitive a life meant for fighting can be. My memories of the world under the surface surrounded by heat and flame are filled with death and destruction as demons consume each other to survive.

A select few saw a future beyond the first stage. We decided to expand our minds in addition to physical and magical abilities. We studied our kind until that was enough, then we moved to the surface. Here, animals and humans are the perfect hosts for demonic energy because they contend for power, which in turn returns to us. I toyed around with possession for years until I became bored with it. What was the point if it consistently became the same experience over and over again? That was when I stumbled upon your Yeluthian father and human mother and decided to wait nearby. When your father fled, you were the closest being to the light-blooded available. I never experimented on one of their kind, so when you were at the age to discover your own magical abilities, I attempted something new by giving you a part of my self, not merely my energy.

This bonding of souls had been unintentional, yet it acts similar to a possession without corrupting the host's body or mind. I kept quiet to take in what I did until your untimely, near-death experience involving a sword through the chest. It was then I revealed myself to you and discovered a balance between our selves. I nurtured this connection over the years, though I have much less of an influence ever since the incident in the southern valley. From what I can conclude based on our connection, a part of your soul has been morphed into mine, making it able to tolerate and wield demonic energy. By sending you to fetch the creatures around the country, I confirmed this. Although, the side effects reminded me you are merely a human. Is there anything else I left out?"

How Soirée could speak so calmly, as if she were lecturing a history course, Coura couldn't understand. The demon had essentially shared more about her kind than anyone in Asteom ever knew while simultaneously admitting how she meddled with Coura's life and soul. Nothing surprised Coura about the story, yet that was all from the past and present.

"What about the future?" she asked aloud when the question lingered in her mind. "You told me what I am, but what do you want with me? Why did you bring me here?"

"In order for me to share what comes next, I want you to prove you're worthy to listen." After those words, the demon's slim blade appeared in her hand without giving any notice.

Coura followed suit, though as more of a defensive response than an actual acceptance of the challenge. It annoyed her to hear Soirée consider crossing blades before sharing her intentions, but there was no helping the situation.

While the demon stood patiently, Coura charged with the full aim to initiate the one-on-one fight. Soirée brought up her sword without much force in response. From there, the dance felt nearly identical to their previous encounter in the meeting chamber. Coura relied on her training from Byron and Marcus and her instincts when facing an opponent of equal or greater speed and strength to dodge, strike, and block whatever Soirée threw her way.

The two only traded blows with their identical weapons, which piqued her interest. The demon usually used physical attacks, such as punches and kicks, when an opening presented itself. She remembered the bruises on her ribs from the last time they fought when Hendal interrupted and distracted her, so she remained on guard despite Soirée's lack of interest in anything other than swordplay.

This left no time for her to notice what took place in the world around them. For however long they slipped around each other, often leaving minor scratches, there was nothing except the need to best the other at what she eventually came to realize was just a game.

***

Byron caught up to the rest of his companions as soon as they reached the center of the palace where the council meeting chamber was located and the crazed high priest presumably waited. No one said a word after Coura took her leave; that seemed to signal the severity of their mission and the limited amount of time left to stop Hendal. He even found his mind going blank when he considered their next steps. So, in the moment of stressful uncertainty while they huddled together outside the final hallway, he relied on those around him to supply ideas.

"With the demon distracted for the time being, I believe there are enough of us to handle whatever is inside," the Yeluthian commander offered, though his thin smile betrayed his doubts. "I suggest we keep together in case more opponents are present. If the lady and I have protection, we should be able to cast the necessary spells."

Surprisingly, the usually compliant assistant general turned down the strategy. "I'm sorry, but I can't do that," Marcus shared and shook his head. "Aaron hasn't been around this entire time, and I doubt Hendal is the type of person to hide the fact that he has a king under his control. My first priority is to keep him out of harm's way, if he is in there."

Commander Detrix frowned. "If that is your decision, I will not attempt to sway you otherwise."

"Leave Hendal to me," Clearshot offered, drawing all eyes. "I assume it would be easier for everyone if he's disarmed and immobilized. Byron, Will, and Marcy can back me up."

"Cornelius," his wife whispered while placing a hand on his shoulder.

"Do you have a better idea? He's the main target."

"Shouldn't some of us guard the spellcasters?" Marcy added warily.

While everyone murmured their own ideas and concerns, Byron cleared his throat to get their attention. "It's too risky to rely on a predetermined plan without knowing what's inside. Commander Detrix and Emilea should begin the spells at a safe distance. Marcus, if Aaron is inside, you can keep him away as well; otherwise, we'll need you for protection. My energy is still significantly weak, so I won't be of much use. Grace, you can keep watch in case anybody follows us inside. I suggest the remaining four of us pair up just in case there are other guards. Marcy, follow Clearshot and his orders. Will, you're with me."

"Yes, sir," Will answered confidently.

For a second, Byron couldn't believe the young man at his side was the same person who cowered in the face of conflict years ago. *In fact, it seems most everyone here has changed*, he reflected until the rest of the group settled on his idea.

"Leave it to Byron to get out of being possessed and drugged yet still manage to plot our best course of action," Clearshot commented with an eyeroll.

The gesture had Byron smiling as he recalled his friend's normal behavior.

"Well then, shall we?" Commander Detrix asked without any of his previous humor.

With the Yeluthian and Clearshot still in the lead, they approached the entrance. No guards had been posted in front of it, so Grace pressed against the nearest wall and nodded to confirm her position.

Then, Clearshot stepped closer, crouched, and pushed the unlocked door open.

This was Byron's first time in the council's meeting chamber since his second assignment to Dala in order to locate Coura. Even after all he heard about what took place in the space during the night of the Nim-Valan's initial welcome ball, he hadn't felt comfortable arousing Hendal's suspicion any further by investigating. He expected a worse scene than what their group found, which was a nearly empty room with several char marks darkening the walls and floor on the opposite side. Only two torches had been lit along with a candelabra sitting at its center. No furniture adorned the room anymore aside from the king's throne, and it held one of the three people lingering nearby.

Clearshot poised his bow at the slouched figure seated in between the familiar face of the young king and a stranger with Yeluthian features. As each member of their group stepped inside, they prepared their weapons without removing their eyes from the target. Byron gripped his own, trusty blade in his right hand while surveying the power resting inside, keeping it at the ready should he need to use magic. His mind continued to consider their options with both Aaron and a guard present and armed.

The quiet within the palace walls grew to become suffocating when no one moved or spoke for minutes. It felt so unnatural that at a deep, rumbling sound, Byron thought he had lost his mind. The noise grew louder until he realized it was laughter coming from the high priest, whose shoulders shook. The man threw his head back with a final chuckle, breathed deeply, then set his eyes on the intruders. Even at a distance, it became obvious he wasn't completely sane despite his priestly attire. The previously smooth, controlled face bore many wrinkles from stress beneath an unshaven chin and cheeks. His eyes looked like black beads, shining with some unspoken desire, and the once smiling mouth turned downward to frown.

"Is this it?" Hendal asked, his hoarse voice teeming with disappointment. "I was hoping for more. You insult me with such underestimations."

Byron considered being the one to respond when Emilea took it upon herself to do so. "Hendal, step off the king's throne at once," she demanded. "We have you cornered. If you give yourself up, the punishment will not be as severe."

The man grunted before rolling his eyes. "You speak as eloquently as ever, Emilea. Why a lady decided to entangle herself with these soldiers is beyond me. Although, I see another person I detest even more among you. Master Byron should still be under my control, or dead."

The venom in Hendal's final sentence as the crazed man said Byron's title with a glare was evident, yet he refused to be intimidated.

"You must not have been paying attention since you released your hold over me once I became immobilized. Emilea's right; this nonsense has gone on long enough."

"Enough!" Hendal shouted above Byron's last word and slammed a fist on the arm of the throne. As if on cue, both Aaron and the presumed angel drew their swords; the former kept his blank stare while the latter grinned without looking away from Commander Detrix.

"Aaron," Marcus called and stepped forward. "Let him go!"

"Quiet!" the man on the throne barked and spat at the king's feet in spite. "He belongs to me now."

"You're nothing but a tyrant," Clearshot added defiantly without lowering his arrow.

His accusation amused Hendal, who chuckled once more. "Tyrant? What a subjective word that is. If I called the king a tyrant, would I be wrong? Both he and his father were cruel before I freed them from the shackles of ruling. Then again, not everyone is born to lead, and those with the skill are tossed aside by people like you, people who think it's honorable to neglect one's freedom for traditional roles. How could you understand? None of you were destined to spend your lives like this.

No matter what any of us do, we *will* serve someone. If I disappear right at this second, you would return to the king. If he were to disappear, you would bow before a new ruler, or tyrant as you like to throw around. If that person ordered you to go to war or pay unfair taxes, or kill, you would obey. All creatures live to serve because it is as the world is meant to be. Ironically, the demon taught me that. The cycle of life thrives on survival by the strongest and the most cunning. So, forgive me for taking a few shortcuts to spare myself from suffering. Once you understand your place, manipulating the world is child's play. Normal creatures want to survive, but extraordinary ones want to *thrive*! I have a vision for the future, and that hinders on remaining here."

As Hendal folded his hands on his lap, appearing as comfortable as ever on the seat, Byron found himself shaking his head. *He's gone insane. It sounds like his exposure to the demon's primitive way of seeing humans has made him think he's above us. We must keep the problem as down to earth as possible, or else he might become more dangerous.*

He inhaled and exhaled in a deep breath to calm his mind before taking a couple steps in front of the others. "This is your last chance. I will not vouch for your safety should you choose to resist arrest."

Hendal met Byron's challenging stare with a violent rage, then he scoffed. At the sound, both Aaron and the angel charged.

Fortunately, neither went straight for Byron; he still didn't feel fully responsive thanks to the sedatives. Marcus leapt in front of his friend, who carelessly ran at the bulk of their group, and held his blade diagonally in a defensive maneuver as the possessed king swung wide. Their weapons collided with a ring as the assistant general shouted.

"He's mine!"

With one opponent taken care of, Byron turned his attention to the others.

Unlike Aaron, the angel had a clear target. He passed by in a blur to strike at Commander Detrix, who somehow expected a direct attack. After blocking and pushing away the enemy, their Yeluthian comrade reminded them all of the plan.

"We need protection!" he shouted while simultaneously holding his ground against the persistent rogue angel.

Emilea stayed back, obviously uncertain of what to do. That was when Byron's mind caught up with him.

"Clearshot, keep that one away," he shouted with a glance over to Will. One look was all he needed to convey the order.

Before he could do the same for Marcy, the woman matched Clearshot's aim. Together, the pair of archers stayed by the entrance and fired at the most threatening enemy, causing the blond figure to back off with plenty of frustration. Will hurried over to stand beside Commander Detrix then.

Byron prepared to join until loud footsteps from behind caught his attention, and from out of the corner of his eye, he saw something white moving closer. In response, he sidestepped in the opposite direction before spinning around to face Hendal, who loomed nearby with a knife in one hand and a scowl.

He has to know the difference in our skill, right? Byron wondered in near disbelief as the man approached. *It would be all too easy to stop him for good, yet I assume he needs to be alive for the light spell to destroy the demon's power.*

With that in mind, he extended both hands outward to craft a shield encompassing Hendal and the throne from as far as the man had wandered. The high priest's face dropped at the unexpected avoidance of a confrontation, then it twisted in irritation before he struck the wall in front of him madly. Byron returned his attention to the rest of the room after.

In those precious seconds, much had happened. The sound of clashing metal echoed in the closed chamber from both Marcus and Aaron, who remained at the back of the space, and Will and Commander Detrix as they traded blows with the snarling angel. He had no idea why the wild Yeluthian acted so hostile toward the commander alone, but Byron realized while he watched the archers holding their shots and Emilea presumably focusing on her part of the spells that they would only get in the way of an enemy intent on attacking with force.

Not only that, but we need both light mages to be near Hendal without distraction.

Byron glanced between the man huffing behind his shielding spell and the trio engaged in combat with only a fraction of a new strategy. Then, he remembered the third Yeluthian.

Grace, can you hear me? he threw out in his mind, imagining the thought floating into the air. The worried response was instantaneous.

{Yes, I am here!}

Commander Detrix and Will are fighting against another angel under Hendal's command. When I give a signal, I need you to tell them to join Emilea near the throne.

{Right. I will be listening.}

Her presence lingered in Byron's mind like a second pair of eyes on the scene. Although he had yet to fully estimate the risks, he hurried away from the shield while calling to Emilea.

"Take Clearshot and Marcy," he ordered and pointed behind once she noticed him. "Begin your spell while they guard you. I'm going to separate the other angel so Commander Detrix can join too."

The woman opened her mouth to either ask for more information or protest the idea, but the two archers were already at her side.

"Let's go," Clearshot urged and grabbed his wife's arm.

If she hesitated, Byron missed it as he released part of the shielding spell and moved forward to stand just out of range of the three swordsmen. Without the speed to keep up with the nonhumans, Will took up a basic, defensive position, one requiring a broad stance, his torso bent forward, and the blade centered with his body. Unfortunately for him, the Yeluthians' combat brought them all over that side of the room, which wasn't nearly wide enough to allow them to move comfortably.

"Will," Byron called when the young man waited while Commander Detrix forced his opponent farther back against the stone wall.

Will turned to stare at him for a moment with concern etched into every feature. Byron pointed toward where the figures of Emilea, Clearshot, and Marcy were attempting to corner Hendal behind the violet veil of energy; at least, he assumed that was what was taking place.

When the young man still didn't move, he reached out to Grace again and asked her for assistance. A brief pause followed, one that brought the angels frightfully close to Will's position, but whatever she said resonated with him, for he sprinted away from one chaotic scene to another. Byron wasted no time by glancing after him.

Instead, he stepped closer to Commander Detrix. Neither Yeluthian bore any visible scratches on their skin or armor, yet something told Byron their style of combat relied on wearing down their opponent, making fights drawn out. His next actions would need to be precise, swift, and most importantly, confident.

Grace, it's time, he thought while bringing up the necessary power for a duplicate shielding spell. Neither angel noticed as he raised his hands and waited.

The second set of eyes on his shoulder faded without any sort of confirmation. After a few seconds, the soft, somewhat nervous voice returned.

{I relayed the message, though Commander Detrix voiced his doubts about leaving such an experienced opponent to you.}

I'm grateful for the vote of confidence, Byron thought sarcastically to himself once Grace's presence slipped away again. *In any case, I have to be ready for the enemy to give chase and probably come after me next. As long as my spell keeps him as cornered to the wall as possible, his movements will be severely limited.*

The combat in front of him required all of his attention to keep up with because of its reliance on the speed and accuracy of their weapons. In the back of his mind, Byron was genuinely curious how the Yeluthians trained; however, he needed to survive before questioning any of them.

Commander Detrix made a new move in the fluid motions by being the first to dodge while retracing his steps for a momentary break between the two. Then, he leapt forward just as his opponent did the same, and their swords connected. The following push with both hands gripping his weapon proved enough to cause the other Yeluthian to stumble backward in a similar manner to the commander's previous retraction. Byron understood then the pause was meant to signal an opportunity to cast a shielding spell and allow for the angel to retreat. If he didn't realize that, Commander Detrix already spun around on one heel and nodded.

While his bronze-clad comrade raced away to join Emilea, Byron released his dark energy and shaped it into a formation similar to the one used to block Hendal's attack. The translucent wall grew firm within seconds and became a half-dome structure rounding out at the ceiling to pin the enemy angel against the stone perimeter. There seemed to be enough room for about three steps forward and five to either side, which he felt would be plenty.

As expected, the opponent trapped within didn't appear pleased with their trick. Bryon kept his arms outstretched while feeding more energy into the shield as he prepared for the many counterstrikes that followed. Unlike Hendal's flailing around with the knife, this angel was experienced with shielding spells and stabbed with full force directly in multiple spots. This required Byron to divide his attention between mending the deeper breaks, as well as keep the entire spell equally fortified.

The first wave lasted long enough to have both him and the rogue Yeluthian breathing harder, though the latter had also faced Commander Detrix. That worked in Byron's favor, yet he felt beads of sweat beginning to slide down his forehead and the back of his neck once his prisoner resumed the attempt to escape. He could give no extra attention to anything else in the room without risking his spell's stability.

When it seemed his cornered opponent was slowing, Grace made herself known with more optimism in her voice than earlier.

{Byron, are you all right?}

At first, the question startled him. *Yes, but I'm concerned about Hendal since I haven't sensed any light energy at work. Can you tell me what everyone else is doing?*

{*Marcus has Aaron pinned to the ground, as if they were wrestling, but I can see the shadows of either blood or bruising on his face. It is difficult to make out what is going on across the room. A few figures are crouching together, and two others are standing nearby. One is Commander Detrix for sure, and I think I can make out Emilea's longer hair as well.*}

Based on what you described, Clearshot, Marcy, and Will might be trying to bring Hendal down to a manageable level where he won't interfere, Byron concluded. *Will you let me know if the situation changes?*

{Absolutely...}

As she replied, a surge of power both familiar and unfamiliar to him pounded a heartbeat-like rhythm within the space. It didn't seem malicious or frightening; instead, it reminded him of drums during a musical performance intended to elicit dancing. The pace sounded consistent, a sure sign of the exorcism to come. Still, he refused to turn his eyes away from his own magic.

The angel noticed this new presence as well. His sapphire eyes went wide in alarm, but he didn't try attacking again.

"What are you doing?" the Yeluthian shouted across the shield.

Byron decided there was no immediate harm in explaining their motives to one of Hendal's followers. "We're here to release the demon's hold on our fellow soldiers and others in Asteom by breaking its connection to the high priest. Only then can we safely arrest him for his crimes."

"Break its connection?" The angel's face relaxed into an expression displaying his confusion, yet nothing more was said, and he made no other attempt to free himself.

Byron wondered if his captive became more curious about the spells Emilea and Commander Detrix were using than interested in obeying orders. With that in mind he chanced glancing over his shoulder to watch as well.

Grace's description of the scene had been accurate as Hendal was pressed to the floor beneath at least two other bodies. Marcy's slim figure stood farther away with her back to Byron, and Emilea and the Yeluthian commander stood side by side with their hands reaching toward the target. A bright, golden glow emanated from them, casting the pair in a warm light. Suddenly, Hendal's muffled voice began screaming unintelligible sentences. His body jerked, but the man could hardly move since Clearshot and Will kept his limbs and torso firmly in place.

At last, after nearly a minute passed by, the light coming from Emilea's hands faded before she graciously dropped to her knees in a fatigued manner. Commander Detrix remained still. Byron felt a surge of power then unlike anything he had ever experienced, reminding him of the purity of a Yeluthian's energy.

Chuckling from behind tore his attention away. The angel he held captive grinned at him, though an unmistakable fear lingered.

"I understand," Byron heard him say. "Using the goddess fire is an interesting move, but that spell leaves the wielder practically useless."

He intends to attack once Commander Detrix exhausts himself after burning the demon's energy away. I'm going to need to be on my guard for now in case he tries to break through again. As if to emphasize the thought, he poured another part of his power into the shield, drawing a less amused look from the angel. Then, he returned to analyzing Commander Detrix's power.

The Yeluthian's unique energy felt different from Byron's; the more he was exposed to it, the greater the divide became. Unlike the demon's, which brought about a sense of danger and hostility, this reflected self-assurance, as if *it* knew the Yeluthians were a different race that needed no influence from the humans. The demon's threatened imprisonment, making him imagine a beastly predator on the hunt while what belonged to the angel seemed more like an intelligible bird of prey watching perceptively from a distance.

That sensation steadily grew fainter, along with the golden light, until Byron could no longer sense the energy. A calming silence replaced any other emotions, and the enemy behind the magical wall began fidgeting but did not go after the shield.

Until someone comes for me, I can't let him go. Who knows how dangerous he is without Commander Detrix's skill holding him back.

Scuffling footsteps and softly spoken words too distant to understand came from multiple places around the room. Soon, someone hurried over in their direction.

"Byron, I think we did it." The tired yet relieved voice belonged to Will.

"Is everyone safe?" he asked with a glance at the young man, who appeared unharmed.

"For the most part. Hendal fell unconscious, but he put up a fight against Clearshot and I. Marcy helped at first, but he sliced open her forearm, so I told her to stay back. Emilea's recovering, but Commander Detrix is about ready to pass out."

"What about Marcus and Aaron?"

"Grace joined us and offered to check on Aaron. From what I can tell, it's the same situation we've seen before; he's just confused and weary. Marcus' face is bruised, but he says he's fine."

Byron released a sigh. "That's good."

"What should we do now?" the young herbalist asked hesitantly while eyeing up the remaining enemy in the room.

He chewed on the inside of his cheek and contemplated their next steps. A dozen ideas passed through his head, including what the troops outside would be dealing with, the remaining rogue angels, and finally the fact that Coura was involved with the demon and waiting for the ancestral weapon.

We need to focus on our immediate problems, he told himself sternly. *The generals and Yeluthians can figure out the results on the battlefield, and our issues here should be addressed before finding Coura.*

"We must convene as soon as possible," he told Will as the words formed in his mind. "Can you bring everyone to me? My shield is the only thing stopping this angel from lashing out again."

Will nodded, returned to the others, and soon joined them in circling around Byron. Clearshot and Marcus supported Commander Detrix, which confirmed the group's assumption that the Yeluthian had drained himself; however, the proud smile stretching across his face projected their victory. It eased a lot of the resulting tension, though Byron noticed the rogue angel frowning, as if seeing the commander alive and beaming was a bad omen.

Emilea stopped at his side to scan the space as Commander Detrix lowered himself to sit cross-legged on the stone floor. "Are you still able to keep the shield up?" she asked.

Byron noticed the lines of strain decorating her thin face and nodded.

"That should do it," their Yeluthian ally announced in an exasperated tone of voice loudly enough for them all to hear. "The demonic power within that human has been burned away. I felt many connections branching from him, but once his center of power was destroyed, they either returned to be burned as well or crumpled as they normally would after a spell's release. Before you bring it up, I cannot confirm any details about the soldiers under that man's possession. There may be unforeseen or lasting consequences. For now, he is nothing to worry about."

"What should we do with him then?" Marcus wondered aloud with a hand on the hilt of his sheathed sword.

No one answered immediately. Then, Aaron reached over to put a hand on Marcus' arm. The king seemed dazed by the situation, yet he voiced his thoughts as surely as if nothing had happened to him.

"Hendal is going to be tried for his actions against Asteom. If he has no more of the demon's power, he should be bound and supervised until he can be put into a prison cell."

The hand on the ancestral weapon fell at the king's order while Marcus visibly relaxed. "How are you feeling?" he asked his friend with a hint of sympathy.

"Like I just woke up from a long, dreamless nap," came the disgruntled answer. "Someone's going to have to explain what else is going on."

"I'm afraid that has to wait," Emilea interjected. "Our problem with Hendal is over, but the demon is still roaming free. Marcus has the ancestral weapon we need to seal the creature away, and Coura's distracting it nearby."

"She's out there alone?" Aaron asked without hiding his disbelief, bringing a little more liveliness into his face in the process.

"Yes, so those of us who can move should get going."

While most of the group expressed their agreement, Byron's arms ached to remind him of their remaining issue. "What about this one?"

Commander Detrix's smile vanished before he replied. "You may remove the shield."

"You can't be serious," Marcy blurted out before everyone echoed her thoughts.

They all glanced at the Yeluthian. His expression shifted into a mask of smug satisfaction so unlike his previous personality it became unnerving to look at.

THE ANGEL'S DESCENT

On the opposite side of his stare, the angel behind Byron's spell squirmed uncomfortably.

"This youngling understands his position," the commander went on in that same persona. "The man he chose to support has been defeated, giving us every right to execute them. He has nowhere to turn and no leader to follow anymore. So, unless he believes he can escape unharmed *or* kill all of us before we kill him, he will save his own life by surrendering. That is the way of our people, valuing life and dignity over anything else."

Byron felt the chill beneath the words as he observed the influence they had on their enemy. He guessed the Yeluthian was around Aaron's age and found himself pitying the angel. The figure dipped his head to hide his face, and his body bent forward in a disheartened manner. Their group continued watching in silence until their final opponent caved in by tossing his sword to the side and falling to his knees.

"I surrender," came the following, hopeless admittance of defeat.

Still, Byron wasn't willing to risk their lives, especially when he considered his past encounters with the enemy. "Marcus, I want you and Will to head to one of the storage rooms and gather some rope to bind Hendal and this angel," he ordered. "When that's done, we can find Coura."

While the two agreed and left, he continued maintaining the shield until their return minutes later. The angel didn't resist the bindings yet kept his face averted. Commander Detrix remained where he was as this happened and only spoke again once Hendal's body was dragged over and bound as well.

"I will keep watch over them," he said in a friendlier manner filled with the exhaustion he showed.

From where she stood at Grace's side, Emilea placed a hand on the youngest Yeluthian's shoulder. "This is the perfect place for you to stay and relay messages."

Grace shot her an alarmed look, but it fell after a moment. "You are right. I should see how the generals are doing and let them know what took place here."

The master light mage offered an appreciative smile in response and thanked her.

"Someone else should stay to guard them," Marcy added and walked to stand beside Commander Detrix. She cradled her right arm, which had been wrapped with cloth torn from part of her undershirt; in the other hand was the knife Hendal used earlier. No one argued with her decision to remain with Grace.

"I suppose we should get going," Byron said as his eyes wandered over his companions. Without wasting any more time, Clearshot was the first to exit with Emilea close behind.

One more problem to take care of, and then we can start rebuilding, he thought as he pushed aside the looming physical, mental, and magical exhaustion while exiting the chamber.

***

Being left behind while others went on to do the fighting was something Grace became accustomed to. Although it meant she was too valuable to send into danger she was unqualified to handle, the slight flattery remained overwhelmed by a desire to be useful to her friends. The only solace proved to be the use of her goddess gift, a trait that made her vital to their group's communication with the outside world.

"Don't worry. I'm sure they'll be fine," Marcy offered to comfort Grace, though her lips were tight with worry to contradict those words.

"I know, but I just wish I could do something else."

"You should focus on doing what you can," Commander Detrix commented from where he lied flat on his back. His merciless behavior when dealing with one of their kind sounded cruel to Grace, yet he spoke true. Obedience had been driven into their people's lifestyle to the point where it would be worse for a traitor to fight back than to continue disgracing their name.

Their enemy had no advantages left without the high priest using demonic energy. She prayed fate would not bring her to be present when he and his remaining comrades were brought to justice by King Arval.

The extreme impact of using the goddess fire spell left Commander Detrix unable to sit up. That was when Grace realized how hard he had been trying to keep up an appearance in front of the humans.

Was I that concerned about what people thought of me when I first arrived at the palace? In any case, I must find King Arval, General Casner, or General Tio and explain our victory. Hopefully that will ease some of their concern.

Firstly, she wanted to heal Marcy's forearm. She asked the woman if she could inspect the wound, earning her a surprised look. The cut didn't seem deep, yet blood seeped through the tightly wrapped cloth.

"While I waited outside this chamber, I remembered what Emilea said about reserving our energy. I promised myself I would do what I could to heal anyone's injuries since both she and Commander Detrix needed their power," Grace explained as she cast the basic spell and sealed the skin closed.

Marcy wiped away most of the blood before thanking her.

"You are welcome. Now, I am going to reach out to whichever leader is available and-"

Any thoughts were driven out of her mind as a blast of demonic power surged nearby to nearly suffocate her, and her whole body began trembling.

What...is this?

"Grace!"

She spun around to where the Yeluthian commander sat up with a grimace and a concerned expression.

"The demon's energy is out of control!" he shouted.

Marcy gasped. "Are the others in trouble?" she asked him.

"I...do not know, but the creature's power is too much for any of us to even think about facing in our current conditions." His eyes shifted to meet Grace's. "You need to send for backup. Find Evern, Isan, or King Arval. If they are not on their way already, tell them the king's, master mages', and others' lives are on the line!"

The commander's arms visibly shook from holding his body up until he gave into the weight and dropped down. When Grace moved to help, Marcy put a hand out to stop her.

"Do as he says," the woman demanded before she hurried to kneel behind his head and place it in her lap in an attempt to comfort him.

This left Grace to concentrate on a message. Despite the additional hours of rest prior to the day's battle, her own center of power had not fully replenished, but it would be enough for her to reach the dozens of human and Yeluthian minds lingering in the southern clearing.

The camp is too far away, she found with displeasure. *Is there someone who can help near the palace?*

Several Yeluthians, both in the air and on the ground, projected their own stress, so she reached out toward the closest one since it would require less energy to speak with them.

This is Grace Zelnar, the ambassador stationed in Asteom. We need help dealing with the demon. Is there a commander or general near you I can speak with?

Unfortunately, the individual she selected had no notion if a leader wandered nearby. Instead of waiting for him to locate someone, she decided to bounce around to those along the front line until she received an immediate response from a soldier with a definite location. She avoided considering how much time she spent on the task in favor of contacting as many Yeluthians as she could.

Finally, she found a lead from a soldier whose thoughts sounded as frantic as hers. They pointed her to their superior, and she established the new connection a minute later.

{*This is Commander Evern. Can you hear me?*}

She replied with a confirmation before summarizing the situation with Hendal, Commander Detrix, and what the rest of her friends were doing. *I am assuming the creature is on the opposite side of the clearing you are in. Please, send help that way as soon as possible!*

A pause followed her words.

{*I must request a favor. Because time is of the essence, I will go to where the demon is before it makes its escape or does any more damage. Can you speak with one of my soldiers so they can repeat the information back at our camp?*}

She gaped but found herself agreeing with his reasoning. *Of course.*

{*Excellent. I am on my way!*}

THE ANGEL'S DESCENT

With that, Grace removed her presence from the commander before selecting another Yeluthian to use as a messenger. Her temples throbbed enough to threaten a headache, yet she understood the importance of sending for aid. She knew it was the least she could do to assist the humans who watched over her during her time in Asteom.

16

Swordplay with Soirée when the demon didn't mix in physical blows was nothing spectacular, as Coura soon figured out. Their previous confrontation had been similar at first, yet after a longer duration, their skills seemed to be evenly matched. Neither could do more than scratch the other's arm or leg.

I can keep up with her just fine, Coura thought as she ducked underneath the matching blade when it swung horizontally for her head. *Our speed feels almost equal, and I believe she knows this tactic won't stop me. Why is she wasting time by playing around?*

The question wasn't necessarily bad since the others were taking care of Hendal, but she wondered what else the demon had planned.

Soirée followed up the swipe with a lunge and back-to-back stabs for her chest, which she deflected with ease. This continued for another minute until Coura grew tired of the motions. With a grunt, she mirrored the demon's lunge while leaning forward to put her weight behind the stab. As she expected, Soirée retreated and poised herself to defend against another attack; however, it did not come. The demon's unreadable expression remained, though she frowned a bit when Coura stood straight.

"Are you giving up now?" the creature purred with amusement soon after.

"What are you doing?" Coura countered, letting her growing temper emphasize the question. "Am I not a worthy opponent anymore?"

The demon let down her façade to giggle and toss her raven hair over one shoulder.

When Coura refused to comment on the obvious attempt to push her emotions, Soirée continued talking in a tone of voice teeming with humor.

"You've grown so much, Dear One. My taunting no longer influences your actions. I must admit, that makes me a bit sad. We were having so much fun together…"

"That's enough," Coura interrupted. "I'm not your toy. You told me about the past, but now I can control my own life, so you better take me seriously."

She expected a laugh after admitting such a claim, yet Soirée's gaze became more intense than ever as she lowered her blade.

"If you are so adamant about this, I suppose I can let you in on a little secret. As many times as I tried, I was never able to fully possess your body unless your life was fleeting. It's most likely because of the soul bonding sharing our energy, but why I could only act as a presence in your mind is still a mystery."

An unsettling shiver ran down Coura's spine as she considered their relationship, or rather, what it could have turned into. *I would have been no better off than those people under Hendal's control. My life would have been tossed aside so easily and my body torn apart.*

"Even if I'm meant to be stuck with you for the rest of my life, I refuse to let you continue to meddle with people like you've been doing."

"Oh? How do you plan to stop me then?"

Coura cursed her tongue for hinting at a means of defeating the demon. As she worked to craft a lie to deter from that subject, Soirée voiced her other intentions, which had nothing to do with the ancestral weapon.

"Really, I'm quite amazed you care so much about anyone else after the way you were treated. A young woman trained to be a mage and a warrior is thrown into conflict with vile angels, disregarded by her peers for being different, then used as a weapon by the leaders of this country. When we separated, no one wanted anything to do with you anymore because of your weakened state. Let me guess, the light-blooded beings don't fully trust you either, do they?"

Coura refused to answer. *Everything she said is true to some degree, but she's only trying to dishearten my spirit. I need to remember why I came to meet her in the first place.*

"While I have been with you, *you* were the one in control, not me," the demon continued. "*You* trained your body and magical abilities, *you* took the brunt of their words, threats, and disdain, and *you* were cast out for possessing more power than they could ever dream of. Even the high priest is afraid of your potential. He understood how the weak are put down when they refuse to submit while the strong forge their own path. Take pride in yourself, because I had little to do with who is standing in front of me. Anyone else would be dead by now."

The direction of their conversation was unexpected. In all her life, Coura never thought she would hear Soirée speak as if they were equals, yet here she stood listening to the creature responsible for so much negativity in Asteom telling her to accept herself. No one, not even Byron, had ever suggested she be proud of her demonic abilities or avoid changing to fit in.

Stop it, part of her ordered. *Demons are known for their sly tongues; that was what got me into this mess to begin with. She always wants something else and sugarcoats it with blunt truths. I have to figure her out, and soon.*

"You never said anything about the future," Coura pushed to buy more time. "You also refuse to tell me what it is you want, so quit dancing around the subject."

Soirée visibly savored the impact of her words. The familiar grin stretched to show her pointed canines, and the violet eyes shone with an unnatural sense of interest. Whatever she kept hidden, Coura wasn't certain she wanted to listen based on that image alone.

"Tell me, do you wish to grow in power still?" The question, like everything else, hinted at more beneath the surface.

Coura swallowed her rising anxiety as her fingers began to twitch. The warm energy in her center steadied any doubts, allowing her to answer from the heart. "I want peace. What you desire is manipulation and servitude, but I believe in serving each other. The world will never be perfect, but if I have the strength to protect those I care about from creatures like you, then that would be enough."

Her response had an odd effect. Soirée's grin deflated into her normal, slight smile, and she crossed her arms in feigned impartiality; however, the crazed interest behind her eyes doubled, and Coura thought the fur-like coat covering her body bristled.

"Well, that is rather noble of you. Offering yourself and the possibility of a comfortable, safe life so others may enjoy that pleasure is admirable. Why don't we put that to the test."

"What do you mean?" Coura asked warily when the demon made no attempt to go on. Even as she voiced the question, she felt the invisible hold tightening.

"I must reiterate my title as a creature of experimentation, one who wishes to explore the limits of demons, humans, and even the light-blooded. The high priest expressed his wish to rule, so I showed him how to use my power to possess his own people. As with any animal, their natural energy became a part of mine indirectly, and when I wish it, that will return to me. This palace is a means to gather strength, nothing more.

On the other hand, our connection is unique. There's so much I could do with an extra source of power, one born with both angelic and human blood. What I'm saying is my curiosity regarding you far outweighs any need for remaining stationary. Here is what I offer. If you join me, swearing to be mine for the rest of your life, I promise not to involve myself with the humans in Asteom anymore." She paused, licked her lips, and continued to hold Coura hostage with her penetrating gaze.

Coura shook her head in disbelief. "What?"

"It is as I say. I will refrain from possessing any living human in this country in order to gather energy and even go so far as to prevent my demonic creatures from harming them. The light-blooded beings I cannot speak for. Ever since they returned to the surface, I desire to rid myself of their presence," the demon admitted, indifferent to Coura's shock.

"You can't be serious." The words tumbled out of her mouth as her mind slowed.

"I considered the idea of humans in the north and even thought about crossing over to investigate, but their low temperatures are off-putting. Unfortunately, my options are limited now that the high priest is steadily ensuring the downfall of his short-lived reign. The Nim-Valan society is different because it does not have the protection of angels or the attention of demons. You would blend in, and with our connection, it can be just like old times."

Nothing about the idea appealed to Coura in the slightest. In fact, she felt disgusted with herself for not dismissing it altogether immediately, instead waiting for Soirée to finish the thought. Now, as the demon again watched her with a stillness only the creature could manage, the deal had been planted firmly between them. If she were to accept, no one else would get hurt by what power Soirée lent to Hendal. The demon offered her an easier way out of the battle. Her life would be forfeit, yet the country would be free.

Coura felt her body relax and weapon lower until both arms rested at her side. She pulled her eyes away from Soirée's to stare at something nondescript behind the shadow-like figure, still unable to turn the offer down without giving it her full consideration.

"Think carefully," the demon added with poorly concealed anticipation.

Turning the issue over in her mind did nothing except bring Coura back into the same cycle of thought, which grew to frustrate her more than anything. Part of her desperately tried to consider what someone else would do, including her former mentor, parents, or friends.

No, a voice from inside replied patiently. *This isn't about anybody else. No one is in the same position or has a connection with the demon. Only my life is meant to be sacrificed, so it's my choice that truly matters. Besides, I already have an answer.*

Although Coura recognized she might regret denying Soirée's offer, and that it might haunt her for the rest of her life should something worse take place, she shared her decision aloud. "I'm not a fool. I understand what you're after and what will happen if I agree to be a host for your power. To put it simply, I would wish I was dead.

My only comfort would be that my friends and family are safe from you, but then again, you would begin to terrorize the Nim-Valans. Why should I agree to spare one country over another? Why shouldn't I at least attempt to stop the pain and murder at its source instead?"

As she spoke, the words grew more confident, giving her the strength to look Soirée in the eye once more. The warm energy in her center hummed in support, and the demonic presence joined soon after.

"You reject my offer then?" The question sounded cold and emotionless, though nothing changed in Soirée's expression to reflect that until Coura dipped her head.

"It's not so much that I reject it. I just can't accept knowing there's still a chance to stop you," she went on after remembering the golden blade in her friends' possession. "My comrades are fighting too. We believe in each other and give one another a reason to continue on. That's a feeling you'll never share with any living creature, no matter how much you try to control them. They put their faith in me, and I do the same for them. If I were to make that deal and spare Asteom, I would have to live with the fact that I turned my back on everyone and betrayed their trust."

A pause followed her explanation before the inevitable laughter came from the demon. Soirée put a hand to her chest, bent her upper half forward, then threw her head back. After a few seconds, she breathed in deeply and exhaled with a grin while tilting her head at Coura, who watched with a surprising amount of pity.

She thinks she's immortal. What does a creature like that really have to lose? She'll never know what companionship means, or trust or love, especially from the behavior she described from demons. In fact, I think I'm the closest thing to that she ever had, though it was barely a mutual partnership.

"Sometimes I wish I could return to being unknown to your kind, if only to watch the human race stumble through life with such naive notions," Soirée said at last. "Now that you revealed where your loyalties lie, I suppose all that's left to do is collect what power the high priest gathered for me, though waiting for him to die would do the trick. Perhaps I might kill you before then. I wonder if my control will finally give me the opportunity to take over your body completely if you're near death. Should we try it out while we have the time?"

The demon stepped forward to initiate the challenge.

Coura adjusted her stance for the upcoming attack as Soirée moved closer. "You're nothing but a monster," she muttered.

The shared memory of the fiery underworld and merciless beings tearing each other apart helped her to see the demon in front of her as the deadly enemy it was. The images also warned her without words that this woman-like creature had more skill than it first let on.

There's no reason for her to try and keep me alive. I need to make sure to avoid her physical blows, or at least prepare for them, because I'm sure that's what she'll rely on.

Just as the thought concluded, Soirée charged, and her quiet footsteps brought the two face-to-face in a heartbeat. After that, Coura practically forgot about keeping the demon's attention while waiting for the ancestral weapon.

It seemed nothing would distract either of them as they slipped around one another, striking swiftly and surely, as if their swords were forged straight into their hands. Soirée became intent on remaining on the offensive by keeping her movements smooth and constant. She swiped across Coura's chest, just barely breaking the skin, and followed with a spin to bring up her foot. Three more times, she continued that ploy of distracting with the most dangerous, weapon-bearing arm only to try landing another blow immediately after. Coura had to force herself to ignore the first strike, which did minimal damage, and defend against the next.

In addition to the pattern, she found herself taking advantage of the demonic healing ability. Soirée lunged after feigning a punch, so Coura accepted the blade into her left side by shifting in that direction. This not only caught the demon off guard, but allowed Coura to stab for the creature's chest. Once the tip of her blade sunk into flesh, Soirée released her sword in favor of leaping backward. The blade in Coura's side disappeared, letting blood pour forth until the wound sealed. As the healing concluded on both sides, Soirée grinned wildly as she understood what just took place.

THE ANGEL'S DESCENT

"Clever strategy!" the demon exclaimed. She opened her mouth to say more, but her next words were cut short by a surge of unknown, foreign power stemming from the palace.

At first, Coura jumped and prepared for some sort of attack as the energy swelled and irritated what belonged to Soirée. When it continued fluctuating without spreading in their direction, she remembered the Yeluthian's plan to use a spell to burn away the power Hendal possessed.

Her lips began twitching upward at the realization. *They're doing it! They should be able to stop Hendal, and Soirée won't take back her energy.*

The interruption had drawn Coura's eyes away from her opponent for a few seconds. When she returned to looking at Soirée, the demon's face had fallen. The rare occasion of catching her completely by surprise with the angelic, secret spell was priceless enough that Coura savored it as they stood motionless until the Yeluthian's energy faded. Even after, Soirée still didn't move for another minute. It grew somewhat uncomfortable for Coura once she realized she was the only person available to keep the demon in one place for the time being.

If she flees, it might be too late for the others to arrive. My guess is she will turn to exact revenge on them. I should also be prepared for her to lash out, especially since I'm alone.

Coura brought her weapon up, bent her legs to prepare for a sudden attack, and waited. Finally, Soirée slid the violet, rage-filled eyes over to stare daggers at her.

"What was that?"

"You didn't recognize it?" Coura countered. Although she intended to feign ignorance, the retort came out in a condescending way.

Soirée's lips parted, and she bared her teeth in anger so her next words sounded like a growl. "The connection is broken. All of *my* power is gone!"

If she had not been prepared for the demon's wrath, Coura knew she didn't stand a chance at surviving. With a shriek unbecoming of the creature, Soirée launched herself fully without much intent to resume her sly, smooth movements. Blow after blow with both blade and fists were wide and easy for Coura to recognize, so she blocked when not returning an attack.

This is it, she thought optimistically as the demon snarled. *Even if she doesn't wear herself out, I can taunt her in this mindset until backup arrives.*

Beads of sweat flew from their faces as the one-on-one fight had Coura at the limit of her speed just to avoid being slashed apart. Unfortunately, she also noticed Soirée's temper settling down. In an attempt to continue the distraction, she charged and chanced a horizontal swing across the demon's midsection only for it to be parried. Instead of responding during the opening, Soirée retreated a few steps to pause the dance once again. Coura was tempted to lunge forward until her opponent began chuckling in a familiar, frighteningly calm manner.

"If I were to guess, I would say you're trying to hold my attention," Soirée started in a carefree tone of voice. As she stood straighter, her entire demeanor returned to the confident presence Coura always knew, emphasized by the demon tossing her raven hair over one shoulder.

How...

"I must apologize for that sudden change in behavior," she continued. "It isn't often I can be ensnared, though what happened is no laughing matter. If you haven't noticed, the power I lent to the high priest, including all he branched out, has been eradicated by some light-blooded spell. All that energy is gone, though you don't appear as startled as I am considering it was indirectly yours."

She knows, Coura realized with dread before silently cursing and gripping the hilt of her sword tighter. Despite being prepared for a repeated fight, a shiver ran down her spine at what was to come.

Like a cruel mirror, the demon's initial smile returned as the ruby lips curved upward. Soirée took a couple steps forward and twirled her sword with a tilt of her head, but something flickered across her face. The footsteps halted, then the demon's eyes began looking Coura up and down.

"I have an idea," she shared suddenly while resuming her approach. "Please, indulge me!"

Instead of a steady initiation into battle, the demon threw herself at Coura, who stepped back involuntarily.

She's gone mad! Why is this-

Any thoughts were cut short as Soirée swept her blade for Coura's throat. The motion proved slow enough for her to block and push away the opposing weapon. When the demon left her body wide open, Coura decided to retaliate, again stabbing straight through the chest. As the sword sank into flesh, she caught the violet eyes meet hers and realized Soirée was copying her previous tactic.

In her mind, she screamed at her legs to carry her away, yet it was already too late. The blade in Soirée's hand had disappeared, allowing the demon to bring up a fist and connect it with Coura's nose. Only then did her feet stumble backward as her empty left hand rose to cover the bleeding, bruised area. Warm blood trickled down her throat and over her lips, but to her horror, Soirée kept moving.

The demon crouched to bring a leg across the ground and sweep Coura's feet away, causing her to fall onto her right side. In the next instant, Soirée pounced. There was hardly a struggle before Coura wound up flat on her back with her opponent kneeling on her chest.

Next, Soirée sank her blade into Coura's left forearm, using it as a stake to pin the limb to the ground. When Coura raised the sword in her right hand, Soirée grabbed her wrist and twisted it sharply until it broke and she released the weapon.

"There, there. Settle down," the creature on top of her teased.

"Get off!" Coura spat while jerking her limbs in a weak attempt to free herself. The blood continuing to pour down her throat made it burn, causing her to cough. Meanwhile, kicking her legs did nothing as Soirée sat farther up and with enough weight to remain firmly planted. Any force on the left arm resulted in stinging pain coupled with gushes of blood while the right remained glued to the ground by Soirée's grip. Fear crept through her when she could do nothing except lie under the penetrating gaze.

"As I was saying, I need you to stay still for a moment."

With her free hand, the demon caressed Coura's cheek, then she traced a finger downward. When it stopped, it hovered above Coura's center.

"Once you refused to join me, you forfeited your life. After all, what use could you possibly serve except to house some of my power? Well, with the high priest's defeat and that spell destroying all of my hard-earned energy, I think it's only fair you return what is mine. Since we share a special connection, it won't be impossible for you to gather more demonic energy if it's expended. At least, that's what I am counting on for the future."

Before Coura could fully comprehend the notion of the creature stealing back her power, the demon began her work. The leash tethering the two together tightened as Soirée rested a palm on Coura's center and reached inside.

The strain was unlike anything she felt before, giving her the sensation of being torn in half without the immense pain. The energies in her center fluttered in distress. Despite how hard she tried to shake away Soirée, the demonic power decreased against her will.

"Stop!" she screamed once on deaf ears before squeezing her eyes shut.

No matter how much she flailed her legs, turned her head from side to side, or heaved her chest upward, nothing pried the hand away. In a last effort, Coura focused solely on her soul space. The invisible hands used to guide the energy tugged against Soirée's invasive force. Although the draining weakened, she lost more with each second than she saved. Still, she refused to give up until the last tendril resting within slipped away.

There was nothing left to try and protect after that. Her Yeluthian power hid deeper at Soirée's presence and remained that way once the demon stood to step off her body. The blade in her left arm disappeared, so she curled up onto that side with her arms wrapped around her stomach.

It's all gone... I can't feel...anything...

During her time in Dala when one of Hendal's rogue angels stabbed her with the golden dagger, the power poured out of its own will. The demonic energy had been freed, yet what remained in her soul space, her Yeluthian power, became active.

This time, Soirée ripped the energy away, leaving Coura's center hollow. Nothing reacted to her inner voice begging for a response or an unseen touch normally used as a trigger into that power. Any remaining, angelic energy felt as though it went into shock from the violent experience, or at least she hoped it was still there.

"That proved to be much less of a hassle than I initially imagined," Soirée said from where she hovered above Coura. She inspected a hand, closed it into a fist, then smiled. "What you provided isn't nearly as much as I would have gained from the Nim-Valan soldiers, but it will do. Perhaps when you recover and again explore the world, you can collect more from the demonic creatures. Until then, I'll try to stay out of your way."

With that, she spun around and proceeded to walk toward the outer boundary of the area. Coura knew it would be hopeless to pursue.

Without my magic, there's no chance of holding her here anymore. If I fight, she already made it clear I'll be thrown aside. All I can do is lie here and wait for someone to notice me. Maybe if we regroup, we can send another scouting party after.

The last sound Coura expected to hear at that moment was the whirl of an arrow, yet one sung above where she remained on her side. Her head popped up just as Soirée stared behind at the shaft protruding from the center of her back. Then, a glasslike wall appeared to block the demon from escaping into the woods beyond. Even though her center went numb, making her unable to sense energy, Coura recognized the familiar pattern.

Two figures sprinted by from the palace followed by a third, though none stopped to check on her or even glanced her way. That didn't bother her in the slightest when she recognized who they were. Help had arrived, and that was enough motivation to join the fight again, no matter how limited her abilities were.

***

Under Byron's orders, once the group reached the training ground, they would surround the demon and wear it down until Marcus had a clear shot with the ancestral weapon. No part of his plan changed when a surge of the creature's power shook even those without the ability to sense magic. One petrified look from Emilea was enough to remind him what they were up against.

This demon knows us already. If we try a strategic approach, it can purposefully act to avoid falling for anything. It's risky, especially without a properly prepared healer along, but I believe charging will hold the creature's attention. The only unpredictable factor is its reaction to the golden blade, which hopefully it hasn't caught on to.

As Clearshot hurried in the lead, Byron's final words were to leave the demon alone if it decided to run.

"Hendal was our main target," he had explained to some disagreeing expressions. "The last thing we need is for someone to get killed now when hundreds of soldiers are waiting to hear from us on the other side of the palace. We'll get the proper resources to find it again later but not the element of surprise Marcus is carrying."

If anyone planned to protest, they didn't have time. Clearshot never slowed, so he rammed straight into the door leading out to the training ground where the demonic energy flared minutes ago. They all blinked to adjust to the brighter, sunlit area, then they took in their surroundings while continuing on ahead. The space proved to be empty except for a shadow-like silhouette near the farthest end and another figure lying nearby.

"Go," Byron ordered when he sensed everyone's hesitation a moment later. In the back of his mind, he remembered Coura's ability to recover, which eased his concern. "I'll make sure she's all right. Emilea, use a shield to keep the demon from leaving. Everyone else, surround it!"

No one needed words to push them on after that. Marcus and Aaron were the first to sprint toward the opposite side of the field with Will close behind. Clearshot already let an arrow loose to sink into the demon's back, drawing its attention, then his wife crafted her spell.

It wouldn't be long before Byron was pulled into the action, but they needed Coura as well. Without taking his full attention away from the creature eyeing up its new opponents, he approached his former student to kneel beside her. He noticed blood on her forearm and under her nose, but she appeared otherwise unharmed and sat up when he put a hand on her shoulder.

"Are you hurt?" he asked as she stared at where the others engaged in wide attacks to keep their distance.

"You made it just in time," she responded without masking her exasperation and moved to stand.

Byron took her arm to assist. When she was on her feet, her wavering made him suspicious. "What happened?"

She turned away from the action to meet his eyes; hers were filled with her characteristic impatience, which matched the tightness of her lips. "We felt the Yeluthian's spell and Hendal's power disappear. Soirée realized what you did and took back what power I held to compensate for what she lost."

Despite what he knew about the demon's hold over her, hearing of such an ability still amazed him. Once the implications of this settled in his mind, Byron began to understand how this would affect their chances of containing the creature.

"Does that mean…" He started a question before she cut him off with a shake of her head.

"She stole all of it. I can't sense any energy, and the last of it healed my arm."

"I see."

Coura didn't appear despondent, though, and shifted her gaze from Byron to the circle of activity nearby. If anything, he thought she seemed more focused.

"Can I borrow your sword?" she asked next. "I'm kind of empty-handed now."

Byron nodded with a grunt, unsheathed his weapon, and passed it over. Although a less persistent part of his mind longed to keep her safely behind, it would be foolish to restrain someone with her skill and personal investment.

Together, the two hurried to join what currently took place at the edge of the area. Because he lent Coura his own blade, all he had in the way of attacking and defending was dark magic. At the moment, Marcus, Will, and Aaron surrounded the demon, who watched them with a visible sense of superiority. The assistant general kept to its back while the two others switched off lunging to swing and stab. Meanwhile, Clearshot had an arrow nocked and waited for an opportune moment when it would be needed.

As Byron slowed to stand alone opposite his friend, he came to the conclusion that if he focused on offensive spells, he would only end up doing the same while endangering the combatants. To compensate for this, he poured whatever energy he could spare into a shield behind Emilea's. His fellow master mage kept her wall fortified, giving it more power when the demon wandered closer.

As long as it doesn't think to come after us or flee in the opposite direction, we can hold it here, he thought while he pushed the energy forth. In the back of his mind, he made sure to prepare for an adjustment to his spell should the creature turn on him, Clearshot, or Emilea. His position not only allowed him to stay directly out of harm's way but also observe the fight.

Just as the second wall behind Emilea's solidified, Coura reached her friends, yet she didn't slow her pace. He was a tad surprised to see her charge in between Will and Aaron without hesitation, then she slashed downward at the demon. It stepped away to dodge but had to twist to one side in order to avoid Marcus and the deadly weapon he carried.

Still, Coura pursued. When Will hurried to support her, they wordlessly formed a strategy. Two pushed from the front while Marcus waited for his opportunity to lash out.

Unfortunately, its simplicity proved to be too obvious to utilize well. When Coura stood at the center, the creature blocked her attack, threw all of its weight into a shove that sent her falling onto her back, then slipped away as both Marcus and Aaron were already moving to initiate the next step. This caused the two to nearly collide while the demon giggled with a sadistic expression. Coura scrambled to her feet, and its smile faded once Marcus raised the ancestral blade as a challenge. Byron sensed the assistant general's irritation sparked by the previous motions meant to embarrass them, though from his position, he had no indication of what was to come.

The four began circling the enemy again before all except Marcus attacked at once. Their tactic looked similar to earlier, except all three would fight to force an opening; however, just as they had to adjust their strategy, the demon did too.

It began using more than just its slim blade, throwing out fists in the opposite direction and kicks at shins, knees, and thighs. The speed with which it struck also concerned Byron since that helped it to land vicious scratches and blows. No one stopped going after the creature, though, and he doubted the severity of each successful strike, no matter how deep it appeared to be inflicted.

Soon, Will stumbled backward after a shove, then Coura wobbled before dropping to one knee. Without the full support of those two, Aaron retreated, signaling for Marcus to do the same. From that angle, Byron could see the sweat dripping down their faces and soaking their clothes as they panted.

He considered joining with magic, but something in the distance near the front of the palace caught the creature's attention. It stood straighter while watching the sky with narrowed eyes. Although he wished to know what became so captivating, Byron refused to glance away with Will, Coura, Aaron, and Marcus in range of a surprise attack he could shield them from. In a heartbeat, the demon leapt in his direction between Marcus and Will as Byron felt rather than saw a bolt of lightning land where it had been standing.

Years of mastering the elemental spells prepared him for the sounds and aftereffects of such occurrences, but those nearby threw up their hands to protect their faces as pieces of earth flew up. He squinted and found the source a moment later. One of the Yeluthian soldiers flew high above directly in front of the sun, covering their bronze armor in shining light.

They used the sunlight to hide their body, he realized with some admiration as the angelic figure descended sharply enough to make it seem as though they were literally falling out of the sky. As soon as their feet touched grass, the demon sprinted over with the fiercest expression Byron had ever seen from it. Then, he could only watch as the two engaged in combat. The demon's speed remained its advantage while the angel had wings, resulting in a spectacle of abilities and evenly-matched skill.

17

Hurried footsteps crunched on the ground next to Byron, drawing his eyes away from the scene, and Coura, with Marcus behind, halted at his side. Red spots of blood from shallow scrapes decorated her limbs while the assistant general's face bore similar marks, yet neither paid any mind to them.

"Who's that?" the former asked in an odd tone of voice, as if both startled and concerned by the Yeluthian's appearance.

He shook his head and returned to spectating the on-going fight. "I don't know, but at least they can hold their own against the creature."

As he watched the angel continue to rise and swoop down with a slicing motion, he was reminded of the young, rogue male in the palace with Hendal. Their movements looked identical, spanning a wider space than what encircled the demon, who needed to tumble away since it stuck to the ground.

Again, he became fascinated by both beings' combat styles.

If I study their actions, perhaps we can learn the best way to approach sealing the demon away, some part of his mind said to justify that use of time.

The Yeluthian dropped down, pulling in their wings tight, and continued striking from above. This kept pushing the lithe creature in another direction. Between swings, it attempted stabs that were either dodged just in the nick of time or deflected by the bronze armor, which created a low-pitched clang. Unfortunately, the angel was in no better position. Any attack swift enough to land left minor damage that healed almost instantly. Without a proper look at the newcomer's face, Byron couldn't tell if they were growing exhausted, though the demon appeared unaffected.

From his left, Coura stepped forward. Another followed to show she prepared to run into the fray. He extended a hand and managed to grab her by the arm, stopping her charge.

"Where do you think you're going?" he demanded when her body jerked back from the unexpected hold.

"We can't just stand here," she protested.

Again, her attitude didn't project anger but a sense of urgency, which intrigued Byron. He told himself that, because of his time in the palace under Hendal's control, he wasn't as familiar with the Yeluthians as she might be.

"If we get near them now, we would only be in the way."

Marcus came to Coura's other side. "What do you suppose we do then?" he countered with a frown. *That* was the tone Byron expected from his former student, yet imagining how much the assistant general put into the battle shed a bit of light on the young soldier's perspective of their situation.

"I know you don't want to hear it, but the Yeluthian is the only one of us who stands a chance of restraining the demon," he replied. "If they can bring it closer, *maybe* you two can assist, especially with the ancestral weapon. Otherwise, we keep at a safe distance."

Marcus glanced behind at where Will and Aaron still stood near the shields, then he turned to study the inhuman beings nearby. Byron followed his gaze toward the first pair.

They're probably trying to avoid getting in anyone's way, he figured. *Aaron is in constant danger because of his status. If I really considered it earlier, I would've made sure he stayed inside. In any case, it's too late to send him away. Also, that barrier might not be necessary anymore.*

With the dangerous creature no longer at the border, he dismissed his spell and focused on the enemy again. Soon, he understood there would be no escaping with the Yeluthian present. Just as the angel in the chamber remained intent on fighting Commander Detrix only, the demon became fixated on this soldier. Its eyes never looked away, and its mouth stretched into a snarl, reminding Byron that the grudge ran deeper than he could imagine.

He heard a growl when the stranger leapt into the sky right before the demon swung twice, missing its target. It raised a hand to release fire upward in an arch across the gray sky as the Yeluthian swerved to the side. Four more times, the creature attempted elemental spells varying between waves of fire, pointed ice shards, and lightning only for each to be avoided by the angel's graceful maneuvering. As it continued, Byron began to consider giving Coura and Marcus permission to sneak up from behind while he created his own offensive, magical attack. He even spoke their names to get their attention before the situation changed for the worse.

By that point, the demon's sword vanished, allowing it to use both hands to double the output of the spells' strength. Still, the angel dodged with a skill making their flight seem carefree. From a distance everyone on the ground could see how the creature's current fire spell lingered above before lowering to bring the bronze-clad soldier closer to the ground. Then, the magic abruptly ended, and a new spell formed, one containing more malice. Byron's body began to tremble once he recalled encountering a familiar sensation outside the Dalan base.

It's a binding spell! His throat felt constricted at the reminder of his previous helplessness in the face of such power and control.

The Yeluthian remained adamant about keeping to the sky and started to ascend once more only for their arms, legs, and wings to snap against their body. The demon's arms had extended to initiate the invisible hold, but they fell to its sides as the angel plummeted. This time, Byron cried out a warning too late to do any good while watching their group's best chance of success crash into the earth. When the dust cleared and he could see the stranger, they were subtly wiggling parts of their body in an attempt to get free. In the distance, the demon laughed maniacally, a sound that echoed across the area while it strode toward the angel.

Before Byron could think about rescuing the Yeluthian, Coura broke away from his side to sprint in their direction. A second later, Marcus was right behind her, leaving Byron alone.

THE ANGEL'S DESCENT

Regroup, before it's too late, his instincts ordered.

He ignored the internal command until the two were nearly upon the creature. *They can support us. This might be our best chance to catch the creature by surprise and save the angel. Once they realize that, I guarantee everyone will come too.*

With the idea driving his actions, Byron didn't move from his location. Instead, he dove into the last portion of his active energy and prepared to help the combatants however he could.

***

Even without any proof as to the identity of the Yeluthian who arrived to help, Coura let herself believe it was her father. Something about their sure, fluid movements reminded her of earlier in the day when Evern held off two of the rogue angels. What she witnessed then looked similar enough to the newcomer's actions against Soirée that she felt convinced.

She attempted to confirm it, yet Byron reminded her of the risks by grabbing her arm, stopping the impulsive, head-on charge. Together, they stood memorized by the two figures moving in ways no human ever could.

About three years ago, angels and demons were still considered legends to most of Asteom, Coura reflected with growing apprehension. *Somehow, I managed to reaffirm my involvement with both in the same evening, but how each is rooted in my life differs dramatically. I've seen where the demons dwell and what kind of a place that is, and I visited Yeluthia and met its people. Each being is the complete opposite of the other.*

She had no notion of how much time passed between when she lost her demonic power and the ongoing, magical attacks Soirée hurled into the sky. The second presence, the Yeluthian energy resting in her center, steadily crept out from hiding, yet she didn't know how to control it. That power certainly wasn't strong enough to compete against a mature demon either.

Because of the consistent numbness resulting from having her power ripped away, Coura was unable to sense what Soirée prepared to do. All of a sudden, the figure in the sky became as rigid as a log and fell, losing their weapon in the process. Byron shouted a warning when that happened, bringing her back to her senses.

A binding spell, she recalled with horror as the bronze armor connected with the ground. *Evern's in danger... Soirée's going to kill him!*

The thought was still catching up with her even after she started sprinting to meet the demon. She wondered what she could do, how she could ever stop the creature responsible for turning her life upside down. Still, nothing hindered her progress across the space.

Soirée stared at her prey below from their side and poised the point of her blade above the Yeluthian's head. Meanwhile, the angel worked to free their body to no avail. Coura, frightened for her father to the point of delirium, threw herself, sword and all, around Soirée's weapon-bearing arm.

"Stop!" she shouted and hugged the creature's limb with enough weight to lower it.

There came a growl as the demon attempted to free that arm with enough strength to pull Coura off her feet multiple times. She held on, as if her life depended on it, squeezed her eyes shut, and prayed the figure on the ground would break the binding spell.

It was no surprise when Soirée pried her leech away with her empty hand shortly after. The demon had Coura by the back of her neck and tossed her to the side like she weighed no more than a rag doll. Her body collided with the only other person on their feet in the immediate area, which happened to be a fully-clad Marcus, who followed behind her. She had no idea if he planned on attacking, rescuing her or the angel still bound in the grass, or anything else; whatever his intentions were, they became no more as the two tumbled to the ground.

When Coura could open her eyes once the world stopped spinning, she wound up on her stomach. An ache arose from the right side of her ribs accompanied by bruising on her right arm. Marcus groaned from beside her where he lied on one side after been knocked down by the unexpected projectile. They sat up at the same time, and Coura winced with a sharp inhale at the new pain.

"Where'd it go?" her friend asked as he rubbed his head, leading her to glance around.

The demon had disappeared from her previous position in front of the Yeluthian in order to stalk over to where Byron, Will, Aaron, Emilea, and Clearshot stood mostly separated near the outer border.

She's targeting the others. Knowing Soirée, she wants to savor killing her main prey, but we're in the way. All of us are a threat to her current goal. She voiced as much to Marcus, who scrambled to his feet and offered her a hand she heartily accepted.

"We need to move," he said and retrieved one of the two swords dropped during their tumble.

Coura searched for the other even as Marcus took off running; however, she froze in the next instant when she spotted the golden blade in the grass.

He grabbed the wrong weapon! she realized with no shortage of panic. *How could he forget about the ancestral weapon?* Her own sense of urgency led her to dismiss the item once the Yeluthian was in danger, so she couldn't entirely blame Marcus for his current, determined pursuit.

Cautiously, she tapped the hilt, fully expecting the stabbing sensation in her veins, yet nothing happened. The lack of a response reminded her of her lost power, meaning the sword had no reason to react to her anymore. She scooped up the weapon and spent no time admiring it once she noticed Soirée move to strike those remaining in the training ground.

The demon manifested her sword again and charged with as much coordination as a feline upon mice, beginning with the nearest pair. Clearshot stood in front of Emilea and fired arrow after arrow at the inhuman creature; if any of his attacks landed, Coura couldn't tell. Soirée easily slipped in front of the archer before initiating a pair of cross slashes. His bow fell in two pieces, the shoulder of his right arm bled, and he gripped it while still shielding his wife. After a slice to his torso, he dropped to his knees while gripping his stomach. The light mage screamed and crumpled as well before being kicked square in the face with enough force to knock her backward.

When Soirée appeared near Clearshot, Will began hurrying over from where he and Aaron stood at the farthest end. By the time he reached them, the demon had already finished disabling the pair and turned to strike again. Coura didn't fully see what transpired next, but one second her friend stood on his feet and the next he collapsed to the ground. Soirée lunged with her sword raised, and that was it.

Byron started releasing several spells then in a similar manner to what Soirée used on the angel when the figure hovered in the air. The demon rolled away to dodge, but Coura noticed the action took some effort and didn't always prevent damage. Meanwhile, Aaron sidestepped in the opposite direction to approach and join from behind. At this point, Coura and Marcus neared the combat again. Unfortunately, the demon started her next maneuver before they could assist, leaving them to watch helplessly.

Their enemy continued moving forward while dodging the blasts of fire Byron threw at her, for he stopped using any other spell. His pained expression projected the strain on his body as Soirée crept closer. Coura expected a strike, yet the demon didn't attack right away. Instead, she lingered out of arm's reach until Byron prepared his next spell. As soon as his palms glowed to signal the magic's release, Soirée lunged, grabbed his wrists, and pulled each hand in opposite directions; one aimed at Marcus and Coura and the other at Aaron.

The three didn't expect the blast of fire, but it was too late for the energy to be retracted. Coura had been far enough behind her friend to see the bright flames and threw herself to one side. The spell flew by in a wave of uncomfortable heat, which steadily sank until it skimmed over the earth and broke apart into sparks above the dead grass.

If it went this far, that means Marcus got out of the way too, she thought a bit optimistically.

Her assumption proved correct as the silver-clad soldier scrambled to his feet; however, a glance across the field made her heart drop. On the opposite side, Aaron knelt and hunched over while smaller flames caught onto the grass and his shirt. His left arm appeared to be smoking worse than the rest of his upper body.

As for Byron, she didn't catch the next attack because of the spell. He lied on one side as the demon stood beside him with a grin. Time seemed to slow while the creature cackled.

"Is this all you humans can do?" Soirée shouted and circled to observe her work. "Pathetic!"

The world went still. Nobody moved, or could move, for a heartbeat that stretched into what felt like hours. Then, the shadow-like figure turned to face the Yeluthian once more. Coura didn't know if the angel broke free or not. Her entire body began to ache from an invisible chill.

What can we do now? she wondered with a glance down at the golden sword, which continued radiating despite their darkening circumstances. *There's no way I can get close enough to even touch Soirée with this, and Marcus and I are the only ones left...*

It was then she noticed her final companion sprinting to meet the demon, and her throat closed.

He's going to get himself killed! Perhaps if we don't resist, she might leave, and I can find a healer. Still, she remembered how intent Soirée had been on murdering the Yeluthian and decided giving up would ensure the angel's death.

As she watched Marcus reach and lunge for their enemy, bringing about a fight he could barely keep up with, Coura considered her few, limited options. When she prepared to join her comrade with a frontal assault, the resting energy within her center rumbled in distress. She managed a couple steps before halting when the feeling persisted.

I appreciate the enthusiasm, but I don't know how to wield that type of magic, she told the chittering pool.

To her surprise, it projected a familiar sensation introduced right after she departed from Yeluthia.

This feeling... I did use a light spell before! Could I lure Soirée away with it? Would she suspect a trick if I push her enough? What if the portal doesn't appear or won't send her elsewhere?

In any case, Coura understood she had to try for her fallen friends.

If I'm able to move us somewhere unexpected, Soirée will let down her guard, giving me a chance to seal her away with the ancestral weapon. She might escape, but everybody here will have a chance to find help. If it doesn't work... I came into this battle fully prepared to put my life on the line. Demonic power or not, I'm responsible for her; the consequences are mine to bear.

The brief reflection steadied her resolve. She gripped the hilt of her sword tighter and thought she felt it humming, as if eager to fulfill its purpose.

Meanwhile, Marcus was getting to his feet for the third time after being shoved, punched, and then tossed away by Soirée, who returned to her normal manner of playing with the inferior opponents.

Coura considered where to have the magical portal exit as she jogged closer to the combat. Anywhere in Asteom would be dangerous, yet the only other place outside the country she knew of was Yeluthia. Several locations came to mind, including the Valley Beyond or the Dalan base's moat, yet they were all too practical, too easy to escape from.

At the idea of a more suitable place to trap the demon, a foggy memory sprang to the forefront. It often invaded her dreams, preventing her from sleeping soundly. When she considered Soirée's feelings toward it, Coura felt confident the demon would have a difficult time returning to Asteom again, even if she died in the process.

Will this work? she asked the Yeluthian power.

The jittering connection made certain the spell would obey her command, though how much of a toll it would take remained unknown.

Her final obstacle was forcing Soirée through the portal once it took form.

If she follows the same pattern as earlier when we fought, then releasing the energy at the right time should do the trick, Coura decided as she watched the demon shove Marcus down once more.

This time, it took visible effort for him to rise to his knees where he leaned on his sword while breathing heavy. Soirée noticed Coura approaching and waved the point of her blade around his head in a gesture of superiority.

"What were you spouting before about humans taking care of each other?" the demon asked in a supercilious tone of voice. "I wonder if they still trust you. Do you think they're useful anymore?" She chuckled after those words, taking obvious pleasure in tormenting Coura.

Marcus groaned, glared up at the pair of violet eyes, and continued panting. As Soirée frowned at him, Coura charged to prevent the creature from getting a chance to strike again. Similar to her friend's attempt, it became an effort to match blades and focus on avoiding stray fists and feet. She was forced back twice yet continued with the ever-present image of the portal spell in her mind.

After all, the right opportunity wouldn't be on her time but Soirée's.

For several bouts, the two clashed, which always paused with Coura being shoved or thrown to the ground, just like Marcus experienced. Even though her opponent taunted and jeered, she pushed herself to her feet with the understanding that she was a toy meant to be played with for the time being.

The final time she rose, she had a new approach in mind. Instead of hurrying in to inevitably block and dodge, she went on the offensive. Each slash carried an intent to harm or kill, though none could land since Soirée slipped just out of reach; however, as Coura suspected, the creature found amusement in acting the part of the untouchable target and danced away from the golden swipes while wearing a smirk.

All the while, Coura patiently controlled her movements until the moment came when Soirée grew close enough to lunge for. Then, the scene played out as she expected. The unscathed demon eyed the edge of the ancestral sword as Coura stabbed forward before the creature leapt back instead of pursuing.

Her previous behavior with Marcus suggested that, as long as we continue to hold her attention, she'll find amusement in weakening our spirits. I had to make sure I seemed emotional enough so when I pretend to lose my temper and charge, it's more for her to mess with. It's her reason to stay here, and now it's my turn to meddle with her!

As the thought concluded, she released the power within to shape the light spell just behind where Soirée's feet picked up.

A flash of alarm crossed the demon's face once she sensed the energy and looked over her shoulder to spot an oval, mirror-like opening form in midair. Even when it seemed Soirée couldn't stop herself from falling through, Coura slammed a shoulder into the creature, just in case. The sickening, falling sensation after the tackle indicated the pair successfully passed through to the other side.

***

For longer than he thought was deemed acceptable for a figure of royalty, Aaron knelt on the ground coddling his injured left side. Nothing prepared him for the demon's tactic to use Byron's magic against the master mage's will to stop his advance. By the time Aaron could comprehend what happened, flames covered his arm, crawling down to his thigh, across his chest, and over his shoulder while licking the skin. Patting out the fire stung every part burned by the spell, nearly causing him to faint from the resulting dizziness.

That was partly why he remained on one knee without moving; the other reason was because he had no idea how to take on a creature with lightning-fast reflexes and seemingly endless strength.

When he felt compelled to observe his surroundings, Byron lied on the ground and Marcus began fending off the demon alone. Even with his friend's skill, Aaron could see they were being toyed with. He attempted to stand then but winced at the uncomfortable pain that resulted from stretching the burns. Already, they started to blister.

Why didn't I better prepare for this? He thought and ground his teeth in frustration.

Marcus had been thrown again and pushed himself to his knees, leading Aaron to sink deeper into his regret. It only grew worse once he heard the demon taunting Coura before the two began to fight. Out of everyone in the area, he trusted her the most when it came to battling anything possessing demonic power, even though she never used her magic the entire time he had been outside with the others. His dependence made him hate himself for leaving the situation to her, especially since he found he cared a lot about her safety.

Finally, after seeing Coura fall for the second time, Aaron roused the strength to bear the pain and wobbled to his feet. The next task became locating his sword, which wound up in a patch of charred grass. The more Aaron moved, the better he felt; at least, his mentality seemed sharp.

As he retrieved the weapon and proceeded to join the only person facing the creature, another, unexpected moment left him gaping as the lone human still on his feet. Like the spells thrown all across the area, something new appeared. It looked to be a mirror made of light that inhaled the demon as soon as it stepped away from the ancestral weapon in Coura's hand. She slipped in after to ram the creature just before the strange spell disappeared completely, leaving no indication the two had even been there.

What just happened? Aaron wondered in a daze until his mind caught up with him. *It took Coura away. The timing was too precise for her to accidentally fall through, meaning it aimed to separate her from us. Is it because they share a connection, or is there another reason? Where could it have taken her?*

A nearby grunt tore him away from the questions that tumbled forth, reminding him of the damage done to those who came into the field. He called to Marcus and began hobbling over to meet his closest friend.

The assistant general somehow had the energy to rise but gazed at the same location Aaron had been momentarily transfixed by. "Where did they go?" he practically demanded.

"I don't know," Aaron answered honestly. "Did you see what happened?"

He had been friends with Marcus long enough to know the resulting expression behind the helmet and tone of voice in the response meant there would be an explosion shortly.

"See what happened? How could I *see* what happened? They vanished out of thin air! We were already beaten down. Why would the demon steal Coura away? Not only that, but we have no way to track her down!" By that point, Marcus had removed his helmet and threw it on the ground to emphasize his internal mixture of anger, defeat, and helplessness.

Aaron said nothing. Rarely did the assistant general make such an outburst, though it usually slipped when he was unable to do more to solve a problem or when the situation turned out in the worst possible way.

Right now, it's both.

He stared at a patch of blue sky around the gray clouds as his best friend paced with glances at where Coura and the demon disappeared.

"How did we not hear about a spell like that? The demon never used it before."

"Because, demonic magic did not cast it," came a male voice from behind. The Yeluthian soldier who joined to face the creature one-on-one walked over with his helmet in one hand and sword sheathed. His demeanor looked calm and projected a sense of relief, but Aaron picked up an underlying sadness too.

"What do you mean?" Marcus asked. He stopped moving to collect the emotions on display and brushed down his messy hair.

The sapphire eyes were richer than any Aaron had ever seen; his father possessed the same sort and used to say they came from a life of difficult decisions. It intimidated him to stare directly into them, so when the man met his, he looked away.

"Crafting portals to travel from one location to another is a characteristic of a Yeluthian goddess gift. Such an ability has not been seen in decades."

"Who are you?" he asked when the stranger didn't go on.

When the angel's gaze shifted to trail over the visible, throbbing burns and blisters, he involuntarily fidgeted.

"You were not with the others who journeyed into the palace when battle broke out," came the response. "I doubt you are old enough to be an experienced mage either."

"This is King Aaron," Marcus interjected with a half-hearted raise of his arm as a gesture.

At that, the Yeluthian's stoic expression softened, and he placed a hand on his breast with a bow. "Forgive me, Your Highness. You may address me as Commander Evern, one of the army leaders. Please, allow me to heal your injuries."

The offer sounded tempting, but a shudder ran through Aaron's body once he remembered the less fortunate members of their group.

THE ANGEL'S DESCENT

When the Yeluthian reached a hand toward him, he shook his head before glancing around.

Byron remained where he noticed the master mage earlier, and he heard the sobbing of a woman in the distance.

Emilea and Clearshot... I don't even see Will at all. I must have been too preoccupied to notice.

"Others in our party are in far worse conditions than I am. If you can, please heal them first."

In that moment, he couldn't sound demanding even if he tried. He had no medical knowledge and no right to order around a citizen of another kingdom; however, the person in front of him with eyes like the sea and hair as golden as the sun possessed the power necessary to save lives.

As Aaron dipped his head to emphasize his plea, the Yeluthian frowned, scanned the open area where the unexpected magic swept Coura and the demon away, then agreed to help. Byron was the closest to their location, so Commander Evern moved there first at a leisurely pace, which drove Aaron crazy. Marcus shot him a sympathetic look but said nothing.

The master mage looked extremely pale on top of a pool of blood with both hands on the lower part of his chest. His eyes were shut in a tired manner as his chest rose and fell in steady, shallow breaths. The Yeluthian kneeled, laid his hands on top of Byron's, and cast the healing spell, emanating a dull light from the afflicted area. For a while, nothing else happened. Aaron prepared to ask Marcus to find more aid until the stranger sighed.

"Your master mage will be fine," he shared, as though he took care of nothing more serious than a splinter. "I closed the opening and supported the inflicted organs just enough for them to begin healing on their own. It will take some time for his blood to be replenished; I would say a few days or close to a week. All he can do is rest until he is well enough to eat. Now, where are the others?"

"I'll show you," Marcus responded before glancing at Aaron. "Stay with Byron."

Aaron felt his eyebrows scrunching to reflect his irritation, yet he didn't comment. In his condition, he would wear out his body for no reason except to be present for the light magic. Both his friend and the angel wandered over to where he could make out two figures in the grass. Emilea, whose faint weeping they heard earlier, had her husband draped across her legs. Aaron lost sight of them when the commander and Marcus stood in his line of sight.

Whatever happened took longer than their time with Byron, but the pair moved to another, seemingly empty spot to kneel again in a matter of minutes. Aaron remembered Will and his friend's attempt to back up Emilea and Clearshot when the demon went to attack them.

For some reason, considering how the people he'd grown to care about had been cut down suddenly weighed heavily on his heart. He began to imagine what the field on the opposite side of the palace was like, and the potential results his imagination conjured made him want to vomit. Thankfully, a weak groan from the man lying in the grass put those thoughts to rest for the moment.

***

The venture through the mirror-like portal Coura crafted felt drastically unlike the first. Either due to the distance it needed to traverse in order to reach the destination she envisioned or transporting more than one person, the spell required just about all of the Yeluthian energy in her center. The falling sensation proved to be similar, if not sharper, as they passed through, but it ended in an instant. The limited power poured into the spell ceased, meaning there was no longer an entrance into their location, or an exit.

Coura made sure to leap at Soirée in order to keep the demon's body within range of the ancestral weapon; however, the physical results amplified after their arrival. Her eyes had been closed to prevent any sort of disorientation during that time, which saved her from a headache. The rest of her wasn't as prepared. Any strength in her legs gave out as they connected with the ground, sending her crashing into dry, warm dirt. As she tried to gather her surroundings and ward off the impending nausea, Coura pushed herself onto her knees. The golden sword slipped out of her grip when she fell, yet it remained within arm's reach, shining brighter against a dark backdrop whose only source of light became a scarlet glow in the distance.

THE ANGEL'S DESCENT

It's exactly how I remember it, she thought ominously and glanced around the location from Soirée's memory.

The image usually twisted in the nightmares as shadows crept in every crevice, but the layout always remained the same. Her spell transported them to a circular-shaped island of sorts spanning about a third the size of the training ground in Verona. It, and any other spaces farther away, were made of rock and dirt surrounded by what she remembered as molten earth, casting the entire area in a fiery glow that dimmed as it stretched upward into an abyss. Multiple trails led to different points from their spot, but none appeared reliable enough to cross without some risk of the structure crumbling. The final pieces of the landscape worth taking note of were several boulders of various sizes scattered across the surface. From where Coura knelt, she noticed each bore numerous scratches and deep cracks to showcase their wear over the centuries.

Soirée had landed closer to the edge of the platform near one of them, using its solid structure as a crutch while she got to her feet.

Coura mustered the strength to grab her weapon first, then she pushed herself into a standing position, albeit a wobbly one. Something strange also impacted her body. Already, her breathing grew heavy despite having a moment's rest, and the air began to burn her throat. That, coupled with a new pressure squeezing every part of her, had her coughing shortly after.

From where she continued to cling to the boulder, Soirée's head turned from side to side before she faced Coura. The unmistakable and psychotic anger filling her face was both frightening and satisfying to witness.

"Welcome home," Coura muttered in between breaths before walking toward that side of the open area.

Soirée hissed and pushed herself away from the rock to stand taller while summoning the demonic blade. "You did this? Take me back!"

The earth rumbled as the demon growled the order, but Coura shook her head.

"Bringing you here was the best decision I could've made," she admitted defiantly. Through the soreness of her throat and raspy voice, she threw out her reasoning with every remaining ounce of certainty. "Even if I can't seal you away now, you won't be around Asteom for a while. Everyone will be safe and prepare for the future."

Soirée's eyes moved to the ancestral weapon, as if she just noticed it for the first time, and licked her lips, which pulled into a thin line. "Do you feel the heat and pressure where we are? Demons become accustomed to them, as well as the air toxic to creatures above the surface. If you stay any longer, you're going to die trying to fight me when we could-"

"I know," Coura interrupted.

The seriousness in her expression and certainty of her resolve visibly startled the demon.

"I've known for a long time that stopping you would mean sacrificing my life. That's why I never wanted anyone else involved. I don't plan on leaving here; I wouldn't even consider it until you're gone."

Soirée fell quiet for a few seconds. It was only when Coura's vision blurred from the ash and smoke polluting the air that the demon raised her weapon without a word.

The blade shook enough for Coura to notice, making her realize the Yeluthian spell did more harm to the creature's sense of balance. *If the disorientation lingers, I have a chance to use it to my advantage. I'm too weak to focus on wearing her down, so I'll need to rely on precision. All it takes is one, sure strike for this sword to end everything.*

With this in mind, she walked over to where Soirée waited; the fires below made the creature's violet eyes shine like gems.

"We'll see how long you last," the demon purred before Coura lunged straight for the chest.

Soirée brought up her blade to push the sword away, stepping backward in response. Coura avoided doing the same since she knew her opponent's lack of complete balance was her best advantage and would recover if enough time passed. She again thrusted the ancestral blade forward only for the demon's slim figure to twist away, though not quickly enough to avoid a scratch on the side. Again, Soirée hissed, put a hand over the spot, and glared.

THE ANGEL'S DESCENT

Maybe there is a way to weaken her, Coura thought. She recalled how merely touching the hilt while carrying demonic energy resulted in a numbing jolt. *If I didn't even break the surface of my skin that time, I can only imagine what pain it causes a full-blooded demon.*

She had no time to consider alternative measures to stopping Soirée since the creature took the offensive. The swings and strikes were as fierce as they'd been in the training ground, yet it became obvious the lingering aftereffects still hindered her ability to move swiftly. This resulted in Coura blocking just about all of the blows, and those that landed were nothing compared to the aching in her chest.

The pair ended up moving in a circular motion around the dirt until Soirée stood with her back to the boulder once again. When the demon paused to grab for the injured side, Coura began coughing until the hand covering her mouth dripped with blood. *That* frightened her.

I'm running out of time...

"Enough of this," Soirée snapped. "Let's return to the surface. You are still of use to me, which means if you cooperate you get to live. Who knows how long your body will tolerate the toxic air."

Coura slowed her breathing to focus and clear her mind; speaking would risk that luxury. *I'm tired of being stuck in the past because of my poor decisions, even if some did change my life for the better. If I die here, that would be enough of a reward for ridding the world of my mistakes, for undoing the wrong I assisted in bringing about.*

Something like pride or satisfaction flashed across Soirée's face, as though she spoke the words aloud. In that moment, Coura understood this would be their final exchange and raised her weapon once again. The underground world around them grew fuzzy except for the demon in her immediate view. Every movement slowed when Coura charged, and the pain in her limbs, throat, and chest dulled into a strangely comfortable numbness. Meanwhile, Soirée remained still with the black blade in one hand.

I'm going to die... I must die to defeat her. It was that resolution, the promise of a fulfilling death, that allowed her body to continue fighting. *It will be to secure a future for others. For the people of Verona, Dala, and all of Asteom.*

Soirée's expression never wavered; it made Coura wonder if the demon challenged her loyalty and determination. The blade rose above her head.

This is for them, and the angels in Yeluthia. For Mother, Father, Jackie, and Odell; the family I'll never truly have.

Coura pulled her right arm up to angle the golden sword horizontally, blocking the demonic sword's straight, downward slice. Unfortunately, she was too weak to push it away.

Grace, Will, and Marcy are the closest people I've known to siblings, Aimes acted like a caring grandparent, and Emilea and Clearshot always treated me with respect and as one of their own children.

Instead of continuing through with the attack, Soirée retracted her weapon, taking a step back in the process. She lunged in a feigned stab, but Coura saw through the ruse.

Aaron never gave up despite becoming king unexpectedly and even let me help him. Without Marcus, I never would have grown as a soldier or learned about what true loyalty means.

Because the strike was meant to draw her farther away, Soirée didn't move from in front of the stone that loomed behind. She brought her arm back and this time stabbed forcefully enough to ensure she would follow through. Nothing about her expression revealed if she intended to kill Coura or merely incapacitate her prey.

Then there's Byron, the one person who didn't give up on me after all these years. He never showed he was afraid of what I am, or what I could be. If staying here means everyone I care about can live in peace, I will gladly pay that price.

Coura mirrored Soirée's position with the intent to finish using a stab to seal the demon away; however, doing so would leave her defenseless. In response, the corner of Soirée's mouth twitched upward.

Her attack is going to be lethal, she realized as the tip of the black blade aimed for her heart. *If I don't stop it or get out of the way, I'm dead. It also means she's leaving the rest of her body open for the same strike. This is a test to see if I commit to my word or give in to fear. If I run, we both still live, otherwise...*

Each weapon grew closer to their intended target. In the heartbeat that followed, Coura raised her eyes to meet Soirée's as a way to say goodbye. A wave of relief passed over her mind then at the resignation; part of her expected to see the same in the violet eyes.

Instead, the demon closed them. Her lips remained curved into a pretty smile with something resembling sadness but too out of character to label as such.

Then, both swords met the other's body.

Coura welcomed the surge of pain, though most of her attention remained on the golden hilt protruding from the middle of Soirée's chest. Its continuous, warm glow appeared to grow brighter before fading. She hadn't realized how much force she placed behind her attack, or how close the pair came to the boulder, resulting in about a third of the blade sinking into the rock and cementing Soirée in place.

The demon never opened her eyes after that final look, but her smile stayed until the ancestral weapon's sealing was complete and its light disappeared. Only then did Soirée's face relax.

The resulting sense of satisfaction was short-lived. Coura felt her arms tremble and instinctively glanced down at the sword sticking out of her own chest, just below her left breast. Any thought of what to do next fled as her mind went blank and body grew cold. With the demon's power sealed away, the spell on Soirée's weapon released, causing the black sword to disappear. The sudden lack of any sort of support caused Coura to let go of the golden hilt and drop forward onto Soirée where her heavy head rested on the limp shoulder. Once her eyes were torn away from the wound pouring out warm blood, she felt better. Soon, she would lose consciousness, and her troubles would be left behind.

That was her last wish until a familiar feeling returned.

From deep within her soul space, the jittering of her recently discovered Yeluthian power jarred her into a more attentive mindset.

What do you want? she asked bitterly after finding her inner voice. *Why aren't I dead yet? I deserve this... Right?*

Coura felt too weak to inhale, and doing so hurt unbearably; everything hurt when she didn't breathe anyway. Still, nothing ended her suffering.

The active yet distant power chittered away.

Tears suddenly welled in her eyes as she prayed for it to end.

The energy, though untrained and pathetic compared to what used to overflow in her center, smoothed out its restlessness, weaving together involuntarily. Coura hardly gave it any mind due to her condition as sleep beckoned her.

Do whatever you want, she said dismissively.

Just then, her legs began to give out, along with any remaining physical strength, causing her to stumble backward. A hand flew up to cover the hole in her chest while the Yeluthian energy scattered.

Coura vaguely heard voices before falling to the ground and blacking out.

***

Aaron watched as Byron cracked both eyes open into slits, blinked a few times, then spoke in a weary whisper.

"What are you doing here?"

Hearing the master mage's voice relieved part of his concern. "Master Byron," he began while attempting to lean forward and speak directly to the man. "You're alive! The demon wounded you, but the Yeluthian soldier from earlier healed your body."

"What happened to the creature?"

"I don't know," he answered with another glance at the place where their enemy and Coura disappeared.

After a pause, Byron let out another groan and pushed himself into a sitting position with one arm. Although Aaron tried to tell him not to, the master mage dismissed the protests.

"Don't worry about me. The demon meant to stab me there, in the center of my power, so my remaining energy would drain out. An injury like that isn't necessarily used to kill, but I bet I was close to bleeding out."

"Yes, you were," Aaron commented sternly enough to draw the man's emerald eyes.

He held them until Byron's lowered in submission, a sign that his concern and the severity of the wound were clear. Then, he released a tired sigh. The burns and blisters became irritated by the cool air, souring his mood further. As he contemplated leaving the area in favor of other, pressing matters, a pair of footsteps crunched loudly in the dead grass.

Marcus had jogged ahead of their Yeluthian ally, who lingered near the now-standing Will, and explained what took place with their friend, Clearshot, and Emilea. The archer had been in the worst condition with two gruesome injuries: a slice across his midsection and an even deeper one through his right shoulder. Luckily, Emilea used the rest of her power to stop him from dying, but the demon hurt her too. From what Marcus was able to make out, it struck her across the face with its foot. The impact cracked her jaw and practically left her nose hanging off her face in a bloody mess.

"Both are in stable conditions now, according to him," Marcus went on with a gesture to the commander. "Unfortunately, he also said the muscles and nerves in Clearshot's arm might be permanently damaged without immediate attention. He also refused to heal Emilea more than stopping the bleeding."

Aaron blinked in disbelief. "Why?"

"I don't know. Will has a concussion, and the angel won't do anything about that either."

"You shouldn't be so rude," came a grumble from Byron while he rubbed his eyes with a thumb and forefinger. "If he hadn't done anything, I would've bled out by now. There may be a reason he's conserving his energy."

Marcus' eyes went wide, and he spoke Byron's name in disbelief to show he didn't notice the master mage until then. Meanwhile, Aaron straightened as the Yeluthian approached.

The commander glanced at the burns and began to extend a hand toward them. "Your Highness, may I address your wounds now?"

Even with his companions healed, Aaron found himself shaking his head, causing the hand to recoil a bit. "Thank you, but I have a feeling others with more life-threatening conditions than this need your assistance. I refuse to let someone else lose their life when all it means is I have to suffer through this a little longer, especially if they're your people."

At that, the Yeluthian's face softened in surprise. "If that is what you wish," he responded after a moment.

"It is. We owe you a great deal already," Aaron responded while Marcus and Byron looked on.

"You owe me nothing," Commander Evern replied, though not meaning offense. He even stretched his lips into some attempt at a smile. "The duties associated with my position require me to serve my king. If he considers Asteom and its people allies, then I will treat them as I would my own kind."

Aaron politely thanked him again and prepared to ask what they should do next when he noticed how distracted the Yeluthian soldier seemed. *Could it be he wants to make sure the demon doesn't return? Perhaps he knows the same spell and plans to pursue. I hope he does, for Coura's sake...*

Thinking of his lost friend only made Aaron more determined to remain in the area, even if he was unable to do much physically. He said Marcus' name and faced the assistant general before preparing to order a search for back up.

Evidently, Marcus already knew the nature of the request. "Don't you dare send me away when she's still missing."

"Who's missing?" Byron asked.

Aaron ignored the question. "You're the only person who can move well enough and maneuver through the palace."

Marcus opened his mouth to protest, but his eyes drifted to something over Aaron's shoulder. The irritated expression fell and was replaced with a mixture of concern and astonishment that had Aaron spinning around. In the open grass near the spot where Coura and the demon disappeared, the air began to shimmer with a white light at the edges and red, brown, and black colors twisting together in the center. Shadows moved on the other side, yet they were too far away to see clearly. Already the Yeluthian commander had sprinted halfway across the space, leaving Aaron, his closest friend, and the master mage gaping after.

"Stay here!" Marcus ordered before he drew his sword and took off on his own.

Although he tried to call out, Aaron's words came second to the nearby scene. He had not gotten a detailed look at the magic that caused the demon to vanish, possibly pulling Coura along, but something within told him this was the same spell and the figure beyond would return to the training ground.

Then, someone did pass through.

He wasn't close enough to discern who emerged, especially since Coura bore dark markings along her arms and shoulders, but whoever appeared through the magical gate did so back-first. They stumbled a couple of steps before falling to the ground just as the glimmering light faded.

By that point, the Yeluthian commander reached his goal and threw himself to his knees beside the figure. His behavior proved to be enough reassurance for Aaron to hurry over as best as he could in his condition. He imagined how ridiculous he appeared hobbling across an open area with half of his shirt hanging off and scarlet skin exposed until he caught up to stand beside Marcus. Every self-conscious thought flew away as he looked on with his friend.

It was Coura who returned through the light-lined opening, though Aaron wanted to weep for her current state rather than with relief. Every inch of her exposed, pale skin had been smeared with what appeared to be ash, hiding colorful bruises and cuts. Her half-closed eyelids fluttered, and underneath, the usually bright, blue eyes were dull, not really seeing anything as they stared up at the sky. The angel placed his hands on the left side of her chest where they could see fresh, crimson blood underneath. More splattered in the grass as she coughed it up multiple times.

Aaron stood helplessly with Marcus at his side until the sky began to sink into twilight and his body shivered from the dropping temperatures. With every passing heartbeat, his stomach tightened as nothing seemed to change, though other people entered the training ground before it grew too dark to see.

Someone called his name and eventually put a hand on his undamaged shoulder to turn him away. The gesture came from General Tont, who lacked any outward afflictions. The man began asking for orders and started to recount the numbers from the battle while more people circled around.

I must return, for the rest of the kingdom's sake.

Before the general dove too deep into the situation, Aaron raised a hand for a pause. In the resulting silence, he looked at the Yeluthian and cleared his throat. "Will she be all right?"

The commander's hands had stopped glowing a while ago, yet they remained hovering over the wound as he hunched forward to hide his face. After a minute, they heard his faint answer.

"I think so."

Despite the room for doubt, his response satisfied Aaron.

18

*A*n unofficially recognized civil war in Asteom concluded after five days of battle between the Dalan troops, including the surrounding towns' forces, part of Verona's soldiers, mages, and citizens, the Sie-Kie warriors, and our Yeluthian allies and the palace's troops and the Nim-Valan guests under the manipulation of High Priest Hendal with the assistance of a creature identified as a demon. This conflict took place in the field southeast of the capital city. A separate group consisting of the palace's master mages, a Yeluthian commander, an assistant general, and various, trained civilians was sent to isolate and apprehend the high priest and demon.

At the high priest's defeat, he was bound and is currently awaiting trial by the king's council in Verona's central prison. He showed no signs of resistance or hinted that the man is not of his right mind. A Yeluthian had also been taken from the council chamber; he and his companions in league with the high priest were turned over to the jurisdiction of the Yeluthian king, by his request. The demon responsible for manipulating the minds of many in the palace, as well as the Nim-Valan troops, is being pursued. Although we are awaiting proof of its escape or death, we have reason to believe it no longer poses a direct threat to the capital city or palace. Casualty results will be assessed until the estimated thirty-day recovery period when a complete report shall be available to citizens of Asteom. Included are the numbers added together during the fighting and after clearing the battlefield during the first week:

One thousand two hundred thirty-six Asteom soldiers, including eight hundred twelve registered to the Dalan base or surrounding regions, three hundred thirty-seven registered to Verona, and eighty-seven belonging to the Sie-Kie tribe. Nine Yeluthian casualties were counted, but no official numbers have been given. Under King Aaron's orders, they are not required to provide such information. Finally, no Nim-Valan casualties were reported before their departure.

The legal implications are still under debate, but the king's council has pardoned the citizens who otherwise would be convicted for treason or murder while under the demon's influence. Any property damage must be brought to the attention of Verona's city council before the end of the thirty-day recovery period in order to receive emergency funding for repairs. At the time of this letter, the decisions presented are subject to change...

Byron set down the report with a sigh and rubbed the bridge of his nose. This was the second one sent to him that week, though he couldn't read the first clearly due to his weary state of mind. Each had been put together from mixed accounts between Generals Tio, Tont, and Casner since they were the most involved throughout the fighting, its conclusion, and the beginning of the recovery stage. He had already been familiar with some items, though, considering his involvement with Hendal's capture and the demon's disappearance.

The worst information to process was the casualty list. The new papers on his unorganized desk were the first to include any numbers. It hurt terribly, thinking of the many people, friends, comrades, and innocents, who lost their lives over such an unprecedented incident. Already, volunteers had come together to send letters to the families so they could claim their loved ones. For the Dalans so far from their homes, the many bodies were individually burned in a pyre made up in the center of the southern field while their recorded names would be brought to Dala via a messenger. The event took place over the past couple of days led by General Tio and Calin, and Byron was amazed to hear how many citizens of Verona remained in attendance throughout the ceremony; some even requested their fallen loved ones be added to the service.

Likewise, the Sie-Kie men performed their own ritual, which took place in private within the woods to the north of the palace. The day after the battle concluded, they gathered their own, fallen warriors, wrapped the dead in blankets, carried them on their shoulders into the trees, and only returned the next morning. Afterward, they assisted the generals diligently.

In the midst of the confusion, the Nim-Valan soldiers demanded answers. They threatened violence when no one could spare the time or felt informed enough to talk until one of the generals sat them down to explain. Then, they packed their belongings and left before the sun rose the following morning without saying a word to anyone in the palace. All the while, the Yeluthian troops remained mostly uninvolved with what transpired, opting to guard the palace and city in its greatest time of need. How that agreement had been reached, Byron didn't know. He missed a lot of the discussion due to his injury and magical exhaustion, leaving him practically useless until that morning. He hadn't been allowed to leave his quarters ever since waking up, which became especially bothersome because of his caretakers' lack of answers to his many questions.

After skimming the rest of the report, which summarized information from the previous letter, he set it down to put his head in his hands. *I'm recovering fine, but what about everyone else? Are all of the mages and soldiers being kept in their quarters as well? What about Aaron, Marcus, and the others who confronted the demon with me?*

When Byron was barely conscious at the conclusion of their fight, he had been led away into a chaotic mess. The woman who acted as his support crutch while they hobbled inside the palace shared too much for him to remember. Once they climbed the staircases to his room, she dropped him into bed, gave him a sleeping potion, then left. Every day since, a new healer showed up around the late morning to check in on him. No one attempted to do more than the Yeluthian man had done, though, and he soon found himself able to move freely without any tightness or pressure. At the moment, the worst part became recovering his lost energy.

With the damage to my center, I don't think I'll be able to get my full strength back until that completely heals, he reflected somberly. *I'm afraid that might take months. The least I can do now is find something to-*

A gentle knock at the door cut his train of thought short. Byron stood and brushed his unclean hair back, then he told the guest to enter. He knew someone would be in to check on his progress at that time in the day, yet he was startled to see Emilea's friendly face as she stepped inside.

"You seem surprised," she said with a slight smile. Her plain, amber-colored dress looked stained with darker spots, and her blonde hair had been tied into a messy bun at the nape of her neck. Because he hadn't interacted with Emilea due to his own injury, the sight of her bruised face felt jarring. The left side of her jawline turned a deep purple, along with the skin around her nose and the lower half of her eyes. A bandage covered the bridge of her nose, yet the rest remained exposed.

Byron realized how rude he was being and gestured to his desk chair before taking a seat on his bed. After clearing his throat, he apologized.

"It's all right," she replied in a quiet, delicate voice. "I forgot we haven't had a chance to see each other since…" The words trailed off into silence.

"Are you my healer for the day?" he asked to change the subject. "They usually spend less time in here. One glance, some medicine, and they leave."

He meant to ease the tension in the room by making the words sound light-hearted and smiling. Thankfully, Emilea caught the hint and visibly relaxed.

"I'm sorry to change up your routine. If you want to keep that attention, I could tell my underlings you need a few more days of rest."

Byron rolled his eyes and chuckled. "There's nothing less comforting than not knowing what's going on around here."

"Some people would say otherwise." She paused while glancing away. "No one told you what happened out there, did they?"

"I only received those reports," he responded and pointed to the desk.

She nodded without raising her eyes to the papers. "They went out to every mage, soldier, and servant in the palace, but I'm sure you realized a lot of details were not included. I thought you might like to hear them."

Byron felt his mouth fall into a frown. "Right now, all I'd like to know is whether or not everybody is safe," he commented. If someone tracked down the demon, or it still lingered in the area, he needed to be involved in its capture.

Emilea raised her eyebrows and met his gaze in an alarmed expression. The seriousness of his question made her eyes glisten with suppressed tears before she looked away again.

"I'm sorry," she began. "I was trying to help, and all I'm managing to do is worry us both even more. The palace is no longer in danger. The Yeluthians swore to King Aaron they would guard the capital for as long as he wishes. No one quite understands why, except they *are* our allies. I spoke with Grace earlier today about it, and she admitted she vouched for the old alliance and voiced her desire to stay."

Byron's concern ebbed, and he silently made a note to thank the young ambassador for her dedication to Asteom the next time they met. "That's a relief to hear. I suppose the rest of the time has been spent cleaning up the mess."

The light mage nodded, then she proceeded to fill him in on the people he was most familiar with, starting with the generals. As she spoke, he got the impression she focused on the update as much to ease her own mind as to inform him of the situation.

General Tio had been struck by a stray bolt of lightning during the previous week, preventing him from participating in any more fighting, so Calin took charge under his superior's order. General Casner also ended up wounded on his right thigh, yet the man managed to remain on the battlefield until the final retreat, according to their plan. The soldiers under Hendal's control, including General Tont, had been freed and pieced together what took place with the general leading the reorganization effort.

Emilea went on to name students of theirs who either died or were seriously injured. She had to pause twice: once at the beginning when she lost her voice to tears and another time when Byron couldn't hold himself together and raised a hand to stop her. At that, she moved to sit beside him, and the two comforted each other.

"I figured it would be better for you to hear about it from me," she said at last when the tears ceased.

Much of the heartache remained, but now he felt he could bear it outside his walls. At least, for the moment. She had yet to mention a few individuals who would change his hardened mentality in an instant.

"How is he doing?" Byron asked in a hoarse voice.

Emilea understood who he referred to, and her pink eyes watered once more. "Oh, Cornelius! I gave everything I had left to heal him…"

He listened patiently as she went down the list of people who were in the training ground that day and their wounds. The demon sliced open Clearshot's midsection, though not deep enough to prevent Emilea from sealing the skin and inflicted organs; however, she exhausted her reserves doing so, leaving the injury on his shoulder to the Yeluthian who saved Byron. When he was assessed by another healer in the palace, they deemed the nerves and muscles permanently damaged. The results shook Clearshot, and he fell into a mild depression. Emilea hadn't left his side until the man pushed her away while demanding she make sure their children stayed safe and she start treating the other soldiers. She hadn't been to see him since.

When she paused, Byron pressed her to continue, piecing together his memories as she went on.

"Will came away with a concussion, a broken kneecap, and a few deep cuts on his hands. He's been ordered to stay in bed, like you. I figured he would be waking up with a desire to read, so I stopped by this morning to warn him against it."

Despite the circumstances, Byron found a dark humor in how the cure for Will's condition was probably more of a punishment than the resulting injuries.

"Marcus is fine, though he won't stop moving around to rest for longer than a few minutes at a time. Aaron's the same, but I heard it took some convincing for him to let a healer tend to the burns on his left arm and shoulder." Emilea sighed. "Those boys, I swear…"

"I suppose they learned it from us," he added. "We aren't exactly the best role models when it comes to taking the simplest path or retreating when the situation seems hopeless."

"You're right."

In the silence following her response, Byron assumed she saved the worst news for last; it made sense when he realized she had yet to bring up his former student.

"It's okay," he began in a reassuring manner at her hesitation. "I can already tell it has to do with Coura."

Emilea's eyes widened a bit while she stared into his. Once she understood his sincerity, she shared all that took place.

*

The two conversed until lunchtime, yet any appetite Byron might have normally had fled as he listened intently before asking too many questions without answers. No one in the training ground could comprehend what transpired. A magical, mirror-like portal appeared, swept Coura and the demon away, then the former returned in a bloody mess. Although her body appeared, the demon's was nowhere to be found. The Yeluthian commander claimed a spell took place, one a part of his people's mysterious power, but he mentioned nothing else. Instead, he proceeded to tirelessly heal her wounds.

"It's baffling!" Emilea exclaimed with a shake of her head in disbelief at the end of her recollection.

He noticed she strayed from revealing more; in this case, it had to do with Coura's current condition. "Why haven't you asked her about it?"

The light mage frowned and brushed a loose strand of hair over one ear. "Because, she hasn't woken up yet. The Yeluthian healed the most grievous injury, but it took time for someone else to help with the rest. She exhausted herself too, which is a dangerous thing to do when we're in the best shape. Worst of all, there's internal damage to her lungs that magic isn't readily able to heal. Her breathing is short and weak, and she was coughing up blood for hours. When I returned to the medical station, I assigned one of my underlings to remain at her bedside."

Byron couldn't think of anything to say. A weariness passed over him upon processing the news, leaving nothing except a heavy, invisible weight on his heart.

Either Emilea hadn't noticed or what she needed to tell him was too important not to mention, for her voice filled the space again. "I must apologize. I meant to inform you of our current position, even the most painful pieces, but I also need to ask a favor. Aside from our personal feelings, Coura is the only person who knows about the demon's fate. She has to wake up in order for us to have a chance at putting this to an end. Please, when you find the strength, go visit her. If she hears your voice or feels your presence, I believe it may bring her mind back."

"Of course I will!" Byron wanted to shout, yet he couldn't muster enough emotion to do more than dip his head. The losses he endured and the anguish he shared with Emilea were a lot to hear at once, but learning about Coura added another droplet to an already full glass. He feared it would overflow if he went to the medical station then.

The light mage must have sensed this. "Take your time," she urged and placed a hand on his back, then she rose from her seat and walked to the door. Before she could exit, Byron told her to wait.

"Emilea, I have a request as well. Tell Clearshot he should come see me sometime."

A little more life came into her face before she slipped out into the hall without giving a vocal response.

***

Behind her closed eyes, flickers of lights and shadows passed over Coura as she relaxed in the unrecognizable yet somehow familiar space. Her body felt like it floated on the air, and no pain came from the many inflictions she knew it bore. Every time she went in and out of sleep, the lights and shadows danced, though nothing interested her enough to open her eyes; she grew content just existing in that place.

Soon, muffled voices became audible and interrupted her lazy mentality. Above them all, one spoke clearer than the rest.

Open your eyes.

Coura obeyed, then she took a moment to let her eyes and mind adjust to the blinding white surrounding her. No end revealed itself beyond the sea of emptiness lacking any sort of features to distinguish what way the world was meant to be. At the sight, she recalled her previous visit and instantly stood without giving a second thought to imagining the ground.

"This is my soul space," she said aloud against a dryness that burned her throat.

That's right.

Even with the confirmation, Coura noticed the scene had changed. Dark lines jutted from every direction, like cracks on a broken window, slithering while swelling and thinning out in rhythm. They were visible at every angle.

"What are those? Is something wrong?"

What you see is the result of opening yourself willingly to demonic energy. You shared your soul with a demon for so long, yet it was never able to taint what belongs to you without your cooperation. Wrong is a less fitting term than unnatural, though.

"Why...am I...here again?" Coura asked next in gasps. While she had been asleep, a numbness blocked any aches and pains from her chest and throat. Now that she began moving around and growing alert, it continually faded.

There was no response from the mellow voice for a while. Soon the pressure brought her to her knees and had her clutching her chest.

The last time you visited your soul space, the power you relied on and nurtured within had been ripped away. Both body and spirit were deeply wounded and needed internal recovery to cope with the changes. That same power is gone again, yet because you made it a part of yourself and altered this place to accommodate, it had more of an effect. Accepting the demon's energy while awakening your

Yeluthian abilities at the same time forced you to exhaust two opposite sources of power.

The words remained audible as Coura passed in and out of consciousness. The slumber that finally came brought a welcomed rush of the numbness, but not before she was left with a final message.

If you ever need to return to this place, meditate. Focus on what you've seen and the energies here. The only harm you will find is what is brought in from the outside world. A soul space should be maintained, just like your body and mind, in order for a safe balance, both for yourself and others.

***

In the week following Emilea's visit, Byron found himself hurled into meetings and appointments that nearly made him want to pretend he wasn't well enough to be on his feet yet. His first obligation had been to keep his agreement to the master light mage by seeing Coura. The most stressful part about that was making his way through the medical stations packed full of patients, their families and friends, mages, and their assistants. Excusing himself through each room took a lot longer than he planned, but his target had been tucked away at the farthest corner of the least crowded area.

Most everyone lying in bed seemed asleep with bandages wrapped around some part of their body. Coura had none, and someone tucked her in up to the chin. The peaceful face showed none of the emotions they experienced during the hectic fighting, though he did notice her breathing didn't even make her chest move up and down as it normally would have.

Byron found an empty stool to bring over, sat at her bedside, and started talking in a low voice so as to not disrupt the others in that station. He spoke about whatever came to mind, which at the time happened to be his intentions to see Clearshot afterward. When a hefty, brunette woman made rounds to refill medicines and change bandages, he bid Coura farewell and left.

Emilea and Clearshot's shared quarters were on the fourth floor in a room expected to house one soldier. He met up with each of them there on separate occasions, but this was the first time he had ever been inside. Two single-sized beds had been pushed together, and a dresser and desk occupied the remaining space. Nothing decorated the walls or furniture, but Byron figured they only stayed in the palace when necessary. Lady Katrina usually welcomed Mace and Lexie to her home during those instances.

Unlike his first appointment, Clearshot sprang to life upon seeing his guest. The two talked about their recoveries, the information in their reports, and what still needed to be done. A shadow passed over his friend's face when Byron tentatively asked about the injured shoulder.

"Emilea forbade me from trying to use it," he responded with repressed frustration and put a hand on the spot. "It really is the darndest thing. I swear the creature aimed for this spot just to hurt me the most."

"It probably did," Byron commented after reflecting on his own wound. "A mage loses their energy if they experience a direct injury to their center of power. The demon didn't accidentally stab me there; I'm sure it intended to strike where it would cause the greatest lasting impact."

Clearshot glared at the wall across from him for a while without commenting on the response.

Byron changed the subject after he heard the city bells indicating late afternoon. "I suppose I should find one of the generals and let them know I'm still alive."

"You're planning on starting work so soon?"

He nodded. "It's not that I don't trust them to handle my business. I just need something to keep my mind occupied for a while."

*

Because of the destruction in the council's meeting chamber, Aaron, the generals, and the individual leaders within Verona opted to set up a temporary area in the private dining hall since there would be no formal gatherings for the time being. Byron learned this through Emilea, who regularly attended to report on the mages' behalf. She didn't even attempt to hide her enthusiasm for his return, and the two made their way to that evening's assembly.

Every day since, they became involved in the decisions.

The main discussion revolved around what to do with Hendal. Byron understood the ex-high priest no longer possessed the demon's power and vouched for Commander Detrix's spell, as did Emilea. Aaron held the most doubt but agreed with General Tont's idea to sentence the man to life in Verona's prison under constant guard. The final verdict passed without a second thought.

Their next and most pressing concern had to do with the Yeluthians.

Some returned home two days ago with their dead soldiers and the rogue angels who would face justice in front of their own people. Winter closed in the next morning, bringing a thin blanket of snow to Verona. The remaining troops had been welcomed heartily into the palace, yet they voiced their desire to depart before the weather made it impossible to travel safely. This time, General Casner favored honoring their request in a surprisingly sincere manner. He argued enough of the palace's troops could continue their duties, and General Tont shared his opinion that the Nim-Valans wouldn't try to attack so soon after returning to their country.

Still, Byron felt reluctant to let the Yeluthians leave without properly addressing the alliance, especially when the general mentioned how no word came from the north on the status of that potential union; however, he found himself outnumbered by the more empathetic members. General Casner offered to share their decision with the king named Arval in the evening.

A few more details were worked out regarding damages to the city and who was owed what, but Byron excused himself since he wanted to visit Coura before grabbing a late lunch with Clearshot. He had been in to see her over the past week, and the business of the stations steadily declined. Emilea mentioned once that the mages had been so worn out after the first couple of days their assistants insisted they rest unless magic became absolutely necessary. This meant their patients needed to relax and recover on their own, which most were capable of without causing trouble. Some light mages, like Emilea, returned to healing in order to empty the rooms, thus leaving only the incapacitated.

THE ANGEL'S DESCENT

Because of the lack of people normally there at the noon hour, Byron was startled to see a trio of people around Coura's bed. Marcus stood facing him while a man and woman sat on the opposite side. Once he entered, the assistant general waved him over with a comfortable smile.

"I didn't mean to interrupt," he began as he approached the foot of the bed and met the strangers' curious stares.

The man's sapphire eyes drew Byron in first, revealing his identity as one of the Yeluthian soldiers; not only a soldier but the newcomer who joined to fight the demon and heal Byron, Clearshot, and others that day. The woman at his side looked like a plain brunette with tired, hazel eyes and a contagious smile.

When Marcus introduced them, Byron appreciated the warm, calming presence they projected; it helped ease some of the shock.

"You're...her parents?" he mumbled as memories of what Coura shared with him about her past unraveled.

"I suppose we owe a lot of people an explanation," the woman named Paulina admitted and rubbed the back of her neck in a familiar manner.

Just like...

Marcus chuckled at that while waving a hand. "It's not like your appearance isn't unwanted. Besides, our kingdom is indebted to you."

"Does Coura know?" Byron asked next.

The woman bowed her head and laid her eyes on the unconscious figure as the Yeluthian, Commander Evern, met his stare and nodded.

An odd, hot anger bubbled in his heart, and before he realized it, he was expressing those feelings aloud. "Where have you been all these years then? You had to have learned what happened to her!"

He caught Marcus turn with wide, startled eyes after. The commander's expression remained unreadable, and Paulina's face scrunched up, though she didn't look away.

The internal strife relaxed when neither attempted to speak again. Byron kicked himself for letting his emotions take hold of his mouth and apologized. "I'm an outsider. I have no right to interject in your familial relationship," he continued.

"No, you are wrong," the woman replied with a kind smile. "You would not make such an outburst if you did not care about our daughter. Both of you, and others I have seen, made an effort to stop by too. We are the ones who should be thanking you for being there when we were not."

Commander Evern kept quiet. The only indication he was listening had been the dip of his lips into a frown. The four of them talked for a little longer, then the pair left. During that time, Byron learned how they met Coura in Yeluthia, believing her to be dead until her arrival, and intended to leave her at their home. He could see the pain hiding beneath their continually calm expressions throughout the conversation and made a point to apologize to Marcus after. The assistant general acted polite, mentioned his own amazement at the situation, and made his exit.

The next day, the Yeluthians prepared to return to their home in the east. Their king was present at the morning meeting to accept Aaron's gratitude and agreed-upon offer of gold and silver, but the real reward proved interesting. Because of the landscape around their home, many crops couldn't grow nor were there animals to hunt. He wished to establish a permanent route with the town of Kercher being their primary location on the surface to initiate opportunities for trading. King Arval also mentioned his desire to return to Asteom, but he didn't specify any details regarding why. The council shared their own details on a spring celebration to make up for that year's missed Harvest Festival, an idea brought up by a merchant representative with information on how much business had been lost from the conflict. Aaron made it a point to invite the Yeluthians back to Verona after this was organized. Everyone parted ways on peaceful terms that morning.

Byron met Clearshot, Emilea, and their children in the southern field where the bronze-clad soldiers gathered to leave together. He decided to share the news about Coura's parents, which surprised them both since Paulina had watched over Mace and Lexie in the midst of the battle. Both she and Commander Evern stood nearby and came over when Emilea waved to them.

"I wish we did not have to leave, but seeing your children reminds us of our own still awaiting our return," Paulina shared after they said goodbye.

The similarities between Coura and her mother's appearances grew more prominent to Byron as the days passed. In that instance, their smiles were identical. What little he saw of her father's personality also seemed frighteningly alike, especially his indifference; however, the bright, gem-like eyes showcased their Yeluthian lineage.

Reflecting on those comparisons managed to remind him of the young woman lying in the medical station. Not even the awesome wave of feathers filling the sky to the citizens' cheering could make him forget that loose tie.

***

The inner sanctuary of Coura's soul space faded piece by piece as she slept and woke to jarring images of bloodshed. Eventually, she remembered experiencing the memories, which helped her to take them in and make them new parts of herself. Once her physical body began to respond and her mind processed what had taken place, she realized what bothered her from the moment she became aware.

Moving proved tiresome, but she felt too stiff to stay on her back for long. Her throat burned as a result of the toxic air she inhaled while under the surface, causing her to cough uncontrollably. Blood splattered onto her hand and the bedsheets until a woman hurried over, shoved a bottle containing some bitter-tasting liquid in her mouth, and forcibly tilted Coura's head to pour it down her throat.

However many times it happened, she didn't know. Every instance seemed identical, including the woman. Sometimes, when she woke without opening her eyes, she could hear voices at her bedside. Most of the time it was Byron, but she also heard Marcus, Marcy, Will, Emilea, and her parents.

Whenever she opened her eyes, no one was around, and all she longed for was the safety of her soul space.

The waves of weariness soon eased until Coura stayed awake for longer durations, though she still refused to move in favor of the pleasantness lingering from a restful sleep. The troubling thoughts plaguing her boiled down to her final encounter with Soirée. The demon in her memories didn't gloat over the final attack, nor did the creature appear frightened or angry with Coura's ferocity as she intended to sacrifice her life to enact the sealing.

The tip of the demonic blade rested on my heart. One straight lunge should have killed me.

The sound of footsteps pulled her mind away from considering the past. She listened and identified her visitor as Byron by the way he huffed when he dropped into one of the chairs next to her bed.

"What a day," he muttered before explaining why he had been so late to see her.

She paid some attention to the talk, though her interest in what took place at the meetings he attended and who left Verona and why ultimately fell short against her deeper, internal struggle. At some point while he was talking, Coura opened her eyes to stare up at the stone ceiling. The blank, gray spot helped her to clear her mind, which in turn made her body relax.

After a while, she realized Byron was silent and turned her head to the side to see his eyes glistening and mouth hanging open a bit.

"Coura, are you really awake?"

She nodded.

"How are you feeling? Can you talk to me?"

She shook her head slightly despite not being certain.

"That's fine. Don't worry about it now. Sleep, and I'll come back later," he replied and rose from the wooden chair.

After a brief conversation with the medical station attendant at the far side of the room, he left. Coura recognized the round-faced woman as she approached, fished out a bottle of the bitter liquid from her pocket, and forced it down Coura's throat without a word.

Night darkened the room when she came to again. Someone sat beside her with one of their hands on top of the sheets covering hers. They were silent for so long that Coura debated opening her eyes to check on them, but the hand slipped off as the person rose and walked away. From a distance, she heard a male voice speaking before the door closed.

THE ANGEL'S DESCENT

The space became quiet enough for a few minutes that she felt comfortable raising her eyelids to blink gingerly in the dim lamplight. Several other bodies wrapped into bundles lied on various cots around the station, and her caretaker was nowhere to be found. Coura strained her limbs in order to sit up, avoiding the urge to cough and clear the grating sensation in her throat. She felt terribly thirsty but dared not push what little strength she possessed by rising for any reason. The usual sleeping potion sat on a nightstand beside her pillow and tempted her until a sudden click from the nearest entrance drew her attention. Byron walked in, shut the door behind him, and sat in the chair beside her all while wearing a satisfied expression.

"How are you feeling?" he asked in a soft voice out of respect for the other patients.

Coura shook her head before deciding to try communicating without hurting herself. "Thirsty," she managed to whisper.

Byron offered to find some water and brought back a pitcher and glass from another table. "I can always replace it before they wake up," he said as he poured and handed her the drink.

Three cups later and Coura could clear her throat with only a mild soreness when she spoke to thank him. "What time is it?" she asked after resting her head against the wooden headboard.

"Around midnight. My dinner with General Tont ran over. We were discussing the best way to restart the troops' training now that it's been…"

At the mention of the general previously under Hendal's hold, Coura stared down at her hands and remembered all the demon had done, even until the very end.

They wouldn't know, she realized as the fiery landscape came to mind. *I brought her there alone. I was supposed to die, and that would be it. Soirée didn't… She lowered her sword…*

Byron leaned in closer. "What's the matter?"

"I shouldn't be here," Coura answered and gripped the bed sheets so tight her hands shook.

"What do you mean? Tell me what happened."

She started on the Yeluthian spell, how the two fought in the demons' home, and the resulting sealing that took place; however, none of it sounded like a victory.

"I brought her there knowing it would mean dying. *She* knew that too," Coura continued. Whatever control she held on her voice wore away, causing it to crack at just about every other word. Tears slid down her cheeks then as any slim chance of keeping herself together crumbled.

When Byron didn't respond, she put a hand over her eyes and sobbed.

"Why am I still alive? She knew I wanted to end it, even if it meant giving my life! I was prepared, but she couldn't allow me the satisfaction. She lowered her sword…"

By that point, Coura's words became lost to hysterics, prompting her former mentor to go to her side and wrap an arm around her shoulders. She accepted the invitation to cry into his chest after.

***

It had been a long time since Byron needed to hold and comfort Coura. When she was a lonely child still new to the world of magic, he helped her through the adjustment process, which sometimes involved her breaking down.

This instance was different. It hurt him to hear her admit to sacrificing herself with the intent not to return to the surface world, yet a part of him thought he understood her distress.

By that point, Coura became certain stopping the demon would end her life as well. It was a dangerous assumption to make, but she never had time to consider otherwise. I guess she's correct, though. From what I can tell, the creature chose not to kill her. Having no control over the changes to her fate, and not understanding why they happened, must be causing her so much pain.

Explaining anything before she calmed down would do no good, so Byron waited until the choked sobs dwindled into calmer sniffs. Coura leaned completely against him, looking frail in front of his wider build, and he gently led her into a sitting position by the shoulders before hurrying over to the nearest medicine cabinet, grabbing one of the cloth rags kept inside, and bringing it back to give to her before taking a seat in the chair.

She wiped her face and blew her nose, then she stared down at her hands while he considered what to say. Byron figured she wouldn't talk again, and shouldn't because of how her voice cracked, yet more tumbled out in fragmented thoughts.

"I bet it's a curse. She saw through me and figured the best form of revenge would be denying me the right to sacrifice myself. Or maybe she wants to keep her precious experiment going after-"

"Coura."

The slim figure jumped, as if she forgot he was still there. Then, for the first time that evening, her head turned and the puffy eyes met his. Beneath their longing for answers shined the same brightness he came to recognize and adore throughout their time together.

"You shouldn't linger on what you'll never know. It can drive a person to insanity."

"I do know," she squeaked with a wince that reflected her condition.

Byron narrowed his eyes. "No, you don't. There's the idea of revenge, but what about mercy or pity? It sounds like you put the creature in an inescapable position where it made the choice to spare your life. Whatever the reason, you should be thankful."

"But...I..." Coura opened and closed her mouth twice before bowing her head in a more thoughtful gesture.

"If the demon is sealed away, that ends its chapter in our lives," Byron went on. "I think you assumed you were going to die, and that would remove the pressure of trying to live after such an ordeal. Well, we won. It's sealed away in a place with only demons, so the ancestral sword will remain untouched for untold generations. With that in mind, do you still *want* to give up with an open future ahead of us?"

During the pause, she contemplated his words. He held his breath and only released it with a slight smile when she shook her head.

***

As chilling as the late fall season became, winter arrived and went without much fuss; not that Coura experienced much of it.

She learned from Byron about the Yeluthians' departure, Nim-Vala's silence, and how the city went about rebuilding after speaking with him a second time. Still, he refused to give many details. Emilea was also hesitant to say more than necessary when she stopped by for checkups. As a master light mage, her approval became Coura's key to being released from the medical station, which didn't happen for another two weeks.

Apparently, her body suffered from a lack of proper nutrients and rest, resulting in the unconscious state of recovery. More sleep and meals built up her strength until Emilea seemed pleased, then the light mage ordered her to remain in her room and have food brought up. Coura found she didn't mind this and shut herself away to reflect on what transpired. Although only a month had passed, it felt as though every muscle weakened severely.

"You relied on the demon's power for a lot, especially healing, and that needed to add up eventually," Emilea explained one afternoon. "The markings on your skin are starting to fade away as proof that your energy is balancing out. I believe it will continue to do so, but I can't tell you how long it'll take or what the results will be."

The master mage also warned against physical training so soon after waking up and threatened Coura with unmentioned punishments if she ignored that. So, her time consisted of reading and resting in between meals and daily visitors, a few secret stretching sessions, and meditating, which often resulted in a nap.

Over the next couple of months, life crept by. When she could do whatever she wanted, Coura found herself uncertain. Marcus and Will each mentioned helping her to start training again on separate occasions, Marcy invited her on walks through Verona to visit Aimes, who found a position as a cook at one of the city's inns, and Grace took up embroidery and offered to teach her. Aaron even wrote brief notes to hint at when he would be in the queen's garden. Essentially, they were trying to make her feel better through inclusion. Each came by when they could, and at least one person escorted her to the mess hall at every meal.

It wasn't until two pieces of news began spreading throughout the palace that she felt compelled to do more than hide in her room.

Spring brought word from the north about the Nim-Valans, who posted guards along the border once again and raised their weapons when any Asteom soldiers approached. This information, coupled by the lack of a response to the palace's many letters sent out from the generals and Aaron, lowered everyone's expectations for peace between the two countries. Training resumed for both the soldiers and mages who held memories, and external scars for most, of the battle fresh in everyone's mind.

On a brighter note, Grace excitedly shared the Yeluthians would be arriving in Verona in a few weeks to participate in the spring festival organized by the nobility and citizens of the capital. Many lost business or gathered to perform for the Harvest Festival without being paid and wished to make up the lost holiday. Coura heard bits and pieces about the new event up until the week before it was scheduled to take place. This lightened the mood in the palace, and eventually her spirits as well.

The world had moved on, so she figured it was time to do the same.

*

The Yeluthians arrived three days prior to the festival, making a camp to the south where the Nim-Valans had stayed. It was surprising to see so many in the sky, yet even more trekked into Verona through the western road. In the midst of the hustle and bustle as they adjusted to the onlookers, Coura snuck into the field alone. No one paid her much attention while she passed through because of the other humans who invited themselves over to greet the strangers, help set up tents, and bring supplies. Her heart began beating furiously as she searched for the familiar faces, then it jumped into her throat when she spotted her parents and siblings handing off supplies between other people.

Evern noticed her approaching first. Once his eyes scanned her up and down, he said something to the man at his right before jogging in her direction. At that, Paulina, Odell, and Jackie ran after him. They slowed enough not to plow over her as they wrapped their arms around her, yet they squeezed so tightly her chest ached.

If Coura didn't love every second of it, she might have cried out.

Paulina asked about her condition while inspecting every facial feature and patting her arms. After, Evern mentioned general pieces of information about the city, steadily hinting at his knowledge of Soirée's fate. The children remained quiet but with a curiosity of their surroundings more than out of shyness.

Coura suggested a tour of the palace and Verona and offered to buy them a meal in the city, which proved to be an enjoyable experience. Although the most entertaining space to her was the garden, and it required more time in order to become a floral paradise, her family adored the architecture of the entire building. Evern raised questions about its history, most stemming from his memories of living in the capital city, but Coura hardly had answers.

Odell begged her to stop at the training ground next since he heard about their fight with the demon. The reminder sent a chill down her spine, yet she hid it behind a smile and agreed. Of course, she didn't lead them to the outer wall because of the soldiers and mages working in the open. Both children became engrossed in the motions, and she even caught Evern eyeing up the maneuvers. Meanwhile, Paulina and Coura spoke about various topics until they took their leave, moving into the grand hall to exit.

The city was bustling due to the arrival of hundreds of newcomers and the ongoing preparations. She brought them to the decorated homes on the western road, along the shops lining the main street, and finally ended at the inn Marcy dragged her to before. By then, it became supper time. As she expected, Aimes came into the common room to welcome them and refused her payment with the hope to cover their meals. Evern and Paulina promised to recommend the place to their people as a way to show their appreciation.

Coura returned them to the camp, bid them a good night, then returned to her room feeling pleased with herself. The experience didn't seem quite as comfortable as she imagined it should be between family members, but it was a start.

*

During the night, something startled her awake. An all too real suffocating sensation stole her breath as she dreamed until she threw herself upward to gasp for air. The spot in the middle of her chest ached, which grew worse when her body continued to tremble, and she remained that way until dawn. Sunlight peeked through the curtain, beckoning her into standing and going to throw the window open. A warm breeze slid past to caress her exposed skin and offer comfort.

It's like when I would fly, Coura thought with some sadness. *I haven't even tried summoning my wings again. If the demonic energy is gone, all my magic should be too.*

Although the notion held true because of the lack of power in her center, she wondered if the Yeluthian energy lingered.

It was there with me in the demonic realm, and the ancestral weapon helped. Soirée even confirmed her power had nothing to do with my ability to manifest wings. If that's the case, I suppose it's worth a try.

Coura moved away to stand in the middle of her room and channeled the familiar spell. Deep down, she felt frightened of what the result would be and wondered what she would do if her power returned.

Despite the doubt, a spark as bright as the sunlight leapt at the invisible touch, springing forth at her command.

With tear-filled eyes, she looked over the wings with a mixture of relief, satisfaction, and no shortage of distaste upon recognizing their normal, dark appearance; however, upon further inspection, they differed from her father's and the other angels' only in color. The previously jagged feathers had softened, smoothing out at the edges to add volume to the top. This set her apart from the other Yeluthians, yet Coura took pride in the one ability that made her wholly unique.

Unlike in Dala, I don't need to give up everything I was just because Soirée's gone, nor do I owe it to anyone to try and alter what took place in the past. I'm still a citizen of Asteom and a member of the angelic race by blood, as well as a soldier who traveled all over the country. Change is in the wind. Life likes to do whatever it wants, whether we're prepared or not. At least I have the wings to ride it through on my own course this time.

Epilogue

"Where could I have put that thing? It's not like I leave a bunch of jewelry lying around."

Coura continued mumbling to herself to express her irritation before resigning to empty her dresser of its few contents for a second time.

That morning, she and Grace explored outfit options for the festival taking place the next day. Her friend had handfuls of dresses prepared over the years since she first began living in Asteom and decided on a bright yellow one with sleeves to cover her arms while leaving the shoulders exposed. On the other hand, Coura had been too preoccupied to acquire a collection like Grace's. The younger Yeluthian then suggested they visit Emilea, who returned home to prepare with her family. Half a day later and the light mage showed them the dozens of gowns gifted to the family by Lady Katrina.

"I usually end up with what she can't use or doesn't want anymore," Emilea explained with a chuckle as Coura and Grace stood in awe. "If I refuse, she throws a fit. She likes to say Lexie will grow into them, but who knows how many more I'll get before then. Take any you like."

After some searching, Coura settled on an evergreen gown and wrapped it into a makeshift bundle so the pair could return to the palace without ruining the fabric. Along the way, they reminisced about Katrina's home and the previous Harvest Festival when the rest of their friends could attend. The conversation reminded Coura that the lady gave her a golden bracelet and emerald necklace after the funeral procession over a year ago.

What happened to the two pieces, she didn't remember, leading to the fervent search, which included digging through her dresser, in between the dusty stacks of books on the desk, and under the bed. Once she checked those spots again, she fell onto the bed in defeat.

"I guess if I cared enough to wear them I would've put them somewhere I wouldn't forget," she said to herself and yawned. "It's time for dinner anyway."

Coura sat up and stretched her back before swinging her legs around the edge of the bed to rise. Her right knee passed too close to the front side, though, bringing it straight into the corner of her nightstand. With a startled cry, she wrapped both hands around the afflicted area while growling curses at the inanimate table. That was when she remembered the thin drawer attached to the top part; the pain ebbed as a hand flew over to open it.

Inside, she found both the bracelet and necklace, still shining as if they hadn't been thrown away for months, along with a pair of ribbons worn in her hair at one point and what appeared to be a patch of cloth. Coura pushed aside the jewelry to pick up and turn over the final item, causing every part of her body to grow tense. The image of wings embroidered on the scarlet patch in silver thread had been engraved in her mind ever since she tore it off her uniform.

I can't believe I never remembered this, she thought while brushing her fingers over the image. *Then again, the last time I even wore the full outfit was in Dala. Speaking of which...*

Every part of her uniform had to be replaced due to the recent tearing it succumbed to. One of the servants added a new undershirt and pants with polished boots to her dresser, as she discovered after first returning to her quarters. The crimson coat hung untouched where she put it away after returning from Dala with Emilea, Byron, and Will. Coura glanced between the badge and the wooden doors hiding the clothing while contemplating whether to throw away the patch and request another coat or not.

I used to believe Hernan assigned this to me out of spite, she reflected. *He thought I would accept whatever he wanted by labeling me as something different. Why he needed to do that, I won't ever understand. Still, ever since I traveled and fought for the kingdom, I don't believe people see me the same way he did anymore. I think this badge has become more meaningful with the time that passed and Yeluthia's arrival in Verona.*

Her most prominent fear after more consideration was what keeping and wearing the uniform would do for her image among the palace troops and the angels. Her wings made her stand out among the human and Yeluthian soldiers, so no matter who she trained and fought with, she would always be an outsider.

After setting aside the predicament to leave for the mess hall, Coura returned with a decision. She took both the badge and coat, went down to the first floor, and interrupted one of the seamstresses bent over a project to request professional mending. Although the request irritated the middle-aged woman, she accepted it with an outstretched hand. How anyone could do such precise work by lamplight astounded Coura, yet in a few minutes, she received the coat back before thanking the seamstress by way of a silver coin and marveling at the work with greater confidence.

I'm a soldier of Asteom, but I refuse to hide my abilities, especially since I can't imagine not flying anymore; it was terrifying to worry about before I manifested my wings. Besides, Marcus once said the badges and stars indicate what type of weapon-users we are. If I train and fight like I did in Dala, I'm already going to be unique to the people here. The best thing I can do now is embrace it.

*

Whatever internal encouragement Coura mustered the previous evening to convince herself to wear her uniform at the festival fell silent when she studied herself in the mirror. The clothing appeared looser on account of the weight and muscle she needed to make up, but it still presented her as an orderly figure with authority from the army. After smoothing down and tying her hair into a ponytail, she took a couple of deep breaths before braving the world outside.

Grace agreed to meet outside Coura's room since it was one floor closer to the grand hall so they could spend part of the morning together. The Yeluthian ambassador had other priorities and appearances with the leaders, but that would all take place closer to noon, leaving them with a couple of hours to roam around the capital. As they found one another and descended to the ground floor, Coura felt a twinge of guilt from Grace's disappointment at her change of outfit after the work that went into acquiring the gown from Emilea. When the Yeluthian didn't comment on the badge, she relaxed.

Because this new event brought hundreds more bodies from Yeluthia and around a wider area of Asteom, specifically the soldiers from Dala who were expected to attend, the city needed another space to use for entertaining. Rumors floated around about how the wealthier citizens on the western main road rejected the idea of setting up booths or another stage near their property because they already had to tolerate people moving into Verona from the south. The central road was out of the question since it already consisted of merchants with wares, farmers bringing in crops and livestock, and street performers squeezing into whatever corners they could find between everybody else. The generals refused to damage the training ground to the north of the palace by having thousands of feet trampling the earth, and hosting anything to the south of the Yeluthians felt disrespectful to the fallen soldiers honored there.

Someone argued for the grand hall, which ended up being the final location for a second, makeshift stage. Extra security would be necessary to avoid strangers sneaking around, but fortunately plenty of people volunteered for guard duty because food and drinks were being brought around by servants throughout the entire day, just like the ceremony for Grace's arrival. That, coupled with the soldiers and mages living in the palace, meant the area would be a comfortable hub for the army by evening.

Coura let Grace take the lead until they stood outside the entrance. The yellow gown stood out among the crimson uniforms and blue or white robes, drawing all eyes. Once those who saw her recognized the ambassador, they parted to let the pair pass, usually with smiles and greetings. The hall wasn't as crowded as they expected since most people stood around to wait for others; however, no matter how hard she tried to stay focused on avoiding everyone else's stares, Coura saw and felt eyes falling on her. In her mind, she dismissed them and reminded herself it would take time for the people who knew what she had once been to accept the person she was trying to be now.

The two had no direction in mind when they moved into the welcoming, spring weather. Already, the chill of winter seemed to have disappeared as sunshine lit the bustling city, which presumably livened at dawn. Together, Grace and Coura followed the flow of people casually wandering from the east to the western edge of Verona, stopping several times to purchase breakfast and other treats for Grace's sweet tooth, observe street performers, and pet some of the docile cattle, goats, and horses kept on that side of the city. On their return route, they decided to visit the inn where Aimes worked and found him too busy to talk for more than a few minutes. In that time, though, he complimented them on their appearances.

"My lady, you're more beautiful than any of the roses, buttercups, or tulips I've seen around," he said to Grace after taking and kissing her hand.

Of course, the young Yeluthian blushed at the comment and shook her head modestly.

When he tried to do the same to Coura, she shot him an unamused look.

"I should have known," he responded with a chuckle. "Ah, but this is the first time I've seen you in uniform! It's amazing how often I notice it all over the place, yet no two soldiers appear the same."

After some conversation, he was called back to work as more people poured in at a consistent enough pace to require every table. Grace noted the time as well, reminding Coura the ambassador needed to return to the palace where the royal procession into the eastern square would begin. They scrambled through the crowds until they finally reached the front gate. Both doors had been thrown open on account of the event, allowing Grace to slip through with a wave behind while Coura remained just inside and out of the way.

The grand hall became packed since the royal council and Yeluthian leaders would take the stage soon. According to Marcus, Aaron would welcome everyone to the festival, introduce the Yeluthian king, mention the kingdoms' reaffirmed alliance, then allow King Arval to speak. A hush indicated the appearance of the group on the raised platform a moment later.

Coura listened to the formalities, clapped and cheered at the end, and watched as the generals led the way into Verona. Evern and the other two Yeluthian commanders took up the rear behind their king, so she decided to follow with the hope of speaking to him since she felt obliged to meet her mother and the children as well. Marcus, Aaron, and Grace wouldn't be available until the evening, Will had been invited to eat and drink with his mage-friends, and Marcy joined Katrina and the other ladies at a private party. The latter two had extended the offer to her, yet Coura rejected them. Not only would Will and Marcy be the only people she knew well enough to feel comfortable around, but neither group appealed to her. The mages liked their drinks to the point of making fools of themselves, and the nobility always acted pretentious.

The procession ended at the eastern square where Aaron, Grace, King Arval, General Tont, Marcus, and one of the commanders climbed to the empty seats at the viewing platform above the main stage. Musicians and dancers were already performing, but they abruptly stopped to collect themselves and welcome the kings. Coura waited for her father to finish conversing with the others before approaching.

"I am glad to see you," he said with a smile before she returned the greeting.

"Do you have free time? I was hoping you know where Mother is. We can watch the performances together or walk around if you want."

Her father gazed upward a bit in thought before shaking his head. "My fellow commanders and some of their soldiers are on guard duty for the afternoon and evening. I left Paulina, Odell, and Jackie at the camp this morning to take the first shift in order to have the rest of the day off. Unfortunately, I am not certain if they remember where I would be."

The two decided to stay where they were for a while, or at least in the eastern square. Evern led her away once to purchase a couple of portable meat pies, which they nibbled on while listening to a trio of singers take the stage to harmonize with one another. After, they returned to the base of the platform before an acrobatic family began their performance. Such athletic acts always impressed Coura, so she remained captivated until their final trick. The audience vocalized their approval as the members took their bows and left.

During the following break, Evern spotted his wife and children nearby. Paulina hugged Coura while Odell and Jackie shared the places they visited. Then, the group decided to leave and explore the main road.

For the most part, the children chose what booths to stop at and street performers to watch. Coura noticed how her mother divided the money while her father's eyes darted around. She thought about reminding him of the dozens of Asteom guards in every direction yet knew from her own experience as a fighter that some habits continued even in areas deemed safe to the public. The afternoon crept by until Jackie and Odell became weary from walking. They managed to traverse the central main road, and Coura planned to join them at the eastern square until the dancing began; however, a stray comment from Evern added another stop to her schedule.

While Jackie and Paulina went to purchase treats, Odell asked Coura about her uniform and pointed out the patch. As she explained, using the same system Marcus and Clearshot gave her, the boy's enthusiasm grew. His positivity comforted her, especially since she spotted her parents catching glances at the clothing over the course of their time together. Even then, Evern turned away with an indifferent expression. When Coura finished talking, Odell expressed his goal to become a commander like their father, who faced them once more with the joy of a parent whose child dreams of following in their footsteps reflecting in his eyes. Paulina and Jackie returned then with a handful of doughy items they passed out before the group prepared to move on. Coura kept ahead of her parents as they locked arms and spoke casually to one another.

"That woman is from Kercher," her mother commented. "I never dreamed we would be able to visit a place that brings people together from all over the country."

Evern huffed a laugh. "Well, that would be the capital city for you. Did you notice the Mintelian dancers a few stations to the left?"

"No. That is a surprise! I did not think they would make such a journey for this."

It took Coura a moment to recall the name of the people who live in the mountains and her encounter with the man whose name escaped her memory. She stopped to ask Evern to repeat the dancers' location, which he did with some astonishment at her familiarity with their people. Perhaps it was her lack of closure with the merchant who lured her friends in during their first encounter or sheer curiosity at his wares, but something piqued her interest enough to separate herself from her family with a promise to meet up at the square. Paulina and Evern shared a confused look with one another before Coura went off alone to retrace their path.

In a few minutes, she caught the bright orange clothing and gold jewelry peeking out from the crowd. Both women appeared as she remembered with lean bodies and caramel-colored skin, and their movements still looked fluid, extending from their arms and hips to the neck and hands. Even the black hair tied into ponytails on top of their heads stretched down to the middle of their backs to add to the elongated effect. It proved to be as stunning as the first time Coura, Will, Marcus, and Grace watched.

As expected, a well-built man sat behind a table scattered with gems and metals shining brightly in the sunlight. Because of the dancers, not too many people laid eyes on him or the available products, allowing Coura to approach. He looked preoccupied with polishing a bronze mug and greeted her without removing his eyes from the object.

"It's about time you showed up."

Coura remained silent and stood awkwardly while the man finished his task, set down the item, and met her eyes with a wide grin.

"Has it been over a year already?" he continued. "Well, don't worry too much. We both needed the extra time. In fact, yours was the final piece I crafted before leaving my home."

"Does that mean you have something for me?" Coura asked without attempting to hide her interest.

This caused the man to laugh, a hearty, genuine sound that had her smiling too. When it faded, mischief replaced his humor. "Yes, I believe I do. Do you recall what I described about the process of Mintelian metalwork?"

Coura shook her head and grew inexplicably anxious at his change in behavior.

"I'll let you in on a secret," he went on while leaning closer. "My people focus on the self. It's something we humans like to wear on our sleeves, no matter how hard we try to hide it. What I explain to curious folks like you is usually the first of two levels to observe. This involves noticing the characteristics of a person and finding a piece to counteract the negative qualities while enhancing the positive ones. We could say this balances their natural energy."

"So?" Coura felt compelled to add when the question sounded partly answered.

He waved a hand in front of his face. "Any basic metalworker among my people can do that. The most difficult part is knowing humans change and understanding no piece will ever truly stay with someone forever, except in rare, unfortunate cases. Now, the second layer I neglected to mention when we first met requires years of training to master. I studied with our town's monk for a decade just to comprehend what it is he does all day. This requires one to look beyond the personality and into the soul, the essence of a person, then craft a piece to compliment it instead of balance it out."

"What does that have to do with me?"

"When we last saw each other, your soul was unreadable. At first, I felt ashamed to admit my lack of talent and thought about the experience often. Only after speaking with my mentor, the monk who specializes in understanding souls, was I able to accept I hadn't been the one at fault. He shared several stories of humans who visited him just for a cleansing because some trauma in their life damaged their soul. It was then I knew what I was dealing with."

The Mintelian bent over to grab something from underneath the table. Coura stood still, too enraptured by the man's experience and knowledge to consider much else beyond how it related to her situation. After digging through a leather sack, he removed a folded handkerchief, which he held out for her. The normal smile returned once she accepted and unwrapped the piece. At the sight of what lied beneath, she became speechless.

A silver brooch glimmered in the sunlight; no gems adorned it, and the metal seemingly pulled to create smooth ropes that twisted into the shape of an angel. An oval rested between two strips folded over one another to represent the head and arms with the bottom stretching down two pieces for the legs. At each side, the metal had been flattened to extend outward, representing the wings, which bore tiny markings to display each individual feather. It reminded her of the decorated armoire in the palace's basement, though more meticulously detailed. Coura also noticed how the wings were slimer and more horizontal, jutting out the feather tips. When she considered an image of a Yeluthian in her mind, it was one of grace and beauty. Somehow, this design projected their strength as well.

"Now that you've had a good look, flip it around," the Mintelian instructed with a twirl of his finger.

Despite her confusion, she obeyed and immediately saw another image take shape. The round head became a hilt, the legs a blade, and the wings an embellished guard. "It's a sword," she muttered in amazement.

Although flamboyant compared to a real weapon, she couldn't doubt the man's foresight when crafting the piece. Coura glanced up to find him beaming with pride.

"One of the best things I ever made! The most difficult part was what I shared about understanding the person who would wear it. Once I had some direction, once I could see the two parts making up your whole self, the metal bent to its own will. Silver is perfect for that because it likes to do the talking." He laughed, as if a joke had been revealed by his words.

At the reminder of silver, she carefully set the brooch on the table and reached for her coin pouch.

"There's no need for that."

She paused as the man stood, bent forward to pick up the handkerchief, and wrapped it once again. Part of her worried he would return it to his sack. Instead, he reached down for a similarly sized, cloth bag to drop the brooch into before extending it over to her.

She stared at it before looking into his face. "Why? After all that work, why are you just giving it to me?"

The Mintelian paused to search for an answer. "I suppose you could say the journey is my reward. In this special craft, we do not focus on the monetary reward as much as the joy in our accomplishments. I learned, and that's enough."

All Coura could do was thank him as sincerely as possible while pocketing the bag. Before she began walking away, though, the strange, sly expression returned.

"If you have the time, feel free to visit my people. The Yeluthians do occasionally, so they can direct you to the mountain. Just ask for Steiner or Sage Vidar. With a soul as damaged as yours, someone might send you to us anyway. That is, if the demonic scent doesn't interfere enough for them to turn you away."

Then, the jolly personality returned to wave and wish her a pleasant evening.

***

Two of the aspects Byron sorely missed during the fall and winter seasons were a later sunset and warmer temperatures at night. A lingering chill remained at the beginning of spring, but the drinks passed around and purchased throughout the evening helped keep it away.

Clearshot found him at some point that afternoon, and the two enjoyed themselves among the soldiers and mages their age. After, the pair moved to the busying square before it would become too packed to get comfortable. Emilea, looking quite cheerful herself, sat at one of the benches reserved for her family while her children played with others nearby. Byron hadn't put himself into a stupor like his friend, who now clung to his wife, but a content lull that allowed him to stay somewhat aware of the people around him. This proved to be in his best interest.

Shortly after taking his own seat, Coura and her parents approached with a blond boy and brunette girl. The children hesitantly separated themselves to join the group running around tagging one another in a friendly game while the adults talked. Emilea stood to greet the trio and began a friendly conversation with Commander Evern's wife, whose name slipped Byron's memory. Meanwhile, Coura crossed her arms, rolled her eyes at him and Clearshot, and half-heartedly scolded them for drinking so early in the evening. To his surprise, the commander came to their defense right away.

"Tonight is a night for celebrating," the Yeluthian countered with a slight smile. His sapphire eyes scanned the area for one of the women carrying the remainder of ale mugs. Once he found his target, Commander Evern slipped away from his daughter's side.

Coura shook her head in defeat after, though not without a grin.

The final performance concluded to much applause before the area in front of the stage cleared for dancing; however, with the additional guests compared to a normal festival, the space had to be emptied up to the main road. Byron wondered if those in the far back could even hear the music and hoped the guards on duty would be able to manage given the changes. The whole affair seemed like a new experience for the veterans like him.

He had little time to spare on considering anything else because Commander Evern insisted on conversing with him the remainder of the time. The angel inquired about simple topics, such as the Magical Arts Academy and what his training consists of, with a kindness and curiosity shown by people who were genuinely interested in a mutual friendship. That felt a bit jarring considering the Yeluthian's position and his relationship with Coura.

Unlike her father, she only threw in comments after Byron's explanations. He knew her reserved behavior usually meant something else occupied her mind. When Clearshot noticed the addition to her crimson coat, he understood what bothered her.

"What kind of badge is that?" his friend blurted out during a pause and pointed to the silver thread on her chest.

She went tense and explained it had been the original design from King Hernan. That was all Byron needed to hear to know how she felt about wearing the uniform.

"I didn't even notice it was missing when I first saw it," Clearshot added dismissively. "Still, it suits you."

Coura's mother shrugged from the farthest seat to his left. "I think it looks nice. Besides, Asteom will soon be getting used to the sight of wings."

Her eyes turned to the commander before she laughed in an innocent manner and chatted with Emilea again. Commander Evern's resulting smile hid his thoughts, but it looked forced enough to give away that he felt differently than his wife about their daughter's position.

Byron sipped at the last of his drink as the music started to initiate the dancing. While Emilea described the event to the newcomers, focusing on the types of moves and partners associated with particular songs, he caught Coura's eye and attempted to send her a look of reassurance.

What a horrible mentality to grow up with, he reflected when she turned away to watch the musicians. *Even before her first venture away from East Hoover, she usually chose to be alone. Many students learn and develop skills with each other through their classes, but her potential had been much greater. I fostered it by training one on one, which ultimately led her to act out. That independence, not to mention the demonic power, made her an outcast, both at the MAA and in the palace. Surprisingly, instead of giving into the negativity, she used it as motivation to get stronger. Every time she met someone, I think Coura assumed they would dislike her. Perhaps that's why she always seems indifferent. Her experiences shaped her into a person who expects backlash for who she is and the decisions she makes. People can be so cruel to one another, even when they don't intend to be.*

He set his empty mug aside with a sigh. Soon, a younger Yeluthian confronted Commander Evern about their king's retirement to the camp and assured his superior of the guards placed around that area. Then, to Byron's surprise, the soldier slipped over to Coura after being dismissed. The two spoke briefly before the Yeluthian offered her his hand for a dance, which she accepted.

"Who is that?" Byron asked her father, who snickered into his own mug.

"One of my underlings named Lavine. If you have not noticed yet, he likes to flirt with the women around his age. The two met during her time in Yeluthia where she practically forced him to watch Odell and Jackie so she could return to Asteom." The commander's following laughter proved contagious.

As the night went on and his former student disappeared into the crowd, Byron settled on the notion that only time and a more positive outlook on life would be the best cure to heal the wounds of the past.

***

During the many songs that played well into the night, Coura's mind pulled away until she simply enjoyed herself without considering every wandering glance or the comments thrown out by others in passing conversations.

Lavine's appearance started that process. The Yeluthian convinced her to dance by claiming she owed him for forcing him to watch Odell and Jackie while she rushed back to Verona. If she really wanted to, she would have ignored the request; however, at that moment anything seemed better than standing around and listening to the older adults. The two stayed together for several songs until the musicians retired and another group took their place.

Before they could sit down, Grace and Marcus appeared out of nowhere, and the latter offered his hand after Lavine led Grace away for a formal dance. Coura listened to her friend ramble about nothing in particular before inviting her to speak. Twice, she caught him eyeing the newest addition to her crimson coat but went on about her day with Grace, her family, and then Byron, Emilea, and Clearshot. They only broke apart when both began sweating in their full uniforms.

After stripping off his coat, Marcus gestured for her to follow him. "Come on. We can keep these up by Aaron where no one's going to notice. King Arval and his company won't be there again tonight."

They scrambled to the highest platform and found the king of Asteom observing the festivities taking place below. It had been over a week since Coura saw Aaron, and she immediately felt comfortable in her friend's presence. In fact, his was the company she preferred the most when it came to forgetting her concerns and savoring the atmosphere. The realization seemed a bit jarring considering his position rarely allowed for them to be alone.

He showed less surprise upon seeing Marcus and Coura than she thought he would and ushered them over to the empty chairs.

"I'm glad you could spare some time. I've been here all day, and it gets boring, especially when all you can talk about is what's appropriate between royal figures."

"I heard King Arval returned to their camp a while ago," Coura mentioned as she recalled Lavine's report to Evern.

She hung her coat on the back of the seat to Aaron's left before dropping into her chosen chair. Usually, she kept her arms and chest covered to prevent drawing attention to the fading, bruise-like markings, but the dim lighting made them hardly visible. Meanwhile, Aaron explained the generals' desire that he avoid leaving his spot when this was the Yeluthians' first appearance in Verona. Not only did they object to projecting a lax attitude around honored guests, but spending time with women emphasized how he remained the only heir to the kingdom.

"I understand their concern, but it's still tedious," he concluded with a shrug.

Coura frowned. "Yeluthia is also our ally, so I would assume they want to protect you too. Besides, who cares about making small talk during a public celebration."

Silence stretched between them before Aaron replied.

"Are you pitying me?" he asked with a sidelong look that made her laugh.

"Well, maybe a little. I hate dealing with people. Doing it for a full day sounds awful!"

Coura remained on the upper platform with Aaron for the rest of the evening. At some point while they were talking, she looked behind, expecting Marcus to share his input on the current topic. She figured he was standing guard by the entrance, as he usually did during these events, but he had vanished. If Aaron noticed, he didn't mention it. The music filled every break in between their words, and the people below soon distracted Coura enough for her to realize how tired she'd grown.

A sudden scuffle and creaking sound from the right made her jump and turn to see Aaron sliding his seat over until the arms of their chairs touched.

"What's wrong?" he asked nonchalantly.

She stared at him before relaxing again. "What are you doing?"

"You looked like you were about ready to fall asleep."

"Maybe you need to learn how to hold a conversation instead of discussing the dull politics of royalty," she retorted in reference to their previous subject.

Thankfully, he understood the joke and laughed. "I don't think it's my job to keep you from dozing off up here."

Coura rolled her eyes and glanced forward again. Before she could settle into a cozy position, Aaron slid his left arm around her shoulders to bring her close and hug her head to his shoulder.

"What are you doing?" she repeated after her heart skipped a beat. The gesture was startling yet not unwelcome.

His head rested on hers, and his following words felt warm in her hair. "This is more comfortable."

While his entire body felt at ease, Coura remained tense until she recalled a moment between the two she found she cherished. *That's right, I held him in the queen's garden after his parents were... Aaron had been hurting, and I just wanted to help by being there for him. I guess he's returning the favor. It's sad I need a reminder that actions like this are common.*

She thanked him in a mumble before closing her eyes and giving into the embrace.

*

A normal Harvest Festival typically lasted until dawn when the weather was fair, or however long the musicians accepted payments to stay; the spring event seemed to be heading down a similar path. Coura never remained in the square late enough to find out what became of the events.

Because Aaron needed to be escorted during his return to the palace, she figured it would be rude to be the one keeping him and his guards there. She sat straighter, stretched, and shook her friend's shoulder to rouse him. When the two finished rubbing their eyes and yawning, Coura wished him a good night and hurried to the ground before waiting for a response. As she expected, the handful of soldiers, including Marcus, stood together nearby. Some had drinks in their hands while others swayed from side to side in a sleepy manner. She snuck around them and through the waning crowd to reach the main road.

A steady flow of soldiers and mages remained around the palace's bridge and open gate since that stage still appeared to be in use as well. In order to avoid the traffic, Coura decided to walk around to the training ground and use the entrance there instead. Some couples or groups of men and women found privacy in the field, which seemed peaceful underneath the clear, star-filled sky. Even with the image in front of her, Coura couldn't help but replay the memory of fighting the demon in her mind, as she always did when she lingered in the area.

The following months of the recovery period had been kind to her, and she found she could be alone with only her thoughts. Before she realized it, Coura managed to stroll near the outer border where she summoned the portal to force Soirée into the realm of demons. Her weary mind went blank as her body, particularly her chest, shivered from a sudden chill.

I need to keep paving the way forward, she reflected against the physical, unnerving sensation. *It's all over now. Yes, even the person I was until that moment is gone. To linger on what I lost and the resulting changes is only going to overwhelm me. I want to continue to be here and see Asteom grow, through both the best and worst times. Besides, my friends and family are relying on me.*

Coura stood in that spot a while longer before sweeping past the other people in the field like a wandering spirit to return to the palace and her awaiting bed.

About the Author

Courtney Lillard was born and raised in Appleton, Wisconsin as the middle of five children. Growing up, she enjoyed music and theater, and participating in both allowed her to develop a deeper interest in the arts. She graduated from Quincy University in 2015 with a B.A. degree in Broadcasting and Public Relations Communications and from Western Illinois University in 2018 with a M.A. degree in Communication Studies.

Outside of writing, Lillard is a fan of reading fantasy stories and the classics. Her other hobbies include cooking, playing video games, relaxing by the pool, and doing puzzles, at least until her cat knocks the pieces off the table.

Made in the USA
Columbia, SC
28 October 2023